Mr. Darcy's

Forbidden

Love

Mr. Darcy's Forbidden Love

A Pride and Prejudice Adaptation

Brenda J. Webb

Other books by Brenda J. Webb

Fitzwilliam Darcy: An Honourable Man

*Dedicated to my betas,
Debbie Styne, Colleen Lane,
Kathryn Begley and Joy Olson.*

*Their hard work helped to make this book
possible. Their friendship made the
project enjoyable. I am indebted to them for
the hours they spent making this story better.*

Chapter 1

MERYTON
April 1812

It was a brisk, cloud-covered day when Fitzwilliam Darcy arrived in the small village of Meryton. He had never visited there before, but his best friend, Charles Bingley, had requested that he come to Netherfield to assess the estate in light of his desire to purchase it, and because William was eager to focus on something other than his growing unhappiness, he consented.

As his elegant black coach rolled slowly through the village, he spotted a small bookshop through the open window and was reminded that he had not brought anything along to read. Knowing Charles as he did, he presumed that Netherfield would have no library to speak of, even though his friend had been in residence for over a month. Thus, he had his driver stop at the quaint shop with high hopes of finding something spellbinding to keep him occupied at night. Nights were especially hard to endure.

As he opened the weathered door of the shop, a bell overhead jingled, alerting the proprietor, who stuck his head out from a door on the left. The balding, middle-aged man smiled broadly, and taking the measure of the tall, elegantly clad man from Derbyshire, he called out, "Welcome to our humble shop. I am Martin Grant. May I assist you?"

William nodded, methodically pulling off his kidskin gloves while simultaneously scanning the shelves of the small but seemingly well-kept shop. He had often found interesting books in places such as this. "I am looking for new editions—poetry especially."

The shopkeeper's crooked teeth gleamed as he responded. "You sound like Miss Elizabeth!" Then, glancing over his shoulder towards the back wall, he exclaimed loudly, "Elizabeth, are you still straightening the new editions?"

A lilting female voice came from somewhere in that vicinity. "I am, Mr. Grant!"

"Good, good! Would you be so kind as to show this gentleman the shelf where they are kept while I finish cataloguing this shipment? Then I shall show the both of you into the back room to look through all that has arrived today. You may each find something you want in the new selections."

Again the melodious voice answered. "I will be glad to assist!"

Addressing his customer, Mr. Grant explained, "I hope you do not mind letting Miss Elizabeth direct you to the section you desire." Before William could reply, he swiftly disappeared through the door from which he had come.

At first, it appeared that only a halo of ebony curls peeked around a tall bookcase in the back, but on closer inspection, William could see a beautiful face with dark, expressive eyes beneath the unruly tresses. Instantly the painting of a wood nymph that he had seen on his tour of the Continent came to mind—only that nymph had been completely nude, her long silky hair her only covering. For the first time in a very long time, William felt the stirrings of desire flood through him—feelings now so foreign they unsettled him.

A young woman of perhaps one and twenty studied him for the briefest of moments before she came forward, all the while trying to tie her unrepentant mane back with a blue ribbon. A smile played on her lips, and by the time she reached him, she had secured her hair and was laughing at the stunned look on his face.

"I must look a fright! I am sorry."

She caught his intense gaze and was lost in his light blue eyes when he finally managed a small smile. Nervously she began to explain. "I was on the way into Meryton when the wind caught my bonnet and I had to run to retrieve it. Soon afterward, I found that I had lost most of my pins. I decided not to worry about my hair until I am nearly home again. I hope no one tells my mother, as she would have a fit of nerves if she knew I had run my errands in Meryton with it loose!"

Your hair is beautiful just as it is! William furrowed his brow. Where had that thought come from? Had he said it aloud?

He was mesmerized—no, he was lost! For two long years he had kept himself under good regulation, not daring to enjoy the company of any woman that he found the least appealing. And now, in this insignificant little shop, he found himself instantly drawn to this beautiful pixie of a woman. Disconcerted, he was unable to utter a word, though he could not prevent his eyes from travelling down and then back up her body, catching the shadow of her figure beneath her thin muslin morning dress.

Elizabeth, coloured at his examination and began anew breathlessly. "In this corner," she gestured to where she had emerged moments before, "are the newest editions."

Turning in that direction, she left William staring after her, then looking over her shoulder, she teased, "You will need to follow me if you are to discover anything you might want."

I have already found what I want! William's heart shouted, startling him from his reverie and causing him to quickly recover and follow.

In a few steps, he stood at the end of a bookshelf, watching her slim finger slide over the titles on a certain shelf full of books as she read them aloud. There was very little room in the aisle, and he considered whether it would be improper to join her as she recited. Not actually listening, he found himself studying everything about her—the tan of her skin, her pert nose, the rose colour of her lips, the curve of her breasts—quite generous considering her petite figure—and the smallness of her waist as compared to her rounded hips. Imagining the joy of having such a woman in his life, he did not hear her question, though he could tell from her expression that she was awaiting an answer.

"I … I am sorry. What was your question?"

She smiled mischievously, her amazing eyes dancing. "I heard you tell Mr. Grant that you were looking for poetry. I am hoping that *A Selection of Irish*

Melodies[1] is in the new shipment, as I have been waiting for months for a copy, and I wondered what poetry you find interesting."

William's entire countenance transformed with his smile, both dimples now clearly visible as he proclaimed, "Ah, Thomas Moore has another admirer. I think highly of his work as well."

For some unknown reason, he felt compelled to step closer and gently lift a curl from her shoulder as he recited a verse from one of Mr. Moore's works. Their eyes locked, and he was spellbound by two dark pools as he quoted the bard.

> "Oh, the heart that has truly loved never forgets,
> But as truly loves on to the close:
> As the sunflower turns on her God when he sets,
> The same look that she gave when he rose." [2]

"That is a favourite of mine," Elizabeth offered, astonished that he would pick that very poem.

William examined her with unconcealed admiration, noting that she had begun to pale. He reached to take both her hands in his and squeezed them gently.

"Are you well? Do you need to sit down?" As he asked, he glanced about for a chair, but she began to step away, pulling her hands from his in an attempt to regain her composure.

"I … I am well. I thank you. I was just surprised that you quoted a poem that I admire, that is all."

Mr. Grant chose that moment to return from the storeroom, and brushing his hands together as if he were well-pleased with his accomplishment, he declared, "There! I have unpacked the entire shipment, and it is on the table awaiting your perusal!" No notice was taken that the two he addressed seemed preoccupied, thus he continued with his mission, waving William ahead of him. "Come! Come! You may find something you like better in my newest order."

I doubt that very much, William's heart whispered. Nevertheless, he turned to enter the other room as Mr. Grant motioned for Elizabeth to follow and then entered after both of them. In only a short while, the bell over the door rang again, requiring the proprietor to return to the front of the shop. Left alone, William and

---

[1] *A Selection of Irish Melodies,* 4 *(November 1811) Thomas Moore, Irish Poet, singer, songwriter and entertainer. (May 1779 – February 1852)*

[2] *Believe Me, if All Those Endearing Young Charms is a popular folksong of early 19th century Ireland and America. Irish poet Thomas Moore wrote the words to a traditional Irish air in 1808. The last verse is as follows:*

> *That the fervour and faith of a soul can be known,*
> *To which time will but make thee more dear.*
> *Oh, the heart that has truly loved never forgets,*
> *But as truly loves on to the close:*
> *As the sunflower turns on her God when he sets*
> *The same look that she gave when he rose.*

Elizabeth continued to peruse the stack of new books.

"I apologise. We were not introduced properly, but if you do not mind, I shall introduce myself—Fitzwilliam Darcy of Derbyshire," William offered, bowing slightly.

"Elizabeth Bennet."

"Do you work for the proprietor, Miss Bennet?"

The giggle that he had expected floated across the air. "Heavens, no! Papa would never allow me to do that! He and Papa are old friends, and he knows how much I dearly love to read." She leaned in conspiratorially. "Do not tell a soul, but Mr. Grant lets me straighten the books after his customers have moved them about in exchange for reading all that I desire." She lifted her chin, and her eyes sparkled in challenge. "It is not a popular notion for women to educate themselves, but I enjoy learning."

William struggled not to smile. "I admire women who do, Miss Bennet."

"Oh?" She looked bewildered, as though she had expected an argument.

"What do you enjoy reading most of all?"

"Why poetry, of course. Thomas Moore, as you know, anything of Donne's, Sir Thomas Malory's *Le Morte d'Arthur* and Sir Walter Scott's *Lady of the Lake*. But I also enjoy Shakespeare's plays and other works of literature."

William suppressed his delight at her choice of works and her enthusiasm. "Such as?"

"Dante's *Divine Comedy*, Milton's *Paradise Lost* and *Paradise Regained*, Homer's great epic poems, *The Odyssey.*" His eyebrows rose higher with mention of every work, while her smile grew proportionately. "And *The Iliad*, to name a few."

He bowed very low now, sweeping his hand across in a grand salute. "I must say I am suitably impressed."

In a few moments, the proprietor returned to find them deep in discussion of *The Iliad*, though each held a selection from the new arrivals in hand. As they returned to the main room, Elizabeth asked Mr. Grant to hold the book she wanted until she had the funds to pay for it, and William purchased the book he had found. Having no more excuse to stay and further their acquaintance, they exited the quaint shop.

At once the enchantress began swiftly pushing her hair under her bonnet with great enthusiasm. William could not help but smile at her zeal, though he much preferred it as it was. While watching her work at the task, he noted the moment that she began to study the emblem on the side of his coach—her face taking on a totally different expression.

"Will you be staying in Meryton?" Immediately she shook her head, biting her bottom lip in a gesture that captured him. "I am sorry! It is none of my business. It was impolite of me to ask."

William answered, ignoring her apology. "I am staying at Netherfield at the invitation of a friend."

She smiled warmly, recognising the significance. "With Mr. Bingley." It was merely a statement, so William did not answer. Looking down at her shoes, she continued a little shyly, "I am invited to Netherfield tomorrow."

"Tomorrow?"

She glanced up to see his reaction. "Yes, Mr. Bingley has invited the entire neighbourhood to a ball."

William rolled his eyes, dropped his head and groaned, making his dark-haired pixie chuckle anew. Smiling in spite of himself at her enjoyment of his unease, it suddenly dawned on him that he had completely forgotten his misery while in her company. At that realisation, his dutiful companion, the voice of reason, whispered its usual warning—*be very careful!*

He was taking the warning into account, when Elizabeth lifted one brow in a delightful manner. "Surely a gentleman such as yourself has attended many a ball, yet you do not want to attend the one at Netherfield? Is it the local society that offends you?"

William noted the wary look now present in her eyes, and for some reason, felt obligated to reassure her, though he had to admit that he probably would have considered attending a ball in this village beneath him two years earlier.

"That has absolutely nothing to do with it, I assure you. I am simply not fond of the rituals of society, no matter the location. Bingley is aware of that, so he must have conveniently forgotten to tell me about this ball."

His answer obviously pleased her, and the sprite of the bookshop swiftly returned as she enquired demurely, "Do you dance, Mr. Darcy?"

He laughed mirthlessly, shaking his head at the remembrance of endless dances he had suffered for the sake of good manners. "Not if I can help it!"

She seemed taken aback as her eyes widened. "Might I ask why?"

"Because I do not dance unless I am particularly acquainted with my partner."

The same eyebrow shot up again. "And would I not be considered an acquaintance now that I have helped you select a book?"

William laughed aloud at her cleverness. "You have ensnared me, Miss Bennet. I shall have to ask you for a set."

Elizabeth began to back away teasingly. "Oh no, Mr. Darcy! I would not dream of punishing you by having you stand up with me! I shall have my share of partners, so never fear that I shall be slighted by other men!"

With those words, she disappeared around the corner, and William found himself staring into empty space with a silly grin on his face. Once he realised she was not going to return, his heart sank and he looked about, embarrassed to be smiling at nothing. Catching sight of the bookshop window reminded him of something he had resolved a few moments before and he returned. Slipping inside, he purchased the book that Elizabeth had asked Mr. Grant to hold for her.

Netherfield

Lost in his thoughts of the impertinent Miss Bennet, the last leg of his journey to Netherfield took little time, and William was surprised when his coach came to a stop. He glanced out the window to see a footman approaching the door, and as he climbed out of the coach, his first glimpse of the estate did not disappoint.

Charles Bingley was standing on the portico of the impressive grey-stone facade with his arms crossed when he arrived, but was now hurrying down the steps with his hand outstretched. Bingley had changed little in the years since he had befriended him at Cambridge, perhaps only getting a bit taller. But with his boyish good looks and flaming red hair, he still looked years younger than his five and twenty years as he approached the coach.

"Darcy! My Lord, it is good to see you!" Bingley grabbed his hand and began pumping it, while his other hand squeezed William's shoulder. "Come in, come in! See what you think of my humble abode."

William was even more impressed with the inside of the house, though it was still sparsely furnished, as was Charles' wont with all the estates he rented. He could not fault the man for that—better to find out if you wanted to buy a place before purchasing furniture to fit. After William handed the butler his hat and coat, he turned in a circle, taking in the foyer, the grand staircase and glimpses of other rooms through the open doors. He did not have time to give an opinion, as Charles instantly suggested they go to his study, and once there, they each sank into a comfortably upholstered chair.

"Well, I must say, Charles, that unlike the last manor house you were so eager to buy, this one is striking. And unless I am fooled by my impressions, it seems well maintained. I can only hope the grounds do not disappoint."

Charles snickered, grinning crookedly. "Oh, yes, that estate. Well, perhaps a certain young lady who lived nearby influenced my delight with the place."

"Yes, *the angel,* Miss Farnsworth, if I remember correctly," William teased.

"Precisely! I am so pleased that you advised me to carefully consider that alliance. I was truly not in love with the woman, though I imagined I was at the time."

"You must learn to guard your heart, Charles. You simply cannot believe you are in love with every woman you meet. If you do, you will be married before you know what has transpired. And you may rely upon my word—an unhappy marriage is something that you will regret for the rest of your life."

Charles watched William's face assume the mask that had been his normal mien for the last two years. He hated the fact that the kindest man he had ever known had formed such an unhappy alliance simply to protect his family.

"I know you speak from experience, Darcy. I can only imagine your pain at being married to someone you despise—feeling that you had no choice. And I know countless others who have married without such noble intentions but are equally as miserable. My own sister married for greed, and I do not wish to end up like Louisa and Bertram—so miserable that they follow me about because they are unhappy when they are alone. Speaking of them, they are upstairs."

"As long as Caroline is not upstairs, I do not care."

Charles' head dropped, and he stared awkwardly at his feet. William challenged, "Tell me she is not here, Charles."

"I … I did not tell her you were coming, Darcy, but I think Louisa must have, as I received a letter just today telling me she would be here in the morning. Supposedly, she feels she must be the hostess for the ball I am giving tomorrow, even though Louisa is certainly capable. She has handled all the arrangements without any help from Caroline."

"Can she not leave me in peace? Is it not punishment enough that I am tied to that—" William rubbed his eyes with both hands wearily. "You would think that after two years your sister would relent."

"You know that I love my sister, but I do not condone her actions. Nonetheless, Caroline is a slave to the gossip of the *ton.* Everyone in your sphere knows that your marriage is a farce. You make it plain by maintaining separate residences. There is even a wager on the books at White's on just how long it will last."

At this William's eyebrows knitted and he growled, "Cannot a man be left in peace? Apparently even men who are supposed to be my friends gossip like old women. And another thing, what is this I hear of a ball? How is it that I was not informed of that either?"

Charles squirmed uncomfortably, not meeting his eyes. "I was cajoled into giving the ball by some lovely young ladies in the neighbourhood, and it was not settled upon until after you informed me of your visit. Knowing that if you learned of it you would postpone your trip again, I said nothing. However, if you want to feign illness, I will not insist you attend. I will even make your excuses."

An image of the pixie of the bookshop came to mind and William smiled unknowingly. "No, I think I shall attend and meet your new neighbours. After all, how am I to judge the estate without judging the neighbours?"

Charles looked stunned, as though he had expected William to decline, and he stuttered a bumbling reply. "Of ... of course! You must meet the neighbours, and this will be a great opportunity. Besides, I was hoping to introduce you to someone that I have met. She is truly an angel, Miss—"

"Charles! What was I just saying about—"

"Bennet."

William's heart skipped a beat. "Bennet? You are in love with a Miss Bennet?" William felt his stomach lurch as he pictured Elizabeth. Had her heart already been taken?

Abruptly, his conscience demanded a part in the conversation. *What is that to you? After all, you cannot have her or any woman for that matter!*

"I think she is the one, Darcy! She is beautiful, funny, kind and not at all like any woman I have met before. She makes me laugh."

William was reeling but tried not to let his emotions show as he murmured, "No, she is not like them."

Bingley's brow furrowed as he overheard the whispered comment. "You know her, Darcy?"

William forced his heart to slow its frantic beat and his voice to steady. "Yes, I met her in Meryton on my way here. She is remarkable, I will give you that."

"And is she not the most beautiful creature—"

William could endure no more. Standing, he hurried towards the door. "I simply must change my clothes and rest before dinner. Can we not talk more of the object of your admiration later?"

Charles called after him. "Of course. Where are my manners? You must be exhausted." As Charles gained the door, he met the housekeeper who had been standing by since William's arrival. "Mrs. Watkins, please show Mr. Darcy to his room."

The elderly woman curtsied slightly and hurried to catch up with William who was had stopped on the stairs. "Right this way, please."

Charles could not see the empty look in William's eyes as he woodenly followed the woman to his room, nonetheless, he did notice the sudden slump of his friend's shoulders the minute he thought he was out of sight.

I have never seen Darcy so unhappy. Even his attempts to appear unaffected are unconvincing. I pray his misery does not get the better of him. If only Caroline had not decided to come!

Dinner had been torture. Charles had tried to bring up the subject of his Miss Bennet several times, only to be thwarted by his older sister, Louisa, who would quickly change the subject. As William pondered how little Louisa looked like Charles or Caroline—she was shorter, heavier and had mousey brown hair—he realised that, despite their differences, he liked neither woman. Louisa did everything she could to forward her sister's schemes and to keep Charles from assuming his rightful place as head of the family.

Ordinarily, William would have been incensed by Charles' sister interrupting his every sentence and would have intervened, but tonight he was secretly relieved that he would not have to listen to his friend expound on the merits of the one woman who had touched his heart, the one he had found so enchanting. Mixed emotions duelled in his heart and mind. While he knew that he could never have such a woman, he wondered if he could continue a close friendship with the man fortunate enough to call her his own.

Thus, shortly after dinner, he made his excuses and went to his room as he needed to think about that dilemma. And now, settled in bed for the night, William's conscience began to challenge him as it always did when he dared so much as to consider any woman.

What are you doing? It is not gentlemanly to trifle with a young woman's affections and especially not if she is Bingley's angel.

I only wish to enjoy her company for a short while.

So you say, but would it not be better to limit your conversation to that at the bookshop?

Knowing that he had never won this debate in the past, William rolled over, pulling the pillow over his head and willing his mind to quiet. It appeared that he was going to have another long and sleepless night.

Chapter 2

Netherfield
The Ball

As anticipated, Caroline Bingley arrived early the next day. Thankfully, William and Charles were out riding the property line when her coach pulled into the drive, and she spent the entire day in her room—first resting and then preparing for the ball. Had she known that nothing she could have devised would have attracted Mr. Darcy's attention that night or any other, she might have spent a little less time with her preparations—or perhaps not. After all, she was quite vain and still hopeful that Mr. Darcy might one day be back on the marriage market. For, thanks to his close friendship with Charles, she had eavesdropped enough to know that his marriage was not a happy one.

And now as the time approached for the ball, Caroline studied her image in her dressing room mirror, quite pleased with the reflection. Though now four and twenty, she comforted herself with the fact that she was years younger than William's wife, who was eight years his senior, and felt certain that her age would not be a detriment to becoming the next Mistress of Pemberley. Taking her time placing two large, orange ostrich feathers in her elaborate coiffure, something she refused to leave to a maid, she then smoothed the burnt-orange silk of her gown with her hands, all the while admiring the quality of the material. Quite pleased with herself for having thought to have yards and yards of silk and several feathers dyed that particular colour, she could not help but feel smug. From this night on, she would easily stand out in a sea of mousy women with mousy gowns. Finally, fastening her mother's pearls around her neck, she was ready to impress not only the wilds of Meryton society, but also the Master of Pemberley with her fashion expertise. She left her rooms and went in search of her brother.

As time for the ball approached, Charles had not been able to locate either sister, so he proceeded down the stairs to take up his position as host, only to find that William was already in the foyer. Stopping midway on the stairs, he watched surreptitiously as his friend paced relentlessly, as though he expected the Prince Regent to arrive at any minute, instead of the good people of Meryton. Occasionally, he would even walk over to the large front windows to peer out at the drive.

Finally, Charles could hold his tongue no longer, and continuing his descent, he called out, "I would never have figured you to be in such a state, Darcy."

William jerked his head around and examined Charles for a long moment before realising that he was teasing. Relaxing a bit, he tried to smile. It would not do for Charles to know just who he was anticipating.

Charles continued, "I hope you do not mind that I asked you to stand with me so I may introduce you to my new acquaintances."

"No, not at all."

"If I did not know better, I would think you are expecting someone."

William decided to tell a half-truth. "I suppose I am eager for the ball to begin. This shall be a diversion for me, as I have not been in company for the last six weeks, and I must admit that I find the idea of watching an entirely different level of society quite intriguing."

"Only you would look at it in that particular way. But you were always much more an observer than a participant."

"Charles, you know why I cannot—"

Two hands held up in apology stopped William's explanation. "I know, friend. Please forgive my intrusive comments on what is strictly your business. I sometimes forget your circumstances, since you are never in each other's company. You are a better man than I to persevere as you do."

William turned towards the window again, not willing for Charles to see the depth of his despondency. Most of the time, he preferred to pretend all was well, but Charles' mention of his situation made the reality of it come flooding back, dampening his spirits.

Charles observed the morose expression on his friend's face as he walked away and was about to say more, when the sounds of a carriage on the gravel drive announced that the first guests were arriving. Mercer went to stand by the entrance while William joined Charles in the receiving line. Just then, Caroline and Louisa came down the stairs as though they were in no hurry to begin the task.

"Oh, my Lord!" William whispered to Charles upon seeing the orange monstrosity that was Caroline Bingley from tip to toe.

But Charles was more concerned with the look in Caroline's eyes when she saw William. "Come, Caroline, stand beside me," he motioned her to his other side, effectively keeping her from planting herself next to William. As Caroline scowled at her brother, Louisa took the position next to William, and Bertram Hurst, who made it a point to sneak into Charles' study for a sip of his expensive brandy every time he could, was the last to take his place alongside his wife. He smelled of liquor.

Later

Convinced that he had already met the entire population of Hertfordshire in little over an hour, William began to despair of seeing the woman from the bookshop as the arrivals dwindled to a sparse few. And that disappointment, along with Caroline's constant stream of criticism of everyone after they had passed out of hearing range, was beginning to grate on his nerves.

Trying not to sound greatly disappointed, he enquired of Charles quietly, "Was your Miss Bennet invited to the ball?"

Charles chuckled without thinking, which instantly drew Caroline's attention, annoying William. He had hoped against hope that no one would take note of his interest in a certain young woman, especially Caroline.

"According to *my* Miss Bennet, they will be among the last to arrive, as she has four sisters and her mother is always busy with last minute preparations. Rest assured that I have it on good authority that her mother will not allow a soirée to pass in Meryton without being in attendance!"

Caroline seethed at Charles' jest, and seeing that all the current arrivals had passed on into the ball room, she murmured loud enough to be heard, "Yes, Charles, Louisa has informed me of the crassness of the entire Bennet family."

Louisa leaned out to catch her sister's eye and shook her head in hopes of silencing her, but Caroline ignored her and continued.

"I do hope you do not embarrass us with your attention to them." She leaned around Charles, as if to confide to Darcy. "It is well known that the entire family is ridiculous. Their mother pushes her daughters on any man that breathes, and their father neglects his duty, preferring to laugh at his wife's lack of decorum and indulge his three youngest daughters—one who quotes Fordyce's sermons and others who are infatuated with redcoats. I had no idea that Charles would be so foolish as to invite them."

Charles addressed his sister quietly with gritted teeth. "You are my guest and can very well leave if you do not like the company I keep." Then he focused his ire on Louisa. "I would appreciate it if you would keep your opinions to yourself. You were performing competently as hostess before Caroline arrived, and I should like you to continue, but only if you can refrain from gossiping about our neighbours."

Louisa cast another unpleasant look at Caroline. She had sworn her sister to secrecy before sharing her misgivings regarding the Bennets, and Caroline had betrayed her. Addressing Charles, she stated with little true remorse, "Forgive me. I am sorry for being so outspoken, and from this point on I will do as you ask."

Caroline stiffened at her sister's apology, but quickly recovered. After all, she reasoned, where else could Louisa and Bertram stay so comfortably without having to pay one farthing out of their own pockets? Caroline had every intention of winning this fight, and she intended to seek Mr. Darcy's help in doing so. He had tried to bring Charles into his circle of friends, and surely, he would know that these women were detrimental to that goal. Thus, she had resolved to hold her tongue just as the family in question arrived. Nonetheless, while she was concentrating on being silent, had Caroline listened, she might have heard the distinct drumming of one wildly beating heart standing in the line.

At the sight of Elizabeth dressed in her best gown—a white silk confection—her hair piled atop her head and interspersed with tiny white pearls, William felt his heart begin a relentless rhythm. A part of him was relieved that, in his loneliness, he had not overestimated her beauty. She was just as perfect as he remembered. But another part, the faction that always reminded him of his duty, was not as pleased.

What does it matter? She cannot be yours.

Reminding himself that she was the object of Charles' affections, he schooled himself not to react as she stepped forward, the first of the Bennets to come through the receiving line. Because of the heartbeat pounding in his ears, William could not hear what Charles and she were saying or what his friend said as he introduced them. But all of a sudden, Elizabeth was standing before him looking slightly bemused. Thinking he had composed himself, he realised at that very moment that he had not. Though he could not formulate a decent sentence, she still smiled—only the smile began to fade as he continued to hesitate.

Finally, he found his tongue. "Miss Bennet, I am pleased to see you again."

Elizabeth's smile returned full force, and he prayed earnestly that no one recognised his discomposure as she responded, "I feared from your silence that you had already forgotten me."

His eyes never left hers as he said very quietly, "You are unforgettable, Miss Bennet."

"I am not Miss Bennet," Elizabeth grinned, tilting her head towards the woman who was now talking to Charles. "My sister, Jane, is Miss Bennet."

William cut his eyes to Charles who was in deep conversation with Jane, and it was quite obvious which *Miss Bennet* his friend was enamoured of—the blond-haired, blue-eyed *angel* whose hand he held. William felt his entire body go limp with the realisation that Elizabeth was not *Miss Bennet*.

Longing to request a dance, he knew that he should not, so instead he ventured, "I cannot wait to see if your boast is fulfilled." Elizabeth's eyebrow rose in question, so he added cheekily, "That your dance card will be full."

Her eyes crinkled with a laugh. "Oh, you shall see that I was not speaking idly!"

She was gone before he could formulate a reply, and once more he found himself staring after her. It was not until Charles began to introduce another of her family that William realised he had not been paying attention.

After being introduced to the rest of the Bennets, he had to admit that Caroline was, unfortunately, mostly correct in her assessments. The mother was strictly interested in making matches for her daughters, but he would grant that she was no bolder than most mothers of the *ton*. The middle sister was boring and the youngest two were totally out of control. Only Miss Bennet seemed to be like Miss Elizabeth in her demeanour. And as for the neglectful father, it seemed to him that Mr. Bennet took an inordinate amount of time studying him when they were introduced, and from the questions he was asked, the man was certainly not neglectful of his second oldest daughter.

"I could not help overhearing my Elizabeth mention that she had met you before, Mr. Darcy. How is it that a man newly arrived in Meryton knows my daughter?"

William noted the raised brow that accompanied his question, and it brought to mind Elizabeth, as she had the same mannerisms. He almost smiled at the realization before it dawned on him that Elizabeth's father did not seem amused in the least. So instead, taking on an air of indifference he replied, "I met your daughter when I stopped at the bookshop in Meryton on my way to Netherfield. She was most helpful in pointing out the section of new editions."

Mr. Bennet's expression relaxed just a bit, and he nodded in understanding. "Yes, my daughter is a great reader and spends many hours going through Mr. Grant's merchandise."

"She is an intelligent young woman. I was impressed with her conversation regarding the authors and works she admires."

Mr. Bennet chuckled though his eyes did not join the merriment. "Most men would be wary instead of impressed."

"I am not most men."

Elizabeth's father studied William with a sombre expression for a long moment. "I shall remember that."

William was not sure if that was a compliment or a warning, but from the look in the man's eyes before he walked away, he was inclined to believe it was the latter. And he did not blame him in the least.

If I had such a daughter, I would be protective of her, too.

As he stood against the wall watching Elizabeth dance, it dawned on William that she was not only one of the loveliest women he had ever seen, but the most unaffected. Not afraid to show emotion, she openly enjoyed the gaiety and even laughed aloud at something her partner said. William was mesmerized—so much so, that he did not see Caroline approaching. Often, he managed to avoid her by circling the room and keeping a few steps ahead of her every machination. Thus, when she spoke from just behind him, he was startled.

"I did not mean to surprise you!" She affected a laugh. Then following his line of sight to see what he found so engaging, she saw Elizabeth. Her face instantly fell into a frown, her voice spiteful as she lashed out, "Oh, you have noticed the spectacle that Miss Eliza is making of herself, too. It is little wonder that one so vulgar is popular with the men."

William turned to study Caroline now, who seemed uncomfortable as his withering glare stayed fixed on her. Before she could make some excuse to leave, he declared, "I have come to the conclusion that Miss Elizabeth Bennet is simply an honest woman without guile. And, I do not believe laughter is evidence of trying to garner attention. I believe it is evidence of a sincere disposition."

Caroline was incensed and remarked, "In any case, I do not see why a married man, such as yourself, should take any interest in her."

William, who had turned back to follow Elizabeth through the next dance, did not bother to look at Caroline as he replied, "Just as I do not understand why you have always concerned yourself with my affairs, especially since I am married."

The rustle of orange silk skirts was the only answer William was to receive as Caroline quickly removed herself from his presence. At that very moment, he met Charles' eyes as he and Jane made another round on the dance floor. As he shrugged, Charles shook his head in understanding. Insulting Caroline was never William's objective, but it always seemed to work out that way.

With nothing to occupy his time, he turned his full attention back to Elizabeth. It was evident as he watched her dance with first one man and then another, that she was a very popular young woman. Strangely it caused his heart to ache.

He had long since accepted that he was never to fall in love, being trapped in this nightmare of a marriage with Gisela. And, never the type to disregard propriety or selfish enough to fulfil his own needs, he had resisted every offer made by the widows and wives in the *ton* who preyed upon dissatisfied men. Nor had he resorted to trifling with single young women's affections or raising their expectations. It went against his very nature, as he had a sister that he loved and whom he would not want to be treated in such a manner.

Until coming to Meryton, William believed that he had subjugated his desires. He had resisted temptation so efficiently and so often that he had begun to think his heart was untouchable. Thus, these unbidden feelings for Elizabeth Bennet perplexed him. What was so different about her that made it painful to contemplate ending their association? Apparently, a force had gripped his heart the moment he first laid eyes on her, and it would not let go. And while he truly desired not to hurt her, he desired to be in her presence even more.

Just for tonight, he told himself. *Just this once I will dance with her and then leave all thoughts of her behind forever and return to London.*

Having made up his mind, he decided that he needed a breath of fresh air first and headed to one of the open double doors that led onto a terrace that ran across the back of the house. The cooler air was invigorating, and he took a deep breath. He noted that the wind had picked up since the ball began, and the moon was now going in and out of ever-increasingly dark clouds. Whenever it was hidden, the night was black as pitch, but as soon as it reappeared, he could clearly make out the fountains and statues that graced the gardens.

Enjoying the silence, he was startled to hear the sounds of young women talking animatedly—whether they were happy or distressed he could not tell. Deciding that he should investigate, he went down the few steps to the ground and headed in the direction of the voices. Rounding a large group of hedges, he could see a smaller terrace that led from the ballroom on another side of the room. It was occupied by Miss Elizabeth and another young woman whom he recognised as Charlotte Lucas from their introduction earlier in the evening. Since they had not seen him and they appeared well, he turned to leave. However, he halted after a few steps, when he heard his name mentioned. Though he knew he should not eavesdrop, he found that curiosity got the better of him.

Elizabeth's voice was unmistakeable. "I do not care how much of Derbyshire Mr. Darcy owns, I refuse to join in the speculation, Charlotte. It is unseemly to talk about people in regards to their wealth. I prefer to judge men in terms of their character and their good nature."

"Only you would choose a man using such criteria, Lizzy. And, you have to admit that he is certainly a mystery. My father was barely able to get any information out of Mr. Bingley regarding his friend, other than the fact that he owns half of Derbyshire. And, we know from what Caroline Bingley said to her sister that she means to marry him. I think she said that aloud so that the other ladies would realise they had no chance."

The melodious laughter he had come to expect from Elizabeth echoed across the wind. "She certainly keeps an eye on him." William could not help but grin at this pronouncement. "But that is his business, I am sure."

"Well, as I tried to tell you earlier, he certainly has been studying you tonight, and you should take every opportunity to put yourself in the path of eligible men. After all, we are alike in that you have nothing to recommend you, either—no dowry and no connections."

Elizabeth sighed, dropping her head. "Must everything be about money or connections? Cannot the most important decision in our lives be about love?"

"Elizabeth Bennet! Have you not listened to a thing I have said for the last two years! Love means nothing! Get your head out of the clouds, or you shall be left behind as a spinster while your sisters marry."

"I do not wish to marry unless it is for the deepest love." She took a deep breath of air, puffing up her cheeks and then blowing it out. "I would rather teach Jane's children to embroider and play the pianoforte ill than to marry someone I do not love!" William covered his mouth to keep from chuckling aloud.

Charlotte huffed, "Well, I see that I have wasted my time trying to advise you about Mr. Darcy, so I shall return to the ball. Perhaps you need time to be alone and consider that you may be alone for the rest of your life, unless you change your way of thinking!"

With these words, Charlotte disappeared back into the ballroom, and Elizabeth stepped down off the terrace and began to walk the gravel path to the lower garden. William continued to watch her from afar. Suddenly, Mr. Bennet stood beside him.

"Elizabeth knows better than to walk out alone in the night."

William did not answer, wondering instead what her father was thinking. They both stood watching her silently. The elderly man finally spoke again. "I am grateful that you were watching over her and not attempting to meet with her alone."

William turned to study Mr. Bennet just as the moon lit up the area. He could see that her father's expression was sincere, thus he nodded at the truth of Mr. Bennet's assumption.

"I saw her walk out, and I was afraid for her. I am the guardian for my younger sister and have a tendency to be protective with any woman I fear may be in an unsafe position."

Now it was Mr. Bennet's turn to study William, whose eyes were still trained on Elizabeth. Satisfied with what he had just learned of this enigmatic man, he nodded though William did not see.

"I know little about you, Mr. Darcy, other than the fact that Mr. Bingley credits you with being a good and decent man, one who has been his friend even in the face of censure from those members of the *ton* who would never accept a man from trade. However, the fact that you seemed to watch my Elizabeth a great deal during the ball and that I find you watching over her now concerns me, though you have acquitted yourself by not going into the garden with her. I can tell from your clothes and your coach that you are a wealthy man of a higher society. My Elizabeth has nothing that could interest a man of your stature other than her quick mind."

William studied the childlike woman still strolling the gravel lanes, her delicate hands outstretched to brush the tops of the flowers planted along the paths. His heart literally ached as he lied, "I have no feelings toward your daughter other than friendship."

"Good. Then I shall concern myself with your intentions no more. If you will excuse me, I shall retrieve my child."

As he watched Mr. Bennet walk down the path towards Elizabeth, William knew what he must do. There would be no dance and tomorrow he would conclude his survey of the grounds of the estate and give Charles his evaluation. Then, he would leave this area of England and the sprite of the bookstore forever.

Chapter 3

Netherfield
The Next Day

Everyone at Netherfield slept late the day after the ball—everyone but William. He had left the soirée after talking with Mr. Bennet and retired early. But sleep would not come, and after tossing and turning until the early morning hours, he had risen, dressed and readied himself to ride over the balance of the estate. He purposely did not disturb Charles, as he wanted to be alone to consider his feelings for Elizabeth. Leaving Meryton as quickly as possible was now his top priority and he needed a clear head if he was going to get the rest of the tenant houses inspected. If Thomas Bennet could *discern* his interest in his daughter, then things were getting out of hand, and the best he could do was put plenty of distance between them.

After he heard the staff stirring downstairs, he located Mrs. Watkins and asked her to have food and drink readied so that he would not have to return to Netherfield until late that evening. She had been most helpful and supplied him with a sack of food and a bottle of water that he placed in a pouch and threw across the saddle of the horse that he was going to ride. It was just beginning to get light as he rode out of the paddock, headed in the direction of the farthest reaches of Netherfield—the border with Longbourn. Little did he know that today would definitely not turn out as he had planned.

"Elizabeth, that goat of yours escaped again!" Mr. Bennet stood looking into the dining room where his second daughter was wrapping two buns in a serviette for her usual morning walk to Oakham Mount. "This time she ran the ducks out of their pen before she scampered off down the front lane."

"Oh, Papa, I do not know what I am going to do with Juliet!"

Mr. Bennet tried not to smile at the name Elizabeth had given the kid. The goat seemed anything but a *Juliet* to him.

"Mama is angry that she got into her flower garden and ate all the blooms from her roses and that she chased the hens until they would not lay eggs. And twice she has run away and I found her near where the wild dogs have begun to gather in the woods. If I cannot keep Juliet in her pen, I am afraid that I shall have to give her back to Charlotte for her own good as the dogs are concentrated in this area. But I would truly miss her if that were the only choice."

Mr. Bennet patted his favourite daughter's arm. "It is amazing how something so small can cause so much mayhem. But, if your Juliet is determined not to stay in the barn or the pasture, we cannot let her destroy your mother's gardens, and it would be preferable to give her back to Charlotte than let her become dinner for the dogs."

Stuffing the serviette in her pocket, Elizabeth declared decisively, "I shall take a rope and find her. I have an idea that she is just where she was last time—in the meadow right below Oakham Mount."

"Do not stray too far. It is going to rain today, and I don't want you to get stranded on the other side of the brook."

"I will be careful, Papa. I did not enjoy having to stay at Lucas Lodge the last time the stream rose. John Lucas seemed to think that I made the brook rise just so I could be in his company."

Mr. Bennet schooled himself not to smile. "You do not care for John Lucas? I thought you and he were great friends."

"We were when we were younger, but now that we are no longer children he assumes too much."

"Such as?"

"Such as assuming that I will marry him."

"He would not be a bad choice as a husband, Lizzy. He is to inherit Lucas Lodge when his father passes, and he is a steady sort of fellow. I believe he would treat you well."

"But I do not love him, Papa. He is like a brother to me."

"Love has little to do with marriage, my daughter. And besides, compatibility is much more desirable than love."

"Why do you say that?"

Her father looked wistful as he explained. "Because you can be fooled into thinking you are in love with someone, only to find out that it was just a passing infatuation. If there is nothing more substantial to bind you—friendship, mutual interests—then you can find yourself very unhappy for the rest of your life."

"Then I will just have to be sure that I marry for the deepest love."

Mr. Bennet smiled. "I hope that you can, my dear. Now, if you are to have any chance of finding that scamp, you had best be on your way. Remember what I said about the rain."

As her father turned in the direction of his study, Elizabeth swallowed her last sip of tea, grabbed her cloak from off the chair and slipped past him. "Do not worry. I shall return before the rain begins in earnest."

When William left Netherfield, there was only a light mist falling, but sometime during the day it had turned into a steady drizzle. Now that it was after noon the rain had begun in earnest with torrents beginning to blow sideways as the wind picked up. In the distance a wall of dark clouds approached with thunder and lightning heralding its severity.

William was very weary, not having slept. Nevertheless, he had managed to visit every tenant dwelling along the northern perimeter, save one, and it was in the furthest corner, where Netherfield's property adjoined Oakham Mount. The last tenant he called on had given him direction for finding the next house, though he informed him that the tenant, an old woman with a teenage boy, had gone to visit her daughter four months before and had not returned.

With the darker clouds fast approaching, William briefly considered returning to the manor, but it was at least three miles back to Netherfield. And knowing that he had only one empty tenant house to inspect before he could leave Meryton forever, he made the decision to continue. Besides, he reasoned, he could wait out a storm at the cottage if necessary, and if he was any judge of the weather, a severe one was brewing. Untying the cravat that had choked him since early that morning, he wiped some of water from his brow and thanked the Lord that he had worn his great coat. There was no doubt that he would need the protection against what was to come. Hence, kicking his horse into a trot, he headed in the direction of the mountain.

Finally, through the blowing rain, he could make out two small structures at the base of Oakham Mount and he found himself sighing in relief. Not one to be afraid of storms, nevertheless he had a healthy fear of the damage they could cause. He had not traversed far in the direction of the cabin, when he caught sight of a small white animal crossing in front of his steed so quickly he could not identify what kind of creature it was. Regardless, it caused the horse to bolt upright, almost tossing him to the ground as he had not anticipated such an event. He had barely gotten the stallion calmed, when he heard what sounded like a woman's voice.

"Juliet! Juliet!"

Was his mind playing tricks, or could that be Elizabeth?

William sat deathly still for several minutes, turning first one direction in the saddle then another, straining to hear the voice again, but gaining nothing for his efforts. Try as he might, the tossing of trees, limbs and brush back and forth with great ferocity masked further confirmation. Beginning to believe that the howling wind may have deceived him, he kicked the horse forward and had gone perhaps another fifty feet when three large, snarling dogs ran past about twenty feet ahead. They were headed in the same direction as the previous creature and almost caused his horse to bolt anew.

Fear welled up. He knew how vicious wild dogs could be towards man or beast, and if the voice was not a figment of his imagination, a woman could be in their path. Turning the horse around, he followed the dogs.

He had not gone far when he came upon an alarming sight. A stream was beginning to overflow its banks, the swiftly moving waters sweeping everything in its path downstream. In the middle of this stream Elizabeth sat on a fallen tree that must have served as a bridge when the water was calm. She had one arm wrapped around a small white goat and the other wrapped around the remains of a large limb sticking up from the log. On the bank were these same grey dogs, teeth bared and growling. One was just attempting to climb atop the log, as the small goat bleated and struggled to break free from Elizabeth's grasp. Each time the frightened animal thrashed about, it almost dislodged her from her insecure perch. His heart leapt into his throat at the realisation that if she were to fall into the rushing water, she would most likely be swept away before he could reach her.

Swiftly, William dismounted, tying his horse to keep it from bolting and pulling his rifle from the sleeve on the saddle. Afraid that he might hit Elizabeth if he tried to shoot the dogs, he fired into the air, causing them to scatter. Then he hurried forward, his eyes locked on her as he neared the log.

"Elizabeth, let the animal go!" She shook her head frantically. Seeing that she was resolute, he commanded, "Then hold on and I will come to you!"

Noticing that another tree's limbs stretched above the fallen trunk, William prayed that he was tall enough to reach one of them. As he climbed atop the fallen tree, he found that he was just able to grab a limb and pull it down to steady himself. Then holding on to it, he began the slow process of edging towards Elizabeth on the slippery log, one step at a time. As he looked down to find where to place his next step, he noted that the water would soon be lapping over the makeshift bridge, but he forced himself not to think on that. Finally, he stood above where she sat.

"Elizabeth, it would be best if you let the animal go."

Elizabeth shook her head insistently, trying to hold the small creature up to him. "Please," was all she could manage to say, but her eyes continued to plead, and he knew he could not refuse.

Taking the kid from her grip by the scruff of its neck, he commanded, "Do not let go, and I shall return for you!"

She watched as he made his way back to the bank with the small animal as swiftly as possible, and using his cravat, secured its feet and lay it over the horse where it bleated in protest. Losing no time, he returned to her, moving as rapidly as he dared until once again he stood over where she clung desperately.

"Give me your hand."

She did not move, her knuckles now white as she gripped the upturned limb. She was shaking violently, whether from fear or cold he knew not. The rain began to intensify, and at that very instant, lightning struck a tree close by, causing them both to jump. The water now began to flow over parts of the tree trunk.

"Trust me, Elizabeth!" he declared as if expecting to be obeyed. "Give me your hand!" Immediately she looked up, her frightened eyes focusing on his outstretched hand. "NOW!"

Instantly, she let go of the limb and reached to take his hand. He grabbed it securely. "I am going to pull you to your feet. Hold on to me and get your balance."

She did as he instructed, swaying a little as she regained her footing and the feeling returned to her numb limbs. Seeing her unsteadiness, William slid an arm around her waist and pulled her closer to him. "Do not look down; look at me. We shall take one step at a time."

She nodded, though she appeared as small and frightened as a child. His heart ached for her. "I promise I will keep you safe."

He waited for the confirmation in her eyes and then began to move a few steps at a time, their feet now mostly underwater as they inched slowly towards the bank. Nearing the end of the log, he stepped down into the water's edge with his tall boots and pulled Elizabeth into his arms. Swiftly leaving the flood behind, he rushed to the horse and lifted her onto the saddle and placed the small goat in her arms. Promptly mounting behind her, he wrapped his great coat about them as he urged the stallion onward. She turned into the warmth of his body as he murmured in her ear, "We shall take shelter in a nearby cottage."

In less than a quarter-mile, the tenant house was in sight, and William manoeuvred the horse into the barn. Quickly situating the animals in the dry hay scattered about the structure, he noted that Elizabeth was beginning to shiver more severely. Sweeping her off her feet, he rapidly made his way to the house, kicked open the inadequate door and carried her inside the bare but dry refuge. Constant flashes of lightning illuminated the room, and spying a chair, he set her on her feet, stripped off his great coat and tossed it aside. Then removing his dry frock coat, he placed it about her shoulders, observing as he did that it hung nearly to her knees. She smiled as she surveyed the makeshift covering and then looked up at him. Gently, he scooped her up and sat her in the chair.

"Sit here while I get a fire started."

Hurrying to the fireplace, he found sparse kindling in a wooden box but tossed it into the grate. Then looking about for more wood to burn, he spied two more chairs. Smashing them against the stone hearth, he began piling the largest parts on the fire and stacked the rest on the hearth for later use.

As he was concentrating on what he wanted to accomplish, he almost missed Elizabeth's quiet murmur. "There shall be a scandal if I do not return home."

Turning to study her, he noted that she looked childlike with her hair wet and lying about her shoulders, a look of apprehension marring her countenance. He was trying to compose words of comfort when she spoke despairingly.

"I know that the bridge to Longbourn is likely under water with the stream so high, so it would be useless to set out for home."

Her eyes involuntarily closed with exhaustion before he could answer, and seeing this, he kept quiet. From then on, Elizabeth was unaware of the progress going on about her until William's touch brought her back to the present. When she opened her eyes, William, clad once more in his great coat, was kneeling in front of her, holding both of her hands.

And as strong fingers clasped delicate ones, William's heart soared with the stirrings of first love. At that precise moment, he was certain that nothing in his life would ever be the same. Swallowing hard, he pushed his newfound emotions back into the secret compartment of his heart and focused on the task at hand.

"I am going to close the barn door in case the dogs come back, and I want to retrieve my rifle and some food I brought with me." A loud clap of thunder shook the house, and a volley of fierce lightning lit the room. Running his thumbs along the back of her hands, he offered reassurance. "Do not be afraid. I shall come right back."

"I ... I shall never be afraid when I am with you."

Her declaration gave him pause, and he leaned in to place his forehead against hers, and for that brief moment, all was right with the world. But such happiness could not last, and William rose and was out the door in another moment.

In minutes, he returned with a horse blanket he had spied in the barn, his rifle and a small leather sack. Opening it, he placed a serviette on the table next to Elizabeth and opened it to reveal a bun, a piece of cheese and an apple. Next, he pulled a half-full bottle of water from the sack.

William squeezed her shoulder lightly as she stared at the offering. "Drink the water and try to eat something. You need your strength."

"What will you—"

"I had just eaten before I found you," he interrupted. "Please, do as I say. Your body needs sustenance to help you stay warm."

Elizabeth was too tired to argue and took several sips of the water before beginning to eat the cheese, sandwiched in the bun. As he watched her struggle to eat while shivering, he realised he must do more. Thus, while she ate, he searched the cottage for blankets. All he found was a poor excuse for a mattress—hay stuffed into a roughly sewn burlap bag—which he threw on the floor in front of the fire. He then proceeded to drape the horse blanket he had found over the mattress and placed his great coat atop it, with the dry side out. By then Elizabeth had finished the small meal and was watching him arrange everything. She said nothing when he lifted her from the chair and deposited her on the makeshift bed, then removed his waistcoat to fashion a pillow for her. Nonetheless, she was taken aback when at last he kneeled at her feet.

Focused on his task, William began to undo one soaked shoe, stopping only when their eyes met. He waited until a silent understanding was reached and without a word, he began anew, carefully removing and placing each shoe in front of the fire. Then he tended to her wet stockings—being careful to pull them down from the bottom instead of starting at the top.

"How … how is it that you have no qualms about divesting a woman of her shoes and stockings?" Elizabeth asked, her voice quivering, though she was not sure if it was from the cold or his touch.

He looked up at her enquiry, noting that she was trying to smile and visibly relaxed. "I have a much younger sister, thirteen years my junior. My mother never recovered from her birth, and my father was absent much of the time, so I took it upon myself to see that she had plenty of attention." His face took on a wistful look. "I took her everywhere I went. I well remember when she was still very young, helping her out of wet clothes after she decided to retrieve a new duckling from the pond, fully clothed. And, as was often the case, I had to help her change clothes to disguise her wilfulness—such as when she played with her paints while wearing her best clothes—which she had been expressly instructed never to do. I must admit I spoiled her."

"Could not a maid have helped?"

"All the maids would have told Mother straightaway."

Elizabeth smiled. "Ah, you were her protector. Nevertheless, it seems that your sister and I are kindred spirits!"

It was William's turn to smile. "How so?"

"My mother thinks me wilful, too. I have not lived up to her expectations of a daughter, much preferring to run through the meadows, climb trees and, yes, even take a dip in the pond on a hot day. Oft times as a child, I had to slip in the backdoor to keep her from learning that I was soaked to the bone." She laughed mirthlessly. "She will be horrified when she learns of my adventure today and will no doubt inform the world that I shall never grow up or secure a decent husband."

William thought of the peril she had been in earlier and he sobered. Choosing his words carefully because he did not want to hurt her feelings, he cautioned, "Miss Elizabeth, you could have been killed trying to rescue that kid. That was very foolish on your part. You do know that?" Their eyes met and after a long silence, she nodded. He smiled lovingly. "And I may not be here to rescue you the next time."

Elizabeth's face crumpled. For a moment, she looked as though she would cry, but she did not. Instead, swallowing a large lump in her throat, she replied, "I thank you for risking your life to save me and Juliet. But please—just for tonight—let us pretend you will always be here." With those words, she closed her eyes, the sign that their conversation was finished. And William said nothing more.

Free to observe Elizabeth now that her eyes were closed, he allowed that the thought of leaving her brought him no pleasure either. Nevertheless, he was resolved that he must, especially now that he was confident that he loved her. Mr. Bennet came to mind, and her father's certain disapproval of their current circumstances made him uneasy. How would he be received when he took Elizabeth home? Seeing that her eyes were still closed, he began to massage the warmth back into her cold, numb feet as he contemplated just that.

Elizabeth was awake but quickly fading into unconsciousness as William's strong hands continued to stroke her feet, bringing warmth to her cold limbs. Never having been touched by a man and certainly not in as intimate a manner, the pleasure produced by his manipulations was almost overwhelming in its intensity. And drifting off into her dreams, she contemplated the truth that she had learned this day—she had met the man she would love for the rest of her life.

Sometime during the early morning hours Elizabeth slowly regained consciousness to the sound of a drumming in her ear and the pleasant smell of sandalwood. She burrowed into the fine scented pillow that lay soft against her face and immediately strong arms tightened about her. Her eyes flew open. Though plainly asleep, William lay facing her, holding her in his embrace. It was evident that the pillow of her imaginings was the fine lawn of his shirt and the continual drumming, his heartbeat. Just as obvious was the fact that, at some point during the night, he had pulled the great coat over her and wrapped his arms about her to keep it in place.

Now fully aware, she reflected on everything that this kind-hearted man had risked for her. At peril to his own life, he had rescued her and Juliet, then spirited them to this cabin to wait out the storm. Clearly he knew the jeopardy he was courting should they be found out; nonetheless, he had thought only of her wellbeing. And as she studied his handsome face, lit only by the glow of the fire, her heart began to swell with love. Though certainly still a young man, deep furrows cut across his forehead and lined his eyes—the kind that usually accompanied great burdens. And being this close, it was easy to discern the scattered grey hairs amongst his black curls. Still, he looked so very handsome with just the stubble of a beard on his strong jaw that she felt drawn to touch him. Shyly she brushed a curl from his forehead, which caused his nose to crinkle but did not awaken him. She smiled.

If we were married, I would see him this way every morning.

At the thought of marriage, her father's disapproving face appeared in her mind's eye, and Elizabeth wondered what he would say once they were found. Would he insist that they marry? While she knew without a doubt that she would not repine such a union, she wondered what the one in whose arms she now rested would think of the prospect.

But alas, knowing the great disparity of their stations, the possibilities were too troubling for her to dwell upon at the moment. Thus, she laid her head back on his chest and felt him pull her closer. The flicker of the still glowing fire and the warmth of his embrace were comforting, and she fell asleep with a smile on her face.

Chapter 4

Netherfield
The next morning

Charles had not been especially worried when Darcy did not appear in time for dinner yesterday. After all, he knew of his friend's propensity for finishing any project he started, no matter the weather. And Darcy's note of that morning stated that he wished to finish the survey of the farthest reaches of the property that day, so he probably kept going despite the storm and found shelter somewhere along the route. The thought that his friend likely preferred a tenant's barn to Caroline's company at dinner brought a smile to Charles' face. And the fact that Darcy also mentioned leaving for London forthwith came as no surprise, either. Once Caroline arrived, Darcy always found some reason to leave—that was how it had always been.

Caroline had protested Darcy's absence from dinner, but Charles brushed aside her insistence that he immediately send men out to locate him. This morning, however, he was beginning to get a bit concerned, though he was certainly not going to bring attention to his disquiet. Better that none of his household learn that Darcy had not returned until he knew what had happened. The less they knew, the less Caroline would likely find out. Thus, he told the servants that he had personally let Darcy into the house very late last night, and he would be spending the rest of the day in his room as he was exhausted. He emphasised that Mr. Darcy was not to be disturbed and instructed them to tell Caroline and the Hursts the same thing when they came down to break their fast.

With his mind a jumble of thoughts and apprehension for his friend, Charles Bingley rode out just before daylight, hoping to find that he was correct, and his best friend had found a safe shelter from the storm at one of the tenant homes.

At the cottage

Watching Elizabeth as she slept, William thought how very beautiful she was with absolutely no embellishment. She needed no finery, sparkling jewels or elaborate hairstyles to enhance her person. Her dark brows and eyelashes lay like silk against a perfect complexion and her hair—her hair was his undoing. The long dark locks, drenched the night before, had dried—the resulting dishevelled ringlets more striking than he had seen that day at the bookshop in Meryton. Against his better judgement, he reached to stroke one long tendril, finding it softer than he had imagined and brought it to his nose, closing his eyes in anticipation of a delightful fragrance. The scent of lavender still lingered, and at that moment, he would have given everything he owned for her to be his.

The pain of this reflection pierced his heart, and he hurled that yearning into the same deep recess where he had tossed his own desires two years before. Stoically reaffirming the acceptance of his fate, he began to focus on what was crucial at this point—getting Elizabeth home to Longbourn before daylight. Well aware that they must return before Mr. Bennet had time to arrange for a search party lest their night spent together become common knowledge, he had already saddled the horse. Since all that remained was to wake her, he knelt down beside her, gently shaking her shoulder.

"Elizabeth?"

She murmured but did not wake, so he reached to cup her face. Immediately he became alarmed—she was running a fever! Now the need to return her to her family's care was even more urgent.

"Elizabeth!" he said louder. Her eyes opened and despite the clear evidence of the fever in her slow, affected speech, she tried to smile at him.

"Fitzwilliam, why are you up so early? Can we not sleep until the household awakens?"

William was taken aback. "The household?"

Sighing lazily, her eyes closed once more. "Have you forgotten already?"

He would have smiled at her misconception, had it not been so painful for him or had she not been sick. "I fear you are dreaming. We were caught by the rain and found shelter in this cabin. But the storm has ceased, and it shall be getting light soon. We must get you home before the waters recede entirely and they begin a search. It would not do for anyone to find us together under these circumstances."

"But what will it matter?" she murmured sleepily, not opening her eyes. "We are married."

William's heart lurched. How he longed to tell her he would gladly marry her, but he could not. Instead, he began to slip his arms under her. "I am going to lift you, and as I do, try to put your arms about my neck."

As he picked her up, she studied him dreamily, murmuring, "My home is with you." Then she laid her head on his shoulder and promptly went back to sleep, no doubt as a result of the fever.

Just as he began towards the door with Elizabeth in his arms, the sound of heavy footsteps announced the presence of someone coming up the small front steps, and a man's shadow filled the doorway. William found himself holding his breath as the front door was pushed open and a familiar voice rang out.

"Darcy, what the devil!" He rushed towards them. "What has happened to Miss Elizabeth, and why are you here with her?"

William had never been happier in his life to see Charles Bingley and he let go of the breath he was holding.

"It is a long story Charles, which I shall be happy to tell while we make our way to Longbourn. But in short, I pulled Miss Bennet from the middle of a raging stream as she clung to an old tree trunk that fords it. We spent the night here due to the severity of the storm, and I have just now discovered that she has a fever. I desperately need to get her home before anyone sees us or her condition worsens."

"Yes, the locals say that even the small bridge between Netherfield and Longbourn is covered with water when it storms as it did yesterday, and no one can cross until it recedes."

"Then let us pray the bridge is passable now and that Mr. Bennet was unable to arrange a search party. It is such a relief to know that you will be accompanying me, as I believe he shall react more rationally."

"I would imagine you are relieved. And I will be most pleased to hear your explanation before he kills you."

William was almost to the barn when Charles made his jest, and he turned to confront Bingley, Elizabeth still in his arms. "I am glad that one of us sees humour in this situation. I do not wish to duel Miss Elizabeth's father."

"I am only trying to lighten your mood, Darcy. It does not take a scholar to see that Mr. Bennet is very protective of her. I just hope he takes the time to listen to your explanation before …" Charles' voice trailed off.

"Yes," William agreed. "Let us pray he is a man who listens before he acts."

**Longbourn
Mr. Bennet's study**

William felt almost like a schoolboy under Mr. Bennet's glare, but he would not be the first to look away. He had done nothing wrong, and he was not about to be treated as though he had. Suddenly a knock garnered the older man's attention, and the impasse was temporarily broken as he looked towards the door with a glare that questioned what interloper dared interrupt his interrogation of the gentleman he held responsible for compromising his daughter. As the door slowly opened, William was stunned to see Bingley's head enter the room before the rest followed. After all, Mr. Bennet had summarily dismissed Charles when he demanded William's presence in his library after seeing his daughter to her room.

"Mr. Bingley," Thomas Bennet began, "I am afraid that I shall have to ask you once more to wait in the parlour."

Charles would not be dissuaded as he shut the door. "I feel that I should have a part in this discussion; after all, it was I who discovered my friend and your daughter at the tenant's shack this morning."

Mr. Bennet considered the red-headed man with great dissatisfaction before he conceded. "Very well, come in. But I warn you that I shall have my answers from this gentleman."

Charles moved forward to take the seat next to William. They both faced Mr. Bennet, who sat behind his desk. Without bothering to speak to Charles, he turned back to William, addressing him sarcastically as he had been doing since the interrogation began.

"Now, you were saying."

William's demeanour was not conciliatory. He took an exaggerated breath, puffing up his cheeks and blowing it out, hoping to convey his displeasure at her father's intimations.

"As I tried to explain previously, I was not at Oakham Mount to meet your daughter. I had no way of knowing that she was in the vicinity, and it was just a coincidence that I was surveying the last of Netherfield's tenant houses and was in the area."

"That is correct!" Charles interjected, causing the two to glance his way. "Darcy set out alone early yesterday morning to survey the last of the structures, as I was too tired to accompany him after the ball."

William was far too weary to object to his friend's attempt to be helpful, so he ignored him and continued. "And the only cottage left to inspect was at the base of Oakham Mount, where the two properties meet. As I arrived in that area, the storm began in earnest, and my only thought was to find shelter. It was a miracle that I came across your daughter at all."

Mr. Bennet rubbed his chin uneasily. Perhaps the man had been telling the truth and was not the scoundrel that he had painted him when he arrived this morning with his favourite daughter in tow. Learning that the bridge was now passable, he had just sent a servant to saddle his horse when he had found himself squinting at the shape of two riders barely visible in the distance, against the backdrop of the breaking dawn. And by the time they entered the drive to Longbourn, he knew that it was Mr. Bingley and Mr. Darcy and that each carried something on his horse.

He stood as if in a trance until he could make out that Bingley transported Elizabeth's small white goat and that Mr. Darcy held his daughter. Moreover, whereas Bingley looked rested and well dressed, he noted that Darcy hardly looked like the man he had met at the ball. He was unshaven, his hair uncombed and his clothes dishevelled. Elizabeth's appearance was equally disturbing. That observation and the fact that she was feverish combined to push his temper to the edge of reason. Consequently, he had not expressed gratitude towards Elizabeth's rescuer, but instead, had fired accusations at him the minute they entered the privacy of his library.

Now as he studied Darcy anew, Mr. Bennet had to admit that having been up all night fretting about Elizabeth and trying to calm his wife might have rendered him swift to judge. However, he was not of a mind to admit that to Mr. Darcy just yet.

"So you contend that you followed some wild dogs, who were chasing the goat, and found Elizabeth stranded in the middle of a stream, trying to shield that kid from the pack?"

"Yes, sir."

"Hmmm." Mr. Bennet studied his desk top for a moment before challenging him again. "And you maintain that you were barely able to rescue her and the animal from the swollen waters." William's head nodded in agreement. "Then somehow you managed to find this tenant cottage in the middle of a driving rain, and you decided it was best if you both spent the night?"

"Yes, sir. Your daughter mentioned that the bridge was most likely underwater, and even had it not been, it would have been impossible to get there during the downpour that followed."

"I would imagine she was soaking wet. How did you manage to keep her warm?"

"I started a fire with the scant firewood left near the hearth and broke up a few old chairs to add to it. There was a horse blanket in the barn that I spread over an old straw mattress. Then I wrapped her in both my coats."

The way the man stared, William was unsure whether Elizabeth's father was impressed with his ingenuity or still very irritated with him. Finally he spoke.

"I suppose you know that Mrs. Bennet is already demanding that you marry Elizabeth?"

Bingley turned to stare at his friend. Noticing his friend's wide eyes and shocked expression, William addressed him. "I will deal with this, Charles."

Mr. Bennet studied both men, wondering what in the world they were speaking of and was totally unprepared for what William said next.

"Were it possible, I would gladly marry your daughter, but I am afraid that circumstances prevent me from doing so. However, Bingley and I have discussed the situation and feel there is no need for alarm. No one at Netherfield knows I was out all night, thanks to Charles' quick thinking. He tries never to let his sisters know anything that may promote gossip, especially about me. Thus, he informed the servants this morning that he had admitted me to the house late last night and that I would be in my room all day and was not to be disturbed. His sisters are to be informed of the same tale once they awaken.

"I was readying to bring Miss Elizabeth home when Charles found us, and we made quick work of getting here. You have apparently not had time to let anyone know that your daughter was missing, thus only you and your family are aware of the impropriety. Therefore, if you tell no one and your servants are trustworthy, there will be no scandal. I shall follow Charles back to Netherfield, where he will assist me in slipping into the house via a back stairwell and then into my room. There will be no compromise and no need to marry."

Elizabeth's father considered all that William had said before responding. "This plan just might work. I trust my servants explicitly—they love my Lizzy and would do nothing to harm her. I will have to make sure that my wife does not ruin it with her loose tongue, however. Now, would you kindly answer one question for me?"

William's jaw tightened and he grimaced, knowing what was to come.

"You have stated that you would gladly marry Elizabeth if you could. I assume from the way that you observed her at the ball and from your pronouncement, that you are fond of her." He waited but William's only response was to study his shoes. "Might I ask why it is not possible for you to marry her?"

"I am already married."

Mr. Bennet came to his feet, his face now crimson with anger. "You ... you are married! You have apparently pursued my daughter the whole time you have been in Meryton, first at the bookshop and then at the ball, and you are already married?"

William stood now, his voice rising. "I never pursued Eliz ... Miss Elizabeth!"

Bingley jumped to his feet interjecting, "This is ridiculous! I know Darcy well enough to know he would never dishonour your daughter, or any other woman for that matter, nor would he knowingly raise their expectations. Frankly, sir, you have no idea what this man has had to endure in the past two years."

The older man's glare swung between Bingley and William. "Then I suppose one of you should enlighten me, as we shall not leave this library until you do! As her father, I see things a great deal differently than the two of you, and I demand an explanation this instant!"

"I am not in the habit of discussing my private concerns," William answered, his voice eerily flat.

Bingley interrupted impatiently, "This is not the time to be restrained, Darcy. He thinks you are a cad of the worst kind! At least tell him that you have never lived with that woman, that she is your wife in name only!"

With Charles' disclosure, Mr. Bennet sat back down, his anger diminishing a bit as he studied the obviously uneasy young man before him. "I pride myself on being able to sketch a man's character, and from our first meeting, I believed you to be a gentleman. If there is any explanation for your behaviour, I am ready to listen to it now."

William sat down wearily, dropped his head in his hands and rubbed his eyes. He was not used to sharing his personal affairs with anyone, certainly not a perfect stranger. Nevertheless, he admired Mr. Bennet's determination to protect his daughter, just as he had always tried to protect Georgiana. They were kindred spirits in that regard and it pained him that Mr. Bennet might think him less than honourable in his intentions towards Elizabeth. Having resolved the issue in his heart, he lifted his head. "I will tell you the situation regarding my marriage, if you will swear never to reveal a word of it to anyone. You have to understand that this is very difficult for me, as I love my parents, flawed though they were."

"You have my word as a gentleman."

Swallowing the lump in his throat, William began. "A little over two years ago, before my father died, I was in London with him. One afternoon while I was at my club, I received a summons to an unfamiliar address, ostensibly to assist my father. When I arrived at this townhouse, I found him being treated by a physician for a sudden heart ailment. The house belonged to a widow, Lady Gisela Grantham, with whom I *was* familiar. I met her about six months before at a dinner party, where she was brazen enough to follow me onto a balcony and suggest we have an affair. I refused but she would not take no for an answer. She began to appear wherever I happened to be—dinner parties, the opera, even Hyde Park—and repeated her offer. That was when I realised that I had to be blunt. I told her plainly that I could never be interested in someone like her, and she was the last woman in the world I would bed. Apparently, she had decided to retaliate against me by seducing my father. I had him transported to our townhouse as soon as it was feasible, and when he was able to travel, I took him home to our estate, Pemberley, in Derbyshire.

"A little over a month later, this woman had the audacity to come to Pemberley. Luckily, I was able to intercept her and direct her into the study where she informed me that she was carrying my father's child. She demanded that I marry her or she would see to it that my mother learned of the paternity of the child. At that time, my mother was in very ill health and would likely not have survived this revelation. I also had the welfare of a twelve-year-old sister to consider. After discussing the matter with my father, I was told that the child could indeed be his. Thus, I felt I was left with no choice but to purchase her silence with marriage, howbeit a marriage in name only.

"Three months after the marriage, my father's weakened heart failed and he died, and my mother expired shortly thereafter. By then it was obvious that Gisela was not with child, so I instructed my solicitor to begin drawing up the documents to annul the marriage. That was when she produced a letter written by my mother that would seal my fate."

William stood quickly, moving to the windows to stare out into the gardens as he continued. "I was shown only an excerpt, but I recognised her handwriting. How Gisela could have come into possession of it is a mystery." He hesitated, his voice barely discernable. "Nothing that I will relate to you now can change the fact that my mother was the most gentle, kind and godly person I have ever known. She put her family's needs above her own, and I will always revere her memory." Looking over his shoulder, he saw Mr. Bennet nod so he continued.

"Before my father's death, he spoke to me of his relationship with my mother, including the miscarriages she had suffered. He credited his fear that she would perish if she had another child as the impetus for his liaisons with other women, although I refuted that justification. In any event, he said that because of his seeming abandonment of her, my mother had sought solace with another man—an old friend that he refused to name and who fathered Georgiana. Apparently the letter Gisela acquired names my sister's father, and she swears that if I attempt to sever the marriage, she will make this information public."

William turned, his voice rising as he walked towards Mr. Bennet. "My parents' deaths were a cruel blow from which Georgiana is just now recovering. As her sole guardian, I refuse to let anything else destroy her."

"So you have no relationship with this woman—your *wife*?"

"Our arrangement specifies that she live at her own residences, an estate in Derbyshire and a townhouse in London that she inherited from her late husband, Lord Grantham. It stipulates that there will be no children from our marriage. I, in turn, pay all expenses for the residences and give her an allowance. She has my name, not my respect or my love."

"And now? Surely you want a son to inherit Pemberley?"

"Georgiana and her children are allowed to inherit Pemberley. That is how it has always been."

The older man studied William intently. "It seems you have taken upon yourself burdens that were not yours to bear, all in order to protect your family. I can respect you for that, but I do not feel you were entirely honest with my daughter or me. Why were you silent regarding your marriage when you arrived in Meryton?"

William stared wistfully at the sun now rising over the horizon. "The question never arose, but had it, I would not have lied." He turned to face his accuser. "From the moment I met your daughter, I was captivated by her intelligence and unaffected manner. Against my better judgement, I convinced myself that we could be friends. Yet, when you and I talked at the ball, it was obvious that you had already recognized deeper feelings—feelings I had not acknowledged. And I knew that if you had discerned my admiration, then she most likely had or would. Rather than hurt her, I determined that I must leave Meryton immediately. That was the purpose of my being out so late yesterday—to finish the survey."

"Oddly, I believe you."

"I am gratified that you do, for it is the truth."

"And you do not want Elizabeth or anyone else to know what you have told me."

William blinked several times, trying to control his widely swinging emotions. "Above all, I do not want *her* to know."

"May I ask why?"

William grew solemn. "I believe that she may harbour feelings of … gratitude for my help last night. And because she is so very young, she may mistake those feelings for more. I have found her to be very kind, and if she knew the truth about my situation, she would likely pity me—want to befriend me."

"She may never suspect you are married. No mention of it was made at the ball, and as far as I know, it has not been made public. Even my wife, who knows all the gossip, believes you are single."

"Bingley and his family are most likely the only ones in Meryton who know, though my marriage and the circumstances surrounding it are well-documented in the gossip sheets of London. However, like the rest of the *ton*, Caroline Bingley prefers to think that I am available, and she perpetrates the lie that I am hers for the taking—thus people believe I am single. Apparently she is under the delusion that I shall eventually be free, and she will be my choice."

Charles groaned audibly and shook his head.

"I apologise, Charles."

"It is the truth, Darcy. Much as I hate to admit it, Caroline is just that foolish."

"In any event, she will not spread that fact here, nor will Louisa, so hopefully there will be no need to inform Elizabeth of my *unusual* marriage."

"You were leaving before this unfortunate incident. Is that still your plan?"

"Yes. I believe that Miss Elizabeth will consider us, at the least, good friends after the ordeal we shared last evening, but it would best serve her interests if she does not. Therefore, I shall leave straightaway."

Mr. Bennet nodded. "I have to say that I am impressed with your concern for my Elizabeth. I am relieved to know that I was not wrong—I did sketch your character correctly the first time. I ask you to accept my heartfelt thanks for rescuing her. You likely saved her life."

"There is no reason to thank me for doing what any man would. And please accept my apology, as it was foolish of me to think we could be friends. After getting to know Miss Elizabeth better, I realise that I would never have been satisfied with so little."

"I believe your foolishness lies in thinking you can instruct your heart whom to love."

"You may be right."

"At some point you will know for certain that I am."

⟡

Chapter 5

Netherfield
The next day

It was early morning, but William's coach was packed and ready to leave. Four footmen and the driver, in their finest livery, stood at attention in the morning mist beside the imposing coach. Matching sets of greys pawed the ground in anticipation of beginning the journey, occasionally shaking their heads and snorting, their breath visible in the chilly morning air. Mr. Foster, William's driver, surreptitiously kept his eyes trained on the portico where the master stood talking with Mr. Bingley.

On the portico, Charles had closed the door as he exited so that the butler and footman just inside could not hear. He tried not to smile as he teased, "By the way, I have to ask. Caroline told me last night that she wants to return to London straightaway so I told her to pack her bags. Would you mind letting her and her maid ride back to London with you?"

William tensed, readying a sharp reply before catching the gleam in Bingley's eye and beginning to smile. "Thank you, Charles. I needed that to brighten my spirits."

Slowly the smile was replaced with a look of remorse. "I feel absolutely horrid for leaving without saying goodbye to Miss Elizabeth. If I have caused her any pain …" Ceasing as his voice cracked, William managed to murmur roughly, "I have never felt this much for any woman, Charles."

Bingley placed a hand on his friend's arm. "I admire your courage and resolve, Darcy. I am not sure that I could sacrifice as you have, even to protect my family."

William's next words were barely above a whisper. "See that she is taken care of—for me."

"You have my word."

William smiled wanly as he turned and began to walk briskly down the steps, Charles sighed. *I pray the future holds more happiness for you than the past, my friend.*

"Mount up!" Mr. Foster called, and in seconds all the men were in place except for Jones, who held the door for his master. By the time William was settled in the seat, the crack of a whip stirred the horses. As he leaned out the window to wave to Charles, William caught a glimpse of Caroline standing in the doorway of a small balcony on the second floor. It appeared that she was clad only in her night clothes, and he pretended he had not seen her. Settling back into the comfortable cushions of his conveyance, William closed his eyes while his mind swirled, revisiting the conversation he had had with Charles in the library late the night before.

"I hate that you are leaving so soon, Darcy. I feel that it is my fault for allowing Caroline to barge in on us," Charles handed William a glass of brandy and watched him walk to the hearth and study the flames. "While I dearly hate Caroline's manoeuvrings, you know I must leave Meryton because of my stupidity. I should never have tried to pursue a friendship with Miss Elizabeth. I knew it would never work, but I let my heart overrule my reason."

"You are just a man, Darcy. Try not to be too hard on yourself."

"I am old enough to know better. Eliz ... Miss Elizabeth is very young and impressionable, and the thought that I may have caused her pain will lie heavy on my conscience. If her heart was touched, as was mine, leaving without saying goodbye will cause her to despise me and rightly so."

"I was heartened at Mr. Bennet's acceptance of your personal physician's assistance, as it appears he believed your account of the incident and has forgiven you."

William chuckled mirthlessly, never turning. "Yes, he was definitely kinder when we left Longbourn than when we arrived. As for Mr. Meacham, I was not about to let the local apothecary attend Miss Elizabeth." He looked over his shoulder at Bingley. "Are you sure that you do not mind that he will be staying at Netherfield? He should arrive late this evening or in the morning."

"Of course not! I am pleased to have him under my roof."

"It is just as well that I received the post from the retired solicitor Mr. Barton hired, requesting my presence in London. Unfortunately, Mr. Lowell has a habit of not explaining anything in his letters, which leaves me conjuring up the worst possible outcome. I do not expect the man to talk of particulars, but he could at least say whether things are going well with his investigation of the joint venture."

"I pray Lowell's news is nothing dreadful, as you have had your fair share of misery. I am still awaiting word from the investigator Barton recommended to look into the ship lost with all my goods aboard. One cannot run a successful mercantile without goods, and the stock in my warehouse in Liverpool is getting sparse, what with the loss. If you would, ask Mr. Barton if he has heard from Mr. Carter."

"I will certainly do that, and my offer of a loan to replace the loss at sea still stands."

Charles walked over to pat William's shoulder. "As we discussed, I have no need for it at this time, but I appreciate the gesture."

William nodded, continuing, "In any event, I got a letter from my Aunt Audrey right before I left London. She will be bringing Georgiana back to Town in another week or so, so I would have returned then in any event."

"At least you can be thankful for your aunt, as she seems to have your best interest at heart. From what you have said, she has been most helpful with Georgiana."

"Yes, she has been a godsend since Mother died. I do not know what I would have done without her."

"She is your mother's youngest sister and is childless, is she not?"

"Yes. She is but five and forty. Her husband died years ago and she never remarried. When Mother died, she moved into Pemberley, putting herself at my disposal to help with Georgiana. She and Georgiana have been in Bath. Naturally I would like to see her while she is in Town, and I know that they are planning another trip to Ramsgate to allow Georgiana to study with the masters."

"I am happy that you do not have to worry for Georgiana. You will let me know if there is a problem after you consult with Lowell. I may not be able to do anything, but I will help however I can. I have some dealings with the mills, you know."

William reached to shake his hand. *"I will certainly keep that in mind. Do not forget your promise. Write me every day with news of how Miss Elizabeth is faring. I want Meacham to concentrate on taking care of her, and I trust you to contact me if she needs anything."*

"Every day, I promise."

"I shall be in London unless I advise you that I have left for Pemberley, so that your correspondence may follow me."

"Go and attend to what you must, my friend. I shall keep you abreast of the news here."

Charles was hesitant but could hold back no longer as William stood and set his empty glass on a table as if preparing to retire. *"Darcy, may I ask your opinion on something?"*

"Certainly."

"We have not had time to discuss this, what with your being stranded in the storm, but what do you think of Miss Bennet? I find myself growing quite fond of her." At William's cynical expression, he quickly added, *"I know, I know. I have often thought myself in love in the past, but I promise that I will take my time and do nothing in haste. I am considering extending my lease on Netherfield just for the purpose of getting to know her properly."*

William considered Charles, noting the eagerness in his eyes and remembering his own desires to know Miss Elizabeth. How he wished he had the right to stay in Meryton and further their acquaintance! Carefully he chose his words, not wishing his own misery to colour his counsel. After all, Charles was like a brother to him.

"You know my advice—proceed slowly, know your mind. Keep your relationship strictly as friends. Stay if you feel you must, but make no decisions without consulting me. Promise me that we will talk before you progress beyond friendship."

"You have my solemn promise," Charles replied eagerly, his face aglow with happiness as he feigned a salute. *"No decision without talking to you."*

"Then I have no objections to your staying or extending the lease, though I would suggest you extend it by only a few months at a time. That way you can vacate the property in short order if circumstances change."

Afterward each man retired for the night as William was determined to leave at the break of dawn.

As the Darcy coach made its way through Meryton on the way back to London, William instructed the driver to stop at the bookshop. With the book he had intended to give Elizabeth in his coat pocket, he stepped into the quaint shop. The now familiar ring of the bell over the door brought Mr. Grant's head around the end of a bookshelf.

"Mr. Darcy! How good to see you again! I am just dusting the shelves. Are you here to find another book?"

"No, sir, I am away to London sooner than I expected, and I need to ask a favour of you."

The gentlemen came forward hastily, brushing his hands against the apron that he wore. "Certainly! How may I be of service?"

William pulled the book of poetry from an inside pocket of his coat. "As you may remember, I purchased this book that Miss Elizabeth Bennet was admiring, intending to present it to her for her valuable help the other day."

"Yes, I remember." Mr. Grant tried not to smile.

"But as I have to leave Meryton forthwith, I have not had the opportunity to give it to her. Would you be kind enough to have it delivered to her home? And, if I may be so bold to ask, would you let her assume that you are gifting her with the tome, perhaps for her assistance the other day? She was very helpful to this newcomer."

The proprietor smiled. "I would be happy to do so. And as for your being a newcomer, perhaps you are to my humble shop, but certainly not to the world of literature! I was not eavesdropping, you understand, but this is a small shop and voices carry, and from what little I heard of your discussion, your knowledge of the best authors and works is equal to Elizabeth's."

William smiled at the recollection of her crooked grin. "I am most proud to be mentioned alongside such an august reader."

With his business finished, William looked about the small establishment, fixing it in his mind. This was where he had first seen Elizabeth, and it would always have a special place in his heart. Taking a deep breath, he turned to leave.

"Oh, Mr. Darcy!" William looked over his shoulder. "I am sure that Miss Elizabeth will appreciate the gift, but is unfortunate that she will never know the true benefactor."

"I believe that she will know … in her heart."

With those words the door closed behind the tall gentleman, and Mr. Grant walked to the front window to watch as he entered an imposing coach. Directly, it pulled away and in a few moments was out of sight. Shaking his head, the shopkeeper turned back to his duties.

Longbourn
Two days later

Mr. Bennet raked the back of his weathered hand across Elizabeth's cheek and was pleased to see her eyes open. It had been two long days since Mr. Darcy had returned her in the early morning hours, and one day since the physician that Darcy had insisted on summoning from London had arrived in Meryton.

He was duly impressed with Mr. Meacham, as he had stayed with his daughter all night until the fever broke and she was greatly improved. Then, after declaring that it would be days before she would recover her strength or that he would allow her out of bed, he had returned to Netherfield to rest. Leaving instructions to send for him if they deemed it necessary, he promised to return in the morning to check on his charge.

"Papa?"

"Yes, child?"

"Why do I feel so weak?"

"You were ill after being caught in the rain and trying to ford the stream with that blasted goat!" Mr. Bennet could not but smile as Elizabeth's eyes widened and then crinkled to see that he was teasing.

She sounded very weak as she enquired, "How is Juliet?"

"Juliet is doing better than you, my dear. Though, I fear she will reside in a pen from now on. I do not intend for her to escape another time, as her rescuer is not in any shape to save her again."

Immediately, Elizabeth pictured an exceptionally tall man with black curly hair, and dark brows and eyelashes which framed sky-blue eyes. His nose was noble and straight and his lips were perfectly formed. And if she closed her eyes, she could once more hear him chiding her as she lay on the makeshift bed.

Miss Elizabeth, you could have been killed trying to rescue that kid. That was very foolish on your part; you do know that. And I may not be here to rescue you the next time.

Trying not to appear hopeful, she enquired, "I hope you were not angry at Mr. Darcy for my foolishness. Had he not intervened, I might not be here now."

"I did not challenge him, if that is what you are asking." Elizabeth tried to smile. "After I calmed down and heard him out, I expressed my deepest appreciation for his assistance to you and for keeping the whole ordeal from being known. Outside our family, only he and Bingley are aware of what happened. I have sworn your mother to silence and Mary, Kitty and Lydia know nothing. Jane figured it out when I brought you upstairs that morning, but the other girls were still sleeping. When they awoke, I told them that you were sick after getting soaked searching for Juliet."

"Has he come to call?"

"Mr. Darcy?" At her nod, he continued. "I understand that he has returned to London."

"He did not even say goodbye," she murmured forlornly.

"Mr. Bingley informed me that Mr. Darcy received a post that bade him return immediately to London. It must be a heavy burden indeed to be so wealthy and have so many lives dependent upon you."

Her reply was barely audible. "I am sure."

Mr. Bennet must have comprehended his child's disappointment, for she sank further into the pillow and turned her face away. He offered, "Would you like to open the package that Mr. Grant brought today? He said it was a book you admired, and he wished you to have it since you were ill and confined to bed. I thought I would read a bit to you, if you wish."

Even the prospect of a new book could not raise her spirits. "I believe I would like to sleep now, if you do not mind."

"Of course, child, sleep will do you good. I shall leave you with Jane. She has been asking to sit with you. All of us have been worried, but you know that of all your sisters, Jane has suffered the loss of your companionship the most."

Elizabeth nodded, closing her eyes as though to sleep. It was hard holding back the tears that threatened until he was out of sight. Mr. Bennet leaned in to kiss her forehead, and then rose from his place on the side of the bed. He stopped in the doorway to take one last look and then quit the room.

Elizabeth took a deep breath, willing the hot tears that filled her eyes not to spill, but they would not cooperate. Instead, they quickly made trails down her cheeks to the pillow below. Despite the tenderness Mr. Darcy had shown her during their ordeal, his heart had evidently not been touched as had hers. And all the gestures she had taken as evidence of his affection clearly meant nothing to him. *Else how could he have left Meryton without so much as a word?*

Elizabeth felt that her heart would break. *Silly, foolish girl!* She chided herself. *You made the choice to care for this man against your better judgement and have learned a hard lesson!*

With the backs of her hands, she began to wipe the tears from her face, but was unsuccessful in removing them entirely before Jane entered the room. Seeing her sister's distress, Jane immediately ran to her. "Lizzy, please do not cry! You will feel better soon! Mr. Meacham has assured us that you will be out of bed in only a few days."

"That is not the source of my misery."

"Then why are you upset, dearest?"

"Promise to tell no one, as I could not abide it if the rest of our family should learn of my folly."

"Whatever you share shall be between us, as always."

So, Elizabeth confessed everything about her friendship with Mr. Darcy— from the moment she met him in the bookstore until the morning he brought her home on his horse. And for a long time after she finished speaking, Jane sat in stunned silence. Finally, taking her sister's hand, Jane squeezed it, forcing a smile.

"I am pleased that you felt you could tell me of your heartache, and I apologise that I was too involved with my own concerns to see that you needed me."

"You assume too much, dear sweet Jane. You are not to blame."

"But, I never realised that you were gone! Papa made us go to bed very early that evening. He dressed in his greatcoat and said that he was going to fetch you and Juliet. It was the next morning before I awoke to find him bringing you into our bedroom. He explained to me what happened, though he told Mary, Kitty and Lydia only that you had gotten sick from being soaked chasing after Juliet. They do not know you were out all night."

"You could not have known of my dilemma, as Papa was protecting me. And you knew nothing of my friendship with Mr. Darcy because I kept it secret." She did not meet Jane's loving gaze.

"I was aware that it was a hopeless situation—that such a man could never care for me, but I misinterpreted his kindness for interest because ..." she took a ragged breath, "because, I fell in love with him the first time we met. It was my lack of prudence that has left my heart broken."

"What will you do if you are ever in his company again? After all, Mr. Darcy is Mr. Bingley's best friend and may very well visit him another time."

"I will just have to avoid his company. But I swear to you that I will never allow my heart to break again. I knew it would be entirely foreign for a man of his stature to consider someone like me." She laughed mirthlessly. "I have no dowry, no connections—nothing to recommend me."

"That is not true! You are lovely and you have a brilliant intellect. Surely, some good man—"

"And you know what Mama says," Elizabeth interrupted, "No man could be interested in a woman who reads too much and has an opinion on everything!"

"Mama cannot speak for every man."

"Nevertheless, apparently she was right. He left without saying goodbye."

<hr />

Rosings
The drawing room
One week later

Lady Catherine de Bourgh looked every inch the imperious matron as she sat in her large, throne-like chair studying the two people she had summoned to Rosings. As she took the measure of the man and woman perched on settees on either side of her, she pondered why she had ever considered them capable of carrying out her plans.

Gisela, tall and regal, and beautiful beyond description with her dark blond hair and emerald green eyes, should have been the answer to her prayers. What man could resist her charms? Only the one man she had hoped to control— Fitzwilliam Darcy. And George Wickham, while a handsome rogue, had proved equally useless after he was tossed from Pemberley. Both had cost her a good deal of money in the past and presently disappointed her greatly. Nonetheless, knowing that it was too late to change her plans, she took a deep breath to calm her nerves.

"You can be at no loss to understand why I have summoned you."

Gisela Darcy, her eyes flashing with ire, glanced across to George Wickham before returning her gaze to her ladyship. "I cannot account for the honour at all. I was supposed to attend a ball in London tonight. Instead, I was practically kidnapped by your lackey here. What gives you the right to order me to Rosings without my consent?"

"Money gives me the right, my dear! If you will remember, I gave you five thousand pounds upon your marriage to my nephew to insure that you voted with me in regards to our joint ventures and to try to influence him to see my point of view. Now, I learn from my solicitor that you did not have the decency to sign the latest papers, seconding my decisions on the future monies to be spent. You are well aware that my nephew thwarts my every move, and without your vote, I am stymied! At least your father and George Darcy had sense enough to allow *me* to control the funds without their interference. It is only after both of them died that I have had to struggle—first with my nephew and now with you."

"My father was your pawn, and George Darcy was too interested in his next affair to worry about his finances! Neither of them cared enough to disagree with you, whereas I have my own opinions. Besides, I was trying to do what you ordered me to do—secure my husband's esteem. I have held off voting, hoping that he would seek me out on the matter. I intended to use my vote to secure his approval!"

"This is not the way I intended for you to secure his approval. You were supposed to do that in his bed! I have it on good authority that Fitzwilliam is questioning the entire stock venture at this point. I relied on your marriage to keep him occupied, and if you had had a child, we would not even be speaking of this now. You would have secured your place as a Darcy!"

"Is it my fault that Mr. Wickham could not accomplish that simple task?"

George rose to his feet, "I assure you, madam, that I have left women with bastards all over England. I would point out that I have firsthand knowledge that you have been with a number of men, even while you were married to Lord Grantham, and you have never been with child. Perhaps you should look in the mirror for the problem!"

Lady Catherine stood to stop the argument. "Enough! If you were going to have a child, you would have done so by now. You are likely barren, which leads me to believe that Fitzwilliam will divorce you once he feels that Georgiana is old enough to hear the truth." She seemed deep in thought. "I suppose I should look for someone to be his next wife!"

Gisela glared at the woman. "That is preposterous! He is so protective of his *precious* sister that he will never tell her. She is not capable of dealing with that kind of disclosure, as I have stressed to Fitzwilliam often enough."

Wickham jumped into the fray. "Darcy is a pansy! I agree that he will never knowingly tell Georgiana, but I have an idea of how to control him, even should the secret be revealed."

"Go on!" Lady Catherine commanded. "I have put enough pounds into your pockets, it is about time you used your brain!"

Wickham glared at the harridan who had begun to buy his loyalty at the tender age of fifteen in exchange for privileged information on the Darcys. If his plan worked, he would get control of a goodly portion of Darcy's money and never have to deal with her again. "I think it is time little Miss Darcy married, and who better for her to marry than me?"

"La!" Gisela laughed. "As if Fitzwilliam Darcy would let his little sister wed a degenerate like you!"

"He married you, did he not?" Wickham sneered. "And I do not propose to ask for his sister's hand. I propose to elope with her, after I gain her confidence. Though I have not been allowed at Pemberley since George Darcy died, she would remember me, as I used to entertain her to impress the old man. He was a dupe for all my schemes. I happen to know that at this time of year she spends weeks in Ramsgate taking art lessons with the *so-called* masters who congregate in that area. I can take steps to renew our friendship there."

Lady Catherine listened intently as he expounded on his plan, continuing to study him long after he had finished. He was beginning to think she was not going to agree when she responded, "It is worth a try. But if my nephew learns of your plans before you accomplish this elopement, God help you! In fact, he may just kill you in any event."

"He would never kill Georgiana's beloved husband! And, besides, I am not afraid of Darcy."

"You should be! He is zealous in protecting my niece."

Gisela interjected, "But she is always accompanied by your sister. It would be hard to talk to her alone."

Lady Catherine considered her younger sister. "Yes, Audrey has been a thorn in my side since she was old enough to talk—always tattling to our father. I loathe that woman!"

Wickham brought the conversation back to his plan. "I have been very busy studying Audrey Ashcroft. I know that she leaves Georgiana alone while she takes the lessons, visiting with her friends in the area until it is time to retrieve her. And I have confidential information that the artist they have chosen this time, a Mrs. Younge, is the sole support of her mother and sister. They live very frugally, and with enough incentive, I believe I could use her for my purposes. Naturally, I would have to travel to Ramsgate and ply her with my attention, so by the time Miss Darcy visits again, I will be a well established visitor to her studio. But alas, as you ladies well know, I do not have the funds to accomplish this. You would have to provide the resources, while I provide the charm."

"Is that not how it has always been?" Lady Catherine scowled. "Very well. You must appear every inch the gentleman."

"I AM a gentleman, thanks to George Darcy, though the old fool forgot to provide the means for me to live as one after his death!"

Darcy's aunt harrumphed. "What of the living he left you at Kympton? We are all aware that you refused to take orders and asked my nephew for the value of the living—three thousand pounds—and immediately gambled it away."

"Three thousand pounds is a pittance compared to what Fitzwilliam Darcy earns in a year's time!"

"But he is a Darcy and you are not," Gisela reminded her nemesis.

"And if the truth be known, neither are you! You may be Mrs. Darcy, but you have none of his regard or any of the prestige associated with the name! How does it feel to walk into a soirée knowing that everyone there is aware that Fitzwilliam Darcy dropped you off at your townhouse on your wedding day, never to darken your door again?"

Gisela seethed, moving to stand within a few inches of Wickham's face. "And how does it feel to know that he will never allow you at Pemberley ever again!"

Lady Catherine stood and moved between them. "If you continue to fight one another, I cannot control my nephew, and I WANT to control him! Now, are we agreed?" She glared at Gisela first. "*You* will sign the papers that I shall have my solicitor bring to your townhouse as soon as you return to London. And *you*," she turned to Wickham, "will go to Ramsgate."

Gisela and Wickham glared at each other, too angry to speak. Lady Catherine addressed Gisela. "I will have my housekeeper show you to one of the guest rooms." Then she turned to Wickham. "You cannot be seen here. I shall have Mr. Crump show you the rear exit which leads to the stables. There is a groom's room that is empty, and you shall have the use of it until I can arrange for the funds. The sooner we have something to hold over my nephew the better!"

With that, the harridan stomped out of the room, her cane striking the floor with every step. She shouted for her servants as soon as she gained the doorway and could be heard calling out orders as she got further away. Alone now, Gisela

Darcy and George Wickham studied each other for a moment before slipping to the doorway to watch *her majesty* disappear down the long corridor.

"It seems she believed our ruse," Gisela stated wryly. "She thinks we hate each other."

"I told you she would! I have known the old shrew for a lot longer than you, and it is better that she believes we are at odds. She does not trust anyone, and I have no doubt that she would have us watched if she thought we might be conspiring."

"But we are not conspiring against her … at least not yet."

"No, but the time shall come when we will have to make a choice between our interests and hers. I care not for what Lady Catherine de Bourgh wants unless it benefits me."

"Nor I! She had the gall to mention finding Fitzwilliam's next wife!"

Wickham motioned for her to be quieter. "Pay her no mind. I shall make Georgiana Darcy fall madly in love with me, and she will be only too happy to elope. Afterwards, when Darcy makes a scene, you shall step into the fray to support her right to choose the husband that she desires. That should sway Georgiana's good opinion towards you. Then we shall control a goodly portion of the Darcy money and influence. And who can predict when Fitzwilliam might die and leave us in charge of everything?"

"And how do I know that you will not betray me?"

"You have the backing of the Matlocks—at least they pretend to accept you in the eyes of society. Why should I alienate you? I wish to be acknowledged as a gentleman, and as Georgiana Darcy's husband, I shall be taken more seriously with the Matlocks approval. Together we have a much better chance of success."

Gisela seemed to contemplate that thought and then nodded. "We should withdraw and go our separate ways before she notices."

With that, they exited the room, heading in different directions, each still distrustful of the other, as thieves and liars are wont to be.

Chapter 6

London
Darcy House
Three weeks after Hertfordshire

*T*he wind howled and whipped the driving rain about violently as tree limbs
fell intermittently on each side of the well-worn path. Airborne debris flew
across William's path, sometimes striking him and his mount. Even the
lightning, relentless and frightening, seemed to target him, striking several places
nearby and causing his horse to rear in protest at being urged forward.

"Steady! Steady, boy!" William soothed the frightened beast, patting the
animal's strong neck as he leaned over its head to keep the driving rain from
hitting him square in the face. Just then, above the howl of the wind, came the
sound of a voice—a woman's voice.

"Fitzwilliam!"

Pulling back on the reins, his head whipped right then left in a desperate
attempt to determine from which side the sound had come. Even so, after only a
few seconds, he sighed in frustration. It was impossible to discern one sound from
another amidst the clatter of the storm. Had he actually heard it at all?

Suddenly he heard it again over the din. "Fitzwilliam! Help me!"

Somehow he was transported to the same swollen creek where he had found
Elizabeth and her pet clinging to a log, his alarm growing as he watched the
water begin to flow over the top.

"Elizabeth! Hold on, sweetheart! I will save you! Do not let go!"

But unlike what had happened in reality, when Elizabeth tore her eyes from
the raging water to acknowledge him, instead of the look of panic that had been
there in actuality, there was a look of extreme sadness. It was obvious that she
had been crying, and when she spoke, it broke his heart.

"You led me to believe that you cared!"

Immediately a great wall of water surged over the tree, washing her and the
small white goat from the log and he watched helplessly as she disappeared
beneath the water.

"ELIZABETH!"

William bolted upright in bed, his arms flailing and heart pounding as though
it would burst from his chest. As he tried to get his bearings, the familiarity of his

surroundings sunk into his consciousness, and he began to settle once more, examining the chaos about him. The counterpane was dishevelled, the sheets wadded into unrecognisable piles and most of the pillows were on the floor. Sweating profusely and in great misery, William had been completely unaware that he had rolled from one side of his large, four-poster bed to the other. His nightshirt was soaked with perspiration, so he slid out of bed and pulled it over his head. Tossing it aside, he grabbed a dry one along with his robe from the large closet. Then donning the clean garments, he moved to sit on the settee in front of the waning fire.

Each night since his return from Netherfield, he had been transported back to that scene in his dreams—a cycle he could neither avert nor control. And with each reliving of the incident, he searched for Elizabeth anew. Tonight was no different. Taking several deep breaths to try and calm his still racing heart, he closed his eyes and whispered her name as though it was a prayer. *Elizabeth.*

Though they were only dreams, the very real likelihood that she had been hurt by his actions caused a familiar dull ache to begin deep inside—an ache that occurred with the mere thought of her. Now fully awake, William searched for his slippers and finding them headed towards his study for a full bottle of brandy. In the days since his return from Meryton, he had come to depend on the amber liquor for some relief from the night terrors and a few hours rest.

⌒⌒⌒

Darcy House
Three Days Later

Upon receiving a note from Mrs. Barnes, William's housekeeper, Richard Fitzwilliam set out for Darcy House almost immediately after his arrival in London. It was with a great deal of unease that he made this call, because her missive indicated that William was not in an amiable mood.

Blast! Richard mused wryly. *Darcy has not been in a good mood since he married that wretched woman two years ago.*

Nevertheless, according to the long time servant, his cousin's usual propensity to withdraw from society had apparently changed into living for the last few days in his study, taking his meals on a tray—what little he ate—as well as sleeping on the sofa. In fact, according to both Mr. and Mrs. Barnes, their master's attitude had deteriorated so dramatically with his return from Hertfordshire three weeks previously that they were at a loss to know what they should do. And with Miss Darcy's imminent return to London, they were very worried that he would remain in his present state. Thus, when they learned that Richard had returned to London, they sent word straightaway.

Now standing out front of the impressive, red brick facade of Darcy House, Richard did what he had always done—stopping to look up and admire the grandness of the full three stories. Spying the third floor balcony, he recalled the many times he and William had slipped up there as boys and tossed small pebbles onto the pavement in front of unsuspecting people. All had gone well until they had almost hit George Darcy's steward. He smiled at the memory of his uncle holding Darcy accountable for them both, the smile quickly fading at the recollection of the punishment his own father had inflicted when he was informed of the incident.

It is time! Taking a deep breath and he steeled himself and threw back his shoulders. *You have faced bigger foes than this. Best get to it!*

Taking the steps two at a time he was pounding on the beautifully carved entrance door in seconds. It was opened almost immediately by a footman who stepped out of sight as the butler and housekeeper came forward. Richard observed that the usually talkative couple were abnormally sombre. Mr. Barnes only nodded as he took his coat and hat, while Mrs. Barnes silently held out her ring of keys, the one to the study noticeably separate from the others.

"You say he has not been out of the study in three days?"

Mrs. Barnes eyes fell to her shoes. "No, sir. He has slept in the study on several occasions since he returned from Netherfield, but never for a number of nights in a row—until now. He barely eats, and he has had several bottles of brandy sent up from the cellar."

"Once I am in the study, bring us coffee—plenty of coffee."

She nodded as Richard took the key from her hand and headed towards the study, the housekeeper on his heels. After unlocking the door, he handed the keys back to Mrs. Barnes and motioned for her to leave, which she seemed eager to do. Slowly opening the door, he stuck his head in to ascertain exactly where William was in the large room. Finding his cousin in the chair behind his desk, feet propped upon the edge and eyes closed, he entered the room as noiselessly as possible.

Making his way to William, he noted an empty bottle of brandy on the edge of his desk, a half-empty bottle on the corner of the liquor cabinet and a full glass sitting in front of him. A few papers were stacked neatly on the corner of the large mahogany desk, as though he had not touched them in some time. As a rule, the entire top of his desk would be a miscellany of papers and folders, each piled upon the other, as well as numerous pens and ink. It did not take much evaluation to determine that William's primary goal of late had been drinking himself into oblivion.

"Am I interrupting anything, Darcy?" Richard asked loudly, dropping smoothly into the chair in front of his cousin.

William, who had indeed been dozing, startled at the sound of his cousin's voice. Promptly turning to put his feet down on the floor, he sat up straight, a pronounced frown on his unshaven face. Richard's impertinent smile instantly reminded him that he was not in the frame of mind to be amused.

"Would it matter if you were interrupting? And where are my servants? That door was supposed to be locked."

"To answer your questions—no, but I enjoy it so much more if I am interrupting —and I sent Mr. and Mrs. Barnes back to their duties. The door was locked, but I had Mrs. Barnes open it for me."

"So my servants answer to you, do they? I suppose then that you should be paying their salaries instead of me."

"Do not be angry because they are concerned for you, Darcy. It does not become you. Besides, if I had money for servants, I would gladly hire Mr. and Mrs. Barnes away from you!"

Ignoring his quip, William rubbed the stubble on his face, realising that his head was aching once again. "To what do I owe the pleasure of this visit?"

"Oh ho! Pleasure is it now? The last time I was here you berated me for keeping you from your business and lamented the fact that His Majesty's army could do very well without me for weeks at a time." Richard's lips curled into a smirk. "I have never felt so unloved and unwanted."

William picked a paper from the neat stack on his desk and pretended to read. "You do not have to stay and be humiliated. You may leave now."

"Very well, if I am only going to be insulted, it is time for you to confess. How has Gisela embarrassed you now? Made a spectacle with Lord Attenborough again? Fallen down drunk at Vauxhall Gardens? [3] Or perhaps she tried to enter your townhouse for the hundredth time, when you have strictly forbidden her to do so."

William just shook his head resignedly as he concentrated on whatever apparently fascinated him on the paper. Richard noted that his hand trembled slightly.

"It is a good thing that she is clearly barren, or she would have had some cad's bastard by now and tried to pass it off as yours."

William groaned, laying the paper down and ceasing all pretence of interest. Closing his eyes, he lifted the glass of brandy and ran it back and forth across his forehead as if to cool his brow. Studying William's haggard appearance, Richard said sympathetically, "I apologise, Darcy. I know that you believe you can do nothing about your situation at this time. It is just that I hate how that woman embarrasses you."

"Gisela's antics are not the source of my present misery, though she is part and parcel of all my despair."

"Then why do you not tell me what is bothering you? I may not be able to do anything but commiserate with you, but at least I can do that."

William downed the rest of the contents of his glass and stood to pour himself another drink just as there was a knock at the door. Before he could say anything, Richard opened the door to Mrs. Barnes, who held a tray with a pot of hot coffee and cups. He stood back to give her room to enter, and avoiding meeting her employer's eyes, the housekeeper set the tray on a nearby table, bobbed a curtsey and turned to leave.

"Mrs. Barnes?" Richard called. The elderly woman stopped and turned slowly.

"Darcy and I shall break our fast in the dining room as soon as you have food prepared."

A small smile played at the corners of the housekeeper's lips. "Very well, sir. I shall send word as soon as it is ready." With that, she bobbed again and vanished out the door.

Richard walked over to William and took the empty glass from his hands. "No more brandy, Cousin. It is time you sobered up and ate something besides biscuits."

Richard handed him a cup of black coffee, and he took a sip before taking it with him to the large floor-to-ceiling windows. For a long time, William stared

---

[3] *Vauxhall Gardens was the oldest of London's pleasure gardens. Its twelve acres, containing shrubbery, walks, statues and cascades, were located in Lambeth, south of the Thames from Westminster Abbey. (The Regency Encyclopedia)*

into the gardens while drinking the soothing liquid. Richard watched him in silence, noting that he was a good bit thinner than when last he had seen him.

"There are two things weighing heavily on my mind," William stated at last. Looking back to see Richard nod, he continued. "I hired a retired solicitor to investigate the joint venture that my father began years ago with Lewis de Bourgh and Jackson Montgomery—I think I told you about the stock in the mills." Richard nodded again. "With my father's death, I am now partnered in the enterprise with Lady Catherine and my *dear* wife, since I allowed her to keep all her assets when we married."

"I never understood your reasoning for doing that, especially in light of the fact that she inherited Lord Montgomery's vote."

"I did not want our lives joined in any aspect. Besides, Montgomery was her father, and he left it to her in trust. I wanted nothing that belonged to her, and she has nothing that belongs to me, except my name and an allowance to support her dissolute habits.

"In any event, the income from the venture has steeply declined these last two years. While that income is not paramount to my portfolio, the supplementary loans have grown significantly. I questioned extending loans to the mills for more equipment until we analysed each mill's viability, but of course, I was over-ruled, as Gisela always votes with Aunt Catherine. I am beginning to think that there is more to this than meets the eye, so at my solicitor's advice, I retained Mr. Lowell to investigate the finances. While I was in Meryton, he asked me to return to London for a conference. When we met, he asked my permission to expand the investigation to include visiting the mills to trace the expenditures for equipment."

"What will our aunt say when she learns of this? Or Gisela for that matter?"

"I care not what either one thinks. They have overruled all my objections, so I am under no obligation to inform them."

William held fast to his vigil at the window, his eyes searching the horizon as though somehow the answers he sought were out there. When the silence continued, Richard ventured, "And the other matter?"

William's shoulders visibly slumped, and with his free hand, he gripped the window frame as though it were necessary to keep him upright. His knuckles turned white with the effort. "I met someone."

No further explanation was necessary. Those words could only mean one thing—Darcy had fallen in love. This was a significant development, possibly disastrous, and Richard could not, would not, make light of it. All of his bravado disappeared and he stood mute as his cousin continued.

"She is entirely unlike any woman I have ever known. She is intelligent without being haughty, full of merriment without being ridiculous and refreshing as a spring rain in her innocence. And beautiful. So beautiful I can only compare her to a painting of a woman I saw on my tour of the Continent."

For a moment William seemed lost in thought, so Richard ventured, "Does this paragon have a name?"

"Elizabeth … Elizabeth Bennet."

"And she hails from Hertfordshire, I presume?" William nodded absently. "Knowing you, *Mr. Duty and Honour*, I am perplexed as to how you were able to form an acquaintance, given how attentively you avoid being in company with women."

Without turning, William began to recount how he had met Elizabeth in the bookstore and again at the ball. Then he explained how Providence had placed him in the role of her protector. Leaving out the finer details of their night spent together, he quickly moved on to his meeting with Mr. Bennet and the decision to leave Meryton straightaway.

A low whistle preceded Richard's reply. "I knew you would not raise her expectations cold-heartedly. And I will not ask what transpired during your stay in the cabin, as you have so studiously avoided telling me that part of your story, but it is obvious that you have strong feelings for her."

William's eyes hardened. He drained his cup, then in one motion turned from the window to fling it into the hearth, where it shattered into tiny pieces. The ferocity of the gesture caused Richard to flinch.

"Duty and honour!" William shouted. "Why must I be the one held to such a standard?" His voice grew louder and he began to pace. "Why must I suffer when I was not the one who carried on an adulterous affair? And why was it left to me to spare my mother and sister from the embarrassment of my father's lust?"

William stopped pacing and stood with his hands covering his face as Richard hurried to him. Sliding an arm across his shoulder, Richard could feel him shaking with fury.

"Because, my brave cousin, you were man enough to step in to protect those you loved. That is more than I can say of Uncle George."

William threw up his hands in frustration, laughing mirthlessly. "I often wonder if it was worth it. Had I known that father and mother would die soon after …" His voice trailed off, as his thoughts returned to what might have been.

"I know you too well, Cousin, and you would have gone through with it regardless. You were always fearless when it came to protecting your family, whereas I would have likely refused, as I am not so fond of mine." Richard replied dryly.

William slumped down in a nearby chair, and for a time he ran both hands through his hair, something Richard has seen him do since they were children whenever he was distressed. Finally, his hands stilled and he murmured roughly, "I was afraid that if I stayed one more day, I would confess my feelings and if I had—"

"Do not torture yourself, Darcy. You are only human. And you deserve more than the misery that has been your lot. Perhaps it is time to put this matter to rest and explain to Georgiana about her birth."

William's head swung slowly side to side. "I cannot. Not when I have no idea who her real father might be." He took a deep breath and sat up straighter. "Do not concern yourself for me, cousin. I have another two days until I have to face Georgiana and pretend all is well. I shall persevere."

"And what will you do if the one woman who has managed to touch your heart is no longer available should you decide to extricate yourself from Gisela?"

William stared into space for some time before answering. "I suppose I shall just have to accept that she was never meant to be mine."

Just at that moment there was a knock on the study door. "Come!" William called and he and Richard watched as it slowly opened, and Mr. Barnes warily stuck his head inside.

"Come in, Barnes," William offered, knowing full well that he had not been the kindest employer since his return from Hertfordshire. Mr. Barnes stepped towards him, a silver salver in his hand and a letter upon it.

"This was delivered a moment ago. It came by express so I thought it might be urgent."

William stood and took the missive. "Thank you, Barnes. You are most perceptive."

"Thank you, sir. And Mrs. Barnes asked me to relay that the dining room is prepared and you may eat when you wish."

As Barnes turned to leave, William added, "Would you tell Mrs. Barnes that the Colonel and I shall also dine together tonight?"

Mr. Barnes smiled slightly, his eyes meeting Richard's before settling on William. "I will be most happy to do so, sir."

Richard's brow furrowed as he turned from watching Mr. Barnes exit the room, to see the scowl on his cousin's face. "What is the matter now, Darcy?"

William kept reading for a moment before he looked up to meet his cousin's gaze. "This is from Mr. Carter—the investigator hired to look into Bingley's lost shipment. He has written that another of his ships has apparently been lost at sea. Carter thought I might be able to locate Charles without delay, as he sent a letter to his townhouse but has not received a reply." William shook his head tiredly. "I told Charles to notify his solicitor when he was not going to be in residence in London, but I imagine he forgot as usual."

"What do you plan to do?"

"I shall send an express to Charles asking him to come to London at once! This makes two ships in the last few months, and he will need to formulate a plan. He cannot operate a business without merchandise."

Longbourn
A bedroom

Lizzy dropped down on the bed next to Jane, who sat staring at the invitation that had been delivered no more than twenty minutes before. Other than Mr. Bennet who was locked in his library, the house was empty, as their siblings and their mother had walked to Meryton.

"Are you actually going to dine with Caroline Bingley? I cannot imagine that she truly wants to get to know you—not after the way she avoided you at the assembly last night."

"Oh, Lizzy, you are too quick to find fault with everyone. According to Mr. Bingley, Caroline did not feel well and almost decided to stay home."

"Would that she had!"

"Lizzy!"

"I am teasing, Jane."

"I pray so. Caroline has never been unkind to me, and since she has been gracious enough to issue an invitation for me to dine with her and her sister, I do not see how I can very well decline."

"I could." At Jane's frown, Elizabeth laughed. "I said that I could! I know that you cannot, dear sister. You are too apt to see good in everyone. I just pray that you keep in mind what I have said."

"I shall keep your warnings in mind. I promise."

"Thank you. So, when is this grand experience to take place? Tomorrow?"

"Yes."

"Now, if only Mama will not try to make more of it than a dinner invitation. I thought she was going to pull Charlotte out of Mr. Bingley's arms when they danced last night." Both young women giggled. Elizabeth continued, "I feared for her life at one point, but after Mr. Bingley asked you for a second set, Mama calmed down considerably."

More giggles ensued until suddenly Jane sobered. She looked wistfully into the distance. "Lizzy, I have a secret." She glanced to her sister who was listening attentively. "Lately I have begun to imagine what it would be like to be married."

"To Mr. Bingley, of course!" Elizabeth declared making Jane blush.

"Yes. He is everything a gentleman should be … sensible, good-humoured—"

"Handsome, conveniently rich—"

"You know perfectly well, that I do not believe marriage should be based on wealth."

Elizabeth's smile vanished as she said cynically, "I agree wholeheartedly. I will marry only for the deepest love. And I shall never again be fooled by a handsome face or pretty words!"

Jane reached to take one of her hands. "I am so sorry, Lizzy. I forgot about your Mr. Darcy. I would not have mentioned it had—"

Elizabeth interrupted, shaking her head vigorously. "Nonsense! In the first place, he was never *my* Mr. Darcy, and in the second, I have completely forgotten everything about him. If I met him today, I doubt I would remember what he looked like. We would meet as just indifferent acquaintances."

Jane studied Elizabeth's smile, but was not convinced. "Lizzy, you do not have to pretend with me. I know that you cared for him."

Elizabeth pulled her hand from Jane's and stood, moving to stare out into the gardens from their bedroom window. She wrapped her arms around her waist. Jane was about to say more when Lizzy offered, "Then let me pretend that it is true until it is so."

"Oh, Lizzy," Jane began but was instantly interrupted as Elizabeth hurried back to the bed to pull her to her feet.

"Come. No more talk of my folly. We shall look through the closet to find something for you to wear to impress the Bingleys. I am sure there is still time to add some ribbon or lace to please Mama."

Jane lowered her voice in warning. "Lizzy!"

In unison the sisters collapsed on the bed giggling.

Later that evening when Jane was in another room helping Kitty with her embroidery, Elizabeth reached under her mattress to retrieve the book that Mr. Grant had delivered to the house whilst she was bedridden. Though she had coveted it for months before its arrival at the bookshop, she had secreted it away because it reminded her of *him*—of their meeting in the bookshop and the fact that he quit Meryton without a word of goodbye. But three weeks had passed, and Elizabeth was determined to let go of the hurt that accompanied his memory. So she crawled onto the bed, piled a few pillows behind her head and reached for the tome.

As she lifted the book, however, a folded paper fell into her lap. Picking it up, she immediately realised that it was a letter written in a woman's script. The recipient of the letter made her startle—Fitzwilliam Darcy. She blinked continuously until it dawned on her what must have happened. Mr. Darcy must have purchased the book intending to give it to her and then had Mr. Grant deliver it after he was called away. Her heart soared. Curiosity got the better of her as she eagerly opened the missive and began to read.

Dearest Fitzwilliam,

Our dear Georgiana is doing so much better in Bath. The change of atmosphere has been like a tonic, and her disposition improves every day. But as it has been several weeks, she longs to see you again. No one can take your place in her heart, and that is the way it should be.

We shall be back in London before the end of the month, and naturally she expects you to be waiting with a present from your trip to Netherfield. How you spoil her! We shall travel to Ramsgate next, but there should be ample time for you to be together in the weeks before we leave.

God bless you until we meet again,

Audrey Ashcroft

The elation Elizabeth had felt moments before turned to trepidation —her smile to a frown. Who was Audrey Ashcroft? And more importantly, who was this Georgiana who missed Mr. Darcy so dearly?

Chapter 7

London
Grantham Townhouse

Gisela Darcy carefully examined her reflection in the large, gilded mirror that hung over her intricately carved dressing table just as she did every morning. With practiced acuity, she leaned closer to inspect her countenance for signs of aging, slowly gliding her fingers over every inch of her face and then down her long, slender neck. She was so proud of her neck that she had had all her necklaces refashioned into chokers to take advantage of what she perceived to be one of her best assets. Relieved to find no discolouration or wrinkles marring her flawless ivory skin, she was equally pleased that she had not found one grey hair among the dark blond curls now woven into an elaborate design, courtesy of her new maid.

Satisfied, Gisela stood and removed her robe and gown to peruse her body, inspecting it with equal diligence. She sought reassurance that her breasts were still pert, her waist still small and her hips trim. Turning this way and that, she smiled at the image in the mirror, pleased that she was still as shapely as a debutante. Many of her friends were overweight now, having given birth to several children and gaining considerable weight with each confinement. A good many others had just let themselves go once they had secured a husband.

At least being barren has its advantages. I shall never be fat like them! And, I shall never neglect myself, as is their wont. If those fat cows only knew the offers that their husbands have made me!

Her green eyes danced with delight, her lips curving into a smile as she recalled the men who had lusted after her. Nonetheless, the smile faded as the one man who had *never* wanted her came to mind. Instantly, she sought to reaffirm her allure.

Do not let Fitzwilliam's rejection affect your attitude. Remember that you are still beautiful—even more so than any of last season's debutantes! It is his loss if he chooses not to partake of your favours, and other men are eager to take his place in your bed.

However, having worked herself into a fury at the thought of her husband's rejection, Gisela slipped on her robe and hurried into her bedroom, heading straight to a large closet, which held a secure chest. Using a key that was hidden in a secret place, she unlocked the chest and began removing several velvet boxes stacked inside. Returning to her dressing table with them, she was determined to think of more cheerful things—such as the Satterfield ball that night. She would choose her jewels for that soirée now.

As was her custom, she reached for the most spectacular of all her jewels and clasped it about her neck, though she did not intend to wear it that evening since her gown was dark green and thus called for her emeralds. Even so, the multiple strands of diamonds sparkled against her skin, and she smiled conspiratorially at the woman reflected in the mirror. The necklace, a choker five strands deep, had been the reason she had accepted Lord Stanley Grantham's proposal of marriage … well, that and a half-dozen equally impressive pieces he had shown her in a bid to win her hand.

At that time, she had been young and naive enough to believe her mother's assertion that the portly Earl of Chesterfield, who had never married and had no heirs, would most likely be dead of his heart ailments within the year. Thus, Gisela had accepted him and, as Fate would have it, he had lived for another decade. But as she fingered the finest of his many gifts, she allowed that she had made the right choice, as he was far too wealthy to refuse. After all, these treasures had been attained with little effort on her part. Grantham had made it clear from the beginning that he was too weak for marital relations and only wished to have a beautiful woman on his arm. He had even gone so far as to hint that he would turn a blind eye to any affairs she might have, as long as she was discreet.

As she exchanged the most expensive necklace for another consisting of emeralds and diamonds, she gloated at her good fortune. She had had many lovers during the ten years she was married and had welcomed widowhood as a chance to do entirely as she pleased with no need to hide her liaisons. It had been amusing at first. Grantham had left her quite wealthy and independent—she clearly need never marry again. Nevertheless, after bedding innumerable young bucks of the *ton* that were off to the next widow soon after leaving her bed, she had tired of the novelty of being merely a convenience.

Yet, due to her noticeable contempt for society during her season of indiscretion, the upper echelons had begun to shun her, and she began receiving less and less invitations. Thus, Gisela had come to a crucial decision. Vowing that there would be no more ugly, old men for her, she set out to find a respectable, wealthy *and handsome* second husband—one who could not only ensure her a place in society, but one she would welcome in her bed. The notion had been simpler than the execution of it, however.

On the whole, the extremely wealthy men she encountered after her momentous change of course were just what she feared—old, ugly or married—in most cases, all three.

She had almost despaired of finding anyone who fit her criteria when she spied Fitzwilliam Darcy at a ball in London two years before. Having been only a boy when she had married Grantham, she had paid him no mind, but now he was every inch a desirable man. And as he walked into Matlock House that spring night, the tall, dark and handsome heir of Pemberley seemed the perfect answer to her predicament. Even now, her heart beat faster at the memory of how he looked that night.

Dressed in black coat and breeches, black boots, white linen shirt and a gold waistcoat, his dark curly hair, tanned skin and light blue eyes had mesmerised her when they were introduced, at her insistence, by her current *good friend*, Lord Norton. But in spite of her arts and allurements, that evening she was not able to coax a single smile from him or even an invitation to dance, though she hinted that she was without a partner. It was as though he was impervious to her manoeuvrings and, in fact, he seemed to grow more unreceptive the harder she struggled to gain his attention.

This she could not tolerate! Men had always been at her beck and call. A little flirting and they grovelled at her feet—but not Fitzwilliam Darcy. Infuriated, she had taken the wrong stratagem by following him onto the terrace and openly propositioning him. Incensed, he had told her in no uncertain terms that he was not interested in anything she had to offer.

Instantly irate at the memory of his insult, Gisela hastily unclasped the emeralds and unceremoniously dropped them back in their case. Then picking up all the boxes, she headed back to the chest, no longer intrigued or entertained with her bounty.

Who is he that he should turn up his nose at me? It is not as though he is a paragon of virtue!

She missed a step and stopped, considering her last thought.

What am I saying? He IS the epitome of virtue! That is the problem! That strait-laced Puritan could never appreciate a passionate woman like me! I do not know why I bother to stay married to him!

Swiftly she hurried on to her task of replacing the jewels. Then returning to her dressing room, she considered the consequences of no longer being Mrs. Darcy—no more invitations to the Matlock's soirées and rubbing elbows with the Countess' friends in the *ton,* no more looks of envy from the women just learning that Fitzwilliam was her husband. She had no doubt that most of them despised her and would shun her without the Fitzwilliam's cachet. Picking up a vase of flowers atop a stand, she hurled it across the room where it crashed into the hearth.

No! I relish being Mrs. Fitzwilliam Darcy, and I love the doors that open to me because of his name. I shall never give that up! After the way he has humiliated me, I shall see to it that he never has another woman or an heir! I shall forever be a reminder of what his arrogance and disdain has cost him.

With that, Gisela pulled the cord to summon her maid, and Jemima briskly appeared in the doorway, looking nervously at the broken vase of flowers. As she moved towards the mess, Gisela's outburst stopped her.

"Help me dress! I have someone important to call on this morning." The maid bobbed her head and started to the closet. "Never mind! I shall select my gown. You shall assist me in dressing."

The young maid, her third in as many months, stopped in her tracks, too afraid to speak. Gisela was caught up in her own thoughts and did not notice the maid's discomfiture. With a smug smile, she walked to the large closet, and slowly began examining the long line of expensive gowns hanging inside. Something mundane would never do for a call on Darcy House.

I shall try once more to talk to my arrogant husband. After all, though Fitzwilliam may hate me, I enjoy reminding him why he can never divorce me.

Finally, she pulled a burgundy gown, cut very low with sequins across the entire bodice, from the assortment. It might have been fashioned for a night at the opera, but she wanted to make an impression and this gown would definitely do that. After all, she mused, Darcy very seldom saw her when she was dressed opulently. She reached for one of her more modest wraps, intending to wear it over the gown and dazzle him when she removed it.

Luckily, as Gisela laid the gown on the bed, she did not see the stunned look on Jemima's face. Her former employer, a great lady who had expired recently, would never have worn such a gown in broad daylight. She stifled a smile.

Lady Gisela Darcy may have a good deal of wealth, but she obviously has no taste!

◌◌◌

Darcy House
William's Study

Lord Landingham stood at the tall windows, taking in the view of the gardens as he enjoyed an expensive cigar. Every so often, he shook his head in agreement with the proposed settlement that William was reading. Finally he turned and marched back towards the desk.

"I do not care how you want to handle it, Fitzwilliam. One way is as good as another, and I trust your men to replace the fence along the correct property lines. Besides," Lord Marshall Landingham smiled mischievously, "if your men do the work, then I shall not have to pay my men to do it."

William laughed aloud at his godfather's remark, then relaxed back in his chair to study the tall, distinguished, grey-haired man that had been like a second father to him. "I suppose I was too quick to offer to manage the problem. The next time I shall wait for you to propose a settlement!"

"Now you sound like your father!" Landingham's smile waned as he offered sadly, "I miss George ... and Anne."

William's countenance darkened. "Yes. I miss them more each day. Just take this matter, for instance. If he had been here, Father would have known what to do instinctively without dragging you into Town to discuss it."

"Nonsense! I had business in London, and as you could not leave, it worked out well for me to come to you! Besides, you handled everything admirably, my boy!" Landingham declared with his usual enthusiasm for whatever William did. "George could not have done a better job of settling the tenant's dispute, and I have thirty years as your nearest neighbour to support my claim."

William tossed the pen he had been fiddling with onto the desk. "Without your valuable counsel the first year after Father died, I think I would have gone mad!"

"I think not! But rest assured that I will always be available if you need me. I believe, however, that you have learned your lessons so well that my services may never again be required—at least, in regard to estate management." At the pleased look on William's face, Landingham changed the subject. "I know you do not like to speak of it, but I cannot help but wonder..."

William coloured, knowing the direction the conversation would take, as Landingham had always played the role of mentor and counsellor. He had taken in his altered appearance when he first entered the study, and Landingham could not have failed to note how much weight William had lost or the new worry lines around his eyes. Other than his best friends, Richard and Charles, the earl was the only person that knew of Gisela's threat to reveal that Georgiana was not a Darcy. And like his true friends, Landingham could always tell when he had slipped into a quiet desperation. "Wonder?"

"Have you reconsidered what we talked of … about telling Georgiana?"

"Yes."

"And?"

"I feel I cannot take the chance of telling her about her father until I know his identity. I have paid too high a price to keep her from learning of that scoundrel's role, and I want to wait until she is older and wiser."

Landingham's face fell at William's description of Georgiana's father. "Fitzwilliam, I was acquainted with your mother from the time she was just a child. I knew her well enough to know that she would not have taken up with a scoundrel. She was a true lady, and if she sought comfort in another man's arms, then it had to have been someone she cared about and trusted."

William stood and walked around to the front of his desk, where he stopped and leaned back on the edge. Cupping his chin with one hand, he considered Landingham's words.

"You are correct. My mother would not have turned to anyone she did not respect, but I will NEVER respect the man who took advantage of her distress."

Landingham looked away. Since William had confided in him about the letter Gisela held over his head, he had wanted to be honest with his godson about his love affair with Anne Darcy. But he was only too aware that William had much responsibility resting on his shoulders and little family he could trust for advice. As it was, William sought his counsel often, and if he must keep the fact that he was Georgiana's father a secret a while longer, he would, if only for the young man's sake. As all of these thoughts were running through his mind, William began to elaborate.

"I suppose I speak of him in that manner because it is easier to blame him than my mother. Yet you know as well as I that there is no certainty that I shall ever learn his identity. And if I tell Georgiana what I suspect—that she is not a Darcy—she will be heartbroken! And how could she ever recover without knowing her true father's identity?"

Landingham stood and put an arm around William's shoulder. When he was in the young man's company, it was never far from his mind that, but for a quirk of fate, he could have been William's father. As it was, Anne Fitzwilliam was the woman he had fallen in love with as a boy, and after she declined his offer and accepted George Darcy, he had never married.

"I support whatever you decide, but I cannot fathom how any young man can stay with a woman he despises—a woman who has trapped him into marriage. It must be very hard not to notice a pretty face or to ignore a young woman to which you might feel an attraction."

The look of pain that crossed William's face was not lost on his counsellor. "Fitzwilliam, is there something I should know?"

William's eyes dropped to his shoes. "There is nothing to tell. I met a young woman I believe I could have loved, but she is lost to me."

"I am sorry. Anne spoke to me often before she died of her belief that you had married Gisela for the wrong reasons, though she had no way of knowing the truth. She would not have wanted you to sacrifice yourself. You realise that."

"I can only pray that, because she never learned about Gisela's affair with Father, she was at least not tormented with that humiliation before she died. If so, I accomplished what I set out to do."

"I understand that she never knew that Gisela was supposedly carrying a child when you married."

"No, she did not. I forbade Gisela from telling her, as mother was so sick."

Landingham squeezed William's shoulder. "While I did not agree with the method you chose, your love for your mother is admirable. You are truly the man she hoped you would be."

"It is kind of you to say."

"No. It is not kind, it is the truth. And there are no words to describe the witch that has ensnared you—first with her lie about the child and then with the letter." William nodded but did not speak, so Landingham offered, "Shall we speak of more pleasant things? When is Lady Audrey expected back from Bath with Georgiana?"

William's face brightened. "In two days."

"Good. Good. I shall extend my stay in Town so that I may escort them to the theatre and the opera while they are here, if you do not mind."

"Of course, you may, if they are willing. What I cannot discern is whether you are fonder of my aunt or my sister." William could not pass up the chance to tease his friend, as Landingham and Audrey Ashcroft had become fast friends after she moved to Pemberley two years before.

Landingham was not perturbed. "I am quite fond of Georgiana, being her godfather as well as yours, and your aunt has, shall we say, grown on me."

Thinking of his aunt's impertinent ways, William chucked. "Yes, she is not easily understood at first acquaintance. Mother always referred to her as a *whirligig*—always animated, especially when she is explaining something, and never staying in one place long."

"I remember that now that you mention it. She was so much younger than Anne that I did not know her well. Then she married and moved to Kent. It was not until she moved to Pemberley to help you with Georgiana that I actually got well acquainted with her. She is quite different than any woman I have ever met— even outspoken and brash when the occasion warrants!"

"I see you have not forgotten Aunt Audrey's altercation with Aunt Catherine when she came to Pemberley after mother died."

"I shall NEVER forget that day! I believe I stood open-mouthed for several minutes after she had Lady Catherine escorted off the grounds of Pemberley! I will admit to being in shock at seeing the two lock horns, but at least the more rational sister won the day."

"Yes, she did. I will forever be grateful to Aunt Audrey for telling Aunt Catherine that Georgiana most certainly would not live at Rosings. I would never have allowed it to happen under any circumstances, but having my aunt living at Pemberley countered any argument for taking Georgiana away from me."

"I think that is when I first began to see that there was more to Lady Audrey Ashcroft than meets the eye. Yes, she is quite a lovely woman, but she is also a woman to be reckoned with."

"That she is," William chuckled. "Definitely not a shrinking violet."

"Well, let me leave and get about my business so you and your steward can finish what I interrupted."

Before William could object, Lord Landingham disappeared out the door and Mr. Albritton reappeared out of nowhere with folders in hand. William shook his head at how fast his steward had determined that Landingham was gone.

"Sit down, Mr. Albritton, and let us see what we can get done before we are disturbed again."

A few minutes later

Lord Landingham had barely left Darcy House when there was a knock at the front door and a newly-hired footman opened it to find Gisela Darcy standing there, smiling benignly. Not being aware of just who was and who was not welcome, the footman dutifully stepped aside as she pushed past him. However, she was not quick enough to dodge Mr. Barnes, who immediately blocked her progress. He noted that she smelled of brandy.

"Madam, I must ask you to leave."

Gisela dropped the modest wrap to reveal her very low-cut burgundy gown. "Nonsense! I am here to speak to my husband. Either he speaks to me inside these walls, or I shall wait on his doorstep and accost him when he leaves—in public!"

Mr. Barnes sighed and glanced at the footman who still held the door open, his eyes large as saucers. "Brigham, shut the door then see that Mrs. Darcy does not move from this spot."

Brigham slammed the door in his eagerness to please and hurriedly moved to stand in front of the flamboyantly dressed woman, his face expressionless, as he had been trained.

As Mr. Barnes continued to address his employer's estranged wife, the tone of his voice was evidence of his disdain. "I shall tell Mr. Darcy that you are here."

With those words, he turned and walked toward William's study, occasionally glancing over his shoulder to make sure that Gisela Darcy had not followed.

A knock on the door tore William's attention from the paper he was reading as his steward, Mr. Albritton, waited patiently for him to finish. "Come!"

The door opened and Mr. Barnes' head appeared before his body followed. Glancing first at Mr. Albritton, his eyes met William's. "Sir, Mrs. Darcy is in the foyer. Our newest footman was unaware of who she is, so she walked right past him. I am sorry."

William signed and rubbed his eyes before standing and addressing his steward. "Wait here. I shall return shortly." Mr. Albritton nodded—his expression confirmation that he was quite used to Mr. Darcy's estranged wife's antics and he pitied the young man.

As William came down the hall followed by Barnes, the delight on Gisela's face was unmistakable. She tried to walk on into the house, only to be stopped by the large body of Mr. Brigham.

"All is well, Brigham," Mr. Barnes declared. "Let her pass."

Gisela walked around the footman with a smirk on her face, the expression increasing as she saw how irritated William appeared.

"Fitzwilliam! So good of you to take time out of your busy schedule to see me."

Without answering her, William took her elbow and not too gently pulled her into the drawing room and closed the door behind them. Slowly she looked about as if admiring the lovely room. William seethed.

No longer able to keep silent, he declared, "Why are you here? Have you already gone through your allowance? If you are here for more money, the answer is no!"

Gisela immediately moved to press herself against William, running her hands suggestively over his chest. Disgusted and smelling the brandy on her breath, he pushed her to arm's length.

"My, my, we *are* irritable!" she exclaimed. "I have no need for more funds. I only came to deliver some good news." William said nothing. Disappointed but undeterred, she continued, "I just wanted you to know that I am going to vote with you on Lady Catherine's request for another loan regarding our joint venture. Her plans to fund more repairs for Strathmore Mill have been thwarted."

The hatred in William's eyes was disconcerting. His failure to react or reply was not what Gisela had expected. Her confidence began to wane. "I … I thought you would be pleased."

"Pleased? The only thing that would please me is if you say that you want a divorce!"

"I have told you often enough that I enjoy being Mrs. Fitzwilliam Darcy! I will NEVER let you divorce me."

"You may have no choice! I have all the evidence I need, what with you flaunting your latest affair all over London!"

"Are you jealous?"

"Never!"

"Then perhaps I should remind you that I can bring your little sister's world crashing down around her if you persist in this matter!"

"I see that you have not changed, so there is nothing more to say. Leave my house immediately!"

"Oh, but there is another reason for my visit! Lady Matlock tells me that dear Georgiana will be back in Town shortly. I hinted to her ladyship that she should invite my dear sister to the theatre. And, if I should just happen to be there and join them in their box …"

William's eyes narrowed as he gripped both her forearms with enough force that they began to ache. "If you are wise, you will stay away from my sister!"

"Oh! I love a passionate man! It is too bad that you will not sample *my* passionate nature in bed."

"I abhor you. I could never desire you!"

"We shall see. After all, at some point you must give in to your baser instincts."

"Not with you! I can assure you of that!"

"So you have said enough times. But rest assured that should I learn that you are satisfying your desires with a paramour, I shall make certain that all of England knows her identity. For anyone that you fancied would, of course, be a lady. Would you be willing to subject her to public shame? And would you want your precious sister to know that you are keeping a whore?"

William began to drag her from the room, even as she spewed even more vile threats. By the time they had reached the front door, Brigham was holding it open, and William flung her onto the portico. Just as she turned to hurl one last insult, the door slammed in her face.

"Humph!" Gisela declared, kicking the bottom of the front door before turning to find that several people had stopped on the walk below to watch the spectacle. Lifting her head as though she were royalty, Gisela descended the front steps, losing her balance on the fifth one. A footman hurried to guide her to the carriage door, handing her inside. She entered as quickly as possible, thankful that she had not come in an open carriage. Ultimately she was able to escape the curiosity of her audience by pulling down the window shade.

"He shall pay for this!" she raged to the empty carriage. "I should have Wickham rape that ugly little mouse Georgiana just for good measure!"

The drive back to her townhouse was punctuated by the sound of loud acclamations of displeasure—nothing out of the ordinary for the two footmen and driver, as they were well-acquainted with their mistress' temper tantrums and drunken rants. Exchanging looks every time she got louder, they shook their heads, hoping that they could get back to the townhouse without her deciding to go shopping. It was difficult at best to keep her from falling down when she drank so heavily. And, of course, she always blamed them for her mishaps.

Chapter 8

Meryton
Longbourn
A few days later

Elizabeth found Jane where she had least expected—sitting on the side of the sprawling oak tree atop Oakham Mount that was her own haven. It was not like her older sister to walk out alone in the mornings or to go this far alone, as she was never as adventurous as Elizabeth. But Jane had not been herself since Mr. Bingley's departure from Netherfield. From behind, Elizabeth thought her sister looked perfectly well, except for a few blond curls that had escaped her bonnet and were blowing in the gentle breeze. It was only after closer inspection that she saw signs of her distress.

"Jane?" Elizabeth stopped, hesitating to come closer as her sister turned her head away. "Jane, you know my heartache, let me share yours."

Jane took a deep breath, her shoulders visibly rising with the effort, then turned to meet Elizabeth's gaze. It was evident that her lovely blue eyes were red from crying, and though Elizabeth longed to comfort her, she did not rush to do so. Truly understanding her sister's wish to be alone, she was determined to honour Jane's privacy, if that was what she wished.

"It is just …" Jane's voice cracked as her face crumpled, and she shook her head in an effort to recover. "Please allow me a moment to compose myself."

Elizabeth said nothing and did not move closer. Finally, Jane was able to control her voice and began speaking. "It is just that he left without a word. After all the time we spent in each other's company, all I was to receive was this." She held up a tear-stained paper. "This note from Caroline!"

Those few words preceded another torrent of tears, causing Elizabeth to edge closer. Under her breath, she cursed the missive that had arrived early on the day Jane was to dine with Caroline and Louisa. Though it was short, and in Elizabeth's estimation meant to wound, she knew it by heart already.

Dear Miss Bennet,

I regret that we must cancel our dinner invitation. By the time you read this, we shall be on our way to London, as my brother has been summoned by Mr. Darcy to come immediately. It seems his sister is returning to London, and he wishes Charles to be there to greet her. We are all looking forward to renewing our friendship with Miss Darcy, who is a lady of the finest calibre. Charles is not sure at this point when, or if, we shall return to Netherfield.

Yours truly,
Caroline Bingley

Seeing that Jane had begun to quietly cry again, Elizabeth came around the other side of the tree and slipped down beside her, threading an arm around her shoulders. "I am sorry. I truly understand your pain. I was not as well acquainted with Mr. Darcy as you were with Mr. Bingley, but nevertheless, my feelings were hurt by his unfeeling departure. However, Mr. Bingley had gone to such great effort to get to know you—all of the dances at the assemblies, the walks into Meryton and his calls at Longbourn—that his departure without any explanation is truly a mystery."

"I must have read more into his actions than he intended," Jane whispered dejectedly. "After all, he never asked permission to court me."

"Apparently Mr. Bingley may be more like his dear friend, Mr. Darcy, than I believed at first," Elizabeth huffed, beginning to consider the similarities. "In fact, since it was Mr. Darcy who summoned Mr. Bingley to London so swiftly, perhaps he learned of his attraction to you from Charles' sisters and did not wish his friend to be attached to a member of my family!"

"Oh, Lizzy!" Jane stood and began to pace. "I am not ready to attribute such cruelty to Mr. Darcy or to Mr. Bingley's sisters. Perhaps there is a rational explanation for his hurried departure and, as I said, he did not ask to court me."

"You are too trusting," Elizabeth retorted. "But never mind the reason for his removal. He is gone, and it is just as well, as we shall be leaving Meryton too! We have been invited to London to stay the summer with our Uncle and Aunt Gardiner beginning next week!"

Elizabeth stood and slipped a letter from her pocket. Then she reached out to grab Jane's hand to pull her alongside as she sat back down. "This came right after you left, and I managed to hide it from Mama. After all, it is addressed to me."

As Jane leaned in to follow what was written, Elizabeth began. "Aunt Madeline writes that her second cousin, Penelope—the one that is married to Colonel Holmes—is returning to London. Holmes' eldest brother, Viscount Moreland, has died, and his father is ill. The Colonel has resigned from the army to become the Viscount, but Aunt says it is only a matter of time until he will take his place as the Earl of Rhodes. Then Penelope Holmes will be a countess! Can you imagine that we shall have connections to a countess?"

"Do not tell Mama!" Jane cautioned, pulling a handkerchief from a pocket to dry her eyes.

"Certainly not! Aunt Madeline was adamant that she did not want Mama to know, for fear she would send all our sisters to London at once."

"She would, to be sure."

"In an event, Aunt enclosed a letter for me to give Papa, which she says explains her wish for us to come. She is eager for us to attend the soirées that are being planned in her cousin's honour, since she and Uncle will be in attendance at many of them. Who knows how many eligible men we shall meet! You shall most likely forget all about Mr. Bingley, just as I shall forget Mr. Darcy."

"Lizzy, you do not have to pretend for my sake," Jane chided. "I know that you are only trying to cheer me. You have always made light of social occasions, just like Papa. How often have you told me how tedious and mortifying it is to be put on display for matchmaking purposes?"

Trying to keep up her sister's spirit, Elizabeth challenged, "Oh, but I dearly love to dance! And besides, maybe I shall not mind being on display if I am in the company of real gentlemen—not those like Mr. Darcy. He has all the appearance of goodness, but it is merely that—appearance. I promise to keep an open mind if you will."

"I will not be going."

"Not going? Oh Jane, why ever not?"

"I do not wish to visit London at this time. I have been so focused on Mr. Bingley that I have not given due consideration to what I really want in a husband. I am so confused at this moment that I do not believe I would know the perfect man even if I were to meet him. Besides, why must I go to London? There are plenty of men in Meryton."

"For instance?"

"Arthur Rice, Walter Gould, John Lucas."

"Arthur Rice is bald and fat. Walter Gould is a dolt and John Lucas is so immature that he has to ask his mother when to breathe!"

"He does not!" Jane exclaimed, beginning to weigh Mr. Lucas' qualities. "I find him solicitous and steady –"

"Boring and predictable!"

"As of now, I have a new appreciation of boring and predictable."

"Please go with me, Jane, or I shall have no confidant with whom to chuckle about the foibles of London society and, besides, we shall never know what fate might await us if we limit ourselves to the gentlemen of Meryton!"

"No. I may join you for a while during the summer, but for the present, I am staying at Longbourn."

Elizabeth sighed. There was no arguing with Jane when she had her mind made up. She stood, declaring a little too enthusiastically as she paced back and forth, "Well, I for one am going! And while I am there, I shall look for a suitable husband for you, so do not make any commitments while I am off regaling London with my brilliant intellect!"

Jane tried to smile but it was not convincing. Elizabeth stopped to gently lift her chin with one finger until their eyes met. "Promise me?"

"After what happened with Mr. Bingley, I cannot imagine trusting another man with my heart in the near future so I believe I can safely promise you that."

"Come then. Let us walk back down the trail together. If we hurry, Hill may find something left in the kitchen to break our fast!" As Jane got to her feet, Elizabeth hugged her tightly before pushing her at arm's length. "Swear that you will not waste another thought on Mr. Bingley, just as I have vowed never to waste another on Mr. Darcy. You shall see—we shall both be better off without them!"

"I swear," Jane murmured, though it was obvious that her heart was not in the pledge. If she had searched her sister's eyes a little longer, she would have seen that Elizabeth's heart was not in her pledge either.

Arm-in-arm, they started back down the well-worn path that led to the bottom of Oakham Mount and then on to Longbourn. Neither was aware of how momentous a decision had been made that day or how their promises would affect them in the coming months. But it was with better spirits and renewed faith in the future that they returned to their home.

∾⌒∾

Ramsgate

For the fourth time since he had arrived, George Wickham admired the view as his rented carriage made its way down the street nearest the beach. As he peered up at the sky, it seemed bluer than he had ever imagined, with fluffy white clouds drifting lazily across the great expanse. On his previous jaunts, he had noted that the weathered old houses that lined the street were evidently well built to withstand the storms that blew in off the sea, and any repairs that did not fit the older, grey portions, were all ornamental—trim and such. Nevertheless, these once stately homes had declined over the years and had long ago been turned into business establishments, such as the one he would call on today.

As abruptly as the conveyance came to a stop, so did Wickham's contemplations of the neighbourhood. He stepped out onto the sandy street, taking a deep breath of the lightly gusting salty air. *Invigorating!* For a moment, he envisioned how pleasant it would be to live near the sea, but dismissed the idea as quickly as it had come. The risk of staying in one place was too great, as he was constantly in flight from one plot or another gone awry. No. There would not be a seaside residence for him.

Consequently, he turned once more to study the facade of the last manor on the street. It was three stories high, the upper floors occupied by family, per the shop keeper's admission, while the bottom floor served as the art gallery. A uniquely painted white sign with a seashell border and black lettering swung back and forth over the top of the stairs—*Younge's Art Gallery*. Underneath in smaller letters were the words, *Lessons Available.*

As his eyes dropped to the entrance, he noted Mrs. Younge peering through the glass so he hurried towards the steps, removing his hat as he went. She opened the door before he reached it.

"Mr. Wickham." Bobbing a curtsey, the proprietor stood back to let the tall, handsome, brown-haired man pass. Sarah Younge was undecided what to think of the gentleman who had already visited several times that week—perusing the same paintings and talking of purchasing one—though he had not bothered to do so as yet.

A widow of five years, she could not help blushing under his persistent gaze. Plain and overweight with no hope of another offer of marriage, she was unaccustomed to attention. After her husband's death, she had continued to run the art gallery, since she, her mother and her sister depended on the income. Her late husband's brother, a merchant, had been a co-owner of the gallery, but upon John's death, he took ownership of not only the business, but the house as well. Graciously, he allowed them use of it, and Mrs. Younge gave art lessons and sold her paintings and those of other artists in order to survive.

"I have to tell you, madam, that I have searched all of Ramsgate for the perfect painting for my cousin and have found none that I admire more than the one you have created."

Mrs. Younge barely smiled at his fawning. "I am pleased that you like the painting. It is one of my personal favourites, as I love the tranquillity of the sea, the grasses, birds and sand dunes. Unfortunately, most people have rejected it as too placid."

"I admire the tranquillity of it as well. I find that I can actually feel myself relax as I take it in. I am sure that it will please my cousin." The widow's mien softened at his compliment. "I suppose, however, that it is not wise of me to praise the painting as the price may increase!"

"Oh, no!" Sarah Younge declared decidedly. "The price is the same as I quoted the first day you came into the shop—five and twenty pounds."

"Sold!" Wickham exclaimed, taking a bank cheque from his inside pocket. "I would like to have it shipped to London so that when I return it shall be waiting for me to present."

"That can certainly be arranged," the woman replied. "We have a friend, a merchant, who delivers to London once a week, and I believe he leaves here again tomorrow. I shall send word to him immediately, so that he may take this painting with him when he delivers his goods." Mrs. Younge motioned towards a room on the right. "If you will follow me, I shall write out a bill of sale and provide paper for the directions to the address where you want it delivered."

Reaching the enormous desk in the office, she opened a drawer for the book of receipts and handed Wickham a piece of paper for the shipping address. While she wrote out the bill of sale, he scribbled directions to Gisela's townhouse in London, and when she came around the desk to exchange documents, he added a cheque for the painting. Thanking him profusely for the sale and assuring him that it would be delivered in a timely manner, she returned to the desk to replace the book. Taking a seat to complete her paperwork, she assumed he would leave. Nonetheless, she glanced up to see that the he was still standing in the doorway with a quizzical look on his face.

"Yes, Mr. Wickham?"

Wickham moved in front of the desk, a practiced air of shyness about him as he fiddled with the brim of his hat. "I am new to Ramsgate and have made few acquaintances, so I was wondering if you … if you might consider a stroll among the nearby shops this evening, after business hours, of course. I noticed that there is an elegant coffee and pastry shop, an ice cream parlour and a shop that sells unique gifts all within walking distance. I must purchase a surprise for my dear niece, and I could use a woman's perspective. Besides, I would heartily enjoy the company."

The widow did not hesitate as her colour rose. "I would be delighted, that is, if you will allow my sister to accompany us."

She noted that Wickham's spirits seemed to fall, although his words did not betray it. "Of course! The more the merrier, I always say!"

"Thank you. As I have already pointed out, I live upstairs," she turned to nod towards a staircase, "with my sister and my mother. We shall be awaiting you this evening at six o'clock, if that time is agreeable."

"Six o'clock it is!" Placing his hat atop his head, he tipped the brim and was out the door before Mrs. Younge could say another word.

She smiled as she watched him enter his carriage. If Mr. Wickham was no gentleman, she had lost nothing by inviting her sister along. And if he were a gentleman, he would understand that she was a proper lady.

Heading straight to the office, she unlocked the drawer of the desk and placed the cheque that Wickham had presented inside and relocked it. Then standing, she smoothed her skirts and went back to the main sales floor with a renewed spirit. This sale would go a long way towards their expenses this month. And with the art lessons to begin in a few weeks, she would be able to placate her brother, as he was not convinced they could live off the income from the shop.

Wickham relaxed into the comfortable seat of the rented carriage transporting him back to the boarding house. He was pleased that he had secured permission to take the object of his plotting on a stroll that evening. Though greatly disappointed that she had insisted on including her sister, he was proud that he had quickly schooled his face not to show any disappointment. And he was certain that, after the first outing, he could prevent it from ever happening again.

I shall see that this is the last time she brings a chaperone! I must have time alone with her in order to secure her heart before Georgiana arrives.

Wickham had long suspected that Lady Catherine would not keep funding him forever, especially if he could not provide any services. She had made no secret of the fact that she was considering cutting off the monthly stipend she had provided since he was a young man living at Pemberley.

This plan must work else I shall be left without a farthing!

His thoughts drifted to the conundrum of how to convince Mrs. Younge to join him in his plans for Georgiana Darcy. In essence, he would be juggling the affections of both women at once—convincing both of them that he was in love. First, he would persuade the unattractive widow that he loved her. Then he would tell Mrs. Younge a tale of how Darcy had denied him an inheritance from George Darcy. If she proved to be sympathetic to his plight, he would allude to the fact that he could marry her if he recovered the money that Darcy supposedly had stolen from him.

Only if the widow seemed sincerely convinced, would he explain his scheme—kidnapping Georgiana by convincing the girl that he loved her. Afterward, Darcy would pay a large ransom for his sister's return, which would enable him and the shopkeeper to marry and be on ship to America before anyone knew they were sailing. He would even promise to take her mother and sister along with them, if need be. With any luck, the Widow Younge would be so infatuated that she would be willing to allow him access to Georgiana while she took art lessons.

The real strategy, however, consisted of taking Georgiana directly to Gretna Green where they would be married. Afterwards, he surmised, Mrs. Younge would keep her mouth shut about her involvement in his deception, either from fear of retribution from Miss Darcy's relations or out of embarrassment at her naivety. With his plans firmly set in his mind, Wickham began to relax.

I have never failed to gain the affections of any woman, so why should I worry about impressing someone as plain as Mrs. Younge? There is no doubt that I can sway her.

Just then, the carriage came to a stop in front of the boarding house, and he exited, turning to give the driver orders. "I shall be leaving again in three hours.

See that you are waiting for me out front." The driver nodded and then drove on, leaving Wickham to study the nondescript house.

I will be married to Georgiana Darcy ere long and living in a mansion instead of places such as this!

Having regained his confidence, he stepped smartly up the front steps and nodded as he passed other customers exiting the building. It was with a better frame of mind that he looked forward to the evening and the beginning of the charade.

London
Darcy House

"WILLIAM!"

Georgiana bounded down the grand staircase, her blond curls bobbing up and down like a child's as she ran straight into her brother's arms. Entering the upstairs hallway from her bedroom, she had heard him address Mr. Barnes in the foyer and had instantly run ahead of their aunt who was now descending the same stairs at a decidedly slower pace.

As William twirled his sister around and set her back on her feet, she continued to talk excitedly. "Where were you when we arrived? Aunt said that you could not wait for my return, but when we got here, you were out, and now it is evening, and this is the first I have seen of you all day! Have you been with Richard?"

William strove to keep his smiling mask in place. He would rather that neither Georgiana nor his aunt find out that he had stayed up most of the night because of the continuing nightmares and his vow to Richard that he would not resort to brandy again in order to sleep.

Still awake at dawn, he was out of the house for a ride in the park before most of London awakened, and then off to his club where he promptly fell asleep in the quiet of the library. One of the staff had found him there in an upholstered chair and had closed off that room for a short while, allowing him to rest undisturbed. And if another member had not finally wandered in and roused him, he might still be sleeping.

"Well, baby sister, I have been working hard to keep you in fine gowns and bonnets! And as for Richard, I have not seen him today."

Georgiana pulled back to take in his appearance. "You look terrible!"

"That is a fine thing to say, especially as we have not seen each other in weeks! What if I said the same to you?"

"Then you would be lying!" Georgiana chuckled, easily diverted by her brother's teasing.

Over his sister's head, William watched his aunt descend the last few stairs, and unbidden tears filled his eyes. Audrey Ashcroft was the spitting image of her older sister, Anne Darcy. Tall, thin, dark-haired and blue-eyed, she could easily be mistaken for his mother when she was younger, which had been both a blessing and a curse for him.

While he and Georgiana were delighted to have her live with them, his sister had more readily adjusted to having their mother's double in residence. For his part, those first few months after she took up residence at Pemberley, the resemblance was often so overwhelming that he would have to remove himself from a room until he could regain control of his emotions. At any rate, he had kept that secret deep within, not able to speak of it to anyone. He was about to greet her when Georgiana interrupted.

"I cannot wait until you take me shopping! I must have some new music, new books and I want us to ride in the park and visit the museums! And ice cream! May we have ice cream?"

At first Audrey had been torn between laughing at Georgiana and reprimanding her for her unladylike behaviour. She had spent the better part of the last two years trying to fashion a young lady out of a decided tomboy. But she found it somewhat amusing that Georgiana lapsed into her former nature whenever she was in her brother's company—especially in light of the fact that she often maintained that she was now old enough to do as she liked. Nevertheless, having instantly taken note of William's dishevelled appearance, his ashen face, and red eyes, her attention was drawn away from Georgiana.

"Of course, sweetling. We shall do everything you want while you are in London. I am at your disposal."

"Oh, Brother, you are too kind!"

His aunt, however, was not so easily pleased. "Fitzwilliam, may I speak to you alone please?"

Both siblings turned to study their aunt, though Audrey gave nothing away by her demeanour—her face remaining as blank as a canvas. William had no choice but to agree.

"Certainly. Shall we go into my study?"

He waved his hand in that direction, and his petite aunt glided past him effortlessly, seemingly floating over the floor as was the custom of elegant ladies. He followed her with his eyes, then turning back to Georgiana, he leaned in to whisper teasingly, "Wish me luck."

Georgiana squeezed his hands in a sign of support, and he kissed her forehead. "Wait in the library and I shall return."

With those words he promptly followed his aunt, catching up to her just as she flung open the door and entered his sanctuary. Stepping to the very centre of the room, she began to turn in a circle, taking every inch of the room into account. By the time she had completed the round, William was sitting behind his desk with his feet propped upon it, trying to look unconcerned.

"Where are your manners? You did not offer to seat me."

"Aunt, I knew that you would not be seated until you had made a clean sweep of the room. So if I had offered to seat you, you would have wondered what I was trying to hide."

The corners of Audrey Ashcroft's mouth lifted, and for a moment, she looked as though she was trying hard not to laugh. Then she chuckled. "When you were younger, I could intimidate you with my disapproval, but now that you are a man … well, let us just get to the point."

She sat down with a flourish in the chair situated directly in front of his desk, opened then closed the cigar box on the corner, then leaned towards him across the great expanse of mahogany. "Georgiana is right, you look awful! What are you trying to hide?"

"I beg your pardon."

"You heard me, young man! The newspapers are neatly stacked on that table where Barnes leaves them every morning. Evidently you have not read one in days. The cigar box is full, and there are no ashes in the trays, so your friends have not been here. That bottle of brandy has not been opened, and no glasses are sitting about or missing from the cabinet—though judging from your appearance, I would assume you had been more often in your cups than not. You have lost enough weight to be noticeable. Your colour is not good, so you have neglected your customary exercise. And even more telling—your eyes have lost their sparkle. So, I ask again, what is it that you do not wish me to find out?"

William's feet came to the floor with much finality as his mask fell from his face. He buried his face in his hands, and seeing his misery, Lady Ashcroft swiftly moved to his side, sliding an arm around his shoulder and kissing the top of his head. Then she ruffled his hair affectionately.

"I am sorry, Fitzwilliam. Having had no children of my own to practice upon, I have no finesse when it comes to parental skills, though God knows I think of you and Georgiana as my own. I can only be honest with you and expect the same in return. Pray tell me, is your present melancholy due to Gisela?"

"She is always a part of my misery, but no more so than usual."

"Then I can only surmise that you have fallen in love."

William's blue eyes were wide as he gazed up at her. "Wha...what makes you say that?"

"I have watched you very closely since your marriage, Fitzwilliam—mainly because I feared for your sanity. I have seen you persevere in the face of tremendous sorrow and heartache, and I concluded long ago that the one thing that would collapse your carefully constructed house of cards would be for you to fall in love. And I see from the look on your face that you have."

William moaned, dropping his head back into his hands. When he finally spoke, it was with mumbled resignation. "I cannot let anyone know—not Georgiana and especially not Gisela. Besides, it can amount to nothing. I am married, and she can never be mine."

"I do not suppose you want to tell me about her?"

"I would rather not. It is hard to persuade my heart not to care when I am constantly reminded of her."

"Oh, Fitzwilliam, my dear, dear boy!" Audrey Ashcroft leaned down to kiss the top of his head again. "You will learn that the heart cannot be persuaded who to love, or not to love, as the case may be. I know because I never met the man that could replace my beloved Joseph. That is why I have remained a widow all these years."

She smoothed William's hair back from his forehead, just as she had when he was a little boy. "It is not too late to divorce that harridan."

"I cannot. Not until I am sure that Georgiana will not be affected by whatever I choose to do."

"Your concern for your sister is honourable, Fitzwilliam, but Anne would never have wanted you to sacrifice your life for Georgiana's." Lady Ashcroft walked back around the desk, sitting down in the chair once more, before leaning forward to take his hand. "Now, tell me what I can do to ease your suffering?"

"You do too much already, Aunt. But if I had a request, it would be for you to continue to keep Georgiana occupied so that she will not notice my melancholy. I do not wish to burden her with my troubles."

"I shall do my best, but you know that she notices everything that affects you." She smiled warmly now. "Lord Landingham has already sent a note asking us to accompany him to the theatre tomorrow. I know Georgiana would love for you to attend with us."

"I shall attend, though I believe Landingham is most looking forward to being *your* escort."

William's aunt chuckled at his tease, "Fitzwilliam Darcy, are you trying to ruffle my feathers, for if you are, you shall be greatly disappointed. I have had many men vie for my hand since I was widowed, and I turned them all down."

"I would not know about that, Aunt. However, I do know that you seem to enjoy his company and he yours. And I can name no man that I think more highly of than Marshall Landingham."

"I agree with you that he is a good and decent man, and if I were looking to marry again, he would be at the top of my list." She stood to leave with a bemused expression. "How is it that this conversation has turned from your love life to mine?"

William was able to smile wanly. "Is love not a fair subject?"

"While love may be a fair subject, love is far from fair," Audrey Ashcroft replied, a trace of sadness in her voice. "I have found that it most often catches us unaware, comes at the most inopportune times and leaves us vulnerable as babes."

At William's bewildered look, she continued. "However, it is the only thing that makes life worth living. It is obvious that you love your family, but you, my nephew, are a rare breed. You are not like the majority of men who care not which woman warms their bed. You love with all your heart and soul, and you deserve to be loved equally. If you have found that kind of love, I beg you, do not wait too long to embrace it. I had only three years with the love of my life before he was taken from me, so I know how fleeting true happiness can be."

With those few words of wisdom, she smiled at him lovingly, squeezed his hand, stood and exited the room. William watched her go as he pondered all that she had said.

Chapter 9

London
Holmes House
The drawing room

Elizabeth could not believe her good fortune. She was sitting in the exquisitely fashioned drawing room of Lady Penelope Holmes, alongside her Aunt Gardiner, paying little attention as the cousins reminisced about their childhood adventures. The Holmes' townhouse was situated in the fashionable section of Mayfair, right across the street from Hyde Park, and after getting a glimpse of the fair prospect when they arrived, she longed to escape her aunt's watch to take a turn about it. But since that was certainly not going to happen today, Elizabeth filed that aspiration away for another time.

Consequently, while the older women were occupied with their memories, she surreptitiously examined the elegantly appointed room and its furnishings more closely as she delighted in such study. The carpets were of forest green, with borders of cream interspersed with multi-coloured flowers and vines which complemented the subtle cream wallpaper, festooned with these same subjects. All the sofas and chairs were upholstered in pale greens and corals, while the wood trim was mahogany, matching the other pieces of furniture. Intricately carved tables were decorated with Dresden figurines, silver pieces and crystal vases of flowers. In fact, Elizabeth noticed that flowers adorned every available surface, many out of season, a sure indication that the townhouse had a conservatory. And as her eyes came to rest on the tall windows which faced the park, Elizabeth had to admit that while she loved the countryside of Hertfordshire, were she to reside in London, this stately home with the large park in close proximity was her idea of heaven.

"Lizzy?" Madeline Gardiner touched her arm.

"I … I am sorry Aunt," Elizabeth floundered, coming back to the present. "I am afraid I was woolgathering."

"My cousin asked how you like London."

Elizabeth turned all her attention to Mrs. Holmes, who looked as though she belonged in one of Lydia's fashion magazines. Very petite—dainty actually—she looked a lot younger than her age, which Aunt Gardiner had mentioned was five and thirty. She had perfect, ivory complexion, light-brown hair that was scattered with gold tresses and hazel eyes which now danced with mirth as she awaited Elizabeth's reply.

"I enjoy London very much. Especially spending time with my aunt and uncle and playing with my cousins."

"That is natural, but surely you enjoy the entertainment. The theatre, the opera, the—"

At that very moment, the door flew open, and a man and a woman entered the room, a frustrated butler following right behind.

Lady Holmes shook her head in mock disapproval. "Never mind, Chalmers. You must know by now that my cousin never waits to be announced."

The man, who had an arrogant air about him, appeared to be about three and thirty years of age. He was of medium height with light brown hair, brown eyes and was somewhat portly. His features were nondescript, with nothing to recommend them. The girl, who was evidently several years younger, had the same colouring and appearance, though she was trim.

"John! Alfreda! You are early! What a grand surprise!" Their hostess rushed to the newcomers, kissing each before introducing them.

"Ladies, may I present my cousins, Lord John Wilkens, Earl of Hampton, and Lady Alfreda Wilkens of Gatesbridge in Kent. They are the children of the late Lord Carlton and Lady Kathleen Wilkens, Walter's aunt and uncle. And if I remember correctly, Madeline, I wrote to you that Lord Carlton died unexpectedly last year."

Mrs. Gardiner, who had stood along with Elizabeth, nodded.

Then addressing the couple, she offered, "This is my cousin, Madeline Gardiner, and her niece, Miss Elizabeth Bennet."

John Wilkens released his sister's arm, walking forward until he stood in front of Elizabeth with his hands balled, resting upon his hips. His eyes stayed fixed on her as he examined her pointedly. Then he bowed slightly, addressing her and her aunt. "I am pleased to meet you, Miss Bennet … Mrs. Gardiner."

Elizabeth appeared somewhat flustered at his marked attention, but was diverted as Alfreda Wilkens moved forward to take her brother's arm once more.

"It is a pleasure to meet you," the girl offered shyly, as she bobbed a curtsey. Recognizing her bashful nature, Elizabeth gave Alfreda a warm smile and received one in return.

Lady Holmes took advantage of the silence to declare, "Now that my cousin has the management of the estate well in hand, he has time to concentrate on procuring a mistress for Gatesbridge!"

"Cousin, how often have I asked you not to play the matchmaker? I shall make my own choice," Wilkens chided Lady Holmes, not even attempting to hide his annoyance.

"I am only informing the ladies," Lady Holmes rejoined, ignoring his irritation and winking at Elizabeth. "Now, before you entered, I was about to enquire if Miss Bennet would attend the ball the colonel and I are giving next week." Instantly she covered her mouth with her hand. "Oh, my! How will I ever get used to calling Walter *the earl*, when I have called him *the colonel* so many years?"

As all the ladies except Elizabeth giggled, as she was still uncomfortable under the earl's gaze. Lord Wilkens took the opportunity to address her again. "Do say that you shall attend the ball, Miss Bennet, and that I may have the honour of the first set."

Feeling a bit trapped, Elizabeth cut her eyes to her aunt who instantly declared, "Of course, you shall attend the ball with your uncle and me."

It was not as though she did not wish to attend, but Elizabeth had a feeling that this gentleman was used to getting his way, and that did not sit well with her. Nevertheless, she was not in a position to refuse. "I accept your kind invitation to dance, sir."

He seemed smug after her consent, which caused Elizabeth even more trepidation. But upon noting her aunt's expression and remembering her promise to Jane to find matches for them both, she forced a smile.

I might as well get down to the business of being all sweetness and light!

Fortuitously, Alfreda Wilkens quickly claimed the seat next to Elizabeth as she sat back down, and they began a conversation, chatting affably while the other occupants of the room talked among themselves. And after almost a quarter-hour, her new friend made a request.

"I would love for you to stay here with me the night before the ball," Alfreda urged as she covered Elizabeth's hand with her own. "My cousin has plenty of room, and I often invite friends to stay when I am in Town. If you will say yes, you and I shall sit up late and talk!"

Elizabeth smiled at the thought. She had really missed her late night talks with Jane since she had come to London. "We shall see if that is possible."

"Marvellous! With your consent, I shall make all the arrangements."

As they rode in the open carriage back to Gracechurch Street, Madeline Gardiner observed as different emotions played across Lizzy's face. She had gone to some trouble to make sure that they were there when Penelope's cousins arrived and was disappointed by her niece's reaction to the earl. In addition, she wondered at her unusual quietness, especially after such a grand adventure as visiting Mayfair, since Lizzy had always enjoyed touring such grand houses in the past. Nevertheless, she felt she must know Lizzy's opinion of John Wilkens, as she had held high hopes of him admiring either her or Jane.

When asked her opinion of the earl, Elizabeth immediately ceased pretending to study the people in the nearby park and met her aunt's gaze steadfastly, not unaware of why she was asking.

"I … I suppose he is a proper gentleman. I really did not have time to sketch his character. His sister, however, is so pleasant that she reminds me of Jane."

"Yes, Alfreda is a sweet girl. I had no doubt that you and she would be fast friends. However, I have heard many good things from Penelope about her nephew, as well. He assumed a great deal of responsibility with his father's death, and as his mother passed years ago, there is only he and his sister left. Nevertheless, I have been told that he has done an admirable job of running the estate, caring for Alfreda and taking his place as the earl."

Elizabeth studied her aunt for a long time. "And you are telling me this because you want me to try to gain his attention?"

"You have already gained his attention, Lizzy. What I am saying is simply give the man a chance and see how things progress."

Elizabeth turned to face the park again, the look on her face and the sigh she released evidence of her misgivings.

Mrs. Gardiner hurried to caution, "You and your sisters have little dowry, no connections and heaven knows your mother and younger sisters behave atrociously at times, all of which will not be overlooked by the *ton*."

As Elizabeth acknowledged these points with barely a nod, her aunt pressed her case. "Most of society will reject you and Jane outright because of these misfortunes, but John Wilkens has no parents or close relations to please, other than Alfreda, and she warmed to you quickly. This is a great opportunity. Do you understand?"

"He can marry whomever he chooses, so I would be wise to accept him if he offers."

Mrs. Gardiner's shoulders visibly relaxed, and she released a breath she had been holding. "Precisely! Why else do you think you are in London but to secure a husband? And if you were to marry an earl, then Jane would have a much greater chance of marrying well and your other sisters would follow, not to mention the fact that a wealthy man can take over Fanny's care if your father should die."

She leaned over to take her niece's hand. "You know that your uncle and I value you and Jane for the fine young women that you are, and we certainly do not wish you to be unhappy. But Lizzy you must be practical. It is just as easy to learn to care for a wealthy man as a poor one, and you will be doing your family a great service."

The mention of wealth brought to mind Mr. Darcy, and Elizabeth's heart ached with the memory of the night spent in his arms. Under her breath she whispered, "I vowed only to marry for the deepest love."

Unfortunately, Mrs. Gardiner heard and chided, "That is the substance of fairytales, and it is not realistic or sensible. Most people learn to care for their spouse once they are married, not before. The idea of marrying for love is clearly something this new generation has embraced. My advice to you is to forget such nonsense."

Elizabeth turned so that her aunt could not see the tears that welled up. Noting her niece's sad mien, Madeline Gardiner said no more. She and Edward had long blamed Thomas Bennet for leaving his daughters with inadequate dowries, an unchecked mother and undisciplined siblings. His failures now threatened the very future of them all, as they would likely be called upon to help Fanny and the girls if Thomas died, and that would strain their own limited resources. Thus, they considered it their duty to instruct Lizzy and Jane in the ways of proper society and pray that this training would be sufficient to secure them a decent offer of marriage.

As she continued to monitor her niece out of the corner of her eye, she prayed that Lizzy's penchant to chart her own course would be tempered by the knowledge that she must obey the rules of society if she was to be of any benefit to her sisters—especially Jane who held so much promise.

I shall speak of it again tomorrow and emphasize the benefit to Jane. Better to let her reflect on all that I have said.

Darcy House
William's Study

Charles Bingley, doing a very good impersonation of his host, paced the floors of the study while running his hands through his thick red curls. Every so often however, he would stop to gesture wildly, a mannerism he did not share with his friend and mentor.

"Well, I for one, think that Mr. Carter is exactly right! In light of the background information on the ship's captain and the West Indies port captain, he believes there is reason to think the vessels may have been diverted to another port, the merchandise sold and the profits stolen. Thus, I have authorized him to expand the investigation to prove his theory."

William turned from pouring two glasses of brandy to hand one to Charles, mainly to stop his pacing, as he was tired of following his progress. "So the captain, this fellow Grier, is a cousin of the port captain?"

"It seems that is the case and the port captain has recently mysteriously disappeared as well."

"Then Carter believes both ships presumed lost at sea were stolen?"

Charles took the offered drink. "Both!"

"What will you do in the meantime for merchandise?"

"I have sufficient goods for now. I shall simply use different routes, as I have other ships and other sources of spices, coffee, silks and fruit—howbeit, they are more expensive. I am off to Liverpool tomorrow to check on my warehouse and talk with my man there. While trying to distance myself from trade, I feel I may have relegated too much responsibility to others who are less capable and neglected my own interests. It is time I took charge again, at least until I can find someone astute enough to whom I may assign the daily operations of the business."

"And you still do not want a loan?"

"Darcy, I appreciate that you are my silent partner and have loaned me the money to expand several times, but I do not wish to borrow more money until I am sure of what is happening. Do not despair, as I shall not think twice about asking if I see the need."

William could not but smile. "I am proud that you have come to this conclusion without my advice. While trying to raise your position in society is a noble quest, still you must be practical, as your fortune is nonetheless still vested in trade."

"It was not entirely without your advice. After all, you recommended I talk with Mr. Lowell, who put me in touch with Mr. Carter."

"That was nothing."

"In any event, I appreciate it."

"How does all of this affect your relationship with *the angel*?"

Charles' face fell. "In hindsight, I am afraid that in my haste to get to London I may not have handled that well at all."

"What do you mean?"

"I was so upset when I got your letter that I left Netherfield forthwith, not taking the time to explain to Jane—Miss Bennet—why I had to depart. Caroline offered to write a letter of explanation and I approved. In hindsight, I cannot help but feel that she might have been disappointed in my manner of leaving."

"Then write her a letter."

"You know I cannot."

"Then write to Mr. Bennet. Tell him a bit of your current situation, and he will no doubt pass it along to his daughter. Surely she will understand that you had to leave Meryton without delay."

Charles seemed to consider that suggestion before murmuring softly, "I do not know if I shall have anything to offer her, or any woman, if I cannot find the source of my losses and recover the goods. I will not, in good conscience, court someone when I do not know what my future holds."

"Charles, I—"

Bingley held up a hand. "You have helped me a great deal, Darcy, but I have to do this on my own."

His friend had come a long way in the last few years, and William knew that he must continue to let him make his own decisions. But, knowing first-hand the agony of loving someone lost to you, he needed to warn his friend.

"Bingley, if you love Miss Bennet, do not wait too long to secure her."

"I do not intend to. I will make her an offer as soon as I have something to offer besides my name."

William nodded, finishing his drink silently.

If only I could offer Elizabeth my name.

❧

London
Bingley's Townhouse
The next day
Dining Room

Caroline was angry quite often these days, and had Louisa known this quarrel was transpiring in the dining room, she would have waited until later to break her fast. For once, she was pleased that Bertram was still sleeping off his overindulgence, as he dearly hated Caroline's diatribes. And lately he complained constantly about them.

"Really, Charles! Must you be the one to go to Liverpool? Can you not send one of your underlings from the warehouse here?" Caroline huffed and stomped about the room, as their brother ate in preparation for his journey.

"If you do not stay in London, then I shall miss the most prestigious balls and parties. Will you leave me bereft of every notable soirée that London has to offer while you gallivant all over England on a witch hunt?"

Bingley stood abruptly, making his chair tilt back precariously, and threw his serviette on the table forcefully. "What you mean is that without me, Darcy's friends will not invite you! You could have ample society while I take care of business, only you think yourself above them."

"They are all tradesmen! Not a one of them has aspirations of bettering themselves as we do!"

"As *you* do! And thus far, your aspirations have only hurt you, dear sister!"

"How ill-mannered! And I thought that you had my best interests at heart. After all, how am I to make a decent match without being included among the best of society?"

Charles laughed mirthlessly. "Make a match? How indeed! You have chased

Darcy these many years, to the exclusion of every other man, and he still would not have you if you were the only woman on earth."

"Do not be so certain, Charles. If he divorces, it will be over Gisela Darcy's dead body! I imagine she will resist strenuously, and it will be quite the scandal. Some, maybe most, will undoubtedly *cut* the illustrious Mr. Darcy after such a breach of decorum, and he may be very grateful for my steadfast devotion. No doubt he will then see me in a different light!"

Bingley heaved an audible sigh, declaring, "I assure you that Darcy already sees who you are, Caroline, and that is why he is not interested." With those words he quit the room.

Caroline looked to Louisa, who had quietly taken a seat during their exchange. "Charles is such a dullard!"

Louisa cautioned her. "I advise you not to talk ill of our brother. After all, it is to his credit that you live well!"

"And you as well!" Caroline huffed. "Without Charles, I dare say you would not be able to maintain your standard of living. Not with Hurst's disdain for actually doing anything constructive!"

Louisa rolled her eyes. "Attacking my husband will not help you. I know only too well his shortcomings and I agree. However, if you continue to push Charles, I fear that he shall rid himself of you at some point—perhaps making good on his threat to send you to live with Aunt Harrison in Scarborough. And I shall not plead your case if he does. When I have in the past, it only served to make him angry at me. So be forewarned!"

Caroline cocked her head as if studying her sister. "When I am Mrs. Darcy of Pemberley, I shall remember your disloyalty."

Louisa stifled a laugh. "If you are ever Mrs. Darcy, I shall just have to rely on my connection to Charles to recommend me to Mr. Darcy."

With those few words, Louisa resumed eating as Caroline flounced from the room, slamming the door soundly behind. After her sister's departure, Louisa began to recall just when her sister had become so missish and concluded that it was after Mr. Darcy befriended their brother at Cambridge. Caroline had instantly been attracted to the handsome Mr. Darcy and had set her cap for him.

I cannot fault her there. Even I thought him the most handsome man of my acquaintance!

Nevertheless, Louisa was not so foolish as to think she had a chance with the Master of Pemberley and had accepted Mr. Hurst's offer shortly thereafter. With Caroline, however, that was not the case. For years she had used Charles' connection to Mr. Darcy at every opportunity—putting all of them in his company whenever possible.

You are a fool, Caroline, to think that man would ever have you!

Just then the door opened and Mrs. Wiggins entered. Seeing Louisa, she nodded and moved to the sideboard to ensure that nothing needed her attention. While Mrs. Wiggins rearranged the dishes and stirred about behind her, Louisa's thoughts returned to her family. Charles was changing and she wondered why Caroline had not recognized that fact. Their brother was becoming his own man, and once married, he would certainly no longer be the easily managed brother of the past.

The implications were daunting. She was terribly disappointed in Mr. Hurst and did not relish spending time alone with him. Furthermore, it was obvious that they could not keep their present standard of living without imposing on Charles for a good part of the year. Suddenly, with that knowledge, her appetite disappeared and sighing with resignation, she took leave of the room as well.

London
Matlock House
Edward Fitzwilliam's Study

The two men stood facing each other not unlike combatants in a ring. The Earl of Matlock, an older version of Richard with sandy hair and brown eyes, had not called his second son to his home for quite some time—not since their last argument months ago.

"Have you seen this?"

Picking up a tabloid from the corner of his desk, the Earl of Matlock threw it in his son's direction. Catching it in mid-air, Richard dutifully perused the days-old paper to find whatever was annoying his father and found it under the gossip section. It was a veiled reference to Gisela Darcy's behaviour at the Satterfield's ball.

"My nephew is too obstinate for his own good. First, he refuses my request that he marry Anne. Then he marries this ... this widow without warning or explanation, escorts her to her own townhouse and makes a show of leaving her there. The whole of London is aware of this!" The Earl of Matlock took a deep draw from his cigar and blew the smoke into the air. "And his dogged refusal to live with that woman has resulted in more fodder for the gossip sheets than a divorce would ever cause!"

Richard shrugged. "Darcy is not concerned with what society thinks, Father. He feels he has done his part in suppressing family scandals by marrying that harridan to keep George Darcy's secret. But he was betrayed in the worst way! She was never with child."

"My sister should never have married that untitled buffoon. I told Anne that he was not good enough for her, but she would not listen to me. NO ONE listens to me, not even you!"

"And what is my fault? I have given up every woman that I have fancied because you did not approve of her lineage or her dowry was not large enough. Is that not sufficient to earn your good will?"

"Do not be impertinent, Richard! It is no one's fault that you are the second son." Edward Fitzwilliam bellowed. "The point is that Evelyn has been furiously working to suppress one scandal after another since Fitzwilliam married that harlot! And yet Mrs. Darcy flaunted Attenborough in public at the Satterfield's ball. No this madness must stop! I shall demand that Darcy consult a solicitor about a divorce immediately!"

"That is not your decision to make, Father," Richard declared. "If you had not championed Aunt Catherine's plans to make him marry Anne, perhaps he would not have married Gisela without your knowledge or approval." Though he knew that was not the case, Richard could not help but taunt his father with the fiasco that resulted from his attempts to control Darcy.

"Just remember, young man, that your allowance can also be affected by your attitude."

"And how long will you remind me of that?" Richard came to his feet as his face reddened. "I am a decorated officer in His Majesty's service, not a boy! And if need be, I will survive on my salary and my inheritance from Grandmother. I am as tired of being threatened as Darcy. He is his own man, and he can damn well do as he pleases and, in addition, I think it is time I did so too."

With those words, Richard headed to the door. His father was shocked into silence as he exited the room and slammed the door behind him. Just outside, his mother stood waiting. She held a finger to her lips as a sign of silence, before she took his hand and led him to her office down the hall. Once they were inside, the door closed and locked, she motioned her youngest son to sit. She then took the seat behind her small desk and studied him earnestly.

"Your father can be very demanding."

Richard laughed mirthlessly. "That is an understatement."

She smiled wanly. "I … I do not like controversy—you know that." Richard nodded. "I have tried to keep peace among our family, even between those members of whom I am not fond."

"Gisela?"

She nodded. "I do not wish to air our family problems for all England to see, so I have treated her with the respect that her marriage to Fitzwilliam warrants. However, she is being more and more ridiculous every day."

"The Satterfield's ball?"

"Yes. She arrived late with Lord Howard Attenborough, who was surprisingly sober, though Gisela was in her cups. Do you know him?"

"Earl of Wiltshire?"

"Exactly. A more pompous, self-serving man I have never met. They paraded around the ballroom, arm-in-arm like lovers! I think he enjoys flaunting it in your cousin's face that he is sleeping with his wife. You know he could never best Fitzwilliam in any other way." His mother began to fan herself with a piece of paper. "I was appalled, and since your father and Edgar were in the card room, I had to summon them. And you know how stubborn your father can be when he is winning. By the time Edward and Edgar appeared, Gisela and Attenborough had disappeared as quickly as they had come. It was almost as though they planned their arrival and departure precisely when your father and brother would be occupied elsewhere."

"I would not doubt it. Gisela is no simpleton. She is calculating."

"I have tried to give Gisela my approbation, if nothing else, since Fitzwilliam has cast her in such a bad light by his refusal to live with her, but I find that I cannot condone such behaviour." She noted that Richard did not reply, but she understood. He had never liked William's wife.

"I know that you and Fitzwilliam are close. Can you tell me what he plans to do about Gisela?"

"I cannot. Nor would I betray a confidence, Mother. I suggest you talk with him."

"He will not talk to me. He resents that I recognise Gisela and invite her to family gatherings."

"I can understand his position."

"Richard, surely you of all people know what I face with the *ton*! I must keep up appearances for your sister's sake. Alicia is still unmarried!"

Richard shrugged. "Perhaps if Father—"

"Do not say it! Your father will never allow her to marry that man!"

"I do not know what you and Father hope to accomplish by denying her the man she loves. Colonel Neilson is an excellent man and has much to recommend him, though he is a second son. "

"Wealth marries wealth, and titled wealth at that, whenever possible—not second sons."

"How well I know."

Evelyn Fitzwilliam reached to take his hand. "Richard, your father and I will find a woman with a large dowry in need of connections. Be patient."

He stood to leave. "Mother, I do not like being treated like a child any more than Darcy. I believe I have just had this conversation with Father. Now if you will excuse me."

His mother stopped him at the door. "I am sorry that you are caught in this conundrum. It is not easy being a second son, but try to understand our position. If my mother had not left you an inheritance, I do not know how you would have survived once your father dies. Your allowance ends with him. Of course, Edgar could always decide to continue the stipend."

"I understand completely, Mother. I am a pawn in the games of the *ton,* and my only worth is my name. I have no doubt that Edgar will cut me off. In any event, I believe I am going to learn how to survive without an allowance even sooner."

With that, Richard opened the door and left the house, never looking back, though his mother followed him to the foyer with a puzzled look on her face. In the background, Richard could hear his father shouting orders to one of the servants about finding him and demanding his return.

London
Holmes House
The Study

As newly promoted Colonel Steven Neilson waited in the foyer at Holmes House with his friend, he studied the other officer in meticulous detail. Observing Richard Fitzwilliam's bearing, he smiled to recall that, with the exception of when they were training new recruits in survival techniques, he had seldom seen his colleague dressed any less smartly than at this moment. Still, regardless of Fitzwilliam's state of dress, he considered him the epitome of an officer—someone who took his job seriously and expected the same from every officer. He was someone Neilson admired enough to emulate.

His thoughts were abruptly interrupted by the butler's return and the invitation for both men to follow as he proceeded down a hallway. Up ahead a door opened and a tall, boyish-looking man with mischievous green eyes and sandy hair peered into the hall before stepping out with a wide grin.

"I am surprised to see you, Richard!" Lord Holmes, Viscount Moreland, proclaimed, grasping his friend's hand and slapping him on the back. He practically pulled Richard through the door, as Neilson followed. "The last time we crossed paths, you were supervising new recruits in manoeuvres near Wales. That was over a year ago!"

"That is because you have spent the majority of your time in the service in Weymouth, relaxing by the sea while I actually had to work!" Richard teased.

"True! But what was I to do? My commanding officer would not issue an order without my assistance!" Still chuckling, he addressed the other man, "Welcome, Colonel Neilson!"

"Steven, please," the officer replied. "After hearing the tales Richard told for the past few months of your shared adventures, I feel that you and I are old friends!"

"Steven it is! Please call me Walter," Lord Holmes declared, shaking the man's hand before chiding his friend. "I hope you did not tell him *everything*!"

"Only the respectable parts!" Richard confirmed with a chuckle. "I said nothing of the adventures we shared on leave in Brighton when I was first commissioned!"

All the men laughed heartily as Holmes motioned for his two visitors to sit. Then focusing on Richard, he challenged, "As happy as I am to see you, I must ask what brings you here today. You have not exactly been a steady visitor in the past."

"I am here to convey my concern regarding your father. I just learned upon reaching London that his health has worsened, and he has returned to Satterfield Manor. He has been like a father to me, and I wondered if there was anything I could do to be of service to him … or to you."

"You are too kind, but I fear there is nothing anyone can do," Holmes murmured, his smile fading as his expression darkened. "His physician states that his heart is weakening, but he cannot say if he will succumb in another month or another year. I wanted to travel with him, but he insisted I stay here and fulfil my duties, as there is no way of knowing how long he may survive."

The Viscount slammed his fist on the desk. "It is so hard to wait, not knowing when to go to him." Richard moved to stand beside his friend, grasping his shoulder and squeezing it in support. Holmes' voice was quieter as he continued, "It was difficult succeeding Harrison as the viscount, but I cannot imagine succeeding Father."

"How does one prepare for that?" Richard said quietly and then remembered his cousin's similar situation. "I have no experience to draw from, but Darcy knows well what you are suffering. He could not be here today but asked me to offer his assistance. He may not be titled, but he is well acquainted with running an estate."

"Darcy is a good friend. Tell him I am appreciative, and I will certainly consult him. By the way, I am not in the frame of mind for such an event, but nevertheless, Penelope and I are hosting a ball Saturday. She insists that we must reciprocate for all the soirées given on our behalf since our arrival. And, if Father is only going to get worse, we must do it now rather than later. I insist that both of you come, as it will be easier for me to bear. And bring that hermit Darcy. I have not seen him in ages!"

"I will try to persuade him, but you know how my cousin hates being on display. And since you," he glanced to the other officer, "and Neilson are both aware of the circumstances, I must caution you that he will not attend if there is the least possibility that Gisela will be present. Are you aware that she is in London?"

"All of London is aware! I cannot imagine why Mrs. Darcy enjoys being the target of jokes, but emphasise to Darcy that she is not invited. I merely want to renew our friendship, especially as I will likely need his advice. Besides, we are now neighbours—I could hit his townhouse with a rock if my arm was still good and my aim true!"

"You once had the best arm among us!" Richard declared, walking back around the desk to take his seat. "Remember the time you broke the window at Matlock, and Father though it was Darcy. It was a wonder he did not turn you in and save himself the tongue lashing."

"Darcy was always too kind for his own good. I do not think I would have been so honourable if the tables had been turned!" He grinned lopsidedly. "Your father always frightened me. He still does."

Richard chuckled mirthlessly. "He still tries to frighten me!"

Just then, the study door opened and Penelope Holmes stuck her head inside. "Walter? I hope I am not disturbing you, but when I learned that Colonel Fitzwilliam is—"

A wide smile split Lord Holmes' face when his beloved wife interrupted the conversation, and when she rushed into the room upon seeing Richard, he began to chuckle.

"Oh, Colonel!" The petite woman gushed, stopping before him. "I was so pleased to learn from your mother that you were transferred to London. You must not be a stranger now that we are in the same town. And you must attend the ball!" She looked over her shoulder. "Tell him he must attend, Walter."

"I am no longer in the military, dear, so I cannot give orders. I may only request."

"Then I shall be forced to give the orders. You MUST come, Richard."

Richard stood to take her hand, bringing it to his lips for a kiss. "Had I more commanding officers like you, Lady Holmes, the army would be a much more pleasant occupation!"

"We are old friends—it is still Penelope."

Richard nodded. "Penelope."

As she turned to study Steven Neilson, Holmes and Richard exchanged amused glances. Both knew what she was thinking—this tall, good-looking fellow with blond hair and blue eyes would make an excellent dance partner for some lady. Nonetheless, before she could utter a word, her husband intervened.

"Penelope, may I introduce Colonel Neilson, and, yes, I have already asked him to the ball. Colonel Neilson, this is my lovely wife."

Before Neilson could reply, she bobbed a curtsey. "Colonel, so good to make your acquaintance. Please tell me that you dance! "

Everyone, including Neilson, laughed. "Yes, Lady Holmes. I do dance, and I shall attend the ball with pleasure."

"Good. Then, that is settled. I shall expect you and Richard!"

Suddenly, she faced her husband. "Oh, I almost forgot. Elizabeth and Alfreda purchased muffins while they were in Town. I had Cook make tea, and we were just going to enjoy them in the parlour. We would love for all of you to join us."

Before anyone could object, Lord Holmes accepted and both colonels followed Lord and Lady Holmes as they led the way to the parlour.

Thirty minutes later, Richard sat mute, astonished by two things—the proficient manner in which Colonel Neilson entertained the room with his tales of life in the army and the identity of one of the young women introduced to him.

While he had certainly found Neilson humorous around a campfire, he had never witnessed the effect he had on respectable company with less bawdy tales. And were he not aware that the colonel was in love with his sister, Alicia, he might have deduced that the man was trying to win the attention of at least one of the eligible ladies in their company. And *that* lady was eagerly paying attention to Neilson's tall stories, her fine eyes sparkling with merriment.

When Penelope had introduced the women earlier, Richard had discovered that he was already familiar with Alfreda Wilkens. Though they had never met, he had seen her about town with her late father. In addition, he was quite familiar with her brother, the Earl of Hampton, having encountered him at White's often when accompanying Darcy. Neither he nor his cousin cared for the earl's attitude of self-importance, nevertheless, Richard had to admit that he saw nothing of that flaw in his painfully shy sister.

In contrast, the pretty, dark-haired woman had him acting like a schoolboy until he learned her name. Had Darcy not uttered that same name, Elizabeth Bennet, only weeks before, Richard might have been in great danger of falling under the spell of the lovely ebony orbs that now studied him. Thus, it was with a great deal of effort that he had mumbled a reply and scurried to the furthest seat from which to observe her while he recovered his senses.

From his vantage point, it was quickly evident that more than just beauty had stolen his cousin's heart. Miss Bennet's complete lack of affectation was as refreshing as her sincerity. Feigning occupation with his food and drink, Richard was free to enjoy her lively conversation, impertinent questions and infectious laugh. Moreover, she impressed him with her attempts to draw Miss Wilkens into the discussion, showing compassion for the shyer lady's feelings. His conclusion? How could Darcy NOT fall in love with her?

Consequently, as everyone readied to leave, he moved in her direction, determined to learn if she remembered his cousin with the same fondness Darcy displayed.

She raised a quizzical brow when he called her name. He glanced at the other occupants of the room. They were talking and would not likely hear what he had to say.

"Lady Holmes mentioned that you live in Hertfordshire, Meryton specifically."

"That is correct."

"Then perhaps you have met my cousin's best friend, Charles Bingley? I understand that recently he rented an estate there."

Elizabeth's expression darkened, causing Richard to wonder if he had touched on an unpleasant subject for the young woman. "Yes. I had the honour. However, Mr. Bingley quit Meryton abruptly a few days ago."

Richard chuckled, trying to lighten the mood. "He does have a tendency to move quickly when my cousin sends for him."

"Your cousin?"

"Fitzwilliam Darcy."

The colour draining from Elizabeth's face did not go unnoticed. "Mr. Darcy is your cousin?" She stared off into space for a brief moment, then met his eyes with a wan smile. "I should have known there was some connection, given the name."

"Yes. It is a bit confusing, for in Darcy's family, the firstborn often takes his mother's maiden name. His mother was my father's sister. Thus he is Fitzwilliam Darcy."

"I ... I see."

Just then, Penelope Holmes came rushing over to put her arm around Elizabeth's shoulder. "Do you not think Miss Bennet a fine addition to the social scene, Richard? She is so lovely that I expect her dance card will be full before the ball begins, what with her uncle, my husband and my cousin already having claimed a set."

Richard addressed Elizabeth. "Lady Holmes makes a good case for not delaying. May I enquire if you have a set open, Miss Bennet?"

Amused, Elizabeth was about to reply when a man's voice boomed across the room. "Miss Bennet has granted me the honour of the first and supper sets,

Colonel Fitzwilliam!"

With that exclamation, the Earl of Hampton strode directly to where Elizabeth, Richard and their hostess were standing. Evidently he had entered the room as everyone was preparing to depart, going unnoticed as he stood just inside to observe Elizabeth's behaviour. Penelope was taken aback by her cousin's manners, but decided against making a show of it openly. Instead, she vowed to take him to task privately and moved to join her husband. Instantly, Wilkens took her place, standing as close to Elizabeth as propriety permitted, all the while glaring at Richard.

Elizabeth was furious! She had promised him only one set and his possessive behaviour was annoying. The look she gave Wilkens did not go unnoticed by William's cousin. However, just as she was about to put him in his place, Alfreda Wilkens appeared at her side, almost as though she had sensed that Elizabeth was about to chastise her overbearing brother.

She commented in a teasing manner, "Colonel, my brother is quite taken with Miss Bennet, I fear. I suggest you secure your set quickly before he demands them all!"

Not one of them smiled along with Alfreda, who tried to put on a brave face. However, upon seeing her anxious expression, Elizabeth endeavoured to make light of the situation. Ignoring Wilkens, she teased Richard, "Do not fear, Colonel. I am unmarried, and I intend to dance with all the eligible men!"

The scowl on Wilkens face was unmistakable as he turned abruptly on his heel and headed to the door. Alfreda sighed, shrugged her shoulders and followed, catching his arm to stop him halfway. This left Richard and Elizabeth watching brother and sister argue, though they were endeavouring to keep their voices down.

Finally, Richard ventured, "How well do you know the earl, Miss Bennet?"

"We met only a few days ago."

"If I did not know better, from the way he behaves I would think you were betrothed."

"He presumes too much. I hardly know the man," she answered, though her eyes stayed locked on the quarrelling siblings.

"Most young women would think him an excellent match—what with his wealth and title. I have heard him described as the most eligible bachelor in London."

"I assure you that such things hold no weight with me. I prefer to judge a man by his character."

From the corner of his eye, Richard took her measure. Judging by the set of her jaw and the way her dark eyes flashed angrily, she certainly looked as if she meant every word.

"I hoped that was the case, as my cousin would be very upset to learn that you are engaged."

Elizabeth's head swung around to examine Richard, her mind beginning to race as fast as her heart. Unfortunately, the rest of the party chose that moment to leave, affording her no chance to ask what he had meant. Everyone proceeded towards the door, then down the hallway in the direction of the foyer. She was attempting to edge closer to the colonel, hoping to whisper her question, when Wilkens grabbed her arm, stopping her progress.

"Per your Aunt Gardiner's request, I am to escort you home, Miss Bennet.

Alfreda will accompany us."

Too upset to enquire of Wilkens how he had arranged to escort her home, all Elizabeth could do was watch as Colonel Fitzwilliam expressed his thanks to their hosts, acknowledged being pleased to have met her and Alfreda, and made his way out the front door. Colonel Neilson echoed his actions, exiting right behind him.

Elizabeth had no way of knowing that it would be quite some time before she would learn the reason for the colonel's statement.

In the carriage

"If you scowl like that all the way to army headquarters, your face may never recover!"

Richard startled, his gaze settling on the colleague he had almost forgotten was in the carriage. "I am sorry. I was woolgathering."

"I will wager that I can guess what your woolgathering entailed."

"I think not!" Richard tried to smile at Neilson's teasing.

"You are thinking that Lord Wilkens is an arse, and you are upset that he is attempting to secure Miss Bennet, whom you fancy."

At first, Richard was stunned. Then he realised that any sane man would think Wilkens was an arse. He began to chuckle. "You only deduced what was easy. Wilkens is an arse, and anyone who has met the man would grasp that very quickly."

"And my other theory? You fancy the lovely Miss Bennet for yourself?"

"*Lovely* Miss Bennet? I thought you were in love with Alicia?"

"I AM in love with Alicia, but I am not blind!" Neilson declared decidedly. "I can still appreciate a pretty woman and so can you, it seems. Now, if I am incorrect and you do not fancy Miss Bennet for yourself, what was that all about?"

"You know well enough that a second son must marry a woman with a large dowry, which evidently is not the case with Miss Bennet. Her open and friendly manner and the style of her clothes suggest a country upbringing, without the money or prestige of the *ton*. That would not be a deterrent if I were wealthy, as I found her demeanour refreshing, but alas, I am not." Left unsaid was the fact that he would never approach the woman he knew his cousin loved.

"I apologise. I was wrong to assume that your marked attention to her at the end of our visit was more than friendship."

"Let that be a lesson. Appearances can be deceiving."

"Such as Wilkens having all the appearance of a gentleman but none of the comportment?"

Richard nodded. "Well said, Colonel. Well said."

"I watched him insinuate himself into your conversation with Miss Bennet. Rumour is that he is desperate to find someone suitable to marry because he has been turned down by three debutants this year. I do find it sad that he has apparently set his cap for such a vivacious woman as Miss Bennet. I cannot imagine her being leg-shackled to that pompous idiot. My own dear father vowed that he would never allow Hampton to court my sisters, so that should tell you something."

"It certainly does," Richard agreed.

And Darcy will be heartsick to learn of Wilkens' interest in the woman he loves.

Immediately he sobered, remembering the anger in Wilkens eyes as he loudly touted his sets with Miss Bennet. A still, small voice that he had learned to value and obey whispered a warning.

Wilkens is dangerous. If Darcy is serious about Miss Bennet, he had best begin to seek a divorce now and secure her heart and hand!

In a separate carriage

Having just left Elizabeth at the Gardiners' house on Gracechurch Street where he had been very charming to the couple, the Wilkens' carriage had barely cleared the next street when John Wilkens began to berate Alfreda.

"Never make light of my feelings again!" he roared, causing his sister to hide her face in her hands. "In fact, I forbid you to ever discuss me or my feelings with anyone, do you hear me!"

Trembling, Alfreda nodded without answering.

"DO YOU HEAR ME?"

"Y…Yes."

Used to her brother's tirades, though lately each seemed worse than the last, Alfreda had dreaded the moment they were alone. Nevertheless, she liked Elizabeth so well that she had only meant to distract her from her frustration with John. He was too presumptuous and well aware that he had never been granted the supper set! Thus, in her eagerness to prevent a repeat of what had happened with the other women her brother had deigned to single out, she had intervened.

"What I say or do is not your business! Nor do I need you to make excuses for my actions!"

"But, Brother, I was only trying to smooth things over. I did not want Miss Bennet to think you overbearing and reject you like—"

"Reject me? No one has ever rejected me! I have rejected them!" Her brother's face began to turn bright red as it always did when he was extremely angry. She took several deep breaths as she tried to think of what to say next.

"But … but you said that Miss Christensen, Miss Hartwell and Miss Norwood all ended the courtship. You told me that they—"

"Enough! I told you nothing of the sort. On closer study, I simply found each of them unsuitable for a wife. It was I who decided THEY were inappropriate! And, furthermore, I am not overbearing!"

Alfreda sighed, turning her head to the window. At least he was unlikely to strike her with the servants just outside the carriage. There was no reasoning with him when he was angry. The best she could hope for was that he would calm down before they got back to their cousin's house.

Suddenly, there was a hand on her arm and she startled. John moved to sit next to her, feigning concern. "I shall need your help to secure Miss Bennet's trust, as it appears that she likes you. Let us forget about your slip of the tongue and move forward. Are you willing to help me convince her of my sincerity?"

There was nothing to do but consent, so she did. He seemed pleased, smiling in the same manner as he had whenever he apologised for hitting her. He knew not the meaning of sincerity, but what could she do? She very much liked Elizabeth Bennet, and it would be comforting to have another woman in the family. In addition, she held out hope that when he married, he would be kinder to her … to everyone.

Suddenly the carriage came to a halt, and Alfreda watched warily as her brother exited the carriage then turned to hand her out. He was smiling as though they had never argued when they entered their cousin's home. After handing coats and gloves to the servants, she moved towards the stairs, intending to escape to her room. He stopped her before she took the first step.

"I suggest you retire early tonight, as you need to be at the Gardiner's early in the morning."

"I have no appointment with Miss Bennet in the morning."

"You do now. I had a good visit with the Gardiners while you and Miss Bennet were occupied. I arranged for both of you to frequent the modiste tomorrow with Mrs. Gardiner going along as a chaperone. You will order six gowns—three will be ball gowns—and insist Miss Bennet place the same order. I will leave it to you to select the correct fabrics and styles as her aunt would not know what is fashionable. Shame our new friend into cooperating if need be by emphasising the unsuitability of her clothes. Mrs. Gardiner will pretend to pay for her purchases, but, in truth, I shall pay for everything. Her apparel is not up to the standard that I shall require if I am to escort her about Town."

Alfreda cringed. All of the ladies who had ended their relationships with her brother had been opposed to his officiousness. She pondered bringing that up, but knew it would only make him angrier. In the end, she decided to confide in Lady Holmes. Perhaps her cousin would have some suggestions for tempering his penchant for being dictatorial. She raised her eyes to find him still talking.

"… and I told Mrs. Gardiner I would send the carriage at ten. I do not want you to be late."

She pretended to smile. "I shall have to take your advice then and retire early."

He looked as pleased as a cat that had caught a mouse. Alfreda shivered anew. Never would she get used to this expression—the one he wore when he was content to have gotten his way.

Chapter *11*

London
Grantham Townhouse
Several days later
The Drawing Room

"**A**re you sure you took every precaution? I cannot risk having you seen going in and out of my residence," Gisela chided her unexpected guest, looking about the well-appointed room as though a spy might be hiding behind an upholstered chair or the exquisite silk drapes.

Wickham sighed in exasperation. "What more would you have me do— assume a disguise worthy of the theatre? Would a wig or a cape satisfy you? I came through the alley, and your butler let me in through the servants' entrance."

"Still, it is broad daylight, and I told you never to come until after dark!" Gisela fumed, beginning to pace. "Do you know what will happen if Darcy's spies see you here? He despises you almost as much as me, maybe more." She stopped to rail at him. "He has a devious mind, and I know he has me watched and my every move recorded in case he decides to end the marriage."

"Then why do you insist on displaying yourself as a wanton woman at every function in Town—on the arm of one man or another! You are the talk of the gossip sheets." He wanted to add that she was rumoured to be *in her cups* more often than not, but he refrained.

"I shall not sit here alone every evening behind drawn curtains just because my husband does not recognise that I AM his wife! Besides, Darcy can only prove that I was seen in public with my friends. What he cannot prove at this point is that I am entertaining men in my home or in my bed! But since you are of no consequence in society, there would be no way to explain your presence here other than as a lover."

"You have said that Attenborough comes here and I am sure that he stays as long as needed to accomplish his goals. Does that not reek of entertaining a man in your home?"

"I make it a point that he is seen arriving to escort me to functions and we leave shortly thereafter. The same can be said of when he brings me home." She smiled deviously. "If he wishes to spend more *intimate* time with me, he comes in the back gate after dark, just as I asked you to do."

Wickham shrugged. "Enough talk of that dandy! Has Darcy ceased speaking to you now? You never mention your arguments anymore."

Gisela moved towards the bank of windows that overlooked the front entrance. "Do not use that term in reference to Howard! He was kind to me when others were too haughty to speak." Then pulling one heavy drape aside to peer out, she added less harshly, "As for Darcy, he barely spoke to me before, but something has changed in the last few months and I do not know what it may be. I do not care to provoke him though. If he suspects we are up to something—"

"We *are* up to something," Wickham smugly replied. Upon seeing his associate's mien darken however, he became earnest. "Do not worry. I kept my hat low over my brow, my head down and I have the carriage stop right at the back entrance. No one could recognise me, and they cannot see me after I enter the back gate, at any rate. You should worry more about your servants gossiping."

Gisela huffed, letting the drape fall back into place. "My servants were hired for their discretion. I pay them well to keep their mouths shut." Motioning to a large package that stood against the drawing room wall, she changed the subject, challenging, "Did you have this package shipped to me? It arrived this morning, and if I had to venture a guess, I would say it was a painting. But why would you purchase …"

Ignoring her prattle, Wickham strode to the item in question while she was yet speaking and began to undo the end of the parcel. When it was completely unwrapped, he stood back to admire the rendering of the sea that he had purchased from Mrs. Younge.

"My word!" Gisela exclaimed. "I have never seen anything uglier in my life! Pray, what did you pay for that?"

"The price was reasonable, and it is not so very bad. In fact, I quite like it!"

"Then it is unfortunate that you do not have a house in which to hang it, as it shall never be displayed in mine!"

"Calm yourself. Can you not see the logic behind the purchase?" Wickham asked, trying to hold his temper. "I had to show my prey some good will, else how was I to gain her trust and, subsequently, access to Georgiana."

He ran his hand along the elaborate wooden frame. "Purchasing this painting was an inexpensive way to further my goal. Mrs. Younge, who is a widow by the way, is becoming quite fond of me." Wickham smirked as his eyes travelled up and then down Gisela's body. "As you are well aware, I have a way with widows."

Gisela bristled at his braggadocio. "If you are doing so well, why are you here? Would it not have been better to press your case? She may find another suitor whilst you are away."

"Be assured, that is not a concern. She is not attractive in the least. Besides, this is all part of my strategy! I explained that I had to return to London for business, but I stressed that I was reluctant to leave, letting her assume I had begun to care for her and subsequently would miss her. By the time I return to Ramsgate, she shall be so relieved that I returned that she will let down her guard. As I had no chance to inform you of the shipment, I hurried here as soon as I reached Town. Since it preceded me, I am pleased you accepted delivery, as it would certainly have raised suspicions had you refused as she believes the address I gave her is my own."

"Seeing that it was from Ramsgate, I assumed that you had sent it. I do hope the woman believes your lies as now, more than ever, I need Georgiana on my side. With her approbation, I would still have a chance of keeping Lady Matlock's support. That fool Darcy was not civil to me the last time I tried to speak to him—not even to gain my vote in our joint venture. Would you believe that he personally tossed me from his house in broad daylight? I would wager that most of London enjoyed a laugh at my expense before day's end."

Wickham shrugged. "Enough talk of that dandy! Has Darcy ceased speaking to you now? You never mention your arguments anymore."

Gisela moved towards the bank of windows that overlooked the front entrance. "Do not use that term in reference to Howard! He was kind to me when others were too haughty to speak." Then pulling one heavy drape aside to peer out, she added less harshly, "As for Darcy, he barely spoke to me before, but something has

Wickham had difficulty restraining a laugh, and if Gisela had bothered to look she would not have missed his amused expression.

"Unbelievable! Simply mindboggling that *prim and proper* Darcy would do such a thing. My how times have changed."

Not paying him any mind, Gisela continued as though lost in thought. "I fear that may indicate that he is finally considering telling that little mouse about her parentage so that he may seek a divorce." She quickly recovered to confront Wickham. "You need to carry out your plan as quickly as possible."

"If Darcy decides to divorce you, he will succeed. With his connections, there is nothing you can do to stop him."

Unconsciously, Gisela stepped to a large, ornate mirror to study herself, running her fingers lightly over her face and neck as she did every morning when evaluating her beauty. When at last she spoke, it was as much to herself as in answer to Wickham.

"**I am Mrs. Fitzwilliam Darcy,** and for the first time in my life, every woman with breath in her body envies me! I have seen their eyes follow him across a ballroom, devouring him, ready to simper if he deigns to look in their direction. Young or old, married or not, they all desire him! My mother saddled me with that old fool, Grantham, when I was young and beautiful—I should have had Darcy then! I could have made him love me if I were still young!"

Slowly she ran her hands down the dark blue, sateen gown—from breasts to thighs, unaware that Wickham was aroused by watching. "I despise him for his disdain! Nevertheless, he is still so handsome that when I am near him my body responds to his charisma in spite of my wishes!"

Jealous that Darcy's looks inspired such passion, Wickham wanted to point out that when she married Grantham, the heir of Pemberley would have been too young to marry her. Instead, he settled on irritating her with another truth.

"Your title is irrelevant. Everyone knows your marriage is in name only. He has never lived with you."

"Not everyone! A new crop of debutants from distant parts of England, Scotland and Wales come to London every year. I love to see their expressions when I inform them that the best looking man in Town is *my* husband! You should see how their smiles deflate and they turn green with envy. Besides, even if they become aware that we lead separate lives, they understand that legally he is *mine*. And he suffers! Oh, how he suffers for rejecting me!"

Wickham sniggered. "You love that most of all—torturing him!"

"Indeed I do! And if I can gain Georgiana's trust by supporting a marriage to you, I may be able to separate her from him. That would be the best revenge! To lose the good opinion of his dear sister would wound him most of all!"

Gisela moved to a nearby liquor cabinet and poured a glass of brandy. She held the bottle aloft, and Wickham shook his head. Though he liked brandy as well as the next man, he was not used to drinking this early in the day. Gisela downed the entire contents of the glass before continuing her speech.

"In addition, it may give me the advantage I need to counter a divorce. Darcy needs the Fitzwilliams' support, and Eleanor is unyielding when it comes to family harmony and she can sway the earl. She will not let scandal besmirch them if she can prevent it. And if Georgiana is *with child,* it would be a bigger scandal not to keep the marriage intact!"

"With child?"

"Either before or after the marriage, I care not!"

"Have you considered that Darcy may not need the support of the Earl of Matlock to seek a divorce? He has other men of influence on his side—Lord Landingham, for one."

"Yes, but if the worst happens, I could retain my social standing if Georgiana accepts me. That would inspire Lady Matlock to continue to acknowledge me. And little Miss Darcy will accept me, if you play your cards right! She will leap at the chance to find someone willing to say that she was not wrong to marry you."

"Do not fear my progress with Mrs. Younge. I understand women!"

Gisela's hand came to rest on the emerald chocker encircling her long, lovely neck. Playing with the beads, she mocked Wickham. "You may understand servants, shop girls and whores, but I assure you that you do not understand respectable women!"

Almost choking at Gisela's use of the word *respectable,* Wickham focused on the expensive jewels as he pulled her into his arms.

I wonder what price these would fetch on the open market.

She tried to pull away, causing him to grumble, "You were not unwilling to suffer my attention when we were trying to create an heir for Darcy. Why are you being so missish now?"

"That was then. I now have a wealthy *admirer* who would not appreciate it if he knew that you and I had been lovers. In fact, he would be quite put out if he arrived to find you here, so I suggest you leave."

"Do you actually have feelings for that arse? I know him well, and he is just as arrogant as Darcy, though not as honourable."

"He serves the purpose, escorting me to the most fashionable soirées, and I am welcomed when I accompany him. I do think it peculiar, however, that you should refer to Darcy as honourable. I thought you hated the man."

"I hate the man because he is honourable! Even as a boy he was always so meticulous about carrying out his duty. Deuce take him, he even married you to satisfy his principals!"

Gisela had had enough of Wickham. "You have insulted me quite sufficiently today!" she proclaimed, reaching for the bell pull. "Do not call here again without sending your card first and come after dark."

As the summoned butler appeared in the doorway, Wickham pasted on a smile and bowed low to Gisela, sweeping his arm in a flourish. "As you wish, madam! And best of luck with your dandy!"

Seething with fresh anger, Gisela heard his chuckles echoing through the halls until he exited the house at last. She was not happy that he had returned to London. Wickham was unpredictable and careless. With him about, there was always the chance that Attenborough would find out about their affair. Huffing, she strode out of the room towards the grand staircase.

Why did he not stay in Ramsgate as we planned? Must he always do the unexpected? Would that I had never met him!

Holmes House
The evening before the ball
A bedroom

Elizabeth sat in the comfortably cushioned window-seat of Alfreda's bedroom, her eyes sweeping the beautifully appointed room. Alfreda had left her alone, dashing to collect something that she wished to share with her, so she took the opportunity to study her surroundings. The blue guest room she occupied was quite lovely, but it did not compare to this one.

Decorated entirely in cream, lavender, fern green and yellow, this room had to be one of the most exquisite of all those she had seen—and she had seen countless on her various tours with the Gardiners. Except for the furniture, all mahogany with gold trim, the colours were as light and inviting as a spring day.

Nevertheless, in spite of the beauty before her, Elizabeth's thoughts kept returning to an earlier conversation with her aunt over her resistance to accepting Alfreda's invitation to spend the night because she did not wish to see Lord Wilkens.

"Lizzy, you cannot be serious! The Wilkens will consider it an insult if you do not accept Alfreda's invitation. Besides, there are more important matters to consider here."

"For instance?"

I understand from my cousin that the Wilkens will be returning to their estate in Kent in about a week to celebrate their elderly aunt's birthday. She resides in a nearby estate and is in poor health, but she dotes on Alfreda, and seeing as how Lord Wilkens is her heir, they try to accommodate her whenever possible. I feel sure that you shall be asked to accompany Alfreda to Kent if you accept this invitation."

"But I do not wish to leave London, Aunt Madeline. Perhaps I shall meet someone I like better than Lord Wilkens if I stay."

"Nonsense! How likely are you to meet a more eligible man—an earl, for heaven's sake! And one who is ready to marry and has no impediments? A bird in the hand is worth two in the bush."

"Even if it is a vulture," Elizabeth said softly to herself.

"What did you say?"

"I said that I shall go."

"Good! Then it is settled. You shall spend the night before the ball with

Alfreda!"

~⚬~

"Here we are!" Alfreda exclaimed, holding up a small bag as she reappeared as quickly as she had left. "I am so happy that we are finally alone!"

"I am happy that we are, too." *At least that was no lie!* While she was very pleased to find that Mr. Wilkens was nowhere in sight when she arrived, Elizabeth's relief was short-lived, as he did appear in time for dinner. But now they were entirely on their own once more.

Her hostess unwrapped a new deck of cards. "We can use these to play Piquet [4] and I purchased a new novel—**The Absentee**—by Maria Edgeworth.[5] Have you had a chance to read it?"

Elizabeth could not hold back a grin at Alfreda's enthusiasm. "No, but I have heard of it."

"I had it ordered." She leaned in to whisper, which raised Elizabeth's suspicions, as they were entirely alone. "John does not know that I purchased the cards or the book. Please do not say a word to him." At Elizabeth's furrowed brow, she continued. "Brother does not approve of anything frivolous."

"He thinks cards are frivolous?"

"Yes. Other than poker, which he plays at his club, of course. He says it is a gentleman's game and it relaxes him."

"And he believes novels are frivolous?"

"He most certainly does! But you recognise that many people do, not just my brother." She laughed. "But now and again I will purchase one when I stay with Penelope. She hides them for me."

"Then he must be one of those who is in favour of reading books that improve one's mind."

"For men perhaps, but he does not see the need for young ladies to read extensively for any reason. He says that since we are to be wives and mothers, we do not need to educate ourselves beyond that goal. He favours women who occupy themselves by playing the pianoforte, painting screens and embroidering cushions—that sort of thing."

One brow rose as Elizabeth's lips formed a straight line. "Do you agree with him?"

Alfreda looked taken aback. "While I may disagree with a few things, he is my

---

[4] *Piquet is a game virtually unchanged since the 16th century and is played by two people using thirty-two cards. The "piquet pack" is made by discarding all cards below the sevens from a full pack. The game takes about a half-hour to play and takes considerable concentration and skill. The Cambridge Edition of Sense and Sensibility. Cambridge University Press (2006). According to the Regency Encyclopedia.*

[5] *Maria Edgeworth (1 January 1767 – 22 May 1849) was a prolific Anglo-Irish writer of adults' and children's literature. She held advanced views, for a woman of her time, on estate management, politics and education, and corresponded with some of the leading literary and economic writers, including Sir Walter Scott and David Ricardo.*

brother as well as my protector, and I assume that he only has my best interests at heart."

"I see. What else does he consider frivolous?"

Alfreda looked as though she was studying the question, and Elizabeth grew more unnerved as seconds passed without an answer.

"I am sorry. It is none of—"

"Comedies, most poetry, the theatre, fireworks, croquet—in fact, most games, besides billiards and whist, though he only plays cards at his club," she added as though it were the most natural thing in the world.

"Let me guess. He approves of billiards and whist because men enjoy them," Elizabeth added.

Not detecting her vexation, Alfreda nodded and, almost as an afterthought, added enthusiastically, "He does not much favour dancing either, although he will participate in order to please *certain* ladies." The latter was said with a knowing smile. "And I am quite sure that the right woman could get him to agree to participate in some other activities—like croquet—if they were clever."

Elizabeth must have appeared taken aback because Alfreda began to ramble on after seeing her expression. "It is simply that such things do not enrich our minds or our coffers. Practicality is my brother's middle name!"

The small smile that appeared when she was done speaking did nothing to relieve Elizabeth's anxiety.

And this is the man I am being persuaded to marry!

Alfreda reached to take her hands. "Oh, Elizabeth, you must understand! My aunt says that John never had a childhood—he was never carefree like other young men."

"Tell me about him then," Elizabeth urged, hoping to understand what inspired such sisterly devotion.

Our mother died years ago." Alfreda's face took on a glow as she stared into the distance. "She was so very kind and good, everything a mother should be. And she doted on John." She smiled. "And on me, I confess.

"Father was more distant—always away on business. Whenever he was not meeting with the House of Lords, the local landowners would seek him out for advice. There just never seemed to be enough time for it all." Her smile faded and she met Elizabeth's eyes. "I am not being totally truthful. Quite by accident, I learned that even while mother was alive, father had a mistress in Town. And when he was not waxing eloquent to impress his fellow lords, he was with her. We were last on his list of priorities."

"And what does your brother think of men having mistresses once they are married?"

"I have never heard him say specifically, but I once overheard him talking to a close friend, and he was unhappy that a 'woman of the street' had done something or other. I could not make out exactly what had happened, but it appeared that he was not happy that she had approached him. So, I concluded that Brother did not approve of them. And I think I would know if he had one."

"Well, I would never approve of my husband having a mistress," Elizabeth declared, though it was not John Wilkens face that appeared in her mind.

"Father's unavailability was especially hurtful to John, I believe—being the heir. One would think a man would have things to teach his son, his successor, rather than spend all his time with such a woman." She sighed. "And then all of a sudden, Father took ill and came home to die. He was bedridden for only a short time before he passed on, and John had to step in and handle his business affairs and all the responsibility that that entailed. Unfortunately, being thrown into the role of Master of Gatesbridge without adequate preparation caused him to become even more serious. That is why I have prayed that a lively, kind-hearted woman would come into his life—and mine. One who could influence him and soften his character."

Elizabeth hesitated for a moment, but decided she must speak. "Why is he even interested in me? I am certainly not of your level of society."

"Do not say that! You are a gentleman's daughter, Elizabeth. And while you may not have our wealth or connections, you certainly conduct yourself as any gentlewoman would."

"But your brother's every glance seems to be one of disdain."

"You do not know him as I do! He is certainly intrigued by you, but he is not disdainful, I assure you."

"And I have to add that I firmly believe that no woman can change a man who is not willing to change. Only a man truly in love would try to improve in order to please a woman."

"My brother is capable of such devotion, I assure you." She looked sincere though her words fell flat. Seeing that Elizabeth was not going to say anything more, Alfreda stood and smoothed her skirts self-consciously. "Why do we not forget about John for the night and have a cup of tea while we play cards?"

Studying the look on Alfreda Wilkens face, Elizabeth was sure that she was not being completely honest regarding her brother's character, but when all was said and done, she had no way of knowing what she might be hiding. Thus, she stood and followed her to the small card table set up in the adjoining room. As they took their places, a maid brought in a tray with tea and cakes without being beckoned, and they began their game of cards.

Night had fallen, and having tired of Piquet and another card game, she and Elizabeth had changed into their nightclothes to be more comfortable. Alfreda searched the bag she had brought into the room for the novel they were to read. Suddenly, both hands framed her face as she addressed Elizabeth, "I forgot!"

"Forgot?"

"I hid the novel when brother came home from his club unexpectedly. I was showing it to Aunt Penelope in the library when I heard his voice, I slipped it in between two books on a shelf. I know exactly where it is."

Quickly she began to don her robe. "Stay right here and I shall slip downstairs and retrieve the book!"

Elizabeth went with her to the door. "What if your brother sees you and questions why you are in the halls at this late hour? He may discover the book."

"John left after dinner to go to his club. I do not expect him to return until after midnight. He never does."

With that said, Alfreda slipped into the almost pitch-black hall. As the door did not latch properly, Elizabeth went to close it, but stopped at the sound of voices. She stepped back to blow out the candles on a nearby table, then peered through the opening. Barely able to make them out, she could see Alfreda, several doors down, speaking with a man. A footman? No! She would recognise John Wilkens' voice anywhere!

It seemed from the tone of their voices that their conversation had escalated to arguing, though she could not make out what was being said. She grew alarmed and her chest tightened. Were they arguing about her? Deciding to take action, Elizabeth slipped into the dark hallway unobserved and slowly inched in the opposite direction, back towards the room that she had been assigned. Holding her breath lest they notice her, she managed to find the door knob and breathed a sigh of relief to find it still unlocked. Slipping inside, she turned the key, locking herself within.

Her heart beat frantically, and she let go of the breath she had been holding as she turned and slumped back against the door. She was not aware of how long she stood that way, but eventually she heard footsteps just outside, followed by soft knocking at her door. At Alfreda's voice, she opened it just enough to see that it was indeed her and that she held a candle. Elizabeth did not see her brother, but she had the feeling he might be listening. "Elizabeth? I was frantic when I could not find you. I thought you were going to wait in my bedroom until I returned so that we might share the book."

"I ... I am sorry. You had not been gone long, when I almost fell asleep in my chair. I decided it more prudent just to go to bed."

"Would you not reconsider and come to my room?"

"I would rather not. I hope you do not mind, but I truly need to sleep."

Alfreda was silent for a long time, and though she smiled when she finally spoke, it was not heartfelt. "I understand. I shall see you in the morning."

Elizabeth closed the door and locked it again. She hated to disappoint her friend, but there was something about the way that John Wilkens looked at her during dinner that made her uncomfortable. Sighing, she checked the lock once again then fumbled her way to the bed. After she had crawled under the covers, it was not long until she was unaware of anything as she drifted off to dream of a man with dark curly hair and light blue eyes.

The Dining Room
The Next Morning

Joining the household the next morning to break her fast was very awkward for Elizabeth. She could not lift her eyes without meeting those of Lord Wilkens, who sat directly across from her, his mien was completely devoid of any expression. Shifting her gaze to Alfreda who sat next to him was no improvement. Whenever their eyes met, Alfreda would lower hers and surreptitiously glance at her brother as though seeking his approval.

After short but polite greetings, neither of the three made an effort to converse, which mattered little, as their hostess carried on enough conversation for the entire table. Elizabeth noted that Lord Holmes continued to eat silently, watching his wife with a besotted expression on his face.

It seemed to Elizabeth that Lady Holmes appeared most satisfied and winked conspiratorially at her whenever she looked in her direction. She attributed that to the fact that her hostess and her Aunt Gardiner thought they had achieved a triumph in introducing her to Lord Wilkens.

Does she actually think I would favour the idea of marrying THAT man?

Her thoughts were interrupted by that very lady. "Miss Elizabeth, are you having an enjoyable time with Alfreda? She was so excited about having you as her guest."

"I...I am enjoying myself immensely," Elizabeth lied. In truth, while she might have enjoyed staying with Alfreda, she had been on guard since she stepped inside the house. Her eyes darted to the man who inspired her suspicions. She noted that he was now sporting a frown.

Timidly Alfreda spoke. "After we are finished, I thought you and I might go to my sitting room and visit. We did not have sufficient time last night due to your fatigue. So I thought …"

Her voice trailed off and her smile faded as her brother shifted in his chair. Seeing her hesitation Elizabeth declared, "I would love to. I am sorry that we did not get to finish our talk last night."

At that moment, John Wilkens stood and announced that he had a meeting to attend. He bid everyone a good day and exited the room. The atmosphere lightened immediately, and for the first time that morning, Alfreda's smile was genuine.

Chapter **12**

London
Darcy House
Before the ball

Richard could not have been more pleased. Not only had William agreed to attend the ball, but he was wearing the newest addition to his wardrobe—a cream-coloured waistcoat with intricate, multi-coloured embroidery. It was something he had suggested his cousin purchase when he had accompanied him to John Weston's[6] on Bond Street. William was well-known among the *ton* for his tendency to wear clothes that he thought would garner him little attention, though it never worked. The truth be known, he would never be overlooked no matter his attire. However, Richard was determined that tonight he impress a certain miss. Attired in the waistcoat, elegantly cut dark-blue coat and matching breeches, William cut a fine figure indeed! Not that Fitzwilliam Darcy needed such enhancements to attract women, but Richard was well aware which woman his cousin would accidently encounter at the ball.

"Come along, Cousin!" Richard prodded. "I do not want to be late again!"

Standing uncomfortably motionless whilst his valet, Martin, finished tying his cravat, William sighed audibly. Finally after the servant had inserted a diamond stickpin into the finished masterpiece, slipped George Darcy's watch in the pocket of his master's waistcoat and handed him his signet ring, William lost his patience.

"I told you that I do not wish to accompany you tonight or any night, Richard! Why do you not go without me?"

"Because, my reluctant cousin, you need to be resurrected into society, if only for Georgiana's sake. She is fourteen and will be old enough for her presentation before you turn around!"

William scowled. "DO NOT remind me! It is bad enough as it is. I find myself staring down men wherever we go—even in the park when we are out for our afternoon walks. She may have the body of a woman, but she is still only a girl! Can they not wait until she is ready—say perhaps when she is one and twenty?"

"One and twenty? Do not be absurd! Georgiana will debut at eighteen like all

---

[6] *John Weston's, a tailor at 34 Old Bond Street, London, who made waistcoats, breeches and shirts and was a favourite of Beau Brummell, the prince and Lord Byron. (The Regency Encyclopedia)*

fashionable ladies, according to Mother, *and* you know how adamant Mother can be when it comes to the dictates of society."

William's celebrated stubbornness emerged. "Your mother is not my sister's guardian. I am! And she will not be out in society until I say she is out! Besides, Aunt Audrey agrees with me that Georgiana should not be pressed and should wait until she feels comfortable with the idea."

Richard chuckled. "Then my cousin will never come out! She is comfortable only when she is at Pemberley amongst woods and glens."

William threw his cousin an evil look before turning on his heel and exiting the room. Richard hastily followed, having to step lively to catch up to him before they began descending the grand staircase. In the foyer below, Audrey Ashcroft glanced up to see her favourite nephews and an expression of motherly affection swept over her face. Each man went directly to her, placed a kiss on her cheek and then stepped back for the inspection they knew to expect.

Their aunt glanced from one to the other, clearly delighted. "Oh my! The ladies will be deliriously happy that you both decided to attend the ball. And I do not believe I have ever seen either of you look more handsome!"

"You say that each time we are dressed like peacocks," Richard teased as William tried to keep a straight face.

"It is true! Would that I improved as much from one soirée to the next!"

Everyone chuckled as she stepped to Richard first. Running her hands reverently over the medals on his regimentals, she brushed a phantom piece of lint from his red coat before straightening a perfect collar and staring into his face for a long moment.

"Richard, you are the most handsome man in uniform that I have ever seen. It is a wonder your superior officers do not order you never to appear at any soirée they are attending, so as not to outshine them!"

Richard kept a straight face, while William's shoulders shook with the effort to contain his amusement. "You are too kind, Aunt Audrey."

"Nonsense! I am just being honest!" She patted his cheek lovingly then moved to stand in front of William.

"I must tell you, Fitzwilliam, that you look so much better than when Georgiana and I returned to London. Thank you for rising to the occasion and taking stock of yourself." She glanced at Richard. "I know that your cousin had much to do with your improvement." Richard silently acknowledged her statement with a slight nod. "And I imagine, with the addition of this lovely waistcoat, he has exerted an influence over your wardrobe. For far too long you have favoured black and white, and it makes you appear too sombre. You are a very handsome young man! You should dress like one!"

"I shall keep that in mind, Aunt."

William's eyes cut to Richard, who was now waging his own struggle not to laugh aloud, as his aunt ran her fingertips over the gaily coloured threads in the waistcoat and reached up to push a stray curl from his forehead. Then, just as she had with Richard, Lady Ashcroft patted William's cheek lovingly.

"Your mother would have been so proud of you. I know that I am."

Tears formed involuntarily in William's eyes, and fearing she was about to cry as well, Lady Ashcroft hugged him and then turned back to hug Richard. "I am prodigiously proud of you both!"

Just at that moment there was a loud knock at the door, and a footman opened it to reveal Lord Landingham. Looking every inch a member of the landed gentry, he strolled in without waiting while Mr. Barnes rushed to assist him.

"Never mind, Barnes, there is no need to surrender my coat or hat!" Landingham declared. "This beautiful young lady and I shall be leaving straightaway!" Lady Ashcroft blushed in spite of herself, while her nephews exchanged knowing glances.

"Oh, Marshall, how you do flatter!"

The Earl of Westcott paused to admire the woman he had come to love since she had become Georgiana's companion. She was still as slim as a young girl, her hair and complexion equally as youthful, but her vivaciousness was easily her best asset. She literally breathed life into a room, and since she had come into his life, he had learned to smile again. No—he had learned to live again. And tonight she simply took his breath away!

Spectacularly arrayed in a silver-coloured satin creation that was trimmed along the bodice and elbow-length sleeves with delicate lace and seed pearls in the same shade, her dark hair was held atop her head by matching silver combs. In addition, she wore a three-strand, diamond and silver necklace with matching earrings. He was thinking that she could easily be mistaken for a royal princess, when he realised that everyone was waiting for him to speak.

"Lady Ashcroft, I do believe I have never seen you look lovelier!"

When everyone chuckled, he looked surprised. Audrey took it upon herself to explain. "Richard just mentioned that I always say the same thing—that he and Fitzwilliam look more handsome than when last I had seen them! He teased that I was insincere."

"And now I am seen as disingenuous? Well, I can assure you, madam, that while I think your nephews presentable, you are most definitely more beautiful each time we meet!"

"Very well said, sir! You should be a diplomat," William declared, turning to take his hat from Mr. Barnes who held both his and Richard's. "Now, I fear we should all be on our way or Richard will have a paroxysm!"

Richard retorted, "Then do not blame our late arrival on me. It is you who scheme to arrive in time to miss the receiving line. That relieves you of having to smile at our hosts and anyone else who might be in the row."

By then Richard and William were leading the way down the front steps, still jesting playfully.

"I do no such thing Richard! It is you..."

Lord Landingham and Audrey had stopped on the portico, and he glanced down at the lady standing by his side to find her smiling affectionately at the quarrelling men she considered her sons. Leaning close to her ear he whispered, "I am quite fond of those two."

Her eyes sparkled as she considered him. "I am as well, sir! I am as well."

He held out his arm and she placed a delicate, gloved hand upon it, and they followed the cousins to the street below, where Richard and William entered the Darcy carriage still engaged in debate.

As Darcy's carriage pulled away, the earl's carriage took its place, and a footman opened the door for Lady Ashcroft. Swiftly, Landingham handed her inside and followed, barely getting situated in the seat before the conveyance rocked as it moved forward—the driver intent on making short work of the trip around the park to the other side of Mayfair.

London
Holmes House
The Ball

Lit up more spectacularly than Vauxhall Gardens[7] on fireworks night, the Holmes' townhouse appeared to be a veritable lighthouse on a hill in the fashionable area of Mayfair. Every window glowed with the light from hundreds of candles in massive chandeliers, and coupled with scores of floor-to-ceiling mirrors circling the ballroom, each reflecting the light, it created a dazzling effect.

Many residents of London, those not among the elite invited to the soirée, stood outside in the shadows, watching the wealthy arrive in fine carriages drawn by matching pairs of thoroughbreds. Some came hoping to beg or steal, while others wished only to see the finery displayed at such times as this. Slipping as near as they dared without drawing the attention of the footmen and Bow Street Runners hired to keep order and protect the guests, this was most likely as close as they would ever come to a night at the theatre.

Inside the ballroom, Elizabeth could hardly breathe for taking it all in. She had thought Holmes House beautiful on her first visit, but never had she seen it polished and preened to this extent or filled with scores of people, each more finely dressed than the next. In addition, the house was a veritable garden with so many flowers in every conceivable vessel and location that she could not identify one scent in particular. Apparently Lady Holmes did not ascribe to the theory of using one type of flower to the exclusion of all others, so roses were mixed with dahlias, peonies, tulips, chrysanthemums, orchids and other flowers, some she did not recognise. The combination of colours and scents was exhilarating!

Overwhelmed, Elizabeth closed her eyes for a moment only to find upon opening them that Alfreda stood before her with a quizzical look. Wilkens' sister had rushed back to her side after standing in the receiving line with her brother and cousins.

"Elizabeth, are you unwell? And why are you alone? Where are the Gardiners?"

The Gardiners had been with her until minutes before, but Aunt Madeline was feeling faint, since she was with child again, so they were forced to move to the terrace for some fresh air. Secretly Elizabeth had been glad for the reprieve, as Alfreda had not let her out of her sight all day, and her aunt was apparently going to monitor her every move during the ball.

"I am well. And as for my aunt and uncle, Aunt Madeline was not feeling well so they went onto the terrace for some fresh air."

"Oh dear! I do hope Mrs. Gardiner is not very ill! Do you think I should notify

---

[7] *Vauxhall Gardens was the oldest of London's pleasure gardens. Its twelve acres, containing shrubbery, walks, statues and cascades, were located in Lambeth, south of the Thames from Westminster Abbey. (The Regency Encyclopedia)*

Penelope?"

"I would give her a chance to recover before you alert anyone."

"I suppose that would be prudent. However, I simply must revisit the subject of your own health. You looked so pale a moment ago when I happened upon you and your eyes were closed. Perhaps you and your aunt have the same malady."

Elizabeth almost laughed aloud, but she could not betray a confidence and tell anyone of her aunt's condition. No, that would be for the Gardiners to announce. "I can assure you that I am not ill. I was merely overcome with the magnificence of everything—the decorations, the food, the people, the number of musicians—everything is on such a grand scale."

The pronouncement pleased Alfreda. She was aware that Elizabeth came from a family of humble origins, and she wanted her to be impressed with wealth—with her brother's wealth in particular.

Elizabeth continued. "And I have already been introduced to so many people. I fear I shall never remember all their names."

"You should not concern yourself with that, as no one expects you to remember everyone you have met. Besides, Brother and I shall be by your side all night, ready to assist. Oh, look! John is coming this way to claim the first dance."

Elizabeth tried to keep her smile pasted in place as the Earl of Hampton approached, a disturbing look of ownership on his face. Soon she found herself opposite him across a line of dancers. And as the music began, she wondered if she would be able to escape his watch any time that evening. If she did not, she knew the night would be endless.

Richard and William entered the ballroom after the first dance had begun, closely followed by Lord Landingham and their aunt. Landingham immediately steered Lady Ashcroft towards some of his associates from the House of Lords, who had acknowledged his arrival. William was grateful that they chose not to stand with him—both well aware of his penchant for anonymity. Landingham was a very popular speaker, and a group always gathered wherever he appeared, hoping to gain some wisdom from his pronouncements on the latest issue before parliament. Breathing a sigh of relief as they walked on, William turned to say something to Richard, only to find him intently examining the assembly.

"Richard?" There was no answer. "Richard!" he called louder.

His cousin stared across the ballroom, seemingly oblivious to his entreaty. Finally William stepped directly in front of him, causing Richard to startle and step back awkwardly.

"Darcy, what the devil!" He glanced around to see if anyone was watching. Seeing a few people eyeing them curiously, he lowered his voice. "Why would you, of all people, make a spectacle of yourself?"

"I was only trying to gain your attention."

With a hint of exasperation, Richard chided, "Well, now you have it, what do you want?"

"I wish you to help me keep watch for Gisela. I fear she may attempt to confront me or flaunt her latest conquest this evening."

The sadness in William's eyes and resignation in his voice touched Richard, and he was instantly remorseful. Darcy was trapped in a truly ghastly situation, never certain when Gisela might materialize to confront or humiliate him.

"Relax, Darcy. Walter assured me that she was not invited."

"Yes, but she was not invited to the last event she attended, either. It appears she may be hoping to catch me in public. I believe her hatred for me has begun to exceed her good judgement. Each time we talk, she makes new threats."

"But she only harms her own character. Hanging all over Attenborough whilst parading about drunk as a sailor on leave does not serve her interests."

"Once she is in her cups, she does not care who she exposes—not even herself! And the *ton* is afraid to reproach her because your mother and father acknowledge her as my wife."

"And as you are aware, I have told them I do not agree with their stance."

"Forgive me. I should not have brought that up."

"No apology necessary. I am only sorry that she and father are so dedicated to pleasing society instead of their own flesh and blood. In any event, I shall keep an eye out for her."

"Thank you. I do appreciate your help." With that said, William resumed his stance beside Richard, who instantly picked up where he left off in his search for Miss Bennet amongst the long line of dancers that stretched the entire length of the ballroom.

Surely she is dancing with that pompous ass, Wilkens, as he had the first set. And though she may be petite, I should be able to spy that ox!

Suddenly, the ladies made a loop around the line, and she came into view! She looked even lovelier than he remembered in a gown of pale blue, with an empire waist that was circled by a dark-blue ribbon embroidered with various colours. The low neckline displayed her womanly curves to great advantage, making jewellery unnecessary, though she wore small pearl earrings. Her ebony hair was pulled into curls atop her head that were interspersed with more of the same ribbons before they cascaded down her back in long tendrils that bounced with every step. For a second, he was awestruck. Then, remembering that she was Darcy's love, Richard chanced to glance at him, eager to see if he had discovered her yet. He had not.

Nevertheless, as he surveyed the young bucks standing about them, it was obvious that a good many of them had noticed Elizabeth. Numerous heads turned to follow her every move, and for a moment, he wondered if his cousin stood a chance with all the obstacles in his path.

Suddenly, the first set was over, and as Wilkens led Elizabeth from the floor, Lord Holmes moved forward to claim his set. Ever mindful of the direction of William's gaze, Richard knew the exact moment his cousin's eyes found the woman he loved. Had he not known what was transpiring, he would have thought that William had slipped into a trance—his body went so rigid that he could have been taken for one of the statues in his own gardens. At length Richard felt compelled to ask, "Darcy? Are you well?"

Only a tightening of the muscles in his jaw belied William's awareness of the question, and when he fixed his gaze on Richard, emotions flashed in his eyes in rapid succession—not the least of which was misery. Without bothering to give an answer, he stalked towards the open French doors that led onto the terrace. Meaning to take to the gardens, his vaulted control collapsed once he was outside, and he halted where the steps began, holding on to a column for support.

Catching up, Richard clasped his shoulder. "Forgive me, Darcy. Evidently I was wrong."

William seemed to struggle to understand his meaning. "Wrong?"

"I met Elizabeth Bennet in this very house when I called on Walter the other day. She was a guest."

"And you recognised her?"

"How could I forget that name? She seemed to signify so much to you. So, I questioned her. Learning that she was from Meryton, I asked if she had met Bingley, and when she said she had, I was certain it was she—the woman you had come to love."

"You knew all along, yet you did not tell me."

"I was trying to *save* you."

William answered with no little sarcasm. "Save me? From what were you trying to save me?"

"From yourself! If anything, you are too good, too decent. I have only to mention your marriage to Gisela as my case in point!"

William's irritation waned as Richard continued. "You analyse everything and put everyone's welfare above your own. You love her! Of that I am sure, and I am just as certain that you would not have come tonight had you known she would be here. All in the name of what is *best* for Miss Bennet ... what is *best* for everyone. I think you feel she would be better off forgetting you. Am I right?"

William did not answer. Instead he looked up into the velvety star-filled expanse, wondering how the same stars he studied from his balcony every night, could appear so much more beautiful now that she was in London. He took a deep breath of the cool night air. Even the air tasted sweeter! Did he dare consider what he desired now that she was close enough to touch?

Richard persisted, interrupting his thoughts. "You deserve her, Darcy! You truly do! And she deserves someone like you, not that pompous arse Wilkens."

"Wilkens? Earl of Hampton?"

"The very one! Mark my words; he has set his cap for your Miss Bennet. He showed his jealousy the evening I met her, practically daring me to ask her for a set."

"But, he is well known for his temper! Most of White's shun him when it comes to games of chance because he is such a poor loser, and there is talk that he cannot keep servants because of his rages."

"I am not privy to all the rumours at White's, but what I do know is that he is an arrogant fool and not someone the fair Miss Bennet should marry."

"Surely, you jest! Eliz—Miss Bennet could never esteem such a man!"

"Come down from your ivory tower, Cousin. Miss Bennet lives in another sphere, and what she desires will matter not a whit! In her world, a lowly squire's daughter with nothing to recommend her but beauty and intelligence is left to the mercy of whoever deigns to offer for her."

At William's glare, Richard held up both hands. "I am only repeating what you related to me—she has little dowry and no connections." As William acknowledged those facts with a nod, Richard pressed his point. "And to her family, John Wilkens would appear an excellent match. I imagine that Wilkens thinks he will incur none of the problems he did in the pursuit of more socially appropriate candidates. I heard Alicia tell Mother that Miss Christensen, Miss Hartwell and Miss Norwood—all the daughters of earls—rejected his request for a courtship. And you are well aware that my sister is never wrong when it comes to tittle-tattle."

William bristled. "Elizabeth was not meant for such a man as that!"

"She was meant for you! And if you cannot see it, I can! Divorce that wench you are shackled to, and marry the woman you want! Marry Miss Bennet!"

William took a deep breath and slowly let it out. "Do you not think that is what I want? That I do not think of it every waking hour? It is very difficult to divorce, as you are well aware, but I believe I have sufficient proof to win a civil trial, and your father's cousin, the Bishop of London, would agree to preside over the ecclesiastical court or appoint someone favourable to me. Of that I am certain. But the worst of it would be getting Parliament to pass the bill allowing me to marry again. It could be a long, drawn-out battle, and if your father opposes me—"

Richard interjected, "I believe, if it comes to that, Father would support you. But if not, you can do this without him! You have Landingham's support and soon Holmes will be in the House of Lords, and there is Lord Houghton, Lord Pearson, Lord Dearing, Greenlow's uncle, Powell's father. Deuce, half your classmates from Cambridge have fathers in the House of Lords. I could name two dozen of my fellow officers that have family members in their ranks. Besides, it will not be the first time you have faced a battle. Is she not worth the fight?"

"She would be worth any trial! But you forget what I am pitted against."

"Pray enlighten me."

"There is still the matter of Georgiana's paternity. How she will react knowing she is not Father's child?"

"Thanks to Aunt Audrey, Georgiana is not the child she was two years ago but a young woman. She is maturing and it is time you gave her credit for being worldly enough to know that these things happen. She is still her mother's child and your sister, and she will survive the revelation. And, frankly, I think she should be informed, especially when Gisela is the one holding the truth over your head as a bargaining tool. Tell her before someone else does."

William began to pace and run his hands through his hair. "And what would my love for Elizabeth accomplish? Am I selfish to want her for my own? I anguish over dragging her into this misery and fear it would be kinder to steer her towards another—some man more worthy than Wilkens."

"And who would that be? Do you have a farmer in mind? A tradesman? An officer? Most gentlemen of consequence—those of the *ton*—will not give her any consideration beyond that of a mistress."

Richard might have been exaggerating a bit, but he wanted to make his point, and the scowl that was William's reply would have cowed most men. However, he stifled a smile as he stated, "Face the truth! No man will ever love her as you do."

"If I take this chance and Gisela learns of my love for Elizabeth, she will do everything to destroy her—drag her name through the mud, embarrass her, perhaps even confront her. And most of the *ton* would be glad to help, as they love a good mud-raking! Elizabeth would be ruined and her sisters with her. And in the end, it could very well be years before we could marry ... if we could marry."

"Mother and Aunt Audrey can handle the *ton*. And Mother would take your side if you took as drastic a step as divorce, I assure you. Furthermore, despite what you may think, your wealth, family connections and status are enough to protect you in the long term. The *ton's* censure moves quickly on to the next victim, the next scandal."

William considered his words, and Richard continued his argument a little less stridently.

"As for Miss Bennet's sisters, you could prove their saviour—providing them with larger dowries and connections. But in any event, why do you not give Miss Bennet the opportunity to decide her future? She may be happier waiting for you than married to another man, or God forbid, married to Wilkens. Speak to her! Find out what she wants."

Hope filled William's heart. "I ... I suppose it could not hurt to speak with her."

"Exactly! And YOU should inform her that you are married. It will not go well if she learns it from someone else."

William's face softened as his heart began to hope.

Richard patted his back. "Come, let us return to the ball before the affair has ended, and you have missed the opportunity to speak to your amour."

With an arm around William's shoulder, Richard led his friend back into the crowded ballroom. They had gotten no more than fifty feet when they encountered the throng leaving the dance floor as the second set ended.

"Richard, I am so glad you were able to come, even if you were late!" Lord Holmes reached to shake Richard's hand, chuckling at the surprise on the colonel's face.

"It was Darcy's fault! You know how averse he is to receiving lines!" Laughter ensued among those observing the exchange, as Holmes turned to study William.

"Ah, Darcy!" he began, reaching out to shake William's hand. "It has been far too long since we were in each other's company. I am pleased that you decided to join us."

William, a little put-out to be the object of so much attention, smiled wanly. "Thank you. I am pleased to have been invited."

At that moment, Penelope Holmes moved to take her husband's arm, declaring, "Mr. Darcy, it is good to see you. Richard said he would try to entice you to join us."

"On the contrary, I am delighted to be here, Lady Holmes."

Lord and Lady Holmes had hindered the crowd departing the dance floor when they stopped to speak to Richard and William. Now as the throng began to move around the four of them, Penelope reached into the crowd to pull someone to her side.

"Oh, Miss Bennet, you simply must meet this gentleman while the opportunity presents. He is so seldom in London or in company when he is here. Let me introduce—"

Elizabeth now stood directly in front of him, looking even more beautiful than when he first spied her in the bookshop. For a moment, William was dumbstruck, his heart pounding in his throat.

For her part, as Lady Holmes pulled her aside, curiosity quickly changed to dread when Elizabeth saw William. Her beautiful smile faded, and in the depths of the ebony eyes he adored, he saw traces of heartbreak and resignation instead of happiness. And both emotions were replaced by a look of defiance by the time Lady Holmes finished, "Mr. Fitzwilliam Darcy."

Shaken by the changes he had just witnessed, William mumbled, "It is a pleasure, Miss Bennet." Then he bowed curtly.

"Likewise, Mr. Darcy," Elizabeth replied woodenly, barely curtsying.

He was about to speak again when her escort, Lord Shackelford, said haughtily, "Come, Miss Bennet! You wished for some punch, did you not?" With a glare at Darcy, the pompous aristocrat directed Elizabeth away, and still in shock, she did not object.

"Well, I suppose Lord Shackelford considers everyone competition for Miss Bennet's attentions. How amusing!" Penelope Holmes observed. "I suppose it should come as no surprise, though, as she is quite lovely and refreshing with her charming country manners."

Jealousy shone from Darcy's eyes as he followed Elizabeth's departure with Shackelford. Meanwhile, Penelope kept rambling. "I do think that Lord Wilkens has the advantage though. I have it on good authority that her family likes him tremendously. I believe that will be the match for her!"

Luckily, their hosts were distracted as more of their guests began to vie for their attention, and they walked on, leaving William and Richard alone once more.

"That was awkward." Richard declared, glancing at his cousin. "Miss Bennet must be angry for some reason. I secured the last set with her, fully intending for you to take it, but I am afraid that may not be enough time to repair whatever grievance she carries. Perhaps you should ask for an earlier set as well, if there is one available."

"I think it best if I leave her alone until the last set. That way, if she is disinclined to forgive me, she may refuse me the set without injury to herself."

Richard sighed. "As I said before, you are far too noble for your own good."

Chapter **13**

London
Holmes House
The ball continues

Only those who knew John Wilkens well would know what the set of his jaw and constant clenching and unclenching of his fists meant. Though he showed no visible expression as he surreptitiously watched the woman he had decided to marry while she performed to strangers, he was livid.

It was not supposed to be that way. Elizabeth Bennet was supposed to be grateful for his attention and take no notice of other men. Instead, she seemed perfectly content to flirt with first one and then another, though clearly each was of such rank as to consider her no more than a diversion. The only man who had not behaved as though he was mulling over her suitability for his mistress was Fitzwilliam Darcy.

Wilkens had watched as Elizabeth was introduced to Darcy and noted that that gentleman had ignored her—not that he expected anything different. Well acquainted with the master of Pemberley, he knew that Darcy would never consider Elizabeth for a tryst because he would never lower himself to indulge in such diversions. They had once had a heated discussion about the merits of mistresses, in particular married men keeping mistresses, and Darcy was adamantly against the practice, saying that it ruined trust between husbands and wives and destroyed families. Wilkens had argued that he fully intended to keep his mistresses when he married, as he saw no need to forego pleasure just to acquire an heir. That pronouncement had garnered the laughter and approval of the majority of the men gathered around them at White's and Darcy had stalked off. The memory made Wilkens smile for the first time tonight, though no one would be able to tell. Anyone with secrets to hide needed to be able to conceal his emotions in public, and he had perfected the art.

As his thoughts returned to Elizabeth, he considered why he was so cross. Of course, he had known she would dance with other men, but he had thought she would appear to be enduring the dances, not enjoying them. Was she so dull as to have no idea that her future hung so precariously—that without his offer, she would never achieve the approbation of higher society? Apparently she was! Thus, while he watched Lord Shackelford escort the object of his obsession to the refreshment table, he found himself filled with disgust at her behaviour. His only solace rested in the knowledge that he had secured the supper set, and once he had escorted her into the dining room, he would have the opportunity to remind her of her place.

Caroline Bingley fumed! If Charles had not gone on that wild goose chase to Liverpool, she would not be in this predicament. He would have been her escort, and *they* would be standing alongside Mr. Darcy. Instead, she stood in all her finery—new coral silk gown, feathered turban and her best jewels—beside one of the ugliest men she had ever met. Short and heavy, he was fair-haired and covered with freckles, which were ironically his best attributes, the worst being his protruding, uneven teeth and huge ears. She began to worry that she would never recover from the humiliation of being seen on the arm of such a man after she noticed the quiet laughter of some women of her acquaintance who just happened to notice her dilemma.

But the worst of it was that she was unable to socialise as she wished without Colonel Hedges being privy to her every word. The idiot was so enamoured that he never left her side! Even when she danced with other men, he would appear the instant she was escorted from the dance floor, taking her hand and placing it on his arm as though they were a couple. His lavish attention meant she was not free to locate Mr. Darcy and engage him in any conversation.

Not that he had looked her way once the entire evening! Every time she found him in this throng, he seemed to be staring in the direction of that chit Eliza Bennet! What was she doing in polite society anyway? The way she has insinuated herself into the Holmes' good graces was positively scandalous, Caroline thought.

Yes, this was all Charles' fault! After exhausting all other avenues, she had cajoled his friend, Colonel Harold Hedges, into escorting her to this ball as his guest. Once she had realized that as a colleague of Colonel Holmes, Hedges was sure to be invited, she had quickly visited his sister in hopes of encountering the man. Though she had no use for Clementine Hedges because she lacked sophistication and was plain, Caroline was not above using her. After all, her mother was a member of the ton, though she had married a second son, and had many connections. And the simpleton had been easily convinced that she wished for them to be friends. After charming the sister, it had been effortless to lure the ugly bachelor into thinking she favoured him. Too easy, actually! He may have been an experienced army officer, but he had little skills with the fairer sex. Consequently, she had played him for a fool and in the process had created a clinging monster! She fully expected him to call on Charles upon his return to London and request to court her.

It will be a cold day in Hades before I agree to that!

Only a few feet away from her brother, Alfreda Wilkens watched his balled fists with growing concern. This was never a good sign. Fearing that his celebrated temper was about to be exposed in public, she made the decision to speak to him, regardless of the repercussions. Taking a deep breath, she moved to stand beside him. Totally focused, he did not notice her at first as she stood silently for a moment, watching the same person.

"Miss Elizabeth is truly the belle of the ball," she offered timidly, breaking his concentration. "I just imagine that if you and she were to marry, you would be envied very much."

Wilkens eyed Alfreda with impatience, before fixing his gaze back on Elizabeth. She and Shackelford were nearby, conversing with a group that included some of the young men who routinely examined every newcomer to London. The gentlemen were obviously vying for her attention, and every so often, Elizabeth's quiet laughter could be heard.

Alfreda tried again. "I can only imagine she is garnering so much attention because this is her debut in London society. The attention will likely diminish once she is no longer a novelty."

He did not reply.

"It is not Miss Elizabeth's fault that she is admired. I believe she is conducting herself with dignity under the circumstances. "

Wilkens turned to study her anew. "Are you implying that I think she is not acting the part of a lady?"

"No, but—"

"But nothing. You will find Penelope Holmes and converse with her. Leave me to my thoughts. Do you understand?"

"Y ... Yes!"

Alfreda took a deep breath to steady her thumping heart and looked about to see if anyone had noticed their exchange. Surprisingly, she found Mr. Darcy studying her with a quizzical expression. She smiled benignly at him before moving in the direction of their hostess, hopeful that she had convinced the gentleman from Derbyshire that all was well.

Later that night
The Dining Room

From his seat across the room, Fitzwilliam Darcy could not eat for watching Elizabeth. The disquiet on her face, especially when Lord Wilkens leaned in as though to speak privately, was obvious. And though he could not hear a word of what was said, it was evident from the way her features darkened and brow furrowed that the earl was not being complimentary. In addition, Wilkens' sister, who sat on her other side, looked as though she expected something awful to happen at any moment.

"Darcy, if you do not stop staring at Miss Bennet, people will realise there is something between you," Richard whispered in counsel. "Fitzwilliam Darcy pays no woman notice, especially not a country squire's daughter. It will raise enough brows when you take my place in the last set, even if we have concocted a good excuse."

William was unfazed. "But there is something wrong. I have been observing them closely, and Elizabeth has not spoken a word in the last half-hour, even though both Wilkens and his sister are still addressing her! She is not the type to be easily silenced, and the earl looks furious."

Richard shifted in his chair so that he could see around those blocking his view, and scrutinized those in question. "While it is true Miss Elizabeth is not responding, I cannot see that Wilkens looks any worse than usual. He always scowls in that manner."

"No. He is definitely cross. I can only imagine that he is spouting something meant to silence her, as Elizabeth is normally gregarious."   Instinctively, he began to slide his chair back.

Richard put a hand on his cousin's arm, stopping him. "Calm yourself! You will only embarrass her. Besides, she is looking this way."

At that very moment, Elizabeth locked eyes with William, the uncertainty therein unmistakable. She was questioning him, and he responded by displaying his feelings more plainly than he ever had. If the ton wished to know how Fitzwilliam Darcy felt about Elizabeth Bennet, the answer lay in his expression at that very moment. By chance, they were too busy eating and conversing with their tablemates to be aware of the significant disclosure taking place right under their noses.

You know me, Elizabeth! Look into my eyes and see my love for you! Trust me again! Please, darling!

For a few precious moments he thought she would be swayed, but her look of uncertainty was soon replaced by one of suspicion. Breaking their connection, she returned to studying her plate silently while Wilkens continued to pontificate.

William sunk into his chair, his hopes dashed as a dull ache permeated his chest. Clearly, Elizabeth's heart was closed to him. His decision to depart Meryton without speaking to her must have wounded her so deeply that it destroyed her faith in him. And of one thing he was certain—she had trusted him during that night in the storm. She had said as much.

I shall never be afraid when I am with you.

"You should keep in mind that I am in a position to choose to marry any woman that I desire. Most men in this assembly tonight are not. They shall marry for large dowries, connections and familial obligations. Oh, these men might toy with your affections, but they would never offer for you."

Elizabeth was weary of Lord Wilkens' argument. First, he had spoken with condescension of her station in life, reiterating her lack of fortune and connections and even the fact that she had four sisters. She had responded by completely ignoring him. This annoyed him, and after repeated attempts to get her to reply, he had turned a deep shade of crimson.

In between his preaching, Alfreda had offered her version of what her brother *meant* to say, which only served to anger him. Elizabeth no longer responded to Alfreda's attempts to soothe her feelings. She had no energy left to feel sorry for his sister, as she could barely manage to keep her disgust and anger under good regulation. What the Earl of Hampton said might be true, but he did not have to remind her at every opportunity!

In the midst of it all, Elizabeth looked up to find Mr. Darcy studying her from the next table with a boldness that caught her off guard. If she were to trust her instinct, she would assume his eyes conveyed tender feelings for her. After all, was this not the same expression Mr. Bingley wore when he observed Jane surreptitiously?

Elizabeth concluded that Mr. Bingley's expression was that of a man in love, but for Mr. Darcy to look at her with the same regard was too outlandish to credit. After all, how could he have tender feeling for her? Had he not abandoned her in Meryton and upon their encounter earlier tonight, dismissed her with little notice? Thoroughly unnerved, she pulled her eyes from his and began examining the food on her plate.

I am done with being amiable to those I can barely tolerate as well as to those I do not understand at all!

The ball concludes

All of her scheming had been for naught. Caroline had gotten no closer to Mr. Darcy than to be seated across the room at dinner. Even then, he had not noticed her, his gaze firmly fixed in Eliza Bennet's direction.

What could possibly interest him about that lowly country dullard? Did he not quit Meryton without even taking leave of her family? That is what I overheard Charles tell Hurst the day after Mr. Darcy left Netherfield. Have they renewed their acquaintance since she came to Town?

As she fixed her gaze on the object of her scorn, she determined she must get to the bottom of that conundrum. There was no doubt in her mind that Mr. Darcy would divorce his horrible wife at some point in time. She just knew it! And when he did, she intended to be his next choice for a wife. She would never allow that chit to interfere with her plans! The wheels in her devious mind began to turn.

As secretive as Mr. Darcy is, I wonder if Eliza is even aware that he is married. Perhaps it is time that I made sure that she knows.

The end of the evening had arrived. As Elizabeth was being led off the dance floor by her partner, Mr. Martindale, she began looking about for the man who had secured the last set—Colonel Fitzwilliam. Thinking he should be easy to spot in his regimentals, she was surprised to find not one red coat in the room.

After supper, Mr. Darcy had positioned himself in an alcove within sight of the dance floor, and though she tried not to care, with every turn of the dance, she stole glances to see if he was still there. And he had stayed in that place faithfully until about a half-hour before, when he had simply disappeared. An uneasy feeling came over her as she realised that since Mr. Darcy was in attendance, he might object to his cousin's partnering her. Had he insisted they both leave?

Fortunately for Caroline Bingley, Colonel Hedges' invitation to partake of cigars in Colonel Holmes' study, along with several other officers, provided just the interlude she needed, and she intended to make good use of it. Seeing an equally alone and seemingly perplexed Eliza Bennet, she sidled in that direction.

"Eliza Bennet, how nice to see you! I had no idea that you were in Town." Elizabeth cringed when she heard that voice. Steeling herself, she turned with a pasted-on smile.

"Miss Bingley. It is nice to see you as well."

Caroline's tone of voice suggested she was not sincere, and the smile on her face confirmed it. Elizabeth was reminded of a cat that had just cornered a mouse. Nevertheless, she resolved to bear the woman's insincerity to learn what she could about her brother.

"Did Mr. Bingley accompany you? I have not seen him tonight, but there are so many people that it would not be difficult to miss someone."

"No. He could not attend. I am here with an old friend."

Elizabeth found it hard to suppress a smile, recalling the man she had seen earlier who had obviously escorted Caroline. He was certainly not the type Charles' sister would have chosen for an escort, had she been given an option. Extremely short and balding, what hair he had left was bright red. His pasty white skin was scattered with freckles. In fact, it seemed there was no place on the colonel that did not sport a freckle, including his ears. Seeing the bemused smile on Elizabeth's face, Caroline immediately bristled.

"My brother had important business in Liverpool that could not wait, but he is eager to return to London and Miss Darcy's company." Elizabeth's countenance fell, though she tried not to let her disappointment show, but Caroline did not fail to notice Elizabeth's reaction. "Yes, he has certainly enjoyed spending time with Georgiana as well as with Mr. Darcy and his dear wife, Gisela."

Elizabeth could not breathe, and she began to feel lightheaded. Had Caroline actually said Mr. Darcy was married? She must have looked incredulous because Caroline leaned in to whisper conspiratorially, "Mrs. Darcy is a well-kept secret. It seems Mr. Darcy loves to appear single, so he never mentions her when she does not accompany him."

Elizabeth struggled to take a deep breath. *I refuse to faint!*

Managing to mumble something about getting a breath of fresh air, she turned on her heel and hurried towards the nearest set of French doors. Caroline could not have been more delighted at the stunned look on Elizabeth's face as she rushed away. But she did not consider her work done for the evening, so she began searching the crowd for familiar faces.

Surely there is someone here with whom I can trade disparaging remarks about Eliza Bennet before Colonel Hedges returns.

Once out on the portico, Elizabeth ran down the steps, following the gravel path that led to a large gazebo. Upon reaching the structure, the tenuous control she had over her emotions gave way and her legs buckled. Dropping to sit on one of the benches, she closed her eyes and let her head fall back to rest against the side. And as the reality of Caroline's revelation sank in, she squeezed her eyes tight against the tears that welled up.

How could he be married? Though he spoke of his sister and his parents, he

never once mentioned a wife. The voice of reason broke through her scattered thoughts. *What does it matter if he is married? He did nothing to raise your expectations.*

Suddenly, a voice floated across the darkness. "Miss Bennet, are you well?"

Elizabeth would know that low baritone anywhere, and her heart began a frantic drumming. She stood up, her back to him, as she surreptitiously wiped tears from her cheeks with the backs of her hands. Afraid that she could not speak for crying, she nodded briskly.

Acutely aware of her distress, William's heart went out to her and he stepped closer. "My cousin has been detained, and he asked me to take his place in the last set. That is, if you will allow me."

"No!" She replied brusquely and then added less stringently, "I thank you, but I have had my fill of dancing tonight, Mr. Darcy. I appreciate your offer, but it is not necessary to fulfil the obligation."

"Eliz—" Darcy moved up the steps to stand behind her, then reached to touch her but stopped short. "Miss Bennet, I know that something has greatly upset you. If Miss Bingley said anything to hurt you—"

Her courage rose and she whirled to face him, her angry expression instantly quieting his protestations. Yet, with William in such close proximity and the moon casting everything in a soft light, Elizabeth found she was in danger of falling under his spell once more. As in her every dream of him, those same dark brows and lashes framed light blue eyes—eyes that were now examining her with such tenderness and love that she was nearly undone. Shaking her head to break free of his spell, she slammed shut the door of her heart.

Taking a step back, she retorted, "How ironic that you worry over Caroline Bingley's words when your own have been so hurtful, so deceptive."

William appeared stunned at the vehemence in her voice and it emboldened her.

"Do you deny that you are married, Mr. Darcy? Or that you purposefully kept that information from me when you were in Meryton? During all the time we spent in each other's company, you never once mentioned having a wife, though you spoke of others in your family. What was your purpose in keeping her existence a secret? And what of the night I spent in your arms? Did you share that experience with your wife? Or was it only for your amusement or that of your friends?"

By now tears were coursing down Elizabeth's face unchecked, though she was not conscious of them. She took a ragged breath, turning away. It was too painful to look at him.

"I swear that it was not as you describe. I never meant to deceive you, and you must believe that I was going to confess everything tonight during our dance."

"Must I? It is easy for you to profess your intentions now that I have discovered your duplicity." She pulled herself up to her full height and turned to face him one last time. "And when were you going to tell me that you ordered Mr. Bingley from Meryton—that you were frightened he might form an attachment to Jane?"

"I have no idea to what you are referring. Yes, I sent for Bingley, but—"

"Apparently, you will not tell the truth, even when confronted with it."

"I can explain, Elizabeth. All I ask is that you give me the courtesy of hearing me out."

"Just as you gave me the courtesy of saying goodbye when you left Meryton, sir? And, **never** call me Elizabeth again. It is Miss Bennet to *you*!"

"I apologise for causing you pain. I never meant to hurt you." William dropped to his knees on the wooden floor, taking her hands. "I deserve all your reproach, but regardless of what you may think of me, please listen to what I say. John Wilkens is not what he seems. He is not the kind of man you deserve!"

Pulling her hands from his grasp, she backed away. "You have no right to kneel before me like a suitor! And who gave you permission to determine what I deserve? Why should I not consider him? At least *he* is honest! He openly declares that I am beneath him and should be grateful for his attention."

William stood to his feet. "That is not true! You are worthy of so much—"

Elizabeth interrupted. "Though, my pride chafes against reminders of my circumstances, everything he says is true! I am beneath his society, but at least he does not care. His intentions are clear—he means to court me, and if we are compatible, to marry. What were your intentions, Mr. Darcy? Since you were already married when we met, were you merely looking for a dalliance or were you seeking a mistress?"

Elizabeth swept past him, down the steps and ran towards the ballroom, with tears still visible on her cheeks. And as his heart took flight with her, he realised that it was he, not John Wilkens, that was to blame for the loss of innocence in those dark brown eyes, the cynicism in her words and the pain in her heart. If Elizabeth accepted Wilkens' offer it would be his fault—no one else's.

Oh, Elizabeth! What have I done?

In the shadows of the gazebo, Audrey Ashcroft's heart was breaking as well. She had been near the French doors when this lovely young woman had practically run from the room and then watched in amazement as her usually self-possessed nephew slipped out to pursue her. Aware of the scandal that could result should they be found alone, she had quietly followed them, discreetly waiting some distance away while they talked. Nevertheless, from that vantage point, she had heard everything they had said, even that which was unspoken.

Obviously they had spent a goodly amount of time together when Fitzwilliam was in Meryton and he had not been forthcoming about his marriage to Gisela. This was the piece of the puzzle that she had been seeking—the person with whom her nephew had fallen in love! Why else would he be reluctant to share his marital state with the woman? Fitzwilliam was not a rake, but she could envision him falling in love so desperately that he would keep his status a secret in hopes of being able to find a solution.

Equally obvious was that despite her anger, this Elizabeth loved her nephew and was devastated to learn that he was married. No one who had heard her speech tonight would think otherwise.

"Fitzwilliam?" William spun around, his disappointment becoming obvious. "I apologise. You were hoping I was her."

William nodded numbly as he sat down, resting his elbows on his knees and dropping his head in his hands. He looked completely defeated.

"I saw you follow the young woman, and I came out to protect you both from gossip. I tried not to listen to your conversation, but neither of you were trying to be quiet."

"No, I suppose we were not."

"I think that I may be able to help you. Will you let me?"

"I do not know if anyone can help me now. She hates me."

"I assure you that her behaviour was not the behaviour of a woman who hates you. She is very young, is she not?"

"Nearly one and twenty, I believe."

"I thought as much. You are likely her first serious love, and to find out that the man she loves is married and has kept it from her is a deep wound. But she deserves to know the truth of your situation and your intentions. I believe she will listen to me. You must tell me everything that transpired in Meryton so that I will be prepared to carry your point."

"I think she no longer cares to hear the truth."

"I can assure you that she wants to know the truth. It is obvious that she still loves you."

His head came up. "How did—are you sure?"

"I am a woman, and I know of what I speak. She loves you. She is upset with you at this moment, but at some point, she will long to hear what you have to say. And I believe that when she learns the truth about Gisela, she will forgive you. You do love her and want to marry her, do you not?"

"I want that more than anything in the world," he whispered raggedly.

She took his hand. "Come. The ball is ending and we must return. But when we get home, we shall have a cup of tea, and you shall tell me everything. Agreed?'

William smiled wanly. "Agreed."

If there was any possibility of reaching Elizabeth, he would tell his aunt everything. For even if she never forgave him, Elizabeth deserved to hear the truth.

Chapter **14**

London
The Gardiner's Residence
One day later

"Elizabeth Bennet, are you listening to me?"

Madeline Gardiner grew more exasperated by the minute. Since her niece had returned from her stay at Holmes House, she seemed to be in another world. More often than not, she would find Elizabeth with a faraway look in her eyes. She would have been pleased if she thought her niece's distraction was the result of fondness for Lord Wilkens, but she was sure that was not the case.

"I...I am listening. You were saying that I should accompany Alfreda to Ramsgate."

"Yes, you should. You will be introduced to the finest families in that area, including their aunt, Lady Hawthorne. I met her once in London and was enchanted by her charm and personality. John Wilkens is her heir, and you shall not only see how wealthy he is—what with Gatesbridge and its surroundings—but how much wealthier he will be when he inherits her properties. Hawthorne Hall is reputed to be even more magnificent, and seeing both estates will prove my assertion that you would be foolish to reject his suit."

"But, Aunt, I truly do not care for Lord Wilkens. He is arrogant and often reminds me that I should be grateful for his notice. Are there no suitable men in London?"

"Should he rejoice in the inferiority of your circumstances? I think not!" Madeline reached out to cup her niece's face and bring her eyes up to meet her own. "Lizzy, the Earl of Hampton is no different than any other man of his station, other than his ability to have a wife of his choosing. Any honest man of breeding and wealth would feel that you are beneath him, so there is no point in seeking another man on that basis. Would you rather that he was dishonest with you?"

Elizabeth countenance darkened as she remembered her argument with Mr. Darcy. "Honesty is the most important thing in any relationship. I could never respect someone who would lie to me."

"Exactly my point! And since it is already decided that you will stay with Lord and Lady Holmes for the short while I will be attending my sister in Bath, it shall all work out perfectly. After all, Penelope says that due to some estate problem

Lord Wilkens is planning on travelling to Ramsgate ahead of his sister, and it would look peculiar if you refuse to accompany Alfreda when she travels there later. You must take advantage of this opportunity to make Lady Hawthorne's acquaintance. I have no doubt that she will approve of you, and her approbation would be a great advantage."

Elizabeth dreaded staying at the Holmes' townhouse while her aunt and cousins were out of town. Lady Holmes presumed that she would marry Wilkens, and it would be unsettling to be so close to Mr. Darcy's townhouse, which she now knew to be just across the park. What if she encountered him on one of her daily walks? Her reverie was interrupted by a hand on her arm. "Lizzy, I asked you a question? Were you daydreaming again?"

"I was only considering your reasoning. What was your question?"

"Did Lord Wilkens find opportunity during the ball to ask permission to court you? Penelope thinks he will call on your uncle before he leaves Town."

"No, but I am certain that he assumes he has my permission." Suddenly an idea came to her and she ventured energetically, "Could I not accompany you to Bath? I would be of help with my cousins, what with the new baby. You will have need of me, as you will be taking care of your sister, I am sure."

"Of course not! Your duty is to secure your future and that of your sisters by being available to Lord Wilkens. Fanny would never speak to me again if I took you with me!"

"Then could I not stay here with Uncle?"

"Your uncle will be out of Town on business several days that week, and I cannot leave you unattended." Madeline Gardiner stood to leave the parlour. "It is time that I looked in on the children."

Elizabeth followed her to the front hall, picking up her bonnet as her aunt mounted the stairs. "I should like a walk in the park. I barely had time while I stayed with Alfreda."

"Make sure Mr. James accompanies you. It is not proper for a young lady to walk out alone."

Elizabeth nodded. She did not mind being accompanied by the elderly footman who, per their agreement, never tried to keep pace with her. As soon as she entered the footpaths that meandered through the small copse and around the ponds, he fell back a good distance so she could walk in peace, pretending to be at Longbourn. With expectations for a match growing unbearable, her feelings in mourning for the carefree days of childhood, when she rambled unaccompanied across the fields and meadows of her beloved home, had increased ten-fold.

Stratton Park
Cheapside

The early morning mist had barely lifted when the carriage pulled up to the main entrance to a small park in Cheapside. Leaping out as only a nimble young man could, Richard Fitzwilliam walked towards his aunt with the self-assured stride of a military officer, gaining the notice of the few female occupants of the park at this hour as he progressed. He had spied her almost as soon as he quit the carriage, sitting upon a bench—Audrey Ashcroft was hard to miss. Every inch the refined lady used to wealth and privilege, she looked as though she hardly belonged in this place. Upon seeing his approach, she smiled and stood, smoothing her skirts. A maid stepped forward to assist, handing her mistress a gaily coloured silk parasol to shade her against the sun's rays which had just begun to push through the haze.

As he got closer, Richard was relieved to find that she was accompanied by two burly footmen of Darcy's employ, who stood guard several feet away. He chuckled to himself. He should have known that his cousin would never allow her to go anywhere alone, much less to Cheapside. This area of Town was known for having its share of beggars and other miscreants on the streets and often in the parks.

"Richard, thank you for coming so promptly."

"When I got your summons, I left straightaway. Now, please explain to me why we were to meet at this ungodly hour and why this venue, when Hyde Park is just across from Darcy House? If you wanted exercise whilst we talked, it would have been much more convenient."

Lady Audrey tilted her parasol in order to see her nephew's face. Noting the glint in his eye and his barely contained smile, she withheld the remark on the tip of her tongue, instead replying, "I have learned that Miss Elizabeth Bennet loves to walk every morning. And since she has returned to her relations and they live near here, this is the logical place for her to accomplish that."

"And how did you manage to glean that information in such a brief amount of time? After all, it was only a day ago that William confessed their relationship to you."

"I have my methods, which shall remain nameless."

Richard grinned widely. "Why do I believe it involves gossiping servants?"

"Since you are so astute, I shall confess. It was merely a matter of having one of my maids enquire of Miss Bennet's habits from a friend who is a maid at Holmes House. I am sure you know of what I speak. My brother's butler tells you every scrap of gossip that he learns from Darcy House, I have no doubt."

"I believe it is you who is astute, Aunt!"

It was now Lady Audrey's turn to chuckle. "That was an easy deduction. How else would you know everything that affects Fitzwilliam, almost as soon as he does? It is obvious that Rutgers respects you, though he has no use for Edgar and very little respect for my brother and sister. He makes the ideal sleuth." Her eyes twinkled. "He is a very wise man. But, alas, we could waste all morning praising our methods and still accomplish nothing."

"You are correct! So we have rushed here in hopes of catching William's love in the park. And I have been included in this adventure because—"

"You have made her acquaintance, and she will be less suspicious if you introduce me. Once you have made the introduction, you shall find a convenient excuse to leave us alone."

Richard feigned hurt feelings, his hand flying to his heart. "How easily I am dismissed." At his aunt's chuckle, he continued. "But have you considered that she may not walk out today for some reason or choose to come later?"

"She will be here this morning. I have a good feeling about it."

"Then shall we walk about the park or sit on this bench?"

His aunt threaded her arm through his. "We shall walk!"

Thus, they strolled slowly along the main paths, ever alert for a glimpse of Miss Bennet. Once they had finished two entire turns about the park, however, Richard was close to voicing doubt about their mission when he caught a glimpse of a young woman in blue out of the corner of his eye. Walking briskly along an intersecting pathway, the brim of her bonnet shielded her identity, though from her height and figure and the few tendrils of dark hair that had escaped, he was confident that it was the object of their search.

"Do not stare, Aunt, but I think that our prey is heading towards the fish pond."

Lady Audrey's surreptitiously observed the petite figure in the simple muslin gown now taking the gravel path around the pond. As she did, Elizabeth stopped to stare into the placid pool, and without warning, stooped to pick up several stones and throw them across the water, making each skip several times in the process. Memories of performing the same ritual when she was a young girl made Audrey Ashcroft smile. *I like her already!*

Though Elizabeth's eyes were hidden, her smile showed that she was pleased with her accomplishment. And just as quickly as she had stopped, she turned and proceeded down the path that led into the woods.

"Come, we shall cross the park and meet her when she exits the copse."

And they did. As Elizabeth emerged from the shadows of the tall trees, her head down in concentration, she almost collided with them.

"Pardon me!" she declared breathlessly, taking several steps backwards. "I was not attending to where I was going."

"Nonsense! It was as much our fault as yours. We were directly in your path," Lady Audrey replied softly, a friendly expression on her face.

Elizabeth laughed, her eyes twinkling in amusement. "I thank you, but my father says that I am too apt to walk with my head down, and I am afraid he is correct!"

Suddenly she noticed the man standing beside the older woman and her smile vanished, replaced by a look of apprehension. Colonel Fitzwilliam had to have known what transpired between his cousin and her at the ball. Could it be that he was here to reprove her? At any rate, her courage rose to the occasion and a look of boldness replaced the one of dread. Performing a quick curtsey, she mumbled, "Colonel Fitzwilliam," then turned this same brave expression on the woman.

Immediately she recognised what she had not seen before—the resemblance to Mr. Darcy. Could this be his mother? The lady looked every inch a member of high society, from her elegant coiffure to her jewellery and expensive gown; even the way she held herself spoke of wealth and privilege. Elizabeth's heart began a furious drumming.

Trying not to smile at the determined expression on Elizabeth's face, Richard declared, "Miss Bennet, how good to see you again. Allow me to introduce my aunt, Lady Audrey Ashcroft. Aunt, this is Miss Elizabeth Bennet from Meryton in Hertfordshire. We met at Lord Holmes' residence several days ago when she and I were visiting. She was also at the Holmes' ball, and you may have met her there."

Lady Audrey could barely disguise the admiration in her reply. "I did not have the pleasure of meeting you at the ball. I am very pleased to make your acquaintance, Miss Bennet."

The name Ashcroft sounded familiar, but Elizabeth could not recall where she had heard it. "Milady," she murmured bobbing another small curtsey.

The older woman's discernible inspection was unsettling, and Elizabeth was about to excuse herself and walk on when Richard spoke again.

"As I was just saying to my aunt, I must return to my office. The general expects a report from me this afternoon. What good fortune it was to meet you here! Would you mind greatly allowing her to continue her walk with you?"

There was no polite way to refuse. "No. Not at all," Elizabeth murmured.

"Wonderful!" Then addressing his aunt, Richard continued, "I suppose I shall see you this evening. You will be present for dinner, will you not?"

Lady Audrey leaned forward to receive Richard's peck on the cheek. "I would never miss the opportunity to dine with you."

Richard's gaze shifted to Elizabeth. "Miss Bennet, thank you for allowing my aunt to continue her walk. I wish you both a good day!" With that, he tipped his hat and started across the large expanse of green towards his carriage. And it was at that very moment that Elizabeth remembered where she had seen the name Ashcroft—on the letter that Mr. Darcy left in the book delivered to her at Longbourn. She turned to her new acquaintance with a puzzled expression.

William's aunt smiled. "I hope my company is not that hard to bear."

At first mortified that her misgivings were so marked, the woman's ready smile caused Elizabeth to calm. "I am sorry if I appeared to be unhappy with your company. But I must confess that I was startled by your resemblance to a gentleman of my acquaintance; the likeness is remarkable. You could be his mother."

"May I ask if you are speaking of Fitzwilliam Darcy?" At Elizabeth's nod, she smiled. "Fitzwilliam's mother, Anne, was my sister, and I am told that we favoured each other a good deal, just as he favours her. Both his parents died years ago. The only immediate family that he has left is his sister, Georgiana, who is but fourteen."

Elizabeth was mortified to feel relief that the Georgiana mentioned in the letter was his sister and hurried to change the subject.

"I must be candid. I have the feeling that our meeting was not happenstance."

"No wonder my nephew is in love with you. You are not only very pretty but very intelligent."

"If you have come on Mr. Darcy's behalf, I must warn you that I do not wish to discuss him." She began walking purposefully and Lady Audrey hurried to join her.

"I confess that this meeting was planned. Forgive my boldness, but I only mean to be of service. I was in the garden that night at the ball and could not avoid overhearing your conversation with my nephew. I am convinced that you are as in love with Fitzwilliam as he is with you."

Elizabeth's pace picked up briskly. "Love built on lies is not love at all. I no longer respect him, so thankfully any tender feelings I had towards him will be short lived."

"Will they?"

Elizabeth halted, seemingly confused.

"And even if short lived, I thought you more inquisitive than that. Do you truly wish to go through life with no understanding of the man? Not even for your own peace of mind? I can assure you that no flaw in your character caused you to trust Fitzwilliam Darcy."

Elizabeth began a slower pace. "I...I wish I could believe that."

"Know this! I would never defend a dishonourable man, even if he were my relation. But I have known Fitzwilliam since his birth. Who better than I to tell you the truth of his situation? If you choose to hate him afterwards, that is your prerogative. Society tries to keep our sex ignorant under the guise of *protection*. I have always ascribed to the notion that it is better to know the truth than to hypothesise for the rest of your life. And I have lived long enough to know that regret is a hard taskmaster."

Elizabeth stopped dead, considering her words. "I am certain that you love Mr. Darcy very much or you would not be here. Do I have your word that you will not embellish the explanation in order to promote his cause?"

"You do. I would never lie for him nor would he want me to! All I ask is that you never repeat what I shall relate to you. I am certain that, once given, you keep your word, otherwise you would not be the kind of woman my nephew could esteem."

"You may trust me. And I shall listen, but only because I want to understand my own foibles."

"I understand completely."

Thus, Lady Audrey spent the next half-hour telling Elizabeth of her nephew's disposition and of his dedication to his family which led to his sham of a marriage. She did not share the part about Georgiana's paternity, something that she had just learned, but simply that Gisela was extorting him with some personal letters belonging to his mother. At some point in time, Elizabeth was so affected by the story that she stopped walking and dropped down onto a nearby bench. She did not try to hide the tears that slid from the corners of her eyes. Lady Audrey took the seat beside her, and once the account was finished, they sat silently for some time.

"He ... he would do all this to keep from breaking his dying mother's heart and to protect his sister? It is hard to believe any man could act so selflessly."

"Not *any* man. My nephew is a special breed."

Elizabeth stood shakily. "I ... I thank you for caring enough to tell me this. And I am relieved to find that his character is not so dissimilar to what I had sketched at the start of our acquaintance. That helps to restore a bit of faith in my own judgement. But why would he not have been honest with me from the beginning."

"Am I correct to assume that he did not lie, but he omitted to tell you that he was married?"

"Yes."

"I surmise that he fell in love with you against all reason, and for once in his life, he wanted to know how it felt to be truly in love, if only for a short while. Everyone familiar with him knows that he has held himself under strict regulation since his marriage, making certain never to be alone with any eligible woman. Your experience in the flood and afterward was something completely out of his control. However, I am confident of my nephew's character. I dare to say that he never meant to harm you, nor did he act the cad while you were alone. He did not take advantage of you."

"No, he did not."

"Precisely! He left Meryton straightaway. If he were a cad, he would have stayed and exploited your feelings, as many men of his station have done to innocent young women."

"You say he is in love with me. Why has he not sought me out to explain?"

"He was trying to protect you by letting you go, but he has not been able to put you out of his mind. Then when he learned that your family was prepared to accept the likes of John Wilkens as a possible suitor, he knew he could not allow it."

When Elizabeth did not reply, William's aunt stood too. "He has resolved to divorce Gisela. It may take years before he is successful, but when he is free, I have no doubt that he will search for you.

"Men like him only love once. I know because my late husband was cut from the same cloth. I would never attempt to give you advice, but I will say that if you truly love him, it would be well worth the wait to have such a man. That kind of devotion comes along only once in a lifetime, if at all."

Lady Audrey reached to take Elizabeth's hand and squeezed it. "It was a privilege to meet you, Elizabeth Bennet. I feared that my darling boy's honour would prevent him from ever knowing the joy of true love. Just to know that for a short time he loved you and you returned that love—well, it restores my faith that if two people are meant to fall in love, they will."

Elizabeth's voice was rough with emotion as she whispered, "I ... I do not have the luxury of choosing my future, and my family is determined I shall make a suitable match whilst I am in London." She raised her tear-filled eyes to Lady Audrey. "I have four sisters, you see." At the lady's nod, she continued. "Will you tell Fitzwilliam that I understand and that I forgive him?"

"Will you not speak to—"

Elizabeth shook her head violently, "Explain to him why I cannot wait and ask him to let me go." Then she ran down the gravel path in the direction of her aunt's house.

As Audrey Ashcroft made her way to the waiting carriage tears slid down her own cheeks. Would it have been better not to have come—for Elizabeth never to have known?

No! At least she knows that he did not mean to deceive her—that he loves her. She deserves that much.

It was with a much heavier heart that she entered the carriage to return to Darcy House. Now she must face the man who loved this intrepid young woman.

The Gardiner's residence fairly buzzed with excitement as Elizabeth returned to find Lord Wilkens' carriage stopped in front. Elizabeth took a deep breath to steady herself as the front door was opened for her, and a very excited Madeline Gardiner immediately hastened her inside. Servants hurried from the kitchen to the parlour, trays of sweets and coffee carefully balanced in their hands.

"Is it not fortunate, Lizzy? Lord Wilkens is in the study with your uncle. No doubt he is here to ask permission to court you! Hurry now! Go to your room and change into your best gown. I should not want him seeing you in this old muslin. What would he think of his future wife should he see how worn this gown is?"

What indeed?

⚭

During the trip back to Grosvenor Square, Lady Audrey reflected on the woman who had stolen Fitzwilliam's heart. She had actually looked forward to meeting the young lady and discovering what made her unlike any other woman of her nephew's acquaintance. Not surprisingly, she had found more than one trait to admire in Miss Bennet.

Though she is not beautiful in the conventional sense, she is striking—with the most unusual dark eyes. More importantly, she practically glows with joie de vivre—something my nephew desperately lacks in his life.

She chuckled to herself. *She is intelligent enough to have realised that Richard and I were not there accidentally and was willing to confront us— something else I admire. In addition, it is obvious that she possesses a kind heart. Yes, I can understand why any man would be in danger of falling in love with her.*

She took a deep breath to calm herself, the dull ache in her heart now almost unbearable. She had to appear composed if she was to be of any use to Fitzwilliam, but since she loved him like a mother, she grieved to envision the results recounting their conversation would produce.

I pray this does not push him over the edge of reason.

⚭

Darcy House
William's Study

"You say you left Aunt Audrey with Elizabeth an hour ago? What could be keeping her?"

"Calm down, Cousin! She is sure to return soon."

William continued to pace back and forth across the room, running his hands through his hair as he was wont to do when he was upset. Propped against his cousin's desk, Richard could barely keep from chuckling aloud.

"You are not helping, Richard!"

Just then the door opened and their aunt entered. She motioned for the butler to leave and turned to close the door behind her. When she faced them, her expression told William all he needed to know, and he sank down in the nearest chair. His entire countenance changed as the truth sank into his heart—Elizabeth would not be his.

Lady Audrey walked over to her nephew, placing a hand on his hair to smooth it as she exchanged a meaningful glance with Richard. "Do not despair, Fitzwilliam. She knows the truth, and given time to think about it, she may change her mind."

"She cannot forgive me."

"She *does* forgive you. She told me as much."

"Then why?" William asked. Noticing his aunt glance to Richard, he assured her, "Speak freely. I have no secrets from Richard."

"She asked me to tell you that she understands and that she forgives you. She also said that she does not have the luxury of choosing her future. Her family has made it clear they expect her to make a match while she is in Town. She cannot wait for you."

His head dropped into his hands. "I cannot let her go."

"You may not have a choice. If they find a suitable—"

"Suitable? That cad Wilkens is suitable?"

"Fitzwilliam, you must calm down. You cannot force her to wait for you. I felt strongly that she should know how you feel about her, and that was my intent in going to her. Now that she knows, she must decide what her course will be."

"It would have been better had I never seen her again—had I never contacted her."

Richard exclaimed, "You cannot believe that! She needed to know your heart. And once she sees that you are determined to divorce, she will change her mind. You will go through with a divorce, will you not?"

"I have determined that I will divorce Gisela, but with Elizabeth's dismissal, there is no pressure to begin quickly. I shall wait until Georgiana has returned to Pemberley from Ramsgate and I have explained everything to her. After she knows the truth about her father, I will begin."

"Why wait? If you start now, it could give Elizabeth hope. She might change her mind."

William raised both hands in surrender. "I know you mean well, Richard, but do not give me false hope. It is probably for the best. Gisela would have ruined Elizabeth had she learned that I love her." He stood up. "If you do not mind, I am going to my room. I need a little solitude."

He walked over to place a kiss on his aunt's forehead. "Thank you for all you have done." Then looking to Richard, "For all the both of you have done. I do not deserve such loyalty. Now, if you will please excuse me."

With those words he walked toward the door, turning to give them a wan smile before quitting the room. Richard hurried to the open door to watch his cousin go down the hall, each footstep appearing to take more effort than the last.

"Is there no hope? Does she not care enough to wait for his divorce?"

"I do not think she feels she has any choice in the matter."

"Are you certain that she ever loved him?"

"That is the one thing of which I have no doubt."

⬅︎❧➡︎

Chapter 15

Kent
Rosings
A Study

Appearing every inch the refined gentleman in his new attire, Wickham drank the expensive brandy he had purloined from Lady Catherine's liquor cabinet minutes before as he inspected the room she used as a study. Admiring the splendid blue papered walls, cream and blue oriental carpets, fine furniture and priceless paintings with envy, he had just begun to calculate the value of a delicate china figurine with gold trim that sat atop the mantle when he was startled by the sound of a slamming door. As he spun around, the Mistress of Rosings walked past him wordlessly, settling herself in a large chair behind the enormous desk. She sat motionless and silent, studying him.

Waiting for me to speak as usual! Why must I always play the subservient fool?

Taking the seat in front of the desk, he reluctantly obliged. "Pray, what is the reason for this summons? I was set to return to Ramsgate when your letter arrived. Coming here has caused me to fall behind schedule."

"I sustain you! Thus, I determine your priorities!" she hissed, opening the middle drawer of the desk as she spoke. Withdrawing a missive, she waved it about as though she expected Wickham to know what it contained. "Apparently I was mistaken to put any trust in Gisela's abilities. First, she failed to produce an heir which would have compelled Fitzwilliam to stay with her, and despite her assurance that their marital difficulties would keep him occupied, that proves not to be the case!"

Wickham swirled the amber liquid in his glass before slowing taking a swallow. *The old bat is getting addled!* He finally replied condescendingly, "I have no idea to what your ladyship refers."

Despite her agitation, Lady Catherine kept her explanation brief. "My solicitor, Mr. Ferguson, had informed me that Fitzwilliam has hired a retired colleague of his to investigate our joint venture. This man he hired, Lowell, has already called on Ferguson to peruse the accounts and indicated he is going to inventory the mills. He was persuaded to undertake the inventory first, thus granting time for Ferguson to complete the quarterly report. I do not wish for him to see any of the records nor will I permit him to ask questions concerning my affairs."

Lady Catherine's eyes hardened, appearing even darker than their usual steely grey. "Is there someone of your acquaintance that can put an end to this?"

It took only a moment for Wickham to realise what she was asking and what it could mean for him. "For the right amount of money, anything is possible. What kind of end do you envision?"

"Follow him from one place to another until the time is convenient for him to have an accident. He is to begin the inventory with Wexford Mill. It would be a simple matter for him to disappear after he leaves that area as the terrain lends itself to highwaymen. Afterward, there should be no one left to tell the tale. Do you understand?"

"Let me see if I fully comprehend. I am to find someone to kill the solicitor Darcy has hired, and once he has done the deed, I am to kill him?"

"Precisely! This cannot be traced back to me."

"I shall do it for three thousand pounds."

Lady Catherine glowered at him. "Must I remind you that it has cost me a great deal to parade you about Ramsgate as a gentleman? Even the clothes on your back came from my coffers. Why should I pay you so large a sum?"

"With your vast fortune, I cannot imagine you will miss a few pounds!" Wickham stood up defiantly now. "It is one thing to spy, lie and steal for you but quite another entirely to commit murder. That means the gallows if I am caught!"

She studied him contemptuously. "Very well, then! But, unlike the fiasco with Gisela, I expect results! If you fail me on this, nothing else will matter. If my nephew were to ever learn—" She halted. "Let me just say that isolating Georgiana at Ramsgate will be a lot more difficult if Lowell is not stopped very soon. If Fitzwilliam becomes suspicious, he will return to Pemberley, taking her with him. Your plans for a marriage will be finished before they have started! Just take care of that solicitor, and if any facts surface after you are wed to my niece, I feel sure that your charm will carry the day. By then, you should be able to convince Georgiana of whatever you wish."

Wickham smiled at the faith she had in his abilities. "I have several acquaintances that can handle such a job."

"Excellent! As soon as the matter is resolved, let me know. Once Lowell is dead, Ferguson will pilfer from his office whatever information he might have there, under the pretence of helping settle his affairs. After all, they are fellow solicitors and in the same building."

"He would not object to being a party to murder?"

"Ferguson has a long history with the de Bourghs. He will turn a blind eye as long as he has nothing to do with the man's death. I pay him well to leave his conscience at home."

"And what will prevent Darcy from hiring another solicitor?"

"By then, Georgiana's hasty marriage and resulting *delicate condition* will be more important than what is now occupying his mind."

Wickham raised his glass in a salute. "I see your point."

London
The Trousdale Townhouse
A Dinner Party

The billiards room billowed with cigar smoke, so much so that John Wilkens had to stop just inside the entrance to get his bearings. The sounds of wooden balls striking one another, along with the drone of constant chatter, almost drowned out his host's acerbic greeting.

"Wilkens, you finally came out of hiding! I was beginning to think you were too busy with the ladies to accept any of my invitations. How many have you declined? Three? Or is it four? And then when you do consent to show, you seem content to remain with the ladies instead of commiserating with those of us in this sanctuary." With those words Frederick Trousdale, the Earl of Dryden, swept his arm towards the other men in the room, a good many of whom overheard the entire conversation and chuckled.

Barely acknowledging those circling the various billiard tables, Wilkens managed to return a weak smile at his host. Dryden was an acquaintance of his late father, as were several others in attendance. None were his friends, but as customary, he pretended otherwise. After all, in their society each must play his part.

"Neither statement is true, I assure you. I have simply been exceedingly occupied with business since I arrived in Town. And while I admit to enjoying the entertainment in the music room, I am here now, am I not?"

"Indeed you are! And just who is that lass on your arm? The one you seem so protective of—Miss Bennet, if I remember the name correctly." The Earl raised inquisitive brows, his expression one of bemused anticipation. "She is a pretty little thing. I will give you that, though I have never heard of the family. Is she someone of import or just a passing *liaison*?"

He was lying, Wilkens knew, as his wife had no doubt passed along the latest gossip while they had enjoyed dinner. So he was well aware that the young woman he was escorting was a country squire's daughter with nothing to recommend her. Wilkens bristled at Dryden's inference. He had no doubt that the entire *ton* had been amused by his humiliation at the hands of the three debutants he had previously pursued. And Dryden clearly saw Miss Bennet for what she was— a poor substitute for a member of their sphere. Nevertheless, Wilkens felt obligated to defend his choice in order to save face.

"Miss Bennet is a gentleman's daughter from Hertfordshire, sir, and I am courting her."

The Earl forced back a smirk though his lips formed a tight line in doing so. "I suppose there are reasons to choose a wife, other than dowry and connections." A guffaw from somewhere behind caused Wilkens to turn, but no one met his eye. His host continued, "I must say she is very ... tempting."

The chatter in the room had quieted, giving way to sporadic chuckles, as he continued to needle Wilkens; all cue sticks were silenced in favour of hearing their exchange. "A lady that handsome might even tempt me!"

With Dryden's last pronouncement, even more scattered sniggers filled the hush, and Wilkens pulled himself up to his full height, his eyes narrowing.

"Unlike some, I have no need to augment my wealth with a woman's dowry. And as for tempting—there is something to be said for not having to settle for an ugly harridan because she is accompanied by a large sum of money."

Thoroughly affronted, Wilkens quitted the now silent room, every eye tracking his progress. The majority of the occupants appeared taken aback, each having felt the sting of his retort as keenly as their host. For they, too, had had to marry plain and even ugly women for their dowries and connections.

The Earl turned to his audience, shrugged and guffawed. "Hell, he could have kept her on the side and still filled his coffers with a stout dowry!"

The renewed sounds of laughter and balls striking one another helped to erase the veracity of Wilkens' taunt. Teasing and bets began anew as the truth was pushed to the farthest corners of their minds. It simply would not do to dwell on the drawbacks of what had always been, and would always be, their lot in life.

The Music Room

As the music played and couples danced, Elizabeth tried hard to attend to what Alfreda was saying. She stood with Wilkens' sister among a small group of ladies that she had never met before this evening. Most of them ignored her whenever she spoke, despite Alfreda's attempts to involve her in the conversation. This did not concern Elizabeth, however, as her heart was not invested in this gaggle of gossips. To be truthful, she was simply tired of it all—trying to please her aunt, to impress the *ton* and deal with Lord Wilkens.

Since that gentleman had received her uncle's permission to court her, he had dominated her every waking hour with one event or another. Apparently his planned departure for Kent in one week made him determined to present her to as many of his acquaintances as possible in the short time he had left in Town. She feared that this whirlwind courtship would mean an equally swift offer of marriage upon his return to London. For her part, Elizabeth was counting the hours until she would be free of him once more, if only for a short while.

Suddenly Alfreda was addressing her. "And what is your opinion, Elizabeth?"

Elizabeth stuttered an answer that she hoped was correct. "I...I agree." She let go the breath she was holding when Alfreda smiled and turned back to the others, never missing a beat.

To be honest, her mind was preoccupied with thoughts of Jane. She was genuinely concerned because her sister had not replied to her last letter. In it Elizabeth had conveniently forgotten to mention that she was being courted by Wilkens. Nonetheless, ecstatic about the earl's declaration, her aunt most likely had written to Longbourn directly after she had posted her letter to Jane. Had her sister learned the news from their mother? Had her feelings been hurt? In truth, Elizabeth had omitted that information because Jane could easily detect any attempt to feign emotions she did not possess. And admitting that there were no decent men of higher society available to either of them, would prove Jane correct in considering the few men that Meryton had to offer.

When the Gardiners spoke to her after Wilkens had declared himself, she was torn between stating the truth—that she would never accept the man—or letting the farce play out to buy time. She chose the latter. After all, her aunt had no intention of letting her pursue other matches so long as Wilkens was already practically in the family. And knowing Madeline Gardiner, she would likely be exceedingly perturbed if she refused his courtship and would send her home unceremoniously. If that were the case, how could she meet other acceptable men? Besides, once at home she would have to face her mother's ire and the sadness in Jane's eyes.

Surely among the many people I meet while on Wilkens' arm, there is at least one kind-hearted, honourable man who will notice me.

Immediately she pictured Mr. Darcy, and it took all her willpower to force his memory into the far recesses of her heart, though she knew full well that it would resurface in the early morning hours when she could least resist. Luckily, at that moment a loud commotion brought a welcome diversion, and she, as well as the entire assemblage, turned to gape as a splendidly dressed couple barged into the room—the butler close on their heels.

"Madam! Sir, you cannot—"

One of the most beautiful creatures Elizabeth had ever seen stood just steps away. There was no doubt in her mind that this woman could command attention in any gathering. Her dark blond hair, topped by a ruby tiara, was swept up into an elaborate style with a few curls left to hang down the back. An exquisite ruby choker highlighted her long, lovely neck and was accompanied by the matching drop earrings. A perfect ivory complexion showcased vivid green eyes, framed by dark brown brows and lashes and while her lips were a vibrant red, her cheeks were only lightly rouged. Her low-cut, crimson satin gown fit tightly from the bodice down to her tiny waist, and displayed her ample bosom. Visually, she was magnificent!

Nevertheless, despite her striking appearance, her unladylike deportment drew far more notice. The distinguished looking gentleman at her side seemed bemused as he tried to keep her steady and the smell of liquor began to permeate the air. Meanwhile, the lively woman met every eye defiantly, practically daring those gathered to censure her.

Ultimately, the butler managed to step in front of her and she snapped, "I do not care if I do not have an invitation. I am a friend of Lord Dryden's and I shall be welcome!"

Seeing that he could not persuade them by reasoning, the butler hurried to find his mistress amongst those gathered in the music room. Elizabeth stood spellbound as the servant and their hostess spoke in hushed tones before he quit the room with his head held high, sniffing disgustedly at the interlopers as he passed them. With a decided frown, Lady Dryden hurried in the direction of the errant pair, presenting a wan smile once she stood before them. The intruders must have been pleased with whatever was said, as the stunning woman looked very smug after the Countess returned to her duties as hostess.

Proclaiming loudly, "Come, Howard, I wish to dance!" the woman practically pulled her partner onto the dance floor and proceeded to hang onto him for balance, much to the entertainment of the *ton*. And they put on a grand show all the while they danced.

Failing to realise that she was still staring, her mouth gapped open, Elizabeth startled when Alfreda whispered, "Do not be shocked. That is the way Gisela Darcy always behaves!"

"Dar...Darcy?" Elizabeth managed to murmur. "But that is not—"

"Not her husband? Yes, *everyone* is aware of that. The rumour is that Mr. Darcy has never had anything to do with her because she trapped him into marriage. I once overheard my brother tell an acquaintance about it when he was not aware that I was listening. It seems Mr. Darcy deposited her on the doorstep of her townhouse on their wedding day and never returned. Brother thought it was simply hilarious."

"Then who—"

"That is her latest *friend*, Lord Attenborough. He is a ne'er-do-well who has more money than sense, Brother says. He enjoys shocking society."

A searing pain shot through Elizabeth's heart! *She is very beautiful.* Her second thought, however, was of Mr. Darcy's pain. *How cruel to embarrass him so publicly!*

"Does she not realise that she is the source of everyone's amusement?"

Alfreda shrugged. "Apparently, her objective *is* to embarrass her husband in any manner possible. I have seen her act like this in public at least twice before and I am seldom in Town. However, my cousin Penelope assures me this behaviour is typical for Mrs. Darcy. She truly has no sense of decency, unlike her husband. I met Mr. Darcy once. He impressed me as a very kind and sensitive man. I know that he cares deeply for his sister, who was with him when we were introduced. One can only wonder what happened to cause him offer for someone as ridiculous as Gisela."

Elizabeth shuddered, remembering what Fitzwilliam's aunt had disclosed. "Yes, one can only wonder."

Shortly afterward, Lord Wilkens returned to their company, and neither woman mentioned the newcomer's arrival. Gisela Darcy was still dancing with Attenborough, as no other man had dared venture an invitation. Upon noticing her presence in the room, however, Wilkens eyes widened as though he had seen a ghost and he coloured. His discomposure was not lost on Elizabeth. Meanwhile, the lady in question had most certainly noticed the Earl of Hampton's return and was smirking at him as though they shared some dark secret.

"What can she mean smiling at you like that, Brother? It is highly improper!" Alfreda exclaimed.

Ignoring her question, Wilkens grabbed his sister's arm, and turned to address Elizabeth with his arm extended as though to escort her. "We are leaving. I have had all the merriment I can stomach for one evening."

And as she was being rushed from the room, Elizabeth glanced back to see Gisela Darcy convulsing in laughter.

"Who are you laughing at so heartily, my dear?" Lord Attenborough asked, more curious as to which man she had spied than surprised at her behaviour.

He enquired because it was to his advantage to keep a tally of those he might be able to blackmail over a past indiscretion with Gisela. Most of the socialites of the *ton* hated the woman, and if they knew that their husbands had sampled her wares … well, Attenborough could make their lives so much more miserable. And now that Darcy's wife drank so heavily, it had been simple to get her to reveal details of her liaisons. It also helped that Darcy was known as the best swordsman in London and an expert shot. Though he knew for certain that the man did not care enough to challenge anyone over his wife's honour, few others were willing to test that assumption. Thus, his threats of exposure were always taken seriously, and his income benefited greatly.

"Just one of those arrogant fools who cut me in public while propositioning me in private!"

Attenborough resorted to his usual flattery. "That could be every man in the room!"

He had pretended great experience in managing investments, making it easy to persuade Gisela to grant him access to her bank accounts. So between the monies he made through extortion and what he skimmed from her accounts, Attenborough was able to continue his usual standard of living, despite the fact that he had gambled away most of his fortune.

Gisela was drunk but not *that* drunk. Thus, she was not yet ready to confess that Wilkens had shared her bed for months before she tired of the novelty of sleeping with one of her husband's enemies.

"Right you are, my love!" she gushed, pleased at Attenborough's statement.

Their affair had taken place right after the marriage. She had felt she was taking revenge on Fitzwilliam, since he and Wilkens had had a public altercation at Whites a few weeks prior. In hindsight, it had been a disaster. The man had been horrible in bed! Only after her hands sought the rubies around her neck, did she acknowledge that his expensive presents were the only thing that made their association endurable.

But it was insupportable to encounter Wilkens now and have him act as though he was appalled at her behaviour. Thus, an idea was born. Perhaps the young woman he was squiring about would like to know what he was really like! She would have to make sure to learn her name.

Her musings were interrupted by Attenborough. "Well, if you are not going to tell me his name, why do we not resume dancing? I believe this is the last set, and you attended tonight in order to dance, did you not?"

"Oh, Howard! You always see to my pleasure!"

"I try, my dear. I try."

London
A Confectioner's Shop

Caroline studied the woman sitting across from her at the small wooden table, her expression eventually transforming into a frown, though she was not conscious of it. Her companion's close resemblance to her brother, Colonel Hedges, with the same red hair and freckles, provoked the alteration. Caroline had not wanted to join his sister on this excursion, desiring no reminders of the horrid man who thought himself her beau, but she felt that she had no choice. After all, while Charles was out of Town, this woman was her only access to the society she preferred.

Both having finished a cup of tea and a biscuit, Clementine Hedges had been observing the people on the street while Caroline surreptitiously observed her. Thus, she was startled a bit when the object of her analysis turned to address her.

"I am so pleased that you agreed to accompany me today, Caroline. I could not stay cooped up in that house one day longer without a diversion. It seems everyone must be out of Town, as I have received no invitations lately."

Who in their right mind would want your company? Only someone like me with no other choice!

Caroline's pasted on smile was getting tiresome. "You were so kind to think of me, Clemmie, and I really needed to restock our supply of chocolates. It is a pity that Colonel Hedges is on duty in Sussex at the moment, and Charles is still out of Town."

"Harold. He wishes you to call him Harold."

"Of course. It is a pity that Harold could not be with us."

Goodness, she is forward! I am just glad he is not here! I must accomplish everything I desire before Charles returns and that idiot asks to court me. At that point, when I refuse, he will know I have no interest in him and so will Clementine.

"You must be aware that I am very pleased that you and he are getting along so well. I would be pleased to call you sister one day." Clementine's gentle face glowed with sincerity.

"How kind of you to say!"

Caroline could not bring herself to echo the other woman's sentiments. That was asking too much. Luckily, at that very moment she spied Mr. Darcy and his sister entering a bookshop across the street. It provided a welcome distraction.

"My dear, I have just remembered that I promised Charles I would purchase something for him in that shop across the street. Unless you are particularly interested in books, perhaps you could pick up your bonnet at Madame Dupree's while I am in the book shop."

"That is a splendid idea. Whoever is finished first shall just walk to the other shop. Agreed?"

Agreed."

Hatchards Bookshop[8]

"Brother, I shall be in the poetry section, if you do not mind. I believe I have had my fill of history and astronomy this week!" Georgiana teased as she pulled away from William's arm. "Aunt Audrey is a hard taskmaster, and I feel the need for something lighter."

William smiled. "That is perfectly acceptable as long as you stay in that

---

8 *Hatchards Bookstore (The Regency Encyclopedia). They are still in business, and this is what they have on their website. "Hatchards, booksellers since 1797, is the oldest surviving bookshop in London. Our customers have included some of Britain's greatest political, social and literary figures - from Queen Charlotte, Disraeli and Wellington to Kipling, Wilde and Lord Byron -and our staff has always had a reputation for knowledgeable and professional service."*

section until I return. I have to enquire as to whether the books I ordered have arrived and then look for one selection in the maps before I join you."

After making her way to the area reserved for poetry, Georgiana was pleased that it seemed deserted. It was only after she hastily turned a corner around a tall bookshelf that she encountered another person—a young woman— with whom she collided.

"My goodness! Please excuse me. I thought I was alone. I was not paying attention," she declared.

A sincere smile mirrored hers. "You have done no harm, and it was as much my fault as yours. My father says I am blind to everyone else whenever I enter a bookshop. And I have to confess that, fascinated by the large selection available here, I have hardly lifted my eyes beyond the book titles."

Georgiana visibly relaxed. "I appreciate your understanding, but it was definitely my fault."

Elizabeth reached out to take her hand. "Let us consider it Fate's way of introducing us. I am Elizabeth Bennet."

Georgiana beamed. "Georgiana Darcy." Her face paled as she watched Elizabeth's smile fade.

"Oh my, I have seen that look often enough. You must have met my brother, Fitzwilliam, when he was in one of his moods. He is really very sweet, but he can appear quite haughty at times because he is so shy. Did he insult you? I will be glad to explain if—"

Elizabeth's smile returned and she interrupted. "No, no. Please do not be anxious. I assure you it is nothing like that. I was just surprised to hear the name—that is all."

No matter her heartache over Mr. Darcy, she would never let this shy young girl think she had hard feelings towards him.

Georgiana quickly rejoined, "Please do not say anything to my brother about my defence of him. He would be mortified to know I spoke to you of such things and so disappointed in me. It is just that I love him so much, and he is so often misunderstood and ..." She stopped abruptly, looking at Elizabeth with a puzzled expression. "For some odd reason, I felt that I should tell you."

Elizabeth smile was warm and sincere as she patted Georgiana's hand. "Your secret is safe with me."

Suddenly, William rounded the same bookcase calling out, "Georgiana?"

He stopped abruptly at the sight of Elizabeth. Nonetheless, no observer, and certainly not Georgiana, could miss the attraction that flowed between her reticent brother and this pretty young woman as they stared at one another, both speechless.

Seeing that neither was going to say anything, Georgiana ventured, "Brother, I came around this bookshelf just as swiftly as you did and—"

"I was right in her way, so we collided," Elizabeth finished cheekily, winking at Georgiana. "I am afraid that your sister is unaware that I am a terror in any bookshop."

William smiled, though it did not reach his eyes. His heart began a relentless drumming and he wondered if his face reflected his feelings. "On the contrary, Miss Bennet, I did not find you a terror, but a delightful source of aid." Then addressing his sister, he explained. "Miss Bennet and I met in a bookshop in

Meryton while I was visiting Charles at Netherfield. She helped me to find the section of first editions of poetry."

"Then you are acquaintances!" Georgiana said effusively. "How fateful that you should meet again in London! You simply must join me for tea tomorrow, Miss Bennet, so we may discuss Meryton and Netherfield. I so want to visit there while Mr. Bingley is in residence. Where are you staying in Town?"

Elizabeth's heart was doing an admiral job of imitating William's and she felt a bit faint. Reaching to steady herself by taking hold of the bookshelf, she smiled as naturally as possible. "I was staying with my aunt and uncle in Cheapside, but this week my aunt is out of Town, so I am the guest of Lady Alfreda Wilkens at the Holmes' townhouse."

At the mention of Wilkens' name, William stiffened, but Georgiana did not notice as she was focused on Elizabeth. She fairly shouted with delight, "Just across the park from where we live! So convenient for our tea party!"

Elizabeth tried not to show any apprehension, though she feared that Fitzwilliam would be mortified to have her as a guest in his home. "I appreciate your kind invitation, but I am afraid I am at Lady Wilkens' disposal since I am her guest. She is just now in the shop next door and will return for me shortly."

"Oh, I am sure my aunt, Lady Ashcroft, can persuade both Lady Holmes and Lady Wilkens to accompany you. Please say you will."

There was no polite way to decline. "I shall be delighted to attend if they accept your kind invitation."

If she had been inclined to glance at Fitzwilliam Darcy at that moment, Elizabeth would have seen great joy and longing reflected in his clear blue eyes. As it was, she was too nervous to look. However, Georgiana had seen his expression and it confirmed her first impression of their encounter only moments before. Her brother cared for this woman.

Searching for the Darcys from the moment she entered the building, Caroline Bingley spotted William near the end of an aisle and quickly moved one aisle over, intending to intercept him at the end of the bookshelves. She hoped it would appear just a coincidence. Instead, upon hearing another woman's voice, she stopped to peer through the small space between some books and was infuriated at what she found—a conversation taking place between Mr. Darcy, Georgiana and Eliza Bennet. And all she could do was eavesdrop as that woman secured the invitation she had desired. Caroline was livid.

That little chit is so cunning! And look how moonstruck Mr. Darcy appears. One would think— instantly her mind flew to the night at the ball when the man she had always coveted had so eagerly stood watch over Miss Bennet. Instantly, she knew what she must do.

Apparently Eliza does not mind that he is married, so it is time I informed Mrs. Darcy of her plans to seduce her husband!

Chapter 16

Liverpool
Bingley's Warehouse

S ilas Kelly watched with great interest as his employer busily gathered the papers scattered across the top of his desk and stuffed them into the open satchel sitting on the chair behind it. Surely, he thought, this signifies that Mr. Bingley is actually going to return to London!

That gentleman had worked very long hours ever since his arrival, which had meant lengthy hours for himself as well. As manager of the facility, he had had to be on hand to explain the entries in the ledgers whenever Bingley had a question. He did not mind, as that was a part of his job, but he had missed his family dreadfully with the schedule he had been forced to keep lately. Still, he held no ill will towards the amiable owner, as he was only doing what must be done. After all, if the business made money, he made money. Charles Bingley was a benevolent master.

Waiting until Charles looked up at him, the young man smiled sincerely and ventured an enquiry, "Sir, are you still planning on leaving in the morning?"

Bingley returned his smile—something Kelly had seen little of in the first days of his visit. "Yes, I think I have everything in hand now. And the letter I received yesterday from Mr. Carter was most informative, but it signifies that I must return to London. You remember Carter, do you not? He is doing a splendid job of investigating the lost ships."

"Yes, we met when he came to inspect the invoices and bills of lading."

"Ah, yes. He was compiling a list of what was supposed to arrive on that last ship. By the way, I must single you out for praise as well. You have done an excellent job of running the warehouse. Your records are meticulous."

"That is very kind of you to say, sir." Kelly flushed a deep red. "I try to look after the business as though it were my own."

"Indeed! That is obvious, and when I have things running smoothly again, do not think I will forget your efforts. Now, it is late, and I know you have scarcely seen your two boys since I have been in Liverpool. Off with you! Enjoy your evening!"

"But there is yet two hours before we close."

"I am fully aware of that. I think I remember how to manage a warehouse," Bingley teased. "Go to your wife and children. I will see you in the morning before I leave."

Kelly hesitated. "Sir, my wife and I would be honoured if you would eat dinner with us tonight. After all, this is your last day in Liverpool, and the missus has enjoyed your compliments on her cooking."

"Tell Mrs. Kelly that I would be honoured to dine with you. The meals she has provided while we have laboured have been the highlight of my trip. I have not enjoyed better cottage pie or apple tart in all of England!"

Kelly chuckled. "She spoke of stewing a rabbit and her rabbit is just as delicious! We shall expect you then at seven sharp."

"Seven it is!"

❦

Meryton
Longbourn

"Jane? Jane?"

Mrs. Bennet pushed the door to the parlour open to find that it was empty. She considered checking in her husband's library, but thought better of that idea when she heard him swear loudly about a missing book, or some such nonsense, just when she took hold of the doorknob. Thus, she headed in the direction of the kitchen.

"Now where has that girl gone? She is getting as headstrong as Lizzy, wandering here and there without a word to me. I shall put a stop to that today! John Lucas will not have a wife who is so flighty."

Entering the kitchen, she found it empty as well, though the smell of bread baking caused her to pause and savour the moment. A noise in a nearby pantry caught her attention.

"Hill? Is that you?"

The elderly servant backed out of the pantry holding a large pan. "Yes, I was just trying to find this—"

"Never mind!" Mrs. Bennet interrupted. "Have you seen Jane today? Do you know where she went?"

"No, madam. I have not."

Mrs. Bennet said nothing more, but continued to huff as she searched the rest of the house looking for her eldest. Nonetheless, Jane was nowhere to be found. Realising that she could just as easily scold her daughter when she came to the table for dinner, she headed upstairs. There were places to go and things to do, and there would be plenty of time to deal with Jane later.

"Lydia! Kitty!" she shouted breathlessly upon reaching the second floor, the effects of hurrying up the stairs becoming evident. "Are the two of you ready? We must be off to Meryton, as I have promised Lady Lucas I would call on her before we return. She and I have much planning to do if there is to be a wedding in Jane's future."

Hill could not help but hear her mistress as she went about the rest of the house seeking Jane and, suffering a pang of conscience, her expression fell. She had not been truthful. She had seen Jane very early that morning just as the girl had started to slip out the back door and she had pressed a piece of bread, with a portion of ham tucked inside it, into her hand. Jane had smiled appreciatively.

There was no doubt in her mind that the eldest Miss Bennet was endeavouring to disappear before her mother awakened and came looking for her.

Meanwhile, Jane was in her usual hiding place—the one she had adopted since Lizzy had deserted Meryton for London—sitting on the backside of the large oak tree on Oakham Mount. Her knees were pulled to her chest, and her head lay across them, eyes closed. It took all her effort not to cry.

Taking a lesson from her favourite sister, she had managed to stay out of her mother's sight for most of the day by walking out just before dawn. Fanny Bennet was nothing if not a creature of habit, and Jane, like Lizzy, had found that if she avoided her for the first hour of each day, she stood a good chance of evading her until dinner.

Each morning, after the family broke their fast, her father would disappear into his library while her mother would instruct the servants before setting out with Mary, Kitty and Lydia for the shops of Meryton. And as usual while in town, she would also call on her Sister Phillips before returning home.

However, lately it was her mother's accounts of frequent stops by Lucas Lodge on their way back from Meryton that caused Jane the most concern. Her mother and Mrs. Lucas talked of nothing else but a match between her and John Lucas. And while Jane liked Mr. Lucas, her heart had never been touched by his attentions. In fact, the more she had gotten to know him, the more disillusioned she had become. He might be the heir of Lucas Lodge but, outside of Mr. Collins, their cousin, he was the most obsequious man she had ever known and completely dependent on his mother's instructions for even the simplest things. No, he was not the man of her dreams.

She had lost track of the times that she had almost written to the Gardiners to say that she was coming to London. *Almost.* Only one niggling aspect to Lizzy's letters had made her refrain—though her sister's missives were always cheerful, it was as though the cheeriness was forced. Then two day ago, her mother had shared news that Lizzy had failed to disclose to her in the last letter—she was being courted by a Lord Wilkens. An *earl,* for heaven's sake! Suddenly all her misgivings had been validated.

Why would her beloved sister not have told her? Why must she learn of it from Aunt Gardiner's letter to her mother? There was only one logical answer. Lizzy was being forced into a courtship she did not desire. A sinking feeling deep inside caused Jane to wonder if she was about to lose what little she had eaten that morning.

Would Lizzy marry someone she did not want in order to further my prospects? And, if Lizzy is willing to sacrifice, should I not do the same and marry John Lucas for my family's sake?

Taking a ragged breath, Jane pulled her knees even tighter to her chest and sobbed in earnest now. There seemed no other course. She must accept her lot in life and give up the fantasies that she and Lizzy had clung to since they were old enough to dream of being married. The next time John Lucas asked if he could court her, she would assent.

There is not going to be a prince on a white horse to rescue either of us!

❦

London
Darcy House
William's Study

While he feigned occupation with his estate problems, every fibre of William's being was aware of who sat merely a few doors down in the music room—*Elizabeth!* With her arrival this morning, it had taken all of his strength not to walk into the foyer to greet her, so eager was he to see her again. But Georgiana had been adamant when they spoke this morning! These were her visitors, and she would brook no interference from him as she and Aunt Audrey entertained their guests.

Interference! He fumed. *As if I would disturb them!*

Directly after Georgiana's spontaneous invitation at the bookshop, a formal invitation for tea at Darcy House had been delivered to Holmes House, but after an answer had not arrived that afternoon or the next day, William had begun to wonder if she would actually accept. Nevertheless, the following day the reply came—Elizabeth, Lady Holmes and Lady Wilkens would be delighted to have tea with Georgiana and Lady Ashcroft.

Forced to stay in his study and attend his affairs, William had nevertheless opened his door in hopes of catching a bit of their conversation when they moved from the parlour to the music room, as was Georgiana's plan. Fortunately, his strategy had worked. When the ladies had made the transition about an hour ago, he had heard Elizabeth's melodious laughter, and it had warmed his heart. Even now, with the sounds of the pianoforte echoing through the house, he was plotting how to *accidently* encounter her when they gathered in the foyer to take their leave. Surely his sister would not begrudge him a chance meeting!

William's deliberations were suddenly interrupted by an enthusiastic greeting.

"Darcy! What luck to find you available! Your servants are tyrants when it comes to interrupting you whilst you are at work. However, even Mr. Barnes could not deny me access with the door standing wide open. Besides, a footman let me in and I got ahead of your dutiful butler!"

The man in question hurried into the room at that very moment, looking very embarrassed. "Excuse me sir, I was answering Miss Georgiana's summons and was not aware that Mr. Bingley had arrived," Barnes cut his eyes to Charles as he was very perturbed not to have announced him.

"There was no harm done! Carry on."

The butler backed to the door, bowing slightly before he exited. "Yes, sir."

Bingley's attention was on the servant and when he turned to see William's scowl, he sobered. "Have I come at a bad time? Would you rather I return another day?"

"No, Charles," William replied, taking this opportunity to stand and stretch his weary body. He had been so focused in his efforts to listen to what was happening in the rest of the house that he was totally unaware of how tightly his muscles had coiled. "I was just shocked to see you; that is all. I thought you were still in Liverpool."

"I left Liverpool so quickly that there was no time to send a letter. I just wanted to get back to London and obtain your perspective on my troubles."

William sat back down and waved towards a chair. "Have a seat."

"Do you not wish me to close the door first?"

"Actually, I would rather you leave it open for now."

Bingley's brow furrowed. It was not like Darcy to talk business with the door open. "As you wish."

Meanwhile William inspected his friend. "From the looks of you, I would say you came directly here without going home. Is it that important?"

"I did and yes it is! Mr. Carter has located the last ship that was reported lost."

"Located it? Where?"

"Docked in Bristol Harbour."

"How singular! So it was not lost at sea."

"No. Apparently it has been in Bristol since it arrived in England under another name."

"Then how was he able to locate it if the name was changed?"

"It seems Humphrey Grier is still the ship's captain. He had not bothered to change *his* name. Carter located him which led to the ship. In fact, Grier was so confident of not being discovered that he was readying the ship for another voyage. Nonetheless, with help from a disgruntled sailor, Mr. Carter was able to prove that the ship had been sailing under another name and got an order from the local magistrate seizing it until all claims are settled."

"And your goods?"

"The ship's manifests were still in the captain's quarters under the original name of the ship—that is the evidence Carter has in his possession. However, as of his last letter, he has not found the bills of lading to ascertain where the goods were delivered."

"I have a distant cousin in Bristol who is a barrister. I am sure that at my request he will assist you. I shall write to him today."

"Thank you, Darcy. I was confident that you would know someone in Bristol that I could rely on. You have friends and relations under every rock in England."

"Not every rock, Charles," William answered dryly.

"Well, very near every one," Bingley declared, his eyes twinkling.

Just at that moment the sounds of lively female conversation caught both men's attention. Without a word to Charles, William jumped up and practically ran to the door and out into the hall. Quickly recovering from the shock of his friend's sudden departure, Bingley followed, catching up with William when he stopped near the grand staircase.

"What is it, Darcy?" Charles whispered, curious as to what emergency spurred his friend to act so swiftly.

"Shhh!" William cautioned, bringing a finger to his lips. His anxious expression did nothing to assure Charles that all was well.

Suddenly, a group of ladies rounded the opposite side of the staircase. Ignoring them, William quickly faced Charles, his back to the group as he proclaimed loudly, "Charles, I certainly understand your desire to get home and rest since you have been on the road for so long. I shall see you tomorrow then?"

Despite being caught unawares, Charles quickly picked up the charade. "Yes, Darcy. I appreciate the invitation to dine, but I must go home and wash the dust off. And our business can certainly wait until tomorrow."

William winked at Charles when Georgiana exclaimed from behind, "Brother?"

He turned, hoping his innocent look was convincing. "I hope I have not interrupted your visit. I was just seeing Mr. Bingley to the door. I believe you have all met." His eyes, now pitch black with longing, unsurprisingly drifted to Elizabeth and stayed on her while he spoke. "I am so very pleased that you ladies accepted my sister's invitation—Lady Holmes, Lady Wilkens … *Miss Bennet*." Her name was uttered in a lower tone, almost as a prayer. "It is a pleasure to have you in my home."

As he addressed each woman in turn, William made a show of taking their hand. He ended up holding Elizabeth's, and held it a little longer than proper. Lady Holmes did not notice his partiality as she was still spellbound by his attentiveness; after all, Mr. Darcy was a strikingly handsome man and cut a fine figure. For her part, Lady Wilkens had felt his magnetism so intensely that she had followed his progress as he moved to stand before Elizabeth. She was perplexed that Elizabeth seemed so affected she could not speak, and was pondering the significance of that when Bingley stepped forward to break the spell.

"Miss Bennet! Upon my word, it is good to see you again. What are you doing in London?" Charles' declaration caused William to let go of Elizabeth's hand and step back. Recovering her composure Elizabeth turned, warily studying the gentleman who had deserted Jane.

"I am visiting with my aunt and uncle in Cheapside, though this week they are out of Town, so I am staying with Lord and Lady Holmes," she swept a hand towards Alfreda, "as a guest of Lady Wilkens."

"And your sister, Jane? Is she also in London?"

"No. Jane has not left Meryton since Mr. Darcy summoned you from Netherfield."

William and Audrey Ashcroft exchanged knowing glances. It was obvious that Elizabeth was testing her theory as to why Charles had deserted Meryton. Oblivious to it all, Charles acquitted himself and William without realising it.

"Darcy sent for me?" He chuckled aloud. "Oh my, I can just imagine it might have looked that way. But, actually he was just passing along a message from my solicitor. You see, one of the ships that transport my dry goods was reported lost."

Elizabeth's voice could barely be heard. "Lost? Lost at sea?"

"Exactly! And this was the second one! In fact, I have spent the better part of the last few weeks in Liverpool, assessing my warehouse there in light of the fact that there will be no new items delivered for quite some time. And, I have just today returned to London."

"I … I see," Elizabeth said hoarsely, glancing nervously at William. She found herself trying to make sense of the look on his face.

Audrey Ashcroft nodded to her nephew before addressing Elizabeth.

"Fitzwilliam often advises his friends on business matters."

Bingley laughed. "Yes, milady. I am afraid I would have made many an error in judgement without his help."

William stiffened at the praise. "Please, that is enough tribute. I did nothing extraordinary. Beyond advising him whom to contact, there was nothing he could not have handled." Then addressing Charles, he stated, "I shall expect you in the morning then, at eight?"

"Eight, it is!" Bingley turned to the ladies. "Lady Ashcroft, Lady Holmes, Lady Wilkens, Miss Darcy, it is always a pleasure. Miss Bennet, I hope to talk with you again soon, as I intend on returning to Netherfield, and I would like to know your thoughts on the matter."

Elizabeth smiled in earnest now. "I would welcome it. However, I am travelling to Ramsgate next week with Lady Wilkens, so you will have to call on me within the next few days if you wish to talk."

"I shall do that!" Charles exclaimed, donning his hat and giving it a pat. "I bid you all adieu."

Only seconds after Charles had gone, the women began their farewells. William was still in a daze, digesting the news that Elizabeth was accompanying Lady Wilkens to Ramsgate, the location of their family estate. He was very aware that this meant that she was most likely going to accept Wilkens offer of marriage.

Audrey Ashcroft was giving instructions for a footman to summon the carriage, while Mr. Barnes came forward with the ladies cloaks and a maid handed them their gloves. She managed a quick glance to a stricken William, as she directed everyone onto the portico. Georgiana led the way and the visitors followed. Elizabeth hesitated only a second before she, too, walked out the door.

William could not let her leave without a word, so he called out, "Miss Bennet, I think you forgot something."

Elizabeth turned, taking a few steps back. His aunt engaged Lady Holmes and Alfreda Wilkens in conversation as she quickly took Elizabeth's place and followed them onto the portico, partially shutting the door behind. Effectively this left Elizabeth in the foyer and out of view and hearing of the others.

William stepped closer, his emotions soaring at the nearness of her. Several dark curls had defied her bonnet and he yearned to untie the offending object and bury his fingers in her unruly mane. Instead, he lost himself in the two dark brown orbs now studying him. Clasping her hands, he intended to pull her into an embrace.

Her voice was breathless as she resisted, "Sir, I do not think that I forgot—"

She ceased speaking when William stopped to bring first one then the other of her hands to his lips, kissing both with great deliberation. His voice was rough with emotion as he whispered, "Forgive me. I know that I have no right, but your presence in my home has made me so very happy, Elizabeth."

Lowering her eyes as they filled with tears, she replied, "You should not call me—"

"Please do not forbid me," He pleaded, bringing her hands to his heart. "I felt I must take this opportunity to tell you how I feel—how I have felt about you since the first time I saw you. I can no longer deny my love for you. I love you ... most ardently."

Seeing his eyes ablaze with hunger, Elizabeth entwined her fingers with his and pressed them tenderly. And as she met and held his gaze, tears escaped despite her attempt to hold them.

"You cannot imagine how deeply those words gladden my heart, Fitzwilliam ... indeed, my very soul. So often my circumstances have caused me to despair, but to be assured that you love me ... love me as I love you—" Her voice softened as his grasp strengthened. "Nonetheless, the truth is that you are married and I ... I do not have the power to choose my future. I hope you will find some comfort in knowing that you will always own my heart." Her voice broke at the last few words, and she pulled from his grasp to hurry from the house.

Her words were like a knife sinking into his heart and unsure if he could endure such pain, William moved unsteadily to stand in the shadows just inside the open entrance. He would bear any anguish just to observe her until the very last moment. And suffer he did, for at the bottom of the steps, Georgiana was embracing Elizabeth in the manner that he had longed to do since he had first laid eyes on her.

Lady Ashcroft stood next to the carriage, addressing each woman before they entered, and when only Elizabeth remained, she gently placed a hand on each shoulder and searched the face of the woman her nephew loved. It was evident that this young lady was suffering just as desperately as Fitzwilliam.

"I am so glad you came, Miss Elizabeth. It was as though you were destined to be here," she said softly. Elizabeth's eyes filled quickly as she turned and entered the carriage. Both hostesses waved until the conveyance was out of sight, and as they mounted the steps, Lady Ashcroft whispered to Georgiana, "I wish to speak privately with your brother, dear."

Entering the house, the hurt on her brother's face was unmistakable, so Georgiana ran to place a kiss on his cheek and, without a word, climbed the grand staircase to her room.

Lady Ashcroft waited until Georgiana was out of sight before walking over to William. Reaching up to cup his cheek, she murmured, "We need to talk."

They returned to the parlour where William walked woodenly to an overstuffed sofa and sat down. Moving to the liquor cabinet, his aunt poured a measure of brandy and handed it to him.

"Drink this."

He complied, drinking it all at once.

"Another?" He nodded, so she poured a like amount into his glass, which he downed in one gulp as well. "That is enough."

She sat next to him, taking his hand in hers. "I know this was not easy for you. But, I was heartened to see that it was not easy for Elizabeth either. Tell me, was she receptive at all?"

"I could not tell. I have no experience in judging women. I told her that I was happy to have her in my home ... that I love her. She said that she felt the same way."

"I knew it!"

"In hindsight, I should not have confronted her. I had vowed to let it be, but the moment I knew she was to be in my home—" He dropped his head with a ragged sigh. "I made her cry."

"Do not torture yourself. Tears are not always a bad sign. At least you are certain that she loves you."

"But, she also reminded me that she could not choose whom to love. Was it cruel to force a meeting?"

"Well, I am a woman, and I know that a woman in love will often do whatever it takes to be with the man she loves. Let her be the judge of what she wants."

"But you heard her say that she is going to Ramsgate with Alfreda Wilkens. That means she will be with *him*!"

"Unfortunately, that is so. Penelope Holmes told me that John Wilkens travelled ahead to handle some estate matters. Alfreda and Elizabeth will leave so as to arrive in time for their aunt, Lady Hawthorne's, birthday."

"Wilkens brags to all that will listen that he will inherit all her wealth when she dies."

"And I can just imagine that he cannot wait until she does. Nonetheless, Violet Hawthorne is an old friend of mine."

"I was not aware of that."

"And since Georgiana and I will also be travelling to Ramsgate next week in order for her to take art lessons, we shall be guests of Lady Hawthorne. So I will be able to watch over your Elizabeth while I am there."

William perked up a bit. "You will see that she is well whilst she is in Ramsgate?"

"I shall make it my business to call on her often. And since she and Georgiana are good friends now, it would not be unusual for them to spend a good deal of time in each other's company."

"I pray you can influence Elizabeth not to succumb to pressure and agree to marry that miscreant! Even if she does not wait for me, she is too good for him."

"I shall do my best, Fitzwilliam." She squeezed his hand. "Now, what say you to explaining your relationship with Elizabeth to Georgiana? She suspects that you have feelings for one another, and it is my opinion that she needs to know what has transpired between the two of you."

"Is she old enough to know of such things?"

"She is a lot more aware than you realise. And it is better for her to hear the truth from you than rumours and gossip from someone else." She stood and reached for William's hand. "She trusts you. Tell her the truth."

William stood and embraced his aunt. "I am told that I do not have a talent for expressing myself well. But I thank God every day that He sent you to me when Mother died. I do not think I could have survived these last two years without your support."

Audrey Ashcroft pulled back to look into his face as tears threatened. "I do not know where you got the idea that you cannot express yourself. You just did very well."

She pecked his cheek and pushed him playfully towards the door. "Go. Before you turn back into the old Fitzwilliam—the one who keeps all his secrets hidden."

William stopped at the parlour door and looked back. "It still uplifts my spirits when you sound just like Mother."

She smiled lovingly. "I am glad."

⚬⚬⚬

In The Holmes' Carriage

Lady Holmes seemed lost in a world of her own as she watched the world from the window of her carriage and reminisced about the pleasant experience she had just had at Darcy House. Alfreda Wilkens' thoughts, however, were of an entirely different nature.

Though she had enjoyed the day with Georgiana Darcy and her aunt, she was not blind to the way Mr. Darcy had looked at Elizabeth when they encountered him in the foyer. Furthermore, she could not help but wonder at his calling Elizabeth back into the house under the guise that she had left something behind.

Was he only creating an opportunity to talk with her alone? And if so, why?

Elizabeth, who was staring out the window on the other side of the carriage, seemed to have suddenly changed moods as well. From being quite gay when they left the music room minutes before, she now seemed sullen, even sad.

"Elizabeth?"

Elizabeth cut her eyes to Alfreda, hoping that if she did not fully turn she might not notice the tears pooled in them. She waited for Alfreda's question.

"What was it that you left in the foyer?"

Elizabeth held up her gloves. "I dropped one of my gloves."

"Oh." Alfreda was almost sure that Elizabeth had both her gloves when she came to the door.

Seeing the unbelief in her friend's eye, Elizabeth offered. "I ... I thought I had them both, but one fell from my grip."

"I see." Alfreda turned to study the view now. Elizabeth was lying. Of that she was sure. But why? After all, Mr. Darcy was married. Ultimately, she decided that she really did not want to know.

Seeing that Alfreda was not going to question her again, Elizabeth breathed a sigh of relief and resumed her study of the park from out the window.

I will not think of him! I will not think of him!

If only her heart did not have a mind of its own.

Chapter **17**

Ramsgate
Younge's Art Gallery

Standing on the veranda that stretched across the entire length of the back of the art gallery, George Wickham's every faculty was engaged. Silently memorizing the landscape, he took a deep breath of the clean, salty air and held it for a moment before releasing it. He also made note of the number of people about at that hour of the day, perfecting his strategy for escaping with Georgiana even as he waited for Mrs. Younge to finish assisting a customer.

While calculating that the sea was only a couple of hundred yards away, his attention was drawn to two figures in a gazebo at the end of a narrow, wooden walk. Intrigued, he studied the ladies under its roof and found that both had easels perched in front of them and were painting. Following the walk's path with his eye, he found that it meandered from the end of this very porch over a multitude of sand dunes and beach grasses before ending up at the structure.

Once at the gazebo, it was possible either to access a wider boardwalk that spanned the entire row of houses or take steps down to the wide, flat beach. In addition, every house had a similar narrow walkway leading to the boardwalk which enabled patrons to access each shop along the way without the necessity of using the front street entrances. The boardwalk itself featured several stations where people could rest, each containing brightly-painted wooden chairs with large umbrellas attached to protect sightseers from the sun. Yet, only Mrs. Younge's walk had a gazebo at the end.

"Goodness!" Sarah Younge exclaimed from behind, causing Wickham to whirl around. "I thought she would never leave! That woman had no intention of buying anything—she never does! But I have to be polite to her regardless, and by some means, she always raises my hopes that today will be the day she makes a purchase." Shaking her head, she smiled wearily. "I do not know why I bother flattering her."

"I can imagine how very frustrating all of this must be for you," Wickham offered sympathetically, waving a hand towards the shop. "For such a talented artist as yourself to be reduced to a shop clerk—well, I cannot wait to take you away from it all."

Mrs. Younge lowered her eyes self-consciously, making Wickham nervous. "You have not changed your mind, have you? God knows that I wish it could be handled differently, but you must realise that I have no choice, given the circumstances. Darcy will never pay me the equivalent of the living that his father left me in his will. And without it, I can never afford to marry."

The widow paused. "I … I have never done anything like this in my life."

"You are not really going to do anything—merely turn a blind eye while I speak to her. What she decides to do will be her choice." He stepped closer, reaching for a trembling hand. "It is for us—for our future."

She studied his face for a long moment before succumbing to his argument. "It only seems fair, since you were cheated of your rightful inheritance. And I have been very lonely running this gallery. It is certainly not the life I envisioned."

Wickham gave her his most innocent expression. "I swear that no harm will come to anyone, and we will only be forcing Darcy to give up what is rightfully mine."

He waited with bated breath as she regarded him. Certainly it had been risky sharing his scheme with the woman, but after her enthusiastic welcome upon his return to Ramsgate, he had been convinced that she cared for him. He was confident that she would not alert anyone, even if she decided not to be a part of it.

Finally, she smiled feebly. "It would be wonderful to be married and leave this horrid place forever. My brother has gradually become a hard taskmaster, in spite of all my efforts to make this shop profitable. The allowance he provides barely covers my needs and those of my family." She immediately questioned, "You do intend on taking my mother and sister with us, do you not?"

"Of course, my dear," Wickham lied, bringing one hand up to place a chaste kiss there. "I would not dream of leaving those you love behind."

Mrs. Younge flushed with his show of affection. "Then it is settled. I shall help you. Miss Darcy arrives in a few days for two weeks of lessons. I shall endeavour to create opportunities for you to be alone with her so that you may speak privately. Since there will be only one other girl taking lessons, that should not be a problem. I often give individual instruction to one student while the other works independently. Then I change over and instruct the other."

Wickham tilted his head in the direction of the outbuilding. "Why is it that you alone have a gazebo? Is it exclusively for your use?"

"My brother had it built especially for my art lessons. We needed a place to sketch the scenery while avoiding the sun's unrelenting heat. And, yes, it is exclusive to my clients."

"I assume then that Miss Darcy will take advantage of that structure part of the time?"

"Yes. I tutor my students in the house in the morning then we move there in the afternoon. This way they can practice what they have learned by creating their own paintings."

"Good. Good. That will work out very agreeably. I plan on convincing her to leave with me by way of the beach. I have found a trail that leads down to the beach several hundred feet to the west of the gazebo. If she will walk with me in that direction, we can take that path back to the street where my coach will be waiting. We shall be on our way to Gretna Green before her hawkeyed aunt discovers she is missing."

"But … but you said that you will not actually go to Gretna Green."

Wickham silently cursed his mistake. "That was a slip of the tongue. As I told you last night, Miss Darcy will be led to believe that we are eloping. But instead I will transport her to a friend's estate in Manchester, where we shall wait until Fitzwilliam Darcy pays the living I was promised. His little sister will be released only after we and your family are well on our way to Scotland where I have relations. Once we are safely out of England, we shall sail on the next ship to the Americas. I have no doubt that we shall be aboard the ship well before the Darcys figure out where we have gone."

Mrs. Younge sighed heavily. "Are you quite sure that the authorities or her family will not suspect I had something to do with her disappearance and arrest me before I can travel to you?"

"There will be no evidence connecting you to the incident. And when you leave to meet me, they will think you have had no choice but to relocate since the business will likely close due to the scandal. They will never be suspicious of you."

The frown lines on Mrs. Younge's face visibly relaxed. "Of course, you are right. I worry too much. Forgive me."

"Come, close up the shop, and let us walk on the beach. I shall not be able to show you any attention nor spend time with you once Miss Darcy arrives. I shall miss that terribly!"

She smiled brightly. "Oh, George! How good it is to have you back."

On the carriage ride back to his hotel, Wickham pondered the only weak spot in his plan—Gisela! It had played on his mind since he had met with Darcy's wife after his sojourn to Rosings. Her conduct had grown even more bizarre, and he assumed her heavy drinking was the likely reason.

Finding her completely indifferent to Lady Catherine's order to kill the solicitor, he was stunned when she suggested he use a long-time servant of hers to do the job—a tall lanky fellow with bad teeth she referred to as Grimsby. She had alluded that this man was very loyal to her and would think nothing of killing Lowell at her command. In addition, she had shown no aversion to the notion that Grimsby was to be murdered after he accomplished the task. Her indifferent attitude had been unexpected. He remembered their conversation.

And you have no problem with murdering Grimsby too!

What is he to me? We do what we must!

But, by your own admission, he has been loyal to you. Does that mean nothing?

As long as I have money, I can buy loyalty.

It was at that very moment that he realised the tenuous nature of their relationship. He had supposed that they were friends or, at the least, business associates who needed one another. But if Gisela had no allegiance to her faithful servant, she would have none to him. This revelation was eye-opening, especially in light of her present frame of mind.

The final proof that Gisela was becoming more unbalanced, one might even say obsessed, was evidenced by what subject occupied her thoughts that day. Instead of attending to his plans regarding Georgiana which would make them both a good deal wealthier, she was preoccupied with having him find the identity of a young woman.

Doubtless, there was not a soul in all of London who had not heard of Wilkens slight of her at the Trousdale dinner party. But that Gisela was willing to spend precious time and pay a goodly amount of money to learn the name of the young woman Wilkens was courting, just so that she could confront her with Wilkens' dissolute ways, was preposterous!

Nonetheless, Wickham felt that he still needed Gisela's help. After the marriage to Darcy, she was supposed to gain Georgiana's trust by championing her right to choose her own course without her brother's interference. Thus, having no choice, Wickham indulged her curiosity, using his contacts to ascertain the young woman's name, Elizabeth Bennet, and the fact that she was of little or no consequence in society.

Gisela had been quite giddy upon gaining the woman's name before learning that Miss Bennet had left London with Miss Wilkens, and they were bound for Ramsgate. Reluctantly, she had acquiesced to his demand that she wait until after their business with Georgiana was complete to continue her mission of revenge against Wilkens.

Wickham sighed heavily. He prayed Gisela kept her word. Thus far, the only part of his scheme that had worked flawlessly was the way the widow Younge had succumbed to his charm.

Nothing is going to hinder my plans to become rich at Darcy's expense, especially not Gisela's petty little vendettas! And after I am secure in my marriage, I shall phase out any reliance on Mrs. Darcy or Lady de Bourgh!

On the Road to Ramsgate

Elizabeth's eyes may have been closed, but her mind was busily engaged, pleasantly recalling Mr. Bingley's call on her two days before.

Are you certain that Miss Bennet would welcome my return?

I am positive that my sister would be delighted to see you again, sir

Elizabeth smiled with the memory of Bingley's wide grin. From the looks of it, at least Jane could count on a love match with a successful gentleman as Bingley had declared his intention to return to Netherfield straightaway. There would be no need for her to send a letter to Jane, as he would be in Meryton long before the post. And with her sister happily situated, it would not be incumbent upon her to accept a man she loathed. If Madeline Gardiner had not already set off for her sister's house, she would have refused to accompany Alfreda to Ramsgate. This dreadful farce was almost finished.

I shall inform Aunt upon my return to London that I shall NOT marry Lord Wilkens under any circumstance!

"Elizabeth, are you awake?" Alfreda leaned over to touch her friend's hand, which brought her eyes open.

"I was just woolgathering."

"We are almost to our destination—the inn where Brother and I always stay. It is half-way between London and Ramsgate and is very comfortable. The proprietors know Brother well and provide the best suites for our use. He made arrangements for our stay when he travelled last week, so all is in readiness. There is nothing to dread in staying here."

Elizabeth nodded at Alfreda before her eyes rested on the older woman to Miss Wilkens' left, Mrs. Armstrong. She had once been Alfreda's governess but now served as her maid and companion. Though pleasant enough, she was not talkative, and Elizabeth hardly realised she was accompanying them at times. Seeing Elizabeth's gaze, the older woman smiled, but it did not seem to reach her eyes.

Elizabeth returned a wan smile, trying to think of something to say to break the silence. Noting horsemen now riding on either side of the coach, she declared, "My goodness! I have not realised until this moment that your brother provided a small army to accompany us."

Alfreda laughed. "Yes. My brother is very protective. We always travel with two footmen, a postillion, a driver and two servants on horseback. He says you can never be too careful, not with all the highwaymen on these roads."

"I suppose he could be right."

"Oh, yes. Brother is always right."

Elizabeth sighed at Alfreda's assertion. Miss Wilkens took her brother's side in every instance, but of late, the adulation had begun to fray her nerves.

"I cannot imagine anyone always being right." Elizabeth offered, trying to get his sister to examine her admiration. "Surely he is capable of mistakes, as we all are."

Alfreda flinched, while Mrs. Armstrong seemed about to speak but thought better of it and held her tongue. Since neither was to reply, Elizabeth continued her exploration of the subject.

"All I am saying is that I have found him to be wrong about a lot of things in the short time I have known him."

The other women exchanged guarded looks before meeting Elizabeth's eyes. From their expressions, one would have thought she had just uttered blasphemy. Alfreda coughed self-consciously, bringing a shaky hand which held a handkerchief up to her mouth.

Then, with a look that showed no mirth, she stated very deliberately, "While I am sure that occasionally you may think him wrong, you will find that my brother is very intelligent and considers things more thoroughly than most. However, may I propose that, until you are better acquainted, you refrain from telling him outright that he is wrong? He is unused to having women speak their mind to him, I am afraid. My late mother always deferred to him, as do I. And I have found it best to let him think you agree and work on presenting your viewpoint in a less threatening manner."

Elizabeth was incredulous. "What is threatening about stating your opinion?"

Just at that moment the coach came to an abrupt halt, and the sounds of the driver issuing orders and the footmen climbing down from the top alerted the passengers that they had arrived at their destination. Unfortunately, it also afforded Alfreda the opportunity to focus on their arrival, instead of answering Elizabeth's question.

Not sure what to make of it, Elizabeth followed Miss Wilkens out the door of the coach, making a mental note to bring up the subject again.

☙✗❧

Longbourn
The Parlour

Jane sat stiffly on the settee, trying and utterly failing to appear pleased. She concentrated on lifting a lukewarm cup of tea to her lips without allowing her hand to shake because of her great disappointment. Across from her sat John Lucas, who had barely said a word in the half-hour since his arrival. He, too, seemed extraordinarily focused on the cup in his hand.

To her right was her father, who sat at a small table pretending to read a newspaper. Every so often, he would peer over the top of the paper, as though studying her. She could not decipher from his expression if he was amused by what was happening, as he had been when Mr. Bingley called, or if he sensed her loathing of Mr. Lucas. Nonetheless, she was near the end of her patience with his entertainment at her expense. Just when she thought she might scream with frustration, Mrs. Bennet burst into the room, startling everyone. She was followed closely by Mrs. Hill, who carried a plate of biscuits and a fresh pot of tea.

"Set it down here, Hill," her mother ordered, motioning to the table where her father sat. Mr. Bennet frowned and moved his paper from atop the surface to his lap. Mrs. Hill had barely quitted the room when she accosted him. "Come, Mr. Bennet. I have something important to discuss with you in the library."

Mr. Bennet lowered the paper and looked over his glasses. "I can assure you, madam, I am not moving from this spot. I have just come from a lengthy meeting with my neighbours regarding a drainage problem and I am exhausted."

"Oh, Mr. Bennet! You try my nerves so!" she cried before addressing Jane's caller. "Mr. Lucas, would you mind escorting Jane to the garden? Then my husband and I will not have to withdraw to the library? I shall be glad to have Hill bring the refreshments to the table beyond the roses."

Lucas eagerly responded to Mrs. Bennet's suggestion by quickly standing. "I would be most pleased to do so." He held out an arm to Jane. Sighing, she glanced to her father, who shook his head in dismay and looked back to his paper.

Jane stood, placing her dainty hand on the proffered arm. Slowly, she and John Lucas made their way out of the house and down the gravel path to a small, white ironwork table. It sat just past the rose garden, next to a brick wall covered with ivy. The place was so lovely that Jane had often dreamed of being proposed to in this very spot. But in her dreams, it was not Mr. Lucas doing the proposing.

Lucas led her directly to one of the small benches on either side. She sat, refusing to look up at him. He hesitated beside her for a moment before taking a seat on the opposite bench.

"Ahem. Miss Bennet?"

Jane forced herself to meet his gaze. Without thinking, she began to analyse why she found him so unattractive. He was not ugly, though he was nondescript. However, as he began another conversation by mentioning Lady Lucas, Jane realised that it was his total reliance on his mother's opinion that predominantly coloured her view of him.

"Several times of late, my mother has spoken to me about the expectations for my future and the future of Lucas Lodge. As you know, I am the heir, and it shall be my estate and my responsibility at some point." He swallowed hard. Jane was not smiling as politely now as she had before they had gotten better acquainted.

"Mother has emphasised the importance of securing a wife and producing an heir. She wishes me to seek a modest, unassuming young woman who will fit well in our family, one who would not cause discord. It is her belief that the sooner I marry ..."

Jane was not listening to the rest of his words, for as he droned on, she stared into the distance. And in her mind's eye, she pictured the one man that she had hoped to be having this conversation with—Mr. Bingley.

Netherfield

As his coach made its way through Meryton, Charles Bingley congratulated himself on leaving his staff in place at Netherfield. Now that he had found an opportunity to return, he was sure that it would not take very long to get the house in order due to his forethought. All that his housekeeper, Mrs. Watkins, should have to do is stock the pantry and retrieve clean linens for his bed, since he was travelling alone. He had made sure not to mention anything to Caroline of his plans to return to this village, instead, letting her assume that he was on his way to Bristol to check on the newly discovered ship.

The truth was that he was not needed in Bristol. Darcy's cousin, Randall Sanderson, a barrister, along with Mr. Carter had everything well in hand. They were in the process of interviewing the sailors and townspeople to discover where the ship's goods had been diverted and had already located a considerable percentage of the wares in a local warehouse. In fact, it looked as though almost the entire shipment that was thought to be lost forever would be recovered. They were even hopeful of finding information about the first ship that had been reported missing as well. The local magistrate was not sure if they would ever ascertain just who the mastermind of the theft was unless Captain Grier decided to talk and, thus far, he had refused. Nonetheless, the magistrate thought that the threat of a hanging might just do the trick.

In any event, Charles was delighted, for the time being, to set aside the circumstances that had occupied his every waking hour for the last few weeks and concentrate on the one who occupied his nights—Jane Bennet. He had just pictured her beautiful face when the coach came to a sudden halt, and he pulled back the curtain to find that they were already at Netherfield. A footman leaped off the coach to open the door, and he found himself staring at an empty portico. No one came out to meet him. He thought it odd, but began to ascend the stairs just as the front door flew open.

"Mr. Bingley. Welcome home, sir," Mr. Mercer said, bowing as low as his arthritic back would allow. "I am very pleased to see you again." As he took his young master's coat and hat, Mercer's expression seemed to belie his happiness at Bingley's return.

"Thank you, Mercer. Have you had everything you needed in my absence?" Charles enquired, all the while absentmindedly removing his gloves. Suddenly he stopped, looking about the house. Something was not right. "And where is Mrs. Watkins?"

"She is in the process of packing her things, sir. After we received the letter from Miss Bingley—"

Bingley interrupted, "My sister?"

Mercer's eyes found his shoes. "Yes, sir."

"Whatever would she write to you regarding?"

Mercer did not respond, though he looked as though he was trying to form an answer.

"Show me the letter please."

Mercer glanced at the footman now coming into the foyer with Bingley's luggage. "May we go to your study, sir?"

Charles nodded and began in that direction with the elderly man following. As soon as they had closed the door, the butler pulled a worn letter from his coat pocket. It was obvious that he had read it often since receiving it.

"I … I wanted to hear it directly from you, sir. But when I tried, I was informed that you were not in London and could not be bothered. I feared taking Miss Bingley's word." He stopped, embarrassed. "I am sorry, but you were the one who hired me."

Charles nodded, taking the letter and silently beginning to read. With every line his colour rose along with his anger. Finally, he stopped and tore the offending missive into tiny shreds, strode to the fireplace and tossed the pieces onto the grate.

"Be assured that my sister does not speak for me! Never listen to anything she says about your employment or the employment of the staff again. Please assure everyone still here that their positions are safe. Now, just who has gone?"

"Mrs. Watkins, as you know, has not left as yet. Neither has Ludlow, the livery manager, two maids, Hilda and Joan, and Hinton, a footman. It was only days ago that the others left. However, they are all local people, and I may be able to reach them in a short while."

"Please try! Then have Mrs. Watkins inform me of any we may have to replace."

As though a huge burden had been lifted from Mr. Mercer's shoulders, he breathed an audible sigh of relief before assuming his usual blank expression. "Very well, sir." He walked towards the door.

"Mercer?" The butler turned. "I apologise for my sister's actions."

"There is no apology necessary. I assure you, Mr. Bingley." For the first time in a long time Mercer's smile was genuine as he vacated the room.

Charles was livid. Why would Caroline tell the servants to prepare the house for closure by the month's end, informing them that they were not going to be paid beyond that date? Was she hoping that having to re-staff the house might dissuade him from returning to Netherfield?

While he was angry enough to ride directly back to London that night to confront her, he determined he would not let Caroline ruin his plans. NO! He was going to see his angel if it was the last thing he did. Thus, grabbing a riding crop from the edge of his desk, where he had left it when last at Netherfield, he headed back to the foyer for his hat and coat. There was no time like the present to get one thing settled—an engagement!

Chapter 18

London
Darcy House
The Study

Richard Fitzwilliam crossed William's study to pour himself another brandy. Picking up the cut-glass decanter, he held it up in a questioning manner.

"No, I do not drink this early in the morning, and I have to wonder at your need for one."

"Nonsense, Cousin!" Richard guffawed, proceeding to pour an even larger glass than he had intended just to make his point. Replacing the stopper on the decanter, he smiled smugly at William as he sauntered over to sit back down in the chair in front of the desk.

"Only an officer would know the advantage of having a stiff drink early in the day. It has kept me going many a time when I felt I could not put one foot in front of the other. Try sleeping on the rocky ground for weeks, often in the rain, I might add, and see how well you function without a drink in the morning!"

"I did not mean to disparage you," William sighed. "It is just that I worry about your ability to consume so much liquor. Besides, it is not as though you are sleeping on the ground at this time."

"And this from a man who practically depleted his entire stock of French brandy when he returned to Town from Netherfield!"

"That was not my usual habit as you are well aware. I was just … disappointed."

"Disappointed? You were crushed! And I had to concern myself with the fact that the best brandy France has to offer was being wasted on a drunken binge." Richard chucked to see a scowl mar his cousin's face. He held the glass of caramel liquid to the light. "I have to admit that those blackguards have perfected the art of distilling brandy."

"And did you come here just to sample my brandy and praise the French?"

"No, actually, I wanted to inform you that my spies have placed Wickham at your wife's house several times in the last few weeks. I thought he had moved on after their first fling."

"What in the world would he be doing at Gisela's now?"

"Other than keeping her bed warm, I imagine conspiring against you."

"I would not be surprised, although I thought she had progressed to more lucrative targets, such as Attenborough. That pompous fool would be aghast if he knew she was sleeping with someone so common. Why would she risk alienating him to be with Wickham?"

"Why indeed—unless she needs his skills as a thief, a liar and general trouble maker?" Richard rubbed his chin. "I do not like the thought of them keeping company again, so I have decided to have her followed in addition to having her house watched."

"I appreciate your diligence, but at this moment, I do not want to be reminded of her. Would it be possible to change the subject to something more pleasant?"

"As you wish. Let us discuss the lovely object of your affection, Miss Bennet. I have just returned from York, and I have yet to hear the latest gossip. Mother and Alicia both left for Bath before I returned. Father and I never talk and Edgar … well, you know how often we converse."

"Edgar and you are still not speaking?"

"Not since I got into an argument with that wife of his over my attentions to Miss Cooperton at Mother's dinner party. The nerve of that harridan, lecturing me on the kind of woman I should pay my attentions to! It is not as though I do not know what is expected of me!" He calmed, wagging his brows. "I was just being charming, as usual. No harm done."

"Frances would never forgive you if you married someone who did not fit well in her little troop of slanderous gossips. She feels it is her duty to guide you. After all, since she married the viscount, she has tried to dictate to all the family, including me."

Richard laughed. "I remember how quickly she learned that you do not take orders! I shall never forget the look on her face when you told her in no uncertain terms that you had no intentions of attending any family events alongside Gisela. And right in front of Father and Mother!"

"Yes, well, I could have been more diplomatic, I suppose, but I was not in the mood for a lecture on family loyalty after what I had endured. I can only wonder why Aunt Eleanor tolerates her controlling ways."

"Mother is only trying to keep peace because she dearly wants grandchildren." Richard paused, and then raised his glass in a salute. "Oh, you are good! You successfully changed the subject! Let us get back to discussing Miss Bennet, shall we?"

William sighed heavily. He threw the pen that he had been absentmindedly twirling down on the desk. "There is nothing to talk about. She is gone!"

"Gone? As in already married? Gone back to Hertfordshire? How is she gone?"

"She has accompanied Wilkens' sister to Ramsgate—to Gatesbridge, his estate. It seems that his aunt, Lady Hawthorne, is having a birthday celebration, and as her only close relations, he and his sister must attend. He is the woman's heir, you know."

"Yes, I remember Father mentioning her name once at White's when he and his cronies were finding fault with the Earl of Hampton. His remarks, if I remember correctly, were to the effect that it was a shame that a fool such as Wilkens would inherit her wealth and properties and effectively double his worth."

"Thank you for reminding me."

"That is still nothing compared to your worth, Darcy."

William shrugged. "In any event, his sister insisted Elizabeth accompany her to Gatesbridge Manor, according to what she told Georgiana and Aunt Audrey when she was here."

"She was here? In your home?"

"Yes. Surprisingly, Georgiana and I were in Hatchards' bookshop, and while I was inspecting one section and she another, she met Elizabeth. They felt an immediate affinity, and Georgiana invited her to tea. I did not expect her to actually follow through once she knew of our connection, but she, Lady Holmes and Lady Wilkens did call a few days later."

"How did you handle seeing her again—having her under your roof?"

"Not well, I fear. I thought I had convinced myself that I could let her go— that it would be for the best. But once I realised she would be near enough to touch, it was all I thought about. I acknowledge it was as though I had lost all reason. I managed to get her alone for a few precious moments when they were leaving, and all my feelings came to the surface. I confessed that I love her … that I had loved her since first we met."

"And?"

"She admitted her love for me." William took a ragged breath as the sting of her words tortured him anew. "But she allows that it changes nothing."

"And she accompanied his sister to Gatesbridge even afterward?"

William sighed, dropping his head in his hands and rubbing his eyes wearily. "Yes."

A low whistle escaped Richard's lips. "That does not bode well, Darcy. It sounds as though she is resigned to doing her duty. Moreover, I do not trust that rogue with Miss Bennet as his prisoner—I mean, guest."

"Neither do I, but Aunt Audrey and Georgiana are on the way to Ramsgate as we speak. You remember the art lessons?" At Richard's nod, he continued, "Aunt Audrey has pledged to keep an eye on Elizabeth in my stead."

William stood, moving to the windows, where he stared into the garden. "I fear that she may agree to marry that … that cad. It takes all my strength not to have my horse saddled and go after her."

Richard moved to stand beside him, clasping his shoulder. "If I thought you could get away with it, I would encourage you to kidnap her and take her to your estate in Scotland." Suddenly an idea popped into his head. "Do you want me to travel to Ramsgate, just to keep an eye on things? I can always get clearance by feigning a need to consult with Colonel Harris, who commands the troops in that sector."

Slowly William's head swung back and forth. "As a friend to Lady Hawthorne, Aunt Audrey contends she will be in the thick of all the social gathering that will no doubt include Elizabeth. She and Georgiana are even going to stay at Hawthorne Hall. I can only pray that Elizabeth will feel comfortable enough with our aunt to confide in her if something goes amiss."

By now, Richard had procured a small glass of brandy for William. As he tendered the drink, he offered words of comfort. "Take heart, Darcy. At least you know she is in love with you, not Wilkens."

William did not refuse the drink this time, but his growing despondency was evident. "I am beginning to wonder if that really matters in the grand scheme of things. Can you name any of our acquaintances who married for love? I cannot."

He downed the contents in one swallow. "Just look at me."

Longbourn

As Charles crossed the creek that marked the separation of Netherfield and Longbourn, his heart began to race. Soon he would see his angel! Purposely not taking the main road between the two estates, he had opted instead to get there faster by way of a shortcut. He was in no mood to prolong the separation from Jane by even a few minutes, and this route would end near the gardens at the back of Longbourn, rather than the front drive.

Weeks of separation had left him worrying that her affections might have waned, though his love for her had never faltered. However, accidentally encountering Miss Elizabeth in London and gaining her assurance that Jane would welcome his return had caused his hopes to soar. He had even spent the greater part of the trip back to Meryton practicing what to say when he pressed his suit. Now nearing her home, he began once more to practice the various ways to begin the most important conversation of his life.

Miss Bennet—Jane, I must tell you how ardently I love and admire …

No! That sounds more like Darcy than me.

Dearest Jane, I have thought of nothing these last few weeks but seeing you again. You must agree to …

No, no. I must ask, not demand.

My love, I am determined that my family shall not dictate …

That will never do! Why mention that my family will not approve when it has no bearing on what I decide. Oh my, I should have settled on a course before now!

At that very moment, Bingley rounded the last copse of oaks near Longbourn and was shocked to find the woman of his dreams sitting in the garden with another man—John Lucas, if he remembered correctly. As he reined in his horse to observe, Lucas leaned across a small iron table, holding out a handful of roses to Jane as an offering. She took the flowers in one hand while her would-be suitor captured the other and brought it to his lips.

Good Lord! He is courting my Jane!

Charles was livid! Despite his practiced professions of love, his reaction was completely spontaneous and nothing like he had planned. He kicked the stallion into a run, charging ahead like a madman going to do battle, his expression determined—face set like flint!

Lucas, whose back was to Bingley, was completely unaware of his approach, while Jane had a clear view of everything. Over Mr. Lucas' shoulder, she could clearly see Bingley galloping towards them, and her eyes grew wide as saucers. Unable to utter a sound, she unconsciously held her breath in expectation of what was about to happen.

Only upon hearing the approaching hoof beats did Lucas turn to ascertain what fool might be leading an assault on their position. Scrambling to get on top of the bench, he was too frightened to decide whether to run or stay on his perch. While he was thus occupied in saving his life, Jane moved to stand on the far side of the table, exactly where Mr. Bingley's stallion was headed. When it became clear that he was not going to stop but only to slow down, she held her breath. Meanwhile, Bingley swooped down to grab her around the waist, pulling her onto the horse, turned the beast and spurred the creature into a full gallop back into the woods.

As Jane and her abductor got smaller in the distance, John Lucas stood completely astounded and rendered mute for some time. Then coming to his senses, he climbed down from the bench and ran towards the house as fast as his short, pudgy legs would take him. By the time he neared the house, he was screaming at the top of his lungs.

"Help! Mrs. Bennet! Mrs. Bennet! Help me!"

Inside Longbourn, Mr. and Mrs. Bennet still occupied the parlour. She had insisted they wait in that exact place for the happy couple to come back inside, sure that Jane's suitor would want to speak to her husband in order to secure permission to marry her. But while Mrs. Bennet occupied herself during the wait by applying lace to Lydia's new bonnet, her husband had finished his paper and moved to the window to observe the goings-on in the rose garden.

Mr. Bennet positioned himself just in time to get a first-hand view of Bingley's acrobatic performance. Had he had time to object to the theatrics because Jane might have been hurt, he would have most certainly done so. As it was, he was left to marvel at the man's audacity, while at the same time, putting aside any doubts he had been having about Mr. Bingley's intentions. He chuckled silently. After all, Bingley had declared himself quite well with that feat!

Upon hearing Lucas' screams however, Mrs. Bennet flew out of the house so quickly that she left Mr. Bennet lagging several yards behind. Rounding the side of the house, she ran straight into her would-be son, causing them both to collapse on the ground. And as he scrambled to his feet and began to assist her in rising, Mrs. Bennet exclaimed with ear-splitting decibels, "Oh, Mr. Lucas! What has happened? What is the matter?"

Mr. Bennet had reached the scene just in time to see both parties struggling to get up off the lawn. Biting his lip, he tried hard not to laugh or even crack a smile, as he offered his wife a hand.

"Have you frightened Jane off as well as crippled my wife, Mr. Lucas?"

Gaining her feet, Mrs. Bennet whirled around to quiet him. "Oh, hush, Mr. Bennet! Do not be ridiculous! Mr. Lucas has done nothing of the kind. I am perfectly fine and Jane is … Jane is …" She began turning in all directions and not seeing her daughter asked, "Where *is* Jane, Mr. Lucas?"

"That is what I was coming to tell you, madam. She has been taken! Spirited away by a man riding a large stallion! I did not get a good look at him but—"

Mr. Bennet fixed a scowl on his face and took a step towards him, hands on his hips. "You mean to tell me that you let someone take my Jane from right under your nose? And from your appearance, it appears without trying to stop him?"

"I … I had no choice in the matter." Lucas stuttered, swallowing hard. "He was like a demon! Huge! At least seven foot!"

"I thought you did not get a good look at him. And if he was on horseback, how would you know how tall he was?"

Mr. Lucas' mind raced. "He ... ah ... he sat tall in the saddle."

"Hmmm."

Seeing Mr. Bennet's skepticism, he continued. "And ... and he wore a black mask, like a highwayman!"

Mrs. Bennet gasped, clasping her bosom. "A highwayman has my Jane? Oh, Mr. Bennet, we must call on Colonel Forster to rally the militia to help us find her!"

Mr. Bennet was enjoying the tale and Lucas' discomposure immensely, but felt obligated to calm his wife. "There, there, my dear. Let us first get the facts before we summon the troops." He patted her back sympathetically as he enquired of Lucas, "Are you sure he wore a mask?"

Wiping the sweat now beaded on his forehead, that gentleman nodded vigorously. "And his steed was equally large, at least seventeen hands—"

Mr. Bennet held up a hand, interrupting his fable. "I think you have given me enough description to successfully find him."

Turning to Mrs. Hill who was now standing a few feet behind, he barked, "Tell the groom to saddle my horse and I shall go see what Mr. Bingley has in mind."

"Mr. Bingley?" Mrs. Bennet parroted. "What has Mr. Bingley got to do with this?"

Lucas wilted under Mr. Bennet's glare and could not answer, so her husband obliged.

"Mr. Bingley is the one who abducted our Jane from under Mr. Lucas's nose."

She rounded on Lucas now. "Why did you not just say so? A highwayman indeed! Why would you make such claims? My nerves shall never recover from this fright!"

Mr. Bennet was almost inside the house before Lucas thought to offer to accompany him to question Bingley. However, once the idea had surfaced, he purposefully delayed trying to catch up to Jane's father. For at this point, the Heir of Lucas Lodge was wondering whether his mother would still approve of Jane if news of today's event reached the gossips of Meryton. After all, Jane had been compromised and was perhaps no longer the best choice for a wife. Seeing that no one was paying him any mind, he slinked towards the front of the house where his horse was tied.

When Mrs. Bennet had finally gotten her wits about her, she turned to find her choice of a husband for Jane riding away. Pulling a handkerchief from her pocket, she began to dab at her eyes.

"My poor, poor Jane! To lose such a good match as Mr. Lucas and heaven knows what Mr. Bingley has in mind. At least Mr. Bennet will find him and demand that he marry her!"

After several minutes of threading deeper and deeper into the woods, Charles reached a clearing and pulled the horse to a halt. He let Jane slip slowly to the ground, then slung a leg over the saddle and slid off to join her. Her eyes were still as big as saucers, and he smiled at her innocent expression. Tenderly he smoothed a few blond curls that had escaped the cluster atop her head. Still she did not speak.

"Miss Bennet," he began. She blinked several times, an uncomprehending expression upon her face. "I have returned to Meryton for the express purpose of—"

Suddenly, Jane brought her hands up to cover her face murmuring, "Oh, my heavens! What will Mr. Lucas tell his mother?" Shakily she turned away from him.

Bingley turned her back around to face him, pulling her hands from her face as he took them in his own. "I hope he tells her that you are taken and that there is no longer reason for him to call on you."

Her lips trembled as she managed to say, "Ta ... taken?"

"Yes, taken. As in engaged to another man ... engaged to me."

She seemed lost in total disbelief so he smiled lovingly, tipping her chin up with one finger. "I love you, Jane Bennet. Say you will be my wife."

She nodded.

"Say it."

"I ... I will!"

Charles cupped the back of her head and began threading his fingers through her golden hair as he guided her mouth to his. Capturing her perfect pink lips, he began a light, chaste kiss. However, as she responded to his urgings and her lips parted, their passion grew. Hearing a sigh, he pulled back to study her, surprised to see tears slipping from the corners of her eyes.

"Jane? Please tell me that those are tears of joy."

She nodded vigorously, whispering, "I am so happy, Charles. I love you too."

He could not resist kissing her anew, pouring every ounce of the loneliness he had felt for the last few weeks into the kiss. His longing grew, and he pulled her tighter against his body—so tight she could feel the evidence of his desire and it inflamed her own. Finally, breathless, he quit the kiss, very much aware of where it was leading.

"I suppose we should get back to Longbourn before your father comes after me with a shotgun."

Mr. Bennet's voice boomed through the glade. "I think it is far too late for that, young man!"

Jane and Charles both jumped, stepping back from one another. They were stunned as her father kicked his horse into the clearing from his hiding spot in the forest. One of his hounds now bounded ahead of him, running in circles around them and providing ample evidence of how he had found them so quickly.

Ramsgate
Gatesbridge Manor

As the Wilkens' coach traversed the last few feet of the gravel drive that led to Gatesbridge Manor, Elizabeth took in the estate. She had to acknowledge that the mansion was very imposing and regal, though not as beautiful as she imagined it would be. It was constructed of a pink-coloured stone and had very little embellishment—no columns across the portico, no shutters or wrought iron around the windows. And her view of the grounds from the coach window showed carefully landscaped lawns but few flowers or areas left as nature intended.

The coach came to a complete halt, and her stomach began to churn, just as it did whenever she chastised herself for agreeing to accompany Miss Wilkens to this place. Would her brother be there to greet them? How would she manage to avoid being alone with him if she was under his roof?

As a footman came forward, her attention was drawn to the small number of people waiting to greet them. Pleased that Wilkens was not among them, Elizabeth breathed a sigh of relief at her good fortune.

Suddenly the door to the coach flew open, and the footman reached inside to hand Alfreda down from the carriage. Elizabeth was next to step out, followed by Mrs. Armstrong. By that time, there was a large woman coming down the steps towards them, and she wondered at the frown on her face.

"Miss Alfreda," the unsmiling woman said while dropping a small curtsey. "We are pleased you have arrived safely."

Alfreda turned to Elizabeth. "This is our housekeeper, Mrs. Cuthbert. She and her husband have faithfully served our family for the last thirty years or more."

Elizabeth smiled at the woman who only nodded curtly and turned to direct the footmen with the luggage. Glancing at the other servants, she noted that they, too, had similar frowns and would not meet her eyes. Having never been introduced to such dour servants, she began to wonder why they would act so coldly or were not corrected. However, her musings were interrupted by Alfreda.

"Come inside, Elizabeth! I cannot wait to show you our home."

Our home?

Elizabeth paused to regard Alfreda who had a very pleased expression upon her face.

"For it will be your home as well, once you and Brother are married."

Chapter **19**

Milton
Ashcroft Park

It was evening by the time the coach entered the long drive to Lady Ashcroft's estate, which was situated almost exactly half-way between London and Ramsgate in the town of Milton. Audrey's keen eye was already examining the manor house as they entered the long front drive to Ashcroft Park.

The exterior of the edifice was beige sandstone, three stories high, lined with pristine white columns across the front and matching shutters on every window. Even the balconies were surrounded by white ironwork, not in a busy pattern as some she had seen, but impressive enough to add to the beauty without overpowering it. One year, while they were in Town for the Season, Joseph had had the balconies redone in the ironwork simply to please her, as she had admired them on another grand house. Lady Ashcroft smiled in recollection of how proud he had been when showing her the results.

This estate had been in her late husband's family for years, and she loved it dearly, though she no longer visited regularly. There were far too many memories to face there, and it was much too easy to leave when she felt overwhelmed. Consequently, after her husband's death, Audrey had taken to residing most of the year in London, even though she preferred life in the country.

When Fitzwilliam had expressed a wish for her to live with him and Georgiana, she had eagerly accepted, knowing they spent most of their time at Pemberley. There had been one point when she had considered selling Ashcroft Park, but she could not go through with it. Joseph had loved it so. No, she would leave it for Richard. Fitzwilliam certainly did not need it, and she doubted her brother would be very generous with his second son in view of how he had stood up to him. Lady Ashcroft smiled, imagining the earl's face when he learned the details of her will. Her thoughts were interrupted as a footman opened the coach door, and she followed Georgiana out, eager to stretch her legs.

As her niece hurried up the steps, she was greeted by the housekeeper, Mrs. Parker. However, knowing what was to come next, the faithful servant did not walk down to meet her mistress. Instead, she waited patiently on the portico while, as was her custom, Audrey Ashcroft ordered the coach on to the stables before slowly making a complete circle where she stood, taking in every aspect of the property. This was her own way of greeting the estate that had been her home with Joseph, and she was very pleased to find it almost the same as when he lived here.

As usual, the realisation that she had last seen her beloved on this very spot produced a terrible ache in her heart, and upon completing the circle, she closed her eyes. It was as though time had stool still, she felt once more the softness of his kiss and heard his whispers of devotion as he bade her goodbye on that fateful day. Promising that he would return as quickly as possible and adamant that she wait at Ashcroft Park since she was great with child, he had entered a similar coach and was lost to her forever. When word had come that his ship had sunk, the shock of it had caused the loss of their child as well.

"Aunt?"

Georgiana's uneasy voice penetrated her consciousness, bringing her back to the present. Her niece had reached the entrance of the house before turning to see that she was still standing where she had alighted from the coach. Pasting on a smile in order to staunch the tears that threatened, Audrey Ashcroft turned and hurried up the steps.

"You know I always make my *turn-about* when I exit the coach."

Georgiana's dark blue eyes were unsmiling as they searched her. "I know. But you always look so sad afterward that it worries me."

Pulling her into a quick hug, Lady Ashcroft released her and pushed her towards the door playfully. "Oh, do not fret over me, child. It is just old ghosts coming to call. I may look sad, but actually, I am very blessed to have so many happy recollections of this place."

As Georgiana entered the house, she began the requests that always accompanied a visit here. "Will you tell me again the story of how you and Uncle met? And how he chased after you until you caught him?"

Lady Ashcroft managed a small chuckle. "I have told you that story a dozen times."

"Yes, but it is so romantic. And will we go to the gallery so you can show me his portrait and tell me once more how he hated standing still so very long and recount how you tried to make him smile so the artist would get angry?"

"If that is your wish."

"You know I never tire of hearing you tell of Uncle Joseph." Georgiana's eyes clouded again. "I only wish I had known him."

"I wish you had too, darling girl. He would have loved you so. He always wanted a daughter."

By then they had entered the large foyer of the warm inviting home, and Mr. Parker, the short, balding butler, was hurrying forward. He greeted them warmly as he took their wraps and gloves.

"Lady Ashcroft, what a pleasure to have you here again!" He could not help beaming at Georgiana. "And you, Miss Darcy."

Georgiana blushed and nodded, while her aunt replied, "Thank you, Parker. I can truly say that it is good to be home once more."

Mrs. Parker had managed to get ahead of them and was backing towards the grand staircase as she recounted all the preparations. "Your rooms are ready, and I have everything in place for your baths. The water is almost hot enough, and Cook will have dinner ready by the time you are finished bathing."

"I can always count on you to have everything in order," Lady Ashcroft commented as the housekeeper beamed with pride. Then she focused on her niece. "What say you to having trays sent to your sitting room after we have bathed? It will be more comfortable than just the two of us occupying the dining room."

"That is a wonderful idea. I am really quite tired, but I was hoping to prod at least one story out of you before I fall asleep."

Her aunt laughed. "Then let us hurry so we shall have the time." Then turning again to Mrs. Parker, she added, "It is settled. We shall have dinner in Georgiana's sitting room right after we finish with our baths."

"Yes, madam."

As the long-time housekeeper watched her mistress hurry up the stairs behind her niece, she recalled that when the Master had brought her here as a bride, Lady Ashcroft had instantly charmed them all and had taken her place as though she had always been a part of the household. Effortlessly carving out a spot in all their hearts, she could not have found a more fitting or more beloved mistress for Ashcroft Park. Their union had been ideal, and all was right with the world until the Master had been lost at sea. But despite the passage of time, his widow had stayed faithful to his memory and remained dedicated to his ancestral home and to the welfare of those who served there. No, not a one of them could complain of how they had fared, though they had known great sorrow.

Mrs. Parker had often dreamt of how life might have been had the Master not perished or had the child at least survived to term. Surely if the boy had lived, their lives would have been so very different. They would have had the joy of seeing their Master's son mature into a man—someone to take his father's place, and the Mistress would not have stayed away so much. But alas, that was not to be. Not only did the child die, but his mother almost perished as well—her sorrow being so great. Only Lady Anne Darcy, who had lost so much herself, had been able to reach her youngest sister.

It was likely due to the fact that Lady Anne brought young Master Darcy with her and he brought laughter back into the house. Then later, Georgiana joined her brother to brighten her life. Even now, these two are a balm to her soul! God bless them!

Suddenly aware that her eyes were pooling with tears, Henrietta Parker took a ragged breath and looked about to see if anyone had noticed. Though several maids were working in that area, none met her gaze. Taking stock of herself, she rose to her full height, put on her usual sober expression and went in search of a footman to carry the pails of hot water. After all, she always found plenty of time to dwell on what might have been when the Mistress left again.

Longbourn
Mr. Bennet's Study

Charles Bingley was beginning to perspire under the steady, unsmiling gaze of Jane's father. Mr. Bennet watched him much as a predator would study its prey.

It was bad enough that the man had taken Jane directly home after discovering them in the woods and ordered him back to Netherfield to await his summons, but he had not sent for him the rest of that day.

Finally, late in the afternoon of the next day, a note arrived ordering him to appear at Longbourn. And after obeying the directive, Bingley had been shown into the study and made to sit in a chair in front of Mr. Bennet's desk for almost an hour before the gentleman actually entered the room. Moreover, after taking his seat behind said desk, his host had stared at him for the next several minutes without a single word passing his lips.

As for the Master of Longbourn, he was having a grand old time and finding it increasingly difficult to keep a scowl on his face. Bingley had gone pale and was squirming in his chair in a display of nerves that almost rivalled those of his wife at her worst. In fact, he had the impression that Jane's suitor might bolt from the room at any moment, and since Mr. Bingley had acted so recklessly, he cared little if he prolonged the man's misery. Unfortunately, to do that would prolong Jane's suffering as well. Despite his instructions for her to wait in the parlour while he met with Bingley, he could hear her soft footsteps pacing the hallway outside. Perhaps, he thought, it was time to give her some relief.

"Mr. Bingley, do you wish to tell me the meaning of the audacious display of horsemanship—worthy of a circus performer, I might add—that occurred in my rose garden yesterday? Have you gone completely mad?"

Charles instantly coloured, faltering just a bit in his resolve. At the time he had not considered what her family would think of his exploits, wishing only to remove Jane from Mr. Lucas' reach.

"I ... I did not mean for things to get out of hand."

"Oh? And did you stop to think that you might have injured my daughter?"

"No, sir." Charles' composure faltered as his head swung slowly back and forth. "I would never purposely do anything to hurt her. I expected to find Miss Bennet alone. I intended to ask permission to court her, but ... but that was not what happened."

"Obviously."

"I was thoroughly engaged in trying to think of how to ask Jane—Miss Bennet— to accept my suit, but when I rode around the trees and there he was courting my ... my ..."

"Your?"

"The woman I love."

"And your love for my daughter provoked your inventiveness?"

"I honestly do not know what came over me. All of a sudden, I found myself racing towards her with the express intent of saving her from that cad."

"Cad? Mr. Lucas is a cad?"

"In my eyes he is."

"And though you made a spectacle of yourself and compromised my daughter, you do not consider yourself a cad?"

Bingley blinked several times before coming to his senses. Rising to the occasion, he squared his shoulders and steeled his resolve.

"No, sir, I am not!"

"Then why did you leave Meryton without declaring your intentions towards Jane and stayed away these many weeks without a word? Was that letter your sister sent not meant to crush her hopes?"

Mr. Bennet had always thought that Caroline Bingley might have embellished the letter in a bid to separate Mr. Bingley from Jane, and though he was not sure why, he had always had faith in the man.

"My sister's letter?" Bingley mumbled, his mien darkening. "Caroline was to send a letter explaining why I had to leave so suddenly."

"After you left, Jane was so despondent that when her mother learned that Miss Bingley had sent a letter, she demanded to see it. After reading the contents, she believed that Jane's affections had been trifled with, so she brought it to me."

Mr. Bennet reached into his top drawer and removed the missive, tossing it across the desk. Charles picked it up to read.

Dear Miss Bennet,

I am sorry that we must cancel our dinner invitation. By the time you read this, we shall be on our way to London, as my brother has been summoned by Mr. Darcy to come immediately. It seems his sister, Georgiana, is returning to London, and he wishes Charles to be there to greet her. We are all looking forward to renewing our friendship with Miss Darcy, who is a lady of the finest calibre. Charles is not sure at this point when, or if, we shall return to Netherfield.

Yours truly,
Caroline Bingley

"That is preposterous! I was not summoned to greet Darcy's sister. My heavens! She is only a child—fourteen years old!"

Charles stood and began murmuring under his breath as he paced. "I shall banish her to Scarborough! Yes! That is exactly what I shall do with that meddling—" Then he caught himself. "Darcy sent for me because my livelihood was in danger of collapsing, and he and my solicitor felt that I had to take charge of the situation. Had I been certain that I was not going to lose my mercantile business, I would gladly have declared myself to Miss Bennet before I left. As it was, I feared that all I could honestly offer her at the time was my name. I was not sure if I would have the means of supporting a wife if things continued as they were."

"What events occurred, Mr. Bingley?"

"It was reported that one of my shipments of goods had been lost at sea three months ago, supposedly during a storm. It was a substantial loss. Darcy and I felt that something was amiss, so he helped me to find a solicitor to investigate. While I was here, I got word that another of my ships had suffered a similar fate, so I was forced to take immediate action. Though I have investments in many other areas thanks to Darcy, I cannot afford to lose my mercantile business."

"Mr. Darcy is your advisor then?"

"He is my friend. And he is very knowledgeable in the ways of business, so, yes, he does advise me."

"What would he advise you to do in light of the spectacular display of last evening?

The corners of Charles' lips lifted in a small smile. "I believe he would tell me to declare myself and ask for Miss Bennet's hand in marriage."

"No courtship?"

"No. He would say that I should quiet the gossip certain to arise and wed as quickly as possible."

For a long moment, Mr. Bennet studied the man who would become his son, savouring the fact that he had been proven correct about Mr. Bingley's character. He offered him a small smile.

"If Jane agrees, you shall have your wedding in two months. I think that is sufficient time to satisfy the tittle-tattle of Meryton and Mrs. Bennet's desire to plan wedding."

Charles jumped to his feet, grabbed Mr. Bennet's hand and began to pump it. "Thank you! Thank you, sir! You shall not regret this!"

Mr. Bennet carefully extracted his hand from the excited young man, eager to urge him from the room and return to his solitude. "Make sure that I do not. Now, I think there is a young lady just outside the door who is eager to learn that I have not eaten you for dinner."

Bingley knocked a stack of books off the edge of Mr. Bennet's desk in his eagerness to get to Jane and began trying to pick them up.

"Shoo!" Mr. Bennet cried, waving his hand in exasperation. "I shall see to that later. Go find Jane!"

Right after the door slammed behind Bingley, Mr. Bennet heard Jane's sweet voice exclaiming how happy she was, and then he held his breath waiting for her mother's reaction. Shortly, loud cries came from the direction of the parlour.

"Oh, Mr. Bingley! I told Mr. Bennet that you would return to claim her! And I always said Jane was not so beautiful for nothing! Whatever was that dolt Mr. Lucas thinking, trying to insinuate himself into our family? Now, where is Hill? Hill? Oh, there you are! We must begin to plan ..."

His wife's voice trailed off the further she moved in the other direction, and Mr. Bennet chuckled to himself as he laid his head back against his chair and closed his eyes. If he were lucky, his wife would be so caught up in gowns, ribbons and planning a wedding breakfast that he would have many peaceful days locked away in his study. All of a sudden, one eye flew open.

Gowns? Ribbons? The breakfast? There will be no end to her spending!

Ramsgate
Gatesbridge Manor
The Dining Room

Lizzy was not fortunate enough to avoid John Wilkens altogether during her stay in Ramsgate; after all, it was his home. In fact, the morning after their arrival when Alfreda knocked on her door and asked if she was ready to break her fast, they made their way downstairs only to encounter the gentleman who was already in the dining room. He was eating and looked at her with an odd expression—one that Elizabeth could not interpret. And as she and Alfreda took their places at the table, he began to speak.

"Miss Bennet. It was kind of you to accompany Alfreda from London. I am also pleased that you shall have the opportunity to see the estate for yourself. Hopefully, being here, you will more readily comprehend the enormous expectations of anyone who aspires to fulfil the role of mistress. It is not to be taken lightly."

He did not look as though he was delighted to have her in his home. In fact, Wilkens looked cross. Elizabeth ignored him as she continued to butter a piece of toast. After all, what could she say that would not make him angry?

She was not impressed with this dark, forbidding house or its dour occupants who, if she was an accurate judge, seemed not to own an ounce of happiness. Gatesbridge Manor seemed to suck the very life out of her, and Elizabeth had no desire to be its mistress. She had not been able to fall asleep the night before, even though she was tired and the bed was adequate. Eventually she had opened the heavy curtains and allowed the full moon to lighten the interior which had lessened her anxiety. Still, she could not shake the feeling that evil resided under this roof. Only recollecting that the book Fitzwilliam had given her was in her bag brought her a measure of peace, and she had retrieved it and read until she fell asleep.

Her ruminations were interrupted by a question directed to Alfreda. "What do you intend today in the way of entertainment for Miss Bennet?" It was obvious from Wilkens' tone of voice that he was not at all worried about Alfreda's plans to amuse her.

Alfreda had blanched when Elizabeth ignored her brother's overture about a mistress for Gatesbridge, but she tried to sound enthusiastic now in her response. "We shall visit the shops of Ramsgate and the artist's shops along the beach and later picnic in the park. Then, if we have time, I shall take her by Hawthorne Hall and introduce her to Aunt Violet so that she will not feel like a stranger during the birthday dinner."

Wilkens' furrowed brow did not smooth as he considered her answer. "Just make sure that you do not go near the older section of town. That area is not safe for men, much less women. And be home in time for dinner. I have several meetings at my club this week, but I hope to be home in time to dine with you every night." He fixed a stony gaze on Alfreda. "Do you understand?"

Alfreda had an idea why her brother did not want them in that area of Ramsgate. Once, she had accidentally overheard him and his friends talking when she had passed his study and the door was left ajar. There was raucous talk of loose women housed in the brothel near their club, and she was certain that she heard her brother boast of visiting someone named Sally, who he referred to as his mistress. At the time, she had dismissed it as utter nonsense—surely a trick of her mind. Over the subsequent months, though, she had begun to wonder if it were not true, as his habits and temper had changed. He stayed away for days without informing her of his whereabouts and, more often than not, one of his friends would bring him home drunk.

Once when she confronted him with his dissolute ways, he had turned violent, squeezing her arms with such force that she had had dark bruises for weeks. And he had begun locking her in her room whenever she did not obey his orders swiftly enough. Fearing that only marriage to a good woman would save him, Alfreda had prayed that he would marry and that the responsibilities of a family would turn him around. But, after several of this year's debutants had spurned his suit and left him embarrassed, he had gotten worse. Elizabeth seemed to be her last hope.

"Yes, Brother. I understand completely."

Wilkens excused himself soon after and quit the manor with the pretext of business to see after. Elizabeth breathed a sigh of relief at his departure and remembered what she had wanted to ask Alfreda.

"Whatever happened to Mrs. Armstrong? I have not seen her since we arrived. Is she not going to break her fast with us?"

Alfreda looked apologetic. "She ... she and Brother do not see eye-to-eye on certain things. So when he is here, she resides with her sister in Ramsgate. However, should I desire to travel a good distance, she will be called upon again to accompany me."

At Elizabeth's look of incredulity she continued. "In all honesty, she is very happy with the arrangement." Then appearing overly eager to change the conversation, she continued, "Are you ready to see the sights of Ramsgate? I cannot wait to show you the beaches and the shops along them. I especially love the art gallery."

Elizabeth nodded. Though she was not satisfied with the explanation of Mrs. Armstrong's disappearance, she would, however, agree to anything rather than occupy this dreary place all day.

"Yes. I love to walk; the long trip was so confining. Besides, staying indoors when the sun is shining is not my idea of amusement."

"You are so lively, Elizabeth! You make me want to walk about too!"

"Then, perhaps we should leave the carriage at one of the businesses along the beach and see what we can discover by walking!"

"Indeed! I think that is a wonderful idea!"

Soon after, Elizabeth and Alfreda were aboard one of Wilkens' carriages and headed in the direction of the shops along the sea.

Chapter **20**

Dismissing the maid with a wave of her hand, Gisela Darcy stormed into her sitting room in a state of agitation. It would be another hour before her escort arrived, and she despised having too much time on her hands. Looking every inch a woman of substance with her elegantly styled hair and the costliest of satin gowns, she took note of herself in the mirror over the hearth, fingering her jewels as she studied her reflection. She had particularly chosen these diamonds and precious stones, worth thousands of pounds, to impress those she met tonight but privately she wondered if any of it mattered. Pouring another glass of brandy, she settled on a nearby settee and steeled herself against another round of melancholy. Lately it seemed to overwhelm her whenever she was left to her own devices, so she began an analysis of the room to occupy her mind.

She had inherited this richly furnished townhouse, filled with every imaginable comfort, from her first husband, Lord Stanley Grantham. And as Gisela studied the surroundings, she recalled having had most of the house refurbished as a new bride. That included this charming sitting room, wallpapered in delicate blue and yellow flowers and various types of greenery. She had simply adored it when it was first completed. Even the royal blue, antique settee with the matching tufted stool, both presents from Stanley, had pleased her for a brief period of time. She sighed, taking a deep swallow of the amber liquor. Such was her life—nothing had ever satisfied for long.

Despite every possible advantage, Gisela had lately come to the conclusion that she was miserable. And though the outward signs of wealth might make her the envy of most, she felt as poor as a beggar within. None of these *things* had brought her lasting happiness. Even Lord Attenborough, who would be here in a short while to escort her to yet another soirée, no longer amused her. She took a deep breath, puffed out her cheeks and exhaled noisily. Where had her life gone wrong?

Her earliest recollections of being entirely content were of childhood. As an only child, her parents had devoted themselves to her happiness. Had it all begun to change when her father, Lord Jackson Montgomery, began to spoil her in earnest? With no little guilt, she remembered flattering him in order to gain whatever she desired, and she reckoned that she could not have been more than ten at the time. It had been a game to get him to agree to her wishes over her mother's objections.

Or had life begun to crumble when she had entered into the loveless marriage with Lord Grantham? There had been other opportunities for advantageous alliances, some with men a good deal younger and more handsome, but she had been determined to marry the suitor with the most wealth, even insisting that her father discuss with her each candidate's worth. And after marrying Grantham for his riches, Gisela had fulfilled her every fantasy with his tacit approval, though it was carried out behind his back.

Then, when Grantham had finally expired, she slipped into the worst kind of decadence—running through a string of lovers, single and married alike, without any concern that the affairs were public knowledge. In fact, she revelled in flaunting her liaisons. It was no wonder that by the time she had set her cap for Fitzwilliam Darcy, she lived completely under the delusion that she could have him. Persuading herself that she could make him love her had been her greatest folly. Fraudulently she had managed to acquire his name, but he detested her and all of England was cognisant of it, making her a laughingstock.

The remnants of her seared conscience whispered, *Why keep him locked in this unholy alliance when you know he will never yield? Would it not be better for both of you if you grant him a divorce without contest?*

Still ambivalent, Gisela reached for the unsigned letter on a nearby table. Left on her doorstep that morning, it had driven home the foolishness of trying to keep him bound to her. From the delicate handwriting, it was obviously written by a woman, and from the contents, it was clear that whoever had written it was jealous of her husband's interest in another. Gisela had received anonymous notes and letters since her marriage, all meant to cause trouble, but this one held a detail that immediately caught her attention. She had heard the name mentioned before. It was the woman John Wilkens had escorted at the Trousdale's dinner party— Elizabeth Bennet!

Why would anyone be stupid enough to engage my help in separating her from Fitzwilliam if she was not a serious threat? Could he actually have fallen in love with this woman?

Recalling an image of Elizabeth from the night of the party, her brows furrowed. From what she remembered of that lady, she was unable to see the attraction.

She is certainly no beauty, and according to Wickham's source, she is a country nobody with nothing to recommend. Still, why would someone consider her such a threat as to write me? And what of her supposed trip to Ramsgate with Alfreda Wilkens? Did that not signify that she was practically engaged?

Downing the last sip of brandy, she threw the glass against the hearth as selfishness won the struggle for her conscience. *If he does fancy himself in love with her, I shall see that it comes to nothing. I cannot be happy, then why should he?*

Having too many unanswered questions regarding this Elizabeth Bennet, however, she rang for the butler before sitting down to draft a note to Grimsby. When he had returned from murdering Darcy's solicitor, she had not had him killed as Lady Catherine ordered and Wickham believed. He was simply too valuable an *ally*. Thus she had sent him back to her estate in Derbyshire instead, knowing Wickham would likely not see him there. Grimsby had, however, mentioned that his grown son, Grady, would be joining him, and she needed someone she could trust implicitly to watch Darcy's house and inform her of who came and went. She determined to ask Grimsby to send Grady to London to do just that.

Finishing with the missive, she walked over to the tray containing the bottle of brandy and more glasses. Pouring herself another two fingers, she raised it in a salute.

To you, my darling husband! To being miserable as long as I live!

Ashcroft Park
The gallery

Georgiana stood in front of the life-size portrait of Joseph Ashcroft, her head tilted back in order to view the entire figure of the man that she had come to admire after listening to her aunt's tales. A dashing fellow, well over six feet tall with curly golden hair and dark brown eyes, she thought him exceedingly handsome, second only to her brother, if she had to say. His expression was almost sombre, until she focused on his eyes. There was no mistaking the twinkle in them, as though he were about to laugh aloud. Recalling her aunt's story of how she had made faces behind the artist's back so that he might lose his composure, she was beginning to chuckle when Audrey Ashcroft came around the nearest   corner.

"Do you still find it amusing?"

"Yes, I never tire of seeing it. Uncle Joseph's portrait is just like every other gentleman's portrait until you notice the crinkling around his eyes and the mischievous sparkle therein. If only Brother had looked more like that when he sat for his portrait! As it is, he just looks older than he is and sad.

Audrey Ashcroft looked up at the portrait of the man she loved. A lump filled her throat as she took in his dear face and gazed once more into the eyes that she had   adored.

"Yes," she whispered roughly. "There is definitely a gleam there. And as for your brother, remember that he was faced with tremendous sorrow when his portrait was painted, as your mother was very ill. Besides, my Joseph was always more cheerful by nature than Fitzwilliam. Joseph very seldom—" Her voice caught and a single errant tear escaped. She could not finish the sentence.

In all the times she had visited Ashcroft Park, her aunt had never refused to recount her love story over again and visit the gallery. But now, mindful for the first time of how much seeing his portrait affected her, Georgiana began to apologise.

"Do not cry, Aunt Audrey. I am sorry that I have asked you to expose something that must still be very painful for you. I have been so selfish not to think of your feelings."

Turning to grip her niece's shoulders, she attempted to ease her worry. "Yes, it is painful, but you do not have to apologise. In truth, my memories are accompanied by pain, but I do not wish to forget anything about Joseph, so I endure what I must." She brushed a tear from Georgiana's face. "In the past, your inquisitiveness has forced me to face my sorrow, and I am stronger for it. I have learned that occasionally I just need to open my heart and embrace his loss once again."

"I … I think I know what you are saying. For so long, I could not bear to think of Mother or Father, but now," she took a ragged breath, "now I can remember them for a short while without feeling that I shall break down entirely."

"Exactly. Our hearts heal as we learn to deal with our sorrows."

"Do you know why I want to hear your love story over again? It is because it gives me hope that there will be such a man for me."

Lady Ashcroft smiled lovingly. "Of course, there will be, child. When you are a good deal older, your brother and I shall see that you are introduced to the finest of men. I have no doubt that the man of your dreams shall walk right through the front door one day. You shall see!"

Georgiana's eyes lit up. "Do you promise?"

"I promise." Audrey Ashcroft was surprised when a moment later the smile left her niece's face and she began to study her shoes.

Hesitantly, Georgiana asked, "Would it be impertinent of me to say that even I know that Lord Landingham cares for you? He is so kind and attentive. Do you not care for him a little?"

"Georgiana Darcy! Where did you ever get the idea—" Lady Ashcroft stopped. "No, I shall not dismiss you. You are correct in your observations, even if it is not polite to ask such personal questions unless someone has indicated your opinion is wanted."

Wide-eyed, Georgiana looked chastised until her aunt smiled, making her courage rise. "But, Aunt, I care for him dearly, and though he is already my godfather, if he were my uncle—"

A hand came up, causing her to quiet. "Since you have brought up the subject, I shall answer. As much as I like him, I have no plans to change my life until you are older and married. I may not change even then." She chuckled. "I am afraid that I am a creature of habit, having lived so long alone."

"But, you changed your habits when you came to live with Brother and me."

"Yes, yes I did." Lady Ashcroft seemed to study that revelation for a moment. "But, changing residences is not like remarrying. I had everything I ever wanted in Joseph. In truth, I think he spoiled me for any other man."

Georgiana took her aunt's hand. "You deserve someone to love you who is here now."

Tears filled her eyes at her niece's concern. Smiling, she turned Georgiana in the direction of the grand staircase, and then slipped an arm around her shoulders. "I promise we shall talk about this again after you are married. Now, what say you to tea and biscuits and the story of Joseph's hound getting locked in our bedroom closet one evening? We shall just have time for a short story tonight, since we must retire early in order to leave in the morning for Ramsgate."

Georgiana giggled. "I never tire of hearing how old General started howling when he awakened in the middle of the night and scared you and Uncle so. It is too bad that he was nearly deaf and could not hear Uncle calling for him earlier."

Mrs. Parker was in the kitchen when she heard the Mistress and her niece descending the grand staircase laughing heartily. She stopped to listen as it was so unique to hear merriment in the house. Ashcroft Park had enjoyed so little of it through the years that it always gave her pause whenever she heard it. And she was very aware of how she would miss the company and the laughter once they were off on their journey again. After a few seconds, she shook off her gloom and gathered the items for which she had come and walked out into the hallway to greet them. Audrey Ashcroft spotted her straightaway.

"We were looking for you, as we would like to know if you have any fresh biscuits that we might have with a cup of tea, Mrs. Parker."

"I think we might have just the kind Miss Darcy loves—vanilla with almonds. And I just had Cook fix a fresh pot of tea. Would you like it served in the drawing room?"

"No, I think Georgiana and I would love to sit out on the terrace while it is still light. This is our last night here until we come back from Ramsgate, and I think it would be nice to watch the sunset."

"Yes, madam," the housekeeper replied. "If you want to go on out, I shall have a tray delivered in two shakes of a lamb's tail."

"Thank you, Mrs. Parker."

With that, the duo turned and hurried down the hallway in the direction of the double doors leading out onto the terrace. As she watched them leave, she noted that they were chattering like two friends instead of aunt and niece.

Thank God for Miss Georgiana! That child has been so good for the Mistress' spirits.

Darcy House
The Study

Both men carried on as they always had, Richard silently entertaining himself with a book on army manoeuvres as he waited for Darcy to go through his correspondence. Afterward, he knew they would discuss whatever was most important to Darcy, or as was often the case, most puzzling—which usually included Georgiana, Elizabeth, Gisela, Lady Catherine and the investigation by Lowell. Since eschewing the Earl of Matlock's advice after he pushed for a wedding to Anne, William had no advisors other than himself and Landingham, and that gentleman was not in London right now.

However, as he turned another page in the boring tome, he was unaware that William had finished his correspondence and was now studying him. He had abstained from his usual glass of brandy in favour of a cup of hot tea with liberal honey, and it did not go unnoticed by his cousin.

"I am very pleased that you are not drinking so early, but why the change?"

Richard looked up. "I thought tea might help this dreadful cold I have been nursing for a week. At least Mother says it will make my head feel less like a bolt of muslin." He chuckled and closed the book. "No doubt she just wants to convince me to drink less alcohol." He stood and walked over to the window before taking another sip of the steaming liquid. "I do suppose tea has a good many benefits, though I doubt it will ever take the place of a stiff drink in getting my day started."

"Perhaps it will be useful in preserving my stock of French brandy!"

"There you go again—always thinking of how to save money. One would think you a pauper to hear you complain."

"'If you do not waste, you will not want,' Mother often said."

"Aunt Anne was a wise woman. I will give you that. I miss her terribly." Immediately he regretted his words, as they cast a pall over William's features. "I am sorry. I should not have said that."

William shook his head. "Do not apologise. You spoke from the heart."

Trying to raise his spirits, Richard enquired. "Have you heard from the deserters heading to Ramsgate? Has Aunt Audrey and Georgiana arrived yet? And, most importantly have they met Miss Elizabeth?"

"Deserters?"

"Sorry, an unfortunate choice of words, owing to being in His Majesty's service—but they are deserting us and the filthy air of London for the seaside."

"Ah." William smiled, nodding as he pulled something from his top desk drawer. "I received this first thing this morning." He held up a letter. "Aunt Audrey says they have reached Ashcroft Park and will stay one day. She feels that they will not be too tired when they arrive in Ramsgate if they rest a day at her estate. So, no, they have not seen Elizabeth yet."

"Odd that you would pay for her to send special messengers from every stop along the way and yet you begrudge me a bit of your brandy. Are you still sending six men along with the coach? That alone must cost you a fortune."

"Money is no object when it comes to the safety of our aunt and Georgiana. They are my responsibility. Besides, Clark, who is the messenger, works for me exclusively and I can always hear from my sister no matter how far she may have travelled. As soon as he delivers one express, he gets a night's rest and heads back to them with an answer. Then he serves as a footman until they need to send another express to me. At least in that way, Georgiana is assured that we are never too far apart to communicate effectively."

"Do not start preaching, Cousin, I was just teasing. I understand completely. I should have known that they would stop at Ashcroft Park. That is truly a magnificent place, though much of the lure of visiting there was lost with Uncle Joseph's death. I barely remember him, but I do recollect that he was a presence when he walked into a room. Bigger than life! The one thing I do recall clearly was that he used to take me riding when we visited." He chuckled. "He insisted on sitting me right in front of him on this big brown stallion. It drove Mother mad."

"I confess I do not remember him at all, as I was so young when he died, but I listened to Mother talk about him so often that I feel that I knew him. He was evidently a good man and quite jovial if you go by those that knew him."

Richard was nodding as he drained his cup of tea. "That is true! I only wish Aunt Audrey had not held onto his memory so tightly that she never made room in her heart for another. I truly believe Lord Landingham would marry her at once if she would only agree and he would be good for her."

William stood and stretched, then went to the side table to pour himself a cup of tea. "Landingham is a good man, and I agree with your assessment. However, we all must do what we feel is right for us, Richard. She must have loved Joseph Ashcroft dearly not to have married again."

Richard studied his cousin soberly. "I can see where you would think her wise. I just imagine that had you married Elizabeth instead of Gisela and, God forbid, she died, you would never replace her."

The cup in his hand stopped halfway to his lips, and William stared into space as though he were contemplating that very thing. Finally, he set the cup down without taking a drink; his voice was barely audible as he replied. "I ... I could never have imagined finding such a woman as Elizabeth and still cannot envision having her as my own. But should that dream ever be fulfilled, I know she could never be replaced in my heart. It would be ridiculous to ever try."

"Not even for an heir?"

William looked at him with an expression of resolve. "Not even for an heir. Why else would I have spurned Gisela these last two years? Georgiana can inherit Pemberley if I never have a son."

Richard walked over to put a comforting hand on his cousin's shoulder. "Just as I said—you, of all people, would understand Aunt Audrey. Now, I think we should put off talking of such sad circumstances and discuss this business with Lowell. Have you heard anything yet from his examination? I worry what Aunt Catherine will do if she learns that he is snooping around the mills."

"Not a word since I received the note saying that he had set out for Wexford. I confess that I am beginning to worry."

Richard made his way back to the chair in front of Darcy's desk, taking his seat and stretching his long legs out in front of him before he responded. "Why is that? I did not think he was supposed to contact you that often."

"We agreed that he would inform me when he had finished at Wexford and was moving on to Stafford. I should think he would have done so by now and written to let me know."

"I would not worry as yet, Darcy. Give him a few more days. If you have not heard by Friday, send me word and I will have some of my cohorts in that part of the country check on his whereabouts. You have to remember that travel in that part of the country is treacherous at best. The roads are nearly impassable especially when it rains and I have seen reports at headquarters of a lot of rain in that area."

William nodded, his spirits beginning to lift at the reminder of why Mr. Lowell might not have corresponded lately. "Perhaps I am borrowing trouble for, as you say, I have gotten reports from Pemberley of unusual amounts of rain and the mills are north of there. The post coaches could be behind schedule too."

Richard rallied to see William's countenance brighten. "Let us do something to take your mind off all this? What do you fancy?"

William smiled cunningly. "What do you say to a round of fencing to see if I am still in shape?"

"You mean to see if you can still best me?" Richard stood and bowed low with a sweep of his arm towards the door. "Why not? If you are still the only man in England who can defeat me, I shall not be too embarrassed. After all, your records at Cambridge have never been surpassed!"

William laughed loudly, proclaiming, "So you say! I doubt anyone would tell me if they had."

"Not to fear, Cousin! Were I to hear of it, I would be the first to inform you!"

They had reached the hall and William halted, studying Richard with a wry smile. "And why is that, might I ask?"

"So as to keep your ego at bay! Do you know how many times you have bested me in the last year alone?"

"My ego!" William protested. "Why I will have you know ..."

As they moved in the direction of the ballroom where they always fenced, each had an arm around the other's shoulder. Hearing their easy banter, Mr. Barnes had taken note of the direction they were headed and smiled. If he hurried, he could convince a few of the newer servants to wager a few farthings on the outcome of the match.

He had never lost a bet, as he always chose first and took the Master's side. Colonel Fitzwilliam was an accomplished swordsman, but Mr. Darcy was in every way his superior. Up ahead he caught sight of the new footman.

"Lyons, are you a wagering man?"

Chapter 21

Ramsgate
Hawthorne Hall

Following a footman down an endless hall, Georgiana twisted her head from side to side as she examined every portrait she could manage while they moved swiftly along. She was aware that Pemberley's gallery was as large, if not larger than this one, however, there were twice as many portraits displayed on these walls because they were hung in two tiers from eye level all the way to the ceiling. Thus some of the upper ones looked positively ancient, and the clothes the subjects wore were quite outlandish. She derived great amusement by trying to choose which was the most bizarre.

My goodness, they have a lot of ancestors—some very unattractive indeed!

I cannot imagine wearing anything that hideous. How did one stand in those shoes?

My, he looks a lot like the new vicar at Kympton, except he has more hair.

Turning to see that her niece was not keeping up, Lady Ashcroft called, "Come along, Georgiana!"

As soon as her aunt turned back around, Georgiana ran to catch up, as she did not wish to lose her way. Luckily, the hall ended just ahead, and as they turned the corner, they did not advance far before the servant abruptly stopped to open a door. Georgiana rounded the corner just as he was showing her aunt into a room and someone shouted out a greeting.

"Audrey, as I live and breathe! What possessed you to come to Ramsgate? Surely you did not travel this far for an old woman's birthday?"

By the time Georgiana reached the doorway, her aunt was bending over someone seated on a magnificent upholstered sofa—obviously Lady Hawthorne. All she could spy from her position was beautiful silver hair, piled high and held with glittering combs. Georgiana's first thought was that the woman looked very petite, almost childlike, sitting on the huge piece of furniture. Her second thought was that the blaring voice certainly did not fit the frail woman.

As her aunt stood straight again, she leaned to the right and set eyes on an elegant older lady clad in expensive clothes and jewellery, not unlike those favoured by her Aunt Catherine. But unlike her least favourite relation, this woman radiated a cheerfulness that reached across the room, enveloping her. She liked her immediately.

"Violet, you never age!" Audrey Ashcroft remarked with a chuckle. "If only I am as keen as you are when I am five and sixty."

"Shush! You must never repeat my age. I believe you are the only one that truly remembers." Laughing loudly as she talked, their hostess continued. "I want everyone who is anticipating my demise to be in the dark about how old I am. And I plan to live a long time just to annoy them."

Both women dissolved into laughter, which caused Georgiana to giggle in spite of trying to act the proper young lady so as not to disappoint her aunt.

"I was surprised to get your letter saying you would visit on your way to Ramsgate. Did you come to town just for my party?"

"I will have to confess that I had forgotten your birthday. It is Georgiana's art lessons that brought us here at this time."

"Since you are in the neighbourhood, you must attend my soirée. I insist. Now, you mentioned Georgiana, where is she?"

Lady Ashcroft stepped aside to give Violet Hawthorne a clearer view of her niece, who had stopped just inside the door. "She is here with me."

Lady Hawthorne grabbed her spectacles from a nearby table, placing them on her nose to study Georgiana. "Can this be little Georgiana? Why, she has grown into a lovely young lady. Come here, child, and let me get a good look at you."

Shyly Georgiana stepped in front of their hostess while her aunt beamed. Aunt Audrey had related that Lady Hawthorne was an old friend of hers and had actually seen Georgiana several times when she was small. As she got within reach, a weathered hand reached to take hers, and Georgiana let the mistress of the house pull her into an embrace. Finally, she was released and stood waiting while two vibrant green eyes examined her.

"You have your mother's eyes," Lady Hawthorne finally said, cocking her head. "Yes, and other than the colour of your hair, you bear a strong resemblance to her."

Georgiana blushed. "Thank you. I love to hear that I resemble Mother in some small way, as my brother looks very much like her."

"And how is that rascal of a brother of yours? I used to see him often when he was still in short pants, but I imagine he would not remember. He was here with your parents one spring, and he picked all the blooms around the terrace to give to his mother. I shall never forget when he came through the French doors with his arms so full of flowers they were dropping everywhere!" She laughed uproariously—not at all ladylike. "George was going to scold him until I intervened. Good gracious, the boy was only three, and he thought he had done something wonderful!"

Georgiana giggled, her eyes crinkling. "I shall have to tease him about that!"

"I just imagine he will deny it, but Audrey would remember!" She glanced to Lady Ashcroft who nodded her agreement. "By the way, I understand that he is still married to that strumpet, Gisela Grantham?"

Georgiana gasped, cutting her eyes to her aunt for some idea of how to respond. But Lady Ashcroft displayed only a wry smile, as if she was not in the least surprised.

Realizing from Georgiana's expression that she might have offended her, Lady Hawthorne declared, "Do not mind me. I am so old and rich that I can say whatever I please. I no longer have to lie and pretend I like people that I despise. I have known Gisela Grantham practically all her life, and since she came of age, she has been a very wicked person. She will never be a Darcy in my book!"

"I … I do not like her either," Georgiana offered timidly.

"Good! Then we agree!" She winked at the girl. "Tell me, how is Fitzwilliam now that he has graduated to longer pants?"

Georgiana laughed at the mention of her brother's clothes. "Brother is well, I thank you."

"I am glad to hear it, though I am sure he would be much better off without that harridan."

At that very moment, a gentleman entered the room and paused when he saw the strangers. He was perhaps eight and twenty, tall with sandy hair and was dressed in a colonel's uniform. Though not handsome, he had a pleasant look about him when he smiled.

"Oh, David, come here!" Lady Hawthorne exclaimed. "I want you to meet some friends of mine."

The colonel walked over to their hostess and gave her a kiss on the cheek. "Please excuse me for interrupting. I had no idea you had company. I came to finish our discussion as you suggested, but I can certainly come back at a later time."

"Nonsense, I am glad you are here to meet my guests. This is my dear friend of more than twenty years, Lady Audrey Ashcroft, and her niece, Miss Georgiana Darcy."

He executed a perfect bow while she continued with the introductions. "Allow me to present my godson, Colonel David Cochran. He is staying with me this week and will be attending my party."

There were acknowledgements all around, and Colonel Cochran exclaimed how pleased he was to meet them.

Suddenly Lady Hawthorne blurted out, "Oh, Audrey, I forgot! When I got your note, I had Mrs. Traywick prepare two guest rooms."

Georgiana's aunt made to disagree. "We are perfectly able to stay in the hotel in Ramsgate. I have already written ahead to secure rooms."

"There is no need to argue. You will stay with me. We have too much gossip to catch up on. Surely you will not refuse an old woman her wish on her birthday?"

Audrey Ashcroft laughed aloud. "Do you use that excuse often to get your own way?"

Colonel Cochran interjected, "I can testify that she has used it a lot lately, as that is why I am staying here as her guest."

Everyone chuckled.

"At my age, I employ whatever method works!" Violet Hawthorne smirked. "Besides, I know you will attend my party, and it will be so much easier if you stay here with me. What do you say?"

"I cannot refuse—not because you use your age to get your way, but because you are the liveliest person I know! I always enjoy your company."

Lady Hawthorne beamed. "It is settled then." Acknowledging the housekeeper now standing in the doorway, she added, "Mrs. Traywick, are the rooms prepared?"

"Yes, madam. I had already prepared several guest rooms in anticipation of whoever might arrive this week, so there was little additional work required."

"Wonderful! Audrey, I just imagine that you and Georgiana are exhausted, so if you will follow Mrs. Traywick to your rooms, you shall find everything you need to refresh yourselves. Dinner is in two hours, so there is time for a short nap. I shall send a servant into town to inform the hotel not to hold your rooms."

She reached out to take her godson's hand. "Meanwhile, the colonel and I will conclude our business, and that will leave plenty of time after we dine for everyone to enjoy a good visit. I hate talking business after dinner!"

London
Bingley's Townhouse

Highly agitated, Louisa Hurst hurried about the house as she tried to recall everything she wanted to inspect before Charles' arrival. Having received his letter only that morning, she knew that he could arrive at any moment. She also knew that whenever her brother was out of town, Bertram eschewed the less expensive provisions in the liquor cabinet and humidor in the drawing room for the fine cigars and French brandy found in Charles' study. With such short notice, she had not had time to replace them. Already she had unlocked the study so that the maids could straighten up, and all that remained was to pray that Charles would not go in there before she replaced everything that had been consumed. A footman had left a half-hour earlier for the shops in order to locate Charles' favourite cigars and another was in the cellar at that very moment, searching for another bottle of his best brandy.

As she continued her assessment, Louisa fretted over the change in Bertram's attitude which had gotten more cavalier over the past year. Her husband had begun to treat Charles' residences as though they were his own, to the point of requesting she unlock the study whenever her brother was gone for any length of time. Afterward, she often found him sitting at her brother's desk, his boots upon the edge, seemingly oblivious to the impropriety of such presumption, and she was well aware that more than one long-time servant had raised their eyebrows at the sight. She lived in fear that one of them might mention his behaviour to Charles. Yesterday, however, things had reached a new level when she found him thumbing through one of her brother's household ledgers that usually sat atop a tall bookcase behind his desk.

Why does Bertram insist on using Charles' private study when he is away? How often do I have to warn him that this cannot continue? My brother may not always maintain us if he keeps to this course. Even Charles has his limits.

Charles' letter had been cheerful, and she prayed that his spirits would not be dampened by the state of the house or by the news that she had to impart. Normally she and Bertram stayed from October to well after Christmas with their Hurst relations, relieving Charles of the responsibility of hosting them the entire year. However, they would not be visiting the Hurst family this winter, due to the argument that her husband had had with his father about his own dwindling liquor supply. Only yesterday they had received notice that his parents would soon be travelling to Scotland to visit Mr. Hurst's sister and would not return to their estate until next spring.

Louisa's troubled thoughts were interrupted by the sounds of the front door opening, and she turned to see Charles step through the entrance and stamp his feet to remove water from his boots. Mr. Gates was already taking his coat and hat but he had not yet spied her.

"Drat! It began raining once we reached London, and I was hoping for the lovely weather I have been enjoying in Meryton, Gates!"

"It has been raining every morning for three days, sir," the tall, grey-haired butler replied. "But it usually ends by the afternoon. In any event, it is good to have you home."

"I hated to leave Meryton, but I have business that must be taken care of in Town. Then I shall be off again."

"Very good, sir."

Louisa's suspicions were raised, and as she stepped into view, she could not hold her tongue. "Charles, it is good to have you home again." She stepped forward to embrace her brother. "Did I overhear you tell Mr. Gates that you were in Meryton? Caroline said that you had gone to Bristol to check on the ship that was lost."

"Bristol? Heavens no! I do not know where she got that impression. Mr. Carter has that situation well in hand, and I was not needed there."

Louisa's mind was racing. If Charles had been in Meryton, then he must be aware of what Caroline had done. Nonetheless, he did not seem angry. She had advised Caroline not to write the letter dismissing the staff at Netherfield from service, but she had no luck in persuading her. She never had.

"Then you were at Netherfield all alone? I ... I mean, apart from the servants?"

Charles studied his oldest sister warily. "I think you are well aware that there were hardly any servants left at Netherfield."

Louisa dropped her head to study her feet. "I tried to intervene, but you know Caroline never listens to me. She has some peculiar ways, Charles, but she means well, I believe. She thought it would save you money to let them go and hire them again when you returned."

"That is very unkind to the servants and no way to build loyalty. Besides, I do not think that was her plan at all. I think she did not want me to return to Netherfield to stay and believed that having no servants there would discourage me from doing so." His brow furrowed. "And, as for your part in this, you should have let me know."

"I am sorry. I did not wish to get caught between the two of you."

"Yet, by being silent you have done just that. I was fortunate, however, in that Mr. Mercer and Mrs. Watkins were able to find most of the servants and convince them to return. In addition, I had plenty of visitors, as my future bride and her family were kind enough to keep me company."

Louisa felt faint. "Bride? Your future bride?"

Charles enjoyed watching her squirm. "Yes, Miss Jane Bennet has made me the happiest of men. She has consented to be my wife."

Louisa looked about for a chair and settled on one of two flanking an ornate table beneath a huge mirror.

Charles tried not to smile. "Are you unwell, Louisa? Should I send for a physician?"

Finally coming to her senses, Louisa took a calming breath. What was done was done, and nothing she or Caroline could say would change his mind. Of that she was sure! Thus, she quickly decided to use the situation to her advantage.

"I wish you joy, Brother! Miss Bennet is a lovely woman, and I am sure you will be very happy."

"Thank you. I am sure that we shall."

"When is the joyous event to take place?"

"We have not set an exact date, though it will likely be the first part of September. I have returned to Town to consult with my solicitor regarding a settlement and that brings to mind something else. Now that Jane will be the mistress of my homes, I think it is time that you and Bertram secure your own residence. As a newly married couple, we will want our privacy. I am sure you understand, being married yourself."

"Of course," Louisa lied, trying not to panic as she pasted a smile on her face. "But what of Caroline? Where will she live?"

"Yes. Dear, dear Caroline," Charles repeated, none too affectionately. "I certainly need to make provisions for her."

The way his expression changed when she mentioned Caroline made Louisa uneasy. Unfortunately, just at that moment her sister appeared at the top of the stairs.

"Are you and Louisa talking about me, Charles? You should have had the decency to wait until I came downstairs and speak to me—not about me."

As she descended the stairs in her usual, irritable manner, Louisa tried to catch her sister's eye and shake her head in warning. But Caroline was paying her no mind.

"Perhaps we should all step into the drawing room. What say you, Charles?" Louisa offered, seeking to move everyone out of the range of the servant's hearing.

Charles shrugged and headed in that direction. They had all barely gotten situated in the room, each taking a seat after the door was shut, before Louisa began.

"Is it not good to have our brother home again, Caroline" she declared with exaggerated cheerfulness. "Bertram and I were just saying yesterday that we missed you terribly, Charles."

Caroline dismissed Louisa's words impatiently. "Oh really, Louisa! Bertram has been in his cups nearly every day since Charles has been away. When would you have had time to talk to him?" Then she addressed Charles. "Louisa and I were talking of how slothful Mr. Hurst has become—doing nothing but eating, drinking and sleeping. He contributes nothing to society."

"And what do you contribute to society, Caroline, other than making my friend Darcy miserable with your meddling?"

Caroline paled as her palms began to sweat. A nervous tic that always surfaced when she was caught in a lie commenced on the right side of her face.

"Surely you do not blame me for informing Mrs. Darcy that that country chit is out to seduce her husband? It was just scandalous how Eliza Bennet chased after him at the Holmes' ball. I even saw her talking to him and Miss Darcy at Hatchards' bookshop several days later, so she must be following him about. I felt that I had to take action to protect him from her distasteful manoeuvrings."

"Protect Darcy?" His eyes narrowed on the twitch in her jaw. "The only protection Darcy needs is from you, my dear sister. Now suppose you tell me all the particulars of what you did, and I shall decide who is to blame."

Caroline swallowed hard, beginning to knot a handkerchief she had absently pulled from her pocket. Gradually she confessed everything she had written in her unsigned letter. The longer she spoke the more crimson Charles' face became, and by the time she was finished, he was so angry he could barely speak. Likewise, Louisa had sunk deeper into the chair she occupied, her face frozen in shock and her mind in turmoil.

No longer able to restrain himself, Charles came to his feet startling both of his sisters. "Caroline Beatrice Bingley! I am ashamed to call you my sister! How dare you compose lies to hurt a kind-hearted, admirable woman like Miss Elizabeth Bennet! She is every inch a lady, which is more than I can say for you!"

"They are not lies! She has designs on Mr. Darcy, and she is acting like a strumpet, trailing him and his sister all over London. I would not be surprised if she calls on him at his house!"

"Enough! If anyone is acting like a strumpet, it is you! Do you know how often Darcy has asked me not to put him in your company? He loathes the way you chase after him. And I know for a fact that he has no relationship with Miss Elizabeth other than friendship."

"You cannot believe that, Charles! She comes from the basest family. Not a one of them has any manners or any qualms about chasing men. Why—"

"I will say this only once. I am betrothed to Miss Jane Bennet, and I will not have you disparaging her or any member of her family ever again."

Caroline let out a piercing scream as both hands came to her face. "NO!"

Charles continued undeterred. "For your arrogance in dismissing my staff at Netherfield and your attempt to ruin Miss Elizabeth's reputation for your own selfish reasons, you shall go and have your maid pack your things. From this day forward, you shall reside in Scarborough with Aunt Harrison. You shall be on your way first thing in the morning. And I warn you, do not give me reason to reduce the amount I have added to your allowance."

With those words, Charles stomped out of the room and up the grand staircase. Eventually, the sound of his boots could be heard echoing down the long hall on the floor above. Caroline stood for several seconds in the same spot, her eyes wide as saucers as she contemplated what had happened.

Louisa rose slowly from her seat, absentmindedly smoothing her skirts before silently heading towards the door. As she was about to exit the room, Caroline found her voice.

"Louisa, you cannot let him do this to me! You have to make him come to his senses and change his mind!"

Louisa did not turn around with her reply. "No, I do not. You have been cautioned often enough that you go too far, and you chose to disregard those warnings. Charles is marrying Jane Bennet, and Miss Elizabeth will be a part of our family. Your actions to do her harm were cruel and could rebound on us all. I am afraid that you have made your bed, and now you must lie in it."

Louisa continued on out the door and up the stairs to the sounds of Caroline's cries.

"How dare you take Eliza Bennet's side over mine!" There was the sound of shattering glass. "I shall not go! You shall see!" More glass shattered. "Charles shall never make me move to Scarborough! NEVER!"

When Bingley's coach pulled away from the house the next morning, a silent and seething Caroline was aboard, along with a very unhappy, howbeit well-paid, maid who had agreed to accompany her as far as Scarborough. Charles doubted the woman would suffer his sister's temper after the trip, and had not extracted a promise that she would stay in Scarborough as Caroline's maid. Nevertheless, he was not worried. After all, the maid's pay would now come from Caroline's allowance and if she wished a maid, she could very well hire one herself. As he watched the coach roll out of sight, he could not suppress a smile.

Now that I have washed my hands of you, dear sister, I shall work on distancing myself from Louisa and Hurst. That should save me several hundred pounds a year. From now on, Jane shall be my first concern. That is how it should be.

Tipping his hat at the retreating coach, he began to walk down the street towards the park. Today was a beautiful day, and he planned to make the most of it.

Chapter **22**

Ramsgate
Younge's Art Gallery

Geolge Wickham stepped out of the hired carriage and onto the hot sand that flanked the walkway in front of the art gallery. Straightening his clothes, he ran a hand through his straight hair before donning his hat and giving it a pat.

Today was the day he would encounter Georgiana Darcy for the first time in years. Many thoughts ran through his head. Would she remember him fondly? Had her brother poisoned her mind against him? Instantly his thoughts flew to the day he was escorted off the property by two burly footmen, and his anger rose as though it were yesterday.

Following his departure from university for several infractions, he had no longer resided at Pemberley and only returned upon learning of Mr. Darcy's death. Certain that the man who thought so well of him would leave him an ample inheritance, Wickham was greatly disappointed to learn that he had been bequeathed three hundred pounds and the living at Kympton. Furious, he had demanded that Fitzwilliam Darcy give him three thousand pounds in lieu of the living. There was no doubt in his mind that he could parlay that meagre amount into a small fortune with his proficiency at cards, however, in less than a year, he was penniless. Then, when he heard that the Kympton living was open once again, he had returned to Pemberley, hat in hand, and practically begged Darcy to forgive his previous attitude and allow him the position. For all his posturing, there was to be no sympathy from the Heir of Pemberley and an argument resulted with him being thrown from the estate.

Today you pay for your arrogance, my old friend! Your precious sister will suffer for your sins against me.

As he approached the front door, Mrs. Younge opened it immediately, and Wickham entered, stopping in the foyer of the modest gallery. Off to one side he could see a golden haired girl through an open door. Her back was turned to him, and she paid no attention to his entrance, no doubt used to customers entering the establishment during her lessons. Mrs. Younge silently tilted her head towards the girl and headed in the opposite direction.

As he approached the doorway, Wickham could tell that Georgiana was working on a watercolour, and he stopped to observe. She must have felt his presence, for she turned to study him. Expecting to see Mrs. Younge, she dropped her eyes. Taking a deep breath, he entered the room with as much confidence as he could muster.

"Miss Darcy?" Georgiana's head came up. "I could not believe my eyes when I saw you sitting here. I believe I would know you anywhere, even from behind. But, even so, you are no longer a girl but a lovely young woman."

Georgiana's voice faltered as her head quickly bowed again. "I ... you have me at a disadvantage, sir. I do not believe that I know you." She turned back around, the set of her shoulders evidence of her discomfort with his presence.

"I am sorry." Wickham removed his hat and walked around the table so that she would have a good view of him. "I did not realise that you would forget me so completely. It has been several years since we were in each other's company, but we were once friends."

Now, Georgiana looked up with a puzzled expression. "Friends?"

"Yes. I grew up at Pemberley."

A thought came to mind. Georgiana recalled someone near her brother's age who used to entertain her with feats of magic. "Are you Mr. Wickham's son?"

Wickham smiled beguilingly and bowed deeply with a sweep of his arm. "Indeed! George Wickham, at your service, madam."

"But, I thought—" Georgiana halted and Wickham held his breath as she glanced about with a bewildered expression. "I do not know what I thought. It seems that one day you were there and the next you were gone." She began to clean the brush she held with great enthusiasm as if scrubbing it would help solve the riddle. "I do remember that Brother would not answer my questions about you."

Wickham hesitated unsure how to answer. Finally, he decided his best option was not to disparage her brother. "He was being kind."

She eyed him suspiciously now, as she dried the brush and placed it in a jar holding several others.

"At that time, I was not the kind of man I should have been, and your brother asked me to leave Pemberley." He walked around the room pretending to focus on the various unfinished pictures that were propped on easels. "I do not blame him in the least. My mother died when I was born, and my father died while I was still a boy. Your father ..." Wickham milked the moment for all its worth, taking a ragged breath and exhaling slowly. "Well, he was like a father to me. When I came home from my first year at university, I learned that your mother's health was still precarious, and your father was showing signs of the heart problems that would claim his life. I am ashamed to say that I did not handle it well at all. I could not fathom life without my mentor."

Georgiana's brow furrowed. "I can fully understand that. I am afraid I did not handle my mother or father's illnesses well, either."

Pleased with her response, Wickham whirled around. "Please, accept my apology for bringing up something that is a reminder of your pain. I should not have mentioned it."

"No, no, there is nothing to forgive."

"It is just that when I saw you sitting here, I knew that I had to speak to you. You are reminder of all that was good in my early years." He smiled, using all his charms to convince her of his sincerity. Then he swept his arm about the room. "This is truly remarkable! Mrs. Younge's late husband was a long-time acquaintance of mine, and whenever I am in Ramsgate, I call on her to see how the gallery is faring and to encourage her. In my opinion, she has done an excellent job with the business since his death."

Georgiana turned to inspect the foyer of the gallery. "Do you know where Mrs. Younge has gotten off to?"

"Just as I entered the shop I saw her leave out the back door and hurried to see where she was headed. She was half-way down the wooden walk to the gazebo by the time I reached the door." He quickly added. "I am sure she will not be gone long."

"Oh, she is never away for too long. I imagine she has left to fetch Margaret— I mean, Lady Strongham—and we shall exchange places." At Wickham's raised brows, she explained, "Mrs. Younge instructs first one and then the other of us. It is my turn to occupy the gazebo and practice what I have learned."

Wickham nodded as though he had not learned this already from Sarah Younge. "Would you object if I accompanied you to the gazebo to continue our visit?" At Georgiana's hesitation, he quickly added, "I would dearly love to hear of Pemberley, as I miss it terribly. I have often wondered whether Darcy convinced Lord Landingham to sell him that black stallion or if Mr. Armistead's son ever returned from Scotland."

She was satisfied with his earnestness and had decided in his favour just as Mrs. Younge entered the room with her other pupil. At that time, the proprietor made a point of introducing Wickham to both young women as her old friend. And because her instructor seemed completely unconcerned that he had been alone with her, Georgiana felt secure in his presence.

Ere long they were ensconced in the gazebo with Wickham captivating Georgiana with tales from her early years and of happier times with her parents. When he ran out of actual stories, he began making them up just to convince her that, had he the time, he could share many more. Naturally Georgiana was mesmerised, as she had never heard these stories, and seeing her fascination, Wickham moved on to his next lie.

"I have to ask, whatever became of Lady Ashcroft? Did she ever marry again?"

"Aunt Audrey has not remarried. She is my companion. In fact, she shall be here to collect me at the end of my session." Georgiana watched the smile fade from his lips and enquired, "What is the matter?"

"I am afraid that if she were to learn that we are talking, she would put her foot down." He smiled wanly, hoping he appeared sincere. "When I was acting out of my sorrow, I am afraid that I managed to anger your aunt, and I fear she will forbid you ever to speak to me again."

"Whatever did you do?"

"I stole a pound from her reticule for a trip to London, set on drowning my sorrows in drink. I owned up to it when it was uncovered, but she was insistent that I was not to be trusted ever again. I believe that was a huge factor in your brother's decision to banish me from Pemberley." Wickham sat down dejectedly on the wooden railing that surrounded the structure. "I deserved her wrath, and I do not begrudge her that opinion, though I have tried to become a better man over the years."

"Then I suppose it would be better if I do not mention you."

Wickham's smile was blinding. "Would you do that? Then we could continue our talks. It is almost like old times learning what has happened to all those I hold most dear from my childhood." He moved to bend down and take both her hands in his. Looking deeply into her eyes, he swore, "I will never do anything to destroy your trust in me."

Hawthorne Hall
The garden

Audrey Ashcroft leaned back into the soft cushions of the large tree swing and closed her eyes. The day was lovely and not too warm, and she was enjoying her stay with her old friend tremendously. She had escorted Georgiana to the art gallery early that morning and would not go back to fetch her until late that afternoon.

On the whole, her mind was fixed on Georgiana from daylight to dark. She was a firm believer in keeping a young person occupied with good pursuits and had taken that path with her sister's child. Anne Darcy was so ill in her last days and Fitzwilliam so burdened with estate issues and his ridiculous marriage that Georgiana had essentially been left to her own devices a good bit of the time. When she had come to live with her niece and nephew, it had taken over six months to get the child headed in a productive direction, and Lady Ashcroft was not about to let her charge slip back into her former laissez-faire attitude. Nonetheless, these few hours with nothing to occupy her mind were a welcome respite, and for the first time in ages, she felt at ease doing absolutely nothing.

"What is making you smile so?"

Her hostess' voice broke through her meditation, and Lady Ashcroft opened her eyes and smiled even more widely. "I was just thinking of how far Georgiana has come in the last two years."

"You have done a fine job; anyone can see that. It is a shame you never had children of your own." Pain crossed Audrey's features and Violet regretted her choice of words. "I am sorry. Will you forgive an old lady for a slip of the tongue?"

Lady Ashcroft slid over and patted the place next to her on the swing. Violet Hawthorne sat down and reached to entwine her friend's arm sympathetically as she continued her request for forgiveness.

"I find that I am constantly apologising lately. I have gotten used to speaking frankly, without thought of how it might affect others. I would never purposefully hurt you, and you know how much I thought of your dear husband."

"I know," Lady Ashcroft said softly.

"Your Joseph was the only man I would have left my husband for!" As Audrey pretended to be shocked, she chuckled. "Not that he ever paid me, or other women, any notice. He was completely and utterly in love with you. That is how it should have been."

They both sat silently for a moment, lost in memories.

"I do believe, however, that he had the most charming personality of any man of my acquaintance. My Horace was not one for being charming, though he was a good man. But Joseph—now he was the ideal man! He was captivating as well as handsome."

"That he was."

"You know that I think it a shame you never married again."

A smile replaced Lady Ashcroft's sad expression. "I should as you have told me often enough."

"And that amiable Lord Landingham is in Ramsgate, and I know for a fact that he dotes on you. He is not short on looks either!"

"Violet," Audrey warned, lowering of her voice. "You know how I feel about your match-making."

"Well, I am just saying—"

"Let us change the subject."

"Very well. Then may I request your help in a conspiracy?"

"And what conspiracy would that be?"

"The presence of my godson, Colonel Cochran, is not a coincidence."

"Oh?"

"I had long suspected that he was in love with my niece, Alfreda. Only recently I learned that he asked to court her last year, and that horrid nephew of mine would not consent. Apparently, John threatened Alfreda if she informed me of the situation."

"What do you intend to do?"

"I intend to put them in each other's company at my birthday dinner. I want to give them a chance to meet again without John's knowledge—to see if Alfreda still desires his suit. David has assured me that his feelings for my niece have not changed. Would you be willing to feign being unwell and ask Alfreda to accompany you into the garden for a breath of fresh air? David will be waiting there."

"Might not Mr. Wilkens follow us into the garden?"

"John always arrives late. He uses business issues as an excuse, but it is likely only his mistress that occupies his time. I have already made my intentions clear to have Alfreda here early, with or without his escort. If all goes as planned, John will arrive later and not realise that David is here until after he and Alfreda have talked. Also, I have enlisted Lord Landingham's cooperation in keeping my nephew occupied once he does appear."

"Marshall—I mean, Lord Landingham is going to attend your party?"

"Yes, and you may call him Marshall in my presence, dear. I know that you and he are very good friends."

Audrey coloured, but did not deny the assertion.

"Now, are you willing to help me with this subterfuge?"

"Of course. I will do whatever I can to help you and Miss Wilkens. I just pray her brother does not discover your plan and cause a scene."

"I will try to handle this discreetly, but make no mistake, if necessary, I will bring the full weight of Hawthorne Hall against my nephew. I happen to know that he gambles to such an extent that he desperately needs the inheritance he is to receive when I die. Between drink, gambling, and the whores that are his mistresses, he is a little more than a pauper. He is already indebted to me for a substantial loan. I even suspect he has spent Alfreda's dowry, and that is why he has not allowed her to marry."

Lady Ashcroft gasped. "What a horrible man! And he aspires to marry a friend of mine, Elizabeth Bennet."

"Yes, Miss Bennet. I heard that she accompanied Alfreda to Gatesbridge and will attend my party. Other than that, I know only the gossip that surrounds her."

"Gossip?"

"That she is gentlewoman with no dowry and no connections and that is why my nephew thinks she will consent to marriage. However, I would caution any woman not to marry that braggart. I have even seriously considered not leaving him a farthing. The only reason I do not disinherit him is fear that he will blame Alfreda and confront her. She could never stand up to him if I am gone."

At Audrey's puzzled expression, she added, "My estate is not entailed, and I may leave it to whomever I wish. In fact, do not tell a soul, but I have changed my will. I have bequeathed fifty thousand pounds to Alfreda, and she will inherit a small estate near London. John is to get Hawthorne Hall and the rest of my fortune. So you see why I would like to see her married to David before I die. He believes that Alfreda will inherit only a small dowry, so he is no fortune hunter. I have no doubt he would protect her and keep John from gaining control of her inheritance."

"Since Wilkens is floundering in debt, I would fear for my life if I were you. Especially should he learn of the change in your will."

"I am certain my early demise would suit him immensely. I have fiercely loyal servants who guard my life, as well as two retired Bow-Street Runners hired for extra protection—bodyguards, if you will. They are rarely seen or heard even by my long-time servants. For instance, if you will look to the roof, you will see a man next to the chimney with a rifle." Audrey scanned the roof, finally setting eyes on the man when the sun glinted off the barrel of his weapon. His dark clothing blended in perfectly with the colour of the roof. "And near the end of the terrace is a guard in the shrubs along the wall."

Finding the other man, Lady Ashcroft exclaimed, "Amazing. I would never have seen either of them."

Violet Hawthorne laughed aloud. "That is the point of protection, is it not?"

"Still, it is a shame to have to be wary of your own kin."

"I am not the first or the last to have that problem. Just look at our monarchs. It has existed throughout history."

"In any event, I am relieved to know that you are safe. Now, I shall have to see if I can remove Miss Bennet from Wilkens' clutches. From your description, I fear that he may not let her leave as easily as she arrived. And I do want to warn her of his dissolute ways."

"I think that is a wise decision. After all, she is not yet engaged to him, as far as I know."

"Thank goodness for that. Now, let us make our plans to put the lovers together and to warn Miss Bennet."

⊙〤⊙

Gatesbridge Manor

As Elizabeth and Alfreda circled the garden, they said very little, each satisfied with the beautiful weather and time away from the master of the estate. Wilkens had hardly been in residence since the first day, staying in Town instead of at Gatesbridge. Alfreda made excuses for him, saying he was occupied with an important business matter that he hoped to resolve before long. This, of course, was no hardship for Elizabeth as she was glad to be free of his company. Finally reaching the end of the gravel walk that led back to the manor, Alfreda broke the silence.

"Would you prefer to go inside or shall we sit on the terrace to have our tea and biscuits?"

"It is such a beautiful day that I would prefer to stay outdoors."

"Then it is settled."

As they took the steps to the terrace, a newly-hired young maid stepped from the French doors that led into the drawing room, a letter in her hand. She executed a perfect curtsy before beaming at her mistress.

"Excuse me, madam, but this letter was just delivered for Miss Bennet."

Suddenly Mrs. Cuthbert appeared behind her, an expression of displeasure on her face. "What are you doing?"

"I … I was just delivering this letter to Miss—"

Grabbing the letter from the maid, Mrs. Cuthbert declared with much indignation, "You should not have assumed that was your responsibility. Go about your duties, and the next time, ask me before you presume anything."

Thoroughly chastised, the girl dropped another quick curtsy and fled in the direction from which she had come, visibly shaking. Meanwhile, Elizabeth had already stepped forward, holding out her hand, as she had been expecting a letter from Jane. Nevertheless, as she waited with palm extended, the housekeeper hesitated. Finally, Mrs. Cuthbert relented. Taken aback at the servant's manner, Elizabeth would not express any gratitude.

Aware that both ladies were eyeing her circumspectly and that Alfreda had already taken a seat, Mrs. Cuthbert changed the subject. "Shall I serve your tea and biscuits on the terrace?"

"Yes, please."

The old housekeeper disappeared as quickly as she had materialized, and Elizabeth looked to Alfreda. If her hostess noted the woman's attitude, she said nothing and Elizabeth's joy at having heard from Jane far outweighed her concerns over the belligerent servant. Thus, she slid a finger under the seal and unfolded the letter.

Already reading, her face aglow, Elizabeth began explaining to her friend. "This letter has been forwarded from the Holmes residence. I suppose Jane had not gotten my letter telling her I was accompanying you to Ramsgate when she posted this."

"What news of Hertfordshire?"

Elizabeth sat down as though her legs had gone weak, her face never leaving the paper though her expression brightened. "My sister is engaged to marry a wonderful man with sufficient means to take very good care of her. Is that not astonishing news?" She glanced up to note that Alfreda was no longer smiling. "Is there something the matter?"

Alfreda was having trouble hiding her disappointment. It was not lost on her that if one of the other Bennet sisters married well, then perhaps Elizabeth would not feel obligated to marry her brother in order to further her family. She was unable to form a reply, so Elizabeth continued.

"My sister is truly a good person, and the man she is marrying is her match in every way—kind, considerate, good-natured. I am exceedingly happy for her."

Alfreda could not control her shaky voice. "When are they to marry?"

"Jane writes that it will be the first part of September." Elizabeth whirled around in a circle, her arms extended as she celebrated. "Oh happy day! I could not be more thrilled."

"May I ask you something personal?"

Elizabeth came to an abrupt halt, the sound of Alfreda's voice an indication of her despondency. She nodded, fearing what was to come.

"You are not happy with my brother, are you?"

Elizabeth's eyes sought her shoes as her head swung right to left. "No, I am not."

"I see." Alfreda stood and walked to the edge of the terrace to stare into the distance. "I can understand why, and I do not fault you. Honestly, I do not. I suppose I was just so hopeful that I would finally have a sister." She turned to examine Elizabeth. "And you are so kind and so full of life. It would have been so nice to be your sister."

Astonished at her friend's openness, Elizabeth walked over to take Alfreda's hands. "We shall always be friends."

"I pray that we shall. But, let me caution you. Do not inform Brother of your decision until we are once again in London, and you are in the bosom of your family. I fear he will not take it well."

Elizabeth nodded even as Alfreda spoke, so she continued. "I am afraid that you may not understand the seriousness of this. He will be very angry. He has courted several women in recent months, all of whom have broken ties with him. To be honest, I know that he presumed, because of your circumstances, that you would not dare refuse him. I fear what he will do if he suspects you do not want to continue the courtship."

"Then I will take you advice and not mention it until we are back in London."

Alfreda sighed as though relieved. "Let us talk of it no more and strive to enjoy our short time together. We shall have a marvellous time at my aunt's party tomorrow. I just know that you will love Aunt Violet, as you remind me a lot of her."

"How so?"

"You have a mind of your own and are not afraid to express your opinions. I admire that."

"Anyone can express themselves."

Alfreda's smile vanished. "No. Not all of us have the courage or the opportunity."

At that moment, the housekeeper returned with a tray of tea and biscuits and their frank conversation ended. Alfreda retreated into her former reserved demeanour, and as they enjoyed their refreshments, Elizabeth was left to ponder all she had heard.

Chapter **23**

London
Angelo's Haymarket Room[9]

Colonel Richard Fitzwilliam stood poised to secure the match, totally oblivious to the uproar emanating from those who were shoving their way into the already crowded room, some still trying to place bets on the outcome. Having spent years maintaining his composure during the height of battle, the clamour did nothing to shake his concentration, though the colonel was certain that his cousin was worried to know that they had drawn such an audience.

Surreptitiously, he had sent one of the attendants to White's to spread the news that he and William were locked in a close battle to prove the better swordsman. He smiled at the bets he heard being placed—ten pounds, twenty—and even laughed aloud when someone shouted fifty and William's brow furrowed. Nevertheless, since there was a case of French brandy riding on the outcome, he was not sorry for the subterfuge he had employed to unnerve his worthy opponent.

Early on, he and William had exceptional luck and neither had taken a clear lead after fencing for the first half-hour. Taking a much needed break and savouring the moment, Richard whipped his blade about in several directions, making swishing sounds in the air as he sought to impress the crowd with his impatience to resume the match and end all speculation. Meanwhile, William finished his glass of water and wiped his forehead, all the while eyeing Richard with something akin to suspicion, due to the large number of spectators that had appeared out of nowhere. Even so, he looked calm as he moved back into position.

Richard winked at his cousin, calling out, *"En garde!"*

Taking advantage of the fact that William had just taken his stance, Richard advanced without further warning, managing to make a hit on his opponent's arm. Nevertheless, William was able to lift his sword in time to thwart the following lunge, and their weapons began clanking against each other in a steady pattern. Both accomplished swordsmen, they appeared as equally matched as they had throughout the early competition, though William's wrist moved the weapon

---

[9] *Angelo's Haymarket Room – A fencing academy run by Henry Angelo and then his sons. In 1770, the salle d'armes was at Carlisle House, overlooking Soho-square; then was moved to Opera House-buildings in Haymarket, next to Old Bond Street. The Regency Encyclopedia and www.georgianindex.net*

effortlessly compared to Richard's bold strokes.

While they parried in a circular direction, lunging and thrusting in turn as the bout escalated, it became clear that William was the more skilled of the two, and he scored several hits as he began to advance, forcing Richard to retreat. For a short while after, the swords clashed rapidly, and the match continued as first one then the other scored more light hits. Suddenly, Richard's sword was whipped from his grip by William's blade, landing several feet away. Richard threw up both hands in defeat and then bowed in a pronounced fashion.

"You have bested me again, Darcy!"

The crowd roared their approval and money quickly began to exchange hands as the noise level increased. In fact, if one wanted to be heard, one had to shout.

"It looks as though some have gotten rich off our efforts. Too bad we were not in for a cut!" Richard declared over the din as he stepped forward to clasp William's shoulder.

"I am afraid we are just a means to an end—entertainment for those who would rather gamble than fence. Let us wash off the sweat and have dinner and a drink at White's. It seems that all the membership has suddenly congregated here, so it should be a simple task to find a table."

Noting William's pointed remark, Richard offered, "You know how fast news travels, and White's is close by."

William swept his arm to indicate the noisy crowd. "And I am confident that you did not send them word of our match so as to arrange this assembly."

"Would I stoop so low, knowing how much you abhor being the focus of attention and how it might affect your performance?"

"In a heartbeat!" William quipped. At Richard's look of chastisement, he chuckled and slid an arm around his shoulder.

Richard brought both hands to his heart. "I am wounded at your insinuation."

"Then to alleviate my fears regarding your trustworthiness, perhaps you will buy my dinner."

"I am not THAT wounded. You should pay for mine, as you are the victor."

"Then perhaps I did not triumph after all."

"You are Fitzwilliam Darcy! You do not need to triumph. You are wealthy as sin."

"And you shall never let me forget, will you?"

"Never!"

White's Club

Enjoying the last bite of his beef and a sip of an expensive wine, Richard leaned back in his chair and sighed in satisfaction. "This is much better than what Mother had planned for tonight. I do not think I could have stood another boring dinner party."

"Oh yes, I forgot about the dinner party. I was invited, but I declined."

"Yes, Mother was not too happy about it either, so I imagine she will be livid that I did not make an appearance as well. And Father is getting quite put out with you. He said something about coming around to see you, so be warned."

"The earl may come, but that does not mean I shall be in!"

Richard guffawed. "Does that old ploy still work? I thought Father saw through that years ago."

"I am sure he has, but he cannot prove I am home, since he never gets past Mr. Barnes." His brow furrowed in thought. "I must remember to increase his pay. Besides, if I need to leave the house, I can still use the tunnel that comes out near the livery."

"I cannot believe Father still does not know about that tunnel after all these years. Uncle George must have used it thousands of times to avoid running into any of the Fitzwilliams he did not wish to encounter."

"He did and he taught me to do the same."

"Well, I, for one, appreciate the fact that you showed it to me. I have had to dodge Mother often enough by going out that way instead of using the front door. But I do think you may want to hear Father out this time. I suspect he wants to speak to you about the joint venture—the one you have Lowell investigating."

"Why do you say that?"

"As his solicitor was leaving the study, I heard the name Wexford mentioned along with our illustrious aunt, Lady Catherine. Wexford is one of the mills is it not?"

"Yes. Wexford, Stafford and Cunningham are the three in the venture started by Gisela's father, Lord de Bourgh and my father."

"Well, perhaps you should see what he wants. Who knows, maybe you will learn something that you did not know about the situation."

"I will think about it. At this moment, I would rather hear from Lowell first."

"You still have not heard from him?"

"No."

"I find that very odd. Do you want me to send a letter to one of my comrades stationed near Wexford to check on the mill? He could enquire if Lowell was still there?"

"That would be a starting point. Now, what say you to retiring to Darcy House and trying our hand at billiards?"

"If I am no better at billiards than fencing, I shall risk losing the rest of this month's pay! Exactly how much is a case of my favourite brandy?"

William laughed. "Do not worry about paying your debt just yet. I have no room in the cellar for more at this time. And let us agree not to bet on billiards, as I imagine we both need the practice. I have barely played since I returned from Hertfordshire."

"My fencing practice did me no favours, so I cannot see how practicing billiards will help. But I am willing if you are."

Both were still chuckling as they made their way out the door of White's, only to stop dead in their tracks at the sight of Gisela Darcy staggering out of a carriage which was at the bottom of the steps.

A large number of club members were exiting behind the cousins, and they too stopped short, anxious to observe what was going to happen. The ill will between

Mr. and Mrs. Darcy was well known in Town, and any meetings of the two had become legendary because of Mrs. Darcy's volatile temper. The steady increase in the noise level behind them heralded a swelling audience, and some patrons were now beginning to congregate on the walk below.

The spectators made William more ill at ease, and just as it seemed all of London was watching, Gisela wobbled precariously up the steps towards him. Her appearance was dishevelled, as evidenced by a gown in need of pressing and hair in want of a maid's touch. She reeked of alcohol.

"My darling husband!" she slurred as loudly as possible. "It looks as though we are destined to meet on the streets, since I am not allowed in your homes and you no longer attend any soirées—not even the Matlocks' dinner parties."

William stepped close to her, answering with quiet fury as he did not wish for all to hear. "If you were invited, then I am pleased I was not there."

"Oh, I was not invited, but as your wife, I could not be turned away. I suppose it makes you feel more of a man to avoid me and pretend I do not exist."

Richard had moved closer as well and put a steadying hand on William's shoulder when he saw his cousin's jaw tighten. William met his eyes before turning back to his nemesis. "You have Attenborough to attend you, or have you thrown him over already?"

"If you were more of a husband, I would not need him."

Richard gritted his teeth and stepped even nearer. In the past, Gisela had gone after William's face with her nails whenever his answers did not suit her.

Hoping to avoid sparring with her in public, William lowered his voice and spoke softly as he brushed past her while moving down the stairs. "Please leave. We have nothing to say to each other."

Gisela swirled around, almost losing her balance on the narrow steps as she followed after him, intent on making him face her. Grabbing his arm just as he reached the street, she declared, "I think we do! All of London knows that you have taken that little Hertfordshire chit, Eliza Bennet, as your mistress! Do you think I shall let that go unchallenged?"

Richard had never seen William so furious. His hands were clenched, and his face quickly coloured as he rounded on Gisela. Even in her inebriated state, her expression betrayed that she realized she had crossed the line, and she shrank back a step as he came towards her. Taking her left forearm none too gently William pulled her towards the still open door of her carriage. The footman attending the door had a peculiar smile on his face and uttered not a sound as he stepped back to allow his mistress to be forced inside. Then leaning into the conveyance, William stopped only inches from her face as he spoke in a forced whisper that only Richard heard because he had moved to shield his cousin's conversation from the now hushed crowd.

"I will say this only once, so listen carefully." The tone of William's warning made Gisela sober, and she wisely kept silent. "I am acquainted with Miss Bennet only because she is Mr. Bingley's future sister and has become good friends with Georgiana. She is a lady— a designation you will never attain. She would by no means become anyone's mistress. Should I hear that you have spread this scurrilous rumour, I shall see that the allowance we agreed upon and your other expenses are no longer paid. If necessary, I shall see that every farthing you have been promised is tied up in court until you are too old and infirm to spend whatever it might purchase. Do you understand me?"

Too numb to speak, Gisela only nodded, and William backed out of the doorway, slamming the door. He walked away leaving her with her jumbled thoughts and an aching arm.

For the first time in her life, Gisela feared that she might have gone too far, and William might make good on his promise to withdraw her means of support. Nevertheless, upon hearing the laughter of the crowd still gathered outside White's, she glanced to see fingers pointing in her direction, and her anxiety was quickly replaced by rage and the need to strike back. Mortified, she lowered the shades as her driver pulled away.

Had she been aware that once they had gotten underway the majority of the guffaws she heard had originated with her own servants, she would have fired them all.

You shall pay for this humiliation, Fitzwilliam!

William slammed his fist against the side of his carriage. "How could she have learned about Elizabeth? I have kept my feelings for her private."

"Perhaps your feelings are an open book, Cousin. It is not hard to read your thoughts when you gaze at her."

"Blast! I should have been more careful! Now I have exposed Elizabeth to gossip and ridicule."

"It is not your fault. Just remember that Gisela was never in company with you and Elizabeth, so she could not have picked up on your feelings by watching the two of you. The only way she could have learned about her existence and your love for her is for someone to have put the suggestion in her head. What you need to do is discover the identity of the informant."

William grew pensive. "You are right in that I have never been in company with them both. Who could have been so diligent as to figure it out and be so bold as to tell her? The only ones that are aware of my feelings for Elizabeth, besides her father, are you, Aunt Audrey, Georgiana and Bingley."

"Bingley— that is it!"

"You think Bingley told Gisela?"

"No, but his sister Caroline would gladly inform Gisela if she thought you had feelings for Miss Bennet, and it would hamper your progress. She would feel it would be to her advantage to stop anything from developing."

"What do you mean?"

"It is obvious from the way she has always pursued you that, in her twisted mind, she thinks she will be your next wife, if you divorce Gisela. Naturally, she would not want any competition for the title of the next Mrs. Darcy."

"If I thought that Caroline—I must find Charles and speak to him."

"Well, you are in luck!"

"And why do you say that?"

"Because he is just now descending the steps of Darcy House."

William leaned over to glance out the window on the other side of the carriage and watched Charles catch sight of them at the same instance. As his carriage came to a halt and the door opened, Bingley stood on the walk with a wide smile on his face.

"Darcy! I am glad you have returned, as I was just about to leave." He glanced at Richard. "Colonel, it is a pleasure to see you again."

Richard only had time to nod before William proceeded out the carriage door and began talking animatedly. "Charles, you must come back inside. I have something important to discuss with you."

Both men were halfway up the stairs before Richard set foot on the pavement. He shook his head at the bemused footman who still held the carriage door. Then straightening his coat, he followed the other men up the stairs and into the house. By the time he reached the foyer, Bingley and William had already gone down the hall towards the study, and Richard headed in that direction at a brisk pace.

Later that evening, William and Richard were enjoying a cigar as they sat in the library watching the sunset through the large expanse of windows stretching the length of one wall. This bank of windows sported sparse curtains on either side so that the view to the gardens beyond as well as the evening skies could be enjoyed without obstruction.

Today had been full—with the fencing match, Gisela's appearance and Bingley's visit—so they were both fatigued, and Richard was not nearly as energetic as usual when he at long last boasted, "So I was right—Caroline Bingley was the culprit."

"Yes, but if she had not confessed to Charles because she thought he was already aware of her ploy, we might never have had proof. Who could have foreseen that she would be so heartless as to send an unsigned letter disparaging Elizabeth?"

"I could and did! I have never liked that woman. She is nothing but an opportunist and a slanderer."

William released a heavy sigh. "But I hate to think she would stoop so low because of her mistaken ideas about me. Elizabeth has never done anything to harm her and never would."

"At least Bingley was man enough to take action. Caroline's reduced circumstances and new residence will likely prevent her from causing further trouble."

"Though I fear she did harm enough by informing Gisela. Nevertheless, Charles acted decisively, I will give him that. He is just as disgusted with Caroline and worried about the consequences of her actions."

"I can hardly believe that Bingley has finally found his *angel* and has requested the hand of Miss Jane Bennet. Now all that is left is for you to secure the same promise from her younger sister."

William stood and moved to the windows, taking hold of the frame and staring into the now fading sunlight as he gathered his thoughts. Richard knew not to interrupt when he was this pensive, so he said nothing.

"How can I pursue Elizabeth now? Even though I threatened Gisela, I know she has already spread that falsehood, and I have no doubt that she will continue to tell it to anyone who will listen as revenge triumphs over prudence. In fact, she has probably told your mother, since they were most likely in each other's company tonight."

"Do not worry about Mother. I will explain to her what is in the cards for Gisela and suggest she defend Miss Bennet to the *ton* if she wants to be on the appropriate side when the dust has settled."

"I hope your mother pays heed this time. I have ignored her support of Gisela in the past, mainly because I did not care to associate with either of them." He glanced at Richard. "Forgive me if I have offended you."

"No offence taken. I am not proud of my parents' choices concerning Gisela."

"In any event, I shall not forgive any slight to Elizabeth. She is everything lovely and decent and God knows that Gisela is good for nothing but ruining lives. How will I ever face her now that my wife is spreading rumours that she is my mistress?"

Richard walked over to stand beside William. "Your Miss Bennet is not a child, William. I imagine that she is a lot wiser in the ways of the world than you suspect. I can also imagine that she will not let any falsehood crush her spirit. She is no shrinking violet and is strong and defiant in the face of adversity. You should know that by the way she confronted you at the Holmes' ball."

William could not stop the smile that came to his face at the remembrance of her actions that night, but it was short-lived. "Still, Elizabeth should not have to deal with problems created by my marriage. Her sister is to marry Bingley, and that will bring her into the company of men of wealth. Perhaps not earls and viscounts, but men of trade who have substantial wealth—like Charles."

"So at the first sign of trouble, you cast her aside like so much chaff—as though she is not worth fighting for."

William whirled around, his features dark with fury. "How dare you say that! I am only thinking of her welfare. Before she met me, she was an innocent—her reputation above reproach. She deserves better than to endure the *ton's* ridicule on my behalf!"

"She already has their ridicule! She is a country girl with values and a good head on her shoulders, but she is nothing to them because she has no connections, no wealth. At least if you marry her, you shall have felicity with the woman you love, and she shall have a good life with a man who worships her."

"But by marrying me, she will be abandoning all hope of acceptance by society."

"Miss Elizabeth does not impress me as someone who holds the *ton* in high regard. I have observed her often enough at events in Town to gauge that already. And you have never cared for the dictates of the *ton*. Marry her, Darcy, and take her home to Pemberley. Raise a house full of children, and let the rest of the world go to blazes."

"You make it sound so easy."

"It will not be easy, just achievable."

"God help me, I want to believe that. I cannot let go of the dream of her. I did not realise how numb I had become—not until she made me feel alive again. If I had to give her up now ..." William could not finish.

"Then, do not give her up. Fight for her."

"Only she can give me that right, and the last we talked she was convinced we had no future."

"That was before she spent the week in Lord Wilkens' company at Ramsgate. The moment she returns to London you must convince her that you have a future together. I, for one, think it not so hard a task. It was obvious to Aunt Audrey that she was in love with you during their first meeting in the park."

"I pray you are right and she still loves me. The thought of her as my wife is all that keeps me sane at this moment."

Grantham House

Gisela stormed through the house, cursing as she picked up various breakable items and tossed them in crumpled piles of porcelain and glass. All the while, as she advanced through the foyer and up the grand staircase towards her sitting room, servants, men and women alike, ran to hide from her wrath—everyone but Jemima.

Being Gisela's personal maid, it was not possible to hide, as the mistress was calling out her name at the top of her lungs, so Jemima waited at the top of the stairs and paled when she noted the condition of the once lovely coral gown that Gisela wore. Jemima tried to remember what day she had retrieved that particular item from her mistress' closet—was it two days ago or three? She could not recall. The one thing of which she was certain was that Mrs. Darcy had not returned home last night or the night before, and the stench of the alcohol on her breath was making her nauseous.

"Where have you been, you sorry girl?"

"I have been here as usual, madam."

"Quiet! I do not wish to hear your excuses!"

Gisela stomped into her bedroom, followed by Jemima, who began helping her mistress out of the gown she was struggling to peel off with no luck. So inebriated that she could not handle the buttons, Gisela quit trying and let the girl finish the task. Finally, clad only in her chemise, she rounded on the maid again.

"Go prepare my bath and be quick about it. Lord Attenborough will be here shortly to take me to a ball." Jemima curtsied quickly and turned to go. "Stop! Do you think you are too good to answer me?"

"No, madam."

"Then execute a proper curtsey and answer me before you leave!"

Jemima had had enough. She had secured a more lucrative job with Lady Carrollton that was to begin next week, and she was certain that the housekeeper there would let her stay in the servants' quarters until her position began.

"I will tell the footman to bring up your bath, Mrs. Darcy, but I will not be helping you with it, as I am no longer going to be your maid. I was waiting until you returned to inform you that I have found another position."

Gisela went wild with anger, grabbing Jemima by the shoulders and shaking her. "You cannot leave me! I have lost too many maids already. You will stay! Do you hear me? You will stay!"

Jemima managed to pull free of her grip and ran down the stairs towards the servants' quarters where she had hidden her already packed bag. Quickly grabbing it, she gave the housekeeper a solemn nod before running out the back door.

Upstairs, Gisela gathered her wits and did not call after her errant maid. Instead, she flopped back on the bed crying loudly. The rest of the household staff tiptoed around the house, ignoring her complaints until she quieted—apparently asleep.

Thus, when Lord Attenborough arrived later that evening to escort Gisela to the ball, he was informed that the mistress was indisposed. Highly agitated, he left in a huff.

Had he seen the lady in question, however, he would have been relieved to have been saved the awkwardness of the situation. Gisela Darcy had finished off the balance of a bottle of brandy that had been sitting on her dressing table. Still clad in her malodorous chemise, she was presently lying face down on the rug in front of the fireplace, snoring as loudly as any man.

Chapter **24**

Ramsgate
Hawthorne Hall
The Dining Room

Georgiana found it hard to contain her excitement. Gazing around the magnificently decorated room filled with hundreds of beautiful people all dressed in their finest attire, she was awestruck.

This was not how she had imagined Lady Hawthorne's birthday party would be when she was first informed of it. In fact, from her aunt's description, she had thought it would be a picnic on the lawn, but the picnic yesterday had only begun the celebration and now she found herself dressed in finery and seated next to the honouree at a lavish dinner party. As she turned to share something with Elizabeth who was seated on her left, she found her conversing with the man sitting across the table. Consequently, Georgiana turned to speak with her hostess and found the free spirited woman leaning in to say something to her as well.

"I am so proud that you accepted my invitation to be my special guest tonight, Georgiana. You look very lovely."

"Thank you. I am delighted my aunt allowed me to participate. This is my first dinner party that was not entirely comprised of my family."

Lady Hawthorne smiled as she glanced across the table to the now empty chairs where Audrey Ashcroft and Alfreda Wilkens had been seated only moments before. She was pleased that her little conspiracy was being carried out according to plan. Outwardly she showed no unease as she glanced back to Georgiana.

"Audrey was kind to grant my request that you be allowed to attend. I know that you are not yet out in society, but I did not want you to miss my birthday dinner. Besides, a young girl has to start somewhere!"

"And what a lovely place to begin!" Georgiana trumpeted, stealing another glance around the room. "I feel like a debutant." Then she began to splutter. "But … but do not tell my brother, or he shall lock me in the attic until I am at least one and twenty."

"Fitzwilliam is a bit old-fashioned is he not? I shall be sure and tell Audrey not to mention how much you enjoyed tonight. She will not breath a word, I assure you."

That statement was followed by the hostess' customary loud chuckles which reverberated across the room, causing everyone to glance in their direction. Georgiana blushed as all eyes fixed on them, but after a few seconds the guests returned to their own conversations, and she sighed in relief. Then she noted the empty chairs and enquired, "Where has my aunt gone? Should I go after her and see if she needs anything?"

"She and Alfreda went outside for a breath of fresh air. Do not worry your pretty head about them as they should return shortly I would imagine.

Georgiana's attention was quickly diverted by a piece of cake now being placed in front of her. She promptly began to devour it, providing her hostess a respite from her questions. Sighing in relief, Violet Hawthorne was about to enjoy her own slice of cake when an old friend stood to offer a toast. The room quieted as he tapped a piece of silverware on his crystal goblet to get their attention.

"Ladies and gentlemen, it is not often that I get to honour someone with a toast who is …" Lord Walter Hornsby stopped to gauge Lady Hawthorne's reaction with a twinkle in his grey eyes.

"Walter, do not dare!" Lady Hawthorne warned, her tone ominous though her slight smile suggested otherwise. "Just remember that I shall have the chance to retaliate at your birthday."

"… the youngest in spirit of any woman of my acquaintance!"

All the guests laughed. And beaming with satisfaction, Lord Hornsby continued. "May you have many, many more birthdays and may they be as joyous as this one."

Violet Hawthorne glowed as he and the entire company lifted their glasses in a salute and Georgiana leaned in to whisper. "I think he favours you."

She was surprised when her hostess blushed without replying.

In the garden, Lady Ashcroft was trying to appear as inconspicuous as possible while standing several feet away from the young couple. She was hidden from view of the house by some ornamental trees and shrubs, but her eyes were trained on the French doors through which they had escaped the house. It was not yet dark, and she could see clearly until the sun disappeared entirely. Very aware that it would not do for John Wilkens to find his sister with the colonel, Lady Ashcroft was determined that he would not. Thus, she acted as a sentry and though she could not hear what Alfreda or the colonel said, just the fact that they had rushed into each other's arms had convinced her that Lady Hawthorne was right—they were still in love, and that made all the danger worthwhile.

As she stood guard, her chest swelled with satisfaction at the thought of thwarting John Wilkens' plans for Alfreda. Reminded of her own intrigues—defying her father and meeting Joseph in the gardens at Matlock during balls and dinner parties—she felt she could do no less. The Earl of Matlock had not been in favour of Joseph's suit, instead pressing her to marry a much older, wealthier earl. Like Fitzwilliam, Joseph was very wealthy but had no title. But her heart had been Joseph's from the moment she had set eyes on him, and she would not be deterred. After spending one entire season dodging the man her father had championed, Edward Fitzwilliam had realized that Audrey would never relent, and he had given Joseph permission for a courtship. She smiled to think that it had come just in the nick of time, as they had begun planning a trip to Gretna Green.

Lost in her memories, Lady Ashcroft was startled to hear the sound of two men talking and peered around the trees just in time to see Lord Landingham walk out onto the terrace. He was arguing with the very man she was trying to avoid, John Wilkens, who had stopped just ahead of him. Wilkens looked upset at first, but whatever Landingham was saying seemed to be calming him, and before long, both men turned and went back into the house. Audrey sighed in relief and glanced to the swing where the two young people, totally lost in each other, seemed unaware of what had just transpired. It was time to spirit Alfreda back into the house.

Stepping towards them, she spoke softly, "Alfreda."

The young woman jumped up from the swing, her eyes wide with fright. "My brother has arrived?"

"Yes, but he has been diverted from the gardens. It is best you accompany me back into the house straightaway."

Cochran had already stood and put a calming hand on Alfreda's shoulder. At Lady Ashcroft's pronouncement, he turned her so she had to look into his eyes. "Trust me, and do not be afraid. Your aunt will see that we are allowed to marry."

Alfreda nodded her head in agreement. "It is just… I know that Brother will be terribly unhappy with me and angry with you when he learns of our plans."

"Remember, he does not know about our reunion tonight, so he has no reason to be angry. He will not be happy to learn of my presence here, of that we can be certain, but he has no idea what we are planning. And he will not learn anything until Lady Hawthorne is ready to take control of the situation."

She reached for his hands. "Please be careful. My brother can be ruthless."

"I do not fear him. It is he who should fear me." The colonel leaned down to place a chaste kiss on her trembling lips. "Be brave, my love. We shall be man and wife ere long."

"That is all that keeps me strong. I love you, David."

Another soft kiss followed. "As I love you."

Audrey Ashcroft reached out to take Alfreda's hand, and with an apologetic smile towards Cochran, pulled them apart, advising him, "Hurry around to the front door and come in as though you are just now arriving."

The colonel nodded and swiftly walked towards the side of the manor. Guiding Alfreda towards the steps to the terrace, Audrey Ashcroft declared, "Remember, you accompanied me to the gardens because I felt unwell."

"I will remember that and Lady Ashcroft—" Audrey turned as the younger woman came to a stop. "Thank you for helping us."

A quick nod and smile were all there was time for as they hurried into the house. Just as they entered the main hallway, they encountered Alfreda's suspicious brother coming out of the dining room, obviously more upset than before. A weary looking Marshall Landingham was right on his heels, his expression one of extreme irritation until he saw Audrey. Smiling slightly, it was obvious that his patience with chaperoning Wilkens was wearing thin.

"There you are! Where have you been?" Wilkens exclaimed immediately upon seeing his sister. "I have been looking for you since I arrived. Miss Bennet never left the dining room, but you—"

Lady Ashcroft rose to her full height, interrupting the ill-bred man. "Your sister was kind enough to accompany me to the garden when I fell ill," she reached to take Alfreda's hand. "I was fortunate to be seated with her, as she was more interested in my health than the dinner being served. Most of the guests were so busy they did not notice my distress."

Wilkens turned to assail Landingham. "I was right! I told you we should have searched the gardens!"

"So you were," was all the older man uttered, though he was having considerable trouble keeping a straight face.

Wilkens studied Lady Ashcroft carefully before fixing his gaze back on his sister. Apparently he believed their ruse and abruptly changed his attitude, though his expression did not soften, and it was evident he was not pleased.

"How fortunate my sister was available to be of service. Now, if you will excuse us, I am certain my aunt expects her closest relations to take part in her birthday dinner. Come Alfreda!"

Lady Ashcroft stepped back to allow the siblings to pass. She followed their progress until they were completely out of sight. "What a pompous—!"

Landingham guffawed. "You have no idea! I was so tired of following him about that I was considering knocking him unconscious, tying him up with a rope and depositing him in the cellar."

She smiled widely. "We are too much alike! I am afraid I have never suffered fools gladly nor minced words, and my disposition has not improved with age."

Her old friend paused, reaching out to lift her chin with his forefinger so they gazed into each other's eyes. "I love that you do not mince words, Audrey. Do you know how refreshing it is to know exactly what a woman is thinking? I am afraid that I have spent most of my life trying to decipher what a lady meant whenever she opened her mouth."

Her expression saddened as her eyes drifted downward. "Even if what I think does not agree with what you desire?"

He took her hand and began pulling her toward the empty library through which they had come from the garden. Closing the door behind them, he pulled her into an embrace.

"Well, perhaps not then. You have known for some time how I feel about you, but I am willing to wait until you feel the same way about me."

She reached to cup his face. "Oh, Marshall, you are too good. I have put you off for so long and yet you remain constant."

"I love you, Audrey. Nothing can change that, and if you never agree to marry me, I shall remain your suitor until I die."

Lady Ashcroft lifted on tiptoes to kiss him lightly. "It is a wonder that some woman did not secure your heart long ago. Was there not one in all these years?"

She could see his expression sober in the waning light that streamed through the large windows. Seeing the heartache in his reflection, she regretted her words immediately.

"I do care for you very much. You know that. But you must also accept that I shall never love anyone as I loved Joseph. Can you live with that knowledge?"

"Truthfully, I am not jealous of what you had with your husband. From the little I knew of him, I thought him a good and decent man. And I understand the difficulty of opening your heart to someone new after experiencing a deep, abiding love. I loved a woman for over twenty years, but she did not return my affection in the same way. That is why I never married."

"Did she marry?"

"Yes. She married a friend, which made it difficult for me, since I had to be in her company often over the years. We did remain friends as well."

"Do you love her still?"

"She died." Landingham looked pensive for a moment before managing a smile. "And then I met you, and in spite of my oath never to love again, I could not help falling in love with you. Perhaps it is a different kind of love, a mature love, but I just want to make you happy for the time we have left." He lifted her hand and placed a soft kiss there. "Let me."

"I feel an obligation to stay with Georgiana until she is married. Afterward, I shall be glad to talk of our future if you still desire it."

Landingham leaned down to kiss her, and this kiss was more demanding than any they had previously shared. Amazed when feelings she had thought long dead stirred deep within, Audrey gladly returned his kiss, and they were lost for a time in each other. Only the sounds of numerous footsteps in the hallway outside reminded them that they were not alone. He broke the kiss, then gently cupped her face and studied it as if memorizing every feature.

Sighing with the realization that she was truly happy, Audrey whispered, "I pray that you will renew your proposal at that time."

The smile that spread across his face was sincere and filled with love. "You may rely on it, my dear."

Slipping into the hall behind the other guests, reluctantly, they released their joined hands and followed the throng moving towards the ballroom where chairs had been set up and entertainment was about to begin. Nonetheless, just before they entered the room, Audrey Ashcroft sought his hand for one last squeeze— recognition of what they both knew had transpired a few moments ago. A fissure in the facade she had built around her heart had occurred and their relationship would never be the same.

Kent
Rosings
Lady Catherine's Drawing Room

Mr. Ferguson, a rotund, balding man of about five and thirty years, shifted uneasily in the ornate, gilded chair as he waited for his client to appear. Trying to focus on the gaudily decorated walls featuring unclothed women, he was not able to keep his emotions under good regulation. Instead, his face twitched involuntarily as he remembered the occasion, five years before, when he assumed his father's practice and began dealing with Lady de Bourgh. Now it was plain that he had been too young and inexperienced to comprehend her manipulations or to stand up to her if he had. And he was certain that he was now too deeply involved in her misdeeds to just walk away. In a word, he feared he knew too much.

She kept nothing from him, including the fact that she paid Mr. Wickham to spy on the Darcys for many years and still used him whenever she needed his expertise. However, it was her decision to murder his fellow solicitor, Mr. Lowell, that proved his client was not averse to disposing of anyone she deemed to be standing in her way, and he knew he could easily be the next object of her ire. Never desirous of being involved in any of the dubious aspects of the woman's business dealings, he was appalled when it took a deadly turn without any consultation on his part. Lady de Bourgh just assumed that he would not object. Moreover, just as he had resolved to escape this very meeting under the guise of being ill, he was interrupted by the arrival of the mistress of the estate. Lady de Bourgh swept into the room, her silk skirts swishing with every step.

"I cannot believe I have not heard anything from that scoundrel, Wickham, in the last week," she complained loudly, not really expecting him to answer. "How am I to know what is happening unless he sends me word?"

Lady Catherine did not sit, but instead paced the room like a caged animal. Finally stopping to pour herself a glass of brandy, she studied Ferguson but did not offer him a drink. Upon their first meeting, she had informed him that she wanted her advisors of sound mind and not addled by alcohol, so she would not provide liquor. Suddenly she lay into him, the swiftness of her assault making him start.

"What have you done about Lowell's affairs? I pay you well, and you have done nothing to my knowledge!"

"He … he has not been declared dead, madam. In fact, I do not think anyone has missed him as of yet. He has no immediate family, you see."

"What is that to you or me?" Lady Catherine exclaimed, downing the rest of her glass. "We KNOW he is dead, so go into his office and see what you can find out about his research on my nephew's behalf!"

"I cannot go into his office until there is some reason to suspect he is missing or dead. If I were discovered there beforehand, it would look suspicious. I could lose my license or worse."

She dismissed his concerns with a wave of her hand. "I care not about such things. Break into his office at night, if necessary. I must know what he has learned and what he has told my nephew."

"Madam, you do not pay me enough to lose my license—my very living. I shall volunteer to look into his business affairs once it is common knowledge that he is missing and not a moment before." He paled to see her eyes narrow.

"You will do well to remember that, by and large, it is I who provides your living." She studied him for a long moment before continuing. "Very well, then you must be the one to raise the alarm about his disappearance. As a colleague and fellow tenant of the building, report him to the authorities as missing. Just as soon as you are taken seriously, offer to take over his cases and inspect his files."

Mr. Ferguson stood, hoping to vacate the place as soon as possible. His knees were knocking, though he tried not to let it show. "You can rely on me, madam."

"I hope you do not disappoint me. Have you finished the report on the joint venture—the one that shows we are making a profit this quarter?"

He flushed to think he had forgotten about the report. "I have changed the account to show a profit, yes."

"Good. Let me see it. I did not have you come all this way just for company."

Fishing in the small case he was carrying, he handed a copy to her as she settled in a chair. He remained standing. Every so often, she would grunt or make some other sound to indicate her approval or disapproval with what she read. Finally concluding, she tossed the paper on a nearby table.

"I hope the profit will convince my nephew to put off further inspection when he learns Lowell is dead. By then, I hope he will be more disturbed by my niece's marriage than business dealings."

"I imagine he already feels he has no say on the joint venture, what with Mrs. Darcy always voting with you." Immediately the solicitor knew he had said the wrong thing.

"Mr. Ferguson, you are treading on dangerous ground. Perhaps it is time for you to return to London and present a copy of this report to my nephew."

Shakily reaching for his hat which sat in the chair next to him, he responded, "Yes. I would like to return home before dark."

Lady Catherine stood, and without another word, exited the room. Relieved, Ferguson hurried towards the front door of Rosings, grateful that he had not given the butler his hat or coat. There were no servants in sight, and he did not wish to wait for either item in order to leave. Clearing the door as quickly as possible, he asked a footman outside to send for his coach and waited on the portico for it to appear.

As once more his coach passed through the imposing gates of Rosings, Mr. Ferguson breathed an audible sigh of relief. He had once again met with the most dangerous woman of his acquaintance and lived to speak of it. He was fortunate indeed.

∞✕∞

Meryton
Longbourn
The Kitchen

"Jane!" Mrs. Bennet screeched as she entered the front door of Longbourn following her morning walk to Meryton. The smell of bread baking wafted through the rooms, as today was the day Mrs. Hill made all the bread for the week. Consequently, her stomach began to grumble in anticipation of a slice as she divested herself of her bonnet and shawl.

Meanwhile, Jane Bennet took a deep breath, bracing herself for what she knew would come next. She had had no trouble hearing the greeting all the way in the far corner of the kitchen where she had gone to collect her baskets. Seeing Mrs. Hill stop her chores to glance her way, she gave the long-time servant a wan smile.

"I am here, Mama," she answered dutifully. The elderly servant just shook her head sympathetically and resumed kneading her bread dough.

Sweeping into the room, Fanny Bennet began immediately, "Hill, I cannot wait to have a piece of your delicious bread with …" Abruptly she stopped and eyed her oldest and most prized daughter carefully. "What is that you are wearing?"

Jane looked down at the faded blue muslin with several patches along the hem. The gown was serviceable and would do for gathering herbs as she had planned. Before she could explain her choice of clothes, however, her mother was expounding on the art of keeping a fiancé as she simultaneously pulled her prize towards the hallway.

"Oh, no, no, no! You should never be seen in anything this old and worn. Heaven forbid Mr. Bingley should return unannounced and see you in this old thing! Without a doubt, he would think twice about his proposal, and what do you think his sisters would do?" She began pushing her towards the main staircase. "They are such fine ladies that they would be appalled to be related to you and who could blame them."

"But, Mama, this old gown is what I wear for—"

Mrs. Bennet grabbed Jane's shoulders and turned her so that they were eye to eye. "Jane, I shall not say this again. Go and change your clothes and then hand me this gown. I shall have Hill burn it."

Before Jane could reply, she found herself being twirled back around to face the stairs. "And come down as soon as you are presentable. I checked the post in Meryton, and there was a letter from your Aunt Gardiner. I hid it from Kitty and Lydia, as I did not want them begging to accompany us to London when we purchase your wedding clothes. In fact, I suggested they visit Maria Lucas so that we could have time alone to make our plans."

Jane was too upset to reply and so she did as she was instructed. She was not about to argue with her mother regarding a gown, sure that there would be more important things on which to stand firm later. However, she wondered about the letter. Quickly donning a better gown with a maid's help, Jane was seated across from her mother at the small table in the parlour in only a short while. She sat in silence as Mrs. Bennet seemed to be re-reading the missive. Finally, she could stand it no more.

"Mama? What does Aunt Gardiner have to say? Does she mention Lizzy?"

"Your aunt's sister has had a difficult delivery, and that has taken Madeline away from London for longer than she had anticipated. However, she is beginning to rally now, and Madeline can see the end of her stay. We were just fortunate that Lady Holmes took Lizzy under her protection and allowed her to travel to Ramsgate with Lady Wilkens." All the while she had been studying the paper, but at this point she met Jane's eyes. "I was upset with your aunt when I first realised that she would not be there to show Lizzy about Town, but it has turned out to our advantage. At present, your sister has caught the eye of a very wealthy man and has become the particular friend of his sister."

Jane showed no emotion, feigning no knowledge of this news. By now she was certain that Lizzy was not enamoured of John Wilkens or his money and would never accept him—certain because of the expresses she received in the morning whilst her mother and sisters were off to Meryton. Receiving these letters without detection had proved invaluable in keeping Lizzy's secret, and Jane was thankful that Lady Holmes had allowed the use of the express rider while her sister resided there. Nonetheless, the expresses had stopped once Lizzy began the trip to Gatesbridge and Jane was beginning to worry. Wishing not to dwell on what might happen whilst her sister was out of touch, she changed the subject, mentioning something dear to her mother's heart.

"Will Aunt be back in London soon?"

"Oh yes! She assures me that she will return in one week and will send word so that you and I may hurry there to begin planning your trousseau." Mrs. Bennet's expression resembled a spider eyeing a fly. "Perhaps, if we are fortunate, there shall be two orders to place by then."

"Mama, I am quite certain that Lizzy would want to be well acquainted with any man before they married, and she is not even being courted as far as I have heard."

"Nonsense! The time to get to know any man is *after* you marry. Beforehand, all you need to know is his income and the amount of your pin money."

"MOTHER!"

"It is true. One man is very much like another. They enjoy horses, hunting, being around other men, good food and plenty of time in their wife's bed. At least until she becomes with child—then they have no use for her."

"You cannot classify every man that way. Some are decent, like my Mr. Bingley. He will love and cherish me, of that I am certain."

"That is what you think, but he will change down the road. They all do. The secret is to develop your own life apart from him and find happiness where you may. That is what I had to do."

Jane huffed as she stood. "I intend to be a helpmeet to my husband and his best friend. We shall raise our children in an atmosphere of love and respect, nothing less."

Mrs. Bennet waved a hand in frustration. "You were always too optimistic, Jane. Life is never a bed of roses. Along with the roses come the thorns. You shall see."

"No, it is you who shall see, Mother. Not all people marry for the wrong reasons or the wrong people. Some people love one another and have happy marriages."

With that Jane stalked from the room, her head held high. Mrs. Bennet shook her head in resignation as she watched her daughter walk away.

You shall learn, my poor, naive girl. You shall learn just as Lizzy will. You and she were always too high-minded to listen to me.

Chapter 25

Ramsgate
Gatesbridge Manor
Wilkens' Study

Navigating the various hallways leading to her brother John's study, Alfreda's heart beat furiously. The three of them—she, John and Elizabeth—were supposed to leave shortly for a trip to Town, but this last minute summons from her brother had dashed any hopes she had for a pleasant outing. Being sent for by him almost always meant trouble, and as she travelled along the corridor, she began to speculate on which of his personalities would be there to greet her. Would it be the kind and conciliatory brother of her childhood who was civil when he needed her help, or would she be met by the irate despot who surfaced most often of late?

Possible developments ran through her mind as she walked. Could he have possibly discovered her meeting with David at their aunt's dinner party? If so, would he lock her in her rooms as he had done when David asked to court her last year? How she wished David had not been called back to duty! Oh if he were still here to protect and comfort her. Her mind raced, and she found that she could not think logically. At last, standing before the dreaded door, there was no alternative but to face him without any strategy. Taking a deep breath, she knocked.

A familiar voice called out, "Come," he said in a stoic voice devoid of feeling.

Opening the door cautiously, Alfreda stepped just inside and closed it without making a sound. John appeared to be reading something and did not acknowledge her presence until he had finished entirely. Then, throwing the paper aside, he motioned for her to sit in the chair positioned in front of the desk. Moving across the familiar space, Alfreda recalled the times their father had been the one sitting behind the elaborately carved oak desk, and despite her determination to show no emotion, her eyes filled with tears. When he had been alive, the rich woods and muted colours of this study had exuded warmth and security; whereas now, these attributes seemed cold and impersonal. With the passing of her father, she had learned that a room—nay, an entire house—could adopt the personality of its owner, for good or ill. Taking a seat before the current master of Gatesbridge, Alfreda folded her hands in her lap and stared at her feet.

"I have a request of you." Alfreda's eyes came up to meet his. His voice was emotionless. "I want you to stay close to Miss Bennet today and see that she does not embarrass me."

"I do not think Eliz—Miss Bennet is capable of embarrassing you. She is a lady."

"Evidently you are not very observant. She is also a very stubborn and opinionated woman, wilful attributes that I plan to curb once we are married, but for now, we must both guard her carefully. What she did at our aunt's dinner party was appalling, and it cannot happen again. My future wife should be above reproach."

Alfreda searched her memory but could think of nothing that Elizabeth had done to bring shame on him or their family. Wilkens must have judged from her quizzical brow that she was struggling to recall.

"There were numerous lapses in protocol, but if you will remember, I had to intervene when she engaged in a long conversation with Mr. Chandler after the entertainment ended." Wilkens stood and faced the cabinet that sat behind his desk. Pouring himself a glass of brandy he took a swallow, unaware of the expression of complete unbelief on his sister's face. "Several of my colleagues were eyeing her warily, and ultimately, I had to escort her into another room to end their little *tète-a-tète*. Why our aunt would invite that man to such an impressive occasion is a mystery to me. He has no connections to speak of and nothing but a crumbling estate now that he has sold practically everything he owns to pay his creditors."

Alfreda pictured the handsome man in her mind's eye. She was certain that his fair countenance was one reason her brother had been irritated with his conversation with Miss Bennet. "Mr. Chandler's father was Uncle Joseph's closest friend, and he has continued to support our aunt. She often mentions his visits to me, saying he is one of a few friends that are genuinely concerned for her wellbeing."

Wilkens studied his sister, apparently not happy with the challenge in her eyes or her tone of voice. "Humph! His father may have been a friend, but Chandler is nothing but a ne'er-do-well and gambler who hangs on to our aunt in order to associate with a society than he can no longer access on his own."

Alfreda continued to object. "Aunt said it was not he who gambled away his inheritance, but his late father. And she championed the son for paying his father's debts after he died."

Wilkens slammed his glass down on the oak desk sending the contents splashing across the polished surface and a few papers. Resting the fingers of both hands on the smooth top, he leaned across the desk menacingly. "Do not argue with me! I know what of I speak! He is of no consequence, do you hear!"

Silently chastising herself for arguing with him, Alfreda said quietly, "Yes…I heard you."

Pleased, he continued his line of reasoning. "Now, as I was saying, this is likely the last time Miss Bennet shall be in public before we return to London, and I cannot allow her to do anything, such as conversing with the lower classes, that might cast a negative light on me in Ramsgate. Much is riding on my ability to induce the upper echelons of society to invest in the venture that my associates and I have designed—an entirely new area of town featuring a luxury hotel, coffee houses, clubs and shops. Suffice it to say that we foresee Ramsgate overtaking London as the most important city in England. After all, we have the seaport to our advantage."

"What could Elizabeth possibly do to hurt your venture?"

"Must I explain everything? The men I must impress will only trust their fortunes to those that are their equals in society, and they must believe my future wife will be among their number. From this point forward, Miss Bennet should be seen and not heard. Once I convince the right men to begin construction of hotels and shops on our tract, I shall be so wealthy that no one will be able to touch me."

"Why have I heard nothing of this before now?"

"There was no reason that you should have been informed. Women are to concern themselves with domestic refinements, nothing more."

Alfreda flinched but did not reply. She had already incurred his wrath by saying too much. Moreover, now that David had returned, she could see how mistaken she had been to encourage Elizabeth to marry John just because she desired her company. It was a selfish goal, as no one deserved a husband such as her brother, and had Elizabeth decided upon the match, her lively nature would be crushed under his iron fist.

Wilkens had ceased speaking. When she became aware of his gaze, she looked down to her feet, a sign he always considered one of submission. "It is settled then? I can depend on you to keep Elizabeth in line?"

Alfreda nodded. At the end of the dinner party, Aunt Violet had opportunity to whisper the plan to inform her brother about the engagement to Colonel Cochran once she was safely ensconced in Lady Holmes' residence in Town. If her brother wanted to inherit Hawthorne Hall, he would have to agree with their aunt's conditions. Alfreda smiled to herself, for she knew how much John wanted that inheritance.

For now, though, she and Elizabeth had to endure only a few more days before they would both be free. They had been in luck as John spent most of this visit in Ramsgate, even the nights, working on his project. Once in London, Alfreda was confident that her friend would put an end to the supposed courtship. Wordlessly, she made a promise to do all in her power to support Elizabeth against the wrath of her brother after he learned her decision. Furthermore, she would earnestly pray that her friend would find a man who would truly care for her—someone as kind and honourable as her David.

Hawthorne Hall

As Barney Giles, a footman of long standing in the household, helped Lady Hawthorne into the waiting carriage, he noted that she seemed to be in an excellent mood. In fact, with all the visitors they had entertained lately, she appeared happier than she had in many months.

Smiling as she settled in the tufted cushioned seat, he offered her the wool rug that he had pulled from beneath the seat only moments before. The Mistress always appreciated something to cover her legs now that she was getting on in years.

"Thank you, Giles."

He bowed. "You are quite welcome, milady."

As Giles looked back to the manor, Lady Ashcroft appeared at the top of the portico and then raced down the steps to the carriage. As he helped her into the seat across from his mistress, Lady Hawthorne chuckled. "Why are you in such a hurry, Audrey? One would think banshees were fast on your heels."

As the carriage began to move, Lady Ashcroft laughed. "Nothing so dramatic, but I was in the foyer before I remembered my reticule was still on my bed. I secreted several pounds and a cheque inside it last night, as I intend to purchase gifts for my family while we shop today."

"You must intend to purchase something quite expensive if you need a cheque."

"That is for a painting of the sea at Mrs. Young's gallery that interests me. If I can strike a bargain with her, I mean to have it in my sitting room at Pemberley. Then I may enjoy the tranquillity of the sea all year round."

"What about Georgiana? Perhaps she has painted a likeness of the sea that you may wish to frame and hang."

"Georgiana has greatly improved, but I would not go so far as to call her accomplished—certainly not in creating large paintings. She does quite well with small landscapes, and her technique is superior to last year. I have no doubt that with more training she will reach her goal of becoming a proficient artist."

"Good. Good. Young women should participate in all those things that interest them. I despise women who while away their time waiting for an offer of marriage. It is evident that Georgiana has a quick mind and willing spirit, and it would be a waste not to allow her to reach her potential."

"Fitzwilliam agrees with us on that matter. He will go to any lengths to fulfil her quest for knowledge." Audrey Ashcroft shook her head sadly. "Would that my father had been of the same mind! Most of my education came after I married Joseph, at least education in subjects of interest to me, such as astronomy and biology."

"You had a good man and so did I. Horace was never jealous of my thirst for knowledge."

Audrey reached to pat her friend's hand. "We were very fortunate. When I think of how your nephew has treated poor Alfreda—"

"He will be her curse no more! I will write Penelope and Walter and inform them of the situation and ask them to take Alfreda under their care until she is married to David. I intend to confront John once Alfreda is safe. I do not believe my nephew is stupid enough to defy me and lose all claim to Hawthorne Hall. I have safeguards in place to make sure he carries out my wishes."

"I pray he sees the wisdom of letting her marry Colonel Cochran and retaining the inheritance you offer him. I am concerned, however, about his plans for Elizabeth Bennet."

"Yes, poor Miss Bennet! I hardly had time to converse with her during my dinner party, but anyone with good sense could see that she is not happy in John's company. And he kept constant guard over her, rushing in to claim her attention whenever she dared to say a few words to my other guests. He is apparently too dim-witted to notice the way she disdains him."

"Precisely. That is why I feel I must ask a favour in return."

"Anything."

"Alfreda confided in me that Miss Bennet is determined to quit the courtship once they return to London. I am greatly relieved, as someone I know is deeply in love with her, and I am praying for a match."

"So Miss Bennet means to toss him over. Good for her!" Lady Hawthorne leaned in as though not to be overheard. "Please, I must know who it is you favour?"

"Promise that you will never repeat this."

Violet's expression changed, and she became serious. "We have been particular friends for twenty years, and I have never revealed any confidence in all that time."

Properly chastised, Audrey shared her secret. "It is my nephew."

"Richard?"

"No, Fitzwilliam! He met her quite by accident several months ago and fell hopelessly in love with her at first sight."

"Does she return his love?"

"I was able to ascertain that she does, though naturally she abandoned all hope after she learned he was married. That is why she agreed to your nephew's courtship and accompanied Alfreda to Gatesbridge. I promised Fitzwilliam that I would keep an eye on her while I was here. Oddly, after seeing the way Wilkens guarded her during your party, I have a strange feeling that he may not let her return to London as planned. I worry that he may begin to suspect that she is going to break the courtship, and he will do something imprudent."

"Granted, John can be quite ruthless if he thinks he is being thwarted. I knew of his dissolute ways, but until I learned of his treatment of Alfreda after David's request for a courtship, I never really comprehended his true nature." She seemed lost in thought for a moment before suddenly addressing Audrey. "I can certainly understand your concern."

"I pray he will let her return to London without incident."

"If not, I shall not hesitate to intervene."

"Thank you. I knew I could rely on you."

"So Fitzwilliam will finally divorce that harridan. I am delighted!"

"He will move heaven and earth to marry Miss Bennet. Only her refusal will stop him."

"Then I pray that Miss Bennet knows a treasure when she meets one. Fitzwilliam is much like my Horace and your Joseph—a man among men."

"I could not agree more."

The carriage came to a sudden stop, and both ladies looked out the window. The streets were lined with various shops and stores filled with all manner of merchandise and products produced in that area of England. As one of the Bow Street Runners leaped down to open the door, Audrey completed her thought.

"Let us pray that both Alfreda and Miss Bennet are allowed to leave without incident."

Lady Hawthorne's eyes twinkled, though she did not smile. "If not, John will learn the consequences of my displeasure."

Audrey nodded, well aware of the scope of her friend's power and influence. "Now, what say you to helping me find something unusual for my nephew? It is impossible to purchase anything for Fitzwilliam, as he had everything he desires, but Richard is another matter. He loves whatever I buy him."

"Then buy Fitzwilliam some serviceable gloves and purchase something for the woman he loves, just as Anne would have done were she alive. We women understand what another woman will cherish. Perhaps some lovely lace handkerchiefs, a silk shawl or opera gloves trimmed with lace." Violet exited the carriage with a youthful vigour. "There is even a shop in the next lane that sells miniature chests. Just follow me."

With that, she turned to enter the nearest shop, Madame Juliette, a modiste. The windows of the establishment featured a bride's trousseau—silk and lace in champagne colours that had been fashioned into every imaginable item of intimate clothing. Audrey could not help but smile at her friend's choice.

As Violet quickly disappeared inside, an animated greeting echoed from the open door. "Welcome, Madame Hawthorne! What brings you to my little shop today?"

⊙~⊙

Younge's Art Gallery

The morning at the art gallery had progressed much as every other had since Georgiana's lessons began. Mrs. Younge started the day by instructing her charges in brush techniques. Then she gave Georgiana personal tutoring while she sent Margaret to the gazebo to practice what she had learned. As the temperature rose, both girls were ushered into a large room in back of the house with windows on three sides. The windows were covered by shutters that could be propped open on wooden supports. An oil lamp burning near an opening in the high ceiling created a draft, allowing the salty sea breeze to be pulled through the open windows, thus keeping their work area cool and comfortable.

Around noon they broke for refreshments—tea with small sandwiches, biscuits and cakes. Next, everyone rested on the shaded back porch for a half-hour before walking to the gazebo, and then strolling down and back along the wide boardwalk that ran behind all the shops to get a bit of exercise. When they returned to the gallery, Mrs. Younge normally would begin instructions in colour composition or something similar. But today was Friday, the one day that lessons ended earlier.

Thus, Lady Strongham was given personal instruction while Georgiana occupied the gazebo. At that time of day, the temperature had cooled somewhat, and the spot provided an excellent opportunity for sketching the sea. Today she intended to draw the various birds that ran after the various insects and sea life along the shoreline. Having just placed a new canvas on her stand, she was leaning down to select a brush from the case containing her supplies when a shadow came between her and the sun. Startled, she gasped and looked up to catch the piercing gaze of Mr. Wickham as he chuckled softly with a bemused smile.

"Did I frighten you? I am sorry. I thought you heard me coming."

Giving him a slightly irritated look, Georgiana began to saturate her brush with a blue the colour of the sky from her palette and then stroked it across the canvas in broad strokes as though annoyed. Wickham noticed. Today of all days a good rapport was essential.

"Truly, I am sorry if I caused you alarm, Miss Darcy. I did not realise that you did not hear my footsteps."

Georgiana's shoulders relaxed, and Wickham breathed a sigh of relief. She continued her preoccupation with her painting, and he feigned interest, making inane conversation, though his mind reeled with his plans. Having learned that this was the least popular day for tourists to visit the area, he felt he had to act now. Less people on the boardwalk meant fewer witnesses to the disappearance, and he had a small window of opportunity to accomplish his objective. Pulling another chair close by Georgiana's, he sat down and leaned towards her as he pretended to study her work.

"I am fascinated by artists. I could never draw, and I am certain that no amount of lessons would improve my poor efforts."

Georgiana smiled slightly. "I think Mrs. Younge could teach anyone to draw a respectable picture, if not paint a portrait."

"Oh, I must disagree. I am talentless when it comes to painting or drawing."

They sat in companionable silence until he felt he had no alternative than to speak. "Georgiana."

Georgiana stopped, her brush in mid stroke, as her eyes flicked to him. "You have always addressed me as Miss Darcy."

"But what I have to say, I would like to say to Georgiana, if you do not mind."

Georgiana shrugged, not realising the importance of his declaration. As she leaned down to wash her brush, Wickham reached to still her hand, making her eyebrows furrow. At the same time, voices were heard coming from the direction of the art gallery. A quick glance told Wickham that several people had walked onto the covered back porch and were now watching them. He strained to see if one was Lady Ashcroft but upon inspection thought that none resembled her. Aware that it was only a matter of time before Darcy's aunt discovered him alone with her niece, he jumped into action.

"Would it be possible for us to walk on the beach while we talk?" At her hesitation, he added, "Only a short walk. This is my last day in Ramsgate, and I have not had opportunity to put even one foot on the sand."

Georgiana studied him, and he smiled widely, making him appear boyish. She nodded. Putting her supplies aside, she stood as he did and placed her hand on his outstretched arm. Guiding her expertly down the steps to the beach, Wickham swiftly led her in the direction of the path he had discovered—the one that led back to the main road where his coach sat poised to spirit her away.

As they walked, Wickham covered her small hand with his, causing Georgiana to peer up at him with an expression of bewilderment. He deliberately avoided meeting her gaze, instead staring straight ahead as he began his soliloquy.

"I cannot adequately express how pleased I am to have found you again. I feel that we have become even better friends in the short time you have been in Ramsgate. In fact, if I might be so bold, I would say that my feelings have progressed far beyond friendship."

Though he kept going in the intended direction, Wickham now glanced to see her reaction and found that Georgiana's expression was not what he had hoped it would be. Instead of appearing to be interested in his romantic assertions, she looked like a puzzled child. His pulse began to race. Was she going to bolt and run?

"I may be several years your senior, but I always admired you, and now that you are a young woman—" He halted to cup her chin. "I must confess that I have fallen in love with you."

He could feel Georgiana's body begin to shake. Her voice quivered as she repeated, "You lov … love me?"

"Most ardently, my dear Georgiana, and I wish to marry you."

Georgiana pulled away from his touch. "I am not ready to marry. Besides, my brother will be the one to determine whom I shall marry."

"I thought better of you," he countered in a mocking tone. "From our conversations, I thought you a young woman of substance, someone in charge of her own destiny. Instead, you sound like all the other women of the *ton*—a mindless slave."

Georgiana jerked away from him now. "Brother told me not to listen to any man that would ask for my hand without asking his permission first."

Grabbing her arm with an iron grip, Wickham pulled her back to his side as he hissed, "Then I suppose that we shall have to do this the hard way." He began to pull her down the beach while she twisted first one way and then another, trying to break free. Stunned at his actions, she did not think to cry out.

Suddenly, shouts came from the gazebo, and he turned to see that a group was congregating there. One young woman in particular seemed determined to catch up to them. As she ran down the steps and began in their direction, Wickham was relieved to see that she was having difficulty negotiating the sand in her fancy shoes and that the man who had been standing with her did not seem inclined to join her, but rather was shouting a warning. In only a few short moments though, she had not only caught up with them but was beating him on the back with her parasol. Annoyed at her interference and smarting from her assault, Wickham backhanded her, connecting with her cheek and knocking her to the ground. The fall almost rendered her insensible, and Georgiana screamed at the sight of her friend on the ground.

As Wickham continued, dragging her towards the path, he glanced back to be sure no one else followed. He was not in luck, for another man, older and taller, had appeared from out of nowhere. Leaping over the rails of the gazebo without bothering to take the steps, he began charging in their direction.

Pulling a small pistol from an inside pocket of his coat, Wickham turned to take aim. At that moment, Georgiana got a glimpse of her second rescuer, and her heart stopped. Her beloved godfather, Marshall Landingham, was Wickham's target.

As though trapped in one of her childhood night terrors, the pistol discharged.

Chapter 26

Ramsgate
Younge's Art Gallery

Mrs. Younge stood in the shadows at the back door of the gallery trying not to be seen as she watched the man she loved flirting with Miss Darcy at the gazebo. For the first time, she considered how effortlessly George could charm anyone he pleased. During the past few days, she had overheard enough of his banter with the young miss to understand how Georgiana Darcy had been swayed into letting him meet with her each afternoon. Were she not a grown woman, one with excellent judgment, she might easily have dismissed her suitor as a silver-tongued rogue when he first appeared on her doorstep. Had she written him off at that point, she told herself, she would never have come to know the true George Wickham. Unfortunately, she overvalued her own judgment.

From their posture, the couple near the beach seemed to be conversing amiably, Georgiana apparently still unaware of what was to occur in the next few minutes. She continued to watch, worried at what might transpire when George's intentions were made clear, when the sound of carriage wheels on the gravel out front broke through her reverie. Quitting her post, she hurried to peer out a window.

Finding Lady Strongham's father exiting the vehicle, she clutched her heart in relief that it was he and not Lady Ashcroft. Always eager to collect his daughter and leave, today would be no different. The fewer people here when the news of Miss Darcy's abduction became common knowledge, the better. There would certainly be enough turmoil when Lady Ashcroft learned that her niece was missing. Taking a deep breath, she stepped forward and flung open the door.

"Lord Strongham, come in, sir! Your lovely daughter is still working on the techniques we studied today. If you will be so kind as to follow me, we shall see how much she has accomplished, as I was just about to check her progress."

The gentleman did as requested, though he began to explain, "I am a bit early, so I am willing to wait if Margaret needs more time to finish her work."

"No!" Sarah Younge exclaimed a little too zealously. Strongham's brow knit in surprise as he came to a complete halt. Trying to recover, Mrs. Younge added, "I meant to say that you are certainly not interrupting, and if your daughter has anything to finish, she will have ample time on the morrow if she wishes to do so."

"I shall ask my daughter what she desires. After all, I have paid for an entire lesson today."

With that, Strongham stalked on ahead, leaving Mrs. Younge speechless. Her heart sank to realise that he might still be here when the abduction commenced. Despite her best efforts, Margaret Strongham had glimpsed George at the gazebo with Georgiana today, and she had taken great pains to convince her that Wickham was a friend who had come to escort her to dinner after she finished today's lesson. In the inevitable melee to come, Mrs. Younge wondered, would Lady Strongham blurt out that she had seen a man with Georgiana—someone who was supposedly a friend of hers?

Taking a deep breath, she steadied herself and hurried to join father and daughter.

⚬◯⚬

A Few Minutes Later

Reaching the art gallery entrance, Elizabeth Bennet rushed inside, closed her parasol and slammed the door firmly. Then she leaned back against it with a loud groan. She was relieved to find no one was in sight, as she was so angry she wanted to scream!

The entire day had been a disaster. There had been one confrontation after another with Lord Wilkens—about her choice of gown, her penchant for merriment, even her insistence on greeting those she had previously been introduced to in Ramsgate. The last straw had taken place at the establishment next door, a pottery shop. While encountering Mr. Chandler, whom she had met at Lady Hawthorne's dinner party, he offered Elizabeth a warm greeting, but she was prevented from acknowledging him. Wilkens had stepped between them, taking her arm as he guided her none too gently out the front door without a word of explanation. Once outside, he declared that she was not to speak to anyone of whom he did not approve, and he definitely *did not approve* of Mr. Chandler. Only Alfreda's sudden appearance and teary eyes had kept her from confronting Wilkens where they stood.

Furious, she had outpaced him and his sister as they headed in the direction of the gallery, their last call on the street. Wilkens was far too stout to keep up with her, and Elizabeth relied on the fact that Alfreda would slow down in order to walk alongside him. At her last glimpse of brother and sister, they were a good distance behind her, though his scowl was unmistakable even from so far away.

Insufferable Man! Elizabeth murmured under her breath as she hurried towards the back of the shop where an inviting covered porch beckoned. *I have no intentions of marrying him nor will I stand his abuse any longer; not even to placate Alfreda!*

At length, Wilkens and Alfreda reached the gallery, and as they entered the front door, they encountered Mrs. Younge and Lord Strongham coming from the back of the house. His daughter had insisted that he wait until her lesson was complete, successfully thwarting the proprietor's plans to send them on their way. As introductions were made, Alfreda seized the opportunity to further delay her brother's mission to catch up with Elizabeth.

"I have so often wished for a painting of the sea to hang in my sitting room," Alfreda declared fervently, whilst her brother looked at her with disbelief. "Mrs. Younge, would you be kind enough to show me the selection, and perhaps, Brother, you and Mr. Strongham will give me your opinions on which one I should choose."

Apparently quite used to his judgment being sought, Lord Strongham did not seem surprised to be asked. "I shall be happy to advise you."

Though he did not reply, Wilkens did not wish to refuse his sister's appeal and appear uncooperative in front of Strongham. Thus, as the entire group headed into a room filled with paintings from ceiling to floor, his expression mirrored his frustration in not being able to find Miss Bennet and chastise her for her childish behaviour.

Meanwhile, on the porch, Elizabeth took a deep breath of the salty air and closed her eyes. *Blessed peace at last! What punishment it would be to listen to that man day in and day out.*

The tranquillity did not last long though, as a conversation at the gazebo drifted Elizabeth's way on the wind. Opening her eyes, she beheld a man and a woman at the structure. On closer inspection, she changed her mind. *No, that is a young girl, not a woman and she looks like ...*

Squinting, she recognized the figure of Georgiana Darcy and instantly stiffened. Why was the child all alone with a man? Furthermore, something about the man's bearing made the hair on back of her neck stand up. *I should go to her.*

She had taken no more than a half-dozen steps down the walkway when a familiar voice challenged from behind. Wilkens had successfully rushed Alfreda to a decision in order to resume his search. "Miss Bennet, where are you running off to now?" His voice dripped venom.

She turned to face him, her expression pitiless and her eyes ablaze. "I am taking this walkway to the beach. Once there, I intend to walk along the shoreline—alone."

Without waiting for rebuttal, Elizabeth turned and walked even more briskly towards the structure. The first thing she noticed was that Georgiana had allowed the gentleman to escort her down the steps to the beach below. As she increased her pace, she heard Wilkens call out, "This is not a race. Wait for me." She paid him no mind.

Had she turned she would have seen him trying to follow her with Alfreda Wilkens right behind. In the doorway, Mrs.Younge still stood beside Lord Strongham. And while her expression had changed to dread, Margaret's father looked pensive, as though he too had noticed the man and girl now heading down the beach.

Meanwhile, the carriage carrying Lady Ashcroft and Lady Hawthorne arrived at the gallery, stopping right behind Lord Strongham's plush vehicle. As the two ladies exited their carriage, another quickly came to a halt behind them and Lord Landingham climbed out as though he wanted to intercept them.

"Ladies! What a happy coincidence. I was hoping to find you here!" he proclaimed, bowing as he doffed his hat. "I came to see how my goddaughter is faring with her lessons, and since you are here, I would like to escort you all to tea at my hotel after she is finished, if you have no other engagement."

Lady Hawthorne was bemused, winking at her friend. "I am always in favour of a handsome escort for tea. What say you, Audrey?"

Lady Ashcroft smiled at her suitor as he stepped forward to offer his arm to both her and Violet and escort them inside. "I would love to join you for tea, and I am sure that Georgiana would as well. Let us see if her lesson is drawing to a close." With that, the three began towards the gallery, totally unaware of the drama that was now playing out on the beach behind it.

⁂

Elizabeth reached the gazebo and could see that Georgiana was now in distress. She was being dragged down the beach, fighting a man who had hold of her arm by twisting first one way then another, but to no avail. Unwilling to stand back and do nothing, Elizabeth ran down the steps and onto the sand with her parasol held overhead as a flimsy weapon. Behind her, John Wilkens shouted out a warning not to be foolish. It went unheeded.

Even though she found it hard to run in the sand in her delicate footwear, at length Elizabeth managed to catch up with the pair. Raising the parasol, she began to beat the man about the back and shoulders as forcefully as someone of her size could manage.

"Let her go! Do you hear? Let Georgiana go, or you shall suffer the consequences!"

The whacks were irritating enough, but soon Elizabeth began kicking at the back of his legs with her pointed shoes. This caused Wickham to turn and grab her weapon, tossing it some distance away. Then he backhanded her. The strike caught her on the cheek and sent her sprawling on the sand. For a moment, Elizabeth lay stunned. Only Georgiana's screams pierced the haze that enveloped her.

Those same screams caught the attention of the party that included Lady Ashcroft and Lord Landingham. Having found Mrs. Younge and Lord Strongham standing spellbound at the back door, they had hurried past them to learn what had captured their attention, praying that whatever it was did not involve Georgiana. Recognising her predicament immediately, Landingham left Audrey behind as he sprinted towards the disturbance. He ran right past Lord Wilkens, who was frozen in place and leapt over the railing surrounding the small building. And as he sprinted after her, he watched as if in slow motion as Wickham backhanded Elizabeth and taking a few more steps, turned and aimed a pistol at him.

Unwilling to give up, Landingham heard the shot and felt the sting of the bullet as it grazed his head. Momentarily staggering, he stopped to feel for the source of the blood now slowly trickling down his face, relieved to find that he had escaped with only a deep gash.

With renewed determination, he continued to pursue the man kidnapping his daughter and in light of her rescuer's tenacity, Wickham pushed Georgiana to the ground and ran. Very swiftly reaching the chosen pathway, he was soon out of sight, hidden by the trees and brush that lay between the sand and his waiting coach.

Reaching Georgiana, Landingham kneeled quickly and gathered her in his arms, soothing her with soft words as she cried. Though seconds ago the most important thing on his mind was pursuing her kidnapper, his duty was clear. She needed him, and he would catch the blackguard later. Glancing back, he witnessed Audrey helping Elizabeth to her feet. Behind them a large group had gathered on the gazebo and the boardwalk, though Lord Wilkens had not moved and was shaking his head as though he thought them all fools.

Soon Audrey and Elizabeth were falling to their knees beside Lord Landingham. The younger woman embraced Georgiana while Audrey reached to examine his wound, her face full of tender feelings. Giving his love a small smile to convey that he was not severely injured, Landingham began untying his cravat. He was not surprised when she took it from his hands and began to wrap it around his head as a bandage. Once finished, Audrey brought one of his hands discreetly to her lips and bestowed a kiss on the back. Then, she turned to console her niece who was enquiring of Elizabeth if she was hurt.

"No, no real harm done," the young woman insisted, giving Georgiana's aunt a reassuring smile over the girl's head.

As he watched the tender scene, all three ladies hugging and crying softly, Landingham fought to hold back his own tears. And when at last he stood, it was with a new determination—for however many years he had left, Georgiana would know the truth of her parentage.

After a time, they all stood to begin their trek back to the gallery, and Landingham insisted on carrying Georgiana. As he swept her into his arms, she did not object but laid her head on his chest, and the heart that was shattered years ago when his child was born, destined to be called by another man's name, slowly began to mend.

On the Road to Rosings

Wickham slumped back, letting his head rest against the tufted seat of Lady Catherine's coach as the vehicle pitched wildly from side to side. Grateful that it bore no insignia to be identified, he closed his eyes and rubbed a still trembling hand across his sweat covered forehead.

How had everything gone so wrong?

Suddenly the carriage hit a deep hole, the road having been rutted by recent rains, and his teeth almost jarred from his mouth. The coach driver had whipped the horses into a fury after Wickham had reached the vehicle, shouting orders like a madman, and had not yet let up on the poor beasts. Though he knew they could not sustain the current pace the entire way to Rosings, Wickham had not ordered the driver to slow. For in truth, the devil would have been more welcome than those who would soon to be on his trail—Darcy, Colonel Fitzwilliam and now, Lord Landingham.

In all likelihood, their coach would be miles from town before anyone at the gallery learned the full extent of the conspiracy that had played out right under their noses. Thus, taking deep breaths and releasing them slowly, Wickham willed his racing heart to calm as he considered all that had happened.

All his carefully laid plans had dissolved in an instant at the hands of that one meddlesome woman. And in failing to kidnap Georgiana, he had shot a man of great import in a moment of madness. In the heat of the moment, he had not recognised Lord Landingham until after the weapon discharged, but had he known the identity of the man, he might have run off sooner and not drawn his pistol. One thing for certain, the shot had not been fatal, and he had created another notable enemy.

It happened so fast. I wonder if he even recognised me. If that stupid woman had not hurried to the gazebo, I would have made off with her! Wickham cursed aloud. *It is no matter. After Georgiana gives them my name, Landingham will not rest until I hang.*

He had ordered the carriage directly to Rosings Park because he knew it was unwise to travel the road to London. Darcy would rush to be with his sister, and the last thing Wickham wanted was to encounter Georgiana's brother. No, he would return the coach to Lady Catherine and hide there for a few days.

Of course, she would be vexed, but what choice did he have? Besides, he reasoned, the old harridan could complain all she wanted; she was just as involved in this affair as he, and Wickham had no intentions of taking sole responsibility if apprehended. He would implicate Lady Catherine and Gisela too, if need be.

The one thing he had learned in his long history with the law was that leverage was everything. When facing prosecution, it helped to have secrets to tell, especially secrets involving members of the *ton*. The law might not care, but if he got word to those involved in the intrigues, they would see that he was treated fairly in exchange for sharing what he knew or, conversely, keeping his mouth shut. And there was a great deal he knew about Lady Catherine—most of it involving Fitzwilliam Darcy. If he was lucky, he would not be hanged but sentenced to prison, or even better—exiled to the penal colony in Australia.

If he had any regrets, it was for being so gullible when he was first approached by Darcy's aunt with an offer of a stipend to keep his eyes and ears open and a chance to earn more for anything *significant* he could pass along to her. Eager to supplement his income, he had invented ways to pry into the Darcy's business, such as eavesdropping and stealing outgoing letters. In hindsight, if he had read them before giving them to Lady Catherine, he would have kept the ones from Lady Anne Darcy to Landingham. Those revealed that he was Georgiana's father. But it was too late. He had learned of it only after Lady Catherine gave them to Gisela to blackmail Darcy.

If I had just one of those letters, I would not have to resort to kidnapping. I could have blackmailed both Darcy and Landingham and left for the Continent years ago. Perhaps I can pinch at least one from Gisela the next time I am in London. Deuce take it, the way she drinks, she would probably have given them to me if I asked!

In spite of fearing that someone could be following right behind, Wickham pounded on the coach roof to order the driver to slow down. It would not do to injure the horses and be stranded along the road. And as he felt the coach slow to a more reasonable pace, he began to practice what he would say to the Mistress of Rosings.

There was a contingent of soldiers nearby, and when Georgiana screamed ...

London
Darcy House
William's Study

William and Richard exchanged looks, each raising a brow in question, as they watched the Earl of Matlock drain the entire contents of a glass of brandy in one swallow, then proceed to the liquor cabinet and pour a refill.

"One more. I think I am going to need it."

More puzzled expressions passed between the cousins. Neither could remember ever seeing Richard's father so upset. When William had received his uncle's note that morning citing an urgent matter regarding Gisela, he realised that he could not put off seeing him any longer. Now both cousins waited with bated breath for Lord Matlock to speak.

As he sat down in the chair opposite Richard and across the desk from William, he began. "I had an unexpected visit from my solicitor last evening."

"And …" William ventured.

"I know about your enquiries into the joint venture started by de Bourgh, Montgomery and your father. It appears the man you hired to investigate— Lowell, is that his name?" At William's nod he continued. "Well, Mr. Lowell is a cousin of my solicitor, Mr. Godbee. And weeks ago he asked Godbee for a second opinion regarding some things he had discovered while going through the files at Ferguson's office."

"Yes, I told Ferguson that I wanted Mr. Lowell to have access to all the records."

Lord Matlock now punctuated the air with his glass. "You do realise that Mr. Ferguson is Catherine's lackey. You cannot trust the man!"

"Yes, I know. He was here a day or two ago, and I did not meet with him. He left another of his questionable financial statements."

"At any rate, Lowell obtained copies of two inventories dated the same date. One showed the new equipment and one did not, and that stirred his curiosity. He deduced that Catherine was in favour of more equipment for the mills, but she was having Mr. Ferguson deposit the funds appropriated from your individual accounts into an account solely for her use. Thus, one inventory for your use showed the equipment, though the true inventory did not. Lowell told Godbee that he had decided to travel to the mills to see for himself if there was any new equipment."

"And what did my aunt do with the purloined funds?"

"Godbee speculates it went to equip a shipyard in Liverpool and some mines in Wales that Catherine has added to her investment holdings."

William looked puzzled. "And how would Godbee know what my aunt owns?"

"Good Lord, Darcy! Do you think unscrupulous solicitors do not spread gossip among themselves when they drink too much? Godbee says there are some that would not be practicing if their clients were apprised of their loose tongues."

"So it was as I suspected. The reason my investment has lost money the last two years is because my aunt has been cheating me."

"Yes, and it is obvious that your wife is privy to Catherine's plan, as she always voted with her. I would not be surprised if my sister was giving her a portion in secret." The earl stood and walked over to look out the window. "But that is not the worst of it."

Richard's frown deepened. "What could be worse?"

"There has been a murder."

Both cousins leapt to their feet, but William was first to reply. "Is that why Lowell has not been in touch...he is dead?"

The earl came back to join his son and nephew in a circle. "Yes...I fear so."

William slowly shook his head and looked away, trying to regain control. Recovering he turned back to his Uncle. "Tell me all you know. What happened?"

The Earl took a deep breath. Clearing his throat he began. "Godbee would not have known to come to me, except that Lowell feared something like this might happen and left instructions in a letter. Godbee was supposed to hear from him at least once a week, and if he did not, he was to read the letter. Since he has heard nothing in two weeks, he did as he was asked. Inside were copies of everything Lowell had uncovered and all his suspicions.

"Godbee was to give us both a copy, and he came to me first. He asked if I would inform you, since the letter implicates your wife. Godbee is an honest man, and he will not let this drop, gentlemen. He is determined to investigate his cousin's disappearance and everything will be public knowledge before long. I asked him to give me two weeks to investigate before he takes action. I felt it best if I questioned Gisela, given your present stalemate."

"You have already confronted Gisela?"

"This very morning, right before I sent the note requesting a meeting."

William poured himself a brandy. "And how did you find my lovely wife?"

"Mrs. Darcy was not in any condition for company. It appeared she had not been out in days. She is drinking heavily."

"That is no secret."

"In any event, when I confronted her, she laughed. Laughed, mind you!" The earl shook his head in disbelief. "It is obvious from Lowell's papers that she and Catherine were cheating you with Ferguson's help. God help that man when I get hold of him! All Gisela had to say in her defence was that Lady Catherine handles all her shares in the venture, as she takes no interest in them. And since you will not speak to her, she cares not a whit if you are being cheated."

"Her usual charming self," William sniffed.

The earl rose to his feet, setting another empty glass down on the desktop. "Well, I shall have her investigated as thoroughly as my sister. I intend to know the truth of it, and I told her as much. However, I do not think she was the instigator. That honour goes to Catherine. In any event, I must insist, Nephew, that you begin an immediate suit for a divorce. I will support you, as will my friends in the House of Lords, and so will my second cousin, the bishop. God knows you have enough witnesses to Gisela's liaisons with other men. You shall have every possible means of support in this quest! I want that woman out of the family!"

Richard began to chuckle. "And how do you plan to rid the family of Aunt Catherine?"

The earl rounded on his son, not amused. "I have my own plans for Catherine.

I think she is completely mad if she ordered this man's murder. If I can prove it, she shall end her days in Bedlam."

"And Rosings?"

"I am executor of her estate in the event she is incapacitated, and I will see that her will is followed. It shall pass to you, Son."

Richard's brows rose. "I never wanted it this way."

"Nor did I, but I shall not let her act as a dictator, able to order murder at her whim. If it is true, it would be better that she be committed than hanged."

"I see your point."

The Earl of Matlock squared his shoulders as he turned to Darcy. "What say you to the divorce?"

William tried not to smile. He did not want his uncle to know that he had been planning to inform him soon that he was going to seek a divorce. And he had no intention of mentioning the lady that prompted his decision. "I could not agree more."

"Good! I shall begin the necessary procedures, if you will notify your solicitor tomorrow to inform that harridan that you intend to secure a divorce on the grounds of her adultery."

"Tomorrow cannot come fast enough," William responded. "I pray my aunt will support me as well."

"No need to worry about Eleanor. She could never stand Gisela though she tried to keep up appearances. This will give her leave to cut her completely."

Richard stood and grabbed the crystal decanter and began to pour two fingers of liquor in everyone's glass. "Let us drink to the truth." He held his glass out to William. "It shall set you free, my friend, and it is about time."

Glasses clinked all around. "To truth."

Chapter 27

Ramsgate
Younge's Art Gallery

Approaching the gazebo, Audrey Ashcroft, Elizabeth Bennet and Lord Landingham, carrying Georgiana close to his chest, were amazed at how quickly a throng had gathered to gawk at the commotion on the beach.

Amidst the gathering, Elizabeth searched for Lord Wilkens' face but was relieved not to find it. Swiftly the crowd parted, the hum of whispered opinions getting significantly louder as Lord Landingham's bloodied visage was now clearly visible. As the crowed moved aside to let them come up the steps and commence down the walk towards the gallery, the natter increased with speculations regarding injuries to the girl in his arms.

Several men stepped up, offering to assist Lord Landingham with Georgiana, still in his arms, but he declined their offers, knowing how timid she would be with a stranger, especially considering what had just happened. Hurrying towards the back door, however, it became evident that a loud argument was taking place inside the building and as they stepped through the door, Lady Ashcroft turned to close it soundly. The crowd following had no choice but to disperse.

"Do not lie to me!" Lord Strongham demanded of an obviously nervous Sarah Younge. "Margaret informed me that she saw this blackguard with Miss Darcy only minutes before the abduction. You told her that he was merely a friend waiting to take you to dinner. Now tell me the truth. Is he an acquaintance of yours?"

Mrs. Younge backed up a step as though she wished to flee the inquisition. Her lips trembled with her reply. "I ... I have met him. I do not know him very well. We were just beginning to get acquainted," she blinked several times, trying not to cry. "I had no idea that he would—"

"You had no idea, madam?" Strongham hissed, taking another step closer so she could not escape. "You let this madman loiter about this establishment whilst my daughter and Miss Darcy were under your protection? It could just as easily have been my Margaret with whom he tried to flee."

"Oh, no!" Sarah Younge hurried to explain. "Miss Strongham was not the—"

Lord Landingham, Lady Ashcroft, Lady Hawthorne and Elizabeth Bennet had entered now and were standing directly behind Strongham. Upon hearing Mrs. Younge's last reply to Strongham, each was eyeing her with equal curiosity and disgust. Their appearance served to remind her that she was suspect and, as such, should probably say no more.

With her sudden silence, Marshall Landingham's demeanour changed for the worse and knowing his temper well, Audrey Ashcroft took hold of his arm, causing him to regard her. His expression was as hard as steel, and she did not have to ask what he was thinking. She turned to her old friend, Lady Hawthorne.

"Would you please ask Clark to come inside and escort Miss Darcy to the carriage while Lord Landingham and I speak to Mrs. Younge?" The older woman hurried to do as she was asked, and Audrey regarded Elizabeth briefly, adding, "Please accompany them, Miss Bennet. We shall meet all of you at the carriage."

Almost instantly Clark rushed into the establishment, his expression mirroring his employer's concern for Georgiana. Lady Hawthorne trailed behind him, and Marshall gently set Georgiana on her feet. He whispered some endearment into her ear that seemed to reassure her and kissed her forehead. Then, with a wan smile, he surrendered her to the trusted footman, keeping watch until she was completely out of sight. He then turned to face Mrs. Younge, the set of his mouth evidence of his fury.

Seeing the intensity in his expression, Audrey took his arm. Strongham was in the process of sputtering something about *ruining* Mrs. Younge, and since he was not above doing the job himself, Landingham stepped between the two, stopping within inches of the gallery owner's face. He observed with satisfaction the fear in her eyes and the difficulty she had swallowing.

"I agree completely with Lord Strongham," he stated. "We trusted you with our most precious gifts—a daughter, a niece, a goddaughter—and you failed us. Whether you acted out of ignorance, wilful disregard or some nefarious reason in allowing that villain near our children is yet to be determined. Oh, but make no mistake, your motive shall be established. I will hold you personally responsible for my goddaughter's ordeal, whatever part you played in it, and I assure you, Lady Ashcroft and Lord Strongham will do likewise."

Margaret's father agreed in a loud voice. "Indeed."

"I suggest you do not attempt to leave this establishment. An armed guard will be assigned to ascertain that you are here to answer any questions the constable may have and those of the solicitor I intend to hire."

"I shall hire a solicitor as well!" Lord Strongham bristled, unable to hold his tongue.

"May heaven have mercy on you, as we shall not!" Landingham added.

The proprietor's face showed very little emotion until Lord Landingham's parting remark, after which she visibly paled.

And as he and Lady Ashcroft stormed out of the business followed by Strongham and his daughter, and for the first time since the debacle began Sarah Younge had opportunity to question the wisdom of trusting Mr. Wickham. Sinking back against the wall, she closed her eyes.

What have I done?

The last to exit through the gallery included Alfreda Wilkens and her brother, who had made their way back inside after the crowd dispersed. Now disdainful of the gallery owner, he ignored her completely. Besides, he was more interested in finding Elizabeth to berate her for getting involved in so sordid a display. He had purposefully stayed in the background, hoping not to be associated with the scandal that was sure to surround the entire incident. As he guided his sister down the steps, he noted the object of his indignation entering Lord Landingham's carriage and his entire countenance darkened.

⟲⟳

Meryton
Longbourn
The parlour

As Jane surreptitiously observed the others gathered in the parlour, each member of her family seemed preoccupied with their own endeavours. Mary was reading a book of sermons while Kitty and Lydia snickered at things only shared with each other whilst trimming bonnets. Her father was reading a newspaper by the light from a window. Her mother was trying to mend a shirt, but whenever Jane glanced in that direction, she seemed to be stitching the same pocket repeatedly.

Since Mr. Bingley's return to Netherfield, Mrs. Bennet had insisted that he dine with them every day. Of course, always pleased to see him, Jane had no objections to his presence, though she worried that even a man as good natured as Charles should not be exposed to her family every day. She feared that he might come to the conclusion that marrying her would not be worth inheriting her family. Thus, whenever he was in attendance, Jane did everything in her power to steer the conversation away from topics that were too rude to mention. Such a topic was his wealth—her mother's favourite subject. Tonight she would fail miserably.

"Mr. Bingley, once you are wed, how many more servants do you plan on employing to serve my Jane?"

Mr. Bennet pulled his newspaper up to cover his face, though the slight jiggle of the paper and occasional snorts revealed that he was laughing as quietly as possible. Jane frowned in his direction but, of course, he could not see. Mrs. Bennet took no notice but hurried on with her enquiry.

"I am sure that you have noticed that Netherfield is badly understaffed, and one needs so many servants these days to keep up appearances. My Jane will want her own lady's maid, of course, and I do not know of any servants that you presently employ that could sufficiently do the job. Perhaps you will want to employ a French maid. I hear they are all the rage in London."

"MOTHER!" Jane finally managed to sputter. "I do not think that is something that Char—Mr. Bingley should worry about now. And he does not need to discuss his servants with you."

"Oh, fiddle faddle! He does not mind, do you, Mr. Bingley?"

Kitty and Lydia's giggles turned into loud guffaws, and they took up their mother's tune. "Oh, do tell us, Mr. Bingley. Will you be hiring my sister a French maid?" Lydia said teasingly, as Kitty chimed in. "Will you have a French valet as well?"

Charles had reddened at Mrs. Bennet's question, but seeing Jane's embarrassment, he reached for her hand and squeezed it reassuringly. Her blue eyes, which had dropped to the floor, came up to meet his kind expression and his smile restored her own. Giving her a covert wink, he focused his attention on his future mother-in-law.

"I can assure you, madam, that your daughter and I shall discuss that matter thoroughly before we make any decisions. The one thing of which I am certain is that she shall have everything that she needs as my wife and mistress of our homes and that includes enough servants."

At his assertion, Mrs. Bennet was effusive. "Oh, I never thought any differently! I had no doubt that Jane would marry well, and with your five-thousand pounds a year, she will have everything she could wish for." She turned to her husband. "That is what I told you, is it not, Mr. Bennet? I said that our Jane could not have been so beautiful for nothing."

Mr. Bennet peered over the top of the newspaper, his mouth now twisted into a slight smirk. "You certainly did, my dear. Quite often, as I remember."

This set off another round of laughter from Jane's two youngest sisters, but Mary huffed in disgust. "It would serve everyone to do without so many servants and give more to the church."

"Bah!" Lydia snorted. "Mary, you are such a bore. What is the harm in living well, if you have the means?"

"I agree!" Kitty chimed in as usual. "Besides, you will need more servants in order to host lots of balls. Netherfield is perfect for having balls."

Mr. Bennet folded his paper. "That is enough girls." Promptly, he went back to his reading as Lydia made a face at her father that only Kitty saw. They both collapsed into a fit of giggles.

Jane just shook her head sadly and glanced back to Charles who was studying her with a sly grin. She could not help smiling at him. "I am sorry," she whispered looking about to see that the rest of her family were not listening.

"Think nothing of it," Charles replied. "Have you heard from your sister? Has Miss Elizabeth returned to London?"

Jane's face lit up. "Lizzy is supposed to return to London in several days. She says that she is homesick for Longbourn. I suspect she wants to come home, though Mama may not be willing to allow it if she has not received an offer of marriage."

"Your mother is determined to see her married?"

"I am afraid so." Jane sighed. "For a while I feared that Lizzy might accept an offer from that awful man that has been courting her."

"Ah, yes. John Wilkens, Earl of Hampton."

"You know him?"

"Yes, I met him at Darcy's club. A rather dour man who seemed to be angry a great deal of the time. Not much for conversation."

"Then you can understand why Lizzy is not impressed with him."

"I certainly can. Your sister is much too lively for him. He is a stick-in-the-mud. I have wondered at his purpose in pursuing Miss Elizabeth. It would certainly not be a good match."

"No. My sister was not formed for such a man. Besides, I have a suspicion that she is interested in someone else."

"Someone I would know?"

Jane glanced sideways at him. "I believe you know him very well."

"Ah yes, my friend, Darcy."

"I have been aware of Lizzy's feelings for him since he rescued her the night of the flood. And she confided in me when she first learned that he was married. However, though the circumstances of his marriage are heartbreaking, it would seem to be an insurmountable obstacle to their union."

"Not insurmountable, but certainly formidable. There are many steps that Darcy would have to complete in order to obtain a divorce—from obtaining the agreement of the church and the House of Lords, to the civil trial." Bingley took a deep breath, exhaling noisily. "Then there is the scandal that would be sure to follow your sister. She would have to be very strong to withstand such disdain."

"Lizzy is strong, but I hate to think of her being pilloried by the gossips. And I have no idea if Papa and Mama would support her decision if she decided to choose Mr. Darcy." Both surreptitiously turned to study Jane's parents who were paying them no mind.

Finally Jane leaned in to whisper to Charles. "I only pray that Lizzy will do whatever is in her best interest. She has been through so much this summer, trying to please Mama and secure an offer for my sake." Overcome with emotion, her next words almost faltered. "I know it was for me that she agreed to the courtship with that horrible man. She wanted to secure a wealthy husband so that Mama would be satisfied and leave me to choose whoever my heart desired."

"And did you find your heart's desire?" Charles' expression was sombre as he held her gaze, barely daring to breathe as he awaited her answer.

"You are everything I have ever desired in a husband and more."

Bingley let go of his breath, his face erupting into a beatific smile. They both knew that had they been alone, he would have kissed her soundly. As it was, all Charles could manage was to squeeze the hand he held.

"You have made me the happiest of men, sweetheart. I can only pray that Miss Elizabeth and Darcy find such happiness as we have."

"As do I, my love."

Outside the Art Gallery

They had no more than cleared the front porch when Alfreda spoke. "John, Miss Bennet has been through so much today. Please do not quarrel with her again."

Wilkens stopped walking, casting a sideways glance at his sister. "By what right do you instruct me?" The volume of his voice increased. "And to make matters clear so that you understand, what I choose to talk with Miss Bennet about is not your concern."

"Shhh," Alfreda whispered as his raised voice brought attention their way. "Please do not let our aunt hear you. You know she does not welcome your show of temper."

"She is a foolish old woman who would not know a show of temper if she saw one. I am simply impatient with people who ignore my advice!" At this declaration, more people stopped to stare, and Alfreda's eyes dropped to the ground. "Now, I will leave it to you to collect Miss Bennet. I wish to leave before the whole of Ramsgate learns what happened today."

Timidly, Alfreda headed in the direction of Lord Landingham's carriage, where Audrey Ashcroft stood at the open door talking to those inside. She remained unnoticed, standing silently behind Georgiana's aunt, until Elizabeth called out from the carriage. "Alfreda, are you looking for me?"

Everyone's attention focused on her and she flushed. "Yes. Brother wants to leave now and asked me to see if you are ready." Her eyes pleaded for Elizabeth to agree.

Meeting the looks of the others in the carriage, Elizabeth knew that it would not do for Georgiana to be upset by another argument. Thus, she began to climb out of the carriage. "Of course. I was so shaken that I was not thinking clearly. I should return to Gatesbridge Manor with you."

Lady Ashcroft reached out to touch Elizabeth's arm as she stepped down to the sand. "In light of this disaster, I am sending a servant to London with an express for Fitzwilliam. I know my nephew well, and he shall demand that Georgiana and I return to London immediately. We shall set out in the morning, and you are welcome to accompany us." She glanced to Alfreda, who was coming closer, and lowered her voice so that only Elizabeth could hear. "I do not think the Earl of Hampton will be pleased with your involvement in my niece's rescue, though I assure you that my family and I shall be eternally grateful." Elizabeth smiled and Audrey squeezed her hand before saying loud enough for Alfreda to hear, "We shall be leaving at first light from Hawthorne Hall."

Being offered a way out of the predicament flooded Elizabeth with relief. "I would appreciate that very much. This ordeal has made me heartsick to see my family in London and to return to my home in Meryton." She looked to Alfreda for assurance. "I am certain that Lady Wilkens will forgive me for wishing to return to London earlier and will provide me a carriage so that I can meet you in the morning."

Alfreda could do nought but agree. "Of course, if that is your wish." By now John Wilkens was coming in their direction, and the look on his face made Elizabeth uneasy.

Forcing herself to focus on Lady Ashcroft, she hoped her eyes conveyed her message better than her words. "Thank you for thinking of me. I shall not *fail* to be there at first light." Unsaid was that if she did not come, she had been detained against her will.

"I look forward to seeing you then," Lady Ashcroft said aloud, leaning in again to whisper, "I shall not leave Ramsgate without you."

Elizabeth calmed, the relief in her face visible. "You are too kind."

There was another whispered secret. "No, I am a stubborn woman who does not suffer fools or bullies."

As John Wilkens watched the women gathered around Landingham's carriage, he pondered what Elizabeth Bennet and Audrey Ashcroft found amusing as they conversed so quietly. Though he strained to hear the conversation, he could not make out the words, and he knew enough not to ask. Darcy's aunt had never liked him, and the feeling was mutual.

⌒✕⌒

Hawthorne Hall
That Evening

As Lady Ashcroft made her way into the library, she did not expect to find Marshall Landingham there, fast asleep. She had assumed that after she tended his wound, he had retired to the bedroom that Lady Hawthorne had ordered prepared. But there he was, still sitting upright, his head resting on the back of a sofa near the fireplace, oblivious to the world. Lady Hawthorne sat across from him in one of two matching chairs, regarding him with great empathy. Upon seeing her confidant enter

the room, Violet smiled and motioned for Audrey to take the matching chair.

"How long has he been asleep?" Lady Ashcroft whispered, sinking into the soft upholstery, her weary body relaxing for the first time in hours.

"He just now nodded off," Violet Hawthorne replied, not taking her eyes from the handsome gentleman. "Just before he fell asleep, I suggested that he retire to the guest room, since I had no intentions of letting him stay at the hotel after suffering such an injury. But he insisted on waiting for you. He also wanted to enquire after Georgiana. I could not bear to wake him, as he mentioned having a headache right before he fell asleep."

It was obvious that though Landingham slept, he found no peace, as his face still held a pained expression. Noting that the bandage she had fashioned when they arrived at Hawthorne Hall was still spotted with blood, she refrained from the urge to check the wound again.

"It has been exhausting for him, what with having to meet with the constable and the solicitor we hired to look into Wickham's actions." Her face darkened with fury. "I could not believe my eyes when I recognised that blackguard! I can only wonder how he managed to get near my niece. Georgiana did not want to discuss the particulars yet, but I shall question her about it in the morning. I must leave details of her remembrances for the solicitor before we depart."

Tilting her head towards the sleeping man, the Mistress of Hawthorne enquired, "Do you suppose he shall be fit to travel?"

"He is resolute that he will escort us to London. I pray he does not suffer from more than those headaches. He refused to let me call for a physician." She seemed to get more annoyed as she continued. "All this time I thought that he was upstairs in bed. I insisted he rest while I was occupied with Georgiana."

"It has been my observation that real men—not those *namby-pambys*[10] who parade as men— are stubborn as can be." She winked conspiratorially. "But well worth the extra effort to allow them into your heart!"

Audrey's lips lifted into a smile, and she turned to study the chiselled features of the one she loved. "He is most definitely a man."

"The servant I sent after his trunk has returned, so your beau is ready to go with you in the morning."

---

[10] *Namby Pamby is a term for affected, weak, and maudlin speech/verse. However, its origins are in **Namby Pamby** (1725), by Henry Carey. Carey wrote the poem as a satire of Ambrose Philips and published it in his **Poems on Several Occasions**. Source: Wikipedia.*

"My beau?"

Violet raised her hand. "Audrey, let us not argue the facts. I have lived too many years not to recognise that you and he are more than friends. Would that I had met such a man after my Horace died. But, alas, it was not to be." Remembering her train of thought, she added, "Men like Marshall do not come along every day, and you, of all people, know how quickly happiness can be snatched from your grasp."

Lady Ashcroft nodded solemnly, her gaze never leaving Landingham. "I shall let you in on a secret."

Violet Hawthorne's eyes lit up. "You know you can trust me not to say a word."

"Marshall and I have come to an understanding. As soon as Georgiana is settled in marriage, we will look to our own happiness. Only ..."

"Only ..." The older woman echoed.

"When I saw Marshall fall today after that blackguard attempted to kill him, I realised that I am unwilling to wait until Georgiana is married, though I am committed to her care, no matter my situation."

"You wish to marry him sooner?"

For a moment Audrey Ashcroft considered the thought. "Yes, I wish to marry him as soon as possible."

"Then marry him! Everything will work out, you shall see. And I am sure that Fitzwilliam will welcome your continued involvement with Georgiana."

"I know that he will. Perhaps Georgiana could reside with us for a few weeks at a time, just as she has always spent a good bit of time travelling with me. It would essentially be no different. And we could hire a trusted companion for when she resides at Pemberley or Darcy House."

"Just let me know when the happy event will take place." Violet's green eyes sparkled with delight and a bit of mischief. "I do not travel much anymore, but I shall make it a point to attend your wedding."

Audrey reached across the divide to take her friend's hand. "I cannot imagine being married without having you in attendance."

"Now that that is settled, are you still determined to leave in the morning?"

"Yes. As soon as we got here, I sent Clark to Town with a letter explaining what happened. Knowing Fitzwilliam would send me a return express asking me to bring Georgiana to London, I elected to save the poor man another arduous trip. I explained to my nephew that we would start to London on the morrow, stopping at Ashcroft Park as we always do. I do not think it wise to tax everyone with a long trip, so we shall take two days."

"Do you really think Fitzwilliam will wait for you to come to him?"

Audrey laughed. "You know him well. No, he will meet us at Ashcroft Park, I am certain."

"Well, I cannot say that I fault him for being so protective of his sister. In fact, it is rather comforting to know that men like Fitzwilliam still exist. Look at the way my nephew treats Alfreda."

"That is another of my concerns—John Wilkens. How could the man refuse to help Miss Bennet rescue Georgiana?"

"He is a coward."

"That is certain, but I think he is most afraid of scandal. And if his expression at the gallery was indicative of his feelings, Miss Bennet is in for a stiff reprimand."

"Do you fear for her safety?"

"You know him better than I. Should I be?"

"I confess that until I was informed of his dealings with Colonel Cochran over Alfreda, I did not think him capable of such cruelty. Now I do not trust him."

"You heard my offer for Miss Bennet to accompany us to Town, did you not?"

"Yes, and I heard her reply. It seemed to me that she was trying to be sure that Alfreda would assist her in meeting you tomorrow morning."

"That was my impression as well."

"Then let us see if he allows her to leave. In the event that he does not, he will see first-hand my ire."

Audrey smiled. "It is comforting to know that you are well able to control your nephew."

"It is not I, but what I possess, that controls John!"

⁕

Gatesbridge Manor
Wilkens' study

Alfreda was trembling as she stood before her brother's desk. From his dishevelled appearance and the smell of brandy on his breath, he had been drinking since they returned from the catastrophe at the gallery. Afraid to confront him and equally afraid not to, she had come as soon as she realised what he had instructed the servants to do to her friend. He paid her no mind as she walked into the room, pouring the last of a bottle of brandy into an empty glass that sat before him.

"Brother, you cannot lock Miss Elizabeth in her rooms. Lady Ashcroft is expecting her to be at Hawthorne Hall in the morning to return to London in their coach. If she is not there, they will likely come here to ask after her."

"Let them come!" he blustered. "I am lord of this house!"

"But ... but what will our aunt say?"

Wilkens stood quickly, his chair tilting back precariously as he picked up the empty bottle and threw it across the room. Striking the fireplace, it split into hundreds of shards of glass that flew over the floor. Alfreda cringed. He was even less rational when he drank, and she feared what he might do to her or Elizabeth.

"Our dear, dear aunt," he mused, swirling the liquor in the glass. "What will she say?"

Opening the drawer to his desk, Wilkens pulled out a small pistol and examined it from every angle, being sure his sister witnessed his inspection. Apparently pleased as her eyes widened in fear at the sight of the weapon, he laughed wickedly.

"What can that old woman do? She has one foot in the grave, and I would gladly give her a little shove if necessary."

"Brother!" Alfreda sank down into a nearby chair as her knees buckled. "You cannot mean that!"

Wilkens aimed the pistol at her and made a sound as though he had fired a shot. "Oh no?"

Alfreda stood and ran rapidly towards the door.

"Where are you going?"

"I … I am going to bed."

Wilkens was too drunk to argue and pleased that he had frightened her. "See that you do. And do not visit Miss Bennet, do you hear? She is to be left alone to consider her actions."

Alfreda did not answer. She knew exactly what she must do, and her mind began to spin with the details of her plan even as her heart raced with the fear.

"Otherwise, I shall have to lock you away, just as I did when Cochran tried to challenge my authority last year. You remember how much you hated that."

She swallowed hard. It would not do if she were locked in her rooms and could not help her friend. "I remember."

Swiftly she exited the study and hurried back to her rooms, all the while praying that she would not encounter Mrs. Cuthbert, whom she had not trusted for some time. The housekeeper had feigned concern for her, even while helping to keep her imprisoned after her offer of marriage from Colonel Cochran.

Afterwards, it had taken all her strength to pretend that she still respected the woman. No, Mrs. Cuthbert was loyal to her brother, and Alfreda was not sure about most of the other servants. As she walked, she considered her options. Mr. Drummond was the only servant she still trusted implicitly. He was the oldest servant in the livery and was still fiercely loyal to her.

Other than Mr. Drummond, I shall be on my own.

Once in her bedroom, Alfreda hurriedly packed a small bag and pushed it under her bed. John was not going to be sensible about Miss Bennet's leaving, so she was forced to take action. Elizabeth's only chance was to escape the house as soon as possible and make her way to Hawthorne Hall. She would slip down the servant's hall to her friend's bedroom and lead her back to her own. From there they would slip out of the house and head to the stables and Mr. Drummond. Hopefully, John would be too drunk to check on them tonight.

Slowly she opened the door hidden in the wall and peered down the narrow, dark corridor. Then, entering it stealthily, she held her hand at the back of the candle to shade the light from anyone who might enter at the other end as she made her way to Elizabeth.

Chapter 28

Kent
Rosings
Lady Catherine's study

Half asleep, having been awakened early, Wickham yawned into the sleeve of his expensive coat. Getting a whiff of the garment, he winced at the foul smell now emanating from his once impressive attire. Obliged to sleep on a small pile of hay in the corner of the stables upon his arrival last night, he now questioned whether it had been as clean as the liveryman claimed. He had expected to stay in one of the rooms set aside for the grooms at the least, but he found himself unceremoniously shown to the stables, without even so much as a blanket. Lady Catherine would certainly hear of his displeasure.

Lady Catherine, he mused. *Why does even the thought of that woman cause my stomach to lurch? It is she who should fear me!*

His thoughts were interrupted as that very individual walked heavily into the room, her ever-present cane marking the cadence. Only this time, she did not take her place behind the huge, imperious desk. Instead, she stopped several feet away from where he stood and studied him with an expression that made his blood run cold. His self-assurance vanished at the sight of her. It was obvious that she was enraged.

"And just what are you doing at Rosings? You should be well on the way to Gretna Green with my niece."

"I—my plans were foiled."

"Foiled!" She slammed the cane to the floor, causing him to jump. Then she punctuated all she had to say with additional thumps as her voice got louder. "Foiled! You mean you failed me again, do you not! I should have known a man like you would never succeed in making Georgiana think she was in love!"

"I was successful in keeping company with Georgiana, but I was unable to convince her to elope with me. That little chit insisted that she would have to have her brother's permission to marry! Can you imagine a young woman of this day and age with no mind of her own?"

"Yes, I most certainly can imagine it—especially if she has been reared by my nephew and my sister! Did you expect her to toss aside everything she has been taught and leave without believing herself in love?" She began to pace. "I was a fool to think you capable of handling something this important. Were you so stupid as to have no alternative plan?"

"I had always intended to take her by force if she would not go willingly. However, just as I abducted her, a troupe of redcoats came down the boardwalk and—"

The Mistress of Rosings used her walking stick to sweep everything off a nearby table. An exquisite china vase flew to the floor, shattering in numerous pieces and causing an enormous racket. Rapid footsteps in the hallway were evidence of her servant's efforts to locate the source of the disturbance. Even so, Wickham's attention was riveted to the irate old woman as she slowly came towards him. He swallowed hard.

"Silence, you liar! I am not to be trifled with, and I do not accept your account! I have no doubt that there were no soldiers about to hinder. You tried to force her and were thwarted." At his silent nod, she continued. "Who was it that found you out?"

"That interfering sister of yours, Lord Landingham and a young woman who has been in their company of late. It was the woman who first noticed me with Georgiana on the beach and came down to investigate. She drew the other's attention to us."

"My sister saw your face? She can identify you?"

"Unfortunately, she did."

"And Landingham as well?"

Wickham coughed, hesitant to tell the worst of it. "He did. As it is, he almost intercepted me before I … I shot him."

"Shot him? You killed a member of the House of Lords?"

"It seems that I only wounded him, as I saw him getting up as I entered the pathway to my coach."

Uncharacteristically, Lady Catherine's face became ashen, and she sat down in a nearby chair, rubbing her face with her hands. "You imbecile! All of England will be searching for you. And what will happen if word circulates that I was involved? My brother will most likely cast me into Bedlam to save face."

"With your help, I shall escape England, and no one shall be the wiser."

Her head came up sharply. "So you are here for more of my money. I should have known you would return penniless."

"I simply need enough to purchase passage on a ship to the Americas and enough funds to stay hidden until it is time to sail. I will need disguises—different clothes, a wig or two—and money for lodging. Shall we say two thousand pounds?"

"Two thousand pounds! It would be less expensive to have you killed!"

"I took into account your logic, and that is why I have left letters explaining our *unique* relationship with one of my associates. He has pledged to deliver them to the Earl of Matlock and Fitzwilliam Darcy should I be *"tucked up with a spade."*[11] Wickham smirked at the stunned expression on her face. "I see that you are familiar with the term. So suppose you just hand over the money and credit the excess to assuring my silence."

Lady Catherine considered him for several moments, her scowl deepening. "I

---

[11] *Tucked up with a spade. One that is dead and buried according to the 1811 Dictionary of the Vulgar Tongue.*

suppose I have no choice. But this is the last farthing you shall ever get from me, and if you are caught and implicate me, I will do everything in my power to discredit you and see you hang."

The feeling is mutual, I assure you.

"Do not worry. No one will find me, and I shall be in distant lands before they realise I am no longer in England."

"You have given me your assurances before, and they have all come to naught. Why should I believe you now?"

"This time I have no choice."

Lady Catherine stood to leave. "And the next time you appear on my doorstep, I shall have no choice. Keep that in mind!"

Wickham quickly added, "I also require one of the groom's accommodations, my meals brought over from the kitchen and my pick of mounts when I leave."

With these added demands she paused at the door and fixed him with a frosty stare. "Return to the stables. It may take a day or more to get the funds." Then lifting her head haughtily, she quitted the room.

Wickham moved to the door to watch her negotiate the long hallway, as was his habit. Her cane tapped out a familiar rhythm as she traversed the slick, polished wood covered by an occasional decorative rug.

I would consider it a stroke of luck if she fell and broke her neck after I leave for London.

As she faded out of sight, he slowly found his way through the house and out the back door to the stables.

❦

Gatesbridge Manor
Elizabeth's Bedroom

Alfreda paced all the while Elizabeth whittled around the lock on the shutter that covered the window. Using the knife she kept hidden in her trunk at her father's insistence, she had hoped to loosen the latch and force it open. However, it was going very slowly as the wood was solid oak.

"Oh, Elizabeth, I am so sorry for bringing you here," Alfreda moaned for the hundredth time. "Brother will likely come back before we escape."

"Hush!" Elizabeth said with exasperation. "There is no time for that kind of talk."

It was taking all her efforts to work on the latch, as they had been up all night and she was tired. Nevertheless, her mind was never far from the madman who could return at any second.

❦

Previously

Earlier that night, Alfreda had entered Elizabeth's bedroom through a panel in wall. Intrigued, she had peered into the dark hallway as Alfreda explained that this was a network that wound throughout the house and the servants used them to access the rooms. Alfreda declared it would be their route to freedom.

All of a sudden, it became clear to Elizabeth that this could explain the nights when she had awakened with the strange feeling that someone was in the room. The thought that it could have been John Wilkens repulsed her, but she had no time to dwell on that as Alfreda was frantically urging her to pack a bag.

All had been in vain, though, for hardly two minutes later, Wilkens had come through the same entrance, and it was obvious that he was drunk. Alfreda tried to stand her ground against the onslaught of her brothers' accusations and anger, but it had served no purpose.

"Brother!" she exclaimed stepping between him and Elizabeth, "How did—" Quickly, she hushed.

"How did I know that you would defy me and go straight to Miss Bennet? Because, I am no fool!" He grabbed hold of a bed post to steady himself. "Your attitude has changed since she came to Gatesbridge. Your sympathy lies with her, not me. And it was simple enough to realise how you would get into her room. I had only to place a servant on the other end of the hall to await the sight of your candle."

"I meant my assistance to Miss Elizabeth to help you as well, John. Holding her in this manner is certain to result in disaster. Our aunt will never tolerate it, and her friend, Lady Ashcroft, is expecting Miss Elizabeth at Hawthorne Hall in the morning. She is to travel back to London with them. And need I mention that Lord Landingham is in their party? I pray you, abandon this madness and let her go!"

Wilkens was not to be reasoned with, and at that point, he had shoved her aside to confront the one he considered his greatest betrayer—Elizabeth. The smell of his body odour and brandy-soaked breath made her nauseous as he stood inches from her face.

"You mean to throw me over just like the rest of those whores in the *ton!*" He spat out, staggering to stay upright as he threw his hands up in exasperation. "Little Miss High-and-Mighty! Who are you to refuse me, the Earl of Hampton?" As she tried to back away, he grabbed her forearms. "You are of no consequence. I could take you here and now, and no one would lift a finger against me, not even my mousey little sister. Then you would be mine, regardless."

Breaking free of his unsteady grip, Elizabeth's courage rose, and she stood tall, declaring, "You are the one who is of no consequence! You are a filthy man who is not worthy of the title or the wealth you possess, and you are certainly not worthy of me."

As he growled and lunged towards her, he lost his balance and fell flat on his face. Cursing, he struggled to get back on his feet by clinging to a table. That was when Elizabeth seized the opportunity to run to the small trunk that she had brought from home. Opening it, she quickly found the hunting knife that was always inside and gripped it fiercely as she turned to face him. Her heart was beating furiously, but she did not let him see her discomposure.

"If you come near me, you shall find out that I am neither afraid of you nor helpless."

Bleary eyed, Wilkens stood deathly still as he tried to gauge whether or not to call her bluff. A threat had always sufficed to make Alfreda fall in line, so he was taken aback by this petite woman standing her ground. Feeling the inside pocket of his coat, he realised that his pistol was still on his desk. Elizabeth blurred into two people and then back into one, a result of all the liquor in his system, and he wisely decided to wait.

"To the devil with your threats! Once I am sober, you shall learn to fear me!"

With that ominous warning, he cast a blistering look at his sister before stumbling back into the servant's hallway and making a show of securing the door from the other side. They could hear him bump into the walls in his haste to leave.

Afterwards, Elizabeth had answered Alfreda's anxious expression with a wan smile. "Let us find a way of escape from this prison before he comes to his senses."

Thus they had broken a window, using a blanket to muffle the noise and then removed the glass and unlocked it. After accomplishing that, Elizabeth had begun using the knife to whittle the wood away from the latch that held the shutter. That shutter was the only obstacle standing between them and freedom, as Alfreda assured her that her brother would not have thought to lock all the doors that led onto the balcony. Once they were free, they could slip through the house using the back passages. Alfreda would then ask Mr. Drummond, the liveryman, to drive them to Hawthorne Hall. She was certain that her aunt would let the old servant work for her if he helped them to escape. Under her aunt's protection, he would be in no danger of reprisal.

Now that several hours had passed, however, and though Elizabeth had made some progress, the lock still held. With the shutters covering the windows, there was no way of knowing if it was near daylight, but she imagined it was. She also wondered what would happen if they could not escape. Would Lady Ashcroft keep her promise not to leave Ramsgate without her? And, if so, would she come to Gatesbridge Manor to find out why she had not come?

Taking a minute to rest and wipe the perspiration from her brow, Elizabeth said a little prayer and then began again with renewed vigour.

Hawthorne Hall
The foyer
The next day

The mistress of the house stood tall and regal, or as tall as the petite woman could while she waited at the base of the stairs for those who were about to depart her home for London. Reflecting on the many wonderful times she had shared with her friend, Lady Ashcroft, Violet Hawthorne smiled in spite of herself. They shared a great deal in common.

Each had married men who loved them and whom they had loved. Both had lost children through miscarriage and been widowed at a young age, left alone to govern large estates. Each had charted her own course through the waters of the *ton* and neither backed down from a fight nor suffered fools gladly. Perhaps, she reflected, that was why they had become fast friends years ago, despite the vast difference in their ages. Audrey's behaviour yesterday served to cement her favourable opinion of the younger woman. Though she could have, Audrey had not left it to Lord Landingham to confront the gallery owner, but had actively participated. That had earned her even more of Lady Hawthorne's esteem.

Her mind thus occupied, Violet did not notice when her friend appeared at the top of the stairs, followed by her niece, Georgiana, and began to descend the ornate staircase. Jarred from her recollections when they came into sight, Lady Hawthorne enquired, "Where is Lord Landingham? Has he changed his mind?"

Laughing softly, Lady Ashcroft responded, "Due to his injury, he is a bit dizzy and having some problems getting dressed. One of your servants proposed his aid, and last I looked, the man was entering Marshall's rooms with shaving implements. I think he is annoyed at having to have assistance. You know how he often boasts of not having a valet travel with him."

"I am sure Landers will have him ready shortly," Lady Hawthorne stated. "He was a valet for many years, and I asked if he would offer his services."

Just at that moment, said gentleman appeared at the top of the stairs and swiftly trotted down them, calling out as he came, "Landers is a godsend! If he would agree, I would gladly take him back to London with me. One cannot find valets like him anymore, and that is one reason I do so much for myself."

"He has lived at this estate almost his entire life, and I fear you will never talk him into leaving. However, I know that he will gladly be of service if you are ever in need of a valet while in Ramsgate."

"And I would be pleased to have him."

The Mistress turned to lead the party into the dining room. "Come, let us eat. We have plenty of time before it gets light, and that will give Miss Bennet time to arrive."

The mention of that young woman brought frowns to all present, and Georgiana spoke for the first time. "Aunt, do you think she will come?"

Audrey took her niece's hand. "She will come, or we shall go find her. In any event, she will be returning to London with us, as that was her desire."

"I … I just wonder why she is not here. Did I not hear you tell her to be here at first light? And it is beginning to get light now."

"I think you are mistaken. It is still dark." Pushing her niece ahead of her playfully, she added. "Let us cease talking and eat! I want to be ready to leave as soon as Miss Bennet arrives. I plan to make Ashcroft Park before nightfall."

As Georgiana hurried on ahead, those left in the circle exchanged worried glances before following after her.

London
Holmes House
The Drawing Room

The two women waited patiently as the maid set the tray of refreshments on the table between them, curtsied and quitted the room as quietly as she had entered. As the door clicked shut, proving that it was indeed closed, Mrs. Holmes resumed what she had been saying.

"I cannot believe that you are with child. You still look so slender."

Madeline Gardiner chuckled. "I can tell a difference, though I can still squeeze into most of my clothes. But my maid is continuing to let out the seams in my gowns so that I may breathe a little easier." With that she sat up straighter, pressed a hand to her stomach and took a deep breath as if to make a point.

Penelope Holmes patted her friend's hand thoughtfully before she began pouring the tea. "Sugar? Cream?"

Two nods of agreement found those items added to the hot liquid before the cup was passed to Elizabeth's aunt. Stirring the tea with the delicate spoon provided, she blew on the contents lightly before taking a sip and then sighed in contentment.

"I believe this is just what I needed today."

"I also cannot believe that you insisted on attending your sister in your delicate condition. It is a wonder that Edward would let you go."

Madeline smiled, "He is very protective, but I am barely three months at this point, and other than some nausea early on, I have felt remarkably well. In fact, while I stayed with Harriet, with all there was to keep me busy, I almost forgot that I am carrying a child."

"Well, I shall not scold you further, as you obviously know your own limitations," she teased before changing the subject. "You were saying that your sister is much better?"

"Harriet gave us quite a scare. For the first few days after Judson's birth, the doctor was concerned that she displayed a slight fever that he could not arrest. But on the fourth day, it disappeared as suddenly as it had come, and she began progressing normally. Before I left, everything was almost back to normal."

"I know you were relieved, as I am to hear about it," Lady Holmes murmured thoughtfully.

Out of the blue, Madeline Gardiner's expression sobered and her brow furrowed. "I truly hate to bring this up, but I must ask about the note you sent regarding my niece. I came directly here once I read it."

A shaky hand came to rest on Lady Holmes' forehead. "I hate to be the bearer of bad news, but I felt sure you would want to know. Alfreda relates that they all shall return to London in a few days, and I could not bear for you to think everything is well when it is not."

"What exactly did Alfreda say? Has my niece completely ruined her chance to better herself?"

"Alfreda is always very vague. I cannot say for sure that Miss Bennet has squandered her chance, but my cousin's letter was not encouraging. She hinted that there had been several disagreements between your niece and my nephew during their time in Ramsgate."

Mrs. Gardiner took a deep breath, puffing her cheeks before releasing it. "I was afraid that Lizzy would not make an effort to be agreeable. Of all my nieces, she is the one most likely to speak up if she disagrees with you. Jane would have been my first choice to meet your cousin, as she is more complacent. She would have heeded my advice and endeavoured to please Lord Wilkens."

"Then why not bring her to London and introduce her to John?"

"Because I had a letter from my Sister Bennet when I returned, and she bragged of nothing but Jane's engagement."

"Engaged? To whom?"

"To a Mr. Bingley, a merchant. But had she come to London with Lizzy, I feel sure she would have impressed your cousin from the start. She would likely be betrothed to him now, rather than the tradesman. While I love my Edward and he has been a sufficient provider, my nieces need to aim higher. Otherwise, if Mr. Bennet were to die, it would place great hardship on us to support Fanny and the girls."

"Unfortunately, from your descriptions of the younger sisters, John would never consider them."

"No, Jane and Lizzy were the only ones that could possibly have fit into London society."

Penelope fiddled with the lace on her sleeves. "I so wanted to help you, my friend, but my cousin will, no doubt, set his sights on another fortunate woman."

Mrs. Gardiner's face brightened. "Perhaps all is not lost. Maybe there is still time for me to convince Lizzy to be more agreeable."

"I am afraid you are being too hopeful."

"Whatever do you mean?"

"There is more you should hear. You realise that I am not one to believe in idle gossip or to pass it along, but—"

The older woman paled. "Tell me."

"Rumour has it that Lizzy has captured the heart of one of the wealthiest men in all of England." She paused, aware that what she next related would hurt deeply. "But, the gentleman's *wife* is most unhappy and very vocal about it."

Mrs. Gardiner almost dropped the cup she was holding. "My Lizzy having an affair with a married man? That cannot be. She has been in my company or Miss Wilkens' since she arrived in London. When would she have had opportunity? Besides, she is not that type of woman; it is simply not in her character."

"I did not think her capable of it either."

"Who is the man?"

"Well, if one is to believe Gisela Darcy, and she is hardly a credible source, it is her husband." There was an audible gasp.

"Fitzwilliam Darcy? I grew up in Lambton, and I remember him and his family as good and decent people. It is no secret that his marriage is a farce, but he has never added to the rumours by carrying on affairs, at least I have never heard of any, whereas Gisela's liaisons are well-known."

"That is true." Penelope Holmes agreed. "Walter, who knows more than I about the circumstances because of his friendship with Colonel Fitzwilliam, has always contended that, in light of how ill that woman has used him, Mr. Darcy is a saint!"

"Besides, it makes no sense. When could he have met my niece? And even if he had met her, why would a man of his wealth and handsome looks be interested in our unruly, outspoken Lizzy? Her beauty is only tolerable, whereas it is no secret that Fitzwilliam Darcy could have his pick of any number of beautiful women if he were so inclined." She made a clucking sound with her tongue. "No! This cannot be true!"

"I am only relating what is being said. However, Lady Matlock, who is a personal friend, denies there is any truth in the rumours. She contends that Gisela has lost her mind to strong drink, and frankly, that is a distinct possibility. Not one person of my acquaintance can remember even seeing Miss Bennet in Mr. Darcy's company, other than when I introduced them at my ball. And I found their conversation awkward—like that of perfect strangers."

"Which I am sure they are!"

"Remember that Lizzy is not the first woman, nor will she be the last, that Gisela has accused of warming her husband's bed. That harridan is obsessed with anyone she perceives as a threat."

"But that will not matter to the gossips! Lizzy will be ruined and so will her sisters!" Mrs. Gardiner stood up, her eyes wide now with fright. "How could this have happened under my watch? Once this gossip reaches Meryton, Lizzy's parents will never speak to me again."

Penelope stood and gently helped her friend back down in the chair. "Please sit and try to calm yourself. Evelyn Fitzwilliam has been very successful in hushing most of the gossip, though there are always a few who will repeat it until she warns them personally. I strongly believe, however, that there is a solution, and that was my purpose in telling you."

"Pray tell me what it is!"

"If your niece were to announce her engagement to my cousin as soon as she arrives in London, that will end all the gossip."

She blinked rapidly as she considered the plan. "You are right. That would quash the gossip, but what if Lord Wilkens is not willing to have Lizzy now? Or what if he hears the rumours and decides she is not worthy of his good opinion?"

"John is awkward with women, and he has not had a lot of luck in the marriage market. I think Lizzy's lower station gives him more confidence in the relationship, and it would be to his advantage not to have another broken courtship. Besides, Walter has said that our cousin is jealous of many men, Fitzwilliam Darcy among them. It would likely stroke his ego to secure a woman rumoured to be sought after by Mr. Darcy."

"Good. Good." Mrs. Gardiner repeated, smoothing her skirts nervously. "My Sister Bennet and Jane will be here the day after tomorrow to order Jane's wedding clothes." She smiled for the first time since learning of Elizabeth's difficulties with Lord Wilkens. "And Fanny is the one person who can force Lizzy to accept your cousin, especially if it is necessary to keep down a scandal."

"Then all shall work out for the best!"

"Thank you for helping me to see my way clear in this matter. You are a godsend, Penelope!"

"Maybe just a fairy godmother!"

Both ladies giggled as the hostess warmed their tea by refilling their cups and held out the platter of goodies to her friend.

"Almond biscuits or gingerbread?"

$$\mathscr{C}hapter \ 29$$

Ramsgate
Hawthorne Hall
The Dining Room

Georgiana grew irritated as she studied the faces of those who surreptitiously stole glances at her over the delicate, flowery rims of Lady Hawthorne's best china. Everyone at the large ornate dining room table had long since finished eating, but each still sipped on a steaming cup of tea. Apparently, being occupied with tea was as good a way as any to keep from talking about the subject presently on everyone's mind: why had Miss Bennet not yet arrived? Finally, Georgiana could hold her tongue no more.

"I think Miss Bennet is being held against her will, otherwise she would have come by now. Should we not go to her?"

Audrey Ashcroft sought Lord Landingham's gaze. She knew that he would be among those protecting them when they confronted John Wilkens, in spite of the fact that he still suffered from the wound inflicted by Wickham. Seeing the resolve in his eyes, she turned and answered her niece. "I believe you may be right. It seems we have no choice but to go to Gatesbridge Manor and learn the truth."

Landingham nodded, but before he could say anything, their hostess stood and addressed the footman standing stiffly against the wall. "Send for my guards, have my driver and four of my best marksmen bring the carriage to the front door without delay."

"You expect trouble?" Audrey enquired as the servant rushed to do the Mistress' bidding.

"If my nephew is drinking, we may face strong opposition. John has been beyond the reach of reason for some time. I should have intervened before now, but today is as good as any to start. As soon as my carriage is ready, you may follow me to Gatesbridge. I shall retrieve not only Miss Bennet but also my niece. I will no longer bear John's foolish behaviour."

With that, Lady Hawthorne quitted the room, leaving the rest to ponder what might happen when they arrived at Gatesbridge Manor.

Georgiana began to sputter, "I ... I am afraid. But only for Miss Bennet and Miss Wilkens, not for myself."

Lord Landingham moved to her, pulling her into a tight embrace. "Of course you are, sweetheart. We all are," he breathed into her hair. "You have always cared more about the welfare of others. That is something I have always admired

250

about you."

Landingham smiled over Georgiana's head at Audrey, who tried to return it, though her heart was heavy. Marshall's words of admiration touched on what she had learned only that morning. George Wickham had insinuated himself into her niece's company at the art gallery by convincing her of his sincerity and persuading her to keep his presence undisclosed.

By keeping that secret, she had almost been taken from them, and her godfather had paid a steep price. If the bullet that grazed Marshall's head had been one-quarter inch closer, he surely would have died. Watching him now with Georgiana, Audrey wondered if, when he, Fitzwilliam and Richard knew the truth, would they still look upon the young woman's soft heart as a virtue, or would they think it a liability.

Reaching the main road, Mr. Drummond whipped the horses into a gallop and soon the carriage was bouncing from side to side over the pocked and pitted surface. Daylight was breaking, but tall trees along both sides of the road cast long shadows, making navigation dangerous. And since the vehicle was devoid of any passengers or luggage, there was no weight to hold it steady. Just the same, despite the danger, the old servant felt that he had no choice but to hurry—not after what Miss Wilkens had divulged that morning. While he had never respected the son, he had not suspected that Mr. Wilkens' heir was capable of such cruelty to his own sister or those under his roof.

His usual habit of awakening early to feed the animals had put him at the stables in time to hear Miss Wilkens' insistent rapping on the door. Years before, he had found her in this same manner—only then, she had come to beg him to give her riding lessons because her father had not the time or patience to do so. The old Master had been more than willing to allow his instruction, and thus, he had spent that summer teaching Miss Wilkens to ride safely and had become very fond of her.

Nevertheless, after that summer, he had not seen her as often, as he had to leave the livery in order to take care of his mother who lived in a tenant's cottage. In fact, he had not seen much of her since his return to the livery after his mother's death. Yet, after she explained why she had to get to her aunt's estate, he knew he could not refuse. He had assured her that a carriage would be ready and waiting when she was.

Mr. Drummond had kept his word. The carriage stood just out of sight behind a copse of trees near the stables when the Mistress and her guest ran out the back door of the manor. He had almost urged the horses forward to collect them but decided to wait until they cleared the manicured lawn. That choice was most fortunate, as the ladies had only gone about a hundred feet when Lord Wilkens and his men emerged from out of nowhere to surround them. At that instant, he knew that they were doomed unless he could bring help—thus, his reason for trying to reach Hawthorne Hall. Lady Hawthorne was the only one capable of controlling her nephew.

Amazed that he and the carriage were forgotten in the hubbub surrounding the capture of the two women, he had raced the horses to the end of the drive the minute the throng entered the house. Now careening down the road, sunlight began to illuminate the way. He breathed a sigh of relief as he caught the sight up ahead of the large, wrought iron gate announcing the entrance to Hawthorne Hall. Turning into the drive, he urged the horses even faster, cracking the whip just above their backs. As he rounded the curve to the main drive, the outline of another carriage appeared, coming towards him at a steady pace. As they closed the gap, he could see two coaches trailing the carriage. Pulling his steeds to a stop, Mr. Drummond jumped from the vehicle and ran towards the woman who was exiting the other carriage.

"Lady Hawthorne! Lady Hawthorne!"

Gatesbridge Manor
Wilkens' Study

Alfreda and Elizabeth, each with hands tied behind their backs and an armed guard on either side, stood before Lord Wilkens. He occupied the large leather chair behind his desk and wore an expression of sneering superiority. At the spectacle of his delight, Elizabeth noted the frightened look on his sister's face and became incensed.

"Untie us this minute you arrogant fool! If you do not allow us to leave, I assure you that I have loved ones who will hunt you down and call you out!"

The smile on Wilkens' face fell as he rose to his feet and walked around the desk. Standing menacingly before her, he noted the discolouration and cut that Wickham had left on her cheek. Suddenly, he drew back and slapped her in the exact place. She did not cry out, though her eyes involuntarily filled with tears. Instead, she glared at him with all the hatred she could muster.

"Maybe that will teach you never again to speak to a man as though you are his equal."

Alfreda cried out. "Stop! If you have no conscience, do you not at least fear her family? Most men would kill you for what you have done!"

Wilkens' turned on his sister. "No one, not even her family, can do anything once we are married."

"Married?" Alfreda exclaimed. "She will never marry you!"

Wilkens eyes returned to Elizabeth. "She WILL marry me! Or she shall have a tragic accident. It is her choice."

Elizabeth spat out, "I would rather die!"

Wilkens reared back to hit her again, only halting when the butler knocked and opened the door without waiting.

"Master, excuse me, but your aunt has arrived unannounced and—"

Wilkens held up a hand to silence the butler. At the same time, he pulled the gag hanging around Elizabeth's neck back up to cover her mouth and motioned for the other guard to do the same to his sister. Then he commanded, "Lock them in one of the guest rooms and stay there. They had better not escape if you understand what is good for you."

As both women were dragged from the room, Alfreda looked back to see her brother taking the pistol from his desk and placing it in his coat pocket. Catching her watching, all expression left Wilkens' face as he ordered, "Get them out of here now!"

It was not until they were alone that he addressed the butler again. "Continue, Cuthbert"

"As I was saying, when I opened the front door, Lady Hawthorne walked in without hesitation. She said to tell you that she would wait for you in the library and that you would meet her there as soon as possible, if you were wise."

"Is she alone?"

"No, sir. There is a lady and a gentleman with her."

The butler made no mention that Lady Hawthorne also had two armed guards who accompanied her to the library and four others who were hidden just inside the anteroom. Nor did he inform him that Wilkens' aunt had threatened to have him and his wife prosecuted as accomplices if anything had happened to her niece or Miss Bennet.

Neither Cuthbert nor his wife had ever failed to carry out Lord Wilkens' orders, even when they did not agree with them. However, they could not help but notice how bizarre his behaviour had become since his father's death, especially when he drank excessively. But in no way did they wish to be held responsible for what he ordered them to do, and all they could hope for was that Lady Hawthorne would make Lord Wilkens behave in a more civilized manner.

Thus the butler's relief was palpable when the master replied, "Tell my meddling aunt I shall be there shortly."

Hurrying from the study, Cuthbert was eager to do just that.

Lady Hawthorne sat directly across from Audrey Ashcroft on matching upholstered chairs, while Lord Landingham leaned against the mantel surrounding the fireplace. As she studied the room, she recalled when her late brother had insisted she come to admire the furnishings, all having been redone in corals, tans and dark greens. They looked so very lovely that day—fine, imported fabrics complimenting the dark mahogany of the bookshelves and tables. She sighed. It seemed ages ago. She had not bothered to visit in almost a year—not since finding her nephew unconscious in this very room. Drinking until he could no longer walk, he had fallen and then vomited on the expensive hand-loomed carpet. It was a painful example of how debauched he had become since his father's death.

Shaking that image from her mind, Lady Hawthorne glanced at Audrey and tried to smile. They hoped that John would focus on them and Landingham, never suspecting that there were two former Bow Street Runners hidden behind the bookshelves on either side. She knew that Landingham carried a pistol, and Audrey was equally armed with a small calibre gun that she hid under the reticule in her lap. But no one knew that hidden in the pocket of her skirt, she too gripped a one-shot pistol that Horace had given her shortly after they married.

Feeling sure that they were as prepared as they could possibly be, she tried to relax and had just exchanged exasperated looks with Audrey when the door flew open and Wilkens stormed in, followed by a meek Mr. Cuthbert. Wilkens' irritation was clear, but equally as obvious was the smell of liquor that accompanied his entrance. He sneered at Audrey Ashcroft and Lord Landingham before turning to address his aunt.

"What can I do for you, Aunt? Lost your spectacles again?"

Lady Hawthorne stood and took a step towards Wilkens, her hold on the gun handle tightening. "I do not need spectacles to see that you are a poor excuse for a man. You stink of strong drink, and you address me like a common blackguard!"

Wilkens fists balled and he, too, stepped closer. "This is my home! Yet you address me however you see fit!"

"My condemnation is no more than you deserve for your actions!"

Reaching into his coat, Lord Wilkens withdrew the hidden pistol. At once, the men stepped from behind the bookshelves with guns drawn and aimed. And as Wilkens' gaze flitted from one weapon to the next, he was stunned to see that even Landingham, his aunt and Lady Ashcroft had guns trained on his heart. Taken aback that he had been ensnared in his own home, he looked about for Cuthbert, but the butler had quietly exited the room.

Landingham walked over to stand by Violet Hawthorne, never taking his eyes from Wilkens. "Put the gun on the table."

Wilkens hesitated only a second before complying. He laid the gun on a small table next to the chair where his aunt had been sitting. However, his posture and demeanour were still defiant.

"So, you felt you needed armed guards to make your point."

"And I was right, since it seems force is all you understand, Nephew. I shall get directly to the point. Where are my niece and Miss Bennet?"

Wilkens chuckled mirthlessly. "I assume they are asleep in their beds at this hour."

Just then Mr. Drummond stepped into the room, hat in hand, gaining his attention. If possible, Wilkens' expression darkened even more as he glared at the old liveryman.

Lady Hawthorne goaded, "Shall I have Mr. Drummond reiterate why he arrived at my estate this morning with an empty carriage?"

Wilkens' eyes fell to the floor, but he did not reply.

"I want Alfreda and Miss Bennet brought here immediately!"

Cuthbert had reappeared at the doorway behind Mr. Drummond, and her command was sufficient for him to act. As the butler hurried to comply, Wilkens taunted his aunt.

"Why do you care about Miss Bennet? She is nothing to you."

"I beg your pardon. She is nothing to *you*! To me, she is a friend. No woman should be treated as a trophy, a piece of property or as nothing more than one step above an animal. Miss Bennet deserves to make her own choices, as does my niece."

At the mention of Alfreda, Wilkens' brows furrowed. "What has my sister to do with Miss Bennet?"

"Alfreda will no longer be under your control. She is going home with me."

"No! I will not allow it!" Wilkens shouted, bringing all the men a step closer.

"You have no choice. I know of your gambling debts, the brothel you and your friends built and fund, as well as all the other losses you have incurred. In other words, I hold all the cards in this game." Glancing to the side, Violet gave Audrey a determined look before continuing, "I do not have to leave you a farthing in my will, as my Horace left all those decisions to me, and as my least favourite relation, it would suit me to leave you penniless."

"You cannot … you will not!" Wilkens sputtered. "Who would be your heir? You have no one left but Alfreda and me?"

Lady Hawthorne's small smile did not waver, and she continued to stare at him until he comprehended.

"No! You cannot leave everything to her! She will only attract some low-life with no fortune, and he will have everything our family has accumulated without an ounce of effort."

"Why should I leave all that my dear husband and his forefathers worked for to a man who would do what you have done to Alfreda and Miss Bennet, let alone one who would threaten to kill me?" Her mien darkened. "I would rather my niece inherit everything. Besides, you will not need it where you are going."

Lady Hawthorne then addressed the two Bow Street Runners. "Hold my nephew here. I shall send for the local magistrate when I return to Hawthorne Hall, and we shall discuss what charges he will face."

Wilkens began sputtering threats only to go uncharacteristically silent as Alfreda and Elizabeth were brought into the room—his recent handiwork now plain for all to view. The women hurried to embrace each other, and through tears, both captives were inspected. The now swollen, darker bruise on Elizabeth's face was duly noted, fuelling Landingham's anger. Acting as though he was only going to inspect the injury, he passed Wilkens then suddenly turned and knocked him to the floor with a steely right hook.

A cracking sound preceded Wilkens' crash to the floor. Cuthbert's eyes grew large, and the old butler swallowed hard as Landingham stepped in front of him and seemed to debate whether to hit him as well. Instead, he grabbed him by the front of his shirt, almost choking him as he pulled him closer and forced the man on the tips of his toes.

"If I hear that you helped this sorry excuse for a man or anyone else abuse another person ever again, I shall hunt you down no matter how long it takes and extract justice. Is that understood?"

The servant's head bobbed up and down like a duck in water. "No, sir! I mean, yes, sir!"

Landingham shoved Cuthbert away, leaving him to regain his balance.

Lady Hawthorne addressed Alfreda as she led her towards the door. "You can tell me what has happened once we are away from this horrible place."

Audrey Ashcroft put an arm around Elizabeth's waist and guided her towards the door as well, whispering, "Let us do likewise, my dear."

Everyone filed past the rotund figure lying on the floor with an obviously broken nose which had begun to stain the carpet a bright red. Ignoring his Master in favour of showing his newfound respect for the man's aunt and guests, Cuthbert bowed low to all who passed.

Once outside, it did not take long to get everyone situated. While Elizabeth's trunks were brought down and secured to Lord Landingham's coach, she was gently settled into the seat next to Georgiana in the Darcy coach, a wet cloth held against her cheek. Lady Ashcroft and Lord Landingham sat together in the opposite seat, and Elizabeth could not help sneaking peeks at the tall, distinguished man who had won even more of her admiration for hitting Lord

Wilkens.

When she finally caught his eyes, she whispered, "Thank you."

He nodded, returning her smile, and a bit embarrassed, turned to watch the goings on outside. Alfreda had already said her goodbyes and was now entering her aunt's carriage which would take her to Hawthorne Hall. Mr. Cuthbert, newly reformed, leaned into the window of their vehicle, promising loudly to send all her clothes and personal items along as soon as they could be packed.

Thus, as the carriage and two coaches pulled away from Gatesbridge Manor, each occupant hoping never to return, Landingham could not help but chuckle to himself as the now obsequious butler bowed over and over until they were completely out of sight.

On the road to Milton

They had not travelled very many miles when the silence in the carriage grew awkward, as first one, then another, stole a glance at the large bruise on Elizabeth's face whenever she refolded the cloth she held against it. Georgiana was on tenterhooks, wishing to know the details of what happened at Gatesbridge Manor. She was well aware that Miss Bennet's injuries were her fault, and she was filled with remorse. Elizabeth had suffered Wickham's wrath, and obviously Wilkens' as well, for intervening on her behalf. Georgiana then caught sight of a bloody bandage tied around Elizabeth's middle finger, an injury she had been hiding by keeping her other hand clasped around it.

"Miss Elizabeth, did you cut your finger?" she asked timidly. She was not surprised to be the recipient of Lady Ashcroft's raised brow, which she pretended not to see.

Elizabeth examined her finger. "I cut it trying to escape the bedroom in which Alfreda and I were locked. I believe it will heal sufficiently without stitches, though."

Lord Landingham's demeanour rapidly altered. His earlier fury at Wilkens returning full force as he mumbled something about *hanging not being good enough*. Audrey placed a quieting hand on his arm, and he inhaled loudly, as though he would have liked to say more but would restrain himself for her sake.

Georgiana touched Elizabeth's arm sympathetically. "Oh, I am so sorry. Would you like to talk about what happened? Brother says it helps to talk about things and not keep them inside." Immediately, she chuckled wryly, her eyes sad. "Though I do not think he takes his own advice."

"Georgiana!" Lady Ashcroft cautioned.

Elizabeth intervened with a wan smile, laying the cloth that covered her injury aside. "I do not mind telling you."

At Audrey Ashcroft's hesitant nod, she began to explain how she and Alfreda had been locked in the bedroom and how she had accidently cut herself by using the knife in her trunk to whittle around the lock on the shutters.

"Why would you have a knife in your trunk?"

"Perhaps I should not say, as it does not sound very ladylike, but—" Elizabeth smiled crookedly, though the exercise clearly hurt. Her eyes crinkled as everyone awaited her explanation. "I have no brothers, so I grew up following Papa around our estate as he hunted and fished. I became quite adept at being his helper, much to my mother's dismay. So when I began to travel, Papa gave me my own hunting knife, suggesting I hide it in my trunk as protection. I do not know that I could have managed the lock on the shutter without it. I would have thought of some other way I suppose, but the knife was a practical help."

"But you were wounded using it."

"Only because I became careless by trying to work faster as dawn approached."

"You were fortunate Mr. Wilkens did not find it in your possessions beforehand." Seeing that Elizabeth had become more sombre, Georgiana tried to lighten the mood. "I think it clever for all women to have such a weapon at their disposal. Do you not think so, Aunt?"

Landingham broke in, retorting, "Would that they all had a pistol and knew how to use it!"

Diplomatically Lady Ashcroft replied, "Hidden arms are useful for those familiar with the weapon and prudent enough to use them judiciously."

Georgiana continued to prod Elizabeth. "The injury to your face …" She hesitated. "I do not remember it being quite that severe when you left the carriage at the gallery?"

"Lord Wilkens saw fit to make it worse because I answered him too smartly."

Georgiana gasped. "You are so brave!"

"I was more angry than brave." Elizabeth cocked her head and again tried to smile though the effort caused her jaw to ache. "My father says that I am too headstrong to be cautious when I should. But I have always found it hard to be frightened when I am furious. It is only later, when I have time to think clearly, that I realise I may have been foolish for acting without first deliberating."

Audrey Ashcroft broke into the conversation. "Georgiana, please allow Miss Elizabeth to rest since, by her own admission, she was up all night. She must be exhausted. Let us all try to do the same, at least until it is time to stop for fresh horses."

Elizabeth tried to smile her appreciation, as she was truly very tired. Georgiana apologised for talking too much, and straightaway each young woman leaned into separate corners, closing their eyes. With no concern for anyone's disapproval, Lord Landingham put an arm around Audrey, pulling her to rest against his chest, and she closed her eyes as well.

Thus as the little group journeyed towards Milton and Ashcroft Park, they were left to their own reflections on the events that brought them together in the coach.

Knowing that she had been the one responsible for the injuries to her godfather and Miss Elizabeth, Georgiana was dreading her return to London and Fitzwilliam. She was well aware that her brother would be greatly disappointed in her for trusting Wickham and causing this entire fiasco. Ever since she had been rescued, his sad, dispirited eyes haunted her whenever she closed her own.

Lord Landingham appeared to be napping, but he was not. Instead, he was plotting exactly what he would do once he reached London. He intended to make sure that George Wickham became well acquainted with the end of a rope for what he had tried to do to Georgiana. And he knew that he would not be alone in his aspirations, as Fitzwilliam and Richard would want to capture that blackguard just as dearly.

Audrey Ashcroft, too, was not sleeping, though her eyes were shut. She could feel the tension in Marshall's body and knew that as soon as he had recovered enough to mount a horse, he would go after Wickham. She worried about that certainty, as he was no longer a young man, and she prayed that he would leave that task to Fitzwilliam and Richard. They were well able to deal with that villain, and with Richard's contacts, they could track him more readily. The thought of something happening to Marshall caused tears to pool in Audrey's eyes, and she opened them to study his dear face.

I pray that very shortly I shall be your wife.

As though he had heard her thoughts, Lord Landingham opened his eyes to find her gazing at him lovingly. Glancing at the two young women across from them, he gauged that he had enough time to give Audrey a quick kiss. And so he did—twice—before pulling her even more tightly to his side. Snuggling in each other's embrace, they both closed their eyes to rest in earnest.

Only Elizabeth had fallen asleep. One might think she would be reliving the horrors of the past two days while she slumbered, but that would be wrong. Her mind was not filled with what had just transpired, but with what had taken place weeks ago.

In her dream, it was storming furiously outside a small, rickety cabin, while inside she was deliciously warm, kept so by two strong arms wrapped entirely around her. There was a beating in her ear that she discerned was William's heart, and she had just realised by the thrumming in her ears, that her own kept perfect tempo with his.

If anyone had been watching, they would have seen her smile unawares.

Hawthorne Hall

As Lady Hawthorne's carriage pulled up to the front steps to her estate, Colonel Cochran came running down them, eager to open the door to the vehicle. First, he helped his godmother from the carriage, planting a kiss on her cheek, and then he leaned in to assist Alfreda. As she stepped to the ground, he could barely refrain from taking her in his arms, but he resisted doing so, addressing them both animatedly.

"Ladies, I came as soon as I got permission from my superiors, and I have been granted two weeks before I must return to duty. I pray that my inability to accompany you to Gatesbridge Manor in no way jeopardised your wellbeing."

Violet Hawthorne looked puzzled, so he continued. "I beg your pardon, Lady Hawthorne, but when I arrived so early and you were not here, I forced Mr. Traywick to reveal where you had gone. I knew immediately that something unpleasant must have happened, and I had just sent a footman to retrieve my horse when your carriage appeared."

"Ah, now I understand the reason for your anxiety," she replied. "But there was no need to fear for us, as we had enough men accompanying us to get the job done. And here is the proof—my niece!"

Alfreda and the colonel were looking at one another as though they were the only people in the world, so Violet interrupted. "Let us go inside. This is no place to discuss all that has occurred today."

Just as they reached the foyer, there was a commotion outside, and the entire party went back onto the portico. Mr. Drummond, the liveryman from Gatesbridge, was trying to climb down from a very agitated horse. His face was bright red from the exertion. One of Lady Hawthorne's footmen stepped forward and endeavoured to assist the man by holding the animal. When the old gentleman finally had his feet firmly on the ground, he wiped his brow and took a deep breath as if to calm his nerves. Then he walked unsteadily up a few steps towards the Mistress of Hawthorne Hall. Another footman ran down to take his arm and keep him steady.

"Lady Hawthorne, you shall never believe me when I tell you what has happened!"

She stepped down a few steps in his direction. "Tell me and we shall see."

"It is Mr. Wilkens, ma'am. Not long after you left, I was at the stables getting my things together, as you had so kindly offered me a job. All of a sudden, the Master was behind me, demanding that I saddle him a horse straightaway. I found out later that he had asked the guards who were watching him to allow him use of the … privy." Colouring with embarrassment, he continued with eyes downcast. "And he escaped through a false wall panel while they waited outside."

The man studied his well-worn boots self-consciously. "I would never have complied had he not begun to whip me with his riding crop." He motioned to some red stripes visible along the side of his neck. "But, having no choice, I saddled old Bailey here." He pointed to the large grey horse now being soothed by the footman. "Now Bailey has always been a well behaved creature, but just as the Master mounted, your men came running down the lawn with weapons drawn. One got off a shot just as Lord Wilkens startled the horse by shouting and beating him with the crop, hence he did something I never expected—he reared."

The man hesitated for a moment for her to understand the consequences of what he was saying. "I am afraid that is when your nephew fell and—" Unexpectedly catching sight of Alfreda Wilkens peering from behind Colonel Cochran, he hushed straightaway.

Wilkens sister's eyes grew wide as she stepped around the colonel to address him. "Please finish, Mr. Drummond. Tell me what happened to my brother."

He swallowed hard, murmuring, "I am afraid that he hit his head on a stone wall and cracked his skull, Miss. He is dead."

Alfreda covered her face with her hands and began to cry as she turned into David's arms. After a little while, he looked to his godmother and nodded towards the open door, then began to lead Alfreda back into the house. Violet Hawthorne said not a word, pensively following the young couple's progress until they were out of sight. Then she turned to meet Mr. Drummond's gaze.

"They that sow to the wind, reap the whirlwind." [12]

---

[12] KJV Bible, Hosea 8:7 For they have sown the wind, and they shall reap the whirlwind.

Mr. Drummond did not reply, but only shook his head in agreement.

Chapter *30*

London
Darcy House

Mr. Barnes hurried towards the kitchen as swiftly as was appropriate for a man of his position and contemplated how abruptly the day had changed. Only an hour before, he had found the Master working in his study by candlelight, as it was still quite dark inside the room though the sun had begun to rise. This was not an unusual occurrence. Since Mr. Darcy's return from Hertfordshire weeks before, he kept late hours and slept for no more than four or five hours a night. When he awoke, more often than not, he would go to his study and begin working on estate matters.

Deeming it his duty to rise early in case he might be of service, Barnes had changed his hours to coincide with the Master's. As a result, every morning he would arise well before dawn, being careful not to wake Mrs. Barnes, since she often kept late hours. Heading downstairs, he would make sure that the footmen who stood guard overnight were replaced. Then he would wait patiently for the Master to appear. Once that took place, he would awaken members of the kitchen staff to make coffee, Mr. Darcy's preferred beverage, and to begin preparing food. When the coffee was ready, he would carry a fresh pot of the hot liquid to the study, delivering it himself, so he could have a few words with the Master before the day began in earnest. That routine served him well for soon afterward the house would be bustling with activity, the silence replaced by the hum of everyday tasks.

This morning, however, Barnes noted that the silence still remained. Each member of the staff moved cautiously and wore a serious expression. Not a one spoke, choosing instead to return his silent nod of greeting. No doubt the news had spread quickly that the Master's mood had changed for the worse since Mr. Clark's arrival, and they were either eager to see Mr. Darcy depart or escape his notice until he had. A customarily kind man, their employer could be quite critical of the smallest infraction when he was worried.

Occupied with these thoughts, the butler almost ran into the kitchen door which swung open with a vengeance directly in his path. Coming out of the room with a tray filled with sausages, cheese, eggs, butter, jam and fresh baked bread was his wife, who managed to stop just in time to avoid dropping the contents. "Mind where you are going, Maxwell!" she declared, trying to regain her balance. Then looking about to make sure no other servants had heard, she sighed heavily and smiled her regret for being so terse.

Aghast at the near miss, Barnes exhaled noisily and feigned wiping his brow as he leaned in to explain. "I am sorry, Matilda. My mind was preoccupied, and I confess that I was not paying attention as I should."

"I apologise as well. It has been Bedlam since you sent Florence to awaken me with the admonition that I should hurry as the Master intended to leave."

"That it has! I have no idea what was in that express Mr. Clark delivered." Now it was his turn to look about suspiciously before continuing. "I have never seen Mr. Darcy's expression darken so rapidly. Immediately he had me send a footman to locate Colonel Fitzwilliam and insist that he come without delay."

"Has the colonel arrived?"

"No, but I pray he does soon. I have never seen Mr. Darcy so upset. He paces across his study, murmuring to himself."

"Then let me hasten with this fare. It may be a welcome diversion."

"I pray you are right." Patting his wife on the back, he enquired, "Would you rather I take it? You know he can be short without intending to be when he is disturbed."

"No, he has never once treated me with less than the utmost courtesy, and I do not expect that to change."

Stepping aside, he bowed, and made a show of sweeping an arm across his body. "Then be on your way, my love."

Returning his endearment with a wink, Mrs. Barnes hastened to her duty. The footman positioned beside the study door leaned over to knock as she approached, and the housekeeper paused for the summons. As she waited, she was surprised to hear Colonel Fitzwilliam's voice echoing in the foyer and turned to see him striding towards her, dressed in his regimentals, immaculate as always.

"That smells wonderful, Mrs. Barnes. I am delighted to find something to eat. I have not had one bite of food this morning. I pray that there is also some of that excellent coffee already prepared."

"As always, we have plenty of food, Colonel, and a pot of coffee was delivered several minutes ago."

She was about to say more, but at that exact moment his cousin called out, "Come."

Smiling, Richard turned the knob on the door and pushed it open, standing aside to allow her to enter first. As he followed the housekeeper inside, he noted that William was clearing his desk of some papers in order to make a place to set the tray. Instantly he began his usual teasing.

"Now, Cousin, what situation could possibly be so dire as to require my attendance at this ungodly hour? Has Bonaparte attacked Pemberley?"

As Richard guffawed at his own joke, William met his cousin's look with a decided frown before addressing Mrs. Barnes. "Thank you, Mrs. Barnes. Please be so good as to have three satchels prepared with enough food and water for a trip to Ashcroft Park. Slattery and Musgrove will travel with me via horseback."

Though her eyebrows rose at the mention of travelling via horseback, the long-time servant executed a perfect curtsey and barely glanced at Richard as she exited the room.

Once the door closed behind her, William walked around the desk without a word and handed Richard the express he had received earlier. Meeting his cousin's eyes briefly, Richard focused on the missive and began to read. As his expression changed from astonishment to anger, he gripped the back of a nearby chair then walked around it to sit down, shaking with fury. Once finished reading, he was immediately back on his feet, mirroring William's earlier pacing.

"How dare that scum try to take our Georgiana! I swear by all that is holy I shall make that cad pay with his life!"

William, who had been leaning against his desk as he waited for him to finish, stopped his cousin by grabbing his arm. "I have no doubt of that, but first we have to find him. Is your man still watching Gisela's residence?"

"Yes. He has not had anything to report lately. By and large, she stays home and drinks. Even Attenborough has deserted her for younger women, it seems."

"Perhaps you should add more men. I would like her observed at all times. I have a feeling that Wickham will return to London, and I would not be surprised if he comes to her townhouse. In fact, I would not discount that she had something to do with this."

"Good Lord, man! Why would Gisela be so cruel as to try to harm Georgiana? She has never done anything to her." At William's pointed look, he answered his own question. "Revenge."

"That and perhaps she thought that she could control Georgiana and, by extension, me, if my sister wed that blackguard."

"I shall strangle her with my bare hands if this is so."

"You will have to get behind me." William snarled, beginning to pour two cups of coffee. He held one steaming cup towards his cousin. "But the priority now is to make sure Georgiana is safe."

Richard took a sip of the hot liquid before replying, "Pemberley."

"Precisely."

"I take it you will travel to Ashcroft Park and escort her to London and then on to Pemberley. Do you need my assistance?"

"I thank you, no. I shall take two men with me. With those already travelling with her party, it should suffice. I want you to head the search for Wickham. With your army comrades, you have useful connections all over England."

"That would be my pleasure. First, I shall dispatch enquiries to my fellow officers in the outlying counties and see what I can uncover. I do not see that rat returning to London via the usual route from Ramsgate. He would fear running directly into you."

"That is my opinion as well. I will rest easier knowing you are on his trail. That leaves me free to focus on Georgiana."

"Of course. When do you leave?"

"As soon as Barnes tells me all is in readiness. I imagine he will avoid giving me clearance until I eat. My servants are very protective."

"You have good people. For that you should be thankful."

"Though I may not always appear to be, I am. And I realise that though I have no appetite, it will not do to ride all day without eating."

"Well, I do have an appetite, so I have no qualms in indulging. Would that we had food like this in the army!"

William relaxed somewhat as he sat down at his desk and began pulling the covers off the dishes. Not hesitating, Richard took a plate and began filling it, unaware of his cousin's amazement at the amount of food he had on his plate.

Once Richard sat down to eat, William forced himself to do likewise.

Later, as the pair stood in the foyer before going their separate ways, Richard moved close so that the servants could not hear. "I can only imagine how torn you are between the desire to be in company with Miss Bennet and the need to focus on Georgiana's safety. It must be very difficult."

"I have no choice, Richard. My sister's safety is at stake, and I cannot fail her." The anguish in William's voice was evident. "I pray that God keeps Elizabeth safe until she is able to return to London and that she refuses that reprehensible Wilkens if he offers marriage."

"One can only hope. I found her very intelligent, but she did not act in her own interest by going to Ramsgate in the first place. You must brace yourself for what may transpire, as she may be willing to sacrifice her own happiness in order to help her sisters."

If possible, William's face fell even further. His shoulders slumped, and his head dropped as he murmured wearily, "I have resigned myself to this one thing—if she is to be mine, it will only be by an act of Divine Providence, as no sane woman would have me under the circumstances."

"Then let us hope Providence is on your side, my friend," Richard said, clasping his cousin by both shoulders and squeezing affectionately. "I wish you God's protection and speed on your journey. Tell my cousin that I love her and will do everything in my power to apprehend that villain and anyone else that may have played a part in his scheme."

"She knows you love her, but I will tell her again." William forced a smile. "Please be very careful, Richard. There is no way of knowing how many are involved. I am certain that, left to his own devices, George Wickham could never have afforded the expense of parading about Ramsgate as a gentleman—hiring carriages, coaches and such or staying in decent inns."

"In addition to locating that rogue, I intend on discovering just who is financing him." Richard straightened to his full height as his hand settled on the handle of his sword. "And heaven help whoever that fool may be."

London
Grantham Townhouse
Gisela's Sitting Room

Gisela's latest maid, Fran, barely two and twenty, moved cautiously into the room trying to avoid waking the woman still snoring on the chaise. In the short while she had been serving Mrs. Darcy, not once had she found her asleep in the large bed in the next room as one would assume. Instead, she was either on the chaise or splayed out on the carpet in front of the fireplace in the bedroom.

Though she had managed to fit in with the downstairs staff since being hired, she was not sure how much longer she would be able to deal with her employer since moving upstairs. It was well known among the staff that her ladyship's personal maids never lasted for more than a few months, and they were not allowed to remain in other positions when they quit; thus, Fran had never been desirous of moving upstairs as she needed to keep the position. But she had been pressed into service forthwith after Jemima left without notice because the Mistress had noted that she had better deportment than the others.

Tiptoeing over to take a closer look at the slumbering woman, Fran shook her head in despair at the sight—dishevelled clothes and a mess of tangled hair, combs and pins. The maid had to wonder if the knots would ever comb out. Furthermore, as she got near the figure lying prone on the tufted seat, she noted a distinct smell, not unlike that of the guttersnipes in the alley—a mix of liquor and body odour. Just yesterday Mrs. Darcy had ordered a bath drawn and then when summoned to the dressing room to bathe, insisted that she had not.

And from the smell, she certainly could have used one!

Sighing at the prospect of another day listening to her mistress whine, Fran spied something on the carpet and stooped to discover bits of broken glass. She quickly surmised that it had come from a broken picture frame lying under a nearby chair.

It is a wonder that she does not run out of things to throw!

Striving to clean up whatever debris she found each morning, it was discouraging to see new items destroyed every day. Picking up the frame, she stopped to study the portrait. It was of Mr. Darcy and his sister, the one Mrs. Darcy had boasted of stealing from Darcy House. That revelation had come yesterday, just as the mistress had begun her evening ritual of complaining about her husband's inattention while drinking until she lost consciousness.

Like the majority of the servants, Fran had never actually seen Mr. Darcy up close. He certainly never darkened the door of the residence, but she had glimpsed him and his sister once on the street, when another maid had pointed them out. She remembered thinking that while the girl was pretty, Mr. Darcy was the most handsome man she had ever seen. This portrait proved that she had not erred in her judgment. Examining the tall, attractive man with dark, wavy hair, light eyes and a chiselled jaw, she recalled the bawdy remarks of one of the kitchen help— *He can leave his boots under my cot any time he sees fit!*

Shaking these improper thoughts from her mind, Fran brushed several small shards of glass from the likeness and then placed it out of sight behind other items on top of the chest of drawers.

Perhaps if it is hidden, Mrs. Darcy will not spoil it. It would be a shame to ruin so fine a likeness.

Seeing Mr. Darcy's picture also brought to mind the servant's gossip about the odd marriage of their employer and the Heir of Pemberley. This topic was often debated below stairs, though she had never added anything to the conversation. She knew the story well and, in any event, she learned more by listening. Nevertheless, the long-time maids and footmen always had some bit of new information to share, including recent reports that Mr. Darcy may have taken a lover. And now that she had been moved upstairs, they were steadfast in their efforts to have her tell them what went on in Mrs. Darcy's private quarters. Nonetheless, Fran knew that a lady's maid was not supposed to gossip about her mistress, so she dutifully kept her mouth shut and hid all evidence that the Mistress continued to destroy everything that reminded her of her miserable state.

That had not endeared her to the rest of the staff, but she did not mind. She was more interested in pleasing Mrs. Darcy to gain her trust.

Picking up several items of clothing strewn about the room, her mind wandered to Mrs. Darcy's friend, Lord Attenborough. At first glance, she had thought him a distinguished gentleman when he appeared at the house on her first day in her new position. However, when she had delivered the news that Gisela Darcy would be delayed a few minutes, he had made her uncomfortable by not answering but continuing to look her over. Then when he had refused to wait any longer, she had been very happy to fly back upstairs to the Mistress' sitting room to inform her that Lord Attenborough had taken his leave and had left her a letter. After reading the letter, Mrs. Darcy had thrown a tantrum, turning over things and breaking objects. It had disconcerted her at the time, but her displays of temper had continued so frequently that Fran had swiftly adjusted and now barely raised an eyebrow when one occurred.

A sudden knock at the door proved to be Mr. Boatwright, the butler, with the post. She glanced at the two letters before laying them on the dressing table. About to quit the room, her employer startled her by sitting up and exclaiming groggily, "Is there a letter from my husband?"

Knowing well not to answer that question, Fran replied, "You have two letters on your dressing table, madam."

Gisela grasped her aching head. "There is no need to shout! Have Mrs. Boatwright prepare one of her headache powders as soon as possible."

"Yes, ma'am," Fran replied, eager to be away from her mistress. "I shall have her do it straightaway and bring it with your tray."

"No. No food! Just have her prepare some strong tea and the powders."

Fran nodded, slipping out the door. Once in the hall, she leaned against the door, closed her eyes and took a deep breath before letting it go slowly. Then she hurried towards the grand staircase to find the housekeeper.

In her room, Gisela slid her feet to the floor and held onto the dressing table to stand. Feeling dizzy, she closed her eyes and waited for the room to stop spinning. Once it had sufficiently, she reached for the letters lying on her dressing table. The one from her solicitor was ignored as she broke the seal on the other. It was not from Fitzwilliam as she hoped, but from Wickham. In it he gave his account of all that had gone wrong in Ramsgate. By the end, when he wrote of heading to London so that she could provide him a place to hide, she was furious.

Why would he think I am willing to help him? That fool will get us both hanged! Thank God, Grimsby's son reports that Fitzwilliam has left London. I imagine he is off to comfort that snivelling little sister of his. Perhaps I should return to Derbyshire until this incident is forgotten.

Throwing Wickham's missive aside, she sank into the chair in front of the dressing table, and for the first time in days, actually stared at her image in the large, ornate mirror. She gasped audibly. *That cannot possibly be me!*

Grabbing a nearby candle, she lit it, holding it near the glass as she leaned in close to study her features. Her fingers flew up to glide over a visage she no longer recognised. Finding the skin rough and dry beneath her touch, she pictured wrinkles where once there were none. Reaching for a jar of some expensive French cream, she began to slather it over her face and neck. The more she applied, the more upset she became until, all of a sudden, she quit the exercise, flinging the jar at the costly mirror while cursing loudly. The glass exploded with an ear-splitting sound, and the clamour of servants running in the hall proved that a good number of the household had heard.

The door flew open and Fran rushed in, stopping abruptly at the sight of her mistress sitting before the broken pane with a layer of something white all over her face.

Lifting her chin in defiance, Gisela bellowed, "Do not just stand there gawking! Call someone to remove this now! And find Mr. Boatwright. Have him bring the mirror from Mr. Darcy's bedroom."

Fran wondered if the woman had lost her mind. There was a bedroom that would normally belong to the master of the house, if there was one. However, since Mr. Darcy did not reside there, it had always been kept locked. As far as she knew, no one ever entered that room, even to clean it. Thus, she had no idea whether it contained a mirror which could replace the broken one.

Gisela noted her hesitation with great irritation. "I do not pay you to stand about like a Drury Lane Vestal!^{13} Do as I say, or I shall have to find another maid."

I wish I could tell you to do so right now, Fran thought as she stalked out and closed the door soundly.

⟡

On the Road from London to Milton

Slattery and Musgrove, trusted footmen of long-standing, nodded at each other as Mr. Darcy nudged his horse into the yard of the small Inn which served as a stop for post coaches. Both had been surprised at the pace their employer had kept since taking the road to Milton that morning and were as weary as the animals beneath them when the familiar landmark came into view. The only respite they had thus far was when they stopped to let their horses drink from a creek, devouring what food Mrs. Parker had packed whilst still mounted. Since their destination was only a half-day's journey from London, they had thought Mr. Darcy would stop at the first small inn along the road, but he passed by it without even slowing in favour of this one further along.

"Let us stop here," William declared, dismounting and throwing the reins of his stallion to an older man who came running from the direction of the stables. "Cool him down, Mr. O'Malley. Give him some oats and do the same for the others." He motioned to the footmen's horses, adding, "Stable them until we return. Please saddle three more from those I keep on the premises."

"Yes, Mr. Darcy!" the man replied, signalling another fellow to come forward to help with the horses. "Right away, sir!"

As William headed into the inn, he waved his servants to follow. Once they were inside, the Master was nowhere to be seen. Unsure of where to sit, as they usually ate in the servant's quarters, Slattery and Musgrove stood looking about the small dining room. Suddenly, a maid appeared, asking that they follow her.

---

^{13} *Drury Lane Vestal - A whore, according to the 1811 Dictionary of the Vulgar Tongue.*

She led them into another section of the inn and pointed to a door.

"The gentleman would have you wait for him here. He said to tell you that he would join you as soon as he settles his account."

Both men did as instructed and found themselves seated in a private dining room, something they had never enjoyed before. A maid quickly appeared, setting plates, cups and forks on the table before leaving. Finally, Mr. Darcy appeared, taking a seat at the end of the table.

"I know that I have pressed you to your limit, but it is urgent that I get to Milton as soon as possible. I appreciate your willingness to ride so hard, and there will be extra in your pay this month."

Both men nodded, and Slattery spoke. "You pay us well, sir. We cannot fault what you ask us to do. Besides, not having to hang onto the back of a coach is a welcome change."

Musgrove agreed, though he added with a smirk, "Aye, it is good to be on horseback for a change, though I fear I am going to be sore for a month after we are finished."

As even William chuckled at his quip, a stout woman appeared at the door with a large pot of stew, while a smaller one followed, carrying a tray with a pot of tea, a bottle of wine, bread and cheese. After the food was spread on the table and the maids had gone, each stared at the bounty before them.

"Let us eat then!" William urged. "This is the last stop we shall make before we reach Milton."

As conversation gave way to eating, William's thoughts drifted for the hundredth time to Georgiana and he took a deep breath, trying not to let his servants see his discomposure. Would she be as traumatised as she had when each of their parents died and be withdrawn for months? He could only pray that Aunt Audrey's influence would make a difference in how she dealt with setbacks now that she was older.

Without warning, Elizabeth invaded his thoughts next and, as usual when she crossed his mind, he was flooded with a different fear. There was absolutely nothing he could do to protect her, for as far as the world was concerned, she was not his to protect—at least not yet. Closing his eyes, the memory of the night she slept in his arms permeated his being like a gentle rain. He opened his eyes to take a sip of the wine, hoping to gain control of the familiar ache that had begun.

"Are you not going to eat?" Slattery asked. "It is quite a good stew."

Musgrove nodded his agreement, though he did not stop eating to comment.

"Yes," Darcy murmured woodenly. "I was just going over some matters in my head."

"Well, you had best eat, Master. It will not do for you to be faint in the saddle, not with those stallions you prefer to ride."

William offered a wan smile before doing something at which he had become an expert—forcing all thoughts of Elizabeth from his mind. That was the only way he had been able to function without going completely mad these last few months. But he had found that even that skill was not without its drawbacks. Suppressing recollections of Elizabeth during the day meant that his nights were fair game for all of them to reappear.

Suddenly no longer hungry, William began to choke down one bite of food after another. Slattery was right. He must be able to maintain his strength with all the miles yet to cover.

Chapter *31*

Milton
Ashcroft Park
The Drawing Room

Audrey Ashcroft watched Lord Landingham pace back and forth across the imported carpet, all the while running his hands through his hair. His actions were very reminiscent of her taciturn nephew, but she had never noticed the similarities before now. Since they were waiting for Fitzwilliam to arrive, she had used the time to enlighten Marshall in regards to Georgiana's confession of keeping Wickham's presence in Ramsgate a secret. There was no getting around the fact that her nephew would have to be told when he arrived, and she hoped that by telling Georgiana's godfather beforehand that he would be of aid in helping Fitzwilliam to see reason when he was informed. She never dreamed that Marshall would need to be calmed himself.

"I am sorry. I did not realise how much this would upset you, Marshall. In your present condition, you do not need something more to make your head ache."

"Please do not apologise," he broke in a little too sharply. His pacing came to a sudden halt as he faced her. "Georgiana is the one with a lapse in judgment, you are merely the messenger."

"Regardless, if you keep treading back and forth, your headache will no doubt return, and all you will have accomplished is to wear a hole in the carpet."

He cocked his head to study her, as though he was not sure if she was serious or not. Audrey read his expression quite easily.

"Yes, I am teasing. But I see I have failed to cheer you. I was counting on you to be the voice of reason—someone to calm my nephew. Only now I fear that you are blaming yourself, just as he will."

Suddenly, Landingham's hands flew to his forehead, and he rubbed his tired eyes rigorously before letting a ragged sigh escape.

"I cannot for the life of me understand why Georgiana would do something so foolish, so dangerous! Why would she acquiesce to that villain's wishes, going directly against everything she has been taught." He stopped and began to shake his head. "No, that is not true. I understand all too well. She may have begun to look like a young woman, but inside she is still an innocent girl who trusts too easily. Her tender heart does not understand the wiles of the wicked."

"While it is true that she has a tender heart that does not dismiss the fact that she knew what she was doing was wrong and has allowed as much. She was properly instructed, but she intentionally withheld information that I should have been made aware of and, in doing so, she not only broke the bond between us, she nearly paid the ultimate price for her error. Not to mention that you were almost killed going to her rescue, and Miss Bennet was injured twice for intervening."

"If only she had had a father who ..." Abruptly Landingham quieted, afraid of saying more.

"She had a father, though George was never an ideal parent. But since his death, she has had an exemplary model in Fitzwilliam. He could not have done a better job of raising Georgiana had he been her actual parent. So I do not consider that an excuse."

Landingham turned away, praying that the guilt on his face would not show. "I agree. No one can fault Fitzwilliam's care of Georgiana."

"No one but him! And we both know that my nephew will blame himself. He will not even include me in the blame, and I have spent the greater part of the last two years with Georgiana."

Landingham stilled, considering his words. "Fitzwilliam always takes the lion's share of the fault. You and I must convince him otherwise. It is not healthy the way he agonises over everything that affects Georgiana. He is not to blame; he cannot control every circumstance and he must accept that."

Audrey rose and walked over to where he had turned to gaze into the gardens. Laying a hand on his back and making lazy circles with her fingers, she said softly, "You sound like his father."

Without turning he murmured, "I have often considered that since I courted your sister before George Darcy, I could have been his father." He hesitated for a second before adding, "And Georgiana's."

Lady Ashcroft mulled over his words, her face taking on a puzzled look as she, too, gazed into the distance. "I had forgotten. It was long ago, and I was so young at the time."

She seemed to weigh that information as she walked over to the liquor cabinet and began pouring two fingers of brandy for herself before doing the same for Landingham. Turning, she held out the glass, and he came forward to take it.

Downing his share in one swallow, Landingham asked, "Where do you suppose Fitzwilliam is? I assumed he would be knocking on the door at daybreak."

"I imagine he would have, had it been possible. In any event, I think he is most likely near and will arrive within the hour."

Noting the slump of Landingham's shoulders, Audrey then began to pull the man that she loved towards a nearby chair, gently pushing him down into the cushioned seat. Once he was seated, she walked around behind him and began massaging his shoulders. Landingham immediately closed his eyes and took a deep breath. Letting his head fall back on the soft cushion, he grew tranquil.

"I swear those lovely fingers of yours can heal any pain I have, my love."

"I pray that will always be so."

He opened his eyes to gaze up at her with an adoring look. Then, reaching for her hand, he brought it to his lips for a soft kiss.

"It shall, I have no doubt. I cannot wait until you are mine."

She returned his smile, lovingly squeezing his hand in return. "Nor can I."

Deep inside, Audrey Ashcroft's heart was at war with her sense of duty. After the fiasco with Wickham, she felt that she could not tell Marshall of her change of heart with regards to their situation just yet. No, she would wait until this crisis with Georgiana was resolved before telling the man she loved that she wanted to marry as soon as possible.

Leaning down, she placed a soft kiss on his head and he sighed contentedly, closing his eyes while she kept up the soothing therapy.

⊙⌒⌒⊙

In Another Part of the Manor

Though her heart was heavy, one would never have guessed that Henrietta Parker had a care in the world as she bustled about Ashcroft Park with her small medicine bag in one hand and an array of papers in the other, performing her job with quiet assurance. As customary, she made copious notes to be certain that everyone was taken care of and all was in order.

Though always pleased to have her Mistress in residence, it was impossible for her to fathom the events that had brought everyone rushing back from Ramsgate. That anyone would try to kidnap Miss Darcy, kill Lord Landingham or hurt the young woman who accompanied them was just unimaginable. Still, those horrible happenings were not uppermost in her thoughts at this moment. What was chiefly troubling her was the fact that Lady Ashcroft had informed her that Mr. Darcy was to arrive today. Other than her mistress and Lord Landingham, no one knew of his eminent arrival, and she had been cautioned not to mention it. Lady Ashcroft did not want Georgiana to fret about his safety on the road and she could understand why. If ever a brother and sister loved one another, the Darcys did. And there was a tender spot in her own heart for them which caused her to dread witnessing Mr. Darcy's reaction to all that had occurred.

While the other servants were oblivious as to why Lady Ashcroft had cut short her visit to Ramsgate, Henrietta and her husband were not. During all the years they had served the Ashcrofts as housekeeper and butler, a strong bond had developed, and they were almost like family. Thus, if anything important happened in Lady Ashcroft's family, the Parkers would eventually be apprised of the circumstances. Naturally, such confidences never passed their lips, but it did help them to anticipate the needs of whatever family members happened to be staying at Ashcroft Park.

For instance, Miss Georgiana had, understandably, not been herself since returning from Ramsgate. Sensing that Lady Ashcroft's niece might not want to participate in her usual activities—playing the pianoforte, crocheting or creating flower arrangements—she had refrained from suggesting them. Instead, she had waited for the girl to indicate what she wished to do. This had worked out well as Miss Darcy was now practicing her charcoal drawings on the balcony with Miss Bennet, who had stopped by her bedroom to enquire after her wellbeing and been cajoled into joining her.

Miss Bennet—now there is a woman to admire, the housekeeper mused as she made her way towards the grand staircase. She began a mental list of all that she liked about her—foremost being her courage. *According to Lady Ashcroft, she immediately ran to Georgiana's aid without any thought of the danger to herself.*

Stopping to add to her load a stack of dusting clothes that one of the chamber maids had set down on a table and forgotten, Henrietta hurried down the hall as though in a race against time. Her chain of thought, however, was unbroken.

Though admittedly at first glance Miss Bennet is not a classic beauty, she is really quite striking once you take a closer look. And though she is not as tall as Miss Darcy, she has a perfectly proportioned figure and carries herself well.

Recalling how she had found that particular guest this morning, she smiled. Thinking that Miss Bennet was already below stairs, she had slipped into her bedroom to leave a quilt in the large closet. Upon hearing voices in the sitting room next door, she quietly moved to the doorway to behold one of the young maids styling Elizabeth's hair. It was obviously one of her best assets as it was dark, unusually thick and curly and had a glossy finish not unlike a fine bolt of satin. The poor maid was having trouble getting her substantial stands to behave and Elizabeth was attempting to console her.

"Oh, do not worry yourself over it too much. A good bit of it shall slip back out of the pins by the time I am fully dressed."

Then Miss Bennet had giggled in her own distinctive way as the maid pretended to throw up her hands in defeat. Not wishing to intrude on this merry scene, Henrietta had slipped back out of the bedroom without letting her presence be known.

Yes, this lass is very personable and laughs easily, unlike most women her age who are conceited and put on airs. And her dark locks are equally matched by those ebony eyes that sparkle when she laughs. Yes, I can definitely see a gentleman falling in love with her.

Instantly, her thoughts flew to Fitzwilliam. She remembered the first time Lady Anne had brought him to Ashcroft Park and how little he had changed over the years. *I have known him since he was but a boy of about four, and if I was to go through the world, I could not meet with a better. But I have always observed that they who are good-natured when children are good-natured when they grow up; and he was always the sweetest-tempered, most generous-hearted, boy in the world.*[14]

Reaching the end of the hall, she halted at the top of the grand staircase to visualize the first and only time she had seen Gisela Darcy. The memory, even now, made her smile shamelessly. Mrs. Darcy had appeared at the estate about six months after the marriage, accompanied by an unknown gentleman and obviously in-her-cups. She demanded to see Fitzwilliam, though he was not there and neither was the Mistress. Moreover, Lady Ashcroft had left word that should that lady ever darken her door, she was not to be allowed inside. Thus, it had been her delight to inform the woman that she would not be offered the hospitality of Ashcroft Park. Gisela had left, but not before berating her as an inhospitable

---

[14] **Pride and Prejudice**, by Jane Austen, Chapter 43. *"If I was to go through the world, I could not meet with a better. But I have always observed, that they who are good-natured when children, are good-natured when they grow up; and he was always the sweetest-tempered, most generous-hearted boy in the world."*

wench.

I have to believe that Mr. Darcy deserves more than that horrible woman, and I pray that he finds true happiness before it is too late. Perhaps Miss Bennet will be the inspiration for him to get the divorce that Lady Ashcroft mentions so often!

Brightening at that thought, the housekeeper hurried down the stairs intent on finding the cook in order to ask for a fresh pot of tea. The Mistress had been exceedingly tired since they had arrived late yesterday blaming it on the lateness of their arrival—rain having delayed them until well after dark. Yet, she felt that the Mistress's ills were more likely due to the stress of worrying over Georgiana's ordeal and Lord Landingham's persistent headaches.

Thus she had prepared powders for the Earl's headache and a draught to relieve her Mistress's fatigue and both had worked remarkably well. Fresh tea was essential for delivering the remedies, and it would be crucial for everyone to feel their best if they were to discuss what happened in Ramsgate with Mr. Darcy. Accordingly, Mrs. Parker was determined to have more tea and remedies on hand just in case the discussion brought a repeat of those complaints and she was asked to provide relief.

Just as she gained the foyer, there was a knock at the front door. Hurriedly, she headed to put the items she was holding where they belonged, while her husband rushed towards the entrance. Though it was earlier than she had expected, she was certain that Fitzwilliam Darcy had arrived.

William was bone tired by the time Ashcroft Park came into view at the end of a long, landscaped drive. Allowing his body to relax, he let his usually straight backbone curve and his shoulders droop with fatigue. The stallion he rode noticed the way his seat had shifted and raised his head in curiosity. Catching sight of the manor house, the animal picked up his pace knowing rest and oats would soon be his reward.

It seemed only a moment until William, Slattery and Musgrove were halting in front of the broad steps that led to the front door, each dismounting with equal degrees of weariness, as well as various levels of pain. Fortunately, several footmen rushed to relieve them of their mounts, these men disappearing around the side of the house by the time all three had climbed the numerous steps to the front entrance. And, before William could raise his hand to knock, the elegant door opened and Mr. Parker's smiling face greeted him.

"Mr. Darcy! Lady Ashcroft told us to expect you today. Come in! Come in, sir! I do hope your journey was not too gruelling."

"Thank you, Parker. The journey was demanding but at least uneventful."

The butler stood back, sweeping a hand in front of himself to direct Mr. Darcy and the two men into the foyer. Once inside and looking about, Darcy was surprised that, other than some footmen, no one was there to greet him. Nevertheless, he began to give orders concerning his men.

"Please see that Mr. Slattery and Mr. Musgrove are given something to eat, a hot bath and a clean bed. They shall need their rest in order to accompany us back to London."

Mr. Parker was nodding his assent, even as he waved a footman over to direct

Pemberley's servants to their quarters. William addressed both men as they turned to follow the servant, "You have served me well. Rest. It shall be an equally tiring journey home."

All three had barely gotten out of hearing range, when Mr. Parker began apprising him of the situation.

"The Mistress and Lord Landingham are in the drawing room and asked that I direct you there as soon as you arrived."

"And my sister?"

"I believe Lady Ashcroft said she was in the conservatory."

William seemed to be considering his options. "If possible, I would rather that Georgiana not know I am here just yet."

Nodding briskly the butler replied, "Of course."

Suddenly, Henrietta Parker was hurrying towards them, smoothing her skirts as she always did when she was anxious. Stopping in front of Mr. Darcy, she dropped a perfect curtsey.

"Mr. Darcy, I am so glad to see that you have arrived safely. Your aunt has been anxious all morning."

"My aunt worries too much," William responded good-naturedly, managing a wan smile in spite of his weariness.

The housekeeper stepped closer, a warm expression crossing her face. "I have your room just as you like it and a bath ready at your convenience. I felt sure that you would wish to wash off the dust of the road."

William gestured to his clothes, "I fear that I am wearing half of the county on my back, so you are correct."

Both Parkers chuckled at William's jest.

"I shall look in on my aunt and Landingham quickly before I go to my room."

Mr. Parker stepped forward. "I shall be happy to direct you."

"There is no need. I know where the drawing room is, and I need no announcement."

Acquiescing, both Parkers stood aside and watched him walk down the hall until completely out of sight, then meeting each other's eyes, they sighed heavily. There was nothing more they could do, so they clasped hands briefly and then went in opposite directions, each with their own chores to accomplish.

The Drawing Room

An authoritative "Come" greeted William's knock on the drawing room door and he entered straightaway. He was not surprised to find his aunt standing right next to the chair that Lord Landingham occupied. The growing closeness between his aunt and his godfather was apparent and, what's more, he welcomed it wholeheartedly.

Now, however, both occupants' furrowed brows made him wonder just what they felt compelled to tell him before he rested.

"Fitzwilliam!" His aunt declared, rushing to take his hands and place a kiss on his cheek. "I was so worried about you."

William pulled back a little. "Do not get close, Aunt. I am filthy. I came here before going to my room to bathe as you seemed so eager to see me."

"I do not care one whit about the dust," she replied. "You never did have an ounce of patience, and I feared you would break your neck trying to get here too quickly. I would not even tell Georgiana that you were coming, as I feared she would fret as well."

"Travelling is no longer the problem that it was when those nags they provide at the inns were the only steeds available. I began to keep my own animals there when you started bringing Georgiana here and to Ramsgate every year and it helps considerably."

Lord Landingham had risen by then and extended a hand, which William shook as he surreptitiously examined the wound at his godfather's hairline. "My aunt's letter told me what you did for Georgiana, and I shall be forever grateful. I pray you are well and your wound is healing properly."

Landingham's hand went instinctively to his injury, and he gently rubbed the place that the bullet had grazed. "I did nothing more than any gentleman would have done."

"There were men there who did not step forward—like Wilkens." Audrey interjected. "Of course, I really do not consider him a gentleman in any sense of the word."

William swiftly added, "Neither do I, but ..." He put an arm around his godfather's shoulder. "You almost died saving Georgiana. That will never be forgotten by her or any of our family." Hesitantly, he added, "And what of Miss Bennet's injuries? Is she well?

"Her injuries are not severe, though they are unsightly," his aunt replied. "I have not told you, but she accompanied us here."

William's befuddled expression became eager as he tried to take it all in. "Eliz ... Miss Bennet is here? Under your roof?"

"She most certainly is. It was not safe for her to stay with Wilkens, and I offered to see her to London."

A look of foreboding crossed his face as his body stiffened. "What do you mean it was not safe for her to stay with Wilkens?"

"I think it best to let Miss Bennet explain that to you. I do not believe she was comfortable telling us the full extent of what happened at Gatesbridge Manor after she returned there from the gallery. Perhaps she will be more forthcoming with you."

William went silent, trying to fit the news that Elizabeth was in this house, and had had to flee Wilkens, into the chaos regarding Georgiana that already spun in his head. Audrey took that as a signal to begin divulging the information she dreaded discussing.

"Fitzwilliam, I hate to be the one to tell you this, but I must alert you to a serious problem regarding my niece. I think it best you know before you see her."

William's face paled. It soon became evident that he was not going to say anything while he awaited her revelation.

"Shortly after the debacle at Ramsgate, I spoke to Georgiana about how it all came about, and she confessed that she had had a part in it."

"Had a part?" William murmured so low it went almost unheard.

"Yes. She confessed that she had met George Wickham at the gallery, and through a series of lies, he gained her confidence. She then agreed to his request not to tell me that he was in her company."

William sank down in a nearby chair, not sure if his legs would suffice to keep him upright while he took it all in. He looked bewildered as his aunt continued with the explanation Georgiana had offered.

"Wickham used some truths and half-truths, as well as memories of your father and mother to draw her into his web of deceit. Unfortunately, she remembered him from when he used to live at Pemberley, so all he had to do was pretend to recall times that involved those she loved, especially her parents. He regaled her with happy tales he supposedly remembered from when she was a child. From those she shared with me, he must have fabricated them, since they all involved her being alone with him while you were at Eton. We both know that your father did not let him keep company with Georgiana alone. But eager to learn more of her childhood, she let down her guard."

William said nothing, but, if possible, his mien grew even more sombre.

"She is very sorry for what happened to Marshall and Miss Bennet because of her disobedience, but above all, she is anxious how you will respond. She now realises that what she has done will hurt you most dearly. I have reassured her that your love for her will never wane."

A pained expression covered William's downturned face, and Lady Ashcroft shot a worried look towards Lord Landingham, who shook his head as though he did not know what to do either. In the end, he decided he should say something.

"Remember, Fitzwilliam, that although Georgiana looks almost grown, she is still a young girl. And because she has been sheltered, she is too trusting and sees only the good in everyone until confronted with the truth of the matter."

Still William sat silent, only now his hands covered his face as he rubbed both eyes tiredly. Landingham glanced to Audrey before continuing.

"We—all of us—should have warned her of the likes of George Wickham or men like him. Though we have tried to protect her from the world, she will be more and more a part of it now that she is becoming a young lady."

William's aunt added, "I think she has learned a hard lesson, and we can only pray that that lesson will keep Georgiana from this type error in the future."

Finally William looked up. "I failed her."

Both jumped to defend him, with William's aunt being the first to reply. "No! You have not! If anything, it is I who failed her. I was her companion for the last two years, and I never cautioned her about this kind of circumstance. My concern was for strangers, not men she had known since childhood."

"Neither of you failed her, anymore than I," Landingham joined in. "I was charged with watching over her. As her godfather, I should have been the one to talk with her about such men as Wickham."

William stood now, his legs a little shaky from riding all day and from what he had learned. "But, I have failed her in the most important issue. If she thinks I cannot or will not forgive her—"

"That is immaturity speaking, nephew. Deep down Georgiana knows that you will forgive her.

"I fear that we shall just argue the point forever." As always, he began to run his hands through his hair absently. "I shall have a bath and try to think of what to say to her. I think she and I should talk before dinner, or neither of us will be able to eat."

His aunt put her arms around him. "I love you so much, Fitzwilliam, and I fear

I failed you and Georgiana in regards to Wickham." She then leaned back to look into his eyes. "Marshall fears he has failed, and you say that you have failed. The truth is that none of us thought of the possibility of this happening at Ramsgate during her painting lessons. We thought she was being supervised. But know this—Georgiana is no child now, and she knew what she was doing was wrong. None of us are guiltless, but we are also not God. We will continue to make mistakes, and we must learn from them and move on. Drowning in regret will help no one."

She cupped his face until he met her eyes. "Do you believe me?" He nodded absently, as though not convinced. "Go. Take your bath and relax. Afterward, you shall talk to her. And I shall be there, too, if you so desire."

"Thank you." He turned to go, his footsteps much heavier than when he had entered. His aunt's parting words stopped his retreat.

"And am I right in thinking that you will want to talk with Miss Bennet before dinner as well?" William looked over his shoulder as she added, "Alone?"

As he turned a wan smile barely lifted the corners of his mouth. The longing in his eyes was heart-rending. "Yes. I would like that very much."

"I shall make arrangements then. Send Mr. Dutton to me once you have dressed and all shall be arranged."

"Mr. Dutton?"

"You might remember him. He was Joseph's valet years ago, and he recently returned here to live out the remainder of his days. He is a dear, dear man, and he offered to be of service to you and Marshall while you are in residence."

"I shall welcome his assistance." William came back to plant a kiss on his aunt's forehead. "I forgot to say that I love you, and I appreciate all you have done for Georgiana and for me." Then with a nod and small smile to Landingham, he quitted the room.

Audrey walked to the door, following William with her gaze as he ascended the grand staircase. Landingham moved to stand behind her, running his arms around her waist and pulling her close. He leaned down to whisper in her ear. "I hope the boy takes what we said to heart."

"I pray he does. He has too many burdens on his shoulders as it is."

A chuckle ensued from deep within her beau as he rested his chin on top of her head. "Why do I have the impression that you believe Miss Bennet can lift some of those burdens, if she so chooses?"

She turned in his arms, then leaned back to look up into his eyes. "When has a woman not been able to lift a man's spirits—at least a man who is deeply in love with that woman?"

"When indeed." Landingham replied, gently pulling her away from the door, before closing it soundly behind them.

Chapter 32

London
The Gardiner's Residence
The Study

Mrs. Bennet and Jane had barely gotten settled on the sofa in Mr. Gardiner's study when Madeline hurried into the room, turning quickly to shut the door and lock it.

"I thought Sarah would never stop talking and finish her lessons. And, as usual, Becky wanted water after I had turned to go. It is a good thing that Nicholas still takes a nap, or I would be even more exhausted."

Then taking a deep breath, she rushed to sit in her husband's oversized chair—the leather one behind his desk. Facing her company, she studied the worried expressions of both her sister and her niece.

"I am so glad that you have arrived as I have learned something that you should know, Fanny, and I feel that it is best that we talk in here." Her eyes darted to the door, almost as though she feared that if she opened it, she might find someone with their ear pressed to the keyhole. "I would not want Mrs. Doane, or any of the help, to hear what we have to say. I appreciate all that she does, mind you, but I have suspected for some time that she likes to eavesdrop," she whispered, referring to the older, rather stout maid who acted as their housekeeper.

Jane's eyes darted to her mother. Mrs. Bennet slid to the edge of the sofa, a look of eager anticipation spreading across her face, an expression not unlike a child awaiting a piece of candy. A small artificial bird that was perched atop her bonnet bobbed up and down with her actions, and Jane reflected that she might have thought it funny had not the situation been so grave.

She and Lizzy had long since learned that there was nothing her mother liked more than spreading gossip, so she dreaded whatever her aunt had to reveal. At least in Meryton, almost everyone knew that her mother spread unproven rumours and even embellished upon them. So the decent folk there did not pay much attention to her reports, while the other gossips took Fanny Bennet's pronouncements with a grain of salt. In London, however, her mother might possibly do irreparable damage.

"Stop fidgeting, Madeline!" Fanny Bennet declared impatiently, interrupting Jane's thoughts and startling her sister. "Just tell us what you have heard. We certainly cannot be found in Edward's study when he gets home, and it is almost the hour of his arrival."

Madeline Gardiner glanced at the old clock on the mantel. "Oh my! You are absolutely correct." Reaching into her pocket she pulled out a letter. "You both know my cousin, Penelope Holmes. Well, when I returned to London after attending my sister, I found this letter awaiting me." She waved it about. "It advised me to come as soon as possible, so I set out that very day to see what could be the matter."

Mrs. Bennet's expression changed, her smile disappearing. She now looked more perplexed than excited as she asked, "Your cousin was supposed to be supervising Lizzy while you were with your sister, was she not?"

"Yes. That is why she sent for me. You know that she allowed Lizzy to accompany her cousins, the Wilkens, to Ramsgate for their aunt's birthday celebration. They were only to be gone a little over a week, and Penelope felt it would be a good opportunity for Lizzy to impress Lord Wilkens and their aunt, Lady Violet Hawthorne of Hawthorne Hall." As an aside, she addressed Jane. "You may not know this, but I told Fanny that Lady Hawthorne is one of the wealthiest women in England, and her fortune will pass to John Wilkens upon her death. And Penelope and I both believed that he was on the verge of offering for Lizzy."

Jane watched her mother's expression change to dread before she blurted out, "Lizzy has ruined everything! That is what this is about, is it not?"

"Will you please listen, Fanny? I have not finished explaining."

The nodding of her pale face gave Madeline Gardiner leave to continue. "Well, Penelope informed me that Alfreda's letters had hinted that Lizzy and Lord Wilkens did not agree on a good many subjects."

Mrs. Bennet jumped to her feet. "I knew it! That ungrateful girl could never keep her ideas to herself." She turned to lecture Jane. "Have I not told you and Lizzy that men do not want a woman who has decided opinions? You took my advice, and you secured Mr. Bingley! Oh why could she not do the same? No, Lizzy is just like her father, so opinionated."

Jane said nothing, knowing that her mother did not expect an answer. Instead, a knot began to form in her stomach as her mother stood to pace the room, murmuring about her second daughter's shortcomings.

Suddenly Aunt Gardiner was on her feet, trying to halt the pacing. "Sit down and hear the solution that Penelope and I have devised."

Dreading to learn what her aunt and Lady Holmes had decided for Lizzy, nevertheless, Jane stood and began soothing her mother. "Mama, you are going to have a fit of nerves if you do not compose yourself. Sit down and let us hear what Aunt Gardiner has to say."

Fanny Bennet slumped into her chair, fanning herself with a folder that had been lying on the edge of Mr. Gardiner's desk. Her eyes were closed as Madeline continued.

"There is more bad news, and I must tell all before Edward arrives. So listen and do not say a word."

At the mention of more bad news, Fanny stopped fanning herself and leaned forward while Jane held her breath.

"Penelope tells me that there is gossip about Town, not too widespread yet, mind you, that links Lizzy with a very wealthy man."

Mrs. Bennet perked up, sitting up straighter as a small smile began. "Wealthy?" Her lips twitched now as they always did when she was eager. "How wealthy?"

"Very wealthy," Madeline Gardiner declared. Mrs. Bennet smiled slyly at Jane, only to have the expression dissolve entirely when Mrs. Gardiner added, "But he is married."

Instantly Mrs. Bennet rounded on her sister. "I sent my child to London under your supervision, and this is how I am repaid! You have allowed this ... this disgrace right under your nose?"

Jane tried to be the voice of reason, knowing that Mr. Darcy was likely the man in question. "Mother, surely you do not believe my sister capable of this type of conduct?"

"It does not matter if I believe it, Jane. What matters is if the whole of London believes it!" her mother exclaimed, beginning to mop her brow with a handkerchief she pulled from her bosom. "My nerves, my poor, poor nerves!" She clutched her chest. "We are ruined! All of you are ruined! What will Mr. Bingley do? Will he still be willing to marry you?"

"Mother, do not worry about Mr. Bingley. He is steadfast in his love for me and he will not waver from it."

"You do not know that, silly girl!"

"Yes, Mother, I do."

Mrs. Gardiner broke into their conversation. "Never fear! Penelope and I have devised a way to put an end to Lord Wilkens' poor opinion of Lizzy and the awful rumours of an affair." She walked around the desk to face her sister.

"Pray tell me straightaway, so that my nerves will quiet and I can breathe."

"Simple enough," her sister proclaimed proudly. "When Lizzy arrives in London, you will make her apologise to Lord Wilkens for her poor attitude of late. John is used to those beneath him seeking his approbation, and Penelope tells me that he needs this courtship to end in marriage. He has not been successful in his last three courtships, and another failed one will be looked upon with suspicion."

"Perhaps he has an irredeemable character, and that is why the other ladies refused him. Surely it would not be wise to force Lizzy to marry him," Jane interjected. She received looks of total disbelief from her aunt and her mother before they turned back to each other, talking as though they had not heard.

"If Lizzy apologises the moment Lord Wilkens comes back to London, he will most likely forgive her lapses, make her an offer and they shall become engaged. Then all the gossip will disappear like fog on a sunny day. No one will care about the rumours if she and Wilkens marry. Then you shall have a rich son, and your other girls will be put in the way of other rich men."

Jane watched her mother's eyes light up. "You are absolutely correct. Lizzy has to marry this Wilkens fellow as expeditiously as possible." She took Mrs. Gardiner's hands. "It shall be done. I shall see to it myself."

Jane's heart sank as her mother and her aunt congratulated each other on finding the perfect solution to the rumours supposedly circulating in London. Pondering all that she had heard and utterly surprised that her mother had not asked **who** the married man was after Aunt Gardiner explained her scheme, Jane tried to think of a way to help Lizzy.

Papa! That is the answer! I have to get a letter to him as soon as possible or

Lizzy will be forced to wed John Wilkens.

"Jane! Jane!" Jane looked up to see both women eyeing her strangely. "You seem to be in another world."

Afraid they might guess that she would try to aid her sister, Jane decided to change the subject, and she knew just the artifice. "I was just considering that I should press ahead with plans for my wedding clothes."

Fanny clapped her hands with glee. "Of course, you should! We shall begin tomorrow visiting the best textile merchants in Town, just as planned. There shall be nothing but the best for you, my dear—laces, satins and silks! Then we shall engage the best modiste in London to transform them into your wedding gown and other necessities."

Mrs. Gardiner motioned to the door. "Let us remove to the parlour and talk more of the wedding, now that we are finished with the *problem*. If Edward knew that we had used his study, he would want to know why and all the particulars. I think it best he is not privy to all the talk concerning Lizzy."

They had just gotten settled in the parlour when the man of the house came through the front door and, after greeting everyone, went upstairs. They had each put on a cheery air for Mr. Gardiner, even Jane, who all the while, was composing a letter in her head that she would slip into the morning post with Jenny's help. Jenny, a young woman of about twenty, had worked for the Gardiner's as a maid for over a year, and Jane liked her very much. More than that, she trusted her. They often took the Gardiner children to the park together, and they had become fast friends.

I pray Papa will leave his library long enough to come to London. Surely he will for Lizzy. He can always leave my younger sisters in the care of Aunt Phillips.

At that moment, the grey-headed, cheerless Gertrude Doane appeared in the doorway. "When shall I serve dinner, madam?"

"I would say in a half-hour. That will give Mr. Gardiner time to change his clothes while I check on the children to see if they have finished their lessons."

"Very good, madam." The taciturn woman did not smile as she turned to return to the kitchen.

Milton
Ashcroft Park
Georgiana's sitting room

By the time William had finished bathing, he felt as though he might possibly survive what still lay ahead. He had washed hurriedly. Perusing his image in the mirror, he noted that he looked more rested than he felt and smiled at the irony.

Entering the hallway from his bedroom, he turned to close the door when his aunt called out. Coming towards him from the other end of the corridor, a large smile crossed her face as she neared. It warmed his heart. She reminded him so much of his mother when she smiled at him in that manner.

"Mr. Dutton told me you were ready," Lady Ashcroft said, reaching to take one of his hands and pull him back into his room, though she did not shut the door entirely. She examined him thoroughly, from the slightly wet dark curls that spilt over the tanned forehead and that highlighted his clear blue eyes, to the black suit with burgundy waistcoat that he wore with exquisite black Hoby* boots, the kind her husband had always preferred.

Swiftly kissing his cheek, she exclaimed, "You are a handsome man, Nephew." At his shrug, she added, "But you look so much better now than when you arrived. Do you feel well enough to forego a nap before dinner so that you may have your talks with Georgiana and Miss Bennet?"

"I fear this is no time to sleep."

She nodded, sighing with understanding before continuing. "Georgiana has just returned to her sitting room from the conservatory. She became even more worried when I told her that you had arrived from London to escort her back. I know she regrets having caused Marshall and Miss Bennet to be hurt, but as I said earlier she dreads facing you most of all." She waited until his gaze met hers. "Remember what we decided when I became her companion—she is not allowed to sulk or to sink into melancholy. She must admit mistakes and move forward. Would you like me to be with you when you speak to her?"

"No, I thank you." William took a deep breath. "I have to deal with her disobedience and I shall, but—" He reflected a moment. "I shall attempt to do it with patience and love, as we have discussed."

She squeezed his hands. "I never doubted that, but remember that Georgiana can elicit sympathy with her tears, especially from you."

A wan smile lifted the corners of his mouth. "How well I am aware of that!"

"Good, then go to her. She is waiting in there." She pointed to a room across the hall. "It should not take long to make your feelings plain. Do not let her go on and on apologising. Afterward, explain to Georgiana that you must speak to Miss Bennet before dinner, as she deserves an apology for the injuries she suffered trying to assist her. Then leave her to consider all you have said. There will be time enough for you two to talk again after dinner, if you think it necessary."

William tried not to sound eager. "Where is Miss Bennet now?"

"She is walking about the property. As soon as you are done talking with your sister, send a servant to find me and then go straight to the library. While you wait there, I shall find Miss Bennet and escort her to you. I think that meeting her again in the library will be less intimidating, since it is such a spacious room and filled with her favourite things."

He smiled crookedly. "How would you know she favours books?"

"Fitzwilliam, I rode all the way from Milton with your Miss Bennet. I know a great many things about her. Besides, if you are enamoured of her, she has to like books!"

His smile faded as his brows knit quizzically, recalling what else she had said. "Do I intimidate people?"

His aunt chuckled and patted his cheek. "Only those who do not know you, my love, and those who do."

Chuckling at his bewildered expression, she pushed him towards the door across from them. "There is no time like the present."

William found himself entering a beautiful sitting room that adjoined the bedroom that Georgiana always occupied at Ashcroft Park. He had been in this room often enough, but it had recently been redecorated in shades of yellows and greens, and he barely recognised it. Calling her name, there was no answer so he walked to the connecting door, intending to knock. Before he got there, he caught sight of Georgiana standing on the balcony. She was staring into the distance, her arms crossed, and she was rubbing her forearms as though to warm herself.

For a brief moment, he took her measure. It had been some time since he had studied Georgiana, and in her present pose, it was plain that she was fast becoming a woman, getting taller and developing womanly curves.

Every hair was in place; that in itself was unusual. Suddenly, he found himself smiling at old memories. As a child she dearly loved to run, even running throughout the house, to their parents' dismay, and her fine hair would always escape the pins and ribbons employed to hold it. Pictures from times past progressed through his mind—Georgiana chasing butterflies on the manicured lawn or pursuing the numerous cats in the gardens and stables, her hair down and in complete disarray. Their mother had been fond of reminding him that Georgiana would outgrow such antics one day, and he would miss them. His smile crumbled as a sharp pain pierced his heart. He missed more than just his sister's childish behaviour—he missed his mother.

As though Georgiana felt his presence, she turned to see him observing her, and it tortured William to see her hands fly up to cover her face. He rushed to her side, pulling her into his arms. Saying nothing, he held her, twisting slowly side to side and soothing her as she cried. At length, she quieted, and he leaned his head back to study her.

"Georgiana, look at me," he entreated softly.

There was a furious shaking of her head, so he used his fingertip to tilt her chin so that he could look into her eyes. She had them closed tightly, and it almost made him smile.

"Open your eyes." A barely perceptible movement of her eyelids revealed two small dark slits examining him. He schooled his face to show displeasure. "Open them wide so you can see me."

She sighed heavily but did as he asked. He stared for so long in silence that her blue eyes began to fill again.

"Now that I have your attention, tell me what possessed you to go against everything you have been taught? Why would you disobey the rules we set in place to keep you safe?"

Her eyes dropped to study the fine lawn of the shirt exposed above his waistcoat. "I thought that I was being mature by deciding something for myself. Lady Strongham often said that I acted much too childishly."

"And do you think it was mature to disregard what people with years of experience have cautioned you?"

More shaking of her head preceded a quietly murmured, "Not anymore."

"You know, sweetling, if I have learned anything in my seven and twenty years, it is that human nature never changes. What our mother tried to instil in me when I was your age has proven invaluable, and that is why I have tried to pass that knowledge on to you. In every generation there are those who stand ready to lie, steal, even to kill to get what they desire. And it is mainly at the expense of those who are naïve," he kissed the top of her head, "or kind-hearted enough to believe them."

He pulled her even tighter, her head coming to rest under his chin. "And even more despicable are those who would prey on a loved one just to have their revenge. I apologise, for I should have warned you about George Wickham in particular. He has much to despise me for and, therefore, a motivation to hurt you. I never dreamed, however, that he could penetrate the wall of protection that I had erected around you."

"You have nothing to apologise for, Brother. I am at fault for not acting on what I knew to be right. Aunt has since told me his history with our family, and I am so sorry that I made a fool of myself by being taken in by his lies. But if he had not first confessed his own faults and failings in regards to you, I might never have thought him sincere."

"You are not a fool, Georgiana, just an innocent. With maturity, you will learn to discern true sincerity. And even when you are grown, you will learn that the advice of those of us who have always had your best interest at heart—Richard, Aunt Audrey and myself—will serve you well." He cupped her face. "Now, there will be no sulking and no melancholy. That is not how a young lady handles setbacks. Agreed?"

"Agreed."

"Good. You know that what you did was wrong. I would like to know what punishment you feel is appropriate? Not that I shall concur with your suggestions."

She sniffled. "I should have to work extra hard on my studies and my music and leave off all frivolities for six months. No trips to museums, plays, operas and ice cream shops when I am in Town."

William tried not to smile at the mention of ice cream shops. "I think your suggestions commendable, only I believe there is one more thing. You shall not have the privilege of having your friend, Lady Ormond, spend the month of September at Pemberley as you had planned. In fact, you will not have friends stay overnight for the same period—six months."

Georgiana nodded, her eyes brightening with new tears as she stood taller. "I have learned my lesson, truly I have. When I saw what happened to my godfather and Miss Bennet, who risked their lives to help me, I wanted to die."

"Unfortunately, the one who almost died was Lord Landingham."

"I know," she moaned, then quickly added, "And Miss Elizabeth was injured. Oh, Brother, have you seen the awful bruise on her face where Mr. Wickham struck her? Every time I see it, I am reminded of my folly. I thought that surely a bone had broken, he hit her so forcefully. And then, to think that that horrid Lord Wilkens struck her in the same place!"

William's eyes narrowed, turning black as night. She felt him tremble just a bit as he grasped her shoulders and tilted his head. "Wilkens hit Elizabeth?"

"Yes. Has no one told you?"

William slowly shook his head and turned to stare woodenly into the distance as she relayed everything that Elizabeth had said about the night of terror at Gatesbridge Manor. Even from the side, Georgiana could see his jaw clench and unclench, while his hands formed fists.

When the tale was done, he challenged even more sternly, "Do you now understand what men like Wilkens and Wickham are capable of? Why we all try so hard to protect you?"

"Yes. And I love you for it, even if I did not show it by my actions."

"And do you understand that I shall always love you no matter what may happen? You shall always be my dearest sister and you should never fear coming to me."

She sniffled. "I do."

"May I count on you to listen to me—to your aunt—from now on?"

"You may. I promise."

William stepped back to her, placing a kiss on her forehead and then embraced her tightly. "I must find Miss Elizabeth and express my appreciation for all that she has done for us."

"Then go, Brother. I am certain that she will be eager to see you again."

"I pray you are right."

Georgiana watched him leave, following his progress through the sitting room and out into the hall. A lump formed in her throat as she considered how diligently he had cared for her since their parents' deaths and how badly she had disappointed him. A fresh pool of tears rolled silently down her face as she vowed never to disobey him again.

⟡

The Library

Since sending a maid after his aunt and entering the vacant library, Fitzwilliam Darcy had employed his usual method of dealing with anger— generating a steady cadence with his boots on the parquet floor near the hearth. As he stalked, his steps kept pace with the pounding of his heart, and he ran his hands through his hair absently. The slow burn that had begun deep inside when Georgiana spoke of Wilkens' assault of Elizabeth had turned into a raging fire.

If he could be thankful for anything, it was that his aunt was not there to tell him to stop pacing, for he did not think it was possible for him to cease. He had tried to keep his anger under good regulation since learning of Wickham's scheme and Elizabeth and Marshall's injuries, concerned that Georgiana would learn just how angry he could become. But learning of additional injuries to Elizabeth at Wilkens' hand had pushed him past his storied control.

Elizabeth, how can I protect you? I cannot claim you for my own, and I cannot bear to see you hurt!

After reading his aunt's account of what transpired that day at Ramsgate, his hatred for George Wickham had consumed him, and he had pondered penalties worthy of that blackguard. But it was one thing to read of an assault and quite another to see the results. Landingham's scalp featured a long bloody crease, evidence of the shot that would have killed him had it been a hair to the left. The sight of that wound drove home just how close he came to losing a man that he loved like a father.

And to think that Elizabeth could have been the one shot and that she bore the evidence of assaults by Wickham and Wilkens made him weak in the knees. Would he be able to compose himself before she came into the room? If not, he was certain that his behaviour would frighten her.

Calm down! You cannot help her as long as you pace about as a madman!

At just that moment, there was a rap at the door, and he stopped dead still. A maid entered, curtseyed silently to him and then began to light the numerous candelabras about the room as daylight was beginning to fade. Immediately when she had finished and was about to depart, he addressed her.

"My aunt—have you seen her?"
"No, sir. Last I heard she was going to the lake to fetch Miss Bennet."
Curtseying once more, she quit the room as silently as she had entered and closed the door soundly. Left on his own, William lapsed into his former activity and was startled when there was another rap on the door.

Chapter **33**

Ashcroft Park

It was late afternoon, and Elizabeth had circled the entire lake and rambled through most of the gardens. All the while, a dutiful footman had discretely followed about a hundred feet behind. She had not protested his presence as she normally would, because she had not wished to argue the point with her hostess. Still, after walking for the better part of three hours, she was just as unsure of her mind as when she had begun. Only now the wind was picking up, a gusty breeze doing its part to impede her progress, and she was quite certain that, had she not held it in place, her bonnet would have taken flight with the last strong gale.

She wrapped her arms around her waist at a sudden chill—whether from the wind or what occupied her mind, she was uncertain. But eyeing the tumultuous sky to the north with its darkening clouds and hearing the distant sound of thunder, she decided that she had best return to the manor and turned in that direction. Perhaps, she thought, she might slip inside and have a few more minutes to herself before anyone noticed her presence. In any event, there was no way she was going to let the footman suffer the weather on her account.

Silence was what she had sought. Ever desirous of evaluating what to do about Fitzwilliam the next time they met, she had no doubt that he would be waiting for her when they reached Town. Having grown quite fond of Georgiana as well as Fitzwilliam's aunt, she knew it would be hard to maintain a friendship with them if she could not foresee a future with him. It would be too painful being near him but not truly being *with* him. Her heart fluttered at the thought.

Be still! She admonished her most traitorous member. *Just because I am in love does not mean I have the right to rush into his arms. I have to remember my duty to my sisters.*

Instantly she pictured him as he had looked that day in London, when he confessed his love for her, and her resolve collapsed along with her stoic expression. For she could not deny that from that day on her efforts *not* to love him had failed utterly and completely. Against all her strength, her very will, he possessed her heart. It was his gentle expression, gazing at her as though she were his whole world, that she imagined whenever Wilkens had belittled her. Moreover, his love had sustained her throughout the horrible ordeal at Gatesbridge. For during that endless night, his voice was the one she heard imploring her not to quit … to persevere … to come back to him.

Despite all your talk of duty, your greatest fear is that you will no longer be

able to refuse him when you meet again. At that realisation, she came to a complete halt. *Then how shall I ever face him?*

In the reflection that followed, a greeting wafted over the wind, and she looked up to see Lady Ashcroft coming in her direction. As the gap closed between them, the Mistress of Ashcroft Park dismissed the footman with a wave of her hand, and when he was sufficiently out of range, she began to speak.

"Goodness! From the strength of the winds, there will be quite a storm."

Elizabeth nodded, inspecting the sky anew. Her wish to be alone a while longer was not to be, and she accepted it with some disappointment.

"I have good news! At least it pleases me. But I want you to tell me truthfully how you feel about it." Elizabeth waited expectantly, so Lady Ashcroft put an arm around her shoulder and began to direct her back to the house. "My nephew, Fitzwilliam, is here." Elizabeth's posture stiffened a little so she offered, "I pray that his presence will not disturb you. He came to escort Georgiana—well, all of us—back to London. I believe you know him well enough to understand how protective he is of those he loves."

Elizabeth took a deep breath and sighed. "He has a right to be protective of his sister, especially after what has happened. It is just …"

"Just?" Lady Ashcroft urged gently.

"I … I care so deeply for him, but I do not understand how our situation can ever change." She blinked to keep from crying. "I will not be his mistress. I could not bear to share so little of his life or the shame it would bring upon me and my family." She added softly, "Not to mention any children."

Audrey turned Elizabeth so that they faced each other. "I assure you that he would never ask that of you. He is not the kind of man to take a mistress, and he loves you dearly. Do you remember the first time I met you in the park?" Elizabeth nodded. "I told you then that he had decided to seek a divorce. Well, he has already taken the first steps. The evidences of Gisela's infidelities are numerous and so are the witnesses. In addition, he has the support of many members of the House of Lords as well as the archbishop, so it will come to pass. It may take years, but eventually, he will be granted a divorce."

Elizabeth's eyes widened. "But what of the letters of extortion used to secure him?"

"The basis for the extortion will no longer exist in a short while, so they will be useless. But let me be perfectly honest. I would be remiss if I did not caution you that it would not be an easy path should you decide to love him. It could mean years of uncertainty and mockery. Nevertheless, as someone who knows him well, I am convinced that you would never regret it."

"I am certain there would be a scandal if anyone so much as suspected we were in love," Elizabeth murmured, searching the distant horizon for answers.

"You are correct. If word reached the *ton* of your relationship, they would rip you to shreds in their parlours as well as in the gossip sheets. And I have no doubt that Gisela would shout it from the housetops if she ever suspected that Fitzwilliam loved you, even though she has had at least seven lovers that I am aware of since their marriage. In any event, in our society, married men are allowed to have mistresses, so long as they are discreet, while the women who are their mistresses are vilified."

Elizabeth tried to correct her. "But, I said that I would never—"

"No one would ever believe that, Elizabeth. You would be branded a fallen woman by society, and regrettably, your sisters would be affected by the scandal. On the other hand, my nephew is very wealthy, well able to supplement their dowries and see to it they are introduced to decent men, respectable men. Despite the consequences, your sisters would probably be better situated than they are at present and much better off than being bartered to men like Wilkens for wealth and connections."

Noting Elizabeth's countenance fall even further at the mention of being bartered, Audrey added sympathetically, "Forgive me if I have offended you, but when we first met, you stressed that you *had* to marry well for your family's sake, so I assumed that none of you have large dowries."

The nodding of Elizabeth's head was the only confirmation.

"Furthermore, if you and Fitzwilliam were to marry, the *ton* would soon lose interest and move on to the next scandal. And you may rely on this—I will stand by you, along with most of our family and those who are our true friends."

"Most of your family?"

"My oldest sister, Catherine, would never accept or support anyone that Fitzwilliam desired." Audrey tried to jest. "But every family has to have at least one aberration. It keeps us from becoming too conceited."

Her ploy worked, as Elizabeth did manage a small smile.

"Fitzwilliam has many powerful friends who value him and would never shun him for seeking a divorce. In fact, a good many, knowing that he was entrapped, have already encouraged him to seek one."

"I assume that he would like to speak to me."

"I am to bring you to the library so you can talk. However, if that is not acceptable to you, you may return to your room to prepare for dinner. Even so, he will want to thank you for helping Georgiana. I will be pleased to accompany you, if you do not wish to be alone with him, and I assure you that he will not seek further contact with you if you do not wish it."

"I do not fear being alone with him," Elizabeth offered. "It is for my heart that I fear."

Suddenly feeling protective, Audrey pulled Elizabeth into a motherly embrace.

"I completely understand. It is a difficult decision. But please consider one other argument. What were the results of trying to please your family? What fate would have befallen you had you accepted an offer from John Wilkens weeks ago? Your lively nature would never have survived under his dominion. I truly believe he would have destroyed you before he would have let you break an engagement, and if the man became so violent while in public, one can only imagine how brutal he would have become in private after marriage. Sadly, he embodies most men of the *ton*. I should know, as I have been an observer of them my entire life."

Her expression softened. "Nonetheless, would you believe me if I told you that in every generation there are a few men who treasure a woman as a gift from God." Her eyes suddenly became shiny. "My Joseph was such a man. So is Fitzwilliam."

Elizabeth's eyes grew wet as well. "I knew that he was very special the first time we met." They stood perfectly still until she whispered, "I shall talk to him … alone."

Audrey Ashcroft hugged her. "I had hoped you would. Now, let us return to the house before we are drenched."

Having decided to change into a more elegant gown before seeing Fitzwilliam, Elizabeth looked truly beautiful in an emerald green sateen creation when she emerged from her bedroom to find Lady Audrey waiting for her in the hallway. Baring her shoulders and designed with a lower bodice than her day gowns, it fit snugly from her décolletage to her waist and drew attention to her generous bosom, small waist and perfectly rounded hips. The garnet cross her father had given her for her sixteenth birthday hung just above the hollow of her breasts. And, while her lush curls were pulled up to form a halo on top of her head, held by combs on both sides, the balance hung in ringlets down her back.

"You look lovely, Elizabeth!" her hostess exclaimed as she took the young woman's hands and then stretched out her arms to examine her. "I am so glad you decided to change gowns. This one is stunning."

Elizabeth's nervous smile went unobserved as a close clap of thunder made known that the storm she had seen earlier was almost upon them.

"Come, Fitzwilliam may fear that you are still out in this weather."

Lady Ashcroft proceeded towards the library, and as they progressed through the manor, Elizabeth began to note the servants busily lighting candles along the way, as the approaching clouds hid the sun. When at length they stood before the elaborately carved double doors, Lady Audrey paused dramatically to take one last look at her charge before rapping loudly, immediately opening one side and entering, leading Elizabeth in by her hand. The combination of the storm and the heavy damask drapes had left the room in darkness, save for the candles reflected in the enormous matching mirrors hung on all sides of the room. Their flickering flames pranced across the walls and ceiling, giving the place a magical appeal.

The sound of heavy footsteps on the other side of a wall of shelves brought her eyes to that area and her breath caught, despite her best intentions, when William came around the end of the structure. Swarms of butterflies invaded her stomach instantly at the sight of him.

He was just as she had remembered—tall, muscular, tanned and devastatingly handsome. He wore black except for a dark burgundy waistcoat, white shirt and cravat. He paused and smiled slightly.

Since both he and Elizabeth stood stock-still, Audrey gently pulled her towards Fitzwilliam, leaving only a few feet between the couple when she halted. Reaching to take her nephew's hand as well, she looked from one to the other.

"This may likely be the only occasion that you will have complete privacy to say what you will, since we leave for London tomorrow. Let me admonish both of you to decide what you want most in life. Keep in mind that, although it is admirable to try and please others, there comes a time when you must consider your own happiness. I am a witness to the fact that life is capricious and far too fleeting to waste. If what you feel for one another is true love, do not let it slip through your fingers."

Having had her say, she pulled each hand towards the other until they met and fingers entwined. "Now, if I know Mrs. Parker, dinner will be served shortly, so I suggest you stop staring at one another and start talking."

Lost in the exquisite warmth of skin on skin, his palm touching hers, Elizabeth was unaware of Lady Ashcroft's departure until the sound of the door closing signified that they were truly alone.

No one had ever looked at her the way he did at that moment—the deepest desires and aspirations of his soul unhidden. His smouldering expression produced a shiver that raced down her spine, and at once her face crimsoned. This heated blush spread down her neck and then across her bosom. As it did, his gaze followed to her décolletage before coming back to meet her eyes. A quick flame leapt into his eyes, as the grip on her hand tightened. Nonetheless, she was very mindful that he made no attempt to come closer.

When at last she realised what restrained him, a great pang gripped her heart. For chivalry would not allow him to press for her love. If their love was to be acknowledged or nurtured, it was to be her choice and at her instigation. That he would not take advantage of her feelings for him was a gesture that erased any doubts she might have had, and the realisation made her both ecstatic and limp at the same time.

As though that were not enough, at that very second William whispered huskily, "Oh, the heart that has truly loved never forgets, but as truly loves on to the close." *[15]

Elizabeth was lost. It would have been far easier to ask her to stop breathing than to refuse so great a love. Watching her expression as it altered to favour him, William began to draw her to himself so effortlessly that it seemed as though a gossamer thread connected them soul-to-soul. Once in his arms, her face came to rest against his rock-hard chest in an embrace so firm that she could hardly breathe.

A heavy sigh escaped his chest, and she could feel his body relax as he breathed her name, "*Elizabeth.*"

One iron hand came up to cradle the back of her head as he buried his face in the velvet of her hair and inhaled deeply of the lavender scent. The other hand slid down to the small of her back, splaying out to pull her close. Lying against his wildly beating heart, she suddenly became mindful that its cadence matched the mad drumming of her own. Gratified that he seemed just as affected as she, without further restraint, she melted into him, her hands sliding around to rest on his back. At this gesture, William groaned and the hand on her back slid a bit further down, urging her hips closer still.

He began to kiss the crown of her head, slowly inching succeeding kisses down her face as he sought her mouth. His lips were exceedingly soft, and Elizabeth held her breath at the realisation that soon she would experience her first real kiss. But alas, the butterflies that had invaded her stomach earlier found reinforcements and her knees began to buckle. As if noticing her sudden frailty, William slipped one arm under her legs and effortlessly picked her up. Carrying

---

[15] *A Selection of Irish Melodies, 4 (November 1811) Thomas Moore, Irish Poet, singer, songwriter and entertainer. (May 1779 – February 1852)*

her towards a large sofa near the hearth, he sat down with her in his lap.

Her eyes were still closed, and she waited expectantly for his kisses to resume. When they did not, she opened her eyes to find him examining her face, in particular the injury now unmistakable in the glow of nearby candles. He ran the back of his fingers gently over the offending bruise, and she watched as his expression sobered.

"How can I ever make amends for what you have suffered for coming to Georgiana's aid?"

"Georgiana is as dear to me as a sister, and I could do no less. There is nothing for which to atone."

His words were strangled. "If only I had the right to keep you with me, to keep you safe."

Elizabeth's heart overflowed at the evidence of his love. "Though it is not possible for you to be with me at all times, even should we marry, I know there will come a time when you shall have the right to keep me close."

Provoked by her declaration, the world was set to right when William, hesitating no longer, hungrily claimed her lips. His own were no longer soft but insistent, seeking that which he had desired for so long, that which was so crucial to his happiness as the air to breathe with.

Unrelentingly he prodded with his tongue until her lips opened, and he tasted the sweetness within. Even the deluge without the manor could not compete with the tempest raging inside him at this moment. Revelling in the feel, taste and smell of Elizabeth, his designs to take things slowly completely vanished and his tongue instinctively darted inside her mouth to tease her own.

At first she sat motionless, as though caught up in savouring each sweet sensation, but in time, she began to replicate his actions. His answer was to caress even deeper with his fingertips, which initiated an entirely different sort of response in Elizabeth. She moaned, threading her hands into his hair, pulling his mouth harder against her own and, for a few brief moments, he forgot that the rest of the world existed.

A sudden knock on the door caused them to pull apart. Breathing heavily, William slipped Elizabeth out of his lap and onto the couch. After he stood, he leaned down to place a kiss on her pale forehead before stepping a few feet away. Straightening his waistcoat, he called out, "Come!"

The door opened and Mr. Parker entered, rapidly making his way to where William stood and examining the floor instead of the flushed faces of the young couple.

"I am sorry to disturb you, sir, but Mr. Mooney has sent a groom to inform you that you are needed at the stables. I tried to explain, but he insisted—"

William's lifted hand brought an end to the butler's explanation. Releasing a disappointed sigh, he glanced over to Elizabeth, who still stared at the floor, her face crimson as she was mortified at the intrusion. "There is no need to explain. Would you be so kind as to send word to Mr. Mooney that I shall be there as soon as I change clothes?"

Parker bowed, "Very good, sir." He quitted the room in seconds, pulling the door shut behind him.

William quickly stepped over to Elizabeth, pulling her to her feet and back into his embrace. Though he feared she might have been frightened by the fervency of his kisses, she made no attempt to resist him. Nonetheless, she was trembling, so he tightened his embrace.

"I love you, Elizabeth. I have never loved any woman but you."

He could feel her relax into him once again and rejoiced in her response. "I love you so very much."

Not able to refrain after that declaration, he leaned in to kiss her yet again with only a little more restraint than before. Then pulling back to adore her, he gingerly fondled one glossy chocolate spiral that had slipped out of the pins and now rested on her shoulder. All the while he memorised her face and after a few moments, he felt able to speak again without his voice betraying him.

"When I arrived, Mr. Mooney was examining one of the mares because he thought she might foal early and deliver breech like her first colt. This mare is Georgiana's favourite; she has ridden her for years. It was evident that Mooney is not well, and he informed me that Mr. Bradford, his assistant livery manager, died last month. Since I have had experience in such matters with my own horses, I told him I would be happy to be of service when the time came. Otherwise, only some completely untried grooms are left to aid in a situation that could prove dangerous to the mare and colt. I could not ignore the situation."

Her words were encouraging, though her eyes begged him stay. "Of course, you could not. I understand completely. Certainly, you must help."

"When I am finished, if it is not too late, I would like for us to finish our talk." He smiled, though it did not reach his eyes. "I fear that I have said very little."

"On the contrary, I think you expressed yourself very eloquently."

At her words, he pulled her into another fierce embrace, kissing her so soundly that she was breathless when he released her, pleading, "Wait up for me?"

"I ... I will," she stammered.

Leading her towards the library entrance, he gave her one last longing gaze and tightly squeezed her hand before opening the door. As they entered the hallway and began towards the foyer, he kept a firm hold on that hand. Immediately, they encountered his aunt hurrying in their direction.

"Fitzwilliam, dinner is prepared, and Georgiana and Marshall are waiting in the drawing room. I was coming to get you when I learned that you have been summoned by Mr. Mooney. Dear boy, you cannot do everything asked of you. You are undoubtedly exhausted, and you have had no dinner. He shall just have to make do without you."

"Aunt, upon my arrival, Mr. Mooney explained the circumstances, and I promised to be of service when the time came. That the animal decided to foal now is no one's fault."

"It is too much to ask of anyone, and for heaven's sake, this is no night to be out of doors!" As if to prove her contention, a low rumble of thunder began and got progressively louder, shaking the entire room while lightning simultaneously lit up the space.

"I fear that I am needed, and there is no putting it off." William's weary eyes crinkled, his dimples cutting deep crevices into his tanned face. "Now, please do as I ask and carry on without me." Glancing to his love, he could not help but smile. "All of you—please enjoy your dinner. Just send a tray to my room, and I will eat later. Now, I must hurry if I am to be of any assistance."

He brought Elizabeth's hand to his lips for a quick kiss, stared into her eyes for a brief moment, then turned and walked towards the grand staircase. His long legs made short work of the stairs, and in a few strides, he was completely out of sight while Elizabeth stood transfixed, staring at the top of the stairs as though she expected him to return at any moment.

Lady Audrey had not missed their joined hands, and when William lifted Elizabeth's hand to place a kiss there, her heart had overflowed with joy. She had prayed so long for her dear boy to find real love and now that he had, all she could think of was how pleased his mother Anne would have been.

She glanced towards heaven. *This woman will be the making of him, my dearest sister, you shall see. You would have loved her, just as I do.*

Laying a hand on Elizabeth's arm, she implored, "Come, Elizabeth. There is no need for us to wait here. He shall likely take the back stairs when he goes to the stables and may be gone for some time. Let us have something to eat while we wait. It will do no good for all of us to be famished."

Elizabeth swallowed hard to suppress the tears that threatened. She did not want to let Lady Ashcroft see how deeply she was affected by his absence. After all, until a few minutes before, she had resisted the deepest desire of her heart to love him. How foolish she would seem to be so upset now. Steeling herself, she walked alongside Lady Ashcroft to the drawing room.

And as they made their way through the house, two sets of prayers were offered. One asked the Lord to spare the mare and colt and for the birth to be uncomplicated and soon done with so that William might get some well-deserved rest. The other contained all of that and more—a request that she be allowed to see him again tonight.

The Stables

By the time William arrived at the stables he was almost soaked to the bone. The winds were howling, small trees bent almost to the ground with the force of them, while lightning and thunder took turns astonishing the night with displays of ferocity. It had been some time since he had witnessed a storm of this magnitude, and while he was not frightened, William was very aware of the potential for damage, especially from the winds. Nevertheless, as he neared the smaller stable where the broodmares were housed along with newborn colts, the door swung open, and he ran inside to be greeted by one of the younger grooms who had been stationed to watch for him.

"Mr. Darcy, sir, I almost missed you! I watched at the window, but it is almost impossible to see anything in this downpour! If not for your great coat flapping in the wind, I would have overlooked you."

"John, is it not?"

"Yes, sir!"

"Well, John, if not for the gravel path, I might never have found the stables!" William declared with a chuckle. "I could only see a few feet ahead of me."

"I am sure Mr. Mooney will be grateful that you came. He is in the last stall on the left."

While they talked, William divested himself of his great coat, hat and gloves and tossed them to the groom. "Please place them across some of the hay bales to dry."

It was not hard to find the precise stall, as there were at least four young men standing around the one in question. They parted as he neared and then gathered again after he entered the spacious stall filled with straw, rags and water. Mr. Mooney and another groom were standing next to a beautiful white mare that his sister had christened Tatiana years before. The mare was evidently in distress, and as he was stripping off his coat and rolling up his sleeves, it laid down. That is when Mooney spoke.

"Thank you for coming, sir. I am sorry for asking your help when I know you are tired. I am just a bit hampered, what with this arm." He tried to move his left arm which was in a sling from having recently been strained. "And without Bradford, I am finding it hard to make do."

"I was sorry to hear about Mr. Bradford. He was a fine man, and I admired his way with horses. There is no need to apologise."

Kneeling beside the animal, he began to run his hands over the ripping flesh of the mare's belly. Everyone watched in silence, their murmurings ceasing as they followed every move he made. Mr. Darcy's reputation as a horseman was well known around these stables.

After a few tense moments, William sat back on his heels, took a deep breath and let it go loudly. The others watched on in silence, as he seemed to be considering what he was going to say. Finally he stood up and spoke.

"Better have more rags and water brought in. If I am correct, you are going to see a rare sight." Mooney's eyes grew larger, but he did not speak. "Have you ever had a mare deliver twins?"

"Not in all my days. Have you at Pemberley?"

"Only once can I recall seeing twins born, and it was at Matlock, not Pemberley. I was just a boy, but I was there during the entire delivery, and I remember what was done."

"And how did it turn out?"

"Both colts were born alive, but one died soon after birth. It was not as large or as strong as the other. But who is to say that will happen with this mare. We shall do our best and pray for the Lord's help. Nothing will happen until her water has broken, so let us each try to relax until nature takes its course."

Moving to sit on a bale of hay and leaning back against the side of the stall, he offered a silent prayer for the animal and her offspring. Then William closed his eyes, hoping for just a moment's respite.

Chapter 34

Ashcroft Park
The Dining Room

The four people sitting at the heavily laden dinner table ate in silence, each glancing from one to the other before quickly looking away when their eyes met. All were troubled at the turn of events that kept William from joining them, but none seemed eager to discuss it, and each had their own reasons for the deafening lack of sound.

Georgiana spent the entire meal pushing her food listlessly around on her plate, quite unaware that the cook had gone to great trouble to change the menu to include some of her favourites at Lady Ashcroft's behest, hoping it would strengthen her niece's appetite. Greatly disappointed that her beloved brother had been called to help in the stables, Georgiana realised she would not likely see him again until morning.

Her hope had been that they would spend the evening together, allowing her to exhibit her skills at the pianoforte and that the music might dispel some of the disappointment she had seen in his eyes. She might have been more accepting of the situation that took him away had Georgiana known that it was her mare that William was attending. But her aunt felt it best not to inform her of that fact, for had she known, she would have been fretting over all three—her brother, the mare and the colt.

Elizabeth tried to feign interest in what little she ate and to give the appearance of having no disquiet. It was challenging, as she had absolutely no appetite—not with Fitzwilliam so soon torn from her arms. However, she was not blind to the covert looks that Lady Ashcroft gave Georgiana as she slid the food on her plate first one way then the other, without actually consuming any of it.

Elizabeth did not want to appear equally ungrateful for the delicious food— and what little she had tasted of it was delectable—but she just could not manage to swallow past that large lump in her throat that appeared the instant Fitzwilliam had passed out of sight at the top of the stairs. Managing to force a smile, she glanced up to see if anyone was looking, and seeing that no one was, she let the smile fade. She was not surprised to see that none of the others had eaten much either.

If one was to study Lord Landingham, it would be plain to see that he was decidedly irritated. Upset that he had not been informed of the situation at the stables in time to accompany Fitzwilliam and chafing under Audrey's insistence that he was not well enough to be out in the present downpour, he was certain that he could have been of help to his godson, if only someone had had the foresight to tell him what was taking place. Even now as he fretted over the situation, he felt a slight twinge of pain, and his hand unwittingly rose to his scalp. Glancing to Audrey, he noted that she was watching him like a cat would a mouse, so he brought the hand back down, and once more focusing on his plate, he silently vowed not to let her assessment of his health prove correct.

I AM better! He affirmed mutely just as a sharper pain struck at the place where the bullet had begun its run through his hair. It was another blasted headache! Sighing, he began to sulk. *Well, I am certainly well enough to help with a mare in foal!*

For her part, Lady Ashcroft was watching Marshall carefully, equally worried about him as well as Fitzwilliam. They were both so similar—each used to pushing themselves beyond his limits. Marshall simply would not accept the fact that he had to relax in order to recuperate.

She had known of one other man who had had this type of injury, a trusted servant years before, and it had taken almost a year for him to return to his normal occupation and good health. At that time, the doctor had been adamant that he be relieved of his duties and to get plenty of rest. Coping with Marshall's reluctance to be a good patient, her anxiety over her nephew's relationship with Miss Bennet, and the entire episode with Georgiana was wearing thin the fabric of her sanity. And somewhere deep inside, Lady Ashcroft feared that one more provocation just might push her past the bounds of her patience and good sense.

Glancing over to see how Elizabeth was faring, the gloom written on that young face was yet another reminder that her nephew was in a dark, dank stable when he should have been with them. It was obvious that he had left London very early and rode hard all day to arrive when he did, thus he had to be weary. And now, while a tempest raged outside, they were all inside a safe and warm home, while he was not. She sent up a silent prayer.

Lord, please help him. If he does not get some rest before long, I fear the result!

Besides being concerned about Fitzwilliam's health, Lady Ashcroft hated that he and Elizabeth had not had more time to talk with one another. Though they both wore a pleased expression when they exited the library, it was clear that they had had little time to discuss their situation. She dearly wished for them to make a decision before morning, when they were to return to London. She had a feeling of tormenting foreboding that something dreadful was about to happen when they returned to Town. Knowing not what it might be, she could only pray it was not as bad as the only other time she had had this feeling—the night her Joseph died.

Shaking those worrying thoughts from her mind, Lady Ashcroft quickly surveyed her guests to find that no one was eating very heartily, so she declared, "If everyone is finished, why do we not retire to the music room for dessert and coffee? Perhaps we might persuade Georgiana to play for us while we wait for Fitzwilliam to return from the stables."

All eyes fixed on Georgiana who blushed but did not refuse. Thus, one and all stood relieved to exit the dining room. As the last to leave, Lady Ashcroft motioned one of the footmen to her side.

"Please notify Cook of our plans, and inform me at once when my nephew returns from the stables."

A loud round of thunder seemed designed to halt any more instructions, so the footman bowed and went to inform the cook of his mistress' orders as the lady trailed after her guests.

The Stables
Two hours later

Though it was long past time to retire for the night, none of the men who had gathered outside the stall to watch Mr. Darcy supervise Tatiana's foaling had stirred. A few had been with the family for decades, but not a one had ever seen a horse deliver twins, and the complexity and novelty of it had kept them riveted to the spot for hours. Yet, even now that the colts had been born without major complications, they had not stirred from their post. It was quite a sight to see—not one, but two identical black colts borne to the solid white mare.

The miracle of new life was not lost on those standing about the stall—the grooms, whose lots in life were to care for the animals and the man whose destiny it was to raise them. And while Fitzwilliam Darcy would always be of a separate sphere, what he had done that night to facilitate the births of the colts had made an impression on each one in the stable. For any gentleman who cared enough about an animal to get on his knees and help deliver a colt, was the kind of man they could admire, no matter his elevated station in life.

The men who had actually assisted with the birth, Fitzwilliam and Mr. Mooney, were sitting on bales against the side of the large hay-filled stall, exhausted but elated at the results. Not only had Tatiana birthed two colts, but both appeared healthy. And the fact that each had stood soon after birth was a good omen. It had been amusing, as always, to watch the newborn colts trying to control their ungainly legs, straining to stand on their spindly limbs only to come crashing down time and again. Nevertheless, no amount of failure could discourage them from their goal, and eventually each small creature was hobbling about the enclosure before, in short order, electing to look for nourishment.

And just as the newborn colts had taken to their legs, the weary gentleman in question finally stood to his feet and stretched to relieve his aching back. The young groom, John, stepped forward, eager to address him.

"Sir, we have heated water for your use. If you will follow me, I shall take you to the room where we wash up."

William looked to Mr. Mooney, who nodded. "Please go ahead, sir. You did all the work, so I am barely soiled. I shall wash after you."

William was too weary to argue, so he followed John to a small room in the back of the stables where a number of large flat stones constituted a floor. Overhead, several boards ran across the middle of the structure and held a line of large buckets. Each pail was secured in such as way as to tip but not fall and was connected to a rope that hung down in the middle of the room. A young man stood upon a ladder pouring water into one of the containers fixed overhead. At William's pensive study of the apparatus, John began to explain.

"This was my idea! We do not have a tub so we stand here and pull the rope, which tips the bucket. It is not fancy, but it is soothing when the water is hot," he smiled as though he had just described the finest accommodations in any manor house. William could not suppress a smile in return.

"Thank you, John. I am sure it will suffice admirably. Now where did you place my clothes?"

John walked over to one wall and opened a small cabinet that was eye level. "They are inside here, Mr. Darcy, along with a clean towel and some soap," he responded. "Now, if you will just give me your boots, while you are bathing, I shall tidy them up for you." He glanced up at the man on the ladder. "Trevor seems to have finished filling the pails now."

William sat down on a small chair near the cabinet, and John helped him off with the boots, then slipped out the door, along with the other fellow. Stripping off his clothes, he positioned himself under a bucket and pulled the rope, sending cascades of deliciously hot water down, and before long, he found himself enjoying the smell of soap and the streams of steaming water. He hurried to finish, not because he thought to see Elizabeth at this hour, but because he knew Mr. Mooney was awaiting his turn, and it was not long until he was clean, dressed and ready to return to the manor house.

"I shall return to the house, John," William offered as he stepped out of the room to find the young man waiting to give him his boots. "Thank you for the hot water."

John nodded with a shy smile and began leading the way back to the large doors on the end of stables. As they approached, William noted that Mr. Mooney stood near the entrance with a lantern. The liveryman addressed him.

"It seems the rain has abated at last, Mr. Darcy. At least you will not get soaked returning to the house."

All three men walked out of the stables and looked up to see that the clouds were now scattered and were moving quickly from one portion of the sky to the other, as the wind was still very strong. "I suppose the worst is over," William sighed tiredly.

The old man handed John the lantern. "Please escort Mr. Darcy back to the manor. It is still quite dark, and the path is not well marked."

"I assure you, there is no need. I shall be perfectly safe."

Mr. Mooney conceded. "Very well, then. Thank you for your valuable assistance, Mr. Darcy." Turning, the liveryman addressed the groom, "Will you please check on the animals in the main stable before you retire?"

John acceded, and as the men resumed their work, William began the trek back to the manor. Since the pathway was lined by tall trees, it was still extremely dark, and he began to wish he had accepted the light. The storm was so fierce it had stripped the trees of leaves. Small limbs and even some dead wood were strewn across the path. More than once, he tripped, almost falling flat on his face. Deciding that he must be more careful, William dropped his gaze to focus on the ground. In doing so, however, he failed to see a jagged tree limb that hung precariously just ahead— right above eye level—until he walked right into it!

The impact knocked William to the ground, and he landed on his backside. His hand flew to his forehead, and he felt the sensation of a warm liquid streaming down his face. The injury was serious; that much was certain. Pulling a handkerchief from his pocket, he pressed it firmly to the wound. Now chuckling in frustration, he considered his situation.

Deuce take it, I should have listened to Mr. Mooney. He climbed to his feet, dusted off the seat of his pants and shrugged. *I shall survive, albeit with a headache, I am sure.*

Downstairs

Rufus Parker had been about to retire for the night, convinced that Mr. Darcy would likely be at the stables until dawn, when the sight of his mistress' nephew entering the back door with a blood-stained shirt and a wound to the head left him speechless. After hearing a quick explanation of the reason for that gentleman's injuries, Parker's mind raced with the question of what to do first—fetch his mistress or his wife? Neither option was pursued, however, as William forbade him from waking either of them. He did manage, however, to coax the gentleman to the kitchen in order to assess the injury.

William had wearily slumped down in a chair next to a table, pulling the handkerchief back for the butler to inspect the gash. Mr. Parker's expression at first sight of the damage did not ease his mind, no more so than the consequent clicking of the servant's tongue in disapproval.

"I wish you would allow me to awaken my wife, Mr. Darcy. I am sure that she would insist that you allow her to stitch up this wound!"

"I do not want anyone awakened at this ungodly hour to see after a scratch! It shall be well."

"Begging your pardon, sir, but based on what I have seen over the years, I do not think it will. You have held a cloth on it for several minutes now, I assume, and the bleeding has not diminished. It is very deep, and without stitches, may not stop bleeding for some time. At the very least, it will leave a horrible scar if it is not sewn up properly."

"I am determined that we will do it my way, Parker."

"Then at least allow me to fetch warm water to wash the wound and your face. I am afraid that blood has run down the side of your face and neck and ruined your shirt. And, I shall also find my wife's bag of remedies, as she has powders for headaches."

"If you insist. I shall wait for you in my dressing room." With that, William was out of the chair and the kitchen in short order.

"Stubborn," Parker murmured to himself as he watched the young man go. Lady Ashcroft would not be pleased with him or her nephew. "The wound will be too swollen in the morning to do anything about it." After sending the footman who had opened the back door for Mr. Darcy to obtain a pitcher of warm water, he set out to find his wife's bag. "Why does this generation think they are experts on everything? A cut on the forehead will never close properly without stitches," he said, still clicking his tongue.

He finally located the bag in a closet next to his wife's office. Turning, he spied the footman coming towards him with the water.

"Thank you, Soames." The footman nodded, as Mr. Parker took the offered pitcher. "You may return to your post." Mr. Parker began to make his way to William's room.

After midnight, Elizabeth had given up her vigil at the window, accepting that there must be complications with the foaling, and she would not see William until the morning. Very disappointed, she changed into her nightgown and crawled into the large bed with the overstuffed pillows, but sleep was not to be found. After reciting every Bible verse and poem she could remember, she was still no closer to falling asleep when she was suddenly overwhelmed with the thought that William was in trouble. She tried to convince herself that she was imagining it—after all, what calamity could possibly befall him in a stable—but she could not free herself from the notion.

Sliding out of bed, she grabbed her silky robe and stepped out on the wet balcony, though her feet were bare. The dampness made her wish that she had her slippers, but she eschewed going back inside for them. The feeling of dread got even heavier as she stared into the darkness in the direction of the stables.

Her eyes were drawn to the heavens when a sliver of moon peeked from behind the clouds, exposing an occasional glimpse of a calmer sky. The wind, still blustering like an ill-tempered shrew, caused the ribbon in her loosely tied braid to come undone, and before she could react, it was flying across the stone floor. She gave chase, almost grasping the ribbon twice, only to watch it fly off the balcony with her last attempt. Frustrated, Elizabeth stood up just as the moon escaped the clouds entirely. It illuminated the night sufficiently to make certain objects appear clearly, and out of the corner of her eye she noted movement on the grounds below. Fearful of looking away, she stood transfixed until she could make out the figure of a man. Her heart lurched at the realisation of just who it was.

Fitzwilliam!

Flying back into the room, she searched for her slippers. Finding them just under the bed, she ran into the dressing room next door where she thought to have a better view of the hallway. Blowing out the candles and hiding by the partially open door, she was perfectly willing to wait until Fitzwilliam appeared, no matter the hour. Fortunately, she did not have to wait long, for in a short while, he appeared in the hallway in shirtsleeves, carrying his coat, a white cloth tied around his forehead. He was focused on opening the door and did not see her as she dashed towards him.

"Fitzwilliam!" she whispered roughly, flinging herself into his arms. Staggered, William ran an arm around her waist and pulled her into the room with him.

Closing the door behind him hastily, William kissed Elizabeth's forehead before pulling back to look at her.

"Sweetheart, why are you still awake? You should be sleeping."

"You told me to wait …" Her voice trailed off and her eyes became wide as she watched the blood begin to soak through the bandage. "What has happened?"

Absently, she reached to touch the dressing, and he hissed in pain. She drew her hand back sharply.

Lowering his voice soothingly, he tried to make amends for scaring her. "I am sorry. It is just sensitive. That is all."

Her eyes clouded as she watched the ever-growing red blot. "How … how were you injured?"

"I hate to admit this to anyone, but I was concentrating on the pathway, since I had already tripped, and inadvertently marched right into a low limb. I suppose the storm made it hang even lower than when I made the trek earlier. I feel sure I would have remembered if I had dodged it beforehand." He looked sheepish. "I pray Mr. Mooney does not enjoy too good a laugh at my expense. He warned me to take a lantern and I refused."

Elizabeth was not amused. "From the way it is bleeding, you will need stitches."

"I see no need to wake Mrs. Parker or my aunt at this late hour to do the deed."

"There is no reason to wake them when I can do it."

William tried not to smile at her determined mien. "Darling, I find it hard to conceive of you doing such a thing, and it would be dreadful of me to ask it of you."

Elizabeth raised her chin defiantly, though she could not be angry with him. "I have helped Papa stitch up our hounds for many years, and I am not afraid. Besides, my courage always rises with any attempt to intimidate me."

William had always been impressed by her intelligence, and this assertion only increased his admiration. Leaning down to kiss the tip of her perfect nose, he murmured, "I was only trying to protect you, my love. There is a difference in stitching an animal and stitching someone you care for. I know. I once had to sew a cut on Georgiana."

She stood on tiptoes to kiss him lightly. "Point taken. And just so you cannot say you were not informed, when we marry, I intend to stitch your wounds whenever I feel stitches are needed."

Her proclamation was what his lonely heart needed to hear! It sent shivers of pleasure through his body, igniting long-suppressed desires. Embracing her, she pressed her body against the hardness of him as he captured her lips possessively and deeply. He felt her full breasts press against the thin lawn of his shirt, and the thin silk of her dressing gown and robe did nothing to mask the hardening of the centres as they moved against him. It was not until one petite hand came up to rest on his cheek, that he remembered himself and loosened his hold, pushing her at arm's length. The love in her eyes totally overwhelmed him, and for a long moment, he was lost in their ebony depths and did not hear her enquiry.

"Fitzwilliam?"

"Yes, love?"

"I asked if you would not do the same if the situation was reversed."

"Do?"

"Stitches? Would you not stitch my wounds if need be?"

He sighed. "I would, though I would rather die than hurt you."

"Then you must understand that I can do no less."

He would have kissed her fiercely again, but at just that moment, there was a knock at the door. "It is Mr. Parker," he whispered, pulling her towards the bedroom. "Please wait behind the door."

Elizabeth did as he asked, and William opened the hall door to reveal the butler, standing with a pitcher and a black bag. He hurried inside.

"Sir, I have brought warm water to clean the wound and my wife's remedies. In this bag, she has whatever items are necessary to stitch a wound, and it would not take—"

"While I truly appreciate your concern, Parker, it is not necessary. You may leave now, as I wish to wash and change clothes, then I shall retire."

Sighing audibly, the servant braved, "Then may I have your coat and shirt, sir. I believe I can remove most of the stains before you leave for London."

William reached for the coat that he had tossed on the dressing table when he entered the room and did as requested and removed the shirt.

With the offending clothes securely in hand, Parker replied, "Thank you. I shall return these on the morrow."

And with those few words, Mr. Parker gave up his quest to change William's mind and was out the door. William locked it securely and turned to find Elizabeth watching him from the bedroom door, her eyes wider and the pupils darker than he had ever seen them.

Completely mesmerized by the beauty of his nakedness, Elizabeth was in a trance. She had never seen any man this scantily clad, and that it was the man she loved with all her heart made their situation all the more precarious. With no will to resist, her gaze travelled from his handsome face to the perfection of his strong neck and collarbone, then to the fine, dark hair covering the solid muscles of his broad, tanned chest.

A small gasp accompanied her inspection of the rippled planes of his abdomen as she followed the line of hair that snaked beyond his tapered waist and disappeared into his breeches. She knew the instant his breathing changed, matching her own, as they stood motionless, facing one other.

"I should find another shirt."

Elizabeth clasped his arm. "Wait."

There were only inches between them, and the blood rushing through her veins was making it difficult to concentrate. "There is no need to spoil another shirt. Please just lie down and let me look at your wound."

"Lie down?" he asked, his voice suddenly raspy with emotion. "On the bed?"

"Yes. If you lie on your back, the blood will not flow so freely, and I can get a better look."

William steeled himself and willed his body to comply. Once he had removed his boots, he climbed upon the counterpane in only his breeches and stocking feet. Positioning one of the pillows beneath his head, his eyes followed her surreptitiously as she scurried about the room, moving more candles to the tables on either side of the bed. At length, she sat down on the edge of the bed and put the bag on the other side of him. Then she moved closer, leaning ever so lightly against his chest while she studied his forehead.

"Take a deep breath."

"Pardon?"

"I need you to take a deep breath and … and close your eyes." He could see her blush even in the candlelight. "I cannot concentrate while you stare at me."

He complied, closing his eyes, and she began to cut away the bandage. "Is that better? I did not realise I was staring."

Elizabeth's quick intake of breath at the sight of the cut caused William to open his eyes once more. It was evident that she was trying hard to swallow as she hurriedly pressed the bandage back down.

"It definitely will need stitches." Refusing to meet his eyes, she busied herself by opening the black bag. "Perhaps there is some laudanum in here."

William reached to still her hand. "No, Elizabeth. I never take that substance willingly. I would rather it hurt."

Her expression was sombre as she met his gaze at last. "Oh, Fitzwilliam, the cut is very wide. I am certain that it shall be quite painful." A tear rolled from the corner of her eye. "I do not wish to hurt you, but it must be attended to now."

William wiped the tear from her cheek. "It is past midnight, and you should be sleeping, not caring for me." He cupped her face. "Go to bed, sweetheart. This can wait until morning."

"It cannot, you know that. You are dear to me, and it is my duty to look after you."

William sat up to kiss her tenderly. "I say it is my duty to look after you."

Elizabeth blinked as though trying not to cry and ran a finger softly down his cheek. "Then we are agreed."

Recovering, she declared a little too brightly, "I saw a decanter of brandy in the other room, so I shall pour you a glass. At least it should afford you some relief."

Without delay, she was off the bed and out of the room. Presently she returned with a full glass of brandy. William complied with her wishes by downing the contents in a very few swallows, though he grimaced at the burn in his throat when he was done.

Taking her position on the bed once more, Elizabeth reached into the black satchel and pulled from it a curved needle with silk thread already attached. She had found it wrapped in a clean cloth as though prepared for use.

"Please know that this shall hurt me more than you."

William grinned though his head was beginning to ache more severely. "My mother used to say that very thing, though I never believed her."

Elizabeth lay across his chest, and began kissing him deeply and thoroughly. His breath was coming in ragged gasps when she drew back.

"What ... what brought that on?"

"I wanted to give you something on which to concentrate on while I stitch you up and to remind you that I love you so very much."

A smile twitched at the corners of his mouth as his dark eyes flashed. "When this is done, I think I shall need more reminding."

Chapter 35

London
The Gardiner's Residence
Gracechurch Street

Jane was up very early, hoping to avoid being discovered by her mother or her aunt before she had time to talk with Jenny, the young maid who had become a friend and confidant. She had tried to surreptitiously slip the letter to her father in with the others to be posted yesterday, but she was unable to do so after her aunt came downstairs unexpectedly.

I must post this letter today, even if I have to slip out of the house to do it!

As she sneaked down the stairs, a noise below startled her and she stiffened, praying that it was not Gertrude Doane, the housekeeper. That woman would tell her aunt the moment she suspected the letter to Longbourn was not to be seen by her Mistress. The door to the dining room opened, and as Jenny appeared with her arms full of clean linens, Jane let go of the breath she had been holding.

"Oh, Miss Jane, it is so good to see you first thing this beautiful morning," Jenny said in a whisper, so as not to wake anyone. "I was fearful that it was your mother." She smiled slyly. "Not that I should be telling you that, but she makes me nervous, the way she talks and waves her hands about."

Jane returned her smile. "To tell the truth, she makes me nervous as well."

Jenny nodded in acknowledgement of their shared amusement. "Is there a reason you are up so early? Something I can help you with?"

Jane took the girl's arm and tugged her back into the dining room. Just to be sure they were completely alone, she peered through the disappearing gap in the door as it closed to make sure no one was coming. Satisfied, she turned to address the maid.

"I need you to do a favour for me?"

"I will help you anyway I can. You know that."

Jane took the letter from a pocket in her gown and held it out to Jenny. "This is why I sought you out. I need this letter to go out in the post today without anyone being the wiser."

Jenny placed the linens down on a chair. Then taking the missive, she glanced at the address before putting it in her own pocket. "Done!"

A small giggle escaped from Jane. "Are you certain that Mrs. Doane will not see it? She would expose me if she knew that I was hiding it from my aunt or my mother."

"I shall be extra careful to see that she does not catch me slipping it in with the others. There is one on the table already, put there last night." Her eyes twinkled with mischief. "There must be something dreadful afoot if you are writing to your father behind your mother's back."

Jane blushed. "I will say this much—I may need your help again before all is settled. My mother intends to force my sister to accept a man she does not want, and only my father can thwart her plans. I have written to insist that he come to London straightaway!"

Jenny raised her brows as she shook her head. "Miss Elizabeth is not one to marry someone she does not fancy. I know her that well."

"Clearly you do," Jane responded. "It would be a disaster to force her to accept a man that she does not respect, and I know for certain that she does not respect this man."

"Well, do not worry yourself about it, Miss Jane," Jenny soothed as she laid a hand on her arm. "Your papa does not seem the type to allow this to happen. Not to Miss Elizabeth or to you."

"I am relying on that, Jenny. So do not fail me, please."

"I will not." That having been said, Jenny picked up the linens once more, just as Mrs. Doane pushed open the dining room door and eyed them with suspicion. Jenny averted her eyes. Jane would not be intimidated and glared at the older woman until she addressed Jenny.

"What are you doing in here, missy? You were supposed to have the bread in the oven a quarter-hour ago."

"I hindered her progress," Jane answered before Jenny could reply. "I was enquiring how her mother was faring. Jenny's mother once worked for one of our neighbours in Meryton, and I know her well."

Mrs. Doane huffed. "That is all well and good, but it will not put food on the table when the Mistress expects it!"

"Well, then I suppose that I shall just have to explain to my aunt why we shall be eating a little later." Jane turned to address Jenny. "And thank you for the information regarding your family. Please tell your mother that I enquired of her health."

Jenny nodded, "Yes, Miss Bennet."

The younger maid hid a smile as she ducked her head and hurried out the door, while the housekeeper watched her go with barely concealed frustration. As Jane made her way out of the room too, she could hear the woman mumbling under her breath about people thinking they were above their stations. She suppressed the urge to say something.

Horrible woman! I do not see why my aunt keeps her about. I pray Jenny will not suffer on my account.

Ashcroft Park
William's Bedroom

Truly happy for the first time in years, a new dream began in William's imagination, and in this one, Elizabeth was the Mistress of Pemberley. In his imaginings, he was standing at the windows of his study which overlooked the rose garden that his mother had designed. He was barely able to contain his elation as he watched Elizabeth who was sitting in a swing amongst the roses and conversing with a small boy playing nearby. Occasionally she would look down to hum a song to an infant that slept in her arms. A breeze stirred the treetops, and his gaze swept across the breadth of the lawn, noting that all the flowering trees, shrubs and flowers were in bloom—springtime was magical at Pemberley!

In his dream, he had just decided to join Elizabeth in the garden when the sounds of a servant shutting the dressing room door penetrated William's awareness. Awakened, he became immediately alert, and the reality of what had occurred between Elizabeth and himself that night came rushing back.

She loved him … truly loved him and had vowed to wait until he was free! Confident that he could endure anything as long as he knew that she waited at the end of the tribulation, he rolled over and reached out to find her gone. Disappointment engulfed him, and he closed his eyes in a bid to relive the ecstasy of their short time together last night.

Elizabeth had completed the task of stitching his wound closed, uttering not a word as her needle moved in and out. He had kept his eyes closed at her request and had barely felt the shift of the bed as she slid to her feet, alerting him that she was finished. Opening his eyes, they acclimated to the dim light, and he noted that she stood at the French doors leading to the terrace. Her hair was dishevelled and reminded him of their first encounter at the bookshop. He could not tell if she was crying, though her head was down and her hands covered her face. Instantly he was standing behind her, clasping both trembling forearms as he pulled her back against his body.

"Elizabeth," he breathed into her hair as he rested his head atop hers. "You are shaking like a leaf. What is the matter, sweetheart?"

Only a strangled sob escaped her throat with her first attempt to speak, but afterward, she was able to say, "I … I was so scared."

"My brave, brave darling," he soothed, kissing the top of her head.

She began to cry as she continued. "It has all been so … draining and so frightening. To learn that you are married … that Wilkens is a madman … to watch as poor Georgiana was almost—" She faltered, swallowing with great difficulty and shaking her head as though that would help to remove the large lump in her throat. At last she whispered hoarsely, "When I saw that you were hurt …"

Instantly, William turned her to face him, pulling her into his embrace. Her head came to rest against the hard musculature of his chest as two small hands slid around to clasp his back. And as her fingertips gripped tighter, striving to pull him closer, he silently repeated his vow to protect her even as his body betrayed his best intentions.

"Shhh, sweetheart, say no more. I should never have involved you in the insanity that is my life. You do not deserve what has befallen you, what will befall you because of me."

She looked up to him. "Please do not think I regret loving you. That is the only thing that makes sense to me in all of this. You cannot help that you were trapped in a loveless marriage or that Providence put us together that night in the cabin. It is   only."

"Only?"

"I came to London to prove my sister wrong, but I fear that I have only proved her right. I bragged to Jane that we would find decent men to marry in London, if only we made an effort. But it is plain that only a madman like Wilkens would settle for a girl with no dowry or connections." Her voice dropped, along with her eyes. "Would you have even cared for me if you had not been trapped in a marriage with a woman you despise?"

William cupped her face, lifting it tenderly so that their eyes met and held. "I am certain of only one thing, Elizabeth. I would have loved you the moment we met, just as I did when I found you at the bookstore. I pray that I would have had the good sense to recognise how precious that love is and to pursue it."

"Tell me about her—about Gisela," she pleaded timidly. "I saw her once at a ball in London. It was evident that she had been drinking, and she was with …" her voice trailed off.

"Another man?" William asked. Elizabeth nodded silently.

"Her liaisons are well known to me. I am aware that my aunt told you that she trapped me into marriage and then blackmailed me with my mother's letters to stay in the union. It began when she tried to entice me into an affair, and when I declined, she decided to seduce my father."

"I do not know the particulars of that situation."

"She told me later that she decided that if she could not have me, she would ruin the Darcy name. My father was a means to an end, though he was more than happy to be used, I fear. Afterward, she claimed to be carrying his child and threatened to tell my mother if I did not marry her. She was aware that the news could likely hasten Mother's death, but she did not care."

"So you married her to keep the secret, and once you realised she was not going to have a child—"

mother's writing. It alluded to the fact that Georgiana is not a Darcy. My poor sister was so devastated when our parents died, that I feared for her sanity if anything of that nature became public then."

Elizabeth gasped. "Poor Georgiana. Do you think it true?"

"I have concluded that it is quite possibly true. My father neglected my mother for years, keeping to his *friendships* in London. The truth came out when I was called to Gisela's townhouse to collect him after he had an ailment with his heart. I condemned his despicable behaviour, and he blamed his actions on the fact that my mother's health prohibited another child. I saw that as no excuse for his infidelity to my mother."

"Your aunt has said that the basis for the extortion will no longer exist in a short while. What is to happen that will make Gisela's threats of no use?"

"I will admit that, at the onset, I sought only to shield Georgiana from more hurt. Then others—Richard, Aunt Audrey, Lord Landingham—convinced me that she deserved to know the truth of her parentage. I wanted to wait until she was older, but she has matured tremendously under Aunt Audrey's care. I truly believe she will be able to bear it now. After all, she is my mother's child, my sister, and forever a Darcy as far as I am concerned."

Elizabeth wore a pensive expression.

"I sense there is more you wish to know. Ask me."

"Even in her present state, Gisela is still quite beautiful, while I am only—"

"Never say that!" William interrupted emphatically. "From first glimpse, I found you to be enchantingly beautiful, Elizabeth. And I never thought Gisela remotely handsome. She never held any sway over my emotions, nor have I ever desired her as I do you."

Satisfied, she whispered, "I love you so."

A quick flame began in his core as he inspected her eyes. Finding the love that he had always desired gazing back, he whispered, "I love you with all my heart and my soul."

Elizabeth laid her head on his chest, closing her eyes. "Then let me stay with you a while. Hold me just as you did that night at the cabin."

"I would hold you forever were it possible, but you know that you should not be found in my rooms."

"I shall not stay long," she pleaded, her voice catching with emotion as she added, "Please."

Swooping Elizabeth off her feet effortlessly, William carried her to the bed and laid her atop the counterpane, quickly taking his place beside her. She turned to snuggle into him, which sent a delicious throng of sensations coursing through his body and surged into his manhood.

He responded by brushing kisses against her temple. "This may not be wise, darling. I fear that my desires could—"

She turned her head to him, and his words were halted by soft lips pressing against his. Further resistance was futile as months of pent-up longing and desire came rushing in, and he surrendered to the yearning to love her. And as their kisses became endless, intensifying and growing more demanding, he was barely aware that he had undone the fastenings of her nightclothes and was now pushing the silky material aside to cup her breast. A low moan escaped her throat, only adding fuel to the fire. No longer capable of halting the hardness that was his body's response, William rolled over, trapping her beneath him. The ecstasy of body against body was so immeasurable that he began to move slowly against her with a rhythm as old as time.

Caught up in their passion, Elizabeth tried to pull him even closer, her nails burrowing into the tanned skin of his back as he feathered kisses down her neck, across her collarbone and down to the softness of her bosom. He kissed the very top of one perfect breast and was just about to capture the hard centre in his mouth when Elizabeth murmured again breathlessly, "I love you." William instantly became aware of what he was doing. Rolling over to his back, he groaned in anguish, uttering an oath under his breath.

Elizabeth looked puzzled by his actions. "Are … are you angry?"

Still trying to recover his self-control, he rolled back to face her. Propping upon one elbow, he began to right her clothes, saying softly, "I am angry at myself, not you, sweetheart."

Nonetheless, Elizabeth's expression showed uncertainty, so he leaned down to kiss her as tenderly as possible before raising his head to meet her gaze. "I should never have allowed myself to go so far. Though I desire to make you my own, I must wait until I can honourably do so."

Her dark eyes seemed to become even darker as she studied him solemnly.

Gently stroking her face with his fingertips, he continued, "Otherwise, you could be disgraced, and your father would run me through, and rightly so."

Her expression changed to one of mortification. "I am sorry. Just because I love you is no excuse to—"

A quick kiss on her lips halted her words. "Never apologise for loving me, Elizabeth. I am a very fortunate man that you have a passionate nature. But you are an innocent, and it falls to me to protect you. I was the one at fault, not you. Forgive me for forgetting myself. I shall endeavour never to let it happen again— until." The corners of his mouth lifted in a small smile. "Until you are my wife."

"I fear that I shall be no help to you meanwhile," Elizabeth confessed. "I find that I love you so dearly that I can be persuaded to whatever you wish the moment your lips meet mine."

William pulled her into a tight embrace, and very much aware of the promise he had just made, he chuckled as he offered a ragged plea. "Please do not remind me again of that, my love. God knows it is hard enough to resist you as it is."

Then, again propping on one elbow, he began to work the signet ring off his little finger. Once it was free, he slid it onto each of Elizabeth's fingers until he ascertained that it would best fit her middle finger, though it was still a loose fit. As they both studied the ring on her hand, he declared resolutely, "You are precious to me, Elizabeth Bennet, and until I can put a proper wedding ring on your finger, I want you to keep this as a symbol of my pledge to you. I have not removed it since my father presented it to me at the age of one and twenty. Now, whenever I notice it is missing, I will smile, for I will know exactly where it is. It will be with you—along with my heart."

"Oh, Fitzwilliam," Elizabeth murmured, pulling his lips down to meet hers. When she had kissed him thoroughly, she added, "Since, I cannot continue to wear it on my finger, I shall keep it on a chain, so that it rests over my heart."

"Then I shall envy it, my love," he responded, placing one last kiss on her perfect mouth. Then reaching for a blanket that was folded at the end of the bed, he covered her. "Now, let me hold you. After tomorrow, I have no idea when we shall see each other again."

Elizabeth said nothing when he pulled her into his embrace, her back resting against his chest, as she was already pondering his last words. Would they be able to see each other once they were in London? And just what would her Aunt Gardiner say when she learned that she had fled the Wilkens estate with Lady Ashcroft? Only God knew what her mother would do when she was informed. Would she be forced to entertain the attentions of another man like Wilkens?

She sighed. *If I ponder these things tonight, I shall go mad! No, I refuse to ruin these precious moments with Fitzwilliam by fearing the future. I shall think only of our love for one another.*

Immediately, her mind skipped to the feelings that he had awakened in her mere moments before. She could not help but blush at the memory, though no one was about to see. *From all the horrors that mother and Aunt Gardiner told me of the wedding night, I have dreaded it so, but surely our marriage bed will be nothing to fear if it is anything like tonight.*

While she relived all that they had shared, Elizabeth discerned the moment that Fitzwilliam fell into a deep sleep as his warm breath against her neck began a steady pattern, and his arms relaxed slightly. It felt so right that, intending to relish this heaven only a short while longer, she inadvertently drifted off to sleep beside him.

Dawn
Ashcroft Park

Other than a few servants, Lady Ashcroft had the house to herself the next morning, since all her guests were still asleep. She was quite content to be alone, as she had wished for some time to ponder the fact that the sorrow she had associated with her home since Joseph's death had slowly begun to diminish. That she had reached a turning place in her life was undeniable, and she wished to share it with the one who had dwelt in her thoughts almost every day since he was taken from her.

Reaching the long hallway that served as the portrait gallery, she walked swiftly to pause in front of Joseph's portrait. Though tears filled her eyes, she could not help but smile at the dear face that looked down on her. Never one to dwell on sadness, her husband would not have been pleased that she had shut herself off for so many years—first unwilling to accept the loss of him and their son, then reluctant to expose her vulnerable heart. She had been mistaken, that she would freely admit, but she was unable to change until she met Marshall Landingham. After they became better acquainted, the void in her life became evident, and following his brush with death, she realised just how very much she wanted to be his wife. All of these thoughts ran through her consciousness as she examined Joseph's likeness and began to speak from her heart.

My darling Joseph, you have always been my ideal. She smiled lovingly. *Maybe even a bit too perfect, for few have compared favourably to you over the years. But I want you to know that I have met someone that I love and admire in the same manner that I loved and admired you. Thank you, my love, for showing me what constitutes a real man. I shall always cherish what we had, and you shall always hold a special place in my heart. I know you would have wanted me to be happy, and that knowledge is what allows me to take the next step. I am going to marry Marshall Landingham sometime in the next few months.*

A sound brought her attention to the end of the hall where a maid was entering a room. Turning back to his portrait, Audrey took one last long look at Joseph before heading towards the foyer. She hoped to find Mr. Parker below stairs and to enquire about her nephew.

When at last she descended the grand staircase, she spied that gentleman coming out of the dining room, and it seemed to her that he tried to hurry in the opposite direction.

"Mr. Parker?" she called out, halting the man's progress. He slowly turned to face her. "I wish to know if you encountered my nephew when he returned last evening. Was he out all night, or did he get some sleep?"

"Milady, I … I did see Mr. Darcy," he stuttered, looking sheepish. "He did not return until the early morning hours, I am afraid."

"I was fearful of that. I shall advise all my guests that we shall postpone our return to London until later this morning. That will allow Fitzwilliam some extra hours to rest before we depart."

Parker seemed to be looking in every direction but at her, and Lady Ashcroft became suspicious. "Is there something you wish to tell me?"

There was an audible sigh. "There is, Milady." He glanced up, meeting her eye. "And I must apologise for not informing you last night."

Lady Ashcroft motioned towards an open door. "Come. Let us go into the parlour."

It took only a few seconds for them to enter the room and the door to close. It took only a few more for the door to fly open and the Mistress to rush out. Though she had not displayed any anger towards Mr. Parker—after all, he could not force her nephew do anything—Audrey Ashcroft was greatly disappointed that she had not been informed last night of what had happened. Her position was that it was inexcusable that her nephew had been injured and she had not been told. Marching purposefully to the family quarters, in short order she stood outside Fitzwilliam's bedroom, though as she lifted her hand to knock, something bid her pause. After all, by Parker's account, her nephew had very little sleep, and she was about to wake him. Deciding on another means of seeing to his welfare, she turned and went in search of Mrs. Parker.

Finding the housekeeper in her office, Lady Ashcroft attempted to regain her composure as she addressed the woman. "Mrs. Parker, may I have the master keys? I wish to check on my nephew, as I understand from Mr. Parker that he was injured while at the stables last night. I do not wish to wake him, however, if he is still asleep."

Mrs. Parker, who had not yet spoken to her husband that morning, stood immediately, beginning to search through a pocket in her gown. "Oh dear me! Of course, madam. Rufus was already on duty when I awoke, so I have not so much as heard of any injury. I pray Mr. Darcy is well."

She found the small key she was looking for and proceeded to unlock the top drawer of her desk. Reaching inside, she pulled out a large ring with a number of keys and handed them to Lady Ashcroft.

"Do you wish me to accompany you?"

"No, thank you. It cannot be too serious, or I would have been awakened," she replied with more certainly than she felt. "I just want to be sure that all is well. I shall return these shortly."

Very soon she was at the dressing room door that adjoined Fitzwilliam's bedroom. Her plan was to sneak into his room through the adjoining room, and if he appeared to be well, to depart. His appearance would determine whether she awoke him for examination. Looking both ways down the hall and seeing no one, she opened the door and stepped inside. There were no candles lit, and it was still early, so the room was dark. Carefully she tiptoed to the door that led into his bedroom, and a slight twinge of guilt came over her at the realisation that she was invading his privacy. Pushing that emotion aside, she opened it and was relieved to learn that a small candle glowed somewhere inside. Stealthily she moved towards the bed until the sight that greeted her caused her heart to skip a beat, one hand flying involuntarily to her chest.

In the large four-poster bed, Fitzwilliam lay asleep atop the counterpane, clad only in breeches and stockings. Miss Bennet lay next to him with her back to his chest, dressed only in night clothes and partially covered by a blanket. Not believing her eyes, Audrey crept closer, almost tripping on Mrs. Parker's bag of remedies which lay on the floor. She blinked in hopes it would prove an illusion, but that was not the case. The stitches in her nephew's head were plainly visible, though he was fast asleep. Taking a deep breath, the Mistress of Ashcroft Park tried to collect herself, knowing that she must work quickly. It was early, and there was still time to spirit Elizabeth back to her own bed before anyone realised that she had spent the night in Fitzwilliam's room.

Nearing the side where Elizabeth lay, she reached to shake her lightly and was relieved to see her eyes fly open. Holding a finger to her lips to indicate that they should not wake Fitzwilliam, she watched as the young woman rose, looked lovingly at him for a moment, and then slipped off the bed. Before long, they were both ensconced in Elizabeth's room without having been found out.

Once the scandal was averted, Elizabeth was left to face William's aunt. Mortified, her head dropped. "It was not as it appeared."

Lady Ashcroft stepped to Elizabeth, lifting her chin with a soft touch. "I know my nephew well enough to believe that. Besides, had anything more scandalous happened, I think you would have been under the covers and not lying atop them fully clothed," she said with a sly smile.

"I confess that something might have happened, had Fitzwilliam not been so honourable. I should not have stayed with him, but I was so worried."

"You love him and he was hurt. Naturally you wanted to be with him ... to see after him." She sank down onto a comfortable settee, pulling Elizabeth down beside her, and for the first time Lady Ashcroft noticed the ring on the young woman's middle finger. She reached out to examine it.

"Fitzwilliam's signet ring."

Elizabeth offered shyly, "He asked me to wear it until he can give me a wedding ring."

Audrey smiled lovingly at the woman who would one day become her niece. "That is so like him." Then she became solemn. "You know it would never do for Gisela to learn that you have his signet. That ring has the Darcy coat-of-arms and is employed to validate letters, contracts and documents of import—it signifies his stamp of approval."

"I understand," Elizabeth hurried to explain. "We agreed that I shall wear it around my neck on a long chain so that it rests over my heart."

"I have a silver necklace that would be perfect." Audrey patted her hand. "Now tell me about Fitzwilliam's injury? Parker mentioned that he had suffered a serious gash and that he could not convince my nephew that he needed stitches, but it is evident that he has them now."

"I ... I was able to convince him of that."

"Thank goodness! But who did the stitches? When I spoke with Mrs. Parker, she was unaware that he had even been injured."

Blushing crimson, Elizabeth focused on her slippers. "I did. You see, I have been stitching up my father's hounds for years and—"

The sound of heartfelt laughter filled the room, and Elizabeth glanced over to see William's aunt covering her mouth as she chuckled. It caused the tension in her shoulders to dissolve, and she began to smile. Then, she shared with his aunt all that had happened since she had seen Fitzwilliam returning from the stables.

Well … almost everything.

Chapter 36

As Charles Bingley neared the front entrance of Longbourn astride one of his favourite stallions, he was surprised to find that no one came running to greet him. Most of the time the younger girls would be the first to spy his approach and alert the rest of the family. With Jane and her mother in London, he felt sure that Lydia and Kitty would notice his arrival and rush to escort him into the house as was their usual manner. However, oddly enough, today no one had appeared by the time he had dismounted other than a groom who materialized out of thin air to take his horse. Nodding at the young man who claimed the reins, Charles was surprised to find Mrs. Hill standing in the doorway when he turned towards the front entrance. She was intently focused on wiping flour-covered hands on her apron in an attempt to clean them.

"Mrs. Hill, how good to see you again."

"And you, Mr. Bingley," the elderly servant replied, standing back to allow him to enter the door she held open. "Mr. Bennet regrets that he is not able to greet you, however, he is waiting for you in his study, if you will follow me."

"No need to show me the way," Charles declared cheerily as he strode off in the direction of Mr. Bennet's study. "You look as though you were occupied with more important things, and I can find the study. Besides," he called over his shoulder with a big smile, "I shall no doubt benefit from whatever delicious item you are baking if I let you return to your work."

Charles had reached the door to Mr. Bennet's study and hesitated for only a moment to reflect on the missive that had arrived at Netherfield that morning. It had been short and to the point, requesting that he come to Longbourn as soon as feasible and gave no explanation of why he was being summoned. Saying a short prayer that nothing important was amiss, he steeled himself and knocked.

A disembodied voice rang out, "Come in!"

Proceeding, the distinct aroma of liniment accosted his senses the moment he stepped inside, causing his nose to curl in protest. Expecting Mr. Bennet to stand as he normally did, Charles was surprised to find that gentleman still sitting behind his desk—his chair turned to the side. His left leg was stretched straight out and cradled upon another chair piled high with cushions, displaying a knee that looked several times larger than natural. It was wrapped in several layers of cloth that, without a doubt, contained the foul smelling ointment.

"Upon my word!" Charles exclaimed, moving closer to examine Jane's father. "What has happened to your leg?"

Mr. Bennet shook his head in exasperation. "I was trying to secure one of the goats when I stepped in a hole and fell, wrenching my knee. Fortunately, I believe it is not as severe as it looks. I can hobble around with the aid of my cane, though it causes considerable pain, but I fear that I shall not be doing any jigs for the foreseeable future."

Knowing Mr. Bennet's reluctance to attend the local assemblies as he did not enjoy dancing, Charles could not help chuckling. "If there was a ball scheduled, you would have a perfectly legitimate reason not to attend. Even Mrs. Bennet could not fault you now."

"Ah," Mr. Bennet concurred, "but unfortunately, this impairment is for naught, as there are no balls to refuse at this time. And as you well know, my wife is in London with your betrothed. That is why I sent for you."

"I wondered why I was summoned," Charles said, before adding a bit worriedly, "Jane is not ill?"

"Oh, no, no!" Mr. Bennet declared, using his arms to lift himself up and shift his position in the chair. He grimaced with pain as he did so. "I did not mean to alarm you, but I have a request to make of you."

Relieved, Charles let go of the breath he was holding. "Anything."

"Take me to London."

"But ... but," Charles stuttered, trying to make sense of the request, his mind whirling with the logistics of taking a man in his condition to London. "Why would you want to travel with your leg in such a state? Surely it needs to heal first or at least improve a great deal before you attempt such a journey."

"I do not have the luxury of waiting." Mr. Bennet said woodenly, opening the top drawer of his desk and pulling a letter from it. He tossed it across the desk to Charles. "I do not think that Jane will mind if I share this with you."

Charles took the letter, and with one last glance at Mr. Bennet, began to read the missive. Other than his eyebrows rising, there was no outward expression of what he was thinking until he was through. Refolding the letter, he handed it back to Jane's father, saying, "I see your point. Do you actually think Mrs. Bennet would order Miss Elizabeth to marry someone she does not want?"

"I believe she would try, though I have serious doubts that she would be successful. Lizzy is undeniably my daughter, and she is not one to be pushed about. However, I will not trust her future to my wife's plots and schemes, not to mention those of her aunt. It seems that Madeline Gardiner is as much a manipulator as Fanny. And apparently, I should not have believed all of my Lizzy's reassurances of her well-being since she reached Town."

Turning to look for a chair, Bingley found one and pulled it towards the front of Mr. Bennet's desk. He sat down and began to run his fingers through his bright red locks as he considered the particulars of a trip to London.

"I suppose we can undertake the trip if we can improvise a way to keep your leg elevated and as motionless as possible—that is, unless you wish to exercise it."

"I have given it considerable thought, and I have a small, square footstool that I believe will just fit between the seats. If I place a pillow or two upon it, it should be just the right height to support my leg. And, if we stop occasionally so that I may walk about with my cane, I believe I shall be able to weather the journey."

Charles smiled. "You must know that I would dearly love to see Jane again, though your wife forbade me to appear in Town while they were ordering her wedding clothes. Mrs. Bennet alleged that I would occupy all of Jane's time, and she would not be afforded the necessary time to visit all the modistes and fabric shops that she had in mind."

"There is not enough time in the day to satisfy my wife when she is spending my money!" Mr. Bennet huffed. Then softening, he added, "However, I shall assure you that Jane shall have all the wedding finery she desires and still have time to spend with you. How else could I repay your generosity in assisting me?"

"I would have aided you in any event, especially to help Miss Elizabeth, whom I already regard as a sister."

"Then we are agreed! We shall leave in the morning, if that suits you."

"My coach shall be here at dawn."

❦

London
Grantham Townhouse

Fran tiptoed to the door of her mistress' sitting room and as quietly as possible, turned the doorknob and peered inside. Breathing a sigh of relief at seeing no one about, she pushed open the door and slipped inside. Her arms were full of clean linens, while in her pocket were the keys she had purloined from the dresser last evening. She proceeded to the large closet to place the sheets and was unnerved to hear Gisela's slurred voice come from somewhere behind her.

"Where the devil have you been? I have been calling for you for over an hour to help me with my toilette! You know that I have a ball to attend tonight!"

Fran was very aware that Gisela had not even been awake an hour, and as she turned to find the lady in question standing in the door that led into her bedroom, she was not surprised to see her still wearing the nightgown she had worn for the last two days. More often than not, Mrs. Darcy no longer changed clothes or bathed unless she intended to go out. And the last time she had left the house, she had returned forthwith, complaining about not being received. From what she had gathered, her mistress had called on a long-time acquaintance who no longer wished to be associated with her.

Fran certainly could not fault whoever it was. She would not want to associate with her mistress either, given a choice. Taking in Gisela's dishevelled appearance, she was pondering how much trouble it would be to comb out the knots from the tangled mess that was her hair, when she realised that her employer was awaiting an answer.

"I was fetching linens, madam. If you had rung, I would have known you needed me. As it is, if you just shout for me, it is unlikely I will—"

"Silence!" Gisela spit out. "Do not be impertinent, or you shall find yourself looking for other employment."

Fran stiffened. This position had turned into a nightmare that she no longer wished to experience, but she had no other recourse at the moment than to endure the abuse. She had a job to complete.

"I need to select a gown for tonight! The Farnsworths will expect me to attend."

Fran had no idea to which ball her mistress was referring. Invitations to soirées and such had almost halted entirely, and Mrs. Darcy had declined to attend the one she had been invited to last. "The Farnsworth's ball was two days ago, madam. You decided at the last minute that you would not attend."

"Two days ago?" Gisela sank into a chair, rubbing her forehead as she mumbled to herself. "That cannot be. Why would I send regrets when I need to be seen at these events?" She stood to rail at Fran. "You failed to keep me apprised of the day, so now you make excuses to cover your error! Why was I not informed in time to attend?"

A knock at the door kept Fran from having to think of an answer, and she opened it to find Mr. Boatwright, the elderly butler, standing without. He looked as though he expected the Mistress to be angry with whatever news he had to impart.

He flinched as Gisela bellowed, "What do you want?"

"Mr. Wickham is in the parlour, madam. He insists that you are expecting him."

"Expecting him? That pompous—" Calming, she said unemotionally, "Tell him I shall be down directly."

Mr. Boatwright bowed and left without further comment. Gisela turned, retreating into her bedroom, calling out, "Quickly, come help me dress!"

Fran sighed and followed her. Unnoticed, she laid the keys back on the dresser as she walked past. However, as she entered the bedroom behind Gisela, she noted that the safe on the wall, where her jewels were kept, was still open from yesterday. Her hopes rose.

Perhaps if she forgets the safe once again, I will find what I have been looking for inside there while she is occupied with Mr. Wickham.

The parlour

George Wickham was tired and in dire need of a bath and a good meal. His appearance had changed dramatically from only a week prior. No longer the image of a confident gentleman, his hair needed cutting, he needed a shave and his clothes were wrinkled and filthy. And if one got close enough, one would soon learn that he smelled of stables and sweat.

He had spent endless hours on the road, hiding from those duty-bound to find him—minions he was certain were employed by Darcy or were colleagues of Colonel Fitzwilliam. He had no doubt that every available means was being used to ensure his capture. Just avoiding those who looked suspicious and the uniformed soldiers at almost every stop on the way back to London had been exhausting. He had not had a decent place to lay his head or a hot meal the entire time, having been reduced to paying scullery maids to slip him a sandwich and stable hands to rest with the horses. Even then, he had often rushed from the stables, fearful of being handed over by those same servants seeking to collect a bigger reward by exposing him. And he had slept many a night in the woods.

Now, as he paced about Gisela's home, he rehearsed his strategy. She would not welcome him under her roof, of that he was certain, though he had no other place to hide. Even his cohorts along the wharfs and back alleys could not offer him a refuge, as they were full of tales of being questioned regarding his location. There was no doubt their quarters were being watched. No, he could not hide with them, and with no other avenue open, he intended to regroup under this roof regardless of Gisela's complaints. Therefore, against his wishes, he decided to include her in his new scheme. That would buy him a sanctuary.

And, he thought, *after I collect the ransom, she will be the perfect dupe to take the blame.* He smiled to himself. *This may work out for the best, after all!*

Suddenly both doors to the parlour flew open, making a huge racket as each slammed solidly into the walls on either side. Wickham turned in time to notice a footman, who had come running at the noise, disappear after seeing that his mistress was the source. He smiled in spite of himself. Yes, Gisela could appear a formidable foe, and if he did not have so much evidence to use against her, he might have feared her reprisal as much as that poor soul.

"I do not appreciate that smirk, Wickham," Gisela said as she moved forward until they stood toe to toe. "What are you doing here after I told you never to come back? Have you not caused enough upheaval with your failure to deliver Georgiana? What do you suppose Darcy will do to both of us when he learns you are under my roof?"

When she finally paused for breath, Wickham answered calmly, "You shall just have to make sure he does not learn I am here, my dear, because I plan to stay until I have secured a way for us to leave England."

"For *us* to leave England?" She laughed derisively, throwing back her head. "What makes you think I want to leave England and if I did, why would I go with you, you vile smelling thing?"

Ignoring her insults, Wickham continued, "What other solution is available for either of us now? You will be in as much danger as I when Darcy finally learns everything about Georgiana's little ordeal."

Gisela's expression changed to one of confused curiosity, which he took as a good sign. "As I see it, there is nothing left for either of us than to extort as much as we can from Darcy and sail on the next available ship!"

Having made that assertion, Wickham went over to the liquor cabinet and began pouring himself a drink as calmly as possible. Once his glass was full, he carefully took a sip before turning to face her. His voice sounded more confident than   he   felt. "You cannot possibly think I am going to let Darcy win. I shall have my thirty thousand pounds, and you can share in it, *if* you play your cards right. You should consider selling as much of your assets as possible and leaving England with me. Together we would make a formidable team, extracting money from wealthy fools wherever they may be. And you know as well as I that Darcy and that blasted cousin of his, Colonel Fitzwilliam, will not stop until they get to the bottom of what happened. And at the bottom, they shall find you *and* me!"

"It is only you they will find. They may suspect I supported you, but there is no proof to implicate me!"

"*Au contraire*, my love. Remember when I shipped the portrait from Ramsgate to this address? Do you really believe they will not find the record once they have interrogated Mrs. Younge?" Wickham tried not to smile as the truth of his assertion dawned on Gisela and her face paled. "That is why I am offering you a means of escape."

Gisela swore loudly and swept the contents of a nearby table to the floor. The sounds of breaking china figurines and candles sliding across the hardwood floor joined the sounds of books finding new places to lie. A maid stuck her head in the door, and seeing her mistress kick one misplaced candle towards the pile she had created, retreated quickly and closed the door as she backed out.

"I should have known you would do something to implicate me." She began to pace. "I was a fool to listen to you."

Wickham stiffened as his face reddened. "You will be a fool if you do not listen to me now! Never mind what has happened; you must consider the future. We both have to leave England, and I plan to leave with Darcy's money."

"And just how do you propose to make Darcy pay you? You do not have his *precious* sister!"

"I shall take someone else he holds dear, someone that is not being guarded so closely. He will not expect another attempt so soon after the other."

"And, pray tell, who is your target now?"

"Surely you have heard that Darcy has a mistress. It is the talk of the *ton*."

Gisela scowled. "I have heard gossip of this sort the entire time I have been married to him, but it has never proven true. You, of all people, should know that he is an honourable prig."

"Well, I have met the alleged amour, and I know that she is returning to Town in company with Georgiana and that nosey aunt of his. That must mean something."

Gisela's eyes narrowed. "Her name?"

"It is the same woman who has been seen with Wilkens, Elizabeth Bennet."

"I was warned about her, but how can she be courted by Wilkens and sleeping with my husband at the same time?"

"Perhaps she has time to spare! How would I know?" Wickham bellowed, indignant at being questioned. "My sources in Ramsgate told me that she spent a considerable amount of time with Darcy's family while she was there, and she is returning to London with his aunt and sister.

Gisela's brows furrowed. "She is travelling with Darcy's family and not Wilkens?"

"Yes. And it is undeniable that she is close to Georgiana, as she is the main reason I failed to snatch her from under Lady Ashcroft's nose. It was she who sounded the alarm when I convinced the *little princess* to walk with me down the beach. Miss Bennet came after me like a lioness, even attacking me with a parasol. If not for her meddling, Lord Landingham would have never gotten to the beach in time to prevent me from abducting Georgiana."

"A woman routed you!" Gisela guffawed, sinking in a nearby chair. "I cannot imagine how you shall live that down! You must be the laughing-stock among your kind."

Wickham huffed. "Make sport of me all you wish, but just remember that she is the one your husband wants in his bed, not YOU!"

Gisela's expression hardened, her mouth forming a thin line, and as she began to give vent to her anger, Wickham wondered why he had ever thought her beautiful.

"If all you say is true, I shall kill that little whore! Then, for once, Darcy will know how it feels not to have what he desires."

"We cannot kill her! If we were to harm that woman, Darcy would track us down to the ends of the earth. No, we shall simply extract a goodly sum from him, turn over the wench and leave the country straightaway. As we speak, I have men looking into where her relations reside. Knowing how proper Darcy is, he will not have her live openly at Darcy House after she returns to London, so she will most likely return to a relative's home. Once she is away from his protection, she will make an easy target."

"And where do you plan to hold her until the ransom is paid?"

"I was hoping you could handle that part."

Gisela slowly moved to the liquor cabinet and began to fill a glass with brandy. Wickham followed her with his eyes, wondering at her sudden composure in light of her recent outburst. She seemed to be as docile as she had been volatile only a few moments before.

"There *is* a place. When I was nearly eight years of age, my father built a hunting lodge he called Stillwater on his property just over an hour south of Richmond. The land is not much suited to farming, so it has lent itself to hunting. Though the lodge was as impressive as any manor house in the country, my mother hated it. She called it crude and said it was too isolated. She hardly ever visited, as she craved the excitement of Town, so Father used it to host hunting parties with his friends in the House of Lords. He would take me with him when he was seeing to repairs and such and there was not going to be a hunt. After he met with his steward, he would take me fishing or riding. We became quite close at those times, and I think mother was always jealous of our attachment." She stared into the distance as though seeing something only she could see. "It was the only time in my life that I was truly happy."

Suddenly she raised the brandy to her lips and drained it in a few gulps. Finished, she slammed the glass on the table. "That is of no import! The lodge is still there, though it has been closed for years. When we married, my first husband liked to go there, though it has not been kept in good repair since his health started to deteriorate years before he died."

"Will Darcy remember it?"

"I doubt he even knows I own it. After all, he showed no interest in my properties when we married. He insisted I keep them all."

"What a fool!"

"Yes ... well, it has worked to my advantage and his detriment. As it is, the lodge sits in the middle of a large tract of land with no neighbours on the surrounding parcels. There is a small village two miles from the front gate, but not much else. It is ripe for such a scheme. I will send a few of my *trustworthy* servants ahead to ready it for habitation. These people are paid not to ask any questions."

"That sounds perfect! I shall employ a few of my cohorts to help me spirit Miss Bennet there. Then I shall direct Darcy to the village to drop off the ransom.

By the time he follows the map I will provide to retrieve her, you and I will be halfway to Weymouth. Your servants can carry the messages, as it will not matter if they are apprehended once we are out of reach."

Wickham smiled inwardly as he offered his plan. He had no intention of taking Gisela with him on the ship or anywhere else. No, he would be nearby when Darcy dropped off the ransom and then rush to Plymouth, NOT Weymouth, while a servant delivered a note to Darcy explaining how to find Miss Bennet. He knew enough of his old friend to know that he would see to her safety first. And if Darcy should find Gisela there with Elizabeth, then that could only work to his advantage.

"I shall send the servants to the lodge straightaway." Gisela's voice cut through his musings, and Wickham assumed a practiced smile.

"Good. They need to take enough supplies for several days, perhaps a week or more, if need be. I intend to snatch Miss Bennet as soon as feasible, but at this point, I have no set day or hour. Meanwhile, you should make arrangements with your bank to close your accounts and retrieve any valuables you store there. I suggest you ship whatever else you wish to take ahead to Weymouth, clothes and such. I can give you the name of the shipping line, and they will hold them until we arrive. We shall be off to the Americas faster than you ever imagined possible!"

My contact at Weymouth can forward her things to me at Plymouth. Gisela will not need anything where she is going, and I may be able to sell the whole lot for ready funds!

Gisela interrupted his thoughts. "Now, you absolutely cannot stay here. I will not take the chance of Darcy finding out you are living with me. Mr. Boatwright may be the answer to our problem." She walked over to a bell pull and gave it a jerk. "He has a brother who runs a pub near the wharfs and rents rooms above it. I am sure that he can arrange a room for you with a little incentive." She walked over to her desk and pulled out a box. Reaching inside she grabbed several pounds and a few odd coins and handed them to Wickham. "Spend it wisely."

At that moment the butler appeared in the door and Gisela went over to converse with him. Counting the money in his hands, Wickham wanted to retort angrily at her miserly offering but instead decided it wiser keep his mouth shut. Nothing could be allowed to foil this scheme. Looking up, he found both parties staring at him.

"Go with Mr. Boatwright. He will give you directions and a note to his brother."

Nodding curtly to Gisela, Wickham followed Mr. Boatwright from the room.

Gracechurch Street
The Gardiner's residence

Beginning to dread another day shopping, Jane had developed a headache while waiting for her mother and her aunt to come downstairs. Nonetheless, looking about the cosy parlour, she tried to distract herself by imagining just how her own home might look when she and Charles married.

Charles. She missed him terribly, but she had had little time to think of him, distracted as she was with her mother's concentration on wedding finery and her own worry over Lizzy's problems.

I hope Charles comes to Town with Papa. At least he will be another voice of reason if Mama and Aunt Madeline have their minds set.

Just at that moment, a voice bellowed from the top of the stairs.

"Jane, are you ready?" Her mother carefully worked her way down the narrow stairs and began complaining the moment she saw her eldest daughter's frown. "I should think you would look happier, after all I am doing for you. We have searched through scores of warehouses and hundreds of bolts of satin, silks and lace, not to mention visiting the best modistes London has to offer—all to assure that you are the most beautiful bride in England. One would think you would appreciate it more."

Jane sighed, trying not to let her frustration show. "I do appreciate all your efforts, Mama. It is just that I was under the impression that we had already garnered all the materials needed and commissioned all the seamstresses necessary. I do not know why we are going to yet another shop today."

Mrs. Bennet harrumphed. "Because, my dear, Madeline has heard of a new shipment of Belgium lace that has been received by another modiste, and if we do not get there first—"

Her words were cut short by two things happening at once—Madeline Gardiner came down the stairs, and there was a knock on the front door. All three ladies stopped short to watch Mrs. Doane hurry to the front entry and each was equally stunned to see who stood without—Lady Holmes. Madeline rushed to greet her cousin with a look of great trepidation.

"Oh, Madeline! You have no idea what has happened!" the well-dressed lady began saying immediately, but stopped abruptly as she noticed Jane and Mrs. Bennet standing in the shadows.

"Penelope, you remember my sister, Fanny Bennet, and her daughter, Jane— *Lizzy's family.*"

The last was said almost as a warning, and Lady Holmes' eyes flicked between her cousin and the Bennets, as though not sure what to do. Finally she replied, "Yes, Fanny, it has been years since I saw you last and, Jane, it is a pleasure to meet you, though I wish it had been under better circumstances."

Madeline seemed anxious, and as an indication that they should remove to somewhere more private, she motioned in that direction. "Let us all go into Edward's study where we will not be disturbed."

Jane felt her stomach twist into a knot. This news had to concern Lizzy. She feared that her mother might know everything in a short while.

What will she do if she learns that Mr. Darcy is the gentleman in question? Oh Papa! When will you get here?

Woodenly Jane followed the others until they were safely inside her uncle's study and the door was closed and locked.

Mrs. Gardiner spoke up immediately. "Please, Cousin, tell us why you have come so early this morning? Has something happened to Lizzy?"

Mrs. Bennet began to fan herself, dropping into the nearest chair as her face paled.

"Fortunately, that is not the case, though it will affect Miss Elizabeth and us all, I am afraid. My news concerns my cousin, John Wilkens. I got an express this morning from Alfreda. It seems that he has died as the result of a fall."

Mrs. Bennet stood up, clutching her chest as her face flushed. "Dead? How can he be dead? He must marry Lizzy!"

Lady Holmes looked shocked, but before she could say anything, Madeline declared, "Sit down, Fanny. This is not the time to speak of that. The man is dead." Turning her attention back to her cousin, she continued. "What in the world happened?"

"Alfreda wrote that he was thrown from a horse and cracked his skull. The funeral is the day after tomorrow, so Walter and I leave in a few hours. I …" She eyed Mrs. Bennet. "I thought that I should inform you, considering his attachment to Miss Elizabeth. I understand that she is on her way back to Town with Lady Ashcroft."

"I appreciate your thoughtfulness in letting me know so quickly," Madeline stated. "Please convey our condolences to Alfreda and Lady Hawthorne."

"I will. Now if you will excuse me, I have a great deal to accomplish before we leave for Ramsgate."

"Of course." The lady of the house moved to open the door. "Let me see you out."

Mrs. Bennet said not a word as Lady Holmes and Madeline Gardiner quit the room. Jane did not like the expression on her face. "Mama?" she ventured. "What are you planning?"

Mrs. Bennet swiftly took to her feet, swirling to face Jane. "I am deliberating what I shall do to that uncaring, irresponsible sister of yours the moment she returns to London!" She began to pace the small space in front of the desk. "Lizzy cares not that she shall ruin us all by her actions! But I shall hold her responsible. Have you ever heard of this Lady Ashcroft?"

Jane shook her head, though she knew who the lady was from Lizzy's letters.

Suddenly, Mrs. Bennet's face lit up with a devious smile. "I have the solution! I shall confront the man she has been cavorting with, the one who is married, and force his hand! I imagine he shall not want his dalliance waved in front of his wife's face. These wealthy men may indulge in affairs, but they do not take kindly to becoming fodder for the gossip sheets. He may be willing to part with a goodly sum to prevent a scandal and keep Mr. Bennet from calling him out." She shrugged dismissively. "Not that Mr. Bennet would do such a thing, but that cad would have no way of knowing. If I can sweeten Lizzy's dowry, perhaps some other poor soul will take her off my hands!"

"Mother!" Jane cried, grabbing Mrs. Bennet's arm. "You sound as though you mean to sell her to the highest bidder!"

"Has she not sold her virginity to a married man already? Why should I care as long as she is married, and it does not affect you or your sisters? I will learn his name and pay him a visit."

Just then, Mrs. Gardiner returned to the room, and Mrs. Bennet lost no time in confronting her.

"Sister, I must know the name of the man with whom Lizzy is having an affair."

Chapter 37

London
Darcy House

It was almost dark by the time the party from Ashcroft Park reached Grosvenor Square and, being used to stopping at the front entrance to discharge passengers, the horses began to slow as they approached Darcy House. Nonetheless, the drivers urged them on, having been instructed to circle the lane in order to enter via the back gate. William wished for as little fanfare as possible to announce their return to Town. Having never forgotten how Gisela had confronted him on the pavement in front of Darcy House in the past, he decided not to take the chance that she would see Elizabeth and make a dramatic scene.

He deeply regretted that he had little time alone with her that morning, only managing to steal a few moments when returning from the stables. All the others had eaten and made the trek to see the rare twin colts by the time he had awakened and were patiently awaiting his declaration of readiness to return to Town. Aware that this might be his last opportunity to have time alone with Elizabeth, he expressed a desire to check on the animals before leaving and asked her to accompany him. The others in the party were not surprised by his request, as the look on his face when he gazed at her was quite easily construed. Even Georgiana thought better of teasing him by volunteering to come along.

Consequently, as he and Elizabeth made their way back to the manor house from the stables, he seized the opportunity to pull her into a small alcove in the garden, which was hidden by tall hedges. Only a stone fountain and bench were witness to their moment of passion, and for a few precious moments, they were lost in each other's arms. All too soon it had to end, amidst vows of love, more tender touches and one last stolen kiss. They entered the back entrance of Ashcroft Park to find no one about.

On the ride back to London, William had insisted that his aunt, Georgiana and Elizabeth make use of his coach, which was newer and had better springs. He had shared his godfather's vehicle so that the ladies would not be overcrowded. As a result, whilst he was never far from Elizabeth that day, by the time the coaches came to a halt on the gravel drive inside the gated compound, William was literally aching with the need to hold her in his arms once more. Thus, he was the first to disembark, intending to be the one to assist her in exiting his coach.

While handing out his aunt and then Georgiana, William paid no attention to their amused glances, as he was preoccupied with reaching Elizabeth. And after he had handed her down, he was equally oblivious to the fact that he was staring at her like a schoolboy while continuing to hold her hand.

Georgiana's tease startled him. "Do you not think it best that we *all* go inside?"

Immediately he released Elizabeth's hand and held out his arm. Being just as smitten, his response brought her out of a similar daze, and she coloured as she placed her hand on his arm. Eager to be of service to his godson, Lord Landingham gathered Lady Ashcroft and Georgiana and began steering them up the path that led through the garden and to the back entrance. The lovers followed at a decidedly slower pace.

During their journey, William had found himself praying that Elizabeth would spend the night at Darcy House instead of removing to Gracechurch Street immediately upon reaching Town. He had decided he was not above enlisting his aunt's support if she hesitated. But once they had disembarked, his mind whirled as he tried to decide which argument he had devised was most likely to be successful. He knew Elizabeth well enough to know that she would not be easily dissuaded once she set upon a course of action.

"I hope that you will agree to stay here tonight, Elizabeth. After all, you mentioned that your aunt had left Town. She may still be gone, I mean, for all we know, and I am sure Lady Ashcroft would be a suitable chaperone, should you choose to stay. There will be time enough in the morning to ascertain if she has returned and where you shall stay. Besides, I would like for us to be together as long as possible. After all, we have no way of knowing when we shall meet again." He knew that he was rambling but could not help himself. "Surely you do not wish to return to Holmes House, in case that cad Wilkens comes to Town in search of you?"

They had just cleared the back door, when the mention of Wilkens' name gave Elizabeth pause, and she stopped walking. Her voice shook a little as she contemplated the ramifications.

"I had not considered that he might follow me to London. I would not want to confront him without speaking to my family first."

Fortuitously, Audrey Ashcroft chose just that moment to come in search of them, appearing in the hallway just ahead.

"Mrs. Barnes informs me that dinner is ready whenever we wish to eat. Marshall and Georgiana have both expressed a wish to have a tray sent to their rooms, as they are exhausted and plan to retire early. I intend to do likewise, so you and Elizabeth are left to dictate your preferences to the staff."

William seized the opportunity. "I intend to eat in the dining room." He looked anxiously at Elizabeth. "And I hope that you will join me." Elizabeth nodded shyly. Hoping to gain another favourable response, he added, "Aunt, I asked Elizabeth to remain here for tonight at least."

Seeing the unspoken plea in her nephew's eyes, Aunt Audrey took up the cause. "Of course, you must stay here tonight, my dear."

She took Elizabeth's hand and continued. "I shall accompany you to your aunt's home tomorrow in order to explain how you came to be travelling with us so there is no conjecture." Elizabeth let Audrey lead her ahead. "Come! Let us get you settled in one of the guest rooms, then you shall have a chance to freshen up before coming down for dinner."

As she escorted Elizabeth up the grand staircase arm-in-arm, they continued to talk, though William could not make out what was being said by the time they passed out of sight at the top of the stairs. The exact moment that he turned, sporting a grin so wide he could not suppress it, the housekeeper appeared in the foyer.

"Mrs. Barnes, thank you for having everything ready upon our arrival. Please prepare the smaller dining room, as Miss Bennet and I will be dining alone. I believe a half-hour should be sufficient for us to dress, but should I find that we need more time, I shall notify you immediately."

Having cared for the Master since he was a child, naturally Mrs. Barnes noticed the stitches on his forehead, which were now accompanied by a purple bruise.

"Sir, may I ask how you came to be injured?"

William's hand flew to his wound at the reminder, and he coloured in spite of himself. Mrs. Barnes tried not to smile. She had not seen him this flustered in years.

"Let us just say that I had a confrontation with a tree that refused to give me due respect. It is not as bad as it appears, so do not concern yourself over it."

With those words, he turned and bounded up the steps towards his bedroom with almost as much enthusiasm as when he was a boy. Mrs. Barnes shook her head in awe at the change in his mood, marvelling at how much younger he looked when he smiled. She had seen his smiles so seldom in the last few years that the sight had caused her heart to catch. As she stood watching his retreating form, a familiar hand on her arm let her know she was not alone. Mr. Barnes had heard their exchange.

"Come, my dear. Nothing is to be gained by staring after the boy. Let us prepare the small dining room so that it appears to the best advantage. I shall see to it that roses are gathered from the conservatory, if you will locate some of the more beautiful linens with lace and such. Between the two of us, Cook and some candles, I think we shall have a romantic dinner ready by the time they come down to dine."

"Romantic?" Mrs. Barnes said, giggling into her palm. "You noticed it too—his interest in Miss Bennet?"

"One would have to be blind not to see it, Matilda."

"I pray this is the incentive he needs to rid himself of that horrid woman," she whispered, looking about to make sure no other servants heard. "He deserves to be happy."

"And happy he shall be, if *we* do our part, my dear."

Mrs. Barnes' hands began to flutter as she looked about. "Oh, yes, yes. Now let me give instructions to Cook and see if I can remember where I had them store that lovely lace table cloth for the private dining room."

She was still talking to herself as she walked away, and Mr. Barnes shook his head in amusement before beginning a search for a footman to go to the conservatory and cut some roses.

Later

By the time Elizabeth made her way to dinner, she found Mr. Barnes waiting at the foot of the stairs to direct her to a room much smaller than the one she had expected. She instantly felt butterflies in her stomach when the stately old butler opened the door to reveal a very intimate space and to find that Fitzwilliam was already inside. The sound of the door closing confirmed that they were alone.

He was so handsome, dressed in black coat and breeches, just as he had been when they met in the library at Ashcroft Park, and he sported the same hungry look. A few dark curls fell over his forehead, leaving her handiwork completely hidden, and creating the illusion that his handsome face was unscathed.

When she entered, William had been leaning against a magnificent hearth with an elaborate marble mantle that took up the entire wall. One boot was propped against the stone surround at the bottom, and upon her entrance, he pushed away from it, straightened his coat and tugged at his cravat uncomfortably. Elizabeth had been about to giggle, as that gesture made him seem so eager, so boyish, but once she met his gaze, she thought better of it. The way he devoured her with his eyes left no doubt that he was *not* a boy!

She looked away to gain control. Now forced to examine the room, she noted that the floors were polished oak covered with intricate rugs, the wallpaper was a pale gold and the furnishings were in shades of crimson, gold and royal blue. In addition to the hearth, a lovely settee and chair, both upholstered in royal blue with gold trim, occupied that end of the room. They were centred upon an oriental inspired rug, along with a few intricately carved mahogany tables filled with books, china figurines and candelabrum. A round dining table with two chairs and a small sideboard with an oval mirror perched above it dominated the opposite side of the room. They were situated on an equally exquisite rug of gold and blue designs on a crimson background. Crystal vases of white and red roses decorated every available surface, including a smaller vase in the middle of the table.

Having waited until she finished her cursory examination, William now walked towards her. She found herself trembling as he reached out to take her hand and suddenly felt vulnerable and a bit scared—not of him but of her desire.

"Miss Elizabeth, I hope you do not mind that we are on our own. Mrs. Barnes has prepared everything so that we may serve ourselves. I hope it pleases you."

He smiled beguilingly, and the sight of perfect while teeth set against his tanned face so unnerved her that Elizabeth almost forgot to breathe. She was certain no stranger would ever be privy to such a treasure as this expression. Barely conscious of what he was saying, she comprehended only the last few words.

"… thus, I did not wish to be disturbed for any reason. I wanted it to be just us two."

Tearing her eyes away, she examined the preparations. The table held place settings for two, while the sideboard groaned with numerous covered dishes, bowls of fruit and trays with breads and sweets.

"I … I am sure it will be delicious, though I doubt I shall be able to eat much. Just being in this magnificent house simply takes my breath away and leaves my appetite sorely lacking."

Bringing both her hands to his heart, he leaned in to rest his forehead against hers, causing them both to close their eyes. For several seconds he said nothing, then raggedly whispered, "Without love, Elizabeth, it is simply a building."

His words were so raw that she was afraid she would cry if she spoke, so Elizabeth only nodded her agreement. He stepped back then and motioned to the table, imploring, "Please try to eat something or I shall surely worry."

She teased him. "Your aunt mentioned that you worry excessively for those you care about."

"I confess that is true. And when I fell in love with you, you became my greatest concern."

Elizabeth's heart thumped so loudly she feared he could hear it. "When did you know that you loved me?"

"If I had to fix the hour, the spot, the look or the words which laid the foundation, I would have to say it was my first glimpse of you at the bookshop in Meryton. When you peeked around that bookshelf, a pixie in a mass of untamed curls, I thought I had wandered into heaven. Only in retrospection did it become clear that I was in the middle of it before I realised that I had begun."*[16]

She rose on tiptoes to brush her lips across his, prompting him to return the kiss by pulling her hard to his chest and kissing her until she was breathless. At length he let go with a wan smile. "Enough of this or you shall starve. There will be time for kisses later after we dine."

He held out her chair, and as she took her place, she ran her fingers over the stunning white lace tablecloth that had been placed atop a deep scarlet one. She marvelled at its intricate design before her gaze moved to the multitude of silverware and crystal glasses, all reflecting the candles in the chandelier overhead.

As she tilted her head to look up at that magnificent fixture, she breathed, "So beautiful."

"Yes … so very beautiful."

The tone of William's declaration caused her to look to him, and she found his gaze fixed on her. From that time on, there was very little conversation, except comments on the food, until they finished dining. When at last they were sated, William offered her another glass of wine and Elizabeth declined. Taking her hand, he then pulled her to her feet and back into an embrace, kissing her tenderly. Then, with one hand on the back of her head and the other splayed across her lower back, he pulled her against his body and rested his head atop hers. Content to hold her thusly, the drumming of their hearts was the only sound penetrating the silence for a long while. Finally, after a deep sigh, he spoke.

"Elizabeth, I cannot fathom how I will survive without seeing you every day. It is as though the moment you are away from me, I die little by little. Tell me we shall find a way to see each other."

Staggered that the misery in his voice matched her own, Elizabeth murmured, "I have also dreaded parting from you." His fingers dug into her back, and his grip tightened. "I do not know what shall transpire after my family learns what has

---

[16] *Jane Austen, **Pride and Prejudice**, Chapter 60. "I cannot fix on the hour, or the spot, or the look, or the words, which laid the foundation. It is too long ago. I was in the middle before I knew that I had begun."*

happened with Mr. Wilkens. I am afraid they were set on our engagement. Then again, his rejection may force me in the direction of another gentleman they deem *suitable*."

William growled into her hair, "NO! I shall not allow it."

Her answer was muffled by his waistcoat. "I fear that you will have no say in the matter." Then she tilted her head to look up into his anxious blue eyes. "They could also send me back to Meryton."

"You know that I will travel to the ends of the earth in order to see you. Even if I do not have permission, I will find a way."

"Our only hope is to tell Papa of our agreement. I believe he, of all people, will understand."

William kissed her gently again. "I pray he will at least give us a chance to explain. Still a part of me—that which thinks of Georgiana as my own child—would completely understand if he forbade me from seeing you ever again, or in the worst case, shot me on sight."

Elizabeth's eyes filled with tears and she pleaded, "Please do not say such things! I could not bear it."

"Sweetheart, I am speaking the truth. We must think of how our love may appear to your father—to anyone that learns of it."

She ran her fingertips gently over one cheek before cupping his face. "Papa has always wished for my happiness. Once he recognises how much I love you, that I do not wish to live without you, he will understand that I have no choice but to wait for you."

William kissed her thoroughly now, his ardour rising with the declaration of her love. Passions escalated rapidly until he pushed away from her, his breath in ragged pants.

"Elizabeth Bennet! See what you do to me. My resolve vanishes the moment our lips meet."

Elizabeth sighed dreamily. "It is the same for me."

"Do *not* tell me that, my love. It will be hard enough having you under my roof tonight without coming to you."

"You will not come? But we may not have another chance to be together after tonight."

Pulling her back into his arms, William savoured the pleasure of her form melding into his. "Last night was torture. Had I awoken this morning with you in my arms—" He stopped to take a deep breath, and she felt his chest swell with the effort.

Unexpectedly he pushed her at arm's length, searching her face for a hint of understanding. "I am only a man, sweetheart. The next time I spend the night with you, I may not be able to resist you. And I want to be able to tell your father the truth when we meet again—that we have never made love. Help me in this."

She nodded despondently.

He tried to smile though his heart was not in it. "Thank you, my love."

After another long, seemingly endless kiss that was more difficult to quit, he led her out of the dining room and up the stairs, stopping outside the door to her room. They stood for some time without speaking, neither wishing to be the first to say goodnight. Finally, Elizabeth took action.

"Please remember that no matter what happens in the future, I shall love you for all eternity, whether we are allowed to marry or not."

"I have never given my heart to any woman save you, my love. Providence willing, you shall be mine in the eyes of God and man one day soon."

A chaste kiss sealed their vows, and as Elizabeth slipped into her room, William stood for a long time with his hand clenching the knob, before retiring to his own room.

⟡

Darcy House
The next morning

The servants were up and about early, all working so quietly below the main floors as to be unnoticed by the occupants of the upper ones. Mr. and Mrs. Barnes had no expectation of seeing the Master or any of their party until much later, as it was their custom to awaken later than usual when they first arrived in Town. In addition, the knocker on the front door had not been put back, as the family never received visitors for at least two days after their return. It would remain off until Lady Ashcroft or Mr. Darcy instructed them to restore it.

Nonetheless, even under those circumstances, someone had the audacity to rap on the front door just after eight o'clock, stunning the staff. Mrs. Barnes was standing in the foyer when the offending noise made her startle.

Mr. Barnes rushed from the back of the house, thinking his wife must be below stairs and had not heard the commotion. Seeing her staring in the direction of the door, he stopped short and addressed her. "No sensible person would call on a house with the knocker removed. Do you suppose there is some crisis?"

Jarred out of her trance, the housekeeper nodded slowly. "You could be right. Even Colonel Fitzwilliam would not call at this hour if he knew the Master was in residence, unless it was urgent." She hurried to grab her husband's arm as he stepped towards the entrance. "But keep in mind it could also be another ploy by Mrs. Darcy."

Mr. Barnes hesitated. Gisela Darcy had tried an infinite number of ways to gain entrance in the past. However, while he vacillated about what to do, the sound of someone outside the door shouting Miss Bennet's name made them both cringe. Aware that the Master would not appreciate anyone making a scene on his doorstep, they tensed with anticipation and dread. Though it was obviously not Mrs. Darcy's voice, neither could place who it might be.

As the shouts increased in volume, Mrs. Barnes shook her head in bewilderment. "We have no choice, but do not let her in until we determine what she wants."

With nods of agreement, both stepped to the door, and Mr. Barnes cracked it open. As soon as it was breached, however, an older, heavy-set woman with red hair generously sprinkled with grey, pushed past them into the foyer. Butler and housekeeper alike were too astonished to react as she continued her rant inside the house.

"Where is she? Where is my daughter?" Crossing the foyer towards the grand staircase, Mrs. Barnes finally came to her senses and hurried to cut her off. Managing to get in front of her, the housekeeper effectively blocked her progress. This infuriated the intruder and she barked, "I DEMAND Mr. Darcy produce my daughter this very minute!"

Meanwhile, Madeline Gardiner and Jane Bennet, who had hurried in right behind Fanny Bennet, were trying to stop her by tugging on her sleeves.

"Fanny, please. I told you we should handle this discretely!" Mrs. Gardiner practically whined, shaken at her sister's daring.

"Mama," Jane pleaded, "Please calm yourself. Be reasonable." She turned to glare at her aunt. "I told you that you should not have offered her the use of your carriage."

Mrs. Bennet rounded on Jane. "I have the right to confront the man who has led my daughter astray!"

Mrs. Barnes had armed herself with a parasol from a nearby stand and rolled up her sleeves in anticipation of keeping Mrs. Bennet from ascending the stairs, when two footmen hearing the commotion came running. They advanced beside Mr. Barnes in anticipation of securing the lady from the rear. Suddenly, out of the blue, the sound of Lady Ashcroft's authoritative voice could be heard coming from the top of the stairs. Instantly, it quieted the melee below.

"Mrs. Barnes, if you will direct our guests into the blue drawing room, I shall speak to them there."

All the uproar in the foyer came to an abrupt halt as the calm, commanding statement prevailed over the pandemonium. Even Mrs. Bennet did not give the lady any argument as she adjusted her bonnet and began to follow Mrs. Barnes towards the drawing room. Mrs. Gardiner and Jane could do naught but follow.

Taking in the exquisite furnishings of the house as she followed the housekeeper, Elizabeth's mother began to calculate Mr. Darcy's worth even before she entered the elegant drawing room. Quite pleased with herself for not listening to Jane or her sister when they tried to tell her to wait and let Mr. Bennet handle the situation, she took a prominent seat and waited for the lady who was obviously in charge to appear. Jane and Madeline Gardiner took their seats in a much more timid manner.

Mr. Bennet! Fanny scoffed to herself. *He would be useless in negotiating with this man. Had not Mr. Darcy fooled him once before when he kept Lizzy out all night in a rain storm? That is likely when this whole affair began. No! I will not leave the negotiation up to my husband! I know how to deal with Mr. Darcy!*

Suddenly the grand lady appeared, her expensive silk skirts swishing as she entered the room. She looked every inch a general in charge of his troops as she passed them and took her seat in a regal chair at the head of the room. All the interlopers tensed as she studied them as though they were mad. Under her piercing blue eyes, even Mrs. Bennet began to pale, wondering at just what she had put into motion and hastily began to introduce herself.

"I am Fanny Bennet, Elizabeth's mother. You cannot be ignorant of who my daughter is, as she is the talk of London. I suppose you are Lady Ashcroft, as my sources say you reside here." Fanny gestured to Jane and Mrs. Gardiner as she introduced them as well.

Audrey Ashcroft's stony gaze was fixed on Mrs. Bennet, but she said not a word. As her eyes flicked in her direction, Jane gave an apologetic look. While Lady Ashcroft nodded slightly in response, she did not smile at Mrs. Bennet or the other woman, ignoring them for now.

Mrs. Bennet noticed that Lady Ashcroft barely acknowledged her introductions and had not called for refreshments. Her ire rose. "I suppose you know why I am here?"

Lady Ashcroft stiffened. "Suppose you tell me."

"I am here because my daughter, Elizabeth Bennet, has been carrying on an illicit affair with Mr. Darcy, who, I understand, is your nephew. In fact, I suspect that she returned from Ramsgate in his coach and spent the night here."

"Mr. Darcy is my nephew, but you are thoroughly mistaken in your assumption of their relationship. Miss Elizabeth returned as my guest and in my coach. She has never carried on an *affair,* as you imply, with my nephew."

"Not according to the rumours circulating around Town. John Wilkens, Lord Hampton, was courting Lizzy, but apparently she had been dallying with your nephew behind his back! Now that Wilkens is dead, there will be no one to save her reputation or her sisters' fate, as Mr. Darcy is married already."

Ignoring the gossip, Lady Ashcroft focused on the information. Her brows furrowed. "John Wilkens is dead? I have not heard of this."

Madeline Gardiner spoke timidly. "My cousin, Penelope Holmes, was at my doorstep this morning to inform me of the awful circumstances. She and Wilkens are cousins by marriage."

Lady Ashcroft barked a laugh. "Awful circumstances? On the contrary, that horrible man deserved whatever tragedy befell him. I only rejoice that Elizabeth was able to escape from his clutches and return to Town with us, or she might have died too!"

"So she is under this roof as we speak!" Mrs. Bennet's voice rose indignantly. "I knew it! I am not a simpleton! I know how these rich men use women such as my daughter and then toss them aside. Poor Lord Hampton probably had a heart ailment after Lizzy left Ramsgate with your nephew."

Audrey Ashcroft was about to answer Mrs. Bennet's dim-witted assertion when the door flew open and Mr. Bennet hobbled into the room with the help of his cane. He was followed closely by Charles Bingley, who was almost out of breath from trying to keep step with his charge. He gave Jane a small smile that was quickly returned.

Having no trouble hearing his wife's accusation through the closed door, Thomas Bennet was livid. "Mrs. Bennet!" he exclaimed. "Be silent!" The woman in question seemed to cower and hushed. Instantly, he addressed Lady Ashcroft. "Forgive me, madam. Mr. Bingley tells me that you are Mr. Darcy's aunt. May I beg your forgiveness for my family's part in disturbing—"

Jumping to her feet, Fanny cried, "Mr. Bennet, you do not know what Lizzy has done, how she has ruined us all. Madeline has just received word this morning that Mr. Wilkens is dead. Who is left to marry Lizzy now? Since Mr. Darcy has been carrying on an affair with our daughter—an affair about which the whole of London knows—he should be made to pay!"

"No more, Mrs. Bennet!" Mr. Bennet exclaimed, turning to Charles. "Please escort my wife and her sister to their carriage immediately!" More softly, he said to Jane. "Please go with your mother. Lizzy and I shall return to Gracechurch Street shortly, and you can see her then."

Her expression was such that it was obvious that Jane wanted to stay, but as was her nature, she acquiesced. Meanwhile, Charles walked over to offer his arm to her mother, but in her anger, Mrs. Bennet eschewed his help. Instead, Bingley escorted Jane and Madeline Gardiner from the room, directly behind that cantankerous woman. Their aunt dropped her head as she was ushered out.

As soon as they were out of sight, Mr. Bennet smiled wanly before addressing William's aunt once more. "Would you mind if I sat down?" He gestured to his cane. "I am afraid that my leg does not lend itself to standing."

Lady Ashcroft nodded. "Certainly, be seated." As soon as he had sunk into one of the sturdy, upholstered chairs, she added, "It is obvious why you are here. To get straight to the point, Miss Elizabeth is under our roof. She accompanied us to London from Ramsgate at my insistence. The man that Mrs. Gardiner has been foisting upon Elizabeth, John Wilkens, Earl of Hampton, proved himself to be a cruel and sadistic person while we were there. Once I learned that he tried to harm Miss Elizabeth as well as his own sister, I insisted she return with us. His sister was placed under the protection of her aunt, a good friend of mine."

Mr. Bennet seemed to lose all colour at her words. "I had no idea. Apparently I have been kept in the dark about a good many things concerning my daughter since she left Longbourn. It appears that I owe you my gratitude for taking her under your protection. My Lizzy means the world to me." He sighed heavily. "Would you please ask her and your nephew to join us? I wish to speak to both of them."

"Certainly." She stood. "If you will excuse me, I shall have my housekeeper bring some refreshments while I locate them."

$$\mathcal{C}hapter \quad 38$$

London
Darcy House
Upstairs

William was not asleep as his aunt had assumed when she encountered Mrs. Bennet that fateful morning. Instead, he had awakened early and dressed straightaway in order to intercept Elizabeth when she headed downstairs to break her fast. Peering through his slightly opened bedroom door for a half-hour, however, had only served to try his patience. Thus, he had slipped into the hallway, looked surreptitiously in both directions to make sure no one was about, then knocked on her door.

When it opened, he was relieved to find her dressed, since he had every intention of going inside. Once within, he captured her in his arms and kissed her deeply before she could even speak. Melting into him as she had before, the sensation of holding Elizabeth intimately was so incredible that he continued the kiss far longer than he knew was proper. When he finally broke away to look at her, her eyes were still closed and she swayed precariously.

"Sweetheart, do you need to sit down?"

"Hmmm?" Slowly Elizabeth opened her eyes. "I fear that I am a bit faint."

He immediately pulled her close again, nuzzling her neck as he growled teasingly. "Faint, is it? I like the sound of that!"

Slowly becoming fully cognizant, Elizabeth pushed him away playfully. "That is nothing to laugh about."

"Of course, it is not, my love." William forced himself to appear more subdued as he added. "I am just pleased that I affect you so."

Just at that moment, the sound of loud voices downstairs reached them, and William stepped to the door and opened it gingerly in order to listen. Elizabeth's hands flew to her mouth.

William turned around, and he gaped at her. "Is that your mother?" Numbly, she nodded.

He took her arm gently and, after checking the hall, led her out of the room and towards the grand staircase. As they neared it, they could see Lady Ashcroft standing at the head of the stairs, and William pulled Elizabeth into another doorway so they would not be detected. Hearing his aunt instruct the housekeeper to take the intruders to the drawing room, he put his finger to his lips to indicate that they should make no sound, then guided Elizabeth to another set of stairs that led to the rear of the first floor.

Once downstairs, the voice now coming from the drawing room was even louder. Both desiring to know all that was being said, William drew Elizabeth into the billiard's room where he opened a wall panel exposing a servant's corridor. Using this means, they swiftly made their way to a point outside the room where her mother was holding forth. Arriving in time to hear most of Mrs. Bennet's strident diatribe and by the end of it, Elizabeth was shaking visibly. So William ran his arms around her waist and pulled her tight against his chest to comfort her. Just as she relaxed against him and laid her arms atop his, Barnes introduced Charles Bingley and Mr. Bennet, effectively ending Mrs. Bennet's tirade. Shortly after that, Elizabeth's father ordered his wife from the room, and when Lady Ashcroft excused herself to go in search of the two of them, he led Lizzy back to the billiard's room and helped her to a seat on a settee.

"Stay here, sweetheart. I shall have Barnes inform my aunt where we are."

Not long after William had quit the room, he returned, and a short time later Audrey Ashcroft appeared in the doorway. Instantly she noted Elizabeth's distress and moved to sit next to her, reaching for her hand.

"Your father wishes to speak to you and Fitzwilliam. If you do not wish to see him now, I shall tell him that you are indisposed, and my nephew shall speak to him alone. However, in my opinion, it would be best if you face him together. I have found that postponing unpleasant conversations oft times makes matters worse. I will add that he seems a fine gentleman and an understanding one at that."

Elizabeth smiled wanly. "Unlike my mother."

Audrey tried not to show any censure. "I am sure she means well, though perhaps she needs to be more circumspect with her words and less accusatory."

"Yes, she does. I ... I apologize to you and Fitzwilliam for her rudeness."

Audrey hugged Elizabeth. "You need never apologise to either of us. You cannot control your relations to any further extent than Fitzwilliam and I can control ours. And believe me when I say that my sister, Catherine, is far worse than your mother."

Elizabeth smiled through teary lashes. "You are too kind."

William spoke up. "She is being honest, Elizabeth."

Giving him a heartfelt smile, she stood. "I am ready to face my father, and no matter what may occur, know that I shall never agree to give you up."

William held out his arm, and she placed a delicate hand there. "I shall hold you to that. Now let us explain our predicament and hope he is as understanding as my aunt believes."

Audrey addressed them. "I shall be waiting in the library in case I am needed to clear any misunderstanding or to be of service in any fashion." She glanced to William. "I feel as though I am your mother, Fitzwilliam, and you," she looked to Elizabeth, "will be my daughter one day. I shall not let anyone disparage either one of you."

"We shall be happy to call upon you if need be," William replied. "Your love and support means everything."

"Yes, to us both," Elizabeth echoed.

After each young person had received a kiss from William's aunt, they proceeded to the drawing room to face her father hand-in-hand, presenting a united front.

❦

Later in the drawing room

Mr. Bennet resembled an older rendition of Fitzwilliam Darcy as he strode back and forth across the drawing room in a steady cadence. The only difference between the two was that his cane punctuated each step, and he did not run his hands through his hair, as it was nearly non-existent. Instead, he used his free hand to toy with his whiskers.

The first subject Mr. Bennet raised with his daughter when she entered the room had been John Wilkens. Elizabeth confessed everything that had transpired while she stayed at Gatesbridge Manor, even revealing some things that William had not heard. As his own anger at the Earl of Hampton was kindled anew, he felt certain that the man that had confronted him in Meryton would be livid over what he had just learned. And when Elizabeth's father rose on his injured leg to stalk about the room, he was not taken by surprise.

William's chief focus, however, was Elizabeth, who sat opposite him. She anxiously observed her father, her dire expression growing more calamitous with every lap and that troubled him. No doubt she knew her father better than he. Even so, when Mr. Bennet ended his incessant pacing abruptly, it gained William's attention.

"I cannot believe that my Sister Gardiner did not know more about that blackguard before she promoted the match or allowed you to accompany his sister to Ramsgate. If he was such a degenerate, surely someone knew of his propensity for wickedness." He trained his eyes on Elizabeth. "And why did you paint such rosy pictures in your letters? Was I to be kept in the dark the whole time?"

Elizabeth's eyes fell. "I am sorry, Papa. To be honest, at first I was trying to prolong my stay, hoping to meet a better prospect than the earl. I knew that if I turned him down arbitrarily, Aunt Gardiner would likely send me home. She made her wishes for a match with Wilkens known often enough. And you know how Mama behaves when she is unhappy with me." She added softly, "Which is most of the time."

"I would never let anyone force you into an unwanted courtship or marriage, and believe me when I say that your aunt and your mother will get a piece of my mind when I return to Gracechurch Street. In addition, if that blackguard was not already dead, I would call him out immediately!"

Elizabeth and William both looked incredulous, simultaneously exclaiming, "Wilkens is dead?"

"According to your mother and your aunt, notice was received this morning," Mr. Bennet continued, unmindful of his audience's shock at the news. "But make no mistake, if he was not dead, I would have no reservations in calling him out for his behaviour. I can still wield a sword if necessary, and while I may be old, I shoot game with the best of them. I may be slower to aim, but I am accurate, which is more than can be said for some of these so-called gentlemen." He waved a hand towards William.

Attempting to demonstrate that there was something on which they agreed, William declared, "I have known him for years, and I tried to warn Miss Elizabeth about Wilkens. After I learned what transpired at Gatesbridge, I was intent on challenging him myself. No man should do harm to a lady without repercussion."

Mr. Bennet's eyes bored into William, and he replied sarcastically. "Do you really want to take that stance, young man? Especially, since I have reservations regarding your own treatment of my daughter?"

William swallowed hard, trying not to appear uneasy. There was no way he would ever raise a weapon against Elizabeth's father, even if challenged. "I look forward to explaining any misconceptions or reservations you may have about my conduct with regards to your daughter."

The older man hobbled towards an upholstered chair, and eased into it, saying to no one in particular, "I should not have let my ire overtax my leg." After he had situated himself more comfortably, he again fixed his gaze on William. "Suppose you begin by addressing the rumours that my wife mentioned regarding you and my daughter?"

Elizabeth swiftly moved to sit down next to William, taking his hand. "Papa, I think I should be the one to tell you how we met again in London and how I came to fall in love with him."

Mr. Bennet's eyebrows furrowed as his eyes narrowed, flicking back and forth between her and William.

"Very well then, Lizzy, please do your best to convince me that I should not run him through once you are finished."

Over one half-hour later, Lizzy's father looked just as pensive as he had when considering John Wilkens' deeds. The only difference was that he had not resumed pacing. He did, however, sit silently with his elbows on the arms of the chair, his head bowed and propped against his tented fingers. Deathly still themselves, William and Elizabeth hoped that this was a good sign. Presently, Mr. Bennet looked up and stared into the distance, as though the answer was to be found somewhere out there. Finally, taking a deep breath that he released noisily, he then began to speak.

"I cannot condone Elizabeth's relationship with a married man, howbeit, one miserably entrapped by a hateful, conniving woman. This situation can only get more unpleasant once it becomes fully known and, make no mistake, it shall. It will affect our entire family—all your sisters, Lizzy, not just you. Have you considered that?"

Elizabeth started to speak but was interrupted by her father. "However, I do not deceive myself that either of you are seeking my approval. And, before you say it, I am aware that you shall turn one and twenty in one month, Daughter, in which case you will not need my consent if you decide to carry out this waiting game or to marry Mr. Darcy in the future. But, until you are one and twenty you WILL follow my dictates."

William and Elizabeth exchanged anxious glances. When he was certain of her steadfastness, William spoke.

"Nonetheless, we both wish to have your understanding, if not your approval." His mien softened as he looked at Elizabeth. "Neither of us meant to fall in love. It was Fate that we met in Meryton and then again here. I did not seek her out when I learned she was in Town, nor did she look for me. On the contrary, we tried our best not to love one another."

Mr. Bennet studied William for a long moment. "I am inclined to believe you, since you left Meryton without asking permission to see Lizzy again in order to explain. I will admit that I was impressed because you wanted her to despise you so as to destroy any attachment that might have developed as a result of your stay in the cabin."

"And I did despise him, Papa!" Elizabeth interjected. "I was so angry when I discovered that he was married that I not only confronted him, I swore to hate him for all eternity."

"Eternity was not so long, eh?" Mr. Bennet offered dryly.

Her eyes fell to her lap. "No, Papa," she whispered.

Sobering, he focused on William once more. "I know what Lizzy wants, but she is young and in love for the first time. What do you wish from me, Mr. Darcy, other than my favourite daughter?"

"As Miss Elizabeth stated, I am seeking a divorce, and though she has agreed to wait for me, we are both aware that it could take years. In the meantime, I shall place all of my wealth and resources at her disposal, just as I would if we were officially engaged. In addition, I shall direct my solicitor to draw up papers that will, in essence, make provision for her care should I expire before our marriage can take place." Elizabeth's hand tightened around his. "It will be very generous, I assure you. In my heart, we are betrothed."

"That is very noble of you," Mr. Bennet said a bit sardonically.

Hurriedly, William added, "I know that Bingley will not be bothered by any gossip nor would he ever forsake Miss Bennet, however, I would consider it a kindness on your part to allow me to augment the dowries of your other daughters— to counteract any contempt that might arise as a result of my circumstances."

"You presume too much, Mr. Darcy. I am not opposed to having my other daughter's dowries considered if your relationship with Lizzy should become well known and affect them conversely, however, they are still years away from being courted. Though my wife likes to think otherwise, I shall not agree to a courtship for any of them until they are much older."

"In that case, with your permission, I shall increase the sum I leave to Elizabeth, should I die before we are married, to include the monies for their dowries. I would not want my dilemma to affect them adversely if I can do something to counteract it."

"Do as you wish," Mr. Bennet replied resignedly. "I have no doubt you will do whatever you feel is necessary." He rubbed his forehead pensively. "On the whole, dealing with Mrs. Bennet and her penchant for gossip will be the worst of this situation, I fear." He began to rise. "I shall need time to consider all that I have heard." He managed to make it to his feet, using his cane for support. "Lizzy, I believe we should return to the Gardiners now and to Longbourn in two days time. That should give my leg ample time to rest from the ordeal of travelling. Mr. Darcy, will you be kind enough to lend me a carriage and a footman to manage her trunks to Gracechurch Street?"

Seeing his resolve, William stood and went over to the door. Opening it, he spoke quietly to a footman standing just outside. As he made his way back to

Elizabeth and her father, he stated, "A carriage has been ordered. A maid will pack Miss Bennet's things, and they shall be delivered later, if that is agreeable to you."

Elizabeth stood shakily, crossing the room to take his hand again, squeezing it as though to gain his attention. Addressing her father, nonetheless, she mainly looked at him.

"But, Papa, I cannot return to Meryton now. Mama will not give me a minute's peace. Will you not allow me to stay in Town with Aunt and Uncle?"

"I do not consider that wise, Lizzy. After all, if you return to Meryton, perhaps these horrific rumours will dissipate as people realise that you are not *with* Mr. Darcy." Then he added knowingly, "Besides, I have no doubt that you will arrange to see one another if you are in close proximity, and that can only add fuel to the fire."

Elizabeth's eyes pleaded with William for support, nevertheless his next words were not what she wished to hear.

"I have to agree with your father, Elizabeth. If the rumours have begun in earnest, Gisela will be in the thick of it, and she will not be content until she finds a way to embarrass and censure you publicly, just as she has me."

Clearly devastated and defeated, Elizabeth entreated her father. "Papa, may I have a word with Fitzwilliam privately?" At his austere expression, she added, "Please."

Mr. Bennet slowly proceeded to leave the room. Once the door was fully closed, Elizabeth fell into William's arms, imploring, "Please do not send me away. I can face anyone's censure as long as I am with you."

William steeled himself for the hardest task he had ever faced. Pulling her tightly against his body, he closed his eyes and buried his face in her glossy hair as he brought one hand up to cup the back of her head. A whiff of lavender that remained there almost caused him to forget his resolve. *Dear God, how I love you! How I yearn to keep you safe in my arms!*

"We have no choice, sweetheart. Your father is determined to remove you from my influence and the fury of wagging tongues." He sighed raggedly. "I cannot say that I blame him. He is doing what he feels he must to protect you and your sisters."

"But should the rumours reach Meryton, our neighbours will shun me, perhaps my entire family. I shall not be able to bear it if I am forced to stay in the house with Mama and my sisters and listen to her denunciations." She tilted her head back to look into his face. Her eyes were darker than he had ever seen them and brimming with tears. "Worst of all, I fear that I shall never see you again once I leave Town."

Her words found their mark, and he felt as though his heart was being ripped from his chest. *So this is the substance of poets' prose—the agony of losing your heart to the woman you love.*

He studied her face carefully. "Please listen, my love. I promise to come to you as often as possible, and I shall position an express rider at Netherfield, so that we may communicate as often as you wish. Furthermore, if the situation in Meryton becomes too unbearable, I shall come for you and remove you to a place far from there. Do you trust me?"

She nodded, though she could not hold back the tears that slipped from the corners of her eyes. "Very well, I shall go. I cannot struggle against you both."

William took hold of the silver necklace that adorned her neck, before gingerly lifting it until his signet ring appeared from its hiding place. He fingered the onyx forlornly.

"A poor trade for all you suffer on my account."

Elizabeth reached for his hand and brought it and the ring to her lips to bestow a kiss thereon. "Never say that! I cherish this ring as it represents your heart … your love."

Capturing her mouth in a kiss with more fire and passion than he had allowed himself previously, he prayed that she would never live to regret those words. Only an insistent rap on the door brought them both back to an awareness of their surroundings.

William tried to tease as he let the ring drop to its hiding place. "It seems your father is anxious to separate you from me."

Lizzy could not be cheered. "Nothing will EVER separate us. Not truly."

Unbidden tears now appeared though he blinked hard to contain them. *How does a man deserve such devotion?*

"Meet me in the park at Gracechurch Street each morning until you leave Town. I shall be waiting for you, no matter how early the hour."

Despite her despair, the corners of her mouth lifted. "I shall count the minutes until I see you again."

With the backs of his fingers, he softly traced the outline of her face. "Until then."

A last gentle kiss sealed their good bye, and they stepped apart. Elizabeth replied brokenly, "Until then."

When she opened the door, her father was waiting. So deeply affected that he could not think clearly, William watched Elizabeth disappear as though it were a dream, and it took several seconds before he thought to follow her.

Rushing to the foyer, he arrived in time to see Elizabeth and Mr. Bennet descend the front steps. Quickly moving to the portico, he observed as she was handed into the carriage and fixing his gaze on the windows of the vehicle, he prayed she might appear in one. Alas, it was not to be, and he stood transfixed as the carriage travelled down the street until it was completely out of sight.

Elsewhere in the house

Lord Landingham had not been asleep either when the early morning visitors disrupted the quiet at Darcy House. He had risen and dressed, apparently just after William and Elizabeth, with plans to return to his own townhouse. He had hopes of finding new correspondence from the detective he hired several months before. It had been two weeks since he received any communication from the man regarding Gisela, and he was anxious. However, once the commotion alerted him to a problem downstairs, he descended the stairs in time to see Mr. Bingley escorting several ladies from the house. While he observed their departure, Mr. Barnes stepped forward, holding out a package that had just been delivered for him.

Looking at the outside of the missive, he could tell that his staff had forwarded it to Darcy House, just as he had instructed. Saying a prayer that the young people he had come to love as his own, Anne's children, and the woman he now wished to marry would understand, he tore open the seal. Inside was a letter addressed to him, along with a bundle of old papers tied with faded ribbons. With eagerness and dread, he began to read—eagerness, because he truly wished to remove Fitzwilliam from Gisela's iron grip and dread because he was well aware of what it could mean for his happiness. If those that he loved most would not or could not forgive, he was not sure how he would carry on.

Looking up he caught Mr. Barnes still watching him from his position near the front entrance. Pasting on a smile, he enquired, "Where is Lady Ashcroft?"

"I believe milady is in the library, sir."

Nodding his thanks, Landingham went in that direction. Once at the double doors, he spied her sitting on a sofa near the windows. He stepped inside and turned to close and lock the doors. What had to be said, no one else needed to hear. Audrey smiled at him when he faced her.

"Locking the door, Marshall? What will my nephew and niece think?"

How he loved her smile! How he prayed she would still smile at him once he finished his confession. Forcing a similar expression, he strolled towards her, stopping in front of her to ask, "May I sit next to you?"

"Of course, you may," she acquiesced teasingly, "I do think, though, that I should unlock the door. Fitzwilliam and Elizabeth are in the drawing room with her father, and I promised to be available if they need me."

His expression darkened. "Do you think he will do harm to Fitzwilliam? Should I go there straightaway?"

She chuckled, reaching for his hand. "No, Mr. Bennet seems a reasonable man, altogether unlike his wife. She is entirely irrational and excitable. I cannot see even the slightest resemblance between her and Elizabeth."

"Was she one of the ladies Mr. Bingley escorted from the house?"

"Yes." Suddenly Audrey began to study him seriously and sobered. "What is bothering you, Marshall?"

He smiled wanly before his expression grew wistful. "How well you know me, my love. It is uncanny."

"As I tell Georgiana, just say what is bothering you. Waiting can only make it harder."

Tears filled his eyes. "I only pray that you care deeply enough for me that you will not hate me once I am done. I do not have the faith to believe that you shall still love me."

Seeing his anguish, Audrey squeezed his hand. "I am no saint, Marshall, and I hope I have lived long enough to have learned that forgiveness is divine, especially when not warranted. I love you very much, and I promise to attempt to understand any secret you have to reveal. Now, just tell me."

"Do you remember when we talked of the woman that I loved for so many years?"

Hesitantly she answered, "I … I do."

"Inside this package are papers that reveal her identity." At her puzzlement, he continued. "When Fitzwilliam told me several months ago that Gisela was blackmailing him with letters that implied that Georgiana was not a Darcy, I realised that I had to act. I hired a detective to see if he could obtain the evidence she claimed. For several months now, I have employed spies who have lived under Gisela's roof."

Taking a deep breath, he held out the package that had been delivered that very morning. Audrey took it, and with one last look at him, began to empty the contents into her lap. After reading the missive from the detective, she began to untie the ribbon around the old papers. She stared at the handwriting, recognising that it was Anne's. Searching through all the letters, there were none from any other. Swallowing hard, she looked back to Marshall.

"You are Georgiana's father." It was not a question.

"Please… let me explain. I believe I first fell in love with Anne when I was a mere boy. We were neighbours, you remember. Later, I asked her to marry me, and she agreed, but we were so young at the time, each barely fifteen, that we agreed to wait to announce our decision until after I finished university. Then, George Darcy came along, and our plans vanished as dried flowers on the wind. He was older, more sophisticated and … well, you know the rest. I tried to be happy for them, truly I did! In fact, I determined that I would remain a good friend to them both. But, for the most part, I confess, that I wanted to be near Anne in order to protect her. I suppose I thought to be there if ever she needed me."

He stood and began to pace. "You have to understand that I did not trust George not to break her heart. I was well aware of his propensity for the ladies during our years at university. Nevertheless, for the first few years after they married, he seemed content. Well, at least until she had Fitzwilliam. Later, there were two children who were still-born, and she lost several others in the early months of pregnancy. That was when the neglect began. He began to stay in London more than at Pemberley. During those years, Anne would cry on my shoulder whenever she heard rumours of a new mistress, a new conquest and there was always some busybody eager to send her a copy of the gossip sheets."

He looked into space, as if recalling. "Meanwhile, Anne was becoming even more broken-hearted, as she still desperately wanted more children. About the time Fitzwilliam was twelve, she sent for me quite unexpectedly one day, saying that it was most urgent. Naturally, I hurried to Pemberley.

"I found her inconsolable. She fell into my arms, crying hysterically. George had told her that he would never come to her bed again, blaming his decision on his fear of losing her during childbirth. Anne, however, felt that he just did not love her, since he never stayed home with her or Fitzwilliam anymore. Only George knew the truth, I suppose. All I know is that I still loved her, and regardless of the reasons, she needed me and sought solace in my arms. Afterward, we both felt such remorse that we vowed never to let it happen again."

During his recitation, Audrey rose and walked to the large French doors that led into the garden. She stood her ground with the most perfect dignity, and his heart swelled with admiration, though he feared what she might be thinking.

"I will say that neither of us ever regretted Georgiana. We loved her. I love her. Nevertheless, Anne swore me to secrecy regarding her paternity. Of course, George knew she was not his child but, in his defence, I have to say that he never rejected Georgiana or treated her any differently than Fitzwilliam. I suppose he felt he deserved what had happened since he had been the first to be unfaithful. If he suspected I was her father, he never acted upon it."

"How do you know there are no more letters?"

"From Anne's account, she wrote me only three times while I was in Brighton. I had gone there to lick my wounds when Georgiana was born. I never received the letters, and for years, we both feared into whose hands they had fallen. If you will note, some of the pages of each are missing. That Gisela acquired any portion of them, however, is a conundrum that I aim to solve. She was not even in George's life when the letters went missing. And God only knows who has the other pages."

"Oh Georgiana, my poor, poor baby," Audrey breathed, her eyes filling with tears and her voice a whisper. "How can she bear this?"

"More than anything else, that fear kept me mute. When I saw how devastated she was after Anne and George died, I vowed to wait until she was old enough to better understand. The last two years, as she has grown stronger with your help, it seemed a fitting strategy. Then, without warning, Fitzwilliam confessed to me about the blackmail."

"You should have told me everything about your relationship with my sister once we began to make plans for our future. For you to delay when you knew it might—"

Landingham interrupted, "By then I was so in love with you that I was afraid I would lose you. I meant it when I said I had not loved anyone but Anne all those years. Until the day she died, I was as much in love with her as the first time I gave her a nosegay of wildflowers as a boy. Until you came into my life, I never felt attraction towards another woman."

Audrey chuckled, though her expression was solemn. "You were most likely attracted only because I resemble her. What a balm to your heart it must have been! To meet someone who looked so much like the woman you had always loved—a veritable twin. You would not even have to—"

"NO!" He reached out and turned her to face him. "I fell in love with you *in spite* of your resemblance to Anne. When you first came to Pemberley, I could not remain in your company for more than a few minutes before I found an excuse to leave."

"I remember."

"Do you know why?" Her head moved slowly side to side. "I could not bear that you looked like her. It was too painful."

"What changed your mind?"

"The day you demanded that Lady Catherine vacate Pemberley, I saw a totally different woman. Not Anne, but Audrey! Anne would never have had the daring to take on her sister as you did. Only you were courageous enough to do that!" He smiled lovingly. "That was the day that I realised what a remarkable individual you are, and as I spent more time in your presence, I realised that, while there were a few similarities to Anne, there were more differences—notable differences.

"Your personality is wholly different. You not only have a clever mind, but you are lively. You laugh easily and when I am with you, you make me glad to be alive. But it was your inner strength, your resolute spirit, which captured my heart and my admiration. You had suffered great losses, but it was obvious that you did not live a defeated life. And I was witness to your steadfastness in protecting Fitzwilliam, Georgiana and even Richard. You are not afraid to stand up to anyone who might come against those you love. In all my years, I cannot say that

I have met a woman I admire more. You are truly a woman of substance.

"After getting to know you well, I find there is, in actuality, little resemblance."

She said nothing so Landingham added, "Please, darling, forgive me if I did not handle things as you would have wished. I thought to capture the evidence from Gisela so that she could hold nothing more over the boy." Sadly he shook his head. "And I confess to hoping that if I recovered the letters, perhaps he might feel more inclined to pardon me. Now, I fear that I have failed, as I do not know what happened to the rest of the pages."

Audrey walked back to the sofa and sank down into the plush fabric. For a long time she said nothing, instead she seemed distracted, fingering the fringe around the edge of a pillow. When at last she responded, her voice was very compassionate though steady. "I must have time to consider all you have told me." Her eyes found his. "Surely you understand."

She held a hand towards him. He moved to take it and knelt at her feet while she explained. "You do not need my forgiveness for being Georgiana's father. That is something that happened years before I met you and concerns only you and Anne. However, I cannot determine if we can have a future together until I know my own heart and learn how this revelation will affect Georgiana and Fitzwilliam."

He said nothing so she continued, "I must be certain that I harbour no reservations. I want to be able to accept your relationship with my sister without regrets. Otherwise, we are sure to be miserable." She squeezed his hand. "I need more time."

Nodding soberly, he laid his head down on her lap. She could not help reaching to brush from his forehead the silver locks that she adored. As she did, he whispered, "No matter what you decide, I shall love you for the rest of my life."

She could not formulate an answer, as the tears began to course down her face, forewarning that she dare not speak. Thus, she continued to stroke his hair and for some time, they remained in that position, both mourning the impasse they had reached.

Chapter *39*

London
Darcy House

Long after Elizabeth's departure, William stared in the direction the carriage had gone. A footman, who held the elaborate front door open, began to look between the Master and Mr. Barnes, questioning what to do. At that point, the butler took matters into his own hands, issuing a discreet cough that brought William's thoughts back to the present. Colouring to see the baffled footman awaiting him, William immediately made his way back into the house, somewhat uncomfortable to have been caught in a trance.

He meant to inform Barnes where he could be found, but changed his mind because of the rising lump in his throat. Therefore, without a word, he took the stairs two at a time in hopes of being safely ensconced in his rooms before encountering another person. Directly, he stood in the hall outside his bedroom, one hand poised on the doorknob. But before opening his door, he noticed that the door to the guest room that Elizabeth had occupied was open. Immediately, he crossed the hall and entered the sitting room. As he continued to the adjoining bedroom door, he was not surprised to find a young maid inside busily packing Elizabeth things.

At her notice, he ordered, "Please leave the packing until this afternoon."

Mumbling her compliance, she dropped a curtsey and vacated the room in mere seconds. He followed her to the door and locked it. Turning around, he was pleased to see that Elizabeth's personal items were still there. Gingerly, he began to examine some objects on the dressing table—a brush which held several long strands of dark hair, numerous hair pins and a small handkerchief. Unfolding the linen square, he noted that it had a different flower embroidered in each corner, though a good many of the stitches were uneven. This revelation brought a wan smile to his face. Naturally *his* Elizabeth was too full of life, too active, to be a proficient at embroidery.

Secreting the few strands of hair in the handkerchief, he hid it all inside his coat pocket before moving to a small table by the window where a book still lay open, a pink ribbon marking the page. Picking it up, he smiled to see notes scribbled in the margins just as was his practice. Turning the book over to discover the title, his heart ached anew. It was the one he had purchased in Meryton—**A Selection of Irish Melodies**—and instantly his first glimpse of her came to mind, causing his heart to ache all the more.

Reaching for a shawl draped over the back of the chair, he brought it to his nose and closed his eyes, breathing in the fragrance she wore on her wrists and in her hair—lavender. Taking the wrap with him, he entered the bedroom, noting that her small trunk still sat open on the floor where the maid had abandoned it. Then the tips of a pair of blue satin slippers, peeking from under the edge of the bed, caught his eye. As he stooped to pick them up, he marvelled at how tiny her feet were and became conscious that he had never really noticed them. His eyes had only been drawn to her own. He placed the slippers where they would not be overlooked by the maid when she returned.

Suddenly, all the emptiness he felt from her departure returned full force, and he lay down across the counterpane, burying his face in her shawl. In this rare instance of complete privacy, he was unable to maintain his fêted self-control. Mourning her loss, a few defiant tears managed to slip from the corners of his eyes, despite his best efforts, and he quickly brushed them away. It would not do for anyone to see him despondent, least of all a servant.

In a short while, he drifted into a fitful sleep.

~∞~

The Gardiner's Residence
Gracechurch Street
Upstairs bedroom

A lone candle sitting on the plain wooden dresser provided the only light in the small bedroom where the sisters retreated upon Lizzy's return to Gracechurch Street. It was enough, however, to illuminate the hurt on her sister's face, and Jane embraced her even tighter, though she said nothing. Their mother's violent reaction to Lizzy's arrival, coupled with the horrifying tales of her stay at Gatesbridge Manor, had almost rendered poor, gentle Jane speechless.

Instead of remaining cowed by her husband's show of force at Darcy House, Mrs. Bennet had become more emboldened with every glass of wine she had imbibed while awaiting her husband and daughter. And when the pair had come through the front door at the Gardiner's residence, she had been ready with a volley of hateful barbs to describe Lizzy's character and her husband's good sense.

For a time, Jane feared that her father might strike her mother in order to silence her as she raged against Lizzy without heed to his warnings. Indeed, though he had never before raised a hand to anyone that she was aware of, he looked angry enough to do so. It took Madeline Gardiner's subtle reminder to Mrs. Bennet of the consequences of defying her husband to make her hush. It crossed Jane's mind then that her aunt might have been worried about having to take Fanny Bennet into her own home.

It was at that point that Mr. Bennet demanded to speak to his wife in the study, and taking her arm, he dragged her in that direction whilst Jane pulled Lizzy up the stairs to the bedroom they always shared.

The horrible acts of which their mother had accused Lizzy wounded her deeply, and she had collapsed on the bed the moment she reached it. As she cried, Jane gathered her into her embrace, gently rocking her side to side. Now, she felt it her duty to try to convince Lizzy that all would be well, though she was not certain of that herself.

"Please do not be so sad, dearest. It shall all work out, you shall see. Mama had too much wine, but in a while she will come to her senses and regret the unpleasant things she said. We shall return to Longbourn, and your Mr. Darcy shall obtain a divorce from that horrible woman and come to fetch you."

"We cannot be sure of that. Gisela is certain to do all she can to prevent a divorce, and even if Fitzwilliam is successful, he cautions that it could take years. What will become of us if the rumours reach Meryton? Then our entire family will suffer, and Mama will never let me forget it. Was I foolish to think only of my happiness, to let myself care for him?"

"You were not foolish to want happiness! And everything you fear now may never occur. You must be resolute above all else. If Mama senses that you regret your choice to care for Mr. Darcy, I fear she will make your life even more miserable. Should she come to the conclusion that you *caused a scandal*, as she says, without truly knowing your own heart ..." Jane's voice trailed off as she considered the consequences. "You do love him, do you not?"

"I love him with all my heart."

Jane relaxed and a small smile returned. Elizabeth, however, looked even more despondent as she crossed to the window seat where she sat down and stared into the darkness at the park across the street. The gate that marked the entry to a trail she followed each morning was visible only when the full moon emerged from behind some dark clouds. Looking up at the sky, she realised that the clouds were increasing, and rain was likely soon. A sudden shiver made her wrap her arms around herself.

"Do you know what I fear the most?"

Jane hurried to the window seat, sat next to her and grasped her hand. "Tell me."

Elizabeth began to blink to keep from crying. "I ... I do not know how I can bear not being able to see him whenever I wish. These last few days have been the happiest of my life."

Jane tenderly ran a finger down her cheek. "I shall help you. We shall stay so busy, he shall return before you realise it."

Elizabeth tried to smile. "Have you so soon forgotten that you are to be wed? A newly engaged woman will not have time for such things, nor would I wish it of you. Your full attention should be directed towards Mr. Bingley now, not me."

"Charles will want to help you and his friend, of this I am sure! We shall both endeavour to lift your spirits. And, after we marry, we shall come to London for a stay, and I insist that you come with us. Then you shall see Mr. Darcy whenever you wish."

"Oh, Jane, do you suppose Papa will allow it?"

Jane smiled indulgently. "You forget. By the time I am married, you shall be one and twenty and able to come if you wish!"

Lizzy sobered, looking bewildered. "In all the turmoil, I had forgotten. Before now, it never occurred to me to go against Papa's wishes, even after I reach my majority. Do you think he would be very angry with you for taking me to London? After all, he will know why I am going, and he has ordered us to stay apart."

Jane looked very pensive before she answered. "I pray not, but I am willing to risk Papa's ire for your sake. You deserve the same degree of happiness that I have found with Charles. Besides, every time I think of what you endured at our aunt's hands, and with Mama's blessing, just to convince me that I am worthy of more than John Lucas—"

Nearly overcome, Jane stood and wiped her teary eyes resolutely. "NO! You are just as deserving of a man like my Charles, and if that man is Mr. Darcy, then so be it! I shall not back down to please Papa or Mama."

Elizabeth stood, hugging her sister. "You are too good to me." Then she pulled back. "I do have something to confess, though. I was too stubborn to admit it before, but you were right about the gentlemen in London not being keen to marry us—at least none that have good sense."

Jane giggled, which made Elizabeth smile. "I know no such thing. If any of them had shown good sense, they would have flocked to you in droves and begged for your hand."

"I am not sure even Mr. Darcy would agree with your opinion. For, alas, he resisted my charms for quite some time," Lizzy countered.

Jane's expression grew solemn. "I must disagree, Lizzy. Charles told me how steadfastly Mr. Darcy resisted falling in love, even before Gisela's entrapment. Apparently, when he was yet at university with Charles, he confessed to having soured on the idea of marriage after seeing his parents' struggles and discontent. Yet he fell madly and irrevocably in love with you the moment he laid eyes on you in Mr. Grant's shop. He confessed as much to Charles."

Joy filled Elizabeth's heart at that revelation and she smiled dreamily. It was the first smile Jane had seen since she had returned.

"Do you remember the moment you met him?"

"How can I ever forget?"

"Then cling to that memory, dearest. Cling to all of your memories. They shall sustain you while you wait for your Mr. Darcy to be free."

Elizabeth took a ragged breath and let it go. "I fear that I shall have to make do with my memories for a long time to come."

Their father joined them a half-hour later to assure Lizzy that their mother was reconciled to his judgment, and she would suffer no more cutting remarks from that quarter. Neither young woman thought it would be that simple once they returned to Longbourn, though they dared not voice their opinion.

Darcy House

It would be late afternoon before anyone saw William again. Still, Audrey knew exactly where he was, as she had gone to find him when he did not come to the parlour after Elizabeth left for the Gardiners' home. They were both so dear to her that concentrating on their happiness allowed her to postpone thinking about what Marshall had confessed.

Enquiring of the head upstairs maid as to William's whereabouts, she learned that he had been seen entering the guest room that Miss Bennet had occupied but not leaving. Concerned, she had obtained the keys and gone inside, only to find him fast asleep on the bed, his face buried in Elizabeth's shawl.

Coping with all she had learned that morning, the poignancy of this discovery had been almost too much to bear. Retreating to her rooms, Audrey vowed not to leave until she could project a serene facade.

The sun dipped low in the sky before Lady Ashcroft once more made her way down the grand staircase. Encountering Mrs. Barnes, she asked, "Is my nephew about?"

"Yes, madam, he is presently in his study with Lord Landingham."

"Thank you."

Aunt Audrey swiftly headed in that direction. When she got to the door, she stood outside trying to hear what was being said, as it was obvious that her nephew and Marshall were having a disagreement. Suddenly, the door opened and Landingham was face to face with her. The tortured look in his eyes made her heart break, but she was unable to speak. When he realised that she was not going to say anything, he nodded and stepped into the hall while she stepped back to let him pass.

Her eyes followed him as he walked towards the foyer, and she wished with all her heart that she could beg him to stay, but, alas, she could not. Not yet. There was too much in her heart that needed sorting out before she could offer him her support.

Suddenly, Fitzwilliam stood behind her. She turned to see the same look of agony in his eyes. "Fitzwilliam, I was coming to tell you that I am available if you need to talk."

"I … I know that you are aware of what Lord Landingham had to say." The use of Marshall's title showed William's unhappiness with his godfather. "I have asked him to allow me to be the one to inform Georgiana. Would you consider joining me when I do? You are like a mother to her, and I think she may need you more than me, once we are finished."

"Certainly, if that is your desire. I love you both, and I am at your disposal."

William indicated that they should walk, and they headed towards the foyer, talking quietly. "Would now be convenient?"

"Yes."

They had no more than reached the foyer, when Georgiana met them at the bottom of the steps.

"Brother, have you heard from Miss Elizabeth since she returned to her aunt's home? Is she well? Will she be visiting again soon?" The pained look on her brother's face silenced her, and her entire demeanour changed. She looked from him to her aunt fearfully.

William reached for her hand. "Sweetling, I have not heard from Elizabeth, and I have no idea if she will be allowed to visit us again. I pray she will, but we shall have to wait and see. However, there is something of great importance that your aunt and I need to discuss with you. Would you be so kind as to come to my study?"

Her brow furrowed. "Your study? What is the matter?"

Lady Ashcroft stepped forward, the palm of her hand caressing her cheek. "Georgiana, dearest, we shall explain all once we are in the study."

A timid smile reappeared. "It seems I have no choice."

William left orders that they were not to be disturbed. This time no raised voices could be heard in the hallway, though they did not depart the room for the greater part of an hour.

⁕

One hour later

Audrey sat in the corner of the large upholstered sofa that faced the windows of William's study. Normally the beautiful view would have lifted her spirits, but not today. In her arms she held Georgiana, the girl's head lying against her chest. She comforted her niece by running her hands through her long curls and whispering endearments. Weeping steadily since learning of Landingham's confession, it now appeared that Georgiana had exhausted her tears, and they were to be replaced by sporadic sniffles.

It had been quite a blow for her to learn that her mother had had an affair with her godfather and that he, not George Darcy, was her father. Upset to see his sister's distress, William had become so overwrought that Audrey had asked him to take a walk about the park to calm himself. It was obvious that he did not want to comply, but reluctantly, he had left to do just that. And once they were alone, Georgiana had poured out her heart, saying those things which would have only further upset her brother were he still there.

"Why? Why would anyone act in such a manner, especially my own parents? To break their marriage vows? And why would Father let Fitzwilliam pay for his sins with Gisela by marrying her?"

She burst into tears, stuttering, "I for … forgot he is not my fa … father!"

"There, there," Audrey cooed, rocking her more vigorously. "You must calm yourself, Georgiana. Try to think rationally. I believe you have seen enough unhappy alliances in your short lifetime to know that most marriages are just that—alliances. They are formed to accomplish a purpose, rather than because of any great love. More often than not, despite managing to birth an heir or more, the parties go their separate ways."

"But I thought my mother and father were in love."

"I remember when they married, and I truly believe that they were then. However, the cares of life sometime cause people to fall out of love. There is a lesson to be learned in this. Marriage is something to be nurtured and not neglected."

"But why did it have to happen to me—to my parents?"

"Should it happen to someone else? Lady Strongham perhaps? Or are you speaking of your friend, Lady Horton, whose father deserted her and her mother to reside with his mistress?"

"Of course not! You know that is not what I meant."

"I am only pointing out that life is not fair and that rain falls on the just and the unjust. You have heard your brother's explanation of what caused their marriage to falter. Your father made a poor decision in regards to your mother's health, which basically was to abandon her. And, Anne, bless her, was ruled by a desire to have more children."

"In my heart I understand all of Fitzwilliam's explanations—Mother's fragile health and Father's weaknesses. I can even forgive my parents' mistakes, but I can never accept them as reason to break their vows."

"If it makes you feel any better, your brother feels the same."

"Does he hate our godfather? For I worry that I shall come to hate him for deceiving me all these years."

Audrey took her niece's face in her hands, searching the depths of her blue eyes for understanding. "I have not had time to talk to Fitzwilliam about his feelings toward Marshall, but I know him well enough to know that he could never hate him." Georgiana looked embarrassed and her eyes fell. "Fitzwilliam would never forget all the years that he has been like a father to him, and you, or that he almost died saving you from Wickham."

A lone tear slipped down Georgiana's face and she sniffled again.

"And you know that Marshall did not purposefully deceive you. Your mother had him swear never to tell anyone he was your father. And in spite of all the obstacles in his path, he managed to be a steadfast presence in your life and has shown you and your brother an unwavering love."

"But ... but he was not forthcoming with the truth."

"Knowing him as you do, do you not think that it must have broken his heart not to be able to tell the world that you were his child? For, if you think of it, he has no offspring but you. And if I remember correctly, Anne said that it was he who taught you to ride and to swim, even to fish, not George. I would say he has tried to be like a father to you all along."

Sitting up straighter, Georgiana began wiping the tears from her cheeks. "I ... I know you are correct, and I am sorry that it fell to you to remind me of his love for me. I do not believe I would have gotten quite as angry if I did not love him, too. I thought he could do no wrong, and I placed him on a pedestal."

"But pedestals are hard places to live— there is so little room to manoeuvre without falling off."

Georgiana saw that her aunt was teasing. She began to smile. "I never thought about it, but I suppose they are. Everything I have learned today has been painful to hear, and it will be hard to contemplate that Lord Landingham is now my father, though I must. Would it be possible not to see him until I sort it all out? Do you think he will understand?"

"I am certain he will. Why not write him a note and tell him how you feel?"

"I shall." She touched her aunt's cheek. "Most of all I regret the effect all this may have on your relationship with him."

"Do not let that trouble you," Audrey interjected. "That is the last thing you should take into account. Instead, concentrate on the bond you have always shared with him and how to establish your future relationship."

"I will."

"Now, what shall you do about your brother? You were very harsh with him."

"I shall find him and apologise. I should not have shouted at him, but I was just so upset that he would ruin his life for my sake! Why did he not just tell me the truth and toss Gisela to the street?"

"You must look at it from his perspective. You were only twelve and deeply affected by your parent's death. He worried that learning you were not George Darcy's child might destroy what little stability you had left. He was not willing to take that risk, so he made a decision that effectively put it off until you were older. Had the roles been reversed, I have no doubt you would have done the same."

She turned to look into her aunt's eyes. "Still, I feel responsible for all his misery, and I love him so much…" She could not finish, but instead bit her lip to keep from weeping anew.

"How often have I said that you are not responsible for the actions of others, Georgiana? We must all answer for our own deeds and nothing more. Other than caring advice, none of us can affect another's decisions once they reach a certain age. That is why it is imperative to 'bring up a child in the nurture and admonition of the Lord.'[17] If they are raised with Godly values, they are less likely to fall into the predicaments that plague those who have no religious foundation."

Standing to her feet, Georgiana began to wipe her face and smooth her hair. "Do I look presentable? I would like to go find Fitzwilliam and apologise."

"After you slip on your bonnet, you will look perfectly fine. I am sure that Mr. Withers would enjoy a walk in the park, he is always eager to walk out when I feel the urge to stretch my legs. Why do you not ask Mr. Barnes to send for him?"

Georgiana smiled shyly, "I shall, and Aunt?"

By this time Audrey Ashcroft had risen and was smoothing her skirts. "Yes?" "Thank you for always knowing what to say. Brother tries hard to understand me, but he is a man, after all. I do not know what I would do without you. You are so dear to me."

Audrey hugged Georgiana, placing a kiss on her forehead. "And you are just as dear to me." Composing herself, she added, "Now, run along if you are determined to locate your brother. It is getting late, and I am sure that Cook has dinner almost prepared."

As Georgiana walked away, Audrey's thoughts returned to the man she loved with all her heart—Marshall Landingham. Could she abide by the advice she had given her niece?

Think of the bond you shared with him and how to establish your future relationship.

Could she accept that he had once loved Anne? Searching her heart, she could not make sense of all the emotions that swirled within it. Recognising the futility of knowing her own heart at this point, she felt she had no choice but to delay talking to Marshall until she did. Slowly, she made her way to her rooms, all the while wondering if she would ever be certain of anything again.

The partial letters that Landingham had purloined from Gisela's house were still lying on her dresser. She had known that she would want to read them again when she was alone. And that is what she did.

---

[17] *And, you fathers, provoke not your children to wrath: but bring them up in the nurture and admonition of the Lord. Ephesians 6:4,* **King James Version of the Bible**.

Grantham Townhouse

Mr. Boatwright made his way gingerly past the Mistress, meaning to place the letter that had just been delivered on her desk without waking her. As usual, Gisela Darcy had fallen asleep on the sofa in her study without bothering to return to her bedroom the night before. A half-empty bottle of brandy sat on the floor next to her.

After he placed the missive in plain sight, he turned to leave, stopping to take one last look at her to be sure that she was breathing. He shook his head, thinking to himself that she looked no better than most of the whores on the Mint.[18]

He was tiptoeing out of the room when she sat up and called out. "What the devil are you doing?

"I … I was trying not to wake you, madam," he answered, disappointed to have been caught.

Gisela placed her legs on the floor as she raised both arms towards the ceiling and stretched. "I was just taking a nap. Why were you in here?"

"There was a letter delivered this morning. I placed it on the desk."

Gisela flew to the desk and picked up the letter. "Who is it from? Why did you not tell me immediately?"

"There is nothing to indicate who sent it, and last night you told me not to—"

"Quiet! I cannot think with all your babbling!"

Boatwright dropped his head and waited while she broke the seal and read the message she recognised as written by Wickham's hand though it was unsigned.

> *Madam,*
>
> *A stroke of good luck! Having my associate watch Darcy's house has been profitable. He observed Elizabeth Bennet leave the residence in Darcy's carriage and followed her. She is now residing on Gracechurch Street. I have moved the surveillance to this residence, which I understand belongs to her uncle, a man named Gardiner, who is in trade.*
>
> *According to my contacts, the maid next door claims Miss Bennet is fond of walking in the park across the street very early in the morning. If this is true, it will make my job almost effortless. Should she walk out tomorrow morning, I shall have her at Stillwater before noon!*
>
> *I suggest you leave town before Darcy finds out she is missing! I will see you again at the estate.*

---

[18] *The most notorious slum of Old London was the Mint, a ten-minute stroll from London Bridge (present day Southwark)--a place of uninhabited buildings, unroofed and in ruins, many shored up by great beams propped up in the centre of the road, blackened timber houses, their upper floors leaning precariously over their foundations, or relics of once-fine mansions now falling down and surrounded by narrow courts and alleys--a place of squalor where some 3000 families lived in cramped rooms where the sewage bubbled up through the floorboards--home to the most desperate of thieves, beggars, prostitutes and outlaws.*
http://www.mmbennetts.com

Finally she looked up at the butler. "Have you shipped those trunks that I had packed yesterday? The ones to Weymouth?"

"Yes, madam."

"Good. Have my coach readied to leave at dawn. Oh, and have that new maid— what is her name?"

"Daisy?"

"Yes, have her pack the rest of my clothes. I shall be leaving tomorrow, but only the usual servants shall attend me—Grimsby, Grady, you know the others."

Boatwright knew the ones she referred to—those that more closely resembled the riffraff that normally loitered outside his brother's pub, without a farthing to buy a pint, than a proper servant. Why she wanted to surround herself with such people was beyond his imagination.

With that pronouncement, Gisela swept out of the room like she was the Queen and proceeded up the grand staircase, halting half-way to turn and call, "Mr. Boatwright!"

Since he had moved to the foyer to watch her leave, he quickly answered, "Madam?"

"I suggest that you and Mrs. Boatwright take that trip you were planning." At his confused look, she added, "Some time ago you mentioned wanting to visit your son. I am going on a long trip and will not be back for several months … perhaps longer. Leave a note with your address, and I shall send for you upon my return." Without another word from either party, she continued up the stairs and disappeared at the top.

The elderly man sighed and went in search of his wife. Perhaps they would do just that. He had managed to save enough to move to Yorkshire where his son lived, and he had had enough of Mrs. Darcy to last a lifetime.

$$Chapter\ 40$$

Gracechurch Street
Gardiner Residence

Elizabeth could not breathe. The air in the bedroom she shared with Jane was stifling due to the humidity and the fact that the window had not been opened because of the rain. She felt she simply must have some fresh air, and the only solution, in her opinion, was to go for a walk. Glancing out the window, she noted that the entire world still seemed cloaked in a drab grey, though it had to be nearly dawn. It was obvious that the sun would not break through the clouds today.

Nevertheless, she was determined that the lack of sunshine would not keep her from the park. At least within its borders she felt liberated, and she had not felt such freedom since she had been placed under John Wilkens' power by her uncle. Shivering involuntarily at the thought of that horrible man, Elizabeth forced herself to think instead of the one who made her smile.

Fitzwilliam did say that he would be in the park no matter how early I walk out.

Donning her white muslin gown, she pulled on a dark green spencer, a pair of tan kidskin gloves and her short, brown walking boots. She stopped to examine Jane's bonnet which lay on the dresser exactly where she had discarded it yesterday. Having no idea where her own had disappeared, Elizabeth thought that it would likely come in handy since it was raining and she had no parasol. With one last glance at her sleeping sister, she placed the purloined item on her head and stole out of the bedroom and down the stairs.

Taking for granted that Mr. James, the elderly footman, would not yet be awake to accompany her, she wondered if she could be so fortunate as not to encounter any servants as she made her escape, especially Mrs. Doane. Elizabeth had no use for that nosy woman, never doubting that the housekeeper would awaken the entire house if she discovered her intentions. Fully aware that there would be a price to pay should her family awaken to find her missing, she decided she must take the chance. She had no reason to believe that her father would let her go out alone, and she simply had to see Fitzwilliam once more ... *and not with Papa looking over my shoulder.*

As she approached the front door, the muffled sound of something being dropped on the thick carpet in the dining room drew her attention. It was followed by an incomprehensible oath sworn by Mrs. Doane. Stiffening, Elizabeth stood absolutely still until she was sure that that woman would not materialise right before her eyes. Then saying a silent prayer of thanksgiving as all became quiet once more, she slipped out of the door completely undetected.

A sombre and breathless calm accompanied the misting rain, and for a brief moment, she stood motionless, profoundly affected by the dreariness. How she wished for a sunny day to raise her spirits! Nevertheless, as she took a deep breath, Elizabeth realised that at least the air smelled cleaner, and that made the dampness a bit more bearable. Beginning to walk in the drizzle, she was also thankful that she had decided in favour of borrowing Jane's bonnet, an item that she normally avoided because it obstructed her view. Smiling to herself, she remembered how Fitzwilliam had begged her not to wear one.

Your face is too beautiful to hide beneath anything, especially a wide brimmed bonnet. I want to see your eyes, nay, your entire face, whenever we are together.

Though she did not think herself beautiful in the least, the remembrance of his entreaty made her heart swell. She could not hold back a smile as her footsteps became lighter, and she almost skipped as she increased her pace towards the park.

Finally having crossed the lane, she reached the gate that led to the trail that she always enjoyed exploring, and as she traversed the familiar territory, her shoulders began to relax. All at once, the misting rain came to a complete stop, so she untied the ribbons that held the bonnet, removed it entirely and began to swing it by the gaily coloured streamers.

Occupied by more pleasant thoughts, she was totally unaware that someone waited only yards ahead, just off the pathway. His clothes were dark, and he blended into the trees, which also conspired to hide his presence. His hat was pulled down over his face which made him look ominous and a sense of foreboding possessed her when she eventually spied him.

"Elizabeth?"

It was not until she realised that the voice belonged to William, that her heart began to beat again. Bringing her hands to her chest, she exclaimed with relief, "Fitzwilliam, you frightened me half to death!"

"Forgive me, my love. I confess I have been propped against that oak for the last hour. I must have closed my eyes for a moment and did not realise that you had come until you were upon me."

While he was expressing his regret, Elizabeth bent down to retrieve the bonnet she had dropped in her surprise, and the ring that she wore inside her décolletage fell from its hiding place. As was her habit, she toyed with it as she rose to face him. The signet was a great source of comfort when they were apart, and she meant to tell him so. However, upon seeing how his expression had changed to one of alarm, all that she wished to say escaped her.

"What in heaven's name are you doing in this park before daylight? And where is your escort? You led me to believe that a footman always accompanied you on your walks. You do realise that Wickham is still free and could be in London this very minute?!"

Elizabeth bristled, slipping the ring back into its hiding place. Indignantly she replied, "It is raining so there will be no daylight this morning. And since it is very early, there was no footman about, and I was not about to awaken one."

William stepped forward to take her in his arms, holding her a little too tightly.

He was relieved when she did not resist. He missed her ardently, so much so that he was almost ill whenever he thought of not seeing her whenever he wished. And since she was no longer staying with him, her safety was a constant worry as well. Nevertheless, the minute she became irritated, he regretted his words. He had no wish to disagree with her today of all days, as this could likely be their last meeting for some time.

Eager to calm the situation, he murmured in her ear, "Please forgive me if I spoke too harshly. It is only because I love you so dearly that I implore you to be careful. I cannot sleep now that you are no longer under my roof. How can I possibly survive if something happened to you? Surely, you realise that that is the reason for my censure?"

Elizabeth relaxed in his arms. "Forgive my fit of pique. I recognize that you are upset because you are worried for my wellbeing. It is only ..." She sighed heavily. "I confess that my mother's attacks have left me sensitive to criticism, any criticism, whether justified or not."

"Was she very unforgiving?"

Elizabeth nodded against his chest, and he kissed the top of her head and rested his cheek there.

"I promise to work as zealously as possible to obtain a divorce, and just as soon as I have opportunity, I shall travel to Netherfield so that we can be together."

Elizabeth sought his face. "Do you suppose Papa will let us see one another once you are in Meryton?"

"I pray that he will. Else we shall have to meet clandestinely. But be forewarned, I shall not be gainsaid on this matter. I cannot live without seeing you." He steadied her chin with one finger, and all the love he felt in his heart now shone in his eyes. "I love you, Elizabeth Bennet. You are precious to me— a light in the darkness of my soul."

She had sworn not to cry, but at this sweet avowal, tears rolled down her cheeks. "I love you just as fiercely."

Relaxing into him, her hands slid inside his coat to his back, while his hands pressed her hips to his. A delicious throng of sensations ensued, and his desire for her became more evident as she sunk her fingertips into his skin, saying softly, "Never stop loving me."

Instantly their lips were joined, the bond becoming more urgent as the kiss intensified. It was as though both sought the strength to survive the coming separation in that one kiss. Freed from traditional fetters, their hands found forbidden places and desire crushed William's vaulted self-control. It was only when his horse whinnied, startling them both, that the spell was broken.

Opening his eyes and finding no one else in sight, he feathered less fervent kisses down Elizabeth's face and throat before laying his head atop hers. With a half-breathless murmur of amazement and incredulity he whispered, "Do you know how much I adore you, my darling? I fear I have not the words to express it."

Her face was buried in the crook of his neck and she placed a gentle kiss there. "In my opinion, you express yourself faultlessly."

Lost once more in a satisfying embrace, it was some time before William walked Elizabeth back to the gate where she had entered the park. Pleased that they had encountered no one, as they reached the wrought-iron gate he leaned in for one last chaste kiss. Then, he stood guard as Elizabeth made her way back to the entrance of her uncle's residence. At the doorstep, she smiled and waved, then entered the house.

For what seemed like an eternity, William did not budge but kept his eyes fixed on the door. Finally, convinced that she was safe, he turned and made his way back to the tree where he had tied his horse. And by the time he was nearing Grosvenor Square, he had come to a conclusion. He would assign several of his servants to keep Elizabeth under surveillance without telling her. Knowing the woman he loved, she would not be pleased, and most likely Mr. Bennet would take offense if he learned of it. But, at least it would give him some peace of mind.

Inside the Gardiner's residence, Elizabeth was resigned to the fact that most likely she would not see Fitzwilliam again before she left for Hertfordshire. There was no doubt that her family would rise early tomorrow, and she would not be able to slip out of the house unnoticed. Thus, with a heavy heart, she entered the empty parlour and sank down onto one of the settees. At least the silence was a welcome respite.

As she reflected on all that had just transpired while her family slept, she began to pine for him and reached for the token of his affection. But it was not there! And neither was the necklace! *Fitzwilliam's ring!*

Instantly, Elizabeth was on her feet. She searched the parlour and retraced her path to the front door. Finding nothing, she ran out of the house, heading towards the gate with her eyes glued to the ground. Once she had gained the park, she immediately set off down the path they had walked only minutes before. When she reached the spot where she had dropped the bonnet, she spied the chain and ring lying next to each other on the gravel path. Relieved, she picked them up and kissed the ring before sliding both into the pocket of her skirt.

Intent on going back to her uncle's home before she was missed, Elizabeth stood and was smoothing her dress, when a hand came from behind to cover her eyes at the same time a rag was shoved into her mouth. Strong arms held her immobile as a scarf was tied around her head, covering her eyes. Though she tried to struggle, she was no match for the blackguards who held her, and a rope was quickly secured around her hands and her feet.

She felt the sensation of being lifted and tossed over a man's shoulder. Kicking and twisting, her heart was beating frantically by the time she was lowered into the door of a coach. Hands from within the vehicle pulled her forward and then shoved her into one corner.

The voice of an old woman exclaimed cheerily, "No need ta be fight'n us, dearie! It will set better if ya mind ya manners and sit still."

Lizzy's mind whirled with possibilities. Was she the random prey of a group of cutthroats that inhabited London? Or was her capture Wickham's doing as Fitzwilliam had predicted? Would she be held for ransom or killed? And how long would it take for her family to realise she was not in the house but taken prisoner? Worst of all, how would Fitzwilliam react when he learned that she was missing? Her heart ached at the thought.

Nearing Hyde Park
Inside a coach

By insisting that they carry out his plans despite the rain, George Wickham had borne many complaints from his cohorts that morning. Reaching the park before dawn, he had been hopeful of catching Darcy's purported lover during one of her usual early morning walks. What he had not counted on was finding her already in the park—with Darcy. In fact, he and Grady, Gisela's servant, had almost been discovered when they stumbled upon his nemesis' horse and spooked the creature, causing it to whinny. At the noise, Darcy had searched the area with his eyes, but they had managed to stay hidden in the shadows. Only the fact that the lovers were engaged in more pleasurable pursuits prevented Darcy from being more inquisitive and discovering them.

Afterward, he had watched helplessly as Darcy walked the woman back to the gate and waited until she was safely inside her uncle's house before leaving. Greatly disappointed, after Darcy rode away, Wickham had given the order to retreat, only to discover in a few more seconds that Miss Bennet had returned to the park. Amazingly, she had run up the gravel path towards him and Grady with her head down as though searching the ground for something.

Quickly, he had signalled the servant to duck behind a row of hedges as he did the same on the other side. Oblivious to the danger surrounding her, it was only when he grabbed her that she comprehended her blunder. Easier than he had ever imagined, she was his prisoner.

All of a sudden, Wickham remembered the chain he had pilfered from her pocket after seeing her pick it up in the park. Pulling it from inside his coat he held it up for examination.

It is most likely a present from Darcy since she was keen to find it, and it looks quite expensive. Slipping it back into his coat pocket, he smiled a sinister smile. *It shall do nicely!*

Darcy House

William had no more than dismounted his horse at the stables when he was confronted by one of the footmen, informing him that his cousin, Richard, and the Earl of Matlock had just arrived. Since Mr. Barnes often helped him avoid the earl's calls, William assumed this was the reason for the notice. Nonetheless, he felt that he had no choice but to see his uncle today, especially since Richard accompanied him.

Sighing at the thought of entertaining company as downhearted as he was at that moment, he assumed his customary mask. "Please inform Mr. Barnes that I shall meet with my relations in a quarter-hour. I need to change into some dry clothes, and then I shall occupy my study. Afterwards, he may bring them to me there."

As the footman nodded and turned to go, William stopped him with another question. "Have my aunt or my sister come downstairs yet?"

"Yes, sir. They are both in the dining room, I believe."

Not wanting to see either of them until he had had time to master his emotions,

William added, "Please ask Barnes to have a pot of coffee and some sweet rolls delivered to the study. I am famished from my ride, but I have no time to eat properly this morning."

"Yes, sir!"

He watched the footman hurry to do his bidding, then slowly made his way to the back entrance of the manor. How dearly he wished for time to savour the memories of Elizabeth this morning, but apparently that was not to be!

I must pull myself together, as there is still much to be done. And heaven knows what news my uncle has come to convey. After all, he promised to report on his investigation concerning Mr. Lowell's death and Lady Catherine's part. I would not be shocked to learn of anything she might have instigated. And I hope that Richard has news of that scoundrel, Wickham.

In short order, he ascended the backstairs to the family wing and was nearing his bedroom door. Just as he touched the knob, Mr. Hobbs, who had been his father's valet, opened it from the inside.

"Hobbs, you startled me!"

"I am sorry, Master Fitzwilliam!" The moniker the valet had used since he was in short pants almost brought a smile to William's face. He had kept the old servant on, letting him act as his valet whenever he was in Town, as he had no family. "I was just putting your clean shirts in the wardrobe." Eyeing his employer's wet attire, he continued, "I assume that you will wish to change immediately."

"Yes, thank you. I should like that very much. Would you mind collecting what I shall need while I divest myself of these damp things? My cousin, Richard, and my uncle are waiting for me downstairs."

Hobbs hurried to do as asked though he sniffed in disdain. "I would not rush to accommodate the Earl of Matlock, sir. He can very well wait for you, since he always shows up unannounced."

Though he was right, William tried not to smile at Hobbs' impertinence. His dislike of the Earl of Matlock was well-known to William, but the valet was loyal to a fault and so old that he got by with saying what others could not. Sitting down to remove his wet clothes, William changed the subject.

"Please find my black boots. They should be in the closet."

Hobbs was not finished. "Lord Landingham left in such a hurry that he did not take his favourite duelling pistols. They are still in the bedroom he occupies when he is here. Should I send them to his estate, or do you expect him to return soon?"

William was wary of Hobbs' reason for asking, but he feigned unconcern. "I think it best if you return them to him. I have no idea when he shall be in residence again."

Not to be deterred, Hobbs continued. "I fondly remember when I was living at Pemberley the occasion when you took it upon yourself to inspect your father's duelling pistols and managed to destroy the stained glass window over the French doors in the music room. You must have been about ten years of age. If Lord Landingham had not claimed that he was responsible for demonstrating how the pistol worked without checking to see if it was loaded, I think you might never have been allowed out of your rooms again until you left for Cambridge!"

William had not thought of that incident in years, and it brought a smile to his face. Quickly he suppressed it. Not meeting Hobbs' gaze, it took a good deal of effort to control his voice as he replied, "He did save me on that occasion."

"Actually, he saved you on several that I remember. Such as the episode with the fire in the hayloft and the time your father's fishing boat ended up at the bottom of the lake?"

William's head swung around. "You are perfectly aware that George Wickham was the perpetrator in both those incidences."

"Yes, but your father was about to blame you before Lord Landingham intervened. Mr. Darcy never laid anything at that sorry lad's feet, always declaring that it was your job as his heir to keep George straight. And I dare say that Lord Landingham taught you most of what you know about shooting and riding. In fact, though I should probably not say so, he was more a father to you than your own, God rest his selfish soul."

Hobbs stopped just before exiting the door. "You owe him a debt of gratitude for all the support he has freely given you throughout your life."

Seemingly satisfied that he had made his case, he quietly left the room.

Hobbs is right. I shall have to meet with my godfather soon and make things right between us.

Darcy's Study

Behind the huge oak desk that dominated the room, William sat as still as a statue in his oversized, custom made chair. The Earl of Matlock and Richard, who inhabited the chairs directly in front of the desk, both marvelled at his calm demeanour in light of what he had just been told.

Suddenly vacating the chair, William moved to stand in front of the desk, sitting on the edge of it as he leaned towards his uncle. "Please repeat that."

The Earl of Matlock looked taken aback, glancing to Richard first. Richard nodded and so the Earl began again to explain what he had discovered.

"Godbee is certain! He has examined all of Lowell's papers and Ferguson's, since I convinced that fool that he would be better off taking our side than Catherine's. My sister ordered Lowell's demise! His remains have just been found half-way between Wexford and Stafford Mills. Richard has already dispatched men to bring his body back to Town for burial.

"Meanwhile I ordered Edgar to Rosings, along with enough men to secure Catherine and bring her to London. While he is there, he is to search the house thoroughly and return with all her personal and business papers. I want everything brought to light in regards to her dirty plots and deals. I have no doubt that George Wickham and Gisela were involved in some of her deeds. There was talk in Town that Wickham had been soliciting someone to do away with Lowell right before he travelled to Ramsgate!"

"And let us not forget Mrs. Younge!" Richard interjected. "The solicitor handling the case against that traitor informed me that they found a receipt showing that Wickham paid for a landscape and had it delivered to Gisela's townhouse in London."

William shook his head, incredulous at what he was hearing. If it were possible, his face turned even more crimson with anger. "No doubt a ploy to ingratiate himself."

"And my sources report that Wickham made the trip between Rosings and Gisela's residence often in the weeks before he arrived in Ramsgate. I would not be surprised if our dear aunt arranged Georgiana's abduction, or at the least, knew of it!"

"Nor I!" The Earl added. "I have made it plain to Edgar that the family shall not suffer for any of the consequences of Catherine's evil. He is to diligently search until he has all the evidence necessary to secure a place in Bedlam for her. I will proceed with my strategy—having her declared insane."

William studied the floor for a long moment. "Do you know if Mr. Lowell left behind a family? If so, I shall help them in whatever manner I can and, of course, I shall see to his burial. He was an honest, decent man. It is the least I can do." He ran his hands tiredly over his face. "After all, I am responsible for his death!"

Richard and his father both tried to protest, but William held up a hand effectively ending their objections. "I appreciate that you do not agree, nonetheless, had I not employed him to look into the joint venture, he would not be dead. I shall have to live with that."

Richard and Lord Matlock exchanged defeated glances before the earl replied, "I shall enquire of Godbee, since he is a distant cousin. He will know about Lowell's relations."

William next addressed his uncle about a different concern. "Though it pains me greatly to say this, I must be forthright. I cannot rest easy knowing that Edgar is in charge of the investigation of Lady Catherine. We have never been close, and since I did not bow to his wife's superior judgement concerning Gisela, he and the countess have shunned me … not that I ever desired their company. But I have reservations about how earnestly he will seek to expose plans meant to harm Georgiana or me."

The earl coughed self-consciously, a twinge of embarrassment making his voice falter. "Well … yes. I understand why you are hesitant to trust him or me, for that matter. I was wrong, Darcy. It was improper of me to use my influence against you because I did not agree with your choices regarding marrying Anne or snubbing Gisela. Eleanor, Edgar and Frances were wrong as well. I have told them that I intended to apologise, as should they."

William looked stunned as the earl placed a hand on his shoulder. "I hope you can find it in your heart to forgive me … to forgive us all. Richard has informed me of your attachment to the young woman who helped to save Georgiana, and I intend to support whatever you decide in regard to Miss Bennet. And if it helps to calm your misgivings, Edgar knows the truth must be exposed in order to save the family!"

"Besides," Richard chuckled, "I sent two of my trusted sergeants with him to make sure that everything that is found is preserved. Quarles and Benedict report only to me, not Edgar!"

William relaxed a bit, enquiring of his cousin, "And what have you learned of Wickham?"

"It is as though he vanished from the face of the earth." Richard lamented. "There is not a pub, an inn or a brothel in England that one of my men has not searched in our quest to find him. Not even the lure of a large reward has brought the cockroaches from out of the walls. I am convinced that if most of these beggars and thieves knew where he was hiding, we would already have him in chains. My guess is that if Gisela is involved. We suspect she is helping to hide him."

William covered his face with his hands, rubbing his eyes in exhaustion as a headache began. "Georgiana is secure, but I fear for Elizabeth's safety. She foiled Wickham's plan to get rich, and Gisela would delight in doing harm to her in order to pay me back. Wickham has the means and Gisela the money. It is a double threat."

"You speak as though Miss Elizabeth no longer resides at Darcy House?" Richard declared. "Surely you can see to her safety here, and with our aunt and Georgiana in residence, there can be no real scandal."

"Her father came for her yesterday. They are now at her uncle's house in Cheapside and will return to Meryton tomorrow. Frankly, I cannot fault the man for removing her as far from me as possible. If it were Georgiana, I would do the same."

"Have you warned her of the danger that surrounds her?"

William began to pace. "I have tried to impress upon Elizabeth the seriousness of my concerns, but she is not easily intimidated." Just at that moment there was a knock on the door and he called out, "Come!"

The door slowly opened, and Marshall Landingham stuck his head inside. Seeing his cautious expression, William offered a slight smile. "You are welcome to join us. We were discussing Wickham and my *dear* wife."

Landingham entered then, crossing the room to where the others were gathered. His expression gave away the fact that his was not a courtesy call. "I thought that I should hurry here to tell you what I have learned just this morning."

No one spoke, so he continued. "The detective I hired to spy on Gisela called on me early today. It seems that she has packed and shipped numerous trunks of household items to Weymouth in the last several days. And she gave a bonus to those servants who had worked for her the longest before dismissing every last one of them. Early this morning she was observed leaving for parts unknown in a coach."

Concerned looks passed between the occupants of the room.

"This does not bode well," Matlock said sombrely. "Why would she dismiss her servants unless she did not intend to return?"

"And why would she not advise you where to send her allowance, Darcy?" Richard added. "After all, she pretends to rely on that stipend."

The door had not been completely closed, and Mr. Barnes peeked inside, knocking on it at the same time.

"Yes, Barnes?"

"This parcel was just left on the doorstep by an urchin, sir. Blakely tried to catch him, but the lad was much too quick. There is no address to indicate who sent it."

Nodding in frustration, William reached for the parcel. There was only the name *Darcy* across the front of it, written in a man's hand—a hand he would never forget. Wickham! A feeling of dread washed over him, and for a moment, he could not move.

His hands shook as he sat down at his desk and broke the seal. A letter and a silver necklace fell onto the desktop. Everyone else exchanged worried glances as he gingerly lifted the chain and his face paled. His voice was barely a whisper. "Elizabeth."

Impatiently, Richard grabbed the letter and began to read silently. Then he read it aloud.

Darcy,

Should you wish to see Miss Bennet again, you will do as I instruct.

Gather two hundred pounds in gold coins and the Darcy jewels. Keep in mind that I know what comprises the collection, as I was often privileged to see your dear mother wear them. If you love this woman, you will not be stingy when you fill the bag.

At daybreak on Monday, proceed to the graveyard at the church near the village of Teddington, an hour below Richmond. A large oak tree stands at the rear of the yard. I will leave instructions in a knothole on the backside of the tree that shall instruct you where to leave the ransom. When you have delivered it, you shall find directions to another site where you will find a map directing you to Miss Bennet.

Do not cross me on this, Darcy. My people are watching you, and if you involve others, I shall know. If you do not come on Monday, I shall be forced to sample the charms of your little minx and then leave her corpse for you to discover.

George

"Teddington? Why the devil would he pick a place as obscure as that?" Richard roared, once he finished reading. "I have been through there, but the village consists of only four or five shops, as I recall, and there are very few estates nearby, as the land is almost unsuitable for farming. Where could he hide Miss Bennet in that Godforsaken place?"

Just then the Earl cried out, "Stillwater! Gisela's father had a hunting lodge near Teddington called Stillwater. I accompanied him there once, and it was the most inconvenient site in all of England. The manor was not grand, but it was sufficient for his purposes, and it sat on a huge cliff, the back facing the valley below. There was only one large attic on the top floor, and Montgomery had the windows removed, a door installed and a balcony constructed so he could walk out on the roof. He called it his crow's nest. From a cousin in the navy, he procured a ship's telescope, and he enjoyed showing his guests the view. He claimed he could see deer in the next county with that glass!"

"I remember hearing tales of his hunting parties, though I never attended. Nevertheless, I do have some knowledge of that area of the country, as my cousin used to live near there," Landingham offered.

The Earl quickly added, "If he is taking Miss Bennet to Teddington, Gisela must be involved. Do you know if she still owns that place, Darcy?"

Every eye focused on William, though he had removed to the window while Richard read the note and remained eerily silent the entire time. As he stared into the distance now, the only sign of his fury were his clenched fists. And just when the Earl began to think he should repeat the question, his nephew answered.

"I confess that I have no idea. I never wanted anything to do with the properties that belonged to her, and I did not bother to learn where they were." He whirled around, his eyes ablaze. "Do you think you could still find this place?"

"Yes, it was isolated, but I can find it, I am sure! In fact, I know a road that approaches Teddington from Hampton. Wickham will likely watch the usual route from Richmond to Teddington, so we could head to Hampton and double back. In addition, I have a friend, Lord Percival, who has an estate between Hampton and Teddington. I have no doubt he will let us headquarter there, and he just happens to be in Town now. Say the word and I shall make the arrangements!"

Landingham walked towards William. "We are with you in this, Son. Whatever you say to do, we will do. But may I be so bold as to make some suggestions?"

"Please do."

"As I see it, you must act quickly before Wickham realises that you know where he is taking Miss Bennet. There is no need to secure the ransom, as we shall surprise him days before it is due. And, if I am correct, the Darcy jewels are probably at Pemberley, which would take too much time to retrieve."

William nodded.

"Obviously, whoever goes with you must not be seen in case he is not lying about the spies, so I suggest that we set out after dark tonight. If we travel together, any highwaymen will be loath to set upon us. It is only a two-hour journey by day, so we should easily make Percival's estate before morning. Wickham expects you to arrive with the ransom in four days, but he will have settled into Stillwater and started to relax. We should storm his hideaway tomorrow evening right before dark. We will have time to plan our execution while we travel."

"I agree," William stated almost too calmly. "I am not willing to wait, and your suggestions make sense. We shall leave in an unmarked coach after dark. As many of us as are able will fit in the vehicle, a few others can ride alongside without drawing too much attention. When we stop for horses, I shall have my driver handle the changes so none of us are seen. Two other coaches will leave an hour later, taking the same circuitous route, and bearing those marksmen we ask to join us."

"Why so many coaches?"

"I wish to transport Miss Bennet back to London by coach, and I just imagine that after we are done, most of you would favour a coach instead of a horse." He turned to Richard knowing that he was an excellent strategist. "What is your opinion of the plan?"

"In truth, I could not have devised a better one. I say we start now to make arrangements. After all, we have only until dark!"

William looked purposefully towards his godfather. "I know that I can rely on you, but you have not fully recovered from your wound at Wickham's hand. I would not have you hurt again. Send some of your men if you wish, but please do not attempt to accompany us. I will not be offended."

Landingham stepped up to William, laying a hand on his shoulder as he looked him directly in the eye. "I never thought that you would be offended if I did not come. You are not that kind of man, I am proud to say. But you must understand that, as part of my family, I wish to be with you. I may not be as young as I once was, but I am still an excellent shot, and I shall not be gainsaid on this matter."

William nodded, trying to swallow the huge lump that had formed in his throat. Then burying his emotions, he addressed the others.

"We need to restrict our recruits to those who are excellent shots. We shall, of necessity, use as few men as possible when we slip through the woods and surround the house."

"I have two trusted footmen with me in Town who are fine shots!" Landingham offered.

"I have three that can hit a fly at one hundred feet!" Matlock boasted.

Shaking his head at his father's claim, Richard stated his plan to have several fellow officers help them, including Colonel Neilson. "My men are good marksmen, used to moving by night and keeping out of sight."

The earl bristled. "Why does Nielson have to be included?"

Richard shrugged. "Just because you do not favour him for Alicia does not mean he is not an excellent soldier and a good man."

William intervened, which silenced the Earl. "I shall welcome his help, Cousin."

Without warning, the door flew open, slamming back against the wall as Mr. Bennet shuffled into the room with his cane. He was followed by an ashen Charles Bingley and an exasperated Mr. Barnes, who threw up his hands, exclaiming with great frustration, "I was going to announce them, sir, but this gentleman—"

Obviously beside himself with fear, Mr. Bennet loudly interrupted the butler as he hobbled towards William.

"SIR, I DEMAND TO KNOW WHAT YOU HAVE DONE WITH MY DAUGHTER!"

Chapter *41*

On the road to Stillwater

The farther from London they travelled, the more the coach settled into a steady rhythm. For the most part, it swayed from side to side in an orderly manner until it came upon one of many deep ruts in the road with teeth jarring consequences. George Wickham paid such small inconvenience no mind, for he had travelled in far worse fashion since leaving Pemberley years before. The more the miles passed with no signs of being followed by Darcy or his minions, the more he began to relax.

Tight knots of tension eased in his neck and shoulders, and he laid his head back against the top of the cushioned seat and closed his eyes. A smile crossed his lips. Extremely pleased would not do justice to describing how he felt at that instant. All that had seemed to go wrong that morning had been made right the minute Miss Bennet reappeared in the park. That had to be a sign that his luck was changing! And after all, he had managed to abscond with Darcy's lover basically right under the man's nose!

It is up to you to take the next step, Darcy! We shall see how much you really care about this woman.

Subsequent to seizing Miss Bennet, it had simply been a matter of stopping across Hyde Park from Darcy House on the way out of town and waiting for the owner to return. He was not about to take a chance with the ransom note. Darcy had to be the one to open it.

There were enough carriages stirring by that time, so their coach went unnoticed, sitting on the side of the park in the steady rain. A quarter-hour later, he observed Colonel Fitzwilliam and Lord Matlock being admitted to the house. When they did not come back out forthwith, he felt certain that Darcy was in residence. Immediately, he sent Grady to find a street waif to deliver the package while he safely observed everything from the window of the coach. The selected messenger did as directed, knocking on the door and dropping the package on the doorstep the minute it was opened. The footman made a valiant effort to catch the boy, only to admit defeat when the lad disappeared into the murky shadows of the landscape.

Imagining Darcy's expression upon opening the package and having the necklace fall out, Wickham's lips curled into an evil smirk as he closed his eyes.

What are you thinking now, old chum? Do you still believe you hold the

winning hand, or has it penetrated that obstinate brain of yours that the woman you love is under my control? Despite your power and wealth, you could not prevent it. All that remains is how much of your wealth you are willing to forfeit for her return.

Opening one eye, he peered at the woman in question—Miss Elizabeth Bennet. He had expected there would at least be some tears shed by now, but not one sound had escaped his captive since she had been tossed inside the coach. And while she sat motionless in the corner, her eyes covered and a gag in her mouth, she did not appear to be overly frightened.

Judging from the way she attacked me at Ramsgate, she is most likely too headstrong to be afraid. Good Lord, Darcy has met his match—a woman as pig-headed as he!

After the show of affection that he had witnessed in the park, he knew Darcy well enough to know that he would track him to the ends of the earth if he dallied with this woman while she was under his power. Thus, he had absolutely no desire to pursue his normal predilection with regard to her. No ... no matter how appealing the thought might be, he would not give Darcy an indisputable motive to pursue him after he fled England.

That bit o'muslin[19] is not worth it! I shall follow my plan to extort what I can from my old friend and flee the country as soon as possible.

Perhaps, he reasoned, if Darcy got Miss Bennet back unharmed, he might be so relieved that he may well forget the ransom paid in favour of spending his time in more pleasurable pursuits. Glancing again in her direction, he studied what little of her face he could see.

Nevertheless, one thing puzzles me. I cannot fathom why Darcy chose her for a lover.

From what he had seen of Miss Bennet at Ramsgate and just now in the park, he would allow that she was pretty, but she was certainly not beautiful. She was definitely not the kind of woman he would have chosen for a lover if he were Darcy. After all, the Master of Pemberley could have his choice of women, all of them as beautiful as Gisela had been in her youth.

There is no accounting for taste!

His chuckles had drawn the attention of Agnes, the old woman that he had brought to watch Miss Bennet. Wickham had known her for years, as her son had been one of his partners in crime until his death at the hands of an unwilling victim. Finding her had been easy, as she always begged outside one pub or another on the seedier side of Town. Eager to make a tuppence without too much effort, she had agreed to the scheme straightaway.

As Wickham closed his eyes again, Agnes proceeded to undertake her own examination of the young woman sitting next to her. Convinced that she was only helping Wickham in order to survive, she was surprised that a small twinge of guilt pricked her conscience, and for a fleeting second she regretted her part in the affair. After all, her father had been a vicar, and he had raised her better than that.

---

[19] *Bit of Muslin. According to The Regency Encyclopedia, a bit of muslin referred to a woman or a girl.*

Then remembering her current station in life, she pushed all kindly thoughts to the back of her mind.

Ain't no need ta dwell on what might' a been. There ain't no goin back. Besides, tha lady ain't gonna git hurt if she don't do nothin' stupid!

⌒✄⌒

London
Darcy House
William's Study

Obviously beside himself with fear, Mr. Bennet loudly interrupted the butler as he hobbled towards William, demanding to know what he had done with Elizabeth.

Landingham and Richard both stepped in his path, causing him to halt and eye them contemptuously. However, unwilling to have anyone fight his battles, William placed a hand on each of their shoulders. When they glanced back at him, he jerked his head to the side in a manner that suggested that they stand down. They complied, and he stepped forward to face his love's father.

"God knows that I wish I HAD Miss Elizabeth, sir, but I do not." He reached into his coat and pulled out the ransom note. "This arrived just before you did."

Mr. Bennet's eyes flicked between William and the others before he took it and began to read. Suddenly overcome, his legs gave way and his knee twisted. He cried out in pain as he went down. William reached for his arms to support him as Bingley pushed a chair underneath him. As they settled him in the chair, he buried his face in his hands with a sob.

"Oh my Lizzy, what have they done?!"

Everyone exchanged worried glances as William shouted for Barnes to send for Mr. Gladstone, the local physician. Shaking his head in disagreement, Mr. Bennet chided the young man he held responsible.

"I need no physician. I need only to recover my daughter!"

Nonetheless, the look William gave Mr. Barnes let the butler know that he should proceed, and he hurried to do just that.

With great exasperation, Elizabeth's father continued. "This man ... this George—"

"Wickham," Richard volunteered.

"This Wickham took my Lizzy in order to provoke you, Mr. Darcy. What befell my daughter is your fault!"

Landingham, Richard and Lord Matlock tried to defend William all at once, but the Earl prevailed.

"It is not Darcy's fault that the blackguard took your daughter!" Lord Matlock challenged. "She garnered his wrath at Ramsgate when she interfered with his attempt to kidnap my niece!"

"Please, Uncle!" William pleaded. "I appreciate your support, but Miss Elizabeth is not to blame for any of this!"

Mr. Bennet glared at Matlock now as he taunted him with the truth. "I realise that my Lizzy courageously risked her life to save YOUR niece, who is Mr. Darcy's sister, but let us be honest with one another. How likely a target was my

Lizzy before she met your nephew? She has no fortune nor connections."

Honouring William's plea, no one replied. So Mr. Bennet turned to the one he had come to confront.

"Is it not obvious? This man found out that you are in love with my daughter. That is why she was his target and why he sent the ransom demand to you. Am I correct?"

Ashamed, William nodded. Mr. Bennet's head dropped despondently with his acquiescence. His voice barely discernible, he added, "I knew my circumstances were too modest to be an inducement. I was not even notified that she had been taken."

William tried to sound confident. "No matter the reason Miss Elizabeth was taken, you must believe that George Wickham shall not prevail. We have already figured out where he is taking her and have devised a plan to get her back unharmed. We are to leave at nightfall and, God willing, she shall be back in London in two days."

The older gentleman raised his head to glare defiantly. "Tell me everything you have planned, but be advised. I shall hold you personally responsible if any harm comes to my child."

"I understand completely. Now this is what we know ..."

◦⌒◦

Later

After everything had been explained, it took some time to convince Mr. Bennet that he should not accompany them to Stillwater. Only fervent guarantees that he would be notified the minute Elizabeth was safe and the fact that his knee had buckled again and would hinder his ability to help caused him to concede. It was unquestionably for the best, as it took several footmen to carry the man to his waiting carriage as he departed. Mr. Gladstone came up the front steps just as Mr. Bennet was being carried down and, at William's request, accompanied the party to the Gardiner's to examine the patient there. Bingley stayed behind, insistent on helping to rescue Elizabeth, so several footmen accompanied the Master of Longbourn to Gracechurch Street in order to help him up the stairs and into bed.

Now all that was lacking was to put their plan for rescuing Elizabeth into action and to try to catch a few minutes sleep, since they would be up all night and most of tomorrow. Richard, his father and Charles left immediately to make arrangements for themselves and their men. However, Landingham stayed behind.

"Fitzwilliam, I wish to thank you for allowing me to accompany you. Not being there—standing with you—against whatever evil you will face would have troubled me exceedingly."

Seeing the love in his godfather's expression, William reached out and Landingham responded by pulling his godson into a hug. Tears shined in both men's eyes.

"I am so sorry," William offered sincerely. "I should have told you sooner that your revelation about Georgiana's paternity has not changed my opinion of you. In hindsight, you have always been a strong influence in my life as well as Georgiana's, and you evidently loved my mother very much. And once I considered what I would have done, had it been Elizabeth—"

Landingham interrupted, "There is no need to explain, Son."

Earlier, William had requested Barnes send for the livery manager, Mr. Fairfax, who happened to knock on the door at just that moment. They stepped apart and as they shook hands, Landingham proclaimed, "I had best get started. Night shall come soon enough."

He opened the door to allow Fairfax access and quickly strode past him and towards the front door. Fairfax entered and William began giving orders concerning the horses and coaches, as well as what marksmen he wished to accompany them. Shortly afterward, the servant left the room to do his duty, and William rose from his chair and stretched. Then, intent on finding Hobbs to inform him of what clothes he needed for the trip, he went towards the grand staircase.

Though exhausted from all that had happened, he did not plan on resting. No doubt sleep would elude him if he lay down. Rest would not come until Elizabeth was safe in his arms again. With these thoughts on his mind, he was looking down at the floor and almost collided with his aunt who had just descended the stairs.

"Fitzwilliam, what in the world has happened? As I stood at the top of the stairs, I saw Marshall practically run out the front door without a hat! With his injury, he should not be running, and I know that he often forgets his hat entirely when he is upset. And you are so preoccupied that you almost ran into me. What has caused you both to be so troubled?"

William could not but smile slightly at how well his aunt knew his godfather. Taking her arm, he gently steered her in the direction of his study.

"Much has happened this morning, Aunt, and there is a great deal to impart. You had better sit down before I begin."

Gardiner's Residence
A bedroom

"Tell me where she is! Has she run off with that dreadful Mr. Darcy?" Mrs. Bennet wailed. "It is just like her to defy us! Headstrong girl! Lizzy shall be the ruin of us all, mark my words."

Mr. Bennet, now lying in bed, his knee throbbing with every beat of his heart, sighed. *At least she waited until the physician departed!*

Then rising carefully on his elbows in order to address his wife, who stood at the end of the bed, he summoned all his strength, replying through clenched teeth, "I am only going to say this once, Fanny, do not ask me again about Elizabeth. All I will tell you is that everything should be settled by tomorrow evening. Now, go downstairs and send Jane to me."

"Humph!" she retorted loudly as she stomped from the room. "I am not surprised at all. You have always placed more confidence in your eldest daughters than in me."

As she disappeared down the hall, he mumbled, "If so, it is because they have good sense, whereas you do not."

Presently Jane entered the room, and he could see the fear in her eyes as she came around the end of the bed. It was the same expression she had worn that morning when she had awakened him to say that Lizzy was not in the house, and the footman reported that he had not escorted her anywhere.

As she took a seat on the side of the bed, he reached out to push a stray curl behind her ear and then ran his fingers down her cheek before patting it in a fatherly expression of love. In doing so, he encountered the tears that silently covered her cheek.

"Jane dear, please try to be brave." She closed her eyes, took a deep shuddering breath and nodded as she released it.

"Now, before I say anything, I am to relay a message to you from your fiancé." Jane's eyes opened and she studied her father. "Mr. Bingley allows that he must handle some business before he calls on you again. He expects to be back by tomorrow night or the next day at the latest. He will see you at his first opportunity."

Her head bobbed up and down obediently, and his heart ached at her hopeful expression.

"I understand that you suffer the most from Lizzy's disappearance, so I want you to know what has happened. I do not want you to discuss it with your mother, aunt or uncle. I will not suffer listening to their opinions as to what happened, or may happen, before your sister returns. I hold them responsible for Lizzy's being in Ramsgate, which brought her to the attention of the man who has taken her."

Jane's eyes grew wide. "Taken Lizzy? Oh, Papa, tell me what has happened."

All the while he explained what had occurred, tears streamed down Jane's face. And when he had finished, he held his breath, fearful that she might collapse. However, her strength surprised him.

Brushing the tears from her face with the backs of her hands, she seemed to gather her composure as she ventured, "I ... I assume that Lizzy is the business that Charles refers to?"

"Yes. If not for this bad knee—"

Now it was Jane's turn to offer comfort. She brushed the hair off of her father's forehead. "You are being unselfish by waiting here. In your present condition, you might only hinder the efforts to save Lizzy."

He stared at the ceiling then, as though to find the answers there. "My mind agrees with you, but my heart will not forgive me for not going. It is so hard to wait here. Lizzy is my child. I should be the one to rescue her."

"But with your injury, you are not able. She will understand. And, from what Lizzy has told me, Mr. Darcy is an honourable man, and I am convinced that he truly loves her. I am certain that he and Charles will take every measure to bring her back safely."

"Lizzy's letters to you must have been more informative about Mr. Darcy than those she sent to me."

Jane smiled wanly. "You know that sisters share everything, especially thoughts of a romantic nature."

"I suppose that by now I should know the habits of young ladies." He tried to tease, but his playfulness quickly faded. "Let us hope that Lizzy's opinion of Mr. Darcy is closer to his character than the one I formed today. That gentleman joins the ranks of those I hold responsible for her being taken."

"How so?"

"It is obvious that this Wickham fellow pursued my Lizzy because of Darcy's wealth."

"Please do not reprimand Mr. Darcy. I believe from what Charles has said that he loves her dearly. Surely this is difficult for him, too."

"As it should be. He brought her into this circle of greed. I shall deal with him as soon as Lizzy is back under my protection. I know that she fancies herself in love with him, but I am not wholly convinced that he is worthy of her devotion."

It was evident that it would do no good to keep pressing her sister's case while her father was so upset, so she quieted on the subject. Standing to leave, she patted his hand. "I have faith that Lizzy shall be returned unharmed."

"I hope your faith is rewarded."

"I shall let you rest and retire to my room. There, I can be alone to pray."

"I doubt I shall rest, but it will be nice to have some silence. I shall attempt to address the Lord myself, as it is the only thing I am good for at present."

"Take heart, for I am fully persuaded that prayer is what shall ultimately save Lizzy and all those risking their lives to return her."

"Thank you for reminding me of that."

She leaned down to place a kiss on his forehead. "Goodnight, Papa."

"Goodnight, child. Hopefully tomorrow shall bring us good news."

Darcy House
Nearly Dark

A few minutes before sunset, Darcy House was full of men dressed in riding clothes and boots, ready for the mission to come. A table in the foyer held an array of pistols, rifles, ammunition, daggers and swords that were being inspected by the marksmen chosen to accompany their masters to Stillwater. Suddenly, amongst the din of conversation, William walked up the grand staircase and turned on the fourth step to address the gathering. His proclamation, which succeeded in quieting everyone, would soon empty the house of all but his kin and closes friend—those riding with him.

"Those of you assigned to occupy the later coaches please gather your bags, take the weapons you have chosen, additional ammunition and follow Mr. Fairfax to his apartment at the stables where food and drink awaits. Your journey will, of necessity, begin an hour later, and you will arrive at Lord Percival's estate behind us."

William tried to jest though it was obvious that he found little humour in the situation. "Do not worry. We shall not start without you!"

Nervous laughter spread among those assembled.

"Now, it is time for some of us to depart. The sooner we get to Stillwater, the sooner we shall return. May God grant our petitions and bring all of us home safely."

Amidst murmurings of agreement, all of the servants departed to occupy Mr. Fairfax's apartments until it was time for them to leave. As the noise level in the house receded, Richard, Colonel Neilson, Sergeants Pugh and Robeson, Lord

Matlock, Lord Landingham, Bingley and Mr. Gladstone, the physician, moved into William's study where glasses of brandy were being poured. At William's request, Gladstone had agreed to go along with them in case there were injuries. Though only five and forty, he had treated the Darcys for twenty years and told Fitzwilliam he was pleased to be of assistance, as the family had always been very generous with him.

After every glass was filled, William held his up, declaring, "We shall assemble with the others at Percival's estate and plan our assault on Stillwater there. I believe we have adequate men to do what is necessary and, with God's help, justice will prevail."

"Hear, hear," rang out as each man downed the amber liquor before slamming his glass down on the desk.

"Does anyone have a question before we depart?" Silence reigned. "Then, we shall be off. Please follow me." Without another word, they left William's study and filed down the hall that led to the back door.

William had already said his farewells to his aunt earlier and had her escort Georgiana to the milliner, with plans to call on a neighbour on the way home. The scheme would keep his sister away while the men gathered, and she would be unaware of what was happening. He had no intention of informing her. However, unbeknownst to him, one of the horses threw a shoe as they left the milliner, and she and Audrey returned sooner than had been expected.

Audrey Ashcroft looked about suspiciously as she and Georgiana gave their bonnets, gloves and shawls to Mr. Barnes. Immediately, she noticed Georgiana eyeing the table that had not been in the foyer before, the one that had held the guns and ammunition.

"Mr. Barnes, is that the table that my nephew wanted moved to the back parlour?"

With a slight nod at Lady Ashcroft, he replied, "Yes, madam, it is. Lyles and Colby are making room for it now and shall return shortly for it."

"Good." She turned to her niece. "Georgiana go to your room and dress for dinner. I have something to do, but I shall look in on you once I have changed."

Georgiana gave her a kiss on the cheek. "Thank you for helping me to find the perfect materials for my new bonnet." Then, she went up the stairs rapidly without awaiting a reply.

Watching her go, Audrey smiled. Then her countenance grew sombre at the thought of what her nephews, brother and the others were about to face. Looking over her shoulder, she found Barnes waiting patiently.

"Mr. Darcy, Colonel Fitzwilliam, Lord Matlock, Lord Landingham and a few other gentlemen are in the study, milady. You almost caught them in the foyer when you returned."

Her brows furrowed. "Lord Landingham? Did you say Lord Landingham was with my nephew?"

"He is, madam."

Her heart sank. Fitzwilliam had not mentioned that Marshall was going to be one of the men going after Wickham. In fact, before he left Darcy House, he was still suffering from occasional headaches and spells of dizziness, so she never considered he might try to insinuate himself in this conflict. He was not well!

Instantly, she decided to speak to him.

Landingham was the last to leave the study, and as he followed the others down the hallway, a hand reached out to grab his arm as he passed the billiards room. Pulling him inside the dark room, Audrey threw her arms around him, burying her face in the crook of his neck. Instinctively, Marshall embraced her, closing his eyes to savour the sensation of her body next to his. Feeling her tremble, he pulled her even tighter to his chest and kissed the top of her head.

"Please do not go," she whispered against his coat.

"I must, my darling."

"I shall chastise my nephew for not telling me that you intended to go. Perhaps if I had more time, I could convince you to stay. You have not recovered sufficiently from your wounds. Let the younger men fight this battle."

He chuckled softly. "Do not be angry with Fitzwilliam. I asked him not to say anything to you. And, as for letting younger men do the job, your brother is included."

"But, he has not been injured recently," she sulked, adding dryly, "Unless you count the times he has tumbled from a chair after falling asleep."

Landingham tried not to laugh. She was upset because she was worried. "All will be well, you shall see." He ran his hands up and down her back to soothe her. "I shall return unscathed."

She leaned back to look at his face, though only half of it was illuminated by the sconce in the hallway. "Promise me you shall return to me."

"I swear it."

And with that promise, he claimed her lips in a torrid kiss, reminiscent of those they had shared before she learned that he was Georgiana's father. Only the sound of his godson calling his name broke the spell, and he stepped back into the hall still holding to her hand. William was standing at the back door when Marshall succeeded in pulling Audrey into the hall, her face a deep shade of crimson.

"Are you going, or have you decided to stay? No one would blame you."

Landingham looked at Audrey, who seemed to be awaiting his answer. "I am going."

Leaning down to place a chaste kiss on her lips, he whispered, "I could not live with myself if I let him go alone. I shall return, my love. Wait for me." Then he walked purposefully towards William.

Silent tears rolled as she followed his progress. *I shall wait for you forever.*

As she touched the knob to her bedroom door, Audrey was surprised to hear shouts coming from the sitting room across the hall. Georgiana was screaming at someone, so she opened the door to determine the problem. Inside her niece was trying to pull her hair back and capture it with a ribbon, while a young maid stood behind her, buttoning her dress as she urged, "Hurry! Hurry!"

"Help me, Aunt," she exclaimed upon seeing her at the door. "I must stop my brother and my... Lord Landingham before they leave! I was on the balcony when they passed below me. I heard them talking about some horrible danger that they are off to face." She whined, "Oh, please, hurry with the dress!"

A jerk of Lady Ashcroft's head dismissed the maid much to her niece's dismay. Then her aunt addressed her as she knelt on the floor, desperately trying to find her slippers. "Georgiana, please, you must stop. It is too late, child. They have already gone. Listen! Do you not hear the coach pulling down the drive?"

The torches in the yard illuminated the scene as Georgiana stood up and ran onto the balcony just in time to see the coach pass the stables on its way to the back entrance. Her shoulders fell and she sobbed as she realised it was too late. "What are they doing that is so dangerous? Can you at least tell me?"

"Miss Elizabeth has been kidnapped by Mr. Wickham." Georgiana gasped, covering her mouth as her aunt continued. "They know where he has taken her and are certain they can return her unharmed. Naturally, they did not want you to worry, but since you have learned it on your own, I see no reason to keep the details from you now."

"How horrible!" she moaned, sinking down in one of the chairs on the balcony. "She has been taken in my stead, has she not? Why must she suffer for helping me?"

"Do not take on this burden. It is not your fault. She was taken because George Wickham learned that Fitzwilliam loves her. He wants to hurt your brother."

"Tell me truly. Do you think she will be returned unharmed? I could not bear it if something happened to her, but I fear most what Brother will do if she is not." Her voice was strangled as she wept. "He is so in love with her."

"I have faith that she will."

"I ... I shall pray that she will as well." A small sigh escaped. "But how I wish they had told me everything before they left! That way I could have told my godfa ... my father that I was no longer angry with him about ... about what he told me."

Audrey pulled her from the chair and into her arms, holding her close as she wept. "He knows that you love him, and you shall be able to tell him yourself when he returns. They all shall return safely, just you wait."

"I suppose because I acted like a child at Ramsgate, they are treating me like a child now—not telling me anything."

"No, Fitzwilliam and Marshall are treating you like a woman. Even if you were grown, a gentleman would never tell you that he is off to do something dangerous if it is in his power. It is the nature of a gentleman to protect a lady, even if that includes protecting us from those things they feel might worry us."

"But it is not necessary!" Georgiana sniffed.

"I agree. But it is so. The best you can hope for is to marry a man who will be honest with you. But I have to warn you that, even then, if he loves you deeply, he may keep secrets to protect you."

"I do not want a man who would keep secrets. I shall not settle for that."

"You may be surprised at what you shall settle for when you meet the man of your dreams." She tilted Georgiana's chin so that their eyes met. "Your brother loves you deeply; therefore, he believes he is protecting you by not having you worry."

"And my ... my father?"

"He loved you so much that he kept a secret for fourteen years because he thought it would hurt you. Why would you think he would not protect you now?"

Georgiana fell into her arms again. "I do not think I shall EVER understand men."

Audrey chuckled as she smoothed her hair. "Even at my age, I do not understand them." Taking her niece's hand, she began to lead her towards the balcony door. "Come. You and I shall eat, and then we shall read the Bible and spend the evening praying for our loved ones and friends."

"That is an excellent idea. At least then I shall feel of some use."

$\mathscr{Chapter}$ **42**

Teddington
Stillwater Manor
The Next Day

A strong, musty odour permeated Elizabeth's senses, so much so, that it caused her nose to crinkle and her eyes to flutter open. Ghostly images of sheet-covered objects appeared in the faint light filtering through the filthy curtains. It unsettled her, and for a brief moment, she could not recall where she was. Then the events of yesterday came rushing back.

Now she remembered the abduction in the park and the long trip in the coach. It had not taken long to learn that Mr. Wickham was her abductor, for while she feigned being asleep, he had proceeded to get drunk on the bottle of brandy he brought along to celebrate. He had immediately begun commemorating his triumph in besting Darcy, and the rogue was very entertaining when he was in-his-cups, if one were to judge by the guffaws of the old woman who rode along with them. So between gloating about the morning's successful events, as well as making remarks about what happened in Ramsgate, Elizabeth was left in no doubt as to his identity.

"I was right!" Wickham had proclaimed to the other occupant of the coach. "All the ridicule I endured when I decided to go to the park this morning, regardless of the rain, was unfounded. Surely you heard Grady grumbling that no one with good sense would be out in the rain, did you not?"

"Aye," the woman replied.

"You would have thought I was ordering him to jump into the Thames instead of endure a little downpour," Wickham had snorted, taking another swig from the bottle. "But I was right in doing so! Darcy was there, and Miss Bennet as well, acting as though they had nothing to fear by meeting in the park in such foul weather! I suppose he, too, thought no one else would be afoot. What a fool he is! I am sure he believed that because I was thwarted in my attempt to grab his sister, I would be too put off to try again—this time with his mistress."

Too absorbed in his braggadocio to await any reply, he continued, "I would give a hundred pounds to have seen the look on Darcy's face when that necklace fell into his lap!" He guffawed, slapping his knee. "That arrogant bastard has always thought himself a step ahead of me. Now he has learned that he is not so smart after all!"

During the time that Elizabeth was forced to listen to his boasts, she did learn where they were headed—Stillwater Manor in Teddington. She knew that

Teddington was south of London, but she would never have known that the estate was owned by Gisela Darcy, had Wickham not blurted it out. That bit of news had caused a shiver to run down her spine, for she realised that she was in the clutches of two people, each having their own reason to hate her.

At length, the coach came to a jarring halt, and she had been dragged inside a building, led to a room and shoved down into a chair. Her feet were tied once more, and she was left alone for the balance of the night. The fright of not knowing where she was, or what lurked beyond her blindfold, had finally given way to exhaustion and, until just seconds ago, she had fallen into a restless sleep.

Fortuitously, as she struggled to sit upright upon waking, the scarf used to blind her slipped, baring the corner of one eye so that she could take in the small room, likely a housekeeper's quarters. She could plainly see the outline of a bed and a dresser under some type of cloth. A glance at the floor next to her revealed a similar fabric had once shielded the chair in which she sat. Glancing to the ceiling, she was aghast at the number of cobwebs dominating the corners of the walls. Involuntarily she cringed, imagining where all the inhabitants of the webs might be.

Just at that instant, a mouse ran towards her feet across the thickly powdered floor, and she stifled a scream. It was then that she realised the gag they had shoved into her mouth at the park was still doing its duty. The offending rag made her mouth dry, so dry that she could barely swallow. She longed for a drink of water, but had little time to dwell on that as she struggled to make sense of it all. *Think Lizzy! You must think clearly in order to help yourself and Fitzwilliam!* She had no doubt that he would come for her.

Suddenly the door opened, causing her to jump. A grey-haired woman, as round as she was tall, shuffled into the room with a tray holding a pot, a cup and some bread. Elizabeth assumed it was the woman from the coach. At the prospect of something to quench her thirst, she tried to swallow but found she could not.

Paying no attention to the captive, the servant searched for a place to set her burden down and settled on a small table. Jerking the sheet from off it, copious dust particles instantly rose to ride the shafts of daylight now streaming through the holes in the window coverings. Though the dust filled the room, Elizabeth tried hard not to cough. She did not wish to draw attention to the blindfold's failings.

Satisfied, the old servant plopped the tray down and turned to study her charge, immediately noticing that Elizabeth's blindfold was half off. She stepped over to pull the entire thing over the captive's head and then removed the gag from her mouth.

"Ain't no point to it now, dearie. We'll be long gone afore they find ya. If ya be quiet, I'll let it be."

Then she proceeded to untie Elizabeth hands. "Just til ya eat what I brung ya." She slid the table before her captive, poured a cup of tea that looked like water and with a toothless grin, stated, "Fixed it fer ya myself."

Elizabeth swallowed hard, trying not to think of how nasty everything in the house was—especially what she was expected to eat. She had seen the dust settling on the bread as it filtered through the air. Nevertheless, she pasted on a small smile.

Her hands now free, she massaged each of her fingers to improve the circulation before carefully taking hold of the lukewarm cup of tea. Starved for water, she drank it down quickly. Seeing how hurriedly she drained the cup, her captor replenished it from the small pot.

"Thirsty are ya? Drink up! I'll make more if need be."

Elizabeth nodded, grateful for any show of concern for her wellbeing. Then she picked up a piece of bread spread with some type of jam and took a bite. While it did not appear appetising, it was edible, so she finished it. Going without food when it was offered was no option. She would need all her strength to face what was to happen. As she ate, her mind wandered as the old woman babbled about being expected to clean up the house and how pitifully inadequate the kitchen was, but she caught Elizabeth's undivided attention when she mentioned Gisela.

A part of her would always be curious about that woman, but a more prudent side cautioned that she was better off not satisfying her curiosity. Nevertheless, Elizabeth knew that if Gisela was at this place, it was not because she had come to welcome her.

Instantly, the ring she had placed in her pocket at the park came to mind. She wondered if Wickham had discovered it when he pulled the necklace from its hiding place. Stealthily sliding a hand inside the pouch, she breathed a sigh of relief to find it still there.

"Ya better mind your manners if the mistress comes in ta see ya. She ain't slow to anger, if ya know what I mean."

Just at that moment, the sounds of people arguing just outside the door reinforced the old woman's warning. The door flew open, hitting the wall behind it with a loud bang. A woman, barely resembling the Gisela Darcy that Elizabeth had seen once at a ball, stumbled into the room. She was followed by a man who was trying to keep her from falling. That man, whom she instantly recognised from Ramsgate, gave up trying to aid Gisela after she latched onto a bed post, disturbing the cobwebs that were attached and causing several spiders to sprint across the sheet that covered the bed. Paying no mind, Gisela struggled to stay upright while simultaneously studying her. And as she did, an expression of absolute loathing crossed her face.

Shocked at Gisela's dilapidated appearance, Elizabeth knew she should not stare, but she could not tear her eyes away. It was evident that the gown that Gisela wore was once very expensive, thought now it appeared wrinkled and dirty, with even a few slashes around the hem. Her hair was dishevelled—half of it upswept, the other half hanging down unkempt. What was more, she smelled as though she had bathed in brandy, though Elizabeth seriously doubted that she had had a bath in days. What little rouge was left on her cheeks was smudged, and she had heavily powdered her face, creating the same pasty look immortalised in portraits she had seen of The Virgin Queen.[20]

Gisela's words were slurred. "So you are the whore my husband keeps in London!" Elizabeth's silence seemed to provoke her. Gisela moved to stand before her. "I am speaking to you! Answer me!"

Elizabeth met her glare. "I am Elizabeth Bennet, and I am no man's mistress!"

---

[20] *Elizabeth the 1ˢᵗ, The Virgin Queen, November 17, 1558 – March 24, 1603*

"Do you think me an idiot? Too stupid to find you out?" She raised a hand as if to strike her, but Wickham grabbed it and twirled her around to face him.

"I told you she is not to be hurt! Darcy will track us to the ends of the earth if she is harmed!"

"I have not pledged that she will go unscathed."

"You had best listen to me in this matter! You are too drunk to be of sound mind!"

"I am drunk? When you arrived yesterday, you were in-your-cups according to my servants!"

"I was celebrating. Now it is time to get down to business. No more brandy! Do you hear?"

He began to drag Gisela out of the room, her shoes streaking the dust on the floor as she struggled to be free. Nonetheless, her present state left her unable to resist, and soon the door slammed shut behind them. Their argument continued outside, the noise level lessening as they moved down the hall towards another part of the house. And as they did, Elizabeth let go the breath she had been holding.

"Like I said, dearie! She ain't one to be crossin'." Agnes reached for the teapot a little more cautiously. "Another cup of tea?"

Percival Manor

As dawn broke over Lord Percival's estate, a dense fog still bathed the ground though the sky was now turning a pearly grey. The sun, which had begun to rise, coloured just the top of the treeline on the horizon in shades of orange and purple. It was at this hour that Richard went in search of his cousin. He found William on the balcony outside his bedroom, standing next to a column, one white-knuckled hand clutching it tightly as though it was all that kept him upright, his head hung in despair.

"Darcy?"

William's head snapped up and turned. Quickly confirming that it was Richard, he turned back to stare into the indistinct, still foggy landscape. All the unknown of the night and the universe had been pressing upon him and he was spent.

Richard ventured, "You thought I was Lord Landingham?"

A nod was his reply.

"He would not think less of you if he knew you were worried."

"I do not want him to worry for me. He is not fully recovered."

"I understand. But, alas, it is only me, your *voice of reason*."

William could not help but smile. "Then my *voice of reason* could not sleep either?"

"It was not *that* duty that kept me awake! It is my training as an officer. We sleep little before a battle."

Doubt tortured William. "This would not have happened had I not made Elizabeth return to Gracechurch Street with her father."

"You do not know that. Knowing Miss Bennet, she would have walked out in Hyde Park, if she had no other choice, and he could have taken her from there.

Besides, you had no say in the matter. Until she is of age, she must obey her father."

William seemed to consider that for a long moment. "Do you think it shall be much of a battle? How many men do you suppose Wickham has recruited?"

"I do not suppose he would have any trouble recruiting the riff-raff that he knows, perhaps as many as twenty, more likely twelve or so."

"There are fourteen of us, not counting Mr. Gladstone. Do you think that enough?"

"Yes. That bunch of misfits will be no match for us. Just the colleagues I brought with me could take them all, of that I am sure."

"I fear they will kill Elizabeth before we can free her." William's voice faded and Richard came forward to clamp a firm hand on his shoulder.

"They did not bring her this far to kill her. I give that snake, Wickham, enough credit to fear what you would do to him if he were to harm her. And we will have the element of surprise."

"But there is Gisela. She has become so ..." William hesitated, trying to find the right word. "Unhinged is the only way to describe her. I fear that she will harm Elizabeth even more than I do Wickham."

"But we have no real knowledge that she is at Stillwater."

"I know her well enough. She is here."

Richard could not concur with his cousin's certainty, but was not willing to argue the point. It was just as likely true as untrue, thus he decided to get William's mind off the prospect of Elizabeth's death by changing the subject.

"Do you smell that? I could swear someone is already brewing coffee downstairs. Mrs. Watwood did say that we could come down to the dining room as soon as it was light, and I made sure to mention that I particularly enjoy coffee in the mornings." His stomach growled loudly. "Come! Let us eat! It shall do none of us any good to be famished when we have important decisions to make."

William nodded, allowing his cousin to push him towards the balcony door.

Once Richard and William descended the grand staircase, they found the downstairs abuzz with servants quietly taking tray after tray in the direction of what was likely the dining room. They also encountered Mrs. Watwood, Lord Percival's housekeeper, who had been awakened to meet them last evening.

"Mr. Darcy, Colonel Fitzwilliam," she exclaimed. "We have coffee and tea prepared already, with sweet rolls, buns, jams, preserves and butter. Bacon and sausages will be ready shortly, along with eggs, if that is more to your liking." She swept her arm towards the double doors through which all the servants were disappearing. "Please help yourself."

All of five feet tall and completely white-headed, Mrs. Watwood had greeted them cordially despite the hour and seen to their comfort seemingly unfazed by the prospect of feeding and housing a number of guests and servants with no notice. Lord Matlock, whom she had met before, had hand delivered Lord Percival's letter of instructions and offered an apology for the lateness of the notice upon their arrival. The epitome of graciousness, even when her guests protested that they did not expect to be treated as guests but only wished to use the manor house as a gathering point, she would have none of it!

"No guests of Lord Percival will spend the night sitting around a fireplace in the drawing room as long as I am housekeeper at Percival Manor!"

Thus they had each been ushered to a guest room in short order. Not only had many of the rooms been at ready for occupancy, others were sufficient for habitation with very little wait. The marksmen who arrived on the later coaches also found clean and comfortable rooms in the servants' quarters.

Now as Richard and William entered the dining room, William found that the wonderful smells emanating from all the trays made his stomach rumble, as he had eaten little yesterday. So they both took a cup of coffee and filled a plate, sitting down at a table made to seat at least fifty comfortably. Not long after, the rest of their party had joined them, eaten and at Mrs. Watwood's suggestion, adjoined to the library. She had insisted that only the library had tables large enough to spread their maps and papers effortlessly.

Teddington
Stillwater Manor
The Stables
Midday

Inside the now crumbling stables of Stillwater, a motley crew of misfits played cards around an old table they had found in a back room. Grimsby, one of those brought to Stillwater by Gisela, had established himself the leader the moment he had arrived. Tall, muscular, dark-haired and swarthy, he looked even more dangerous now that he sported an ugly red scar that ran the length of the left side of his face. And when he threw one of Wickham's recruits from the best room in what was once the grooms' quarters, he went unchallenged. Of course, most of the chaps that Wickham had talked into this adventure were more interested in the few pounds promised than trying to best Grimsby, so they deferred easily.

Another round of cards had just ended with Grimsby winning, when one of the younger men threw his cards down on the table and began to stand as he picked up what few coins he had left. Suddenly, a knife came crashing into the top of the table, spearing a card and causing everyone to jump.

"You ain't quitting, are ya?" Grimsby growled as he worked the knife free. "Cause I don't like men who quit when I'm winning."

The man swallowed hard and sank back down on a crate. "No."

"I didn't think ya was."

Just at that moment Grady, Grimsby's son, came into the stables, leading a horse that he had saddled that morning for Wickham.

"Wickham has returned from the village, Pa," Grady declared as he simultaneously unsaddled the horse. "Do ya think ya had better get out of sight?"

"I won't hide unless he comes here!" Grimsby shoved the man sitting next to him on the shoulder. "Go to the door and watch for 'em!"

The man grumbled as he threw his cards on the table. "Why me?"

"Cause I said so, that's why!" Then Grimsby addressed his son. "Get back to the house. Keep yer eyes and ears open. The mistress said she might be needing me if Wickham gets too troubling."

As Grady made his way out of the stable, Grimsby eyed those now watching him warily. "And don't none of ya be telling *his lordship* that I'm here!" Heads nodded obediently. "He thinks me dead. Keep it that way! Do I make me'self clear?"

There was a chorus of frightened "ayes" and then absolute silence.

"Now, Doolittle, deal again. I feel lucky!"

⌒⌒⌒

Inside the manor house, Elizabeth was considering a plan of her own that included the old woman who waited on her.

She has been kind—not unlike any other maid I have known. Perhaps, she thought, *she will agree to help me with just a bit of encouragement. I shall just have to take the chance.*

While she was coming to that conclusion, the door opened, and the woman in question backed into the room with another tray of tea and what looked like a plate of biscuits. Before she could turn to face her, Elizabeth spoke.

"I am so relieved you have returned. I am so thirsty! I do not know if it is the dust in these rooms, but my mouth feels as though it is full of cotton."

"Likely the result of the rags they stuffed in yer mouth, dearie, but ol' Agnes is taking care of it. I have a fresh pot of tea, and I found some biscuits that the Mistress stuffed in a bag what she brought from Town."

By then Agnes had set the tray down and was proceeding to untie Elizabeth's hands. As she did, she noticed that the ropes were chafing her wrists leaving ugly red marks and bruises.

"I shall try to find some salve for ya to put on that. I wish I could leave 'em untied, but they'd have my hide if I did."

Elizabeth nodded as she flexed her hands. Realising that she must take action sooner rather than later, while Agnes poured the tea, she ventured, "I have noticed that you are not like the others."

The only reaction from the old woman was that she stopped pouring for a brief second, but then swiftly continued as though she had not heard.

"You have a kind heart, Agnes."

"Pa taught me to be so, Miss," she murmured, adding, "though I do things he wouldn't approve of just to eat. It ain't easy being on me own."

"I believe you," Elizabeth consoled. "But surely, you must know that there are powerful people who are trying to find me. And if they find me here with you, you might be held just as accountable as the others. I could help you—they could help you— if only I could tell them that you were kind to me."

Her hand shook as she handed Elizabeth the weak tea. "I have been kind to ya."

"But, if I could tell them that you helped me to escape—"

"Oh no, Miss! This place is in the middle of nowhere. We rode for miles through nothing but woods. If ya were to set out afoot through the forest, ya'd surely die. The only way to escape would be by horseback and the stables are full of men."

"I would rather take my chances in the woods than be used by Mr. Wickham, and I fear Mrs. Darcy shall see that I do not survive."

"You needn't worry! I was told that ya'll be set free as soon as the ransom is delivered. So don't cause no trouble and ya'll live."

Just at that moment, the knob turned and the door began to open. It had not moved more than a few inches when it was pulled shut and another loud argument ensued just outside.

"I told you to stay away from this room!"

"I want her upstairs where I can keep an eye on her! You may think Darcy will not come until time to collect the ransom, but I am not that gullible! I would not doubt he is without the estate at this very hour, just waiting to seize the house and kill us all!"

"I believe you are wrong, nonetheless, we have men posted around the house. And if Darcy is stupid enough to try it, he will be met with force. If I put Miss Bennet under your control, I shall end up with a dead hostage."

"Why not? Darcy would love to see me dead! Then he would be free to marry that whore!"

"Why do you care what he does after we escape with the ransom?"

"Let me be plain. I shall never allow her to be reunited with Darcy! She must pay for stealing my husband!"

"How idiotic you have become! And to think I once admired your mettle! There was a time that you cared not a whit about anyone but yourself—ready to do battle with the devil to further your interests. *That* I could admire! Now you act the part of the pathetic wife, crying over a man you knew never loved you and never will!"

Gisela lunged at Wickham's face with her nails, but he caught her hands and held them as she screeched, "If only that woman had not been so eager to warm his bed, he would have loved me in time!"

"If it comforts you to believe your account, go ahead! But hear this! I am in charge of this operation, and you shall do as I say! Leave Miss Bennet alone, or I shall have you bound hand and foot and confined to your room until we are ready to leave!"

Wickham opened the door to address Agnes. "Keep this door locked, and do not let Mrs. Darcy inside!"

Catching the glare that Gisela gave her behind Wickham's back, Agnes' eyes became big as saucers as she nodded her consent. The door was pulled shut again with a loud bang, leaving both women staring at it. Then Agnes stepped forward to turn the key in the latch.

"Stand guard here and make sure my orders are followed!" Wickham demanded of someone they could not see before addressing Gisela again. "Now go upstairs to your room. Stay there until I tell you to get ready to depart!"

With his parting words, Wickham's heavy footsteps could be heard stalking in the opposite direction. Next the sound of something crashing to the floor was followed by Gisela's fiery response.

"WE SHALL SEE ABOUT THAT!"

After a few minutes of complete silence, Agnes turned to find that Elizabeth was watching her wide-eyed. Swallowing hard, the lump now in her throat making it a more difficult task, she considered what to do next. She had not signed on to be a party to murder.

"Maybe I was wrong to think Mr. Wickham will be able to keep ya safe, after all."

Percival Manor
The Library

All of the men who were to be engaged in the rescue gathered in the huge library, one and all circling a round table which held a map and a crude drawing. The map of the county had been fetched by Mrs. Watwood from Lord Percival's study, while the drawing was a configuration of the grounds of Stillwater Manor as Lord Matlock remembered them to be. There was also a smaller drawing showing the inside of the house as he recollected it as well.

Due to his experience developing strategy as a decorated officer, William felt that Richard could best determine how to breech the manor house and free Elizabeth. More to the point, William was well aware that his own thoughts were so disjointed that he should let someone with more objectivity take charge. Thus, he had entrusted his cousin with planning the execution of their mission. And plan he had—dividing everyone into groups.

Once they had all reached the estate, each group was to make their way around the mansion and attack from a different direction. Bingley, Lord Landingham and Sergeant Pugh would advance from the east, while Lord Matlock, Colonel Neilson and Sergeant Robeson would do the same from the west. Matlock's three best shots, Hocutt, Ross and Marris, would make their way to the rear of the manor and move forward from the area of the stables. As everyone advanced, they would join with the others. This would likely sweep the perimeters of any of the enemy in the process.

While the others created a diversion, Richard, Darcy and Darcy's men, Milligan and Burke, would slip into the house via the front entrance and try to secure Elizabeth as well as capture Wickham and Gisela, if she was there. That left two of Lord Landingham's men, Marks and Sampson, to watch the front of the house in case some of Wickham's crew managed to slip in behind those who went in the front. If they were not able to get a clear shot with their weapons, they were to follow and take them by surprise. Mr. Gladstone insisted on coming, so Richard had put him in charge of the horses, saying he was too valuable to risk getting killed, and his service lay in treating those that might be injured.

"We have no way of knowing if the cloudy skies will hold and the moon will be hidden, nor do we know if Wickham will think to light torches around the perimeter of the house. No moon and no torches will help our efforts, but remember what I say—no shots in the dark! We are most vulnerable to being shot by each other. Know your target before you squeeze that trigger. Better still, if possible, take them down with a knife!" Richard held up a knife with a curved blade. "Does everyone have one of these?" Heads nodded. "Good! My experience with this type of low-life is that most will run at the first sign of trouble, as they are not trained to fight. That is not to say some will not stand their ground if confronted. There always seems to be one who will take you on when you least expect it."

Richard stood, took his glass of brandy and downed it in two gulps before motioning to a muscular, middle-aged man who had entered the room quietly and taken a seat in the back without notice. "Mr. Carver, would you come forward?"

The man stood and took his place next to Richard. "Mr. Carver is the local constable. Mrs. Watwood sent for him at my request. I thought he should be aware of what was occurring in his jurisdiction. He has agreed to join us, and I have asked him to assist Marks and Sampson in covering the front door after Darcy, Milligan, Burke and I go inside."

There were nods and murmurs of agreement around the room.

"Are there any questions?"

Sampson ventured, "How do you propose to get inside—knock on the door and ask politely?"

Laughter eased the tension in the assembly. Even William smiled, though it faded almost as quickly as it had formed.

"I do not expect they shall welcome us so warmly," Richard answered. "If we cannot slip inside easily, we shall force a window or two. It would be better to have the element of surprise on our side, but it is not an absolute requirement. In any event, once we are found out, there is nothing to do but act and act fast!"

"Any more questions?" Silence reigned. "Then I suggest you try to get some rest. It will be dark before we know it."

$$\mathcal{Chapter} \; 43$$

Stillwater Manor
That evening after dark

As the carriages, horses and men headed towards Stillwater Manor that evening, Richard was uncharacteristically silent. Being a military officer, it was his custom to rehearse every aspect of what was to occur right up to the last minute. He had been in enough skirmishes to know that even the best laid plans often depended on factors one could not control, and as he pulled back the curtain at the window to gaze up at the sky, a slight upturn of his lips was the only indication that he was pleased. He had asked God to hide the moon that night, and it seemed that prayer had been answered in his favour. The clouds that had gathered earlier in the day had not abated, but increased. A misting rain now accompanied them on their mission.

When they arrived at the ironwork gate to the estate, the three carriages, brought to transport any injured back to Percival's home, were emptied of their occupants and were hidden with cut limbs and brush. The group then continued down the long, winding drive via horseback. It was not an easy trek, as most of the gravel had been lost long ago, a sign that it had not been used in years. When they got within two-hundred yards of the manor itself, the signal was given to dismount, and they began to walk their horses the rest of the way, hoping to be undetected.

Approaching the once beautiful front lawn, now equally overgrown and unkempt, it was clear that Wickham had remembered to light the torches and, unfortunately, they were doing their job in spite of the mist. Richard led his stallion into the trees, tied him and waited for the others to do likewise before voicing his concern.

"We must eliminate the torches. Each group will take a horse blanket and smother the flames on your side of the house." As the men proceeded to strip blankets from their horses, he added, "Remember, no shooting wildly in the dark. These blackguards will likely panic, but we must not. All of you, except those approaching from the rear, keep watch on the front lawn. When that torch goes dark, that is your signal to begin. For you in the back, just bide your time. If we are detected, those in the stables should rush out to discover what is happening and, if so, take them from behind."

Richard looked around the group of men one last time, meeting every eye but lingering on his father's at the end. He prayed that the anxiety he felt for the oldest members of their group, his father and Landingham, was not plainly evident. He knew he must appear confident of their ability to do the job and not be killed in the process. When he spoke, his voice was unusually rough with emotion.

"Take your assigned positions, and may God be with you."

Inside Stillwater Manor

George Wickham sat at the old kitchen table sipping a cup of watery tea and cursing the fact that all the brandy had been consumed. He now deeply regretted having ever met Darcy's wife or having brought her into his plan to capture Elizabeth Bennet.

The sinking feeling in the pit of his stomach whenever he thought of how enraged Darcy would be if Miss Bennet died, rushed back full force, and he almost lost the contents of his stomach.

I want what Darcy owes me, but I do not want him trailing me to my grave to exact retribution. I hope Gisela will listen to me and leave the woman alone—at least until Darcy comes to collect her. By then, I should be miles away with the ransom in hand. Damn the woman! What a mess she has made of a simple kidnapping.

Suddenly the sound of a door being battered caught his attention, and he drew his pistol as he stood to investigate. *Foolish hoyden, what is she up to now? Gisela is going to do something stupid. I just know it.*

Clearing the kitchen door and beginning across the foyer, he stopped when the barrel of a gun was pressed into his side. Turning his head in that direction, he squinted, trying to make out the face of the one holding the weapon. That was impossible with the faint light provided by the lone candle in the room.

"Just you be standing still, *your lordship*!" Grimsby warned, chuckling as he brought the cold steel up to Wickham's neck. Wickham stiffened at the sound of his voice and it cheered Grimsby. "Yes, it's me, gov'ner! The one what was supposed to be killed, only the Mistress didn't have it in 'er to carry out yer orders. Now, lay yer pistol on the floor and kick it away."

Wickham shivered at the realisation that Gisela had betrayed him over a murderer, but did as he was told. His jumbled thoughts were quickly replaced by fear as she walked out of the room where Elizabeth was being held.

Grady followed, dragging their prisoner behind, while Agnes seemed just as determined to hang on to the young woman. As she tugged at Elizabeth's arm, she pleaded for them to stop at the top of her voice, "Ain't no need to move her. Mr. Wickham ain't gonna be pleased!"

Increasingly irritated at the old woman's cries, Gisela screeched, "Silence!"

His mistress' outburst was taken as an order by Grimsby, thus he took aim and squeezed off a shot, sending the maid crashing to the floor. Instantly, he returned the barrel to Wickham's neck. Elizabeth screamed, trying to break free in order to go to Agnes, but she was unable to break Grady's grip.

Infuriated, Gisela walked over to Elizabeth and stood as though inspecting her. Then with a cold gaze of hatred, she slapped her across the face before pushing her back towards Grady. "Take her to the roof and secure her there! Then return."

Grady did as he was told while Wickham tried to talk sense into Gisela. "Do you not see? You will ruin everything, and we shall end up with nothing. In the end, Darcy will kill you if you harm her!"

"Then that shall be my problem, not yours."

Grimsby shoved Wickham to his knees. "Let me kill him! He would'a had me killed long ago if you hadn't stopped 'em."

Gisela scowled at Wickham. "You should not have threatened me, George. We were supposed to be partners." Then she addressed Grimsby. "Do whatever you wish with him. I do not care."

Wickham's shouts of protest were met with a single shot to the back of the head, and he slumped to the floor just as the sound of gunfire was heard outside the house. It left no doubt as to what was happening. They were under siege.

Grady ran back downstairs just as Gisela stooped to pick up the pistol that Wickham had carried and shouted, "Smother that candle! Both of you stay here, and shoot anyone who comes through that door!"

With that pronouncement, she hurried up the stairs towards the one person she now despised most in the world. She had no doubt that her husband would get past Grimsby and his son at some point, but then he would have to deal with her!

That revelation had both consumed and sustained her since her first glimpse of Elizabeth Bennet. From that instant, Gisela had known what path she would take and that Wickham would never be of the same mind. In her heart, revenge was more precious than the Darcy jewels and safe passage to the Americas. The man she had desired against all logic must know what it felt like to die inside. Elizabeth Bennet would perish before his eyes. Only then would he comprehend unrequited love.

Reaching the balcony, she found Elizabeth struggling to break free of the ropes that circled her waist, strapping her to the rusted flag pole still fixed against the house. Moving to her, Gisela switched the pistol to her left hand and slipped a knife from the pocket of her gown. With it she freed Elizabeth from the pole, leaving her hands tied. Then she re-pocketed the knife and pointed the pistol at her nemesis.

"Climb up there!" Gisela demanded, jerking her head towards a rickety wooden bench that had once been an integral part of the railing that enclosed the balcony. A small crate lay in front for a step, and Elizabeth's gaze dropped to it before returning to the bench. Observing that the entire structure was decayed and completely missing in spots, she refused, shaking her head vigorously.

"Climb upon that bench, or I shall shoot Darcy between the eyes the minute he shows his face. Surely you know that all the commotion is because he has come for you? But you have a chance to save him."

It took only a second for Elizabeth to decide to comply. Gingerly stepping upon the bench at the strongest point she could determine, she balanced, trying desperately not to glance down the steep slope of the roof behind.

The torch directly in front of the manor had been extinguished, and Richard and William crept towards the front entrance with Milligan and Burke close behind. They had trailed one of Wickham's guards across the lawn, intent on going inside if he did. Suddenly, a shot within the manor broke the silence and when he heard Elizabeth scream directly afterward, it propelled William into action. He bolted towards the front of the house, right behind the guard who was now running up the steps to the portico. Shaking his head at William's impulsiveness, Richard jumped up to follow just as another shot rang out inside the manor.

At the same time, to the west of the manor, Lord Matlock had just smothered the torch on that side when someone pressed a knife to his back. Colonel Neilson, who was close behind Matlock, squeezed off a shot killing the miscreant. Simultaneously, Sergeant Robeson eliminated two men who had responded to the sounds of gunfire.

On the east side, Sergeant Pugh was in the process of extinguishing the torch there when a bullet slammed into the wall beside it. Pugh was then tackled to the ground, but killed his assailant with a knife. Simultaneously, two of Wickham's men came running from out of the woods. One was shot by Lord Landingham, while Bingley knocked the other down and then completely insensible with the butt of his rifle.

The three marksmen in the rear of the property got the best of the skirmish as they had only to follow Richard's instructions and wait patiently for the men in the stables to run out as the first shots rang out. They captured the lot of them with little resistance.

Meanwhile, totally unaware that Grady's gun was trained there, the guard William was following bounded through the front door. He had barely made two steps before he was felled. William grabbed the man as he slumped, using him as a shield as they both sank to the floor. Grimsby called out a warning to his son just as Richard, Milligan and Burke burst in the room behind William. All three hit the floor as shots flew at them from different directions. Richard waited until he saw the flash of a gun being fired light up the darkness. Returning fire in that direction, he hit Grady, who pitched forward, dead. At that instant, Grimsby jumped up and ran towards the kitchen with Burke on his trail.

William was instantly on his feet, calling to Milligan, "Help him!"

Taking very few steps, William encountered a body, clearly a man, judging by the size. This afforded him some measure of relief, knowing that it was not Elizabeth, however, as he turned the body over, his heart lurched to discover that it was George Wickham. If he was dead, where was Elizabeth?

Fear completely overwhelmed him and gaining his feet, he rushed ahead blindly, nearly tripping over yet another body—this one much shorter. As he dropped to his knees to ascertain once more if it was Elizabeth, unknowingly he held his breath. Severely wounded and breathing raggedly, Agnes managed to murmur, "She took her to the roof."

William's throat tightened, and he found it hard to swallow! *She?* It had to be Gisela!

More shots rang out from the direction Grimsby had gone. Milligan reappeared shortly thereafter. "We have him! Burke is tying him up!"

"Move this woman to safety, and go for Mr. Gladstone," William declared. To Richard he added, "Follow me, but stay hidden. I fear Gisela has Elizabeth."

Richard nodded and they both hurried up the grand staircase and then up yet another set of stairs that led to the third floor attic. Once there, the balcony was visible through a wide door at the back. Richard moved to stand behind the door while William stepped through it.

Elizabeth was perched upon an obviously unstable bench, her hands tied in front. Their eyes met and instantly a deep anger began to simmer inside him at the same time a painful thought flooded his mind. *If she loses her footing she will fall to her death.* Fear held him in a vice. There was no way he could live without her.

While William was focused on Elizabeth, Gisela unsteadily climbed onto the bench beside her. She wobbled when she made a show of placing the pistol to Elizabeth's head. Her actions made William pale. At the sight of his ashen face, Gisela laughed uncontrollably.

"So, you have come to me at last!" Her lips curled cruelly. Half choked by a rising spasm of rage she added, "I finally have something that you desire! How delicious!"

William tried to appear unaffected, though his heart beat so soundly he could barely hear his own words. "Let her go. She has done nothing to you."

"Done nothing? Done nothing!" Gisela exclaimed. "This whore has stolen your affections, my dear husband, affections that were due me as your wife. She is a thief. Why should she not pay for her sins?"

"She is not now nor has she ever been my mistress," William began, but was promptly interrupted.

"Do not lie to me! You are a man, and men have needs. All this time you have bragged of having had no women, when you have been whoring around behind my back. That is what men like you do."

William decided to try another approach. "Just let her go, Gisela. I give you my word that I will never see her again. In turn, I pledge never to divorce you, and we shall live as man and wife. Whatever you say, I will do. I swear it."

A hurt expression crossed Elizabeth's face, but he steeled himself to show no concern for her feelings.

From the look on her face, Gisela seemed actually to be considering what he had proposed. "You will live with me and treat me as your wife?"

"Yes."

"Why should I trust you to do that now?"

"You know that I am a man of my word. If I give my word, I will keep it. You will have what you wanted all along."

Gisela stood transfixed. Though she was long past thinking rationally, it was obvious that she was struggling to make sense of William's offer. However, just when he thought she might concede, she began to laugh and turned the gun from Elizabeth to him.

"You are quite the actor, Darcy! You almost had me convinced! I shall hang for kidnapping your precious lover and for killing Wickham. Nothing you say will change my destiny, so your offer is of little use to me now!" Her blank gaze was chilling as she cocked the pistol. "I was going to let you watch your little tart fall to her death, but I have changed my mind. I have decided to kill you first. That shall assure that you shall not be able to interfere with my plans to see you both in Hades today."

Elizabeth had been steadily working to free her hands and suddenly one slipped from the tangled knots. Stealthily reaching into her pocket for Darcy's signet ring, she pulled it from its hiding place and dropped it on the floor. Being quite heavy, it made a loud thump when it hit and even more noise as it made several rotations on the wooden floor before coming to a stop. Distracted by the sound, Gisela's scowl deepened when it dawned on her just what it was and to whom it belonged. She fixed her gaze on it, seemingly about to pick it up, when Elizabeth gathered all her strength into a passionate act of courage and pushed the arm with the pistol away from William.

Elizabeth's feat caused Gisela to lose her balance and the weapon to discharge to the left of the balcony door, hitting the wall. Seizing the opportunity, William rushed to grab Elizabeth around the waist and pull her from the bench. As he did, he turned his back to Gisela, effectively shielding Elizabeth with his body.

Gisela regained her balance in time to grab William's arm. While she tried to retrieve the knife in her pocket with her other hand, he shook free of her grip, causing her to fall backward onto the disintegrating railing. The wood gave way, and she screamed as she tumbled onto the roof.

Richard rushed out of the attic when the gun went off, but had to go around William and Elizabeth to get to Gisela. He was not fast enough to catch her, however, and as Elizabeth buried her face in William's chest, he and Darcy watched as she rolled down the steep roof and over the edge.

For some time, they all stood motionless, then a great shuddering seized Elizabeth and she wept. William and Richard continued to stare at the edge of the roof as though they could not believe what had transpired and expected Gisela to reappear at any time.

Later, William would learn that Gisela's neck, the attribute she always considered her most beautiful, had snapped when she landed upon the ground. She had died instantly.

"I could not reach her," Richard murmured tiredly. Then noticing the ring next to his boot, he leaned over to retrieve it. After examining it, he held it towards his cousin.

Taking the ring and sliding it back onto his little finger, William replied, "Her death is not your fault." Then he looked down at Elizabeth, gently lifting her face to peer into her eyes. "I shall send for the physician."

Elizabeth was crying and shaking her head no at the same time, so William kissed her forehead before he slid his hands under her knees and picked her up. She rested her head under his chin as they followed Richard off the balcony. Just inside the attic, the constable and Lord Landingham stood, both having arrived just as Gisela began her fall. They stepped back to allow the couple to pass.

As the entire party descended back down the series of stairs, William enquired about the others, and Lord Landingham began to recount how the rest of their party had fared. To his knowledge, a few men had sustained cuts that needed stitching, but no wounds were life-threatening. Mr. Ross' shoulder had been grazed by an errant bullet, Sergeant Pugh suffered a flesh wound to one arm and Colonel Neilson had suffered a broken rib, possibly two, but all were being treated.

Reaching the foyer, lit by the same poor candle as before, eerie shadows made those who had died appear a ghostly shade of grey. The dead, Mr. Wickham and Grady, had been moved to one side of the room, while Mr. Gladstone knelt over Agnes on the other, nearest the light. He caught William's eye and shook his head, just as he clasped the end of a cloth and began to pull it over her body. Elizabeth, who had scanned the room until she found the maid, sobbed and looked away. At once, William fled the house while Richard stayed to take control of the situation.

Outside, Lord Matlock and Charles Bingley guarded the prisoners along with those who were to help transport them to the local jail until they could be transferred to London. Constable Carver had just joined that group when William appeared still holding Elizabeth.

Both Lord Matlock and Bingley were visibly relieved to see that she appeared unharmed. Nevertheless, the determined look on William's face and his short, clipped answers to their enquiries soon led them to understand that what he desired most was to leave Stillwater behind as quickly as possible. He made an excuse and headed towards the horses.

Finding that none of the carriages had been fetched, William asked some men to bring them to the house, which sent riders racing in that direction. And since he had no choice but to wait, he found a stone bench near a walkway where he proceeded to sit down, careful to keep Elizabeth in his lap. Taking advantage of the dark, he pulled her even more tightly to himself and kissed the side of her face, before feathering kisses downward until he reached the juncture of her neck and shoulder. She sighed and he felt her hands slide to his back, her fingers digging into his skin. Unfortunately, their moment of solitude was interrupted by Richard, who had come to locate them.

"Good news, Darcy! We have come out relatively unscathed while the majority of Wickham's men are dead. Of the ones taken captive, only a few need medical attention, and Mr. Gladstone is seeing to them. With so few injuries, we have adequate room for all the wounded in just two carriages, so you are at liberty to take the third and go on ahead. There is no need for Miss Elizabeth to suffer further by delay. Take her to Percival Manor."

William offered his hand, and Richard clasped it, shaking it heartily. Almost overcome by the magnitude of all that had happened and the reality that Elizabeth was safe with him, William murmured roughly, "Thank you. I shall never forget your courage and skill in planning this undertaking. I could not have done this without your help."

"Is that not what family is about?"

Elizabeth reached out to touch Richard's arm. "I thank you."

His face softened as he smiled at the young woman his cousin loved. "You are indeed welcome. I swore to bring George Wickham to justice after he accosted my cousin, but it seems one of his own kind has done me the favour. That I could be of service to you, while at the same time being a witness to his demise, made it all the more gratifying."

The sound of carriages arriving and the voices of the servants as they rushed to open the doors caused William to stand. With a nod to Richard, he carried Elizabeth towards the first one in line. Richard hurried to catch up, grabbing the door and holding it open for his cousin. After placing her inside, William climbed in to take the seat next to Elizabeth.

Slamming the door shut, Richard spoke through the open window. "Take care of her, Darcy. I shall see the both of you tomorrow."

As the carriage began to roll, William slid Elizabeth back into his lap. Instantly she pushed his unbuttoned coat apart, clasped the lapels of his shirt and buried her face in his chest. The familiarity of his cologne, the hardness of his body and the vice-like feel of his arms brought her immense comfort. And though she had sworn not to cry anymore, she could not suppress the flood of tears that ensued. They continued for several minutes while William whispered words of love and planted kisses in her hair.

"When I thought you were going to die," she sniffled, closing her eyes, "I was so afraid that I could not breathe and then ... and when you offered never to divorce Gisela, my heart stopped." With a voice breaking with emotion, she asked, "Would you have kept the vow never to see me again, Fitzwilliam?"

Her doubt pierced his heart. Smoothing an errant curl behind an ear, he ran his fingers gently from there to her chin before caressing her face. "Surely you know that that was just a ruse to gain her trust. I would never have kept that vow.

"Elizabeth, look at me." Her teary eyes opened. "I would have promised her anything to save your life, but I could never have kept that vow! You are my world, my life. Do you not know that?"

Big tears rolled down both cheeks. "Where is my ring?"

Instantly William pulled the signet ring off his little finger and slid it on Elizabeth's middle one. She examined it lovingly before entreating, "Show me that you love me."

It began tenderly, but Elizabeth's responses became more demanding and William's passion rose to match. They kissed deeply for many long, wonderful minutes, their tongues meeting and their hands gently caressing each other until he breathlessly drew back to study her. In the darkness, her eyes now resembled two black pools, pools in which he would gladly drown. And when she ran her hands into his hair and pulled his mouth back to hers, all thoughts of self-control were lost.

The trip back to Percival Manor was free of any concern of what society or their families might think. Too much in love to care one whit about either, the circumstances of the last twenty-four hours had reduced them to nothing more than a man and a woman—a man and woman intensely in love and hungry for each other. Even if their flushed faces, red lips and dishevelled clothes and hair had not suggested what had transpired in the carriage, by the time Mrs. Watwood greeted William as he carried Elizabeth into the foyer of Percival Manor, it was plain to see that this couple was utterly in love and, without proper chaperoning, would likely end up in each other's arms that night.

Fixing on William, the housekeeper declared brightly, "Mr. Darcy! I am delighted that your mission was successful. Only seconds before your arrival, a servant returned to inform me of the outcome and to report the scope of the injuries. It seems the Lord has protected all of you."

Anxious to be alone with Elizabeth, William did not want to encourage her to talk, so he kept his answer brief. "Yes, God was on our side it seems."

The older woman addressed Elizabeth next. "I am Mrs. Watwood, the housekeeper for Percival Manor. I prayed for your safe return, Miss Bennet, and I cannot say how very pleased I am to be able to welcome you here now. It is a blessing to know you are safe within our walls." Elizabeth smiled wanly and nodded.

Shifting his feet with the weight of her, William looked to the top of the stairs.

"I know that you will understand when I say that we are both very tired. So if you could just show—"

"Of course! Where are my manners! You both must be exhausted, so I shall delay no longer. If you will follow me, I ordered the bedroom that adjoins mine prepared for Miss Bennet." She looked directly at Elizabeth. "I intend to sit with you tonight, my dear. I would not be surprised if you suffer night terrors after all that has transpired."

Elizabeth tried to protest, "Oh, I have never suffered from—"

She patted Elizabeth's arm. "You poor thing! We will not be sure until you try to sleep, will we?"

Smiling innocently, she went towards the grand staircase, being careful to address the young maid who waited at the bottom with both her voice and a nod of her head. "Have you finished preparing the *blue* bedroom, Lois?"

Lois' eyes widened in surprise. "I ... I do not recall being—"

Mrs. Watwood cut her off. "You did find the new nightgown in the dresser, did you not?" Since the housekeeping was nodding, Lois nodded her agreement.

"Good, good! Then, bring some towels to the dressing room and then locate Mr. Lawrence. He is still upstairs, I believe. Tell him to bring up the rest of the hot water."

Lois curtseyed. "Yes, ma'am." She then hurried up the stairs to prepare the blue bedroom since it seemed that is what the housekeeper wished.

Mrs. Watwood fixed her gaze on William just in time to catch his scowl. She almost laughed. "I took the liberty of having Cook fix a tray for each of you with soup, bread, cheese and a pot of fresh tea. I thought you might want a little nourishment before you retire."

William tried his best to intervene one last time. "I intended to stay with Miss Eliz ... Miss Bennet tonight. Just to be sure that—"

"A gentleman in a lady's room? Oh no, that would never do! Besides, her bath will be ready shortly, and there is much to do before she is settled in for the night. I have plenty of hot water boiling, so you may have a bath if you wish. That should afford you some relaxation after the ordeal that you have endured."

William could not think of another argument, so he became mute as the petite woman ascended the grand staircase. A few steps up she turned to declare, "Are you coming?" At William's nod, Mrs. Watwood continued without a backward glance.

Terribly upset that their plans had been thwarted, William locked eyes with Elizabeth, and her gaze lifted his spirits. For there, shining in her ebony orbs, was the same love and desire that he felt. Somehow, knowing that she was just as disappointed made it a little easier.

Leaning in for a soft kiss, he pulled back, offered her a frustrated smile and whispered, "I wish we did not have to part like this. Another time, Elizabeth, and soon, I promise, very soon. I love you so much."

"I know. I love you just as fiercely."

Sighing heavily, William dutifully began to follow Mrs. Watwood to the second floor. After depositing Elizabeth in the room that the housekeeper designated, he walked to the door and paused for one last glimpse of her. Mrs. Watwood stopped whatever she had been saying to address him, making it clear that he must leave.

So he did, closing the door behind him as he walked woodenly down the hall. As he progressed, arms now bereft of the woman that he loved, he contemplated whether the housekeeper had any idea how much strength it took for him to walk away.

Alone with Elizabeth, Mrs. Watwood began to undo her buttons, since Lois had not returned as yet. Hearing the young woman take a ragged breath, she decided to speak.

"That young man loves you dearly."

Elizabeth blinked back tears. "Can you tell that I love him just as much?"

"Oh, yes, my dear, it is evident. I may be old, but I once experienced a love like that."

Elizabeth turned to consider her. "What happened?"

"We got married, of course! And we were in love for one and twenty years, until his death parted us."

"I ... I am sorry. I did not mean to pry."

"Nonsense! I do not mind speaking of it." She took both Elizabeth's hands and looked into her face. "Please allow this old woman to pass along a bit of wisdom I have gleaned in a lifetime."

Elizabeth nodded.

"If it is true love, it will stand the test of time. Losing yourselves in a moment of passion may seem the thing to do, but it often creates more problems than it solves. Waiting until you are husband and wife is so much more fulfilling."

Elizabeth blushed but said nothing. The point was taken.

Chapter 44

Darcy House
London
The Drawing Room
The next morning

Georgiana glanced to Lady Ashcroft, who stood to move nearer the windows and took a seat on a sofa where the sunlight would help her see with greater clarity. She knew that would be her aunt's destination when she pulled a small embroidery frame from the generous bag that always followed her from room to room. It was filled with her current projects, and Georgiana never failed to marvel at how accomplished her companion was—either knitting or embroidering whenever she sat still for longer than a moment. But it was the portable frame that her aunt seemed to employ the most, as it allowed her to embroider the smaller pieces when she was not in the music room. It was in that room that she kept her largest project, a tablecloth, in the huge standing frame. That was the endeavour she worked on whenever she had time to listen to Georgiana practice.

Now firmly ensconced on the end of the upholstered piece of furniture, Audrey had discarded her slippers, as was her custom, and wrapped her stocking feet and lap with a knit coverlet. Georgiana would have sworn, if she were asked, that her aunt was completely untroubled at that moment.

As for herself, she had been unable to rout the anxiety that threatened to overwhelm her whenever she pictured all that might have gone wrong when her brother rescued Miss Elizabeth. Were they all unharmed, as Fitzwilliam had written, or was that a ruse used to placate the child he still considered her to be until he could deliver the news himself? Was her father still alive? Was Richard or her uncle?

Now studying her aunt more closely, Georgiana realised that while her eyes were focused on the linen napkin in the frame, her mind was assuredly not, for her needle did not move with its normal alacrity. Instead, she watched as she made a few stitches before abruptly stopping to remove everyone of them. This was something she had never seen. Her aunt's stitches were always perfect! That was the exact moment when it dawned on Georgiana that she was not alone in her concern.

"Aunt?" Lady Ashcroft looked up to meet her niece's gaze as she walked towards her. "May I please read it again?"

Audrey smiled in the motherly way that she had come to treasure. "Dear girl, I do not think it has changed since the last two times you read it."

"I know," Georgiana pleaded, "but I just want to read what Brother said again."

Indulgently, Audrey pulled the missive that had been delivered only an hour before from her pocket and held it towards her niece. Georgiana rushed to take it, plopping down beside her on the sofa. She read silently, and once finished, smiled widely and handed the paper back to her aunt.

"Satisfied?"

"I shall only be satisfied when they arrive. Do you suppose they are close by? If they left as early as Brother said they might, would they not be here by now?"

"Perhaps, but they could have been slowed by the roads. You know it has rained more than once since they left to rescue Miss Elizabeth, and that means more ruts in the road. I am sure they will not press the horses under those circumstances, and it is possible that Fitzwilliam will stop often to rest them."

"Oh, I do pray they get here soon! I am too excited to practice my music or give thought to what I read. I find myself scanning the same page over again and still not remembering what it was about. I shall go mad if they do not come until late today."

Lady Ashcroft laughed. "I doubt you shall go mad, Georgiana, but—"

Just at that moment, Mrs. Barnes appeared in the doorway, and they both looked her way. "Madam, there are two visitors here to see you—Mr. Bennet and Miss Bennet."

Audrey leaned in to whisper to Georgiana, "I expected this when I sent the note to Gracechurch Street." Then she addressed Mrs. Barnes. "Thank you. Show them in, please."

She quickly replaced her slippers, and she and Georgiana stood, awaiting Elizabeth's family. As they entered the room, Audrey noted that Mr. Bennet was not limping as badly as he had previously. Therefore, after the usual greetings and after they had all been seated, she mentioned it.

"It appears that your injury has improved, sir."

Mr. Bennet nodded, offering an artificial smile. "Whenever I am able to lie down for a number of hours it improves significantly." Then his demeanour became as sombre as the first time she had met him. "Jane and I appreciate that you notified us of Lizzy's recovery. It seems that you, at least, have our interests at heart."

The slight to William did not go unnoticed, and as Georgiana gasped, Audrey reached to take her hand.

Mortified, Jane grimaced, stammering, "I am sure that no slight was intended by Mr. Darcy. I can only imagine he was greatly occupied with getting my sister safely back to London."

Mr. Bennet looked to Jane, his expression leaving no doubt that he did not agree with her view of Mr. Darcy. However, it was to him that Audrey made her point.

"Indeed, my nephew had only one thought on his mind and that was to return Miss Bennet as quickly as possible. Due to the injuries and having to leave men behind to escort the prisoners back to London, Fitzwilliam had only one servant to spare. Thus, he sent him directly here while expressing his desire that I inform you immediately, sir. He did the same for my brother's family who did not receive separate notice, either."

Sheepishly, Mr. Bennet nodded. "Forgive me if I have offended. I am deeply grateful for Mr. Darcy's successful rescue of my child. In light of the gossip circulating about him and my daughter, I have not been in the best frame of mind since coming to London. Then, after I learned that my Lizzy had been taken—"

Lady Ashcroft intervened sympathetically. "No apology is necessary. Moreover, your injury cannot have made all that has happened any easier to bear."

Georgiana relaxed with the new tone of the conversation, and when her eyes met Jane's, they exchanged smiles.

"You are too kind," Mr. Bennet pronounced. "Now, I have calculated that my daughter should be here within the hour. Is that your judgment as well?"

"Yes, and you are welcome to wait with us. My nephew has an extensive library, and I am confident you shall be able to find something of interest, if you care to read while you wait."

Not able to hide his eagerness at the prospect of an excellent library, Mr. Bennet smiled sincerely for the first time. "If it would be no bother, I should like that very much."

"No bother at all." Lady Ashcroft said. "I shall call for refreshments to be brought to the library then, and we shall all retire there to wait."

On the road to London

Just as William's aunt had foreseen, the deep ruts in the roads made the trip back to London from Teddington longer than normal. In fact, the channels were so burdensome that one of the horses on their coach had thrown a shoe, which caused yet another delay, as they had to stop and exchange that animal for another. Thus, the other two coaches, those containing Lord Landingham, Lord Matlock, Colonel Neilson, Mr. Gladstone and all the men who had not stayed behind to help Constable Carver, were most likely a half-hour ahead of them.

This state of affairs had caused William to ponder Mr. Bennet who, no doubt, would be waiting at Darcy House. What would be his reaction upon learning that Elizabeth was not among the first to return? Would her father think that he had spirited her away for, if the truth be told, the notion had crossed his mind, but William had rejected the idea, as it would only serve to further discredit Elizabeth. However, he had been selfish enough to order the driver to slow the coach even more on the last portion of their trip.

Though he had not been able to sit next to or touch the woman he loved for the entire trip, William sat across from her and had the joy of drinking in her beauty and enjoying her blushes whenever their eyes met. Though their coach was shared with Charles, who sat on the side next to Elizabeth and Richard, he barely heard a word of the gentlemen's conversation. For shortly after the trip began, Elizabeth closed her eyes as though trying to rest, and William assumed his normal role of silent observer. On the few occasions when Charles or Richard prodded for his opinion, he only murmured something vague, which seemed to satisfy, and they were on to a different subject.

Nonetheless, he was well aware that Elizabeth was not actually asleep, for occasionally, he would catch her fingering the ring under her glove or peering at him though barely opened lids. This served to stir the fire that had smouldered inside him since the carriage ride to Percival Manor last evening. It took all of his self-control to remain seated, and briefly he pondered what his friends would think if he pulled Elizabeth into his lap and kissed her soundly. Would they condemn him as a rogue, or would they think him a man hopelessly in love?

The unmistakable sound of coach wheels mounting a wooden bridge penetrated his consciousness, and William glanced out the window in time to see the extraordinarily large waterwheel that served Stretton grist mill. It was an exhilarating sight as the water was scooped up on one side and then spilled over the other, causing the wheel to revolve in an endless pattern.

"It seems Stretton Mill[21] is busy today! I do not think I have ever seen so many wagons waiting to be loaded," Richard observed.

"Stretton?" Bingley added. "That mill has been around for ages! My father talked of coming here to buy grain for the warehouse when I was but a lad. He claimed their corn meal was the finest."

With the realisation of how close that establishment was to London, William's heart sank further. His time with Elizabeth was quickly coming to an end, and the evidence brought him misery of the cruellest kind. Lost in his thoughts, he did not hear her soft inquiry.

"Are we near to London?"

Seeing that Darcy was not listening, Richard responded. "Yes. We should reach Darcy House in less than a half-hour."

Elizabeth tried to smile, though her eyes did not concur with her lips. "Thank you."

Encouraged by the fact that she was now apparently ready to talk, Charles brought up a subject that he thought Elizabeth might enjoy. "Jane and I have talked, and we are hopeful that you and Darcy will stand up with us at our wedding."

Instantly the facade of cheerfulness fell and her brows knit. As Elizabeth looked away, her answer was barely audible. "Mr. Bingley, I fear that what has transpired in Teddington, as well as the gossip that already spread in regards to me, might well ruin your special day. I would not want my presence to be a source of embarrassment or a hindrance to my sister's happiness or your own."

"I assure you, Miss Elizabeth, that nothing so unimportant will affect our happiness or our wish to share our wedding with you and Darcy. One cannot stop people from talking; one can only choose to associate with friends and family who do not rejoice in hearing the worst that can be said against us. I intend to have Darcy stand with me, and I can assure you that Jane means to have you."

William slid forward clasping both of her hands and causing her to look at him. "Listen to Charles, Elizabeth. Our true friends and family will not care and neither should we."

---

[21] *Stretton Watermill is a working historic watermill located in Stretton, Cheshire, England. For the purposes of this story I have moved it to near London. Wikipedia.org*

For a brief moment Elizabeth seemed hopeful and smiled wanly. "I would love to stand with Jane. It has always been our dream to stand up with each other when we married." Then her face crumpled as though she would cry. "It is just—how can you bear to stand with me, Fitzwilliam? My mother disparages you, and my father has not decided in your favour. And he may be less inclined to do so after what has transpired. In addition, your family will be disgraced if you marry me." She sighed raggedly. "Not to mention that most of London probably thinks me a wanton!"

Richard could not stay silent. "I must put your mind at ease at least as it pertains to our family. They are on your side already. Even my parents, the Earl and Countess Matlock, have pledged their support, and if they stand with you, no member of the *ton* will dare defy them. Please do not put much stock in what those harridans of the *ton* think. Mother says that their likes and dislikes change day-to-day as new scandals replace the old. I imagine that when word gets out that Lord Landingham is Georgiana's father it shall overshadow everything else. I know that I was shocked to hear it."

"As was I," Bingley added. "The *ton* would rather have a good scandal to talk about than a couple in love who wish to marry."

"Besides," Richard teased, "my mother can control the gossip with a crook of her little finger."

Elizabeth could not but smile a bit at Richard's antics, so William took that opportunity to cup her face, meeting her gaze without flinching.

"I can assure you, Elizabeth Bennet, that not only do I intend to stand up with Bingley, your sister and you, I intend to stand with you on our wedding day, which shall take place as quickly as I can arrange it. In fact, we shall marry before your sister and Bingley."

Charles and Richard exchanged looks of incredulity, stunned at William's plan. Nonetheless, they uttered not a word.

Elizabeth, however, had no such reticence. She sputtered, "Surely you cannot rush into another marriage! Your—Gisela has just died. Is not a period of mourning required?"

William instantly scowled. "You cannot be serious."

By the way the muscles of his jaw flexed, Richard understood that his cousin was on the brink of losing control. Thus, he interjected, "Do not get overwrought, Cousin. Miss Elizabeth is only stating what is customary in such cases."

Bingley tried to soothe him as well. "Yes, Darcy. She fears another scandal if there is no mourning period."

William turned to slowly study his cousin and then Bingley, wondering if they had gone completely mad since leaving Teddington. When next he spoke, his voice was strained but eerily calm.

"What do you suggest I mourn? Being set free from a woman I despised? While I never wished for her death, I cannot bring myself to mourn her passing. For the last two years, our ridiculous pretence of a union has provided fodder for the gossips, yet I did not yield to society's dictates. What could possibly make you think I care one whit what the *ton* will think now?"

Addressing Elizabeth again, his expression and tone softened. "I am seven and twenty, Elizabeth, and I had never been in love—until you. You are everything that I have ever desired in a woman, and I love you more than life itself. In two weeks, three at the most, everything should be settled so that we may marry. Will you consent to be my wife? Will you marry me then?"

Flabbergasted that the reticent, private man they knew would make such a tender declaration in their presence, Richard and Charles sat spellbound, unable to look away.

Elizabeth was already nodding before he finished. Unable to hold her tears, she proclaimed, "I love you too. Whenever you say, we shall marry."

William broke into a wide smile, his face beaming with her affirmation. He almost forgot himself completely, leaning in as though to kiss her but stopped when Elizabeth blushed and tilted her head towards their companions.

Disappointed, nonetheless, he recovered and posed a question. "Do you suppose Aunt Audrey and Aunt Evelyn will be able to plan a wedding and a breakfast in a few weeks, Richard?"

"A public wedding? So it is your intention to meet the *ton* head on!" Richard declared, grinning widely.

Bingley laughed out loud. "That should cause quite a stir."

"I am not ashamed." William brought both of Elizabeth's hands to his lips, kissing first one then the other. "I want all of England to know that I love this woman!"

While Elizabeth blushed crimson, Richard scratched his chin, pretending to concentrate on answering his previous question.

"I would wager a month's pay that Aunt Audrey and my mother could plan the ordination of the next monarch in less than a week, so why should a simple wedding and a breakfast be difficult? Besides, Darcy, you are wealthy and money is a great persuader. I dare say that if you offer enough incentive, you can command an abundance of flowers, food and even wedding clothes in as little time as you wish."

"What a mêlée shall ensue when word gets out!" Bingley crowed, "The *ton* will vie for invitations just to see the woman who has captured the heart of the elusive Fitzwilliam Darcy!"

"I could probably make a goodly sum selling tickets!" Richard parroted.

Elizabeth's brow furrowed at Charles' jest, and when Richard added his teasing remark, she paled.

"Do not fret, Elizabeth." William leaned forward to assure her. "The majority of those invited will be our friends and family—at least, those family members who have supported us."

As an aside, he chided Richard and Charles. "Your teasing goes too far. You frighten her."

"Forgive us, Miss Elizabeth!" Richard exclaimed. "We were trying to have fun at Darcy's expense and did not mean to scare you! I am sure that my cousin's scowls, whenever things do not progress as he wishes, will be frightening enough for you."

This made even William chuckle, and everyone else joined in. Seeing the man she loved so happy warmed Elizabeth's heart. He had laughed very little in the few short months she had known him, and the sound of it lifted her soul. She was looking at him with an expression of such love that once he noticed, his entire being transformed.

I love you, he mouthed.

I love you, she said in return.

Bingley and the colonel pretended not to see their last display of affection. After all, they had been too meddlesome already. For this reason, Richard began to speak quite loudly to Charles of other matters.

"Bingley, do you still have that red stallion that I admired when I encountered you in the park?"

Stumped as to why Richard was now talking about a horse, a nod towards the blissful couple finally caused Charles to comprehend. "As a matter of fact, I do! Are you still interested in purchasing him? A squire from Lancaster has recently written me regarding a price, but I would rather give you first choice."

They kept up a steady conversation until the coach arrived at Darcy House a quarter-hour later. Meanwhile, on the other side of the coach, William and Elizabeth communicated entirely without words.

Darcy House
The Library

For the poor souls waiting in the library at Darcy House, the atmosphere in the room had changed considerably from what it had been when they had entered. Having prepared themselves for the imminent arrival of William and Elizabeth, when that couple did not appear forthwith, it was perplexing and, for Mr. Bennet, a bit suspicious.

Consequently, where once a feeling of eager anticipation permeated the room, fear and doubt was now paramount. And though nothing untoward had been said, Lady Ashcroft could not help but wonder if, from the look on his face, Mr. Bennet might utter a sardonic criticism at any moment.

In fact, she noted that Elizabeth's father had become so uneasy that he actually laid down a book on astronomy that he had been pleased to find earlier, in order to walk over to the tall floor-to-ceiling windows that faced the road. There, he positioned himself with his hands grasped behind his back, as though fully expecting to observe the coach's return from that vantage point.

As he stood in silent vigil, Audrey's eyes happened to meet Jane's. Without uttering a word, Elizabeth's sister pleaded for understanding, and Audrey obliged, nodding almost imperceptibly and offering a faint smile. Of the Bennets she had met, this young lady seemed most like the woman her nephew loved, and that alone made Audrey predisposed to like her. While she considered this truth, her niece's voice penetrated the stillness.

"Aunt," Georgiana whined, "when do you think they shall—"

Sounds in the hallway, heavy boots and men's voices, instantly silenced her, and she stood up and turned towards the door, gasping. Suddenly, it swung open, and her father stepped into the room with Mr. Barnes close on his heels. Smiling from ear to ear, the butler seemed well pleased as he pulled the door shut and backed out.

"Father!"

Instantly, Georgiana ran towards him, crying and laughing at the same time, totally unconcerned with how unladylike she might appear. Crashing into him, it took all Landingham's strength not to stumble as he caught her. Closing his eyes against the feelings that engulfed him, he kissed the top of her head and soothed her with gentle rocking motions as she cried.

"Shhh, none of that, darling girl! All is well." Inside his heart sung—*I have my daughter at last!*

While still holding Georgiana, he opened his eyes to search the room for Audrey. Half dreading that she might have changed her mind since declaring that he would return to her, he was thankful that genuine love shone in her expression. Holding out a hand, she came forward to grasp it.

"I ... I am so thankful you are home."

It was clear that if they were alone she would have been in his arms at that moment, but having given the room a cursory glance, he knew that Elizabeth's father was present and a young woman, perhaps her sister. Therefore, fixing his gaze on the woman he loved, Landingham answered, "I thank God that, in His mercy, He has brought me home." Whispering, "To you," he was hopeful that she heard.

A loud cough from the vicinity of the windows demanded his attention, and as he focused on Thomas Bennet, he stiffened. Obviously unapologetic for interrupting, that gentleman's posture shouted of distrust. It seemed to Landingham that he was spoiling for a fight, and he began to fear what that could mean for Fitzwilliam.

"Sir, may I interrupt your *merriment* to ask the whereabouts of my daughter?"

Not one to take kindly to being spoken to in that fashion and by a visitor, no less, Landingham's ire rose. However, he felt gentle pressure as Audrey squeezed his hand and forced himself to answer civilly. "She occupies the coach with my nephews and Mr. Bingley. They should all be along presently."

"And why did that coach not arrive with yours? Surely, they left at the same time."

"They were detained when one of their horses threw a shoe. We decided not to wait, as they are close to Town, and we were transporting one of the officers who had been injured. The Earl of Matlock insisted Colonel Neilson recuperate under his roof, so they brought me here before making their way to Matlock's townhouse."

"Would that not have been justification to transfer my daughter to the coach that would arrive first? Obviously, her sister and I are frantic to ascertain her welfare."

"Having seen her, I can assure you that Miss Elizabeth is well. As for having her change coaches, I dare say there was no conspiracy to keep you apart longer than necessary. It was just never taken into account."

Mr. Bennet faced the windows again, mumbling under his breath, "Never taken into account! Humph!"

Trying to restore a modicum of gentility, Jane addressed Landingham, "Sir, I am Elizabeth's sister, Jane Bennet, and I wish to thank you for your service in affecting her release. We—all my family and I—are grateful beyond measure."

Jane's statement garnered another *humph* from Mr. Bennet, though he did not turn. Ignoring her father, she smiled wanly at the others.

Lady Ashcroft spoke up. "Forgive me for not making a proper introduction,

Miss Bennet. I was so overcome to realise that Lord Landingham had returned safely that I forgot my duties as hostess."

Simultaneously, Jane and Landingham both began to defend Audrey and ended by talking over one other. Chuckling, each bade the other to continue.

"Ladies first," Landingham said.

Jane blushed, performing a small curtsey. "I just wished to say that no introduction was necessary, Lord Landingham, as I immediately knew who you were from the descriptions in my sister's letters. Lizzy is very good at describing those she admires!"

"Thank you, Miss Bennet. I am just as fond of Miss Elizabeth, I assure you." Landingham then let his gaze fall on Audrey. "And I, too, wish to set Lady Ashcroft's mind at ease, for at a time like this, proper decorum is often overlooked, and no one thinks a thing about it."

Audrey smiled her appreciation at Marshall then proceeded to return to the sofa she had abandoned earlier. He followed her lead, escorting Georgiana and helping her to the seat next to her aunt. Then he sat down on the opposite side of his daughter.

Jane sat back down as well. Then her expression became serious. "Lord Landingham, if it is something you feel that you can share, would you tell me what transpired in Teddington? I find myself both eager and fearful to know, though I dare not ask Lizzy. I would not want to upset her by asking her to recount the ordeal."

Lord Landingham's face sobered. "I shall try to remember everything that I observed, just as it happened."

And with that, Marshall Landingham began to speak of what had taken place at Stillwater Manor. During the narration, Mr. Bennet moved from his position by the windows to stand behind Jane. By the time Landingham had reached the part describing Gisela's demise, everyone was spellbound.

"So, Mr. Darcy put himself in jeopardy to save Lizzy." It was a statement made for her father's benefit, as Jane was well aware that he blamed that gentleman for her sister's ordeal.

"Yes. I have no doubt that Fitzwilliam would have died saving her, were it necessary."

Mr. Bennet was preparing a retort, when the door flew open and in walked Richard, Charles, Miss Elizabeth and Darcy, in that order, each of them scanning the occupants of the room with trepidation. Immediately, Jane stood and hurried to Elizabeth, motivating her father to do likewise. Jane reached her first, falling into her sister's embrace. Tears, kisses and laughter were shared before Jane moved aside to let their father have his turn.

Charles waited patiently for Jane, knowing that greeting her sister took precedence. Immediately after relinquishing Lizzy, she allowed him to take her hands and pull her towards him. Subsequently, he kissed the knuckles of each of her small hands while their eyes devoured one another, both aware that a more satisfying reunion would have to wait.

Of course, Lady Ashcroft and Georgiana hurried to welcome Darcy and Richard, each in turn bestowing hugs and kisses on their loved ones. Georgiana, being already emotional, began to cry anew while simultaneously laughing with relief.

William pulled her into an embrace. "There, there, sweetling! No need to cry!" All the while he kept one eye on Elizabeth's reunion with her father.

From the relieved look on that gentlemen's face, it was obvious that he had been terrified of losing his child, and that touched William deeply, for he understood the fear of losing Elizabeth. However, once Mr. Bennet opened his eyes to see that William was watching him, his manner altered and his expression became stormy again.

Feeling his entire posture change, Elizabeth pulled back to look at her father and noted that his gaze was fixed on someone behind her. His expression, now a stone-like mask, left no doubt who it was.

"Papa, all is well. I am unharmed. And, to be truthful, I never despaired, as I knew that Fitzwilliam would move heaven and earth to find me." Mr. Bennet did not reply, so she continued, "Had it not been for him, I would likely have perished."

"If it had not been for *him*, you would never have been kidnapped in the first place!" Mr. Bennet snapped.

"You cannot know that!"

"I can and I do!" Thomas Bennet declared as he began to pull her towards the door, calling over his shoulder, "Come Jane! It is time I took you and your sister home to Longbourn. At least there I shall be able to keep you both safe."

Elizabeth pulled away from him and stepped back. "No, Papa."

The room went silent, and Richard glanced to Darcy. Noting the fierce look in his cousin's eyes, he took a step closer. Lord Landingham rose to his feet but, almost imperceptibly, Lady Ashcroft shook her head, effectively halting him.

"Georgiana, I have no doubt that your father and your cousin would love to hear the new song you learned yesterday," Audrey said amiably. Her inflection, however, implied that it was an order, not a request.

Georgiana was in a daze, nevertheless, under her aunt's firm gaze, she stuttered, "I ... I should be happy to play for Father and Cousin Richard."

Landingham held out his arm for his daughter, and they walked towards the door. Immediately, Lady Ashcroft threw a pointed look at Richard who had not decided whether to obey or stay and support his cousin.

William settled it. "I think you shall enjoy hearing her play as well, Richard."

Overruled, Richard followed sullenly after his cousin and Landingham, but not before gaining Bingley's attention and tilting his head toward William. Then scowling at Mr. Bennet, he vacated the room. Charles whispered something to Jane and let go of her hand to stand next to William as she moved to take her sister's hand. Lady Ashcroft was satisfied. Those left behind were Bennets or soon to be part of the Bennet family.

Mr. Bennet had frozen in place at Elizabeth's boldness and watched wordlessly as the number of people in the library dwindled. Astonished at Lizzy's refusal, his voice was less confident when he spoke again. "Are you defying me, Elizabeth?"

"I do not wish to defy you, but I feel that I must! I cannot go back to live with Mama or the Gardiners. They shall never forgive me for what has happened. I wish to reside here until Fitzwilliam and I can be married."

"Married? Oh, so now that his wife is dead, you think you shall just marry and all will be well! A proper mourning period must be observed, and even then, there is no guarantee that the scandal will die. In the meanwhile, you cannot just live with him. I forbid it."

William took a step towards Elizabeth, though Charles' hand on his arm kept him from going further. "We cannot account for what others will think or say, and we do not intend to live our lives trying to earn the approbation of the *ton*. We do not want to be apart longer than is absolutely necessary. We plan to marry as soon as may be."

Elizabeth's father looked as though he was about to have a fit of apoplexy, so Lady Ashcroft interrupted, "Mr. Bennet, might I make a suggestion."

He viewed her warily, fully expecting that she would champion her nephew's cause. Nevertheless, he recognised that he had few choices. Thus, he nodded.

"Miss Elizabeth is almost one and twenty, am I correct?"

Before her father could answer, Elizabeth said, "I am."

Audrey continued. "It would seem pointless to force her to return to Meryton against her will, when she can choose her own course in a few weeks. And since Elizabeth's presence would serve to remind your wife of all the unpleasantness that kindled her ... *distress*, perhaps it would be advantageous for her if Elizabeth stayed here.

"If you would be so kind as to agree, I should like to offer myself as a chaperone for your daughter until she and my nephew can be married. She may stay here at Darcy House with me and my niece, Georgiana, while my nephew removes himself to Lord Landingham's residence." She looked to William and saw that his brow was furrowing as he tried to understand her plan. "My sister, the Countess of Matlock, and I will take your daughter under our protection and see that she is well cared for, introduced to the proper people and, with your permission, take her shopping for her wedding clothes. Naturally, you shall be kept informed of everything in regards to your daughter in order to share in her happiness and also to be on hand to give the bride away once a wedding day is set."

All of Mr. Bennet's resentment seemed to deflate, and he simply looked old and defeated. Feeling remorse for refusing to give in to her father's wishes, Elizabeth stepped forward to gently touch his arm.

"Please, Papa?"

Their eyes met and his voice was gentle when he spoke. "Whether you believe me or not, I have only your best interests at heart, and I must give voice to my reservations. Mr. Darcy is rich, to be sure, and you may have more fine clothes and fine carriages than Jane. But will they make you happy?" [22]

"I am convinced that worldly goods could never make me happy. I love him, Papa. You do not know what Mr. Darcy is truly like or you would not say such things, and it pains me to hear you speak of him in that fashion."

"But you told me that when you learned he was married you hated him! That was only weeks ago. Can you trust feelings that change so hastily?"

Elizabeth gazed at William. "I was deeply hurt, and pretending that I hated him was my defence against that pain. I understand now that he never meant to deceive me. He tried valiantly not to love me or allow me to love him. His affection for me was not the work of a minute, an hour or a day, but many months

---

[22] *Some excerpts from **Pride and Prejudice**, Jane Austen, Chapter 59.*

of agony, as was mine. He is a man of remarkable character who tried nobly to keep his marriage vows, even though he had been entrapped by them."

"Well, my dear," Mr Bennet said wearily, "I have no more to say. If you are bound to have him, I shall not stand in your way."

Instantly, Elizabeth was in his arms. "Thank you, Papa! I shall write to you and tell you when we are to marry. I would not want to be wed without you there to give me away."

A tear slipped from his eye, and Thomas Bennet swiftly wiped it away. In a voice heavy with emotion, he replied, "You may count on that, my Lizzy."

Then he faced William, considering him for a moment before acknowledging defeat with a small nod. William nodded in return.

"Well!" Mr. Bennet declared a little too merrily, "Jane, if you are ready, I should like to return to Gracechurch Street and put my leg up for a few hours." Elizabeth had moved to stand next to William and was holding his hand. To her he added, "I would dearly love to see you again before I leave London."

"I should like to see you too."

William interjected, "I wish for all of Elizabeth's family to feel welcome at Darcy House."

Mr. Bennet's lips twisted into a wry smile. "Be careful what you wish for, … Son." That appellation, which came after a brief pause, marked the turning point in his relationship with Lizzy's choice. "I shall come tomorrow morning, as will Jane. I am sure you and your sister will have secrets to share before she leaves, and Mr. Darcy and I will have time to discuss other things, such as a settlement."

Then to Jane, he added, "Since you have made arrangements for your wedding clothes, perhaps Mr. Bingley will accompany us back to Meryton. His presence will mean that your mother will be able to escort the two of you around the neighbourhood, boasting of the wealth of her future son. That and her recitation of all the finery she ordered in Town should stir up a good deal of interest. Perhaps it might even keep her occupied until your wedding, if I am fortunate."

Even with Mr. Bennet's sketch of his wife's plans for him, Charles seemed delighted at the prospect, and he grinned from ear to ear. "I will be pleased to return to Netherfield, and I should like to return to Gracechurch Street with you now." Addressing William, he added, "All of this has been quite an adventure, Darcy, but one that I do not care to repeat anytime in the near future."

Everyone smiled at Bingley's pronouncement, which delighted him, as he had hoped to lighten the mood of those assembled. He then proceeded to hold his arm out to Jane. As she laid her small hand thereon and beamed up at him, he asked, "Shall we?"

Chapter *45*

Matlock House
Three weeks later

Three weeks after the confrontation with Mr. Bennet at Darcy House, the stately townhouse of the Earl and Countess Matlock was the setting for the marriage of Fitzwilliam Darcy and Elizabeth Bennet. The epitome of everything well-mannered society admired, it was the consensus of those members of the *ton* who had been fortunate enough to receive an invitation that there was more silver candelabrum, more crystal vases of exotic flowers and more servants on duty than anyone had beheld since they had attended one of the royal soirées. None were surprised, however, for after all, the countess had made it plain that no expense would be spared for the wedding of her favourite nephew.

The ballroom had been transformed into a chapel and was replete with white tulle strategically draped from the corners of the room to connect with several tall, arched, white columns which created an aisle down the middle. On either side, chairs had been placed for the convenience of the guests. Had one not seen the room beforehand, one could easily have imagined that they had entered a church, so complete was the alteration. The centre walkway led to an impressive white trellis completely covered in white roses and greenery. It was at this altar that the couple took their vows before the Bishop of London, Rt. Hon, William Howley[23], the earl's cousin. Richard and Charles had stood with William, while Jane and Georgiana attended Elizabeth.

When the ceremony concluded, the couple, the bishop and their witnesses retreated to a room nearby in order to sign the register, causing those left in the ballroom to begin to mingle. It was at this point that a sudden sense of triumph filled Audrey Ashcroft, rendering her as near to succumbing to her emotions as she had ever been.

"Was not the ceremony lovely?" Audrey asked Marshall, her blue eyes filling with tears as her voice broke. "I do not think it could have been any more beautiful." She glanced towards the door through which the wedding party had disappeared. "I cannot wait to congratulate them."

---

[23] *I appropriated this name from a list of bishops in 1815 for this story. Bishop of London, Rt. Hon, William Howley. Official trustee of the British Museum. Dean of Chapel Royal, Visitor of Sion College. Provincial Dean of Canterbury. Income exceeded £15,000. From Nancy Mayer Regency Researcher,*
www.regencyresearcher.com/pages/bishops.html

Landingham smiled lovingly. "It was, my dear. Now remember, you promised not to cry again. You should be happy. Smile!"

William's aunt sniffed. "I am happy! I cry when I am happy, you know that."

"I know that very well, but I do not want your eyes to be red and puffy. It has not escaped my notice that since you began planning this wedding you look even more youthful. When I entered the ballroom, I almost mistook you for the bride."

Audrey blushed. "You were always one to flatter, Marshall."

"I am not teasing." He added quietly, "In fact, right before Elizabeth appeared with her father, I was debating taking your hand and escorting you to the altar!"

"With no special license? I think not."

"Are you sure of that?" Landingham teased. "Do you remember when I asked you to move our wedding date closer, and you said that you could not marry until after Fitzwilliam and Elizabeth were settled?" She nodded. "Well, to be honest, I had already obtained a special license beforehand. It has resided here," he patted his coat, "ever since, in the small chance that you might change your mind."

Her expression sobered. "I did not know. Were you terribly disheartened by my answer?"

"Heartbroken," he confessed in all honestly before managing a small smile. "But, do not fret. It shall still be valid when we marry in September."

"Then, we could marry sooner if we wished?" she teased, half considering the idea.

"We can marry whenever you decide. My affections and wishes are unchanged, but one word from you on the subject will silence me forever." His grin widened. "Well, perhaps not forever! I do wish to marry before the end of the year!"[24]

Audrey smiled at the man she loved. "That is one of the virtues I admire most in you. You are not only steadfast; you are unafraid to say what you want."

Landingham slid his hand slowly down the exposed skin of her forearm to her hand, entwining his fingers with hers as their eyes locked. "And in case I have not made it clear, what I want is you as my lover and my wife."

A few feet away from William's aunt and godfather stood some of the patrons of Almacks.[25] Since Amelia Stewart's late mother was a good friend of the Countess of Matlock, she had had little trouble gaining an invitation for herself and her fellow patrons. After all, who were more capable of taking the measure of the woman who had not only stolen Fitzwilliam Darcy's heart but gained Evelyn Fitzwilliam's unwavering support than she and her associates? Moreover, now

---

[24] *Pride and Prejudice*, Jane Austen, Chapter 58.

[25] *Almacks. From the time it opened as exclusive assembly rooms in 1765, it was governed by an elite group of Lady Patronesses who determined who was permitted entrance and who was not. Patronesses came and went over the years, but always wielded social influence that bordered on despotism.*
http://en.wikipedia.org/wiki/Almack's

that they had been witness to the exchange between Lord Landingham and Lady Ashcroft, they had even more *information* to consider. Accordingly, when Lady Ashcroft's colour rose with Landingham's confession, the patrons' eyes met, and they nodded at one another meaningfully.

"Well!" Amelia Stewart, Viscountess Castlereagh, said shrewdly, "It appears we will soon be attending another Matlock wedding."

"Now I understand why Lord Landingham never saw fit to respond to any of our invitations. It is a pity, as he dances divinely," Maria Molyneux, Countess of Sefton, maintained. "However, it seems that his heart was already engaged!"

"I, for one, think he could have chosen more wisely," Sarah Villiers, Countess of Jersey, chided. Her opinion came as no surprise to the others, as they were aware that she had tried to solicit Landingham as a lover without success. "After all, he need not marry again to enjoy a woman's *company* and a *much* younger one, at that."

Countess Esterházy, ever the romantic, sighed. "I think it is marvellous that he pursued a woman nearer his age. It is obvious that he is in love with her!"

"Humph!" Lady Jersey declared. "Love does not exist in a man's vocabulary! Lust perhaps, but never love!"

"I beg to disagree!" the viscountess interjected. "Otherwise, how do you explain what we witnessed today? One of the most eligible men in the country has married a woman with no connections and little dowry. And while I found her pretty enough, Elizabeth Bennet is nothing like the woman I imagined Fitzwilliam Darcy would choose for a wife. One would not call her beautiful and certainly not on the same level as Gisela at that age."

Lady Sefton volunteered, "I met Gisela Darcy twice. First, when Lord Grantham had just died and she was cavorting with the young bucks of the *ton*, which made me pity Mr. Darcy all the more when she ensnared him. The last occasion was a few months ago. I did not recognise her, as her appearance had degenerated   so   severely.

"And now that he had a chance to start again, would you not assume that he would choose someone more suitable? After all, despite the scandal, he could have had his pick of the ladies—beautiful women with excellent connections and magnificent dowries. That is why I sat spellbound throughout the ceremony. It was only at the end that I truly understood!"

"And what did you conclude, pray tell?" Lady Jersey demanded sarcastically.

"That when a man is truly in love, all else is irrelevant! And I have no doubt that Fitzwilliam Darcy is in love with that woman. I saw his face transform when the bishop pronounced them man and wife. Her back was to us, but I could clearly see his face, and his expression became almost—I can only describe it as ethereal. He looked like an entirely different person!"

"I agree. I saw the transformation too. He is certainly besotted!" Countess Esterházy said. Then taking a deep breath and letting it go, she added, "How very romantic!"

"Mr. Darcy is very handsome!" Lady Sefton declared. "I know that *I* would not shirk my marital duties if he were my husband."

Everyone giggled except for the Lady Jersey, who exclaimed, "Bah! His expression was likely the result of a sour stomach. Nothing more!"

The others laughed all the harder. They knew that when the Countess of Jersey was not in the mood to agree, no amount of cajoling would convince her. Besides, she knew the truth just as they did.

◞✤◟

Inside the Drawing Room

It was with great pleasure that Bishop Howley observed Fitzwilliam Darcy and his bride signing the register. At the age of eight and fifty, he had presided over his share of arranged marriages where it was obvious that neither party felt any affection for the other. In fact, he believed that if he never officiated over another *merger* of two families, he would have no cause to repine. Clearly, however, this wedding was different—a true melding of hearts. The joy of it refreshed his soul.

In addition, the look on the groom's face as he watched his bride sign the book almost caused him to laugh aloud. It was clear that the groom feared that something might go wrong at the last minute and, as it would not do for a bishop to be irreverent at such a dignified juncture, he bit his lower lip. Afterward, when Elizabeth looked up to him after she had signed, he managed a broad smile for the lovely bride.

"Wonderful, wonderful!" he exclaimed, motioning for their attendants to come forward. "Now, if the witnesses will sign, we shall make this wedding official!" William's look of surprise at his jovial manner was amusing so he continued, "Or I should say *more* official!"

Richard stepped up to sign the book. "I should think that having a member of His Majesty's Army as a witness should suffice, rendering all other signatures unnecessary."

"*Richard*," William warned playfully. "You are too clever at times. Just sign the book, please."

"I am NOT too clever, Cousin!" Richard retorted. "Just ask my father, or better still, ask Edgar!" That brought a round of guffaws, and even the bishop could not restrain himself.

When the signing was done, Bishop Howley picked up the book to examine it before tucking it under his arm and heading towards the door. "I shall immediately put this register with my personal possessions so it does not get lost."

He glanced back over his shoulder to see that his teasing had gone unnoticed by William and Elizabeth. The newlyweds were holding hands and staring into each other's eyes, completely oblivious to the other occupants of the room, so he addressed the witnesses while gesturing towards William and Elizabeth with a tilt of his head. "I cannot wait to sample the repast that the countess has prepared. I understand that there is food enough for all of London. Would anyone care to join me?"

Taking the hint, Jane, Georgiana, Richard and Charles exchanged amused glances and followed the bishop from the room.

William and Elizabeth did not notice their departure.

◞✤◟

Though both William's aunts had their say regarding her wedding gown, the final decision had been left to Elizabeth, and she had settled on a simple empire style. It featured a white satin slip, cut low and square at the bust and covered with an overlay of English net. The net was embroidered with delicate vines and roses, the roses fashioned with white silk ribbons. The puffed sleeves were entirely net and trimmed on the edge with Belgium lace, and a deep flounce of the same lace graced the hem. Above the lace hem were four white satin pipings, fashioned in waves, and interspersed with satin roses in pale pink and white. White spotted silk slippers with identical satin roses peeked from beneath the hem.

Her dark hair was piled upon her head, except for four long ringlets left to hang in the back. A sprig of pale pink roses was placed at the back of her head, just above the ringlets. Lastly, she wore a pearl necklace with pearl and diamond earrings that William had given her as a wedding present. In truth, at first sight of her that morning, William had thought her the most beautiful creature he had ever seen.

Lost in examining every nuance of Elizabeth's face, hair and gown, William was oblivious to the fact that they were alone until a sudden noise in the hall caught his attention, and he glanced in that direction to find that they had been deserted. He was delighted. They had had little time alone since Elizabeth had moved into Darcy House, and he had gone to live with his godfather. In fact, had the wedding not been this very day, he could not say with certainty that he would not have scaled the walls to her bedroom that night. The thought kindled a fire deep inside.

As Elizabeth watched his every move, the look in her eyes changed from curiosity to amusement, and William could not help but smile as well. "What amuses you?"

"If I have correctly discerned that gleam in your eye, it seems you may wish to forego the breakfast, but if we were to do that, your aunt would surely send out a search party to find us."

He chuckled though his eyes darkened with desire. "Had I a choice, I would steal you away to Darcy House this very moment!"

"What a scandal that would create!" she teased. "Dare we risk another?"

He pulled her tight against his body, moving his hips in such a way that she felt the evidence of his desire. "You know how little importance I place on such things, Elizabeth. Say the word and we shall disappear."

"The desire to throw caution to the wind is very tempting, Fitzwilliam, but you know we cannot. We owe your family so much. We must stay and greet our guests."

"My mind concurs, but my heart does not. I do apologise, though, that our wedding has been inundated with so many guests I did not wish to suffer today, of all days. I promised that it would be mainly our family in attendance, not the *ton*."

"Aunt Evelyn has apologised to me already, and I am not upset. I know that she is only doing what she feels is best for us and for Georgiana's future. And though you and I do not care to perform to strangers, we can make the effort for my sister's sake."

"Your selflessness is only one reason I love you so much."

William captured her mouth in a searing kiss, and it was some time before he remembered that there were things he wished to say to her before they faced the *ton.* He leaned his forehead against hers in a bid to gain control. "I have not yet had an opportunity to tell you how beautiful you are today."

Her face radiated happiness as she pulled back to look up at him.

"I am happy that you are pleased," Elizabeth answered. "I have never had the opportunity to commission such a lovely gown."

"The gown is lovely, but I speak of you. *You* are beautiful, Elizabeth."

She dropped her head, but immediately, William framed her face with his hands and brought her gaze back to his. "You are the most beautiful woman I have ever known. Now, in the future, whenever I say that you are beautiful, I want only to hear you say 'thank you.'" He grinned. "But you may add 'my darling husband,' if the notion strikes you."

"Thank you, my darling husband."

"You are most welcome, my beloved wife."

Raising her hand to study the ring that he had placed there only minutes before, William tenderly fingered the wide gold band inset with emeralds and diamonds in a floral pattern.

"This was my mother's and my grandmother's before her, but if you wish for something entirely your own, you have only to say. I confess that I did not have time to consult with you before I chose it. You may have another ring designed or there may be others in the Darcy collection that you prefer to this."

"I do not wish for another, Fitzwilliam. It is lovely and it means so much more because it was your mother's and your grandmother's. I feel a part of the Darcy legacy because it fits my finger perfectly."

William pulled her into his embrace, his eyes closing as all the emotions of the last few months washed over him. When he was much younger, he had dreamt of being married to someone he adored, but Gisela had cruelly crushed that dream. And by the time he met Elizabeth in Meryton, he had given up hope.

Yet the answer to his prayers was now in his arms—his wife! It was a miracle! He buried his face in her hair, moaning softly, "My wife, my precious wife."

Threading his fingers through her ringlets, he gripped them and pulled her head back to look into her face. He captured her lips fiercely, and for a brief moment, he wondered how she would be able to appear in public after he was done with her hair. Nonetheless, lost in the feel of her body and her mouth, in only seconds, he no longer cared.

William slid his hands down to cup her bottom and pull her hard against his hips. As Elizabeth strained to melt into him, a small sigh-like whimper escaped, causing him to study her. She looked magnificent with her eyes closed and her lips open, waiting for him to resume their kiss. And for a split second, he almost began anew. Only a knock at the door caused him to pause. Sighing, he took a step back.

"Do not forget where we were, sweetheart."

Instantly, his waistcoat was straightened, and he cracked open the door. At once Aunt Audrey entered, closing the door behind her.

"Fitzwilliam, you and Elizabeth *must* appear at the wedding breakfast." She smiled understandingly. "You need not stay for the entirety, but you do need to greet those assembled. Evelyn has gone to a tremendous amount of trouble putting this together. It is the least you can do."

William nodded. Then taking a deep breath, he responded. "We appreciate her efforts as well as your own. We shall be there shortly."

She patted his cheek. "I knew you would."

With a quick smile directed at Elizabeth, she was gone. Rushing back to his wife, William looked so much like a child that had a piece of candy taken from him that Elizabeth wanted to laugh.

"Fitzwilliam, do not pout!" she teased. "It will not be so horrid, and we do not have to stay long. Aunt Audrey said we may leave early."

"That is easy for her to say. She will not be the one that every *so-called* gentleman wants to salute just so he can murmur something bawdy regarding our wedding night."

Elizabeth looked taken aback. "Do they really say such things?"

"Those who are dissolute take every opportunity to goad those who are not. There have been times that it took all of my will not to react when they teased me at the club."

"It makes me proud that they recognise that you are different."

William smiled mischievously. "If it makes you proud, I shall gladly suffer their barbs."

She pushed at his chest jovially. "But since we shall have the next few days entirely alone at Darcy House, you may quickly tire of my company and wish you had spent more time listening to their taunts."

William gathered her hands and kissed them, desire written on his face. "You shall soon learn that it is the other way around, my love. Now, come, let us see if we can repair your hair. It seems I have disturbed some of the pins."

"I shall fix it. Just help me locate them."

It took longer than promised for the happy couple to finally appear in the dining room. They received polite applause as they entered and took their places at the table reserved for the family.

As they were seated, Jane looked across the table at her father, smiling as he rolled his eyes. Just moments before, he had joked about the inordinate amount of time that signing the register must take, causing their entire table to chuckle.

Jane had been anxious at first, since they were the only Bennets in attendance, but the Earl and Countess of Matlock had been very welcoming, and she was beginning to relax. Her mother and younger sisters were not in attendance, since they did not have Lizzy's best interests at heart, and neither were the Gardiners, as they were part and parcel of every scheme her mother had ever devised for marrying off her sister.

Reflecting on her new brother, Jane looked towards the newly wedded couple, who were sharing a private word.

You have found your knight in shining armour, Lizzy, just as I have found mine in Charles!

The Earl of Matlock laid a hand on Richard's arm and nodded towards the hallway. As they slipped away from the table and vacated the room, Richard warned quietly, "We had best hurry. Mother will be unhappy when she notices we are missing."

"This will not take long, and since you have been away on duty, I have not had the chance to impart the latest news."

Quickly entering a small parlour, Lord Matlock closed the door soundly before beginning. "I have heard from the magistrate, and he has ordered Catherine to be transported to Bedlam. She will never again harm our family, or anyone else, as long as she lives." He rubbed his face with his hands wearily. "I did not want to mention this in front of Fitzwilliam, today of all days, so he is unaware. I need for you to arrange a military escort to the facility from the local jail."

"She is in jail?"

"Yes. It seems that lately she has spewed such venom and hatred against the entire family that your mother has been fearful of having her close at hand, especially as the wedding neared. Although I had her locked in the liveryman's cottage, I had to remove her a week ago."

"I would say she is fortunate to be confined in Bedlam after having Mr. Lowell murdered."

"Yes, I could not imagine her capable of murder, though from all that Edgar found among her papers, I learned much more. She had paid George Wickham to spy on George and Anne since he was a boy! Not to mention that she had the other pages of Anne's letters, plus years' worth of correspondence stolen from Pemberley. And there was proof that she funded Gisela's schemes against Fitzwilliam as well as Wickham's stay in Ramsgate."

"How could anyone do that to our family?" When his father started to answer, Richard held up his hand in protest. "I am beginning to see what you meant about Bedlam being appropriate. And what of the money Darcy was cheated of in the joint venture?"

"My solicitor is determining the exact amount, which will be returned to him. By the time you take over Rosings, Mr. Godbee will likely have traced all the wrongdoings."

"What will happen to Mr. Ferguson? After all, he colluded with my aunt to fool Darcy."

"That has not been decided. There is no proof that he was involved with Mr. Lowell's death, though he did compile false financial records. We did make some promises for his cooperation, so I think the barrister is waiting until he talks with your cousin to try the case."

"Darcy is too kind. I do not think his decision regarding Mrs. Younge was stringent enough."

"I agree, but knowing that she was the only support of her mother and sister, he was determined to show mercy. She and her relations will be relocated to Dublin. As you know, Fitzwilliam has a small estate there. He intends to set up a portraiture business next to the widows and orphans home that he built. All three women will be required to live there and assist however needed. In addition, Mrs. Younge will continue to paint as well as instruct the children in painting. Any income from the sale of her works will support the entire enterprise."

"I suppose that will at least aid the less fortunate of Dublin as well as keep her relations from being thrown into poverty. By the by, I have given my commander notice, and my resignation shall be final month after next."

"Excellent."

Richard's expression became mischievous. "Not to change the subject, but my brother and the viscountess looked almost human today. I even saw Frances smile at Mrs. Darcy."

Lord Matlock laughed in spite of himself. "Yes, well, your mother had a little talk with them, so I imagine they are on their best behaviour. And now that Rosings is to be yours and Audrey has decided that Alicia will inherit Ashcroft Park, perhaps Frances will not be so conceited. After all, she is not so far above you now."

"Conceited?" Richard guffawed. "I would never have thought you would admit as much."

"There are quite a number of things I would not admit before the ordeal with Miss Bennet. Like Colonel Neilson, for instance. Has Alicia told you that I have given my permission for a courtship?"

Richard smiled, trying not to look too pleased. "Yes. You will not be sorry. He is a good man."

"I learned a great deal in the past few weeks. I hope I am a better man for it."

Suddenly the parlour door opened and Evelyn Fitzwilliam peeked inside, her face a mask of concern. "Edward, there is a time and a place for everything, but today should be for celebrating our family!"

"Yes, dear."

As she closed the door, he looked sheepishly at his son. "Never argue with your wife when she is upset, Son. It will do you more harm than good."

"I shall try to remember that, Father."

With arms around each other's shoulders, they headed back to the dining room.

Darcy House
A little later

The day was as sunny and beautiful as anyone could remember for the middle of July in London. It fact, the morning temperature had been so pleasantly mild that many of the residents of Grosvenor Square had decided it would be a good day for a walk about Hyde Park. Consequently, when the carriage transporting William and Elizabeth stopped in front of Darcy House, a goodly number of these same residents were returning to their homes.

Several of William's neighbours were on the walk in front of Darcy House, and they all halted at the sight of the Darcy Crest, eager to see who was inside. With the window shades drawn, there was no way of knowing the identity of the inhabitants until they emerged. Even the least important members of the *ton* had heard of the wedding and were eager for a glimpse of the couple.

"Fitzwilliam, have you ever known such a crowd to stop in front of the house before?" Elizabeth queried, after the footman had opened the door.

"No, but today I am happy for it, as I wish to make a statement." With those words, he hurried out of the carriage and leaned back in to help her down. "Watch your step, darling."

Just as soon as both her feet were on the ground, he swept Elizabeth into his arms. It took all her willpower not to cry out, as he had caught her unawares. He swirled her around in a circle before starting up the steps as though she were light as a feather. At the top, Mr. Barnes opened the door. He was smiling ear-to-ear.

Looking back over William's shoulder, it was evident that the crowd was not going to disperse. Elizabeth became self-conscious, burying her head in his neck. "Fitzwilliam, we still have an audience."

"Good," he responded as they reached the portico. "It is as I hoped." Then turning so that everyone below had a clear view, he captured her lips in a solid kiss. It was not a fleeting demonstration, but continued for some time as the hum of the chatter on the walk below grew even louder.

Once he was satisfied, he ended the kiss to smile lovingly and proclaim, "Welcome home, Mrs. Darcy!"

His declaration was easily discerned by those watching and, with that, he carried her over the threshold. The sound of the door closing behind them reminded Elizabeth to breathe again.

Chapter 46

Matlock House
After the Wedding

The garden at Matlock House was renowned for its beauty—from the layout of the flowers, trees and shrubs, to the artistry of the statuary and fountains that accented them. In fact, there were few more attractive landscapes in London located on such limited acreage. However, today the beauty of the gardens paled in caparison to the woman standing before Marshall Landingham. He had meant every word he said to Audrey that morning. She looked so lovely that she could have been mistaken for the bride. Enchanted by her loveliness, he almost did not hear what she was saying.

"… So I told Edward that we would likely marry in August, after Georgiana returns to Pemberley. Of course, I would want a very private affair, held in Derbyshire, so that the children could attend."

What was that? Marry in August?

"Wait! What did you just say? Please repeat it!"

Smiling, Audrey restated what she had just said. When she was finished, Landingham laughed out loud and cradled her face in his hands. "Next month you will be mine, truly?"

Seeing the eagerness in his eyes, Audrey Ashcroft nodded. "Yes, I see no reason we cannot be married some time after the fifteenth of August, when Georgiana will return to Pemberley to be with Fitzwilliam and Elizabeth. After all, I shall be totally without occupation then. With Elizabeth in the family, Georgiana will not need a companion. Perhaps, if Fitzwilliam does not mind, I shall occasionally take her under my wing and escort her to Brighton or Bath or even London. But, I know that I shall most likely see her at irregular intervals and that will take some getting used to on my part."

He patted her hand sympathetically. "And on Georgiana's, I am sure."

She smiled bravely. "But that is how it should be, and I have no regrets. Life is about changes, and when they come, we simply must adjust. I am just so pleased that the children have found the perfect wife and a sister in Elizabeth. She will be good for the both of them!"

"I agree. Elizabeth is a godsend." Landingham looked as though he was going to say more.

"Marshall, is there something else?"

"I … I have thought a lot about Georgiana since she learned that I am her father. I would dearly love to spend more time with her before some young buck comes to claim her hand. I hoped to propose something to my godson that would make that possible, though I know he is fiercely protective of my daughter and rightly so."

"And what would you propose?"

"I wish to ask him if, after we marry, he would allow Georgiana to live with us for six months of the year. I would suggest every other month, if that would be agreeable to him. After all, my estate is next to Pemberley, and we both have homes in Town, so it is not as though she would be very far away. In so doing, I pray that she and I will have a chance to strengthen our bond and, as a result, that would give Fitzwilliam and Elizabeth a bit more privacy as they begin their married life. It would depend on both Fitzwilliam and Georgiana agreeing, though, as I would never want to impose my will on either of them."

"I think that is a wonderful idea. Georgiana has expressed an eagerness to know you better. And I agree that it would give Fitzwilliam and Elizabeth time to establish their relationship."

Landingham pulled her into his arms. "Do you know how wonderful it is to find someone so well-suited to me? And most especially, one who knows my faults but loves me still?"

"Yes, I do, for I have found the same in you."

Losing the struggle to control his emotions, Marshall glanced towards the imposing windows of the house. He knew that it was possible that the earl was standing behind them, and knowing that Edward might not take kindly to seeing his sister thoroughly kissed in the garden, he swiftly began to lead Audrey down the path towards the more secluded section.

Reaching the vine-covered gazebo, he had barely pulled her inside when he captured her mouth hungrily. The kiss was thoroughly enjoyed by both, until a deep male voice sounded.

"I think it would be to your advantage to find another location, Landingham. This one is already taken!"

Startled, he jumped back, promptly scanning the surrounding landscape and only honing in on the interlopers after his hostess waved. The earl and countess, half-hidden by foliage, were sitting on a stone bench under a large willow tree not thirty feet away. Their expressions were such that it was obvious that both were greatly amused at his discomposure. Flustered, Marshall was searching his brain for a credible reply, when the countess spoke.

"Never mind, Marshall, Edward and I were just leaving. Carry on!"

The sounds of laughter wafted through the trees as the earl and countess made their way back to the house. Audrey, who appeared totally unperturbed at their detection, noted the perplexed expression still on Landingham's face and smiled sympathetically.

"Do not be so shocked, Marshall. I think we are all of an age to appreciate that we should not postpone any happiness we may find. My brother spoke to me of our plans directly after the breakfast. It is he who convinced me that if you were the man I loved, I should not wait any longer to marry."

Landingham's posture relaxed as his face lit up. "He did? Remarkable! Then I owe him a debt of gratitude." He pulled Audrey back into his embrace. "However, I shall thank him later ... much later. Now where was I when we were so rudely interrupted?"

He had no trouble remembering.

Darcy House

The first thing that Elizabeth noticed when William set her on her feet in the foyer was that the house seemed bereft of servants, the only ones visible being Mr. and Mrs. Barnes, who eagerly stepped forward to greet her with unrestrained joy written on their faces.

"Welcome back, Mr. and *Mrs.* Darcy!" They parroted one another.

Elizabeth blushed with the use of her new title, nodding shyly while William acknowledged their greeting warmly. "It is good to be home again. Landingham's home is perfectly adequate, but it does not compare to Darcy House or to my capable staff. By the way, Mrs. Barnes, were you able to accomplish all that I asked?"

While William was speaking, the housekeeper took note that Elizabeth looked about with a perplexed expression. "Per your wishes, most of the servants are on holiday. Only those attending you and Mrs. Darcy will be allowed above the first floor until you leave for Pemberley. Those remaining have been instructed to do their jobs swiftly and without notice as far as possible. To that end, beginning tomorrow, if you ring for us from your dressing room, we will assume that you wish for a bath to be prepared. If you ring from the sitting room, it will signify that you wish for meals to be brought up instead of coming down to dine. A subsequent ring from either room will signify that the room is ready to be cleared."

Suddenly, she remembered something significant. "Oh, and lest I forget, the new copper bathtub was delivered two days ago and was installed in your dressing room."

William could not hold back a huge grin at the news. "Excellent."

"It certainly is … *large*," Mr. Barnes offered, a restrained smile the only indication that he might be teasing. His wife stepped on his toe in retaliation.

Fortunately, neither of the young couple noticed. When making his plans, William had never doubted that the servants would be curious as to why there was only to be one bath drawn each day.

Elizabeth's curiosity, however, was another matter entirely. After listening to his discussion with Mrs. Barnes, she had turned to regard him with her head tilted, one eyebrow raised in the inquisitive manner that he had come to adore.

"Let me clarify for you, my dear. Since I did not have time to whisk you away on a wedding trip, I wanted our stay here to be as private as possible. Therefore, I asked that only those servants necessary for our convenience be on duty. After tonight, I shall have no valet and you shall have no ladies maid unless we summon them. In fact, it is my hope that it shall seem that we are the only two people in London, if not the entire world."

Elizabeth could not help but flush again with the implications and was reluctant to meet the eyes of Mr. or Mrs. Barnes, so she sought to examine her shoes. Seeing her discomfiture, William swept her off her feet.

"Fitzwilliam!" she exclaimed, giggling despite her best efforts, "How am I to act the dignified mistress of Darcy House. You have already carried me over the threshold!"

"I am well aware of that, Mrs. Darcy," he retorted cheekily, "but I know of no rule that says I cannot carry you up the stairs as well." With his wife in his arms, William turned to address the servants. "We shall dine downstairs tonight. Please notify me when dinner is ready."

Without another word, William scaled the staircase effortlessly, and while the housekeeper and butler watched them ascend, in only seconds the Darcys disappeared at the top of the stairs.

"Well, Matilda," Mr. Barnes offered, staring at an empty landing, "I suggest we go see what Cook is preparing for their first dinner as man and wife."

Mrs. Barnes, who had lifted her apron to dry some happy tears, was now smoothing it back down. "Oh, Maxwell, were we ever that much in love?"

Putting his arm around his wife's shoulders, the butler leaned in to give her a peck on the cheek. "We still are, Lovey!"

"Indeed we are!" she declared and patted his cheek in return. It had been a long time since he had used that endearment. Then she sighed. "I am so proud that our dear boy has found a good woman to love him. I spent many a night praying over his situation. It is such a relief to know that the Lord has finally answered my prayers."

"He answered a lot of people's prayers, Matilda." With that the butler took his wife's hand. "Come. We do not have any time to dawdle. I imagine our dear boy will want to eat quickly and get an early start on tonight."

"Maxwell!"

"Well, it is the truth!"

They walked towards the kitchen, chuckling and talking about how the entire atmosphere of the house had changed now that the Master had found the one woman who truly completed him.

A sitting room
Later that evening

When they were reunited in her sitting room later that day, it was not far from Elizabeth's mind that she and William had shared a similar evening at Darcy House only weeks before. On that occasion, the uncertainty of when they might meet again had caused Elizabeth great anxiety, but tonight she had a different kind of apprehension.

Just as before, both were well turned-out—William, dashingly handsome in a dark blue suit with matching breeches, dark gold waistcoat, white shirt and cravat, while she wore a celestial blue crape[26] frock over a white satin slip, ornamented around the bottom with a deep border of tulle lace, embroidered with shades of dark blue silks and chenille. The gown was trimmed around the bodice and sleeves with the same embroidered lace.

---

[26] *A transparent crimped silk gauze. The Regency Encyclopedia.*

During the weeks leading to the wedding, Lady Ashcroft had insisted on ordering several gowns for Elizabeth from her personal modiste, though she specified that only three must be completed before the wedding, this being one of those. At the time, Elizabeth had protested that her current wardrobe was sufficient, but William's aunt had been adamant. And tonight, seeing the look of admiration on her husband's face, she was glad that Lady Ashcroft had carried the argument.

After thoroughly inspecting her gown, William's eyes were drawn to her face and hair. The maid had swept up the sides, incorporating them into several thick braids which she entwined with blue ribbons. She then fashioned the braids into a stylish top knot, leaving the back to hang in loose ringlets. From the look in his eyes, it was obvious that her husband was pleased.

"Elizabeth, you look very beautiful."

Elizabeth blushed. Nonetheless, she had learned her lesson well. "Thank you, my darling husband."

William laughed. "I hope I have as much luck with my future requests, Mrs. Darcy."

"You may or may not," she teased. "It shall depend on whether I think them worthy of agreement."

He bowed, making a sweeping gesture with his arm. "I concur with your reasoning, my love." Then, tilting his head towards the door, he held out his arm. "Shall we?"

⌒⌇⌒

The dining room

Both Fitzwilliam and Elizabeth had tasted enough of the dinner to know that it was excellent. After all, Cook had gone to the trouble of creating a memorable meal—turtle soup, a salad of fresh greens and ripe pears with roasted and sugared nuts, a prime cut of beef with potatoes, onions and carrots and William's favorite dessert, pound cake with pineapple-rum sauce. Upon proclaiming the pineapple sauce superb, Elizabeth was told that Pemberley not only boasted a conservatory but also a pinery—a special hot house for growing pineapples.

"I am amazed at all I do not know about Pemberley, Fitzwilliam. Your home must be a magical place."

His expression became solemn as he reached across the table to take her hand and give it a squeeze. "It is *our* home. And it will be magical now that you are its mistress. I cannot wait to acquaint you with all that I admire about it."

Despite the excellent food, neither party seemed to have much of an appetite. In fact, Elizabeth scarcely ate at all, and by the time the last course was served, she had begun to glance surreptitiously at the clock on the mantel. Wishing to ease her mind, William asked that a bottle of his best wine be brought to the library while he escorted her in that direction.

Once again alone with his wife, William popped the cork on the chilled Constantia[27] and poured a glass for Elizabeth. "I have waited to share this with

---

[27] *Constantia Wine comes from the beautiful Constantia Valley in South Africa's*

you, Elizabeth."

She gave her husband an angelic smile as he offered her the glass. She swirled the liquor, raised it to smell the aroma and then started to take a sip.

"Please wait. I wish to make a toast."

Pouring himself a drink, he sat next to her on a small settee. Elizabeth seemed mesmerised as he touched her glass with his.

"To the woman I shall love for all eternity. It was your love, Elizabeth, that made me whole again. I adore you."

Overwhelmed by emotion, they each sipped the sweet vintage. Then regaining composure, she touched his glass, declaring tenderly, "To the man I shall love and cherish until I die."

As they drank to her toast, their eyes locked over the rims of the glasses and William's grew shiny with tears. Blinking, he set his glass on a nearby table and took the one from Elizabeth, placing it next to his. He stood and pulled her to her feet, capturing her face in his hands. He kissed her as tenderly as possible, his lips moving over hers as gently as butterflies' wings, before showering similar soft kisses over the rest of her face. Content for the moment, he quit the kisses to hold her tightly, letting his fingers caress her back in slow, circular motions and causing her to press more intimately against his body. Her deep sighs filled the silence until at length he whispered his deepest thoughts.

"Words are inadequate to convey the joy that fills me, Elizabeth. You cannot fathom how much I despaired after leaving you in Hertfordshire. That is the closest I have ever come to giving up completely. After I returned to London, I could not sleep or eat for weeks on end. My body ached for love of you. I paced the floors incessantly. I began to sleep in my study or in this library in hopes that my pacing would not awaken the household." He smiled wryly. "After several glasses of brandy, I still could not sleep, but at least I could imagine the sprite of the Meryton bookshop sitting across from me."

"Me? I am a sprite?"

"You are my sprite." She closed her eyes as he smoothed an errant curl behind her ear. "I read many a love poem to your phantom."

"I have married quite a romantic man," Elizabeth whispered, her voice rough with emotion. Then standing on tiptoes she brushed his lips with hers. "I treasure that about you."

His expression suddenly became sombre. "I have been lonely much of my life, and I worry that my desire for your companionship may weary you."

"In time, you will learn that I will never tire of you."

"My heart is gratified to hear that." He kissed her pert nose as his cheerfulness returned. "I have a gift for you."

Elizabeth's eyes lit up. "How sweet of you, but you do not have to give me presents."

Cape Peninsula. It is a golden and aromatic wine with an intense and lingering sweetness. It is considered one of the top dessert wines of the world. So little was produced that it was very expensive and purchased mainly by the aristocracy and royalty of the world. The Regency Encyclopedia.

"Here is another directive, my love. Do not protest when I give you presents, as it will not deter me in the least. I intend to shower you with gifts as long as I live. Come!"

Taking her hand, he led her to the far corner of the library where he removed a

certain heavy tome off an upper shelf. Behind it, a secret lever was imbedded in the woodwork, and upon pulling it, an entire section of the bookshelf opened to reveal a safe in the wall that was almost as tall as she.

Unlocking the vault, he pulled it open then reached inside to remove a blue journal from a shelf. "I wished to show you this book. It records the exact point when I began to live again."

Elizabeth took the tome and opened the cover. At the top of the page, recorded in a masculine script, was *Fitzwilliam Darcy, April 29, 1812.* "You wrote this about three weeks after you left Meryton." Then beginning to read the passage, she added, "This tells of our meeting in the book shop. You are speaking of me."

"Yes. You must understand that I was desperate, Elizabeth. So desperate that I thought that by recording my despair, I might purge myself of it. Instead, as I recounted my recollections of you, something began to stir inside me. Something I had not allowed myself to feel in years. It was hope! Hope that there could be more to my wretched life. There could be you."

"Oh, Fitzwilliam ..." Her voice faltered as he embraced her, kissing her silky hair as she leaned into him, still clutching the book.

"I had a history professor who encouraged us to keep journals, arguing that history and our posterity would be better served if we did. So I kept a diary for many years. At some point, I surmised that no one would benefit from reading page after page of misery, so I left off. Besides, by then, having an heir seemed an unattainable dream, and there would be no one to read them."

Gently he took the book from Elizabeth, examining it thoughtfully. "Somehow this journal taught me that even sad memoirs can inspire hope." Then, he looked at her. "I know that, after the early years, my parents did not have a loving marriage. Mother stopped keeping journals by their third anniversary. In view of that, I have a special request of you."

He continued eagerly once Elizabeth nodded. "Would you begin a journal for our children and grandchildren? I wish to have at least one story of genuine love and devotion amongst the memoirs at Pemberley."

"Yes, *our* love story!" Tears could no longer be stayed, and this time they rolled down her cheeks unchecked. Pulling a handkerchief from his pocket, William began to dry her tears.

"Please do not cry, darling. I did not mean to make you sad today of all days."

Elizabeth shook her head, laughing as she replied, "I am not sad, Fitzwilliam. I am happy. You shall have to get used to seeing me cry."

With a soft touch, he removed the last tears from her cheeks. "In that case, I shall look forward to making you cry for joy, my love. Now, I promised you a gift."

Turning, he laid the journal back in the safe and pulled out a package wrapped in cream-coloured paper and tied with red ribbons. Silently he offered it to her. Taking it, she swiftly pulled the ribbons and opened it to find a red leather journal.

Embossed in gold across the front was *Elizabeth Rose Darcy*.

Opening the cover, she discovered that something was written on the first page. Her expression grew serious, and a lump formed in her throat as she read.

> *Presented to my darling wife, Elizabeth Rose Darcy, on our wedding day, July 15, 1812.*
> *Only God knows the times and seasons and the number of days He has allotted us, but I shall thank Him each and every day that I am privileged to call you my own, no matter how short the measure. For eternity would not be long enough.*
> *Forever your loving husband,*
> *Fitzwilliam*

Laying the book down, she threw herself into his arms. "Oh, Fitzwilliam, it is lovely! I will treasure it. I know that we shall have more than enough love to meet whatever the Lord sends our way." She sniffled, shaking her head vigorously in order not to cry anew. "Today you have made me the happiest woman on earth!"

He captured her mouth in a kiss that quickly intensified from tender to torrid. His hunger for her soared, and in seconds he had backed them against the wall. His desire was evident as he pressed his body into hers while exploring the softness of her breasts. Feeling her back arch as she melded into him, his passion grew. Sliding one hand down to lift the hem of her gown, that same hand moved slowly back up her stocking-clad leg until it reached the silky skin of her naked thigh. Elizabeth moaned softly, bringing him to his senses.

Breaking the embrace, he stepped back as they both gasped for air. She looked so innocent, her eyes darker and wider than ever before, and he was reminded anew that she was not yet one and twenty. Resolving to be very gentle, he brushed his fingers over her cheek.

"My love, I believe it is time we retired."

Elizabeth nodded and in mere seconds their clothes were righted, the safe was secured and they exited the library. Shortly afterward, they stood outside the door to Elizabeth's sitting room.

"When should I return, my love? Will half an hour suffice?"

Too affected to answer, Elizabeth nodded. With that, he kissed her forehead, turned the knob and pushed the door open. She walked just inside and stopped to look over her shoulder.

He murmured hoarsely, "Soon, Elizabeth."

The instant the click of the door signaled that he had departed, Macie came rushing into the room from the dressing room. An accomplished lady's maid at five and thirty, she had been hired by Lady Ashcroft to care for Elizabeth when she moved into Darcy House.

"Let me assist you, Mrs. Darcy. We have much to accomplish before your husband returns." In a daze, Elizabeth followed her into the dressing room where Macie began to help her out of her clothes. Once down to her shift, the servant picked up a pitcher and poured some water into a large bowl. "The water is still warm, and here is a fresh towel."

Elizabeth smiled, took the towel and walked to the bowl where she began to wash.

"While you are occupied, I shall collect your clothes from the wardrobe in your bedroom. I hung them there earlier. Oh, and Lady Ashcroft left you some of the lovely cream she swears by." She motioned to a jar on the dresser. "It makes the feet and hands very soft, according to her."

Before very long, everything had been accomplished, and Elizabeth was dressed in her new nightgown.

"You look lovely!" Elizabeth blushed as the maid held out the robe. "Do you wish to put on the robe or shall I take down your hair first?"

"The room is quite warm, so I shall wait."

"Then if you will have a seat, I will begin."

As Elizabeth moved to sit in the chair in front of the dressing table, Macie began to search the surface of the dresser as though looking for something. Apparently not finding it, she turned to examine the room, her expression one of puzzlement.

"I seemed to have misplaced the hairbrush. Perhaps I laid it down when I was retrieving your gown from the other room."

With those words, the maid disappeared into the bedroom, and in the peaceful interlude, Elizabeth closed her eyes and tried to remember Aunt Audrey's counsel of only a few days prior.

"Remember, Elizabeth, the marriage bed is a marvellous gift from God and something to look forward to! Give no weight to foolish old wives tales, but listen to one who has known a love like you share with Fitzwilliam. There may be some pain, but it is quickly forgotten with the passion that follows. Where each is dedicated to the happiness of the other, there is great satisfaction to be had in your husband's arms.

"And, if I may share something that I learned years ago, a man does not want to be kept ignorant. Let him know when he gives you pleasure, and that you desire him as much as he desires you. It will make your union all the sweeter."

Several minutes passed before Macie reappeared. "I apologise that it took me so long," she declared, holding up the brush. "It had fallen off the bed and was hidden beside the table."

"No apology is necessary," Elizabeth said, pleased to have had a few minutes of quiet reflection.

Laying the wayward item on the dresser, the maid quickly set about the task of taking the pins from her mistress' hair. Only then did Elizabeth take time to inspect herself in the mirror. Instantly she crimsoned, embarrassed at how little of her body the gown concealed. Though she had selected the design of her wedding gown herself, William's aunts had insisted on choosing the fabrics for her nightgown and robe. Both were fashioned of the sheerest, champagne-coloured silk, and the diaphanous material clung to her every curve.

When her aunts had selected this fabric, she had pondered how any trim could be affixed to something so sheer, but trimmed it was with the palest blue satin piping around the hem and sleeves and the plunging neckline. Several gathers were fashioned from bosom to waist, each edged with the same piping and laced with blue satin ribbons. The ribbons tied in the front, closing the gown. Once they were freed, the fabric was so flimsy it would simply float unfettered to the floor.

Crossing her arms in a bid to maintain some modesty, Elizabeth was watching the maid work on her hair when a knock on the door caused them both to jump.

Macie's eyes grew large. "He is early! I have only just now removed the pins!"

"It will do as it is," Elizabeth assured, patting the maid's arm. "You may go now." Macie curtsied and instantly disappeared through the servant's corridor.

Alone now, Elizabeth frowned at the image in the mirror. Very quickly she undid the braids and removed the ribbons before shaking her head to unleash a head full of untamed curls. She watched as they fell down her shoulders. Unfortunately, when she reached for the brush she found that Macie had taken it with her when she rushed from the room. Sighing, she ran her hands through the strands in an effort to tame the natural curl without success. With no choice, she gave up all efforts and stood to face the door.

"Come in," she said as steadily as she could muster.

William stepped inside the room, looking simply magnificent in a black, satin trimmed robe. A very handsome man, he had always cut an impressive figure with his broad shoulders and slender waist. Just seeing him could twist her stomach in knots, but the way he looked at this moment caused the blood to rush through her veins. Captivated, she could not keep her gaze from dropping to his robe. It was so loosely tied about the waist that it stood open, exposing his naked torso. Elizabeth had dreamed of seeing William shirtless again since the night she spent with him at Ashcroft Park, and tonight proved no less intoxicating. It was impossible to keep from following the fine, dark hair covering his toned chest as it trailed down the chiselled muscles of his abdomen, only to disappear under the belt about his waist. Her gaze dropped to his bare legs and feet and it became clear that he was completely naked under the robe. Her throat suddenly dry, she swallowed hard.

Again meeting his eyes, she resisted the urge to cross her arms when his own gaze drifted downward to her breasts. Instead, she tried not to appear disconcerted as he carried out his inspection. When their eyes locked again, his were smoldering with hot, fierce desire. Yet he did not come any closer. Her brows furrowed.

"Fitzwilliam, is anything the matter?"

Instantly she was enfolded in his arms. "No, my darling! Forgive me if I caused you to think otherwise. I was just stunned to realise that you look exactly as you did the first time I laid eyes on you. Your hair—"

Elizabeth's hands flew to her wayward curls. "Oh, my hair! Macie took the brush when she left and—"

William captured her fretful hands, bringing both to his heart. "You will learn that the more tousled your hair, the more I love it."

She giggled nervously. "You will be easy to please then, for when I wake in the morning, it is always wild."

"I love wild," he murmured in a way that bewitched her. Then he captured her lips in a searing kiss and picking her up, began to make his way through the door to her bedchamber.

Once inside, he set her on the thick carpet and both of their heads turned to examine what had been accomplished since she had gone downstairs earlier. Startled at the transformation of the room, she gasped.

The room was heady with the scent of roses. Tall crystal vases, filled with red roses interspersed with baby's breath, sat on every possible surface. Rose petals were strewed about, including the floor and the bed. Candles had been lit and gave the room a warm glow. The red and gold damask counterpane had been turned back to reveal luxurious cream-coloured silk sheets. Extra pillows had been fluffed and placed against the elaborate headboard.

Turning back to face each other, Elizabeth smiled a little nervously. It was only a moment before William's hands worked their way down her back to pull her hard against his arousal. He groaned and began undoing the ribbons fastening her gown. Once they were almost all undone, he hesitated.

"Do you know how much I love you, Elizabeth?" She nodded, and he smiled as his fingers traced gently over her jaw. "On my fourteenth birthday, I knew for certain that my parent's marriage had begun to crumble. I was broken hearted, so I asked God for a glimpse of the woman He had destined for me. It was then that He placed your image in my heart. I had no idea of your name or where you were, but I knew without a doubt that someday you would come, and when you did, I would recognise you. When we met in Meryton, I knew that you were the one destined for me.

"Circumstances and fate had delivered a cruel blow, and I had made a decision that went against my better judgement. Instead of trusting God to handle the situation, I took action. Consequently, I found myself trapped in a spiteful marriage, convinced there was no hope. But God forgave my pride and redeemed my mistakes. In His mercy, He has even given you to me, and I intend to do everything in my power to make you happy for the rest of your life. I want tonight to be a beautiful memory."

"I know that you shall be gentle. I am not afraid, and I want to be your wife in every way."

Pushing the sides of her gown apart, the silky material slipped off her shoulders and to the floor. His breath hitched at the sight of her, and for a moment, he could not move. Then driven by his growing need, William picked her up and moved to the bed where he gently laid her atop the pillows. Swiftly untying his robe, he shrugged it from his shoulders and climbed into the bed beside her.

Whispering words of adoration, he placed hot kisses over every trace of her softly scented skin. "I shall love you forever … my love … my world."

The evidence of his passion was visible on her fair skin as he gently nipped down her neck to the juncture of her shoulder, causing her to writhe. Pleased by her response, he kissed across her décolletage and then to her generous breasts. Unable to resist any longer, he captured one hard centre in his mouth while his hands caressed every inch of her body.

"Make me yours, Fitzwilliam," Elizabeth murmured, entwining her fingers in his hair. "Love me."

Without hesitation, William lay atop her, a groan of pleasure escaping his throat as their bodies melded one into the other. He felt her flinch the moment they were joined and opened his eyes in concern. Her dark eyes were full of immeasurable love as she pulled his lips back to hers, murmuring, "Oh, how I love you."

Torn between the pleasure of loving the woman he adored and trying to be gentle, William found it progressively difficult to concentrate on anything but reaching fulfilment. Pleasure built upon pleasure, and just as he began to feel as though he might surrender to the chaos pent up in his body, a quivering deep inside her signalled that she had reached completion. Self-control forgotten, he closed his eyes to absorb wave after wave of ecstasy, crying out, "Elizabeth!"

For some time afterward, they still lay joined, unwilling to sever the connection. When at last he rolled over, he took her with him, so she lay on top. He pulled the sheets over them, and their breathing slowly returned to normal as they floated down from the pinnacle of love.

At length, he bestowed a soft kiss atop of her head, whispering tenderly, "Your love is sweeter than my soul ever imagined, my darling Elizabeth. All that I am or shall ever be, I owe to you."

Overwhelmed, she could say nothing. Instead, she placed a kiss on his bare chest before embracing him even more tightly and drifting off to sleep in his arms.

Chapter 47

London
Matlock House
The garden
Several days later

Holding open the wrought iron gate that led to the rose garden, Mr. Meadows, the Matlock's gardener, removed his well-worn hat and stepped aside to allow the two women coming down the gravel path access to the fenced section. Through the years, the master's sister, Lady Ashcroft, had always treated him with the utmost respect and kindness, and as he bowed a slight bow, Georgiana gave him a large smile. He returned the smile. *She seems to be following in her aunt's footsteps.*

"I do believe the garden is more beautiful this year than ever before, Mr. Meadows," Audrey Ashcroft remarked, stopping just inside the gate and causing Georgiana to almost run into her.

"Thank you, madam. I try my best to keep it so."

"Well, if you should ever decide to retire to the country, you always have a position waiting at Ashcroft Park. And I shall tell my brother as much, so do not worry about his hearing of my offer. If he is not careful to keep you satisfied, you shall be working for me."

Shaking his head at her words of praise, he chuckled. "Oh, I cannot complain, your ladyship! Lord Matlock has been most kind to me."

"I am glad to hear it. He should, you know. This garden is the talk of London!" Mr. Meadows, bent now with age, actually crimsoned with her continued praise. The colour contrasted starkly with his mop of white hair. "Do not let me disconcert you, Meadows. You are an excellent gardener."

He dropped his eyes. "Thank you, madam."

At that moment, a kitchen maid came into view, coming towards them down the same path and carrying a large tray.

"Come, Georgiana! Let us hurry and be seated. That tray Meggie is carrying cannot be light, and I am sure she wishes to rid herself of it as soon as possible."

Lady Ashcroft and Georgiana hurried towards the round table located in the middle of a large, flat stone patio. The old gardener waited at the gate for the young maid, tipping his ragged hat as he acknowledged her.

"Morning, Miss Meggie."

"'Morning Mr. Meadows," was her reply. "Thank you!" she added as he held open the gate.

Watching as the maid reached the table and set the tray down, he sighed when Lady Ashcroft poured a cup of the hot liquid for Georgiana. Memories of when he was a boy came rushing back. Oh, his family might not have had tea, but he had fond memories of his mother serving him a cup of milk. Having never married, he had no family left now. Thus, oft times he would try to catch a glimpse of the family taking refreshments in the garden, as the domesticity of the scenes always filled his heart with warmth. Just knowing that he had provided a pleasant setting to enjoy the out of doors made him feel, in a small way, that he was a part of them.

Satisfied with the prospect presented by aunt and niece, Mr. Meadows hurried in the direction of the garden shed, eager to rid himself of the hoe that he still carried and return to the kitchen. Aware that he had been up since daybreak, since they were always the first two to rise, the cook, Mrs. Mulvahill, always saved a bun and a piece of bacon for him to have at this time of day.

"But I do not understand why we cannot just go over there!" Georgiana complained, dropping a half-eaten biscuit on her plate. "It will only take a few minutes, and I promise I will leave whenever you say."

"Your brother and Elizabeth should be afforded privacy on their honeymoon. I have no intention of disturbing them!"

Pouting, her niece did not look up as she replied petulantly, "Millicent Mooneyham is to accompany her sister when she leaves on her wedding trip. In fact, she tells me that taking a sister with you is not uncommon. Why could I not go with my brother and Elizabeth to Pemberley? After all, it is my home, too."

"Your brother deserves to focus on his happiness now! He has looked after you in every fashion, even before your parents died. You should not expect to be asked to tag along. One day, when you are older, you shall understand why. I dare say you will not wish to be disturbed on your honeymoon, either."

Ignoring her aunt's arguments, Georgiana continued. "But if they truly wanted to be alone, why did they stay in Town?"

"You know that Fitzwilliam did not have time to plan a wedding trip, thus their decision to stay here for a short while before going to Pemberley. He did not wish Elizabeth to spend her first night as Mrs. Darcy in an inn surrounded by strangers."

"But if they are to leave for Pemberley on Thursday, I should, at least, be allowed to say goodbye."

Audrey Ashcroft leaned across the stone table to lift her niece's chin. She waited until Georgiana's eyes met hers before speaking. "In the past you have been away from your brother for weeks on end and, though you missed him, you certainly did not fret about seeing him after so short a time. What is this about?"

"It is not Brother that I wish to see; it is Elizabeth. Surely she expects her sister to wish her joy and a safe journey!" Her face crumpled as though she was going to cry. "I have never had a sister, and I wish to get to know her."

Audrey could not help but smile at Georgiana's argument. "And you shall, but all in good time." She patted her hand. "The next few weeks belong to them and them alone. Let them get to know each other without the intrusion of family or friends."

"I thought they knew each other well enough. After all, they agreed to marry."

"Being engaged is not the same as being married. However, since you are so upset, if you wish—"

Georgiana's eyes lit up. "I can see her?"

"No. You may write a note to Elizabeth, and I shall have a footman deliver it tomorrow. That way you may wish her joy and say goodbye before they leave!"

"Oh, Aunt!" Georgiana declared, her face falling. "That is not what I wished for and you know it."

"I suppose not, but it shall have to suffice!"

Matlock House
The Library

Standing at the large floor-to-ceiling windows in his father's richly appointed library, Richard chuckled at the scene unfolding in the garden just outside. Georgiana had complained to him only minutes before of being unable to see her brother and her new sister.

"What is so funny?"

Richard looked over his shoulder and seeing that it was his sister, Alicia, turned back to watch the spectacle. "It is Georgiana! She wants to pay a call on Darcy and Elizabeth!" He laughed aloud. "I told her she might be able to persuade Aunt Audrey."

"Richard!" Alicia declared, chuckling as she hurried to stand next to him. "You knew her appeal would be fruitless! Our aunt would never let anyone interfere with our cousin's happiness at this time."

"Yes, but it is far better for Georgiana to be angry with Aunt Audrey than with me! I am her wonderful, doting cousin, and I wish to stay that way."

"I did not know you were so devious!"

Richard turned to her with a smirk. "Yes, you do, for I have been such all my life. You realise, of course, that if I were not so devious, you would not be engaged to your colonel as we speak! After all, it was my idea to take Steven with us to Teddington so that father could learn what a fine fellow he is, though I had no idea your beau would end up saving his life."

Alicia slipped her arm through her brother's and laid her head against him as she offered, "Fortunately, your deviousness is mainly a ruse to help others." Richard patted her hand and she continued. "Steven and I owe our happiness to you, and we shall never forget it."

"I hope not!" he retorted cheekily. Then, continuing to stare into the gardens beyond, he asked more circumspectly, "Could I request something of you?"

"Anything."

"I … I am not one to manipulate social situations. In fact, I do not have the faintest idea how to arrange *coincidental* meetings as you ladies do."

"You wish me to arrange a meeting?"

"First, I do not wish for mother to learn of this. Do you promise not to say anything to her or anyone else, for that matter?"

Alicia let go of his arm and stepped in front of him, her expression sombre. "I promise. You may tell me anything you wish, and I shall keep it in strictest confidence." Suddenly, Richard seemed self-conscious as he studied his boots. "Richard, tell me. You have nothing to fear."

"Lady Tierney."

"Colleen Tierney? I met her at a dinner party at the Swansons a few weeks ago. I found her to be very sweet and intelligent." She smiled wryly at Richard. "I dare say that she is also very beautiful, though I imagine that you are aware of that. Else, why would we be discussing her?"

"I have always been drawn to green-eyed young ladies with red hair," he smirked. "It is my greatest weakness."

"Are you aware that our mother and Lady Swanson were good friends with Colleen's mother years before that lady was married Lord Tierney?"

"I had no idea."

"That evening, after talking with her, Mother realised who Colleen was and told everyone who would listen loving stories about the Tierneys. But how do you know of her? You were out of London the night she dined with us at the Swansons."

"When returning from Southhaven, Sergeant Powell and I came across a coach on the side of the road with a broken wheel. I sent Powell to the nearest town to secure a replacement coach and stayed with the occupants for several hours because I feared for their safety. Their party included only Lady Tierney, her elderly uncle, and a driver and footman who looked equally old. I was afraid a highwayman might take advantage of their situation."

"Then, surely you know her well enough to call on her?"

"One would think so, but she and I barely exchanged two words, as her uncle talks more than I do! He and I waited outside the coach and discussed everything from Bonaparte* to brandy. Just think, my charming personality was wasted on a man old enough to be my great-grandfather while a beautiful woman sat just inches away!"

"She must have made some impression if 'barely two words' inspired you to seek my assistance."

He looked sheepish now. "I confess that she did. But if I decide to pursue an acquaintance, I will need a formal introduction."

"If? Brother, you have never shown that much interest in a woman as far back as I can remember!" She laughed out loud. "This has to be serious if my confirmed bachelor brother is considering calling on a young woman!"

At just that moment, Lady Matlock entered the room unbeknownst to them. "Who is calling on a young woman?"

Richard and Alicia each startled, turning in tandem to face their mother. Alicia glanced to her brother whose face was flushed.

"I am, Mother!" Alicia declared a little too brightly. "I was telling Richard that I had met a lovely young woman at a dinner party, and I wished to further my acquaintance with her."

Her mother's face lit up. "And who might that be, dear?"

"Lady Tierney."

"Oh, that is a wonderful idea! I meant to ask her to tea before now, but with all the commotion surrounding Fitzwilliam's marriage, I forgot."

Alicia looked at Richard out of the corner of her eye. "Then I shall send an invitation for tea tomorrow, if that meets with your approval. You will be available then, will you not?"

"I shall indeed! And you should be here to meet her too, Richard. I suppose Alicia has told you that she is beautiful as well as intelligent."

Acting the part of the reluctant suitor, Richard sighed heavily. "You know how I feel about your matchmaking, Mother."

"Surely you cannot object to an introduction if you are here when she arrives?" Lady Matlock declared.

"Of course not!" Richard said, hoping to sound properly offended. "If I happen to be here when she comes, I shall gladly suffer an introduction. I am a gentleman, after all."

His mother patted his cheek condescendingly. "Of course you are!" Then her expression became pensive as she began plotting the menu in her head. "I shall meet with Cook immediately regarding what to serve."

And with those words, she completely forgot her children and headed back out of the room. Used to being abandoned when their mother became distracted, Richard turned to Alicia and winked.

Laughing, Alicia said, "As I said before, you are devious! Mother is on a mission and has no idea that you instigated the entire thing."

"But, it makes her happy to think she is in charge," Richard retorted. Then he took his sister's hand. "Thank you for not giving me away."

"Even if you had not done so much for Steven and me, I would do whatever in my power to help you. You have been the best of brothers."

"It is not hard to best Edgar!" he laughed.

Alicia's expression softened. "Do not make light of my compliment, Richard. You are everything a brother should be."

Richard pulled her into his arms and kissed her forehead. "I have told Darcy numerous times that sisters are not so bad after they are full grown."

Alicia exacted her punishment by pinching his arm.

"Ouch!" he declared, vigorously rubbing his injury. "Perhaps I shall have to amend my opinion on that subject!"

Darcy House
The Mistress' Bedroom

As faint light was beginning to filter through the French doors into the bedroom, from his perch on the rail that surrounded the balcony, William watched patiently while the sky transitioned from gray to shades of blue and orange. Having stirred Elizabeth from her sleep last night, kissing her until she woke in order to make love again, he was determined that she should sleep at least until morning. Judging by her response, she had not minded being awakened, but it was evident that she needed rest, as she had not roused when he had. So, unable to quell his rising passion, William had slipped from the bed and taken up his vigil almost an hour ago.

However, seeing that the sun's appearance was imminent, he took several deep breaths of the invigorating morning air and re-entered the room, taking a cautious seat on the small sofa placed nearest the bed. There he observed her silently. Most of the candles lit last night had burned out leaving only a few producing a dim glow, but he was content. His wife's pleasing form was easily discernible from the light now invading the space.

As William watched her sleep, he felt for the first time that she was his. Certain that nothing could surpass the happiness he felt at this very moment, he was jolted from his contemplations when Elizabeth suddenly rolled from her side onto her stomach. The picture that she now presented tormented his passion anew, for she lay sprawled across this huge bed almost completely exposed. The sheets had slipped during the night and lay across her buttocks, while only her hair covered her back.

Instantly, his eyes flew to the mass of ebony curls that ended just above her perfectly rounded bottom. Reminiscent of a nude he had seen in a Renaissance painting, he envied Georgiana's ability to draw. He would have given anything to capture Elizabeth's likeness just then. Occupied with this new deliberation, he failed to see that she had awakened and was watching him through hooded eyes.

"Fitzwilliam," she murmured sleepily, gaining his full attention.

Instantly he was sitting on the edge of the bed, one hand eagerly interlacing with the chocolate ringlets. "Good morning, my darling. Are you well?"

"A bit tired," she offered. The corners of her mouth lifted in a drowsy smile. "I think I could lie here forever."

Disappointed with her reply, William tried not to show it. "If that is your wish, then you may. I shall not insist that you rise."

The regret in his voice was so palpable that Elizabeth instantly detected it. Thus, she rolled over on her back, making no attempt to cover up or to flinch under his gaze.

Staring open-mouthed, he said not a word, so she began to tease. "Then you would not care if I slept all day?"

William murmured, "I did not say that you should sleep *all day,* Elizabeth." Gently he cupped one soft breast with his large hand, palming it until the center hardened. "In fact, it is my theory that exertions of a pleasurable nature can greatly improve sleep afterward."

"I fear I have not had enough *practice* to concur with your theory. Would you be willing to put it to the test once more?"

Instantly William was on his feet, discarding his robe as rapidly as possible. Falling on the bed and rolling over to trap her beneath his body, he heard her giggle, exclaiming, "Fitzwilliam, your feet are cold!"

Ignoring her protest, he made quick work of warming her, and as their love-making took on a steady rhythm, her protestations became moans of pleasure. Afterwards, having proven his theory beyond all doubt, they slept in each other's arms.

And so it was that the servant's bell, signaling the Darcys' wished to bathe, did not ring until nearly midday. If there had been more servants on duty, undoubtedly more eyebrows would have risen, other than those of Mr. and Mrs. Barnes and the footmen summoned to bring water.

The huge tub was perfect. It was large enough that William could stretch his legs out completely and, if he was not sharing the tub with her, Elizabeth could lie completely down if she wished. As it was, the steaming, scented water barely rippled as he slid into the tub behind her and Elizabeth stopped running a cloth over her legs to lie back against his chest. William smiled contentedly. As she made a pillow of his shoulder and closed her eyes, he took the soap-filled cloth and began to glide it over her body. Unable to imagine a more pleasurable pursuit, his thoughts immediately flew to transporting the tub to Pemberley and ordering a new one for Darcy House.

Elizabeth was full of curiosity. "Fitzwilliam, are you sure this is quite proper? I have never heard of a man and a woman bathing together."

"Would you prefer we bathe separately?"

Elizabeth giggled in the delightful way that he adored. "Of course not, but I have to wonder what the servants will think or, more importantly, what they will say."

"The servants will say nothing, Elizabeth. I have dedicated people who are paid well not to gossip. I can assure you that nothing that happens in either of our homes will ever be discussed."

She ran a hand along his leg, unaware of the effect it had on him. "I confess that I enjoy imagining the shocked faces of the ladies of the *ton,* should they learn our secret. It almost makes me want to spread the rumour."

"Eliz—"

"I am only teasing," she interjected. "But surely, the glares of jealousy at our wedding breakfast did not escape your notice. Most of the ladies acted as though I had stolen you out from under their noses."

"I saw no one but you, my love."

She sat up and turned to kiss him. They settled in each other's arms, her head resting on his shoulder.

"If we are leaving for Pemberley on Thursday, should we not say our farewells to the family beforehand?" she whispered dreamily.

"I believe that our family has seen enough of us to suffice until the end of our honeymoon. I have no wish to interrupt our privacy to bid them farewell."

"I know that Jane and Papa have returned to Hertfordshire, but Georgiana—"

"Georgiana has accompanied our aunt on trips for weeks at a time. Believe me when I say that she shall survive this separation."

Taking a few moments to consider his argument, Elizabeth replied, "Still, I would not wish for her to think I had ignored her."

"You are too kind to worry over your sister at a time like this, but to ease your mind, if you will write her a note, I shall have it delivered tomorrow by a footman. Then, she shall know that you were thinking of her. I shall also send a greeting for her and one for the rest of the family from us both."

"What an excellent idea!" Suddenly she sat up, her brown eyes twinkling deliciously. "How shall I thank you for thinking of it?"

William's eyes were trained on the trickles of soapy water drizzling from the tips of her firm breasts. "Oh, I imagine that you will be able to think of something."

Elizabeth erupted with peals of laughter, falling into William's arms. And it would be much later that day before she realised that she had made a valuable discovery. If it was large enough, a tub could be used for so much more than just bathing.

Just before dinner on the morrow, Elizabeth received a note from Georgiana, and about the same time, Georgiana received a note from her new sister. As both read the missives they smiled, content to know that although it would be over a month before they were together again, they had acquired a sister who thought of their feelings regardless of the circumstances.

So it was that first light on Thursday morning found the newlyweds beginning their journey to Derbyshire. Elizabeth was eager to set eyes on the home that her husband loved so dearly, and Fitzwilliam was just as keen to show it to her. For he was convinced that his ancestral home would be set to right the minute his wife stepped inside.

After all, with Elizabeth's arrival, the true mistress of Pemberley would be in residence at last.

Chapter 48

Pemberley
Seven weeks later

As the coach approached the circular drive of the manor house, Lady Audrey Ashcroft leaned out the window, eager to see if there were any changes to Pemberley since she had last been in residence. Pleased that everything looked just as she remembered, she smiled as she sank back into the cushioned seat of Darcy's coach. Then remembering what had brought her back to Derbyshire sooner than expected, her face took on an entirely different expression.

Elizabeth's note had been terse, offering no real explanation as to why she needed to talk to her so hastily. But considering that she had to return in a few days in order to prepare for her wedding, it had been no inconvenience to come earlier. Since receiving the letter, she had prayed diligently that nothing major was amiss; however, she was apprehensive that whatever the problem, it just might concern Georgiana. After all, her niece had returned to Pemberley two weeks before and she, of all people, knew how demanding Georgiana could be. Naturally, Elizabeth would have been eager to please her new sister, and that could have served to create the perfect disaster.

Why did I not think of this before? I should have had a good talk with my niece regarding Elizabeth's priorities before I let her return to Derbyshire.

Her thoughts were cut short by the sudden halt of the vehicle and the opening of the door by a colourfully dressed footman. As he reached to hand her out, she nodded and offered a polite thank you. Peering up as the front door flew open she relaxed to see the servants who had been at Pemberley the longest step out on the portico to greet her. Mrs. Reynolds had been with the Darcys since Fitzwilliam was in knee pants, and Mr. Walker had been hired not long after. Their presence was comforting. Nothing too dreadful could be amiss if they were on watch.

As she ascended the steps, the housekeeper declared, "How good to have you back, Lady Ashcroft!"

"It is good to be back!" she answered truthfully.

As they continued into the foyer, the white-haired butler took her cape, bonnet and gloves while Mrs. Reynolds exclaimed animatedly, "Mr. Walker and I wish you joy and felicitations on your upcoming marriage. We have always thought very highly of Lord Landingham."

"Thank you. I think highly of him myself."

Everyone shared a laugh as Audrey began to look around as though expecting some of the family to greet her.

"Where is everyone?"

Mrs. Reynolds' smile waned. "Mr. Darcy has been gone several days, Miss Darcy is having her music lesson as we speak and Mrs. Darcy ..." Audrey thought she heard the housekeeper sigh as her voice trailed off.

"Mrs. Darcy?"

"I do not know exactly where she is at the moment. She was in the rose garden earlier, but when I checked a few minutes ago, I could not find her. I have learned not to get overly concerned, as she loves to walk and often takes the path around the lake with the slightest impulse."

"She is alone?"

"Mr. Darcy has commissioned several footmen to follow her whenever she leaves the house, so she is never alone." Lowering her eyes the housekeeper added, "We were not expecting you, or I am sure she would not have walked out."

At that point, Audrey was certain that her new niece had not informed the rest of the family or the servants that she had asked her to come early. She was equally convinced that Mrs. Reynolds was not *at all* unconcerned.

"Then let us keep my presence here a surprise for a little while longer, shall we? When do you expect Mr. Darcy to return?"

Butler and housekeeper exchanged anxious glances before Mrs. Reynolds answered. "At present we have no idea. From the note he sent to Mrs. Darcy, he was about to commission the rebuilding of a bridge that was near collapse, when another storm came through and finished the destruction. That bridge was in the far northwest corner of the estate where the river divides the property."

Audrey's eyebrows rose at this information. "And how long has my nephew been resolving estate matters?"

"A little over a week now. He spent three days settling tenant disputes from dawn to dark and then made the trip to assess the bridge. After the collapse, he has not returned."

"I see," Audrey murmured quietly.

Mrs. Reynolds clarified further. "Mr. Darcy explained that though it would be possible for him to return via a circuitous route, it would add twenty miles of rough road to the normal five. Thus, he decided not to come home each night but to stay and get it done sooner. Mr. Pickering, the new steward, is in residence. If you would like, I can send for him, as he is more knowledgeable of the problems the Master is facing in rebuilding the bridge."

Already woodenly walking towards the hallway that led to the back entrance, Audrey's mind was racing with the significance of all she had learned. Finally, she remembered the servants and turned to address them.

"I shall greet Elizabeth first, and then I will speak to Pickering. See that he is waiting for me in the yellow drawing room when I return. Lastly, I shall greet Georgiana. Would you make sure that her music master knows that I wish for him to keep her occupied until I send word?"

"Of course."

Mrs. Reynolds followed Lady Ashcroft's progress until she was completely out of sight, then she turned to Walker. "You had better hurry if you are going to catch the music master before he concludes the lesson for today."

As she watched Walker dash towards the music room, the long-time servant felt the stirrings of hope for the first time in days.

Apparently I was right. The letter that Mrs. Darcy posted was a plea for help. Everything was so lovely before Miss Georgiana returned to Pemberley. I pray that the Master's aunt can make it so again.

With those words, she glanced to the tall clock standing against the wall. Seeing that it was nearing the noon hour, she began to make plans.

I shall have Cook prepare a fresh pot of tea and a tray with bread, meat and cheese. Mrs. Darcy has barely consumed anything the last three days, and if she continues this pattern, she will be sick. Besides, I could use some chamomile tea to soothe my nerves too.

Just as Abby Reynolds had said, Elizabeth was not to be found in the gardens, thus Lady Ashcroft began to walk the gravel path circling the lake. One section, which turned back towards the house on the far side, meandered into the edge of the woods. It was at the beginning of these woods that she found a footman sitting on a large boulder, waiting patiently.

"Good day, Mr. Wheatly," Audrey said softly as the elderly footman stood. "I assume Mrs. Darcy is nearby." He raised his brows and tipped his head in the direction of the trees.

Silently following his line of vision, she spied Elizabeth sitting on a wooden bench near the path. Nodding her thanks to the servant, Audrey entered the tree shaded haven and stealthily moved towards her niece. Because she was focused on a book in her hands, Elizabeth seemed not to notice her.

"Elizabeth?"

Dark eyes flashed with surprise and then relief. Instantly Elizabeth was on her feet, placing the book on the bench and launching herself into her aunt's arms. She did not make a sound, but it was evident from the way she shook that she was crying. Lady Ashcroft rocked the younger woman back and forth.

"There, there, my darling niece. All will be well. All will be well."

Elizabeth stepped back, hurriedly drying her face with the backs of her hands. "Forgive me. I did not mean to cry. Grown women should not cry at every little thing. In truth, I have no idea why I am so prone to tears with the least provocation these days."

Audrey pulled a handkerchief from her pocket and held it out to Elizabeth. She took it gratefully, dabbing at her eyes.

"Please do not apologise. And do not let anyone tell you that grown women do cry! Now and again it helps to let our emotions out. Now, tell me what has happened to make you so unhappy? Has my nephew been unkind?"

"Oh no, Fitzwilliam could never do anything unkind!" Elizabeth began to sniffle anew. "It is my fault! I have ruined everything!"

"I do not believe that for a minute." Audrey patted her hand. "Now, my presence at Pemberley cannot be a secret for long, so tell me, what has Georgiana done?"

Elizabeth looked incredulous. "How—"

"Georgiana is the reason for your letter, is she not?"

Elizabeth's face crumpled. "I love my sister dearly, but I am finding it difficult to please her as well as Fitzwilliam."

"I understand."

"It started so innocently. I wish for us to be close, so when she began asking me to do certain things with her, I admit to being pleased."

"But, of course, she wanted you to do them with her alone, not including Fitzwilliam."

Elizabeth's eyes went wide at her aunt's effortless comprehension. "She insisted that I come alone to her room at night, just to chat before she went to sleep. But each night the conversations got longer and—"

"And meanwhile your husband was patiently waiting for you to return to him."

"Yes, you see, before Georgiana came home, we would dine early and then enjoy a quiet time in the library." Teary eyes smiled at the remembrance. "Fitzwilliam enjoys reading, and I love to listen to him."

"Yes, he does have a marvelous voice," Audrey smiled. "So your evenings were altered with my niece's return?"

"Yes, and of a morning, he and I would break our fast and then spend the majority of the day exploring Pemberley." Her voice brightened. "Fitzwilliam talked me into riding with him on Zeus, so Mrs. Reynolds would pack a picnic and off we would go. I could never have dreamed of the beautiful vistas reachable only via horseback. We swam, fished, hiked and even went shopping in Lambton." She sighed longingly. "I love the fudge at the confectionery shop and Fitzwilliam indulges me. Late afternoons would find us in the gardens or the library if it rained."

"Let me guess. Georgiana wanted you to break your fast in her sitting room, just the two of you, and then she suggested that you practice the pianoforte or walk or shop in Lambton without her brother."

"How did you know?"

"I know my niece well. Because of her upbringing she can be quite needy if that impulse is not curbed. When I became her companion, she demanded my undivided attention. She became jealous if I spent any time with Fitzwilliam. Unfortunately, it seems she has repeated this behaviour with you."

"While I cannot be with her constantly, I do not wish for her to think I have no time for her."

"Of course, you do not," Audrey said understandingly. "However, your concern for her has made you the victim of the green-eyed monster. Georgiana wants your company for herself, while Fitzwilliam must feel lost that she has gained so much of it."

"I did not mean to."

"I know. And believe me when I say that Fitzwilliam knows this too. He comprehends full well that you need time to establish a relationship with Georgiana, and the guilt of wanting to keep you all to himself must be tremendous."

Elizabeth wrung her hands. "A few days ago it became unbearable! I missed Fitzwilliam so dearly! That was when I realised that I have been trying to please my sister to the detriment of my husband. I explained to Georgiana that I no longer wanted to do things without Fitzwilliam, at least not consistently. I also explained that, on occasion, Fitzwilliam and I would like time alone. In fact, I sent for her music and French masters to resume her lessons to keep her occupied part of the day."

"Elizabeth, you have handled the situation admirably—exactly as I would have advised. But, tell me, how did Georgiana react?"

"Not well, at first. Initially she pouted. That lasted for about a day, though now she seems to have forgotten the entire episode. However, by the time I realised that I had created a monster by catering to Georgiana, Fitzwilliam had found other things to occupy his time." Her face crumpled. "I am mortified to speak so bluntly, but before Georgiana came home we made love often. Yet this morning marks the seventh day since ..."

She was unable to finish, and Audrey used two fingers to lift her chin so their eyes locked. "Tell me about his new preoccupation."

"He began to handle the estate issues that had been neglected while he was in London. I understand that that is his duty, truly I do. It is just that the tenant disputes seemed to take all his time. He would not return until long after I was asleep, and he began sleeping in his bed alone. According to his valet, he did not wish to disturb me. Since he left in the dark of early morning, I had no chance to speak with him then either. I kept thinking that all this madness would end and our lives would return as they were before. In hindsight, I should have written him a note and asked him to awaken me when he got home."

"Unfortunately, hindsight is always clearer."

"Now, with the bridge, I have no idea when I shall see him again." She stared at the lake peeking through the trees in the distance. "My greatest fear is that our first weeks of marriage were an anomaly—something only starry-eyed lovers experience. What if now, given the choice, he would just as soon do his duty as spend time with me?"

"You know that cannot be true. By your own admission, he was a passionate lover before Georgiana came home. I think that when you became preoccupied with Georgiana, he sought an outlet to suppress his desires. That outlet was the estate."

"If he felt neglected or missed me as much as I missed him, why would he not just say so—or at least try to gain my attention again?"

"Men are strange creatures, Elizabeth. Perhaps he worried that since you had so easily been swayed by Georgiana, you were not as, shall we say, *enthusiastic* about marital relations as he was."

"But I was enthusiastic," Elizabeth offered without thinking. "Could he not just ask if he had any doubts?"

"You will learn that something in a man's nature will not allow him to dwell on that possibility. To learn that it is so would destroy him, thus he keeps those fears to himself. Now, may I ask another personal question?"

"You may ask me anything."

"I was wondering if you have had your courses since you and Fitzwilliam married."

Elizabeth's brows knit as she concentrated. "I have not thought about it, but they should have begun about the time Georgiana returned. That was two weeks ago."

"I see," Lady Ashcroft said, smiling perceptively. *That explains the urge to cry so readily.*

Elizabeth looked a little dazed. "Is it possible that I—could I be with child so soon?"

"It only takes one time, my dear, and from your description of your husband's devotion, one time would not accurately describe it."

Elizabeth could not help but smile, though she blushed furiously. Audrey slipped an arm around her shoulder. "Let us start back to the house, and I shall explain how we are going to resolve all your worries."

"Let me fetch my book," Elizabeth said rushing back to the bench. "I would not want to lose it. It was Fitzwilliam's first gift."

Taking her place alongside her aunt, they headed in the direction of the manor house. And as they walked, her aunt laid out her plans.

"First of all, Georgiana shall accompany me to Westcott Manor this evening. She shall reside there with me until my wedding. It shall be just as easy for her masters to meet with her there as here. When she is idle, I shall let her help me with the preparations, which should make her happy. She loves to feel that she is in charge of everything."

Both ladies laughed.

"Afterwards …"

ᢏᠵᡞᢏᠵᡃ

Just before dusk

William let go a sigh of relief and allowed Zeus to slow as soon as Pemberley came into sight. Since receiving the note from his aunt requesting that he come immediately, he had ridden the stallion at a full gallop much of the way. Fearing something had happened to Elizabeth or Georgiana, by the time he reached his home, his stomach was in revolt and, as he slid from the saddle, he prayed that he would not lose what little he had eaten.

His thoughts thus occupied, he happened to pull back on the reins a little too forcefully, causing the horse to rear after he halted. Instantly, the head footman, Mr. Douglas, hurried to take the stressed animal.

"Good evening, Mr. Darcy, sir," Douglas exclaimed breathlessly as he held onto the reins of the skittish animal. "It is good to have you home."

Absorbed with learning the reason he had been summoned, William only nodded, rushing past the old servant and up the steps without a word. And as the front door opened and his master disappeared inside, the man's brows raised curiously. "Mr. Darcy must have something on his mind; he is normally more sociable."

The younger footman seemed unconcerned to have been overlooked. "He is likely just tired." Taking the reins from the older man, he ran a hand down Zeus' damp chest. "I had better get this chap to the barn. He needs a rub down and some oats and I shall instruct one of the grooms accordingly."

Douglas laughed. "If you wish to handle him, I shall gladly defer. That horse has more fire in his belly when he is worn-out than most do when they are rested!"

Striding purposefully into the foyer, William was not surprised to see Mr. Walker coming towards him. The butler began to take his hat, coat and gloves.

"Good evening, sir. Welcome home."

The butler's serene attitude seemed out of place, and William looked about in disbelief. Why was his aunt not rushing to explain the urgent need for his presence?

"My aunt summoned me. Where is she?"

The voice of Lady Ashcroft came from somewhere behind. "I am right here, Fitzwilliam!"

Turning, he watched her float towards him in her usual elegant manner, seemingly unperturbed. Her steps were unhurried, and she had a slight smile on her face. When she reached him, she placed a kiss on his cheek.

He was thoroughly perplexed. "You do not look troubled in the least. Have I taken your missive more seriously than I should?"

"If you took it seriously, it served my purpose, Fitzwilliam. Now, if you will follow me, we must talk."

At the new gravity in her voice, his heart jumped into his throat again. "Please tell me now. Has something happened to Elizabeth or Georgiana?"

"Neither one is ill or injured, but if you will be so kind as to come with me, I shall explain why I sent for you." With those words, she turned and went in the direction of the parlour.

Letting go of the breath he had been holding, William's colour returned and he glanced skyward. *Thank you, Lord!* Then he hurried to follow his aunt.

Once the parlour door was shut, he began to get a bit irritable because he was exhausted. "If they are both well, why the urgency in your message? From what you wrote, I thought the worst."

"Just because neither of them are ill or injured, does not mean all is well, Nephew. Do you not wonder why I am here today instead of next week as planned?"

With all that had occupied his thoughts of late, William had completely forgotten when she was to return. At his look of complete confusion, Audrey Ashcroft's face softened. Smiling, she went to him and cupped his face with both hands.

"My poor darling boy, you look completely done in. Sit down and I shall tell you what has happened while you have been so diligently occupied with things best left to the supervision of others."

Later
William's Dressing Room

Almost an hour after his aunt and sister had removed to Westcott Manor, William was standing in his dressing room. He had bathed and was now clothed in the black silk robe that Elizabeth liked him to wear. Had he not reeked of dust and sweat, he would have rushed to her side directly after his aunt's lecture. However, for what he had in mind, a bath would refresh his body and help to stave off the fatigue of his journey.

Spying the small bottle of sandalwood cologne that was always on his dresser, he reached for it. Instantly, his eyes were drawn to his image in the mirror. His brow furrowed as he considered the man staring back. How could he have been so naive as to think he was being reasonable—even sacrificial—in allowing Elizabeth and Georgiana so much time alone? Perhaps it resulted from not wanting Elizabeth to think him so jealous as to complain about his own sister. Yet, his aunt had completely disabused him of the notion that he was being generous by relating Elizabeth's feelings on the situation as well as her own.

Elizabeth loves Georgiana, but she is wholly devoted to you. Too late she recognised that she had erred in giving her sister her complete attention. She deeply desires that your relationship be as it was before my niece came home. Though she has every intention of spending time with Georgiana, she intends the better part of it to be done together as a family.

Now, Nephew, you need to draw a line with Georgiana. While you may have thought you were being noble by allowing her to have so many private tête-a-têtes with Elizabeth, you were wrong! She is your wife, not Georgiana's companion! That is not to say they shall not spend time alone, just not continuously.

And with regards to your duties and responsibilities as Master of Pemberley, there may well be instances when your presence is needed, but I have learned that the majority of estate problems can be handled by a good steward. You have not seen me rushing to Ashcroft Manor whenever something was amiss. That is because I let Mr. Wainwright do his job. You pay Mr. Pickering a good salary, I imagine, so tell him what you want and authorize him to act in your stead.

Most importantly, never be away from home so long that Elizabeth begins to doubt your devotion to her. She is your strength, Fitzwilliam! If you forget that, you shall fail in all things, but especially in your marriage!

The sting of her rebuke was crushing! Not because he had been proven wrong, but because he had not realised how deeply his fixation on other matters had affected Elizabeth.

Why did you not ask Elizabeth what she thought about your being away? I know you are used to making decisions without consulting anyone, but you are married now. Stop trying to 'guess' what she is thinking and discuss it with her. Communication is the key to a successful marriage!

Properly humbled, he was certain that the only good portion of his aunt's dressing down was learning that Elizabeth missed him as much as he had missed her. Praying under his breath that she would accept his apology, he noted that his hair was unkempt and searched the dresser for a comb. Raking it through his still damp hair, when the usual strands fell across his forehead, he shrugged in defeat. Then heading to the door that led into their joint sitting room, he entered to find it empty.

Fully expecting Elizabeth to be in her bedroom, he was crossing the room towards that door when he spied her out of the corner of his eye. Though night had fallen, a full moon revealed her on the balcony and that she was wearing the transparent silk gown she had worn on their wedding night. As he stood transfixed, a strong breeze began to tousle her hair, causing the gown to cling to her every curve. In an instant he was behind her, pulling her against his body, one arm resting under her breasts, the other around her waist. Burying his face in the crook of her neck, he placed moist kisses over every inch of silky skin visible, begging forgiveness between each scorching caress.

"Forgive me, Elizabeth! I love you so much! I never meant to hurt you. Please say you still love me."

"I *do* love you, but it is you who should forgive me. I was so very blind. I—"

As she turned her head to address him, he could resist no longer and captured her lips. Without breaking the kiss, she turned around to face him. Their bodies melded as his hands slid down to urge her closer.

And as their ardour grew, Elizabeth's legs began to buckle. William reached down to pick her up and swiftly made his way to the bedroom. Once inside, he set her on her feet, and after undressing them both, urged her backwards toward the bed and placed her there.

Knowing now how wrong he had been and how much he had hurt her, his relief at her forgiveness stirred a desire to claim her in every possible way. Thus, the rest of the night was marked by very little sleep, and William made love to Elizabeth as though he were a man possessed. After their last particularly satisfying union, she literally collapsed atop him, unable to move while she caught her breath. William stoked her back while she recovered.

"Are … are we to make up in this manner whenever we disagree?" Elizabeth said breathlessly. Then she giggled. "I would almost be willing to force a quarrel if this is the consequence."

William rolled over, taking her along so that she now lay beneath him. "You will have no need of creating quarrels, my love. I intend to make love to you in this manner for the rest of our lives!"

And with those words, he proceeded to prove his boast.

It was well after noon the next day when a very exhausted but contented looking couple greeted Mrs. Reynolds as they descended the grand staircase, informing her that they were ready to break their fast. She smiled, nodded and then rushed to the kitchen to inform Mrs. Lightfoot, the elderly cook, that a meal was needed without delay.

Mrs. Lightfoot exclaimed in her customary straightforward manner, "They must be starved! Half the day is past! I cannot imagine anything so important as to keep the master away from my scones!"

Mrs. Reynolds did not reprimand her, as it would have served no purpose. Mrs. Lightfoot carried a courtesy title, but she had never been married and simply had no idea what Mr. Darcy might consider more important than food. Chuckling to herself as she headed to her office, the housekeeper took a deep, satisfying breath and let it go.

It is so good to see the Darcys happy again! Thank God for Lady Ashcroft!

Westcott Manor
One week later

The morning had dawned clear and beautiful, the rain from the last few days disappearing as swiftly as the butterflies that flit about the flowers in the gardens. It was almost as though God was determined to show the newlyweds that He approved of their union. At least, that was what the new Countess of Westcott, Lady Audrey Landingham, chose to believe. After all, last night there had been no reason to hope their wedding day would be any different than the previous three. Nevertheless, as Marshall led her across the rain-washed brick terrace, she peered up through a canopy of oak trees at a brilliant blue sky —proof enough that God answers prayers.

As she was contemplating divine intervention, Marshall suddenly stopped walking and turned to pull her into his embrace. He kissed her tenderly before whispering, "You are the most beautiful woman in the world, Audrey."

She smiled a bit teasingly. "You may be in need of spectacles, but I shall not be the one to point it out! Instead, I shall just accept that you are blinded by love and refuse to disagree."

"I mean it, my love. Each time I look at you, you take my breath away."

Instantly she was being kissed! A kiss entirely unlike any she had shared with Marshall in the past and clearly meant to demonstrate the depth of his desire. For a moment, she pondered just who might see them via the floor-to-ceiling windows or the French doors that spanned the length of the terrace, for if ever a kiss was not suitable for witnesses, it was this one. Even so, mesmerized by her husband and losing all ability to think, the passionate embrace continued for some time, in full view of any guest who might look.

Suddenly, the orchestra began to play a German[28] waltz, and the music wafted through the open doors. Audrey looked up at Marshall, surprise written across her face. The rift created when the waltz was introduced at Almacks was a frequent subject of some of their closest acquaintances.

"Is that a waltz?"

"Yes, it is. I gave the conductor a little something extra to play it."

She chuckled. "I cannot wait to hear what the *ton* will say when news reaches London."

"Frankly, I do not care, love. I happened to be at Almacks[29] when Countess

---

[28] *The German Waltz was introduced in England in 1811. The earliest waltzes were not as we think of them now, but more like the dance between Maria and Captain Von Trapp in **The Sound of Music**. "A waltz in Austen's novels refers to a tune and time signature for a country dance, which might have included a landler-like figure, in which the lady danced under her partner's raised arms." The Regency Encyclopedia.*

[29] *Almacks. An exclusive assembly room opened in 1765. The dancing was decorous and dull until the wife of the Russian Ambassador, Countess Lieven, caused a sensation by introducing the waltz and whirling round the floor with Lord "Cupid" Palmerston." Note: Since Lieven did not become a patron until*

Lieven danced a waltz with Palmerston. I was captivated by the gracefulness of the movements. I confess to asking a good friend to show me the steps in hopes of waltzing with you," Marshall declared, kissing the tip of her nose. "Now, what say you? Shall we waltz?"

She laughed. "I have no idea how it is done."

"It is a very simple step. Just follow me!"

Pulling her tight against his body, in no time at all they were floating around the terrace as though they had been waltzing all their lives.

When the waltz began, William was waiting for Richard to return from a private conversation with his father. The few couples brave enough to venture onto the ballroom floor to perform were being watched by the majority. Several ladies nearby remarked loudly that they would love to waltz, but had no partner. Having no intention of accommodating them, most certainly not during a waltz, William concluded he should forget Richard and find Elizabeth. Spying his wife standing with the Countess of Matlock and Alicia near the French doors, he quickly fled into the hallway, only to re-enter a doorway closer to Elizabeth. As he moved towards her, he was pleased when she spied him and smiled lovingly.

Nearing the women, he bowed slightly, "Ladies." Then he turned to Elizabeth, devouring her with his eyes as he kissed her hand. "My love."

"Fitzwilliam, where have you been? It is not like you to leave your lovely bride alone," his aunt teased, winking at Alicia.

Without being distracted, he replied, "I have been trying to find my bride since the music began, in case she wished to dance. I would never allow her to waltz with anyone save me."

Evelyn Fitzwilliam teased her niece. "A very wise man, your husband."

Elizabeth beamed. "I think so." Then she assured William, "I would never waltz with anyone but you, and since I do not know how to waltz, you have no worries that I shall require you to do so."

The last word was barely out of her mouth before she paled and reached out to William as though to steady herself. Naturally, William panicked, pulling her into his embrace.

"Elizabeth?"

Recovering just a bit, she began to reassure him. "I am well, Fitzwilliam, but a little fresh air and something to drink would be welcome."

As he led her out the door, he beseeched Alicia, "Please—a glass of punch." His cousin rushed to do as he asked, while his aunt followed them onto the terrace.

Seeing them enter, Audrey's attention was instantly drawn to her niece. Quitting the waltz with Marshall, she rushed to join the countess at Elizabeth's side.

1814 it would actually have happened after that date. I have moved the date for this story. The Regency Encyclopedia.

"What has happened?"

"I … I felt faint, that is all. I am almost recovered already."

"Send for Mr. Basset immediately!" William ordered, knowing the local physician would move heaven and earth to help. After all, the Darcys had constructed his clinic in Lambton in order to help him serve the community.

"I do not think that is necessary." Lady Landingham countered, giving her niece a look that asked if she had told William her suspicions.

In answer to her aunt's unspoken enquiry, Elizabeth barely shook her head no.

Lady Matlock happily declared with great confidence, "Most likely you have an heir on the way! I remember feeling faint for the first weeks with all my children." Then seeing the perplexed look on her nephew's face and the guilt on Elizabeth's, she apologised, "Oh dear! I fear I should not have voiced my opinion without thinking. I am sorry if I have invaded your privacy."

Elizabeth reached for her hand and gave it a squeeze. "All is well." Then she turned to William. "I was not certain, so I did not say anything. I was being overly cautious, I fear, because all the signs indicate that we are to be blessed with a child."

William picked her up and twirled her in a circle before setting her down. Immediately he declared, "Forgive me! You are faint, and I have likely made it worse. It is just that I am so thrilled with the news!"

Elizabeth smoothed a curl from his face. "I knew you would be."

And then, in front of his family and all the guests who had come to see what was occurring on the terrace, he kissed Elizabeth so fiercely that the hum of the resulting chatter rivaled the volume of the music.

Amused, Marshall whispered in Audrey's ear. "I do not think we need worry about the *ton's* reaction to the waltz, my dear. Once again our nephew has managed to divert attention from anyone save himself!"

Chapter **49**

London
Darcy House
Three months later

Now that November was nearing an end, the weather had turned cold and bitter with intermittent snow and ice. For this reason, Elizabeth had been housebound since she and William had journeyed to Town a week before. If truth be told, she had been indoors on most days, since William insisted she not walk out unless he was available to go with her.

Today was sunny and the paths were clear, and she dearly wished to enjoy Hyde Park. Even the knowledge that her most beloved sister was in Town and could arrive at any minute did little to temper the disappointment she felt of not taking a walk because Fitzwilliam had to meet with his steward.

I am pregnant, not an invalid! A footman would do just as well, if he is not available. Fitzwilliam is simply too cautious.

She had had only two fainting spells in the first weeks of her pregnancy, but she well knew that William would not be dissuaded in his precautions. Thus, growing tired of staring at the park through the tall windows of the library, she sighed and went to her sitting room in defeat. Once inside the light green and lavender sanctuary, she went directly to the window seat and sat down, pushing aside the curtains.

I can at least see the garden from here.

As she watched with increasing melancholy, she absently fingered a new ring that adorned her right hand. It was an exact replica of Fitzwilliam's signet that he had secretly commissioned just before they wed. Stopping to peer at it anew, her temper began to wane as she thought of how often her husband had lamented the fact that he felt responsible for leaving her unprotected in the park that fateful day. Her hand stroked the slight roundness of her belly, and she smiled to think of the child within.

I suppose I cannot expect him to be any less vigilant with you on the way.

A knock on the door brought her thoughts back to the present, and her heart began to beat faster. Was Jane downstairs? Standing, she called, "Come."

The door slowly opened but instead of a servant, Jane peeked inside the room. Seeing that Elizabeth was alone, she pushed the door back and rushed into her sister's arms.

"Oh, Lizzy, I have missed you so much!"

They hugged back and forth, in their usual joyous manner.

"And I you," Elizabeth replied, "but why did you not just come right in? I told Mrs. Barnes that you were expected and did not have to be announced."

"I shall never again rush into a room after what happened at Netherfield." Jane's hands flew to her face. "I do not think the colour in my cheeks has returned to normal ever since."

Elizabeth's own face flushed at the remembrance of what happened the day before the Bingleys' wedding, though she tried not to show her discomfiture. "I told you that you were not interrupting! Fitzwilliam was merely ..." Her voice trailed off and she looked away, trying to think of a good explanation.

Jane smiled at her inability to continue. "Merely?" She smirked.

Elizabeth slapped her sister's hand teasingly. "You know I cannot think of what to say."

Her sister laughed and Elizabeth could only do likewise. The memory of Jane rushing into her dressing room to find William quickly turning to straighten his breeches while she slid from her perch on the edge of the dresser, madly pulling down her skirts, was still vivid.

"Let us just say that I learned my lesson!" Jane said impertinently. Then changing the subject, she added, "Where is Georgiana? From your last letter, I expected she would be here."

"She decided to stay with Fitzwilliam's aunt and uncle last night. She was most upset at not being granted permission to attend the ball, but Fitzwilliam and Lord Landingham both think her too young. Besides, she was allowed to attend the dinner party for Richard's engagement."

"I think it is a blessing that she has so many family members who love her and wish to spend time with her."

"It has worked out well for everyone concerned. Is Charles downstairs?"

"Yes. Fitzwilliam was just coming out of his study when we arrived, and they were speaking when I left." Jane indicated that Elizabeth should sit back down, and when she did, Jane joined her on the window seat. "Now, I need your advice. I need your help to decide what to wear to the earl's ball tomorrow. I have no wish to embarrass you in front of your relations."

"You could never be an embarrassment, Jane. Think of what Mama said when I was in Meryton for your wedding," Elizabeth teased. "If I remember correctly, her exact words were: 'You have always been an embarrassment to me and to this family, whereas Jane has always shown exemplary behaviour.'"

"Oh, Lizzy, that was my fault! If I had not been so careless, she never would have learned that you and Fitzwilliam were going to arrive two days before the wedding. Then she would not have hastily arranged that dinner party in order to show off for our neighbours. Why she would want to pretend that you and she are close, I cannot begin to know."

"It is not your fault. The news would have reached her the minute after our coach rolled through Meryton. After all, Aunt Phillips would have known and hastened to inform her. Looking back on it, I suppose I should have convinced Fitzwilliam to dine at Longbourn in order to appease her."

"I do not think you would have been successful. I cannot see Fitzwilliam feigning good relations with Mama. He is very protective of you, and does not take kindly to our mother's manipulations."

"He is very protective," Elizabeth said with a slight lift of the corners of her mouth. "But by him not accommodating Mama, she almost ruined your wedding. I thought she was going to stand up and denounce Fitzwilliam and me just before the ceremony began. If not for Papa—"

"Yes, fortunately he was able to curb her tongue," Jane interjected. "Though I only imagine she had plenty to say on the way back to Longbourn after the ceremony."

"I still regret that we could not stay for the breakfast."

"Think nothing of it. We shall have ample opportunity to share each other's company in the future. After all, we are to be at Pemberley for Christmas."

"Yes. Sharing the holiday with you and Charles will be a blessing. And I am so happy that you were invited to Richard's engagement ball."

"I was surprised by the invitation. I suppose we were invited because of my connection to you."

"Your Mr. Bingley has always been a favourite of my husband and a good friend to Colonel Fitzwilliam. So, I can safely say that you and Charles would have been invited no matter who Fitzwilliam Darcy had married."

"That is kind of you to say, but I am of a different opinion. In any event, I am glad that it was YOU who married Fitzwilliam Darcy!"

From the doorway a deep voice broke in. "I am profoundly glad as well!"

Immediately Elizabeth was on her feet, hurrying to her husband to receive a hug. With her in his embrace, William smiled at Jane over his wife's head. He had learned of the Bingley's arrival the minute he dismissed his steward and opened his study door. After installing Charles in the billiards room, he had excused himself in order to speak to his wife.

"Elizabeth has been ecstatic since learning that you were going to be in London to attend Richard's engagement ball."

"As I just told Lizzy, I am so pleased to have been included in the guest list."

"Wait until the ball is over and then we shall see if you are still pleased," William teased. "There are many members of the *ton*, along with a few family members, that I could do without seeing."

All three occupants of the room laughed. "I am done with estate business and shall be in the billiards room, sweetheart. If you need anything, do not hesitate to send for me." Then addressing Jane he added, "Charles and I intend to see just who is the most unpracticed." With that, William smiled and left the room.

"He is certainly very happy, your Mr. Darcy."

"We are both happy," Elizabeth said, still staring at the empty door. "And he is even more attentive since he learned of the baby."

Jane reached out to touch her sister's stomach, saying wistfully, "I wish I were expecting a child."

"Aunt Audrey said it will happen when you least expect it, and she was right in my case. She also said that fretting over the situation is never a good way to accomplish it."

Jane smiled. "I shall try to remember that. Now tell me, when can I expect to become an aunt?"

"At the end of April."

"The end of April," Jane repeated thoughtfully. "I cannot believe that we are married, Lizzy, and you are to be a mother! It seems only yesterday that we lay in our bed at Longbourn and plotted our future."

"I do not think either of us plotted anything as wonderful as we have found."

"We are the most fortunate of women! Agreed?"

"Agreed!"

"And now that we have settled that, let me see the illustration you mentioned in your letter. Your description was unclear, and I fear I could not imagine how the hair would be styled."

Elizabeth went to the dresser, opened a drawer and pulled out the latest issue of *The Lady's Monthly Museum*[30] which featured two elegant, coloured plates portraying the latest fashion.

"The minute I saw this illustration I knew your hair would look lovely styled in this manner!"

The sisters spent the rest of the day planning their mission to dazzle the *ton* at Matlock Manor the following evening.

Downstairs

The clack of billiard balls hitting one another replaced most conversation until the end of the game, which ended with another win for William. Charles Bingley tossed his cue stick on the velvet table in defeat.

"I cannot believe how soundly you trounced me, Darcy. Three games out of three and you say you have not played in months?"

"It has been at least three months, perhaps longer," William smiled wryly. "My attention has been taken by more pleasurable activities lately."

"As a newly married man, I understand completely," Charles said, grinning widely. "I am just glad that I did not wager more on this game." Sighing, he reached in his coat pocket to retrieve a shilling and tossed it to William. "What say you to retiring to your study for a glass of that brandy I am so fond of? At least that shall not cost me anything!"

"No, that shall cost me! That is the finest brandy being smuggled out of France and it costs a king's ransom!" Tossing an arm over his friend's shoulder, William began walking towards the door, "But you are worth that and more. I shall never forget your steadfast help during Elizabeth's rescue."

As they continued down the hall towards the study, Charles tried to protest that he had done nothing extraordinary but to no avail. Once they were seated inside William's sanctuary, glasses in hand, his host's expression became solemn as he brought up another subject.

"Richard informs me that Caroline has recently married Colonel Hedges, who is one of his oldest army acquaintances. The colonel has already been invited to

---

[30] *The Lady's Monthly Museum, first published in 1798 by Dean and Munday in Threadneedle Street, London. A "Polite repository of Amusement and Instruction," it was designed to "please the Fancy, interest the Mind, or exalt the Character of the British Fair." Each issue had one, sometimes two, "elegantly coloured plates" portraying the latest fashions.*

the engagement ball and now Caroline will, no doubt, accompany him."

"Yes, I only learned of it just last week from Louisa. I intended to tell you in person, as I knew you would not be pleased."

"Bloody awful development," William said dryly. "I despise that she managed to capture someone with connections to my family. How did it come about?"

"Hedges' father died suddenly, and he resigned his commission in order to run the family estate. Rumours abound that the father was quite a gambler and sold much of the land to pay his debts. It is now half the size of Longbourn and provides roughly a thousand pounds a year. In any event, Hedges had escorted Caroline around Town a few times before I banished her to live in Scarborough. Once he became master of the estate, he sought her out and made an offer. Now that she is no longer my responsibility, the decision was entirely up to her. The only advantage to the match is that she will not end up a spinster, as there is little income and no title. She will never be received in the circles she has always coveted."

"Except those where her husband's army connections gain her entrance—such as my cousin's engagement ball."

Charles looked sheepish. "Yes, exceptions will occur on occasion, I imagine."

"I do not relish seeing her again or exposing Elizabeth to her vitriol."

"It would be foolish of her to ruin a chance to be in polite society again, especially while a guest at the earl's home," Charles replied, sitting his empty glass on the top of William's desk. He stood and paced nervously. "But prudence was never one of Caroline's virtues." Then he stopped in front of the desk. "I apologise, Darcy. If I could forbid her to come, I would."

"She is no longer under your protection, Charles. Let us hope that if she attends, she surprises us all with good manners." William stood to stretch his legs. He walked around the desk and stopped in front of a map of England on the wall. "Have you given more thought about moving farther from the Bennets?"

Charles's expression became pensive. "I have but I have not discussed it with Jane as yet. Why, have you come across a property already?"

"I have it on good authority that there is one within ten miles of Pemberley and another within thirty that shall come on the market after the first of the year." He pointed to the map. "The one closest to Pemberley is located here." Charles walked over to see where William was indicating. "And this is the location of the other."

Charles was pondering the map and had not replied, so William continued. "If you want me to inspect them and I find them satisfactory, when you and Jane come for Christmas you may inspect them yourselves."

"I would be obliged for your help."

"Good. Elizabeth and I would love to have you both close by."

"Yes, I expect you would so you can whip me at billiards whenever the mood strikes you!"

The sounds of boisterous laughter startled Mrs. Barnes as she passed the study on her way to the conservatory to gather some flowers. She stopped to listen and smiled.

It is so good to have the family back and to think a child is on the way! With such handsome parents he is sure to be a fine-looking boy! She quit walking to reconsider. *It could be a girl. Yet, Mr. Darcy's mother said all the Darcys have a boy first! So this child is sure to be the heir!*

Satisfied with her logic, the old housekeeper continued down the hall.

Matlock House
The Engagement Ball
The next evening

Once again, the stately townhouse of the Earl and Countess Matlock served as the setting for a gala occasion. Every surface was polished and shined as it had for the Darcys' wedding, but this time it was in celebration of the engagement of their younger son, Richard, to Lady Colleen Tierney. Never known for sparing expense when it came to entertaining, the sky was the limit when family was concerned.

As the Darcys' carriage approached the front of Matlock House, every window of the manor was glowing, thanks to hundreds of candles in every room as well as in the huge chandeliers. The sounds of chamber music could be heard on the street below, and the night seemed alive with people. Some were being helped from expensive carriages, while still others gathered across the street to witness the spectacle. There were even a few poor souls hiding in the shadows, hoping to beg a farthing when the men hired to secure the house were not looking.

William instinctively leaned over to peer out the window at the three storey facade and sighed.

"Any regrets?" Elizabeth said with concern. At his look of confusion, she added, "I heard a sigh. Are you sad that Georgiana was upset at not being allowed to come?"

William smiled and took her hand. "No. She was allowed to attend the dinner, and that was sufficient for her age. I am not sad at all. I was remembering our wedding day—the happiest day of my life."

She squeezed his hand. "Being here makes me remember it too. But you have been so subdued all day, as though you were not eager to attend tonight."

"While I shall never relish attending balls, I no longer dread them as long as you are with me." He lifted her hand and softly planted a kiss on the back of it.

"So you think me your charm—something to rescue you from the schemes of the *ton*?" she teased.

His eye grew dark. "You are so much more than that. You are my salvation, Elizabeth."

A passionate kiss ensued before the door swung open, and they were forced to leave the privacy of the carriage. Still holding hands and exchanging loving glances, they entered the foyer to find it empty of all but a few servants. At that instant, the band struck up a minuet.

"Oh dear," Elizabeth said. "We have missed the receiving line, and the ball has begun in earnest. I do hope our family will forgive our tardiness."

"Do not worry, love. I informed Aunt Evelyn that we would arrive after everyone else, as I did not want you on your feet all night. I also informed her that we are leaving directly after supper. She had no objections to my plans."

"Fitzwilliam!" Elizabeth declared, her brows furrowing with concern. "You will have them think me an invalid. I am perfectly able to stand for long periods of time. In fact, I plan to dance often tonight."

William stopped, bringing her to a halt as well. "With whom do you intend to dance in your condition?"

Elizabeth tried not to smile. "Both our aunts assured me that the way my gown is designed my condition is not obvious. I dare say most may not realise I am with child. And I intend to dance with whoever cares to ask!"

With that, she let go his arm and boldly walked towards the ballroom. By the time she reached the door, he had caught up with her. Taking her arm, he again wrapped it around his own, causing her to look up and smile. And as they stepped inside the ballroom, every head turned to observe the handsome couple.

"Come, Mrs. Darcy," William whispered, "if you wish to dance, I am your willing partner."

After supper, the ballroom became so congested that it was almost impossible to keep track of the family though, in his usual manner, William tried. He and Richard stood to one side, waiting until Lady Colleen and Elizabeth were through dancing with Lord Matlock and Edgar respectively. He had seen Alicia accept Bingley's offer to dance, while Colonel Neilson partnered Lady Ashcroft, and glancing to his left, he watched as Lord Landingham led Jane to the dance floor. Still in the far corner, his Aunt Evelyn seemed to be holding court along with several of the ladies of Almacks.

William's eyes narrowed when he caught sight of Caroline standing near the countess. Every so often, she tried to insinuate herself into the group with a remark, but she was having no success. It was little wonder as her usual attire—a burnt orange coloured gown and a turban covered in ostrich feathers of the same shade—stood in sharp contrast to the pale gowns worn by the *ton*. The deepening frown on her face each time her efforts went unrewarded caused her usual pinched expression to be even more pronounced and William chuckled aloud.

At the sound of William's laugh, Richard looked in the direction of his cousin's gaze. Seeing the spectre in orange, he laughed as well, which caused William to begin anew. When those standing nearby turned to see what was so amusing, they both struggled to calm and keep a straight face.

Finally able to speak again, Richard whispered, "I am relieved that she has had the good sense not to approach you or Elizabeth. Still, I find it hard to believe that Colonel Hedges married that worrisome gossip, though I suppose Caroline is a step up for him. Do not mistake my meaning. He is a good man, just not the most handsome of men."

"Your mother remarked that Caroline has the advantage when it comes to height and that Hedges has the advantage when it comes to freckles! She noted that while Caroline has a few freckles across her nose, the colonel is covered in them from head to toe—or at least all the visible parts."

"That is undisputable! Well, I can only hope the man knows what he has signed up for by marrying her. As for me, I would rather face Bonaparte! And as for Caroline, Mother has no intention of recognising her, now or in the future. You can rely on that."

Once more turning his attention to the woman he loved, Richard searched the crowd on the dance floor until he found Colleen. After watching her graceful moves for a few seconds, he asked, "So, what is your impression of Lady Colleen?"

William glanced to his cousin. "I have only just met her tonight."

"I know, but you are quick to take the measure of new acquaintances, and I wish to hear your first impression."

"Other than being very beautiful, intelligent and good natured, I see nothing to recommend her," William teased.

Richard punched his cousin on the arm. "I knew you would like her. She is a lot like your Elizabeth, though she is not as lively. I think that shall come in time, as she becomes accustomed to all of us."

William studied his cousin seriously. "In all these years, I have never known you to misjudge anyone's character. If you love her, then we shall all love her, of that I am certain. It is obvious that every woman in the family is already enchanted with her, even Frances. A man can easily be charmed, but not another woman."

"Yes, even Frances seems to like Lady Colleen, though one can never be sure what Edgar's wife truly thinks. As long as she acts in a friendly manner, I am satisfied."

"I feel the same about her actions toward Elizabeth."

With the mention of his wife, Darcy rose on his toes to locate her on the dance floor. Seeing her laugh as she twirled about the floor with Edgar caused him to frown. Having had two dances with her already, it was irrational to be envious of Edgar's set, but he was. Not insensible to his cousin's feelings, Richard noticed his discomfit and, as usual, decided to make the most of it.

"Edgar is a very a good dancer," he ventured. "I think he has bested you and me at the art, would you not say so, Darcy?"

William took a deep breath but refused to comment, so Richard tried again.

"Though he has never been my favourite person, I will give him his due! He is light on his feet! I can certainly see why Elizabeth, well, all the ladies, love to partner with him."

Just then the dance ended, and William tired not to smile as he whispered to his cousin, "I suppose Lady Colleen is fortunate then, for since Edgar has exhausted his sets with Elizabeth, he will most likely impress your fiancée next."

Richard's brow furrowed as he turned to see Edgar leading Elizabeth off the floor and in the direction of Colleen. "I think I shall see if my fiancée would care for some punch."

William chuckled as Richard rushed to collect Colleen and lead her towards the refreshments. Then straightening to his full height, he went to collect his wife. The viscount was still talking with Elizabeth when he stepped forward to claim her.

"Your wife is a lively conversationalist as well as a wonderful dancer, Darcy. I cannot say when I have enjoyed a dance so well."

"I agree that she is both," William remarked taking her hand and wrapping it around his arm. "Now, if you will excuse us, Edgar, I think Elizabeth could use a respite from dancing."

Edgar nodded, following the Darcys with his eyes as they walked away.

That woman is extraordinary. Darcy is a damn lucky man! I wish I had had

the courage to marry for love instead of money.

"Are you not going to ask me to dance, Edgar?" His wife's whiny voice broke the spell, and Edgar turned to display a pasted on smile.

"I had no idea you wished to dance with me, Frances. After all, most of the time you had rather partner one of those dandies who populate every social occasion."

"But you seem so in demand tonight that I thought I should like to see what I might have missed. After all, you seem to be a most sought after partner."

Thus, the viscount spent the rest of the night being shadowed by his jealous wife.

Wearier than she had imagined she would be at this hour, Elizabeth was glad to reach the corner of the ballroom where Fitzwilliam helped her to a seat on an upholstered bench. Wishing for some fresh air but knowing that William was unlikely to let her go outside with the temperatures dropping, she made another request.

"I would dearly love a glass of punch, Fitzwilliam."

William leaned down to say quietly, "If you will promise to wait right here until I return, I shall be happy to be of service."

"Of course."

He had walked only a few feet when he encountered Lady Ashcroft. Elizabeth smiled as she watched them both look in her direction. Afterward, William continued on his way while her aunt hurried to sit beside her, patting her hand as she did.

"How is one of my favourite people?" As she got a better look at Elizabeth, her expression changed to concern, and she reached to tilt her niece's face gently from side to side, as a mother might a child. When she spoke, it was just loud enough for Elizabeth to hear. "You look a little pale, my dear. Has the evening been too strenuous?"

"I would never tell Fitzwilliam, as he has been after me to leave since supper, but I am just a bit fatigued," Elizabeth confessed, smiling wanly. "I was never this tired so early in the evening."

"You must make allowances for your condition, and you must not overtax yourself. Bless him, Fitzwilliam is right in that regard." She chuckled quietly. "Not that you should always let him know that he is right."

"Now, from one who thinks of you as a daughter, I believe you should listen to your husband tonight. You have done your duty to the family and endured long enough. Go home and get some rest." She thought for a moment and then added, "And I do mean for you to rest! Do not let Fitzwilliam persuade you into other activities. I happen to know he can be quite charming when he wants something very much."

Suddenly, William was standing before them with a glass of punch and a small plate of biscuits. As he presented the refreshments to Elizabeth, he declared, "Sweets for my sweet!"

Elizabeth and Audrey both began to chuckle, covering their mouths so as not to be heard by those nearby.

William's brows furrowed in confusion. "I am sorry if I said something amiss. I was only endeavouring to be charming."

This caused them to laugh even more.

Chapter *50*

Pemberley
June, 1813

A s the sun rose over the peaks, casting faint light on the old Pemberley Chapel at the top of the hill and dispelling the morning mist, Fitzwilliam Darcy made his way up the familiar stone steps. He had slipped out of bed before dawn so as not to awaken Elizabeth and then walked the short distance to this place in hopes of accomplishing what he wished before she discovered he was no longer in their bed. He felt drawn here on this particular day.

Departing the manor stealthily, only a few servants were aware that he had risen, much less left the house, but Mrs. Reynolds knew. Whenever he was in residence, she seemed to have a sixth sense about where he was at all times. And just when he thought he had escaped her detection, she appeared in the foyer with a small bouquet of flowers collected from the conservatory. Without a word, she offered it to him, waiting until he shifted the blanket-wrapped form tucked securely under his chin in order to grasp them. He nodded his appreciation though his heart was too full of emotion to form a proper smile of gratitude.

Sometimes she knows me too well.

The chapel was now plainly visible—a small but regal stone building, utilised for centuries for baptisms, funerals and private devotions by his relations, most of whom were buried in the tree-canopied acreage next to it. At some point in time, an elaborate wrought-iron fence, featuring a grand lych-gate*[31] with a cross atop it, had been erected around the cemetery and ordinarily, he would stop to admire the gate's ornate workmanship before slipping inside the sacred plot. But not today—today he was of a singular mind.

Weathered headstones, which had been lost in fog only minutes before, now appeared to rise out of the haze—silent sentinels marking final resting places. Silently threading his way through the hallowed ground, he spied the stone marking the gravesite of the one person he missed most sorely since the birth of his first child.

Anne Fitzwilliam Darcy
Beloved Wife and Mother

---

[31] *Lych-gate is a gateway covered with a roof found at the entrance to traditional English or English-style churchyard. Wikipedia.org*

June 25, 1761 – March 3, 1810[32]

Unbidden tears filled his eyes at the sight, and he blinked to keep them at bay. Kneeling on the soft grass that covered his mother's grave, he carefully laid the flowers near the stone and then began to open the top of the securely wrapped bundle. One arm, covered with a soft knitted coat, waved wildly as it was set free and his heart swelled with love at the sight. Continuing the task, the other arm was soon liberated along with an angelic face that was almost lost beneath a matching knit cap of blue. A fringe of black hair framed the beloved visage while light blue eyes, ringed by equally black lashes, squinted against the sunlight now spreading across this place.

"Do not fret, little one. Papa is here."

Hearing his father's voice, the baby focused on William and he smiled a toothless grin. That expression garnered several kisses across his cheeks before William turned the boy to face his grandmother's headstone. Then taking a ragged breath, he began to speak.

"Mother, may I present your grandson, Fitzwilliam Alexander Marshall Darcy, who is ten weeks old today. I intended to bring him here before now, however, immediately after his birth, we had unseasonably cold weather, and Elizabeth feared taking him out of doors. She is very protective of our son. You, of all people, would understand. After all, you were equally as protective of Georgiana and me."

He glanced down at the baby who was now unusually quiet as he took in his surroundings.

"Elizabeth had an arduous labour, and her welfare has weighed heavily on my mind these past weeks. I thank God that she is greatly improved and that Alexander is thriving, allowing me to bring him here today." He smiled as he described his son. "Elizabeth is delighted that he favours me, while I would have been pleased if he looked more like her. Nonetheless, he has my hair, eyes and the Darcy nose. Mercifully, I believe that he has inherited her personality. After all, he is a very lively and contented little fellow."

As if agreeing, Alexander gurgled loudly once more, this time waving his arms simultaneously and causing his father to smile in earnest before focusing on the headstone again.

"Alex has quite the appetite, as Elizabeth can barely finish with one feeding before he cries for another and, yes, she insists on nursing him against my wishes. I felt it was too much for her to bear during her recuperation, but she would not listen." He smiled lovingly at the headstone. "Aunt Audrey tells me that she is much like you in that regard."

Then William became pensive as he considered that truth. "Truly though, her spiritedness in standing up for what she believes is what I admire most about my wife. You would have loved her, Mother."

At that point, he turned Alexander back around to face himself, running a finger down a chubby cheek which caused the baby and his father to smile at each other before William continued.

---

[32] *Dates are fabricated to fit the story.*

"There is hardly a day that goes by that I am not reminded of you, especially as I attempt to recall everything you taught me about infants when Georgiana was born. And be assured that I shall tell Alexander and all of our children stories of their grandmother, so your influence will be felt in their lives for years to come."

Carefully he began to rewrap the baby in the blanket as though preparing to leave. "I should return, for I do not want to frighten Elizabeth. She might awaken and wonder where her husband and son have wandered." As he stood and gathered Alex under his chin, he added, "I … I just wanted to tell you that I miss you sorely on this day—your birthday. You were the best of mothers and I love you."

A soft voice came from behind, "Fitzwilliam?"

Whirling around, Elizabeth stood only a few feet away. At once, his eyes flew to a figure standing several feet behind—Mr. Spruill, one of the footmen entrusted with her safety. Acutely aware of how independent his wife was, he surmised that the guard must rise very early in order to stay ahead of his wife. Mentally, he made a note to give the man an increase in wages, even as he schooled himself not to show any concern that she had walked so far without the doctor's authorization.

"Mr. Booker will not be pleased that you have undertaken a walk of this magnitude without his permission. This hill is not an easy climb for me, much less someone who has recently given birth."

"Fitzwilliam, you know that Mr. Booker would likely give his permission at my next appointment, which is only two days hence, and I have regained a good deal of my strength by walking the halls of Pemberley. In any event, when I awoke to find you gone and Alexander missing as well, I became a bit concerned. I had just decided to begin a search, when Mrs. Curry awoke. When she insisted that you had never taken Alexander without informing her, I began to imagine all sorts of things."

"I am sorry, my love. Please accept my apology. I did not intend to worry you or Mrs. Curry. She was sound asleep on the bed in his room, and I did not wish to disturb her. I fully expected to have him back before he was missed."

Elizabeth's face softened. "I know you did not mean to alarm anyone. But thank goodness Providence bade me glance out the window to see you walking in this direction. It was then that I recalled the significance of this day."

Properly chastised, William turned to look across the great expanse of Pemberley visible from this vantage point. For a long time he said nothing, though the expression on his face made it plain that he was struggling with what he said next.

"I realise that Mother is not here—that she is with God. However, I feel close to her in the silence of this place." Nodding towards a stone bench under a tall oak, he added, "I often found her there. Father had that bench made so that she would not have to sit on the ground. She often said that being amongst our ancestors gave her a different perspective on her problems, recognising that one does not live forever."

"She was very wise." Elizabeth replied, stepping closer and bringing a bouquet of flowers from behind her back. They were very similar to his offering.

He smiled. "Mrs. Reynolds?"

Elizabeth nodded. "I decided to follow you in order to pay my respects to the woman who gave birth to my wonderful husband and provided me the opportunity to give birth to his son."

William's eyes were suspiciously shiny as he stepped aside for Elizabeth to place the flowers next to his. Then, still holding Alexander securely to his chest, he pulled her into his embrace as well. For a long while they formed a circle around their son, while William alternately kissed the top of Elizabeth's head and then Alexander's. Afterwards, he began to guide them back towards the path that led down the hill. And as they slowly made their way towards the front of the manor, Alexander decided he was hungry and made the fact known by beginning to cry.

Elizabeth laughed. "We had better hurry, or your son shall awaken the entire household before we are even inside. When he wants to be fed, he is not very patient."

They stepped up their pace, and William began to coax Alexander by jostling him up and down and soothing him with words of love. For a brief time, it worked. In fact, they were already inside the foyer before he began to cry in earnest and would not be comforted. Instantly, William led Elizabeth towards his study.

"You can feed him in here just as comfortably, and it is much closer. No need to awaken the whole house by trying to gain the nursery."

She proceeded to comply, taking a seat in her usual chair. While she opened her gown in order to feed their son, William searched a drawer in his desk where he kept a supply of clean handkerchiefs. Draping one across Elizabeth's shoulder in case she needed it, he sat down in a chair across from her. There he watched, utterly contented, as she fed Alexander.

"From the noises he makes, one would think he has not had nourishment in days," he offered, bemused at the loud sucking sounds coming from the small child.

"He was fed not long ago, though he fell asleep halfway through," Elizabeth offered, smiling. "Besides, he always sounds as though he is starving."

William's expression sobered. "Do not judge him too harshly. I know a small bit of how he feels."

One eyebrow rose wryly. "Oh? Pray tell what do you know about starving, Mr. Darcy?"

"I starve for your love constantly. Nevertheless, I have thought of never having another child if it means you will not suffer as you did with Alexander's birth. I would never sacrifice your health. You and Alexander are all I shall ever need."

"Fitzwilliam, I intend to be your wife in every way and to have many more children. The rigours of childbirth are great, but they are well worth the outcome. And Mr. Booker said that we could resume our ... *activities* ... after the eighth week."

"But, you were not well at eight weeks. You are barely stronger now."

"You are mistaken. I AM well. And I know from experience that you can be a very gentle lover. Please, do not make me wait any longer."

And with that pronouncement, William was on his knees before Elizabeth's chair. After running a hand over Alexander's soft curls, he leaned in to kiss her in such a way that there was no doubt that they would resume *activities* as soon as their son was asleep.

It was not long afterward that they encountered Mrs. Reynolds at the top of the grand staircase as they took a sleeping Alexander to the nursery.

"Mrs. Reynolds," William said quietly, "after Mrs. Darcy and I take Alexander to the nursery, we plan to rest for a short while, since we both rose so early. Besides, our guests are not due until later."

Well aware that the Bingleys, the Fitzwilliams and the Landinghams were expected to arrive that afternoon, the housekeeper was not bothered in the least.

"Everything is in order for their arrival, sir."

"Excellent."

It was a struggle, but the housekeeper managed to repress a smile. She had seen that look on William's face enough times to know what he was about. If the master felt that he and the mistress needed ... *rest* ... then who was she to thwart their plans?

"I shall see that the maids do not disturb you. They can always clean those rooms later."

As she watched her employers go down the hallway towards the nursery, Mr. Darcy's arm protectively around his wife, she could no longer hold back her smile.

Mrs. Curry had waited anxiously in the nursery for her charge to return, staring at the door the entire time. Upon the Darcy's appearance in the doorway, she leapt from her chair, rushing to take the sleeping figure from his father. Without hesitating, she hurried the child back to his bed, kissing his cheek as she lowered him down to the mattress. William and Elizabeth watched her pull a coverlet over him and gently ruffle his silky curls in a loving gesture.

"Elizabeth?" William whispered.

"Hmmm," she replied, still staring at the scene. Chuckling, he gently employed two fingers under her chin to turn her head.

"Come, darling, I have something I wish to show you." Instantly he began to lead her down the hall, past her bedroom towards his own suite of rooms.

Elizabeth giggled. "Fitzwilliam, you know that I think the bed is too high."

By then they stood before his dressing room door, and he opened it, pulling her inside. "We shall be in here only a moment." He continued through that room and into his bedroom, letting go of her hand once they stood in front of a certain picture on the wall. Lowering the painting, he exposed a safe, which he opened immediately.

"I have a present for you."

"Another? You are too good to me."

"I can never be good enough. And there is nothing I can offer that can rival your gift to me—our son. Nonetheless, I commissioned a small token to commemorate Alexander's birth."

Then pulling a long, blue velvet box tied with a white ribbon from the safe, he held it out to her.

Elizabeth's eyes flicked from the box to him and back again, before she took it. Then, holding her breath, she opened the lid and pulled back a layer of delicately thin paper. She gasped as she carefully removed a gold, heart-shaped locket strung on a delicate chain. One side was engraved with Alexander's name and date of birth—the other was embedded with diamonds, emeralds, and citrines in a daisy motif. Threaded on either side of the locket were small rings of gold, each embedded with diamonds.

"Oh, Fitzwilliam, it is so beautiful!"

"The flowers represents the month of April, when Alex was born. There is also room for a small portrait and a lock of his hair."

As he sat the box back in the safe in order to show her how to open the locket, a small paper fell to the floor. Elizabeth stooped to retrieve it and found that it was a commission for that locket and more.

"Fitzwilliam, this order is for six lockets."

He looked penitent. "I instructed the jeweller to prepare several, as I intended to present you with one upon the birth of each of our children. Then, all that would have been required is to add the child's name, date of birth, and the flower that represents the month they were born. Each heart was to fit between one of the diamond rings. "

Elizabeth giggled. "And you decided on a half-dozen."

"I ... I ordered them before you had such trouble with Alexander's birth."

"Oh, Fitzwilliam, a long labour with your first child is not unusual according to Mr. Booker, and he said that I would likely not have such a long labour with our subsequent children. Even if that were not the case, is our son not worth every second of the pain?"

"Alexander is truly a blessing, my love, but for me to see you in pain is agony itself! I do not wish to ever see you go through that again."

Elizabeth squeezed his hands. "I understand that you love me and that you suffer when I suffer. I would feel the same way if you were in pain. Nonetheless, the grief of knowing I would have no more children would be more unbearable than the pain of childbirth. And just as you were there for me with Alexander, I will need your support with our future children. I can bear anything as long as you are with me."

"Then you are not averse to having another child?"

"On the contrary, holding Alexander only serves to make me desire as many children as God will allow. And with your help, all shall be well. You will see."

"You are so brave, Elizabeth," William whispered as he pulled her into his arms. "If only I were half as fearless."

"So, tell me, my fearful husband," she replied with a wicked smile, "if there are any lockets left when the last of our children are born, what shall become of them?"

"I had not thought of that possibility."

Elizabeth ran a hand playfully over the hard muscles of her husband's chest, before continuing upward to caress his cheek.

"Then I suppose we shall just have to make it our duty to ensure there are none left."

That afternoon
The Parlour

The atmosphere in the house was electric with anticipation. This was the first gathering of most of the family at Pemberley in many years. Elizabeth's health had been so unstable immediately after Alexander's birth that William was consumed with worry. So it was not until after she improved significantly, that his thoughts turned to inviting the rest of the family to see his son, and as soon as the invitations were extended, they had been accepted. In addition to the Bingleys, Elizabeth's father and the Landinghams, who were bringing Georgiana, Richard and his new bride, Lady Colleen, were accompanying the Earl and Countess of Matlock to meet the new heir of Pemberley.

Having missed Richard's wedding because she was advised not to travel, Elizabeth was especially eager to see Lady Colleen. William had attended the wedding, consenting to travel to London to stand up with his cousin only at Elizabeth's insistence. Not surprisingly, he had arrived and departed Town in the space of three days, so anxious was he to return to her.

Being their nearest relations, the Bingleys and the Landinghams were already frequent visitors to Pemberley, while Georgiana stayed at Westcott Manor and Pemberley in equal measures. In fact, Aunt Audrey and Jane had just returned to their own homes two weeks before, having removed to Pemberley for Elizabeth's lying in and stayed until her recovery was assured. However, both the Bingleys and Landinghams had consented to stay at Pemberley during the Fitzwilliam's visit, in order to fellowship with the rest of the family. Thus the stage was set for a lovely gathering.

When the Bingleys, Mr. Bennet, the Landinghams and Georgiana arrived, right behind one another, William, Elizabeth and Alexander were on the portico to meet them. As Georgiana emerged from the carriage, she ignored her brother who had started down the steps in order to rush towards her sister and Alexander.

"Please, may I hold him, Elizabeth?"

"Once we are in the parlour and you are seated, you may."

So after all the greetings were done and they were all ensconced in the parlour, Elizabeth motioned for Georgiana to sit beside her. Gingerly she laid Alexander in her sister's arms and swiftly Georgiana arranged the baby so that he lay facing her. Then she began to remove the blanket in order to see his legs and feet.

"Oh, Elizabeth, he has gotten so big since I last saw him!"

William chuckled. "You saw him four days ago, sweetling. I do not think he could have changed that much."

"Yes, he has! You see him every day so you would not notice." She looked to Audrey Landingham for agreement. "Do you not think he has grown significantly, Aunt?"

Lady Landingham immediately took the seat on the other side of her niece, smiling down at the child who had captured her heart as well.

"I certainly do!" She winked at Elizabeth who had leaned over to hear her answer. "And he seems much more alert! See how he follows me with his eyes when I speak?"

As though on cue, Alexander gurgled.

"He knows we are talking about him!" Georgiana exclaimed, her eyes still glued to her nephew. All the other occupants of the room exchanged knowing smiles.

Just at that moment, Mr. Walker appeared at the door again. "The Fitzwilliam's coach has been reported at the first gate, sir."

Knowing that it would take about a half -hour for the coach to reach the manor, William did not move from his perch near the hearth. "Thank you, Walker. Please summon me in time to greet them."

The servant nodded, disappearing out of the room and leaving the door open as they had requested earlier. From that moment on, a jumble of conversations ensued in all areas of the room. William, Charles and Marshall were conversing near the hearth while surreptitiously watching the women ogle the baby. Meanwhile, Mr. Bennet constantly inched closer to the sofa, eventually coming to stand behind it where he had a better view of his grandson.

He had visited Elizabeth twice since her marriage, always by himself. He used the opportunity to visit Jane as well, insisting to both daughters that he travelled alone in order to escape the hysterics of his wife and other children for a brief time. Left unsaid was that Mrs. Bennet would not have been welcomed at Pemberley in any event. Neither daughter brought up the subject of their mother, for they well remembered the vitriol directed towards Lizzy at Jane's wedding.

"Would you like to hold him?"

Thomas Bennet was startled from his thoughts by Elizabeth's question. He began to mumble, "He is so small. I do not think I should be trusted—"

"Nonsense!" Elizabeth declared.

Instantly, he was being pulled around the sofa to take the place alongside Georgiana. Across the room, he heard the men laugh just before Alexander was placed in his lap. Not knowing what to say, he could only smile at the child and chuck him under the chin. That was good enough! Alexander smiled and waved his arms in his usual manner.

"He is pleased!" Georgiana declared.

Leaning over to kiss her father's cheek, Elizabeth added, "He feels safe with you."

Just then, Mr. Walker reappeared at the door, and without a word, William nodded. The servant left as William walked over to take Elizabeth's hand.

"If you will excuse us, Elizabeth and I shall greet my other relations and escort them here." Addressing his aunt, he added, "Will you see to Alexander if he begins to fret?"

Audrey nodded. "I shall be glad to, though I think he is quite content at present."

Mr. Bennet looked up to wink at Elizabeth. "I think we shall be just fine until you return."

⟡

Later

The food and drink was magnificent and the conversation stimulating, thus the entire group found themselves enjoying the fine hospitality of Pemberley. After the ordeal they had endured to rescue Elizabeth and learning of Catherine's treachery, the opportunity to welcome a new Darcy into the family was seen as a chance for them to acknowledge what was truly important—family.

After dinner, the men all assembled in William's study to enjoy some newly imported cigars, while the ladies retired to the music room. As William passed out the cigars, Lord Landingham asked the Earl if he had heard anything more regarding Lady Catherine.

"In fact, I heard from the gentleman in charge just last week. It seems Catherine tried to force several of the other incarcerated women to address her using her title. All she got for her trouble was a black eye."

"I thought Aunt Catherine had separate quarters," William said, his voice sad with concern.

"But she shares the courtyard with everyone," Richard interjected. "If she is to get any sunshine or fresh air, she has to do so with all the occupants of her building."

"I regret that she is reduced to such circumstances," William began, only to be interrupted by his uncle.

"She put herself in those circumstances! I have no sympathy for someone so eager to see you and Georgiana destroyed and to have a man killed. While I see to it that she has clean clothes, bedding and decent food, even a maid on occasion to wash her hair, my sister will never again live like a queen."

"I, for one, am glad that she is not free to harm anyone," Richard declared.

The Music Room

For a long time, the women listened silently as Georgiana, who had been prompted, exhibited on the pianoforte. Finally Jane leaned over to speak privately to her sister. Since they occupied the settee nearest the door their conversation would not be a disruption nor could they easily be overheard.

"I have some wonderful news to share with you, but I do not wish for anyone else to know as yet." Elizabeth's eyes grew large as she waited for Jane to continue. Seeing that she had her sister's full attention, Jane whispered excitedly, "I believe that I am with child!"

Elizabeth wanted to shout, but instead, she quickly glanced about the room to find no one paying any attention to them. Squeezing Jane's hand, she whispered in reply, "I am so pleased I want to do a jig."

"If you do, you will give away my secret. I have not even told Charles as yet because I understand that only the quickening is a sure indication. I do not want to raise his expectations, only to be disappointed."

"I understand your reluctance. I was resolved to wait until the quickening as well, but my secret was revealed straightaway when I nearly fainted. Now I am pleased that it was. It was so sweet sharing the entire experience with Fitzwilliam right from the beginning. I well remember the night we were lying in bed and felt the baby move. It is a sweet memory that I shall always cherish."

Jane looked thoughtful. "Perhaps I shall tell Charles sooner."

"Do what seems best for you, Jane."

Just then Georgiana ended a song and stood to address the room. "I would love to hear someone else. Would you consent to exhibit, Elizabeth?"

Elizabeth laughed. "I am willing to sing if someone is willing to accompany me."

"I will," Colleen volunteered, "if we can find something we both are familiar with, of course."

Thus, when the men joined the ladies in the music room, Elizabeth's lilting soprano greeted them, accompanied by Colleen's wonderful skills on the pianoforte. She was as proficient as Georgiana, and seeing her at the instrument made Richard's heart swell with pride.

"Your wife is an accomplished musician, Richard," William offered. "Does she sing as well?"

"No. She allows that she cannot carry a tune, though I am not convinced of that. However, I am content to enjoy her playing."

"Just as I am content to hear Elizabeth sing!"

"We are both blessed," Richard added, patting his cousin on the back.

"That we are, Cousin. That we are."

⌒ↃᏟↃ⌒

Later that night

Now attired for bed, Audrey Landingham decided to join her husband on the balcony. Marshall looked very handsome in his dark blue robe, his grey hair shining in the moonlight as he admired the canopy of stars in the clear, night sky.

"A penny for your thoughts."

At her voice, he turned to pull her into his arms, burying his face in her soft dark hair. For a long time he did not speak, content to hold her. Then he pulled back to look into her eyes.

"I was thinking of how perfect my life is now. I have a wonderful woman to love." He leaned down to kiss the tip of her nose. "And I have my beautiful daughter in my life, not to mention Fitzwilliam, who is like my own son. I thought that I could not want for anything more, but somehow Alexander's birth has made me even more content."

"I know what you mean. It is as though he is my own grandchild."

"And the fact that Fitzwilliam has chosen to have his heir carry my name is not only a complete surprise, it is very humbling. I thought he would name the boy after George."

"My nephew cherishes the time you spent with him, giving him guidance. That was far more than George Darcy provided."

Marshall nodded absently. "I did not do anything significant. I only meant to be available to him if he needed a friend, a mentor. But I have learned that things done with the right attitude do not go unrewarded."

"I have learned that as well."

"When that little boy peers at me with that solemn expression—you know the one."

"The one where he looks just like his father?"

"Yes, that is it, he looks like Fitzwilliam. When he looks at me with that expression, I find myself willing to go to the ends of the earth to protect him. I did not expect to feel so close to a child again—at least not after Georgiana was taken from me."

"If one's heart is open, there is no end to the number of people who will fit inside."

Marshall pulled Audrey tighter in his embrace, kissing the top of her head. "You are a very wise woman, Audrey Landingham, and I love you dearly. If not for you, I would still be lost."

"And I would not be fully alive again after all these years. In your arms, I find the will to love and be loved."

"Then suppose we take advantage of that feeling, darling, for I wish to love you again."

Instantly she was in his arms and he was carrying her back into the bedroom. Without bothering to stop, he kicked the door shut as he went through the door from the balcony. It made sufficient noise to awaken Richard and Colleen in the next bedroom, and would have, had they not been engaged in amorous activities of their own.

The Darcy's Bedroom

All of the guests retired early since they had travelled for some part of the day—with the exception of Mr. Bennet. William and Elizabeth's father talked for a short while after everyone else had excused themselves, and though he did not believe he would ever be Mr. Bennet's favourite son, William was content that they now respected one another. Alexander's birth had broken down the last barrier between them, it seemed. Thus, as he wearily ascended the grand staircase, William relived their conversation.

"I must admit that I was concerned for Lizzy when she married you. I feared most that I might have erred in raising her to be inquisitive and to speak her mind. The thought constantly plagued me that no man would want her without wanting to change her personality. But I have seen firsthand that you have let her flourish, Son. She can be who she is—no matter how outspoken and opinionated."

Mr. Bennet laughed as William shook his head in amusement.

Then Thomas Bennet sobered, his gaze falling to his shoes. "It is important to know beforehand that you can live in harmony with the one you marry. I have learned this lesson well." His smile returned as he looked back to William. "It gladdens my heart to see my Lizzy in a marriage where she is cherished. I owe you a heartfelt apology for anything derogatory I might have said about you."

As he held out his hand, William reached to shake it. "No apology is necessary. It is good to know that we both hold Elizabeth's happiness sacred."

Mr. Bennet's eyes became shiny and he tried to recover his composure. "Yes, well it seems my grandson has greatly added to her joy."

They talked of Alexander until the elderly man allowed that he was tired and followed the others example by retiring to his room, thus by the time William reached the bedroom he shared with Elizabeth, he was fatigued. Fully expecting to find her already sleeping, since she had come upstairs over an hour before to feed Alexander, he was surprised to find her awake. She was lying in their bed on her side, propped up on one elbow. The baby lay beside her almost asleep.

William entered quietly, and so concentrated on their son was Elizabeth that she did not notice his entrance. For a while, he stood in the darkness drinking in the sight of the two people he loved most in the world, reminiscing of the nights he had longed for Elizabeth to be his wife. The realisation that all his dreams had come true was almost overwhelming.

Elizabeth quietly cooed words of love to her son while gently rearranging the dark tendrils on his forehead. "He is Mama's boy. Yes, he is ... and such a good boy ... he lets Mama sleep longer each night ... yes, he does."

In between her murmurings, she kissed his cherubic face. Finally, she looked up to see William watching her and smiled, motioning him forward.

"Is he not the most beautiful baby?" she whispered looking down at the child as she spoke. "Aunt Audrey and Aunt Evelyn both say he is the most beautiful baby they have ever seen, and I imagine they have seen plenty of babies in their time."

William's lips twitched as he tried not to smile. "Yes, he is very handsome." He began to take off his coat and unloosen his cravat. "Now that he is asleep, do you want me to summon Mrs. Curry to take him back to the nursery?"

"No, I told her he will sleep in the cradle tonight," she answered, motioning to the item by her side of the bed. "With our guests here, I missed seeing him today as often as I normally do."

In only a few minutes, William had undressed and retrieved one of the night shirts that he kept in the closet. Pulling it over his head, he joined his wife in the bed, each lying on their sides facing a sleeping son.

"Do you know what I fear most?" Elizabeth offered, her face becoming solemn as she ran a finger down Alex's soft arm.

William reached for her hand and kissed it. "Tell me."

"Being so busy living that I fail to take the time to enjoy my family—you and Alexander. My home was not the safe haven I want for our children and from what little you have said, I fear yours was not either."

"No. Though I felt my mother's love, our home was in turmoil most of the time."

"Precisely. I felt my father's love, but my home was equally chaotic. And while I know what duties are expected of me as the mistress of Pemberley, I do not wish to leave my children for others to nurture. It is my opinion that if one fails in raising their own children, anything else they may accomplish is for naught."

William leaned over to kiss her, replying, "Though I knew that you would make a good mother, darling, I had no way of knowing how wise you were for one so young. Your thoughts reflect my own, as I wish to enjoy our children. After all, they will be our legacy, not this estate."

"Oh Fitzwilliam! You are exactly the man I prayed for when I asked God for a husband. He could not have formed you more perfectly."

William could not suppress a wide smile. "We are blessed to have found one another."

"So very blessed."

In a few minutes, Alexander was sleeping soundly in his cradle while Elizabeth lay enclosed in her husband's arms.

"I cannot imagine marriage being anything other than this. How do people live without love and respect?"

"They do not live, Elizabeth, they exist. It was only after I met you that I had the courage to reach for more. Thank you for showing me the way."

Elizabeth propped upon his chest. "Thank you for loving me and giving me Alexander."

Instantly she was drawn into a fierce kiss. "I shall love you eternally, Elizabeth Darcy. Record that in your journal just as truly as it is written upon my heart."

And they made love as gently as two people madly in love could manage.

Epilogue

It was indisputable that the union of Fitzwilliam George Darcy and Elizabeth Rose Darcy was richly blessed by all standards. That was not to say that they did not have their share of heartaches and sadness over the years, but the joys always outnumbered the sorrows.

Their lives were, as one might expect, entwined with those of their relations. The Bingleys, the Landinghams and the Earl and Countess of Matlock all saw one another frequently, as they resided near one another in Derbyshire. And although Richard Fitzwilliam and his family lived at Rosings in Kent, they spent copious amounts of time visiting their relations in the north.

The number of lockets that William purchased when their first child was born proved to be prophetic, for the Darcys used the entire collection with the six children that God entrusted to their care. Their firstborn, Alexander, had been the perfect child to carry the mantel of heir. Instinctively aware of his duties and responsibility at a young age, he was also blessed with his mother's lively personality, thus he did not fall into the melancholy that had so often plagued his father before he married.

An expert horseman like his father, Alexander's interests lay in the study of animal husbandry. In later years, his expertise would result in the stables at Pemberley becoming renown throughout England, Wales, Scotland and Ireland for their superior stock. Even His Majesty's stables featured stallions and mares gleaned from Pemberley, and the Darcys acquired a standing contract with the army to produce animals for their officers.

Two years after Alexander was born, they were blessed with a daughter they named Audrey Anne in honour of William's beloved mother and aunt. The image of her mother, Anne, as she was called, was completely spoiled by her father. Very inquisitive and bright like Elizabeth, she would become quite an academic. Her interests tended towards botany and the science involved in improving the soil in order to improve the yield of the crops. The vast knowledge she acquired through studying the latest techniques of crop rotation and soil enrichment proved her a valuable ally to the tenants, who depended on the land to feed their families and to her father and older brother, who relied on her knowledge of the subjects.

Almost three years later another son, Thomas Edward Fitzwilliam Darcy was born. Thomas' name honoured Elizabeth's father and William's uncle, the earl. With a temperament that was quiet and reflective, he was the one in the family who listened to every side of an argument before opening his mouth, and the person to whom his siblings would turn when they needed an unbiased opinion. In later years, because of his interests in science, he would become a respected chemist as a direct result of the influence of Michael Faraday,[33] a chemist he met at a lecture at the Royal Institution in London.

Barely a year after Thomas' birth, the Darcys welcomed another daughter, Evelyn Jane, named after William's aunt and Elizabeth's sister. She was the most like her brother, Thomas, in temperament, and though known to the family as Eve, her mother often teased her by calling her Jane because of her tendency to see the good in every situation. Moreover, she resembled her aunt, her hair being only a shade darker. Nonetheless, the sky blue eyes of her father proved her a Darcy, and her interests in books proved that she was her mother's daughter. Inspired by her mother's journals, she became an accomplished writer of novels before she was thirty.

During the year of 1821, Elizabeth experienced a miscarriage, losing a baby boy in the sixth month. Though she and William were deeply saddened, they had only to consider the children God had given them to realise that they should not despair. Vowing not to allow this tragedy to defeat them, it served only to force them closer as a couple and as a family.

It would be four years before another Darcy would join the family. This time it was another daughter, Claire Elizabeth. Claire was a miniature of her sister, Anne, who was now a young lady of eight. Anne, feeling sufficiently grown, took the nurturing of her younger siblings seriously, especially since her mother was busy with the baby. Under the governess' supervision, she became quite adept at helping to instruct the younger Darcys, either by reading to them or helping with their numbers and letters. So dedicated was she, that her parents often insisted that she go riding with her father or pursue her own music and art, otherwise she would have been perfectly agreeable to spend all her time with her brother and sisters.

After several years, the Darcys began to believe that God had no more children in mind for them, but He indeed had other plans. The year that Elizabeth was eight and thirty, she learned that she was again with child. William was ecstatic upon hearing the news, but she secretly worried that she might not be able to carry the child to term. But God was faithful and Sophia Rose was born on the 24th of December, 1831, a perfectly healthy girl and a wonderful Christmas present. She would provide much joy for the family, living at home far past the age when her older brothers and sisters had married and moved away.

In fact, Rose did not marry until she was five and twenty, though she had her share of admirers. She was quite handsome, having her father's black hair and her mother's dark chocolate eyes. Taller than her sisters, a trait she inherited from her father as well, she was a fearless horsewoman and enjoyed competing against any who dared to challenge her. For years, only her father could keep up with her as she raced across the pastures, jumping fences and creeks one after the other.

---

[33] *Michael Faraday, 1791- 1867. British chemist and physicist who contributed significantly to the study of electromagnetism and electrochemistry. Professor of Chemistry at the Royal Military Academy in Woolwich (1830-1851) and frequent lecturer at the Royal Institution.*

And so it was that the Darcy children lived a fairytale existence, anchored by a father and mother determined that they would know that they were cherished. And though they never had much contact with the Bennets other than with their grandfather, who lived long enough to see their third child enter the world, and Aunt Jane, they were not without a great number of relations who loved them and with whom they shared their lives.

Georgiana Darcy was barely two and twenty when she married the handsome Earl of Cheltham, Arthur Findley, who was eight and twenty. She and her husband resided in the county of Cheshire, their home being approximately thirty miles from Pemberley. They had two sons, Arthur Darcy and Roland Harold, though Georgiana also became the mother of Findley's two daughters when they married— Mary, aged two, and Melanie, aged four. Their mother had passed away the year before Findley met Georgiana and both little girls became extremely close to their new mother, who treated them as her very own.

Charles and Jane Bingley had three children, all girls—Charlene Jane, Rebecca Elizabeth and Marjorie Kathleen— born within the space of six years. The oldest girls had bright red hair and dark blue eyes, the image of their father, while the youngest was a miniature of Jane.

Richard and Colleen became the parents of four boys, the first being his namesake, Richard Edward. The second and third sons were identical twins— Joseph Martin and James Marshall. They were so similar that it was impossible for most of the family to tell one from the other and strangers were completely baffled. Colin Spencer was born two years after the twins.

The birth of each successive son resulted in a ceaseless stream of teasing from the men of the family, as it was common knowledge that Richard wished for a daughter. And though content with his boys, nevertheless he added to the dilemma by teasing Colleen.

"And what happened to the girl I ordered?" he would taunt whenever the family gathered to greet the newest addition to the family.

Colleen always replied with a smile. "You are not in His Majesty's service any longer. Surely you do not expect your orders to be carried out."

Nonetheless on their 15th wedding anniversary, Richard was rendered speechless by the birth of a beautiful red-haired daughter, Penelope Colleen.

Thus, as the decades passed and the children matured, there was no end to the number of coaches travelling between the estates as one cousin or another decided to spend time with their personal favourite amongst the multitude of offspring.

With the exception of Edgar and Frances Fitzwilliam, who kept to themselves in London, they were by and large a contented bunch. Years later, after the Matlock title had passed to Edgar, he and Frances died when influenza swept through Town. Thus, the title passed to Richard, along with the estate of Matlock.

Not in good health, the Earl of Matlock expired before William and Lizzy's fifth wedding anniversary and the Countess the following year. They were sorely missed, as they had chosen to live in Derbyshire in their final years. So it was that Lord and Lady Landingham, who were already considered grandparents by the Darcy children, stepped in to fill the void by becoming surrogate grandparents for all the children and were an influence on them all until most were grown.

Over time, the small chapel at Pemberley was enlarged to accommodate the burgeoning Darcy family, and the vicar at Kympton began to hold services two Sundays per month. The new building witnessed many christenings, several funerals and a plethora of weddings during William and Elizabeth's era, while the small stone bench under the oak in the cemetery became a haven just for the two of them. It became a tradition that on certain anniversaries, just as dawn was breaking, one would hurry to the spot only to discover that the other was already there.

And that is exactly as it happened on Anne Darcy's birthday in the year that William turned seventy. He was first to arrive and was already seated on the stone bench in anticipation of Elizabeth's soon appearance. She had every intention of meeting him there, but seeing that he arrived first, she chose to do what she had begun years before—she stopped in the foggy mist to admire the man she had loved for the greater part of her life. It never failed to amaze her how her heart still burned with love at the slightest glimpse of Fitzwilliam, whether across a great distance or merely across the dinner table.

When she spied him, his head was bowed in prayer, and for a second she was disappointed. Though his attractive silvery hair still caused her heart to beat faster, she longed to peer into the sky blue eyes that twinkled whenever he looked at her.

He is just as handsome—no, more so—than the day I first met him in the bookstore!

Suddenly William looked up, smiled and stretched his arms in her direction. Unable to hold back a grateful smile, she hurried to fill his embrace when he stood.

"Why were you smiling so smugly?" she teased, running her hand along his cheek. "Were you surprised that I can still move so fast?"

"Not at all! I was just mulling over how a man who had destroyed his future by assuming he could fix everything, found redemption and then was so fortunate as to marry the most amazing woman in England."

"Only in England?"

The giggle that accompanied her question was so reminiscent of the pixie of the bookshop that William's heart swelled with love and melancholy at the same time. Her hair was still just as unruly as ever, having escaped her combs even now, but it was now almost completely white. He smoothed one long tendril behind her ear and kissed the tip of her nose. "In truth, you are the most amazing woman I have ever known."

Elizabeth laid her head back on his chest. His arms enclosed her tighter, and she sighed. "Do you have any regrets, darling?"

"Only that I did not wait for God's deliverance instead of marrying in haste to hush a scandal. If I had, I would have been free to offer for you when we met. I knew the moment you came around that bookshelf that you were the one God meant for me."

He felt her nodding. "I knew too." When she looked up at him, her eyes were shiny with tears. "I shall love you for all eternity, Fitzwilliam George Darcy."

His voice was rough as he whispered a reply. "And I shall love you for all eternity, Elizabeth Rose Darcy."

The dawn found them sitting, hand in hand, watching the sun rise over their beloved Pemberley.

Finis

CPSIA information can be obtained at www.ICGtesting.com
Printed in the USA
LVOW012051090413

328375LV00032B/2740/P